SEASONS OF LOVE

A COLLECTION OF MAY-DECEMBER GAY ROMANCE NOVELS

ANA ASHLEY

COPYRIGHT

Novels included in this collection

How to Catch a Biker - Chester Falls Book 5
© 2021 by Ana Ashley
First Edition: March 2021

Breakthrough - Dads of Stillwater
© 2022 by Ana Ashley
First Edition: Oct 2022
Dragonfly design <a href='https://www.freepik.com/vectors/nature'>Nature vector created by freepik - www.freepik.com</a>

Love Again - Finding You Book 3
© 2020 by Ana Ashley
First Edition: May 2020

Christmas Bubble
© 2022 by Ana Ashley
First Edition: Nov 2022

The Resort - Room for 3, book 1
© 2021 by Ana Ashley
First Edition: July 2021

Join Ana's Facebook Group Café RoMMance (facebook.com/groups/CafeRoMMance) for exclusive content, and to learn more about her latest books at anawritesmm.com!

DEDICATION

To everyone out there to whom age is just a number.
Keep loving as you do,

Ana

CONNECT WITH ANA

Connect with Ana on social media:

Hang out in my FB Group Café RoMMance
(facebook.com/groups/CafeRoMMance)
Follow me on Instagram (@anawritesmm)
Follow me on Bookbub (bookbub.com/authors/ana-ashley)
Sign up to my newsletter (bit.ly/AnaAshley)
Become a member of Ana's Attic (anawritesmm.com/attic)

CHECK out more of Ana's books:

Dads of Stillwater series
Chester Falls series
Room for 3 series
Finding You series
Christmas Bubble
Midnight Ash
Stronghold

And for an overview of all my books and audiobooks, visit my website (anawritesmm.com/books)!

Chester
FALLS
how to catch a
BIKER
ANA ASHLEY

ABOUT HOW TO CATCH A BIKER

What do you do when you meet the tall, gruff silver fox of your dreams?
You flirt, pretend it didn't happen, and secretly admire his assets.
For research purposes, of course.

I came to Chester Falls to find my voice and save my publishing career.
Instead, I find him.
Slade's story is kept under a lock so strong I don't know if there is a man out there that can break it.
But I'll be damned if I won't give it a try.

A biker with a past
A down-in-the-dumps author
A kitten with a tiger attitude
Two guys that discover there isn't that much mileage between reality and fiction.

How to Catch a Biker is the fifth book in the Chester Falls series and features a May/December story between two guys who have more in common than they think, a group of friends who think everyone needs to be in love, and a small town like no other.

1

SLADE

"Hey, baby."

What the fuck.

I glanced at the screen on my phone to double-check that I hadn't been stupid enough to answer a call from my ex.

Unknown Number.

"Slade, honey? Are you there?" he asked in that sweet, deep voice he thought still worked for me. It had, once upon a time, many times over.

"What do you want, Mike?" I tried to keep my voice flat. I knew he'd pick on up the slightest hint of emotion and latch onto it.

"Now, now, baby. That's no way to greet your husband—"

"Ex-husband, Mike. Ex. Husband," I said, failing to take the bite out of my voice.

"That's why I'm calling," he said.

"What do you mean? And make it quick, I have work to get to."

"It's our anniversary."

"I'm hanging up."

"Wait," he said. "Please..." His voice changed, and I knew I was going to regret it, but I waited until the silence became too heavy, even for me.

"Mike…"

"I just…do you remember that day? Can you believe it was twenty-five years ago? It was so hot and sticky. The hottest day in Atlanta that summer. I was running late for work, but when I saw you, leaning against your bike wearing that leather jacket as if you were too cool to feel the heat…" he chuckled.

How could I not remember? It was the day my life changed forever, and not just for the reason he liked to remember.

"It was a good day," I confessed.

Mike's memory of the guy across the road from where he worked in his uncle's garage couldn't be further from reality.

I'd been scared and unsure. I'd wanted to cross the road and trust that the promises I'd been given weren't as empty as the tank on my trusted Harley.

Instead, I was given a job, and I'd met the man that taught me my life could be good, or at least better than it had been until then. That is until he broke my heart and my trust.

"You were always a mystery, Slade. It was exciting at first, but then…"

I sighed. "Why are we having this conversation? You were the one who left, and not before you took everything you wanted and more."

"Slade…"

"Look, I don't know what you want from this trip down memory lane, but I've moved on. I live on Reality Avenue, where I have a business to run. I suggest you go back to whatever twink you're fucking this week and leave me alone."

I ended the call before he could say anything else.

These days, the only person I kept my mouth shut for was my bank manager, so it was definitely a good idea to end the call.

It was the hottest day of the summer so far, making the glass walls of my office feel like a fishbowl under a UV light, but Mike's interruption only delayed the work I needed to do today, so I grabbed a bottle of water from my small office fridge and drank it all in one go.

The satisfaction of closing my spreadsheets one hour later was only matched by the information they contained within. My business was doing well. So well, in fact, that maybe I could offer Liam a few more hours and consider finally taking the time to work on my bike restoration.

I stepped outside the office. Liam was in the garage working under a car and whistling a tune I didn't recognize.

The familiar smell of oil, grease, paint, and sweat calmed me down, and since there were no customers in the shop, I allowed myself the moment to enjoy the feeling of rightness whenever I was in my workspace. The garage, *not* the office. That was merely a necessary part of running a business.

When I'd seen this building only around the corner from the Chester Falls main square, I knew I'd found my perfect place.

The vintage bike shop with the adjacent garage had direct access from the main street, attracting curious passersby as well as my loyal customers.

Cars weren't really my thing, so when Liam had walked in asking for a job, just a couple of months after I'd opened the shop, I hadn't cared that I had no clue how to pay him.

As it turned out, he'd worked for the previous owners, and since there was no other garage in town, we had a captive audience. As much as I'd wanted to run an exclusive vintage bike repair and restoration shop, I knew it was smart to diversify.

I'd been dumb too many times in my life to not know when to smarten up.

The shop was exactly how I'd always wanted. Paved flooring, a few display cabinets, a leather couch, and several blown-up photos of vintage bikes on the walls.

It was big enough to have a good range of bikes on display, mostly Harleys, but it still felt cozy and personable. Most of all, the long glass wall behind the bikes gave my customers a direct view of the garage.

"Hey, boss," Liam said, sliding out from under the car. "I put the new alternator in Mrs. Mason's car. I'll just give it a quick once over and it'll be good to go."

"That's great. Thanks, Liam. You can head home when you finish."

"You sure? I can hang around," he said, wiping his greasy hands on a rag.

"I'm sure."

"You know Maggie will bring you coffee whether or not you let me off early."

Liam was a good ten years younger than me, and after losing his first wife at a young age, he'd found love again in the girl that seemed to come by a little too often for someone who didn't own a car, bike, or even had a driver's license.

Maggie was a sweet girl in her mid-twenties, and as long as she kept bringing us coffee from Spilled Beans, she could pop by to visit Liam any time. Or have him home early as the case may be.

"I have no ulterior motive. Just being nice," I said, raising my hands.

I wasn't kidding anyone. Indy's coffee was the best and, on most days, we were so busy that Maggie's treat was a lifesaver.

"All right, then. Will we see you at the book fair later?" he asked.

I'd almost forgotten about the fair. These days, reading was my only form of relaxation, usually before I fell asleep after a long day at the shop.

"Maybe," I said. "I want to catch up on some things, but I'll drop by."

I went over to the main shop while Liam finished up. Working with cars and bikes was a messy and smelly business. Just because the scent of oil got my engine running, it didn't mean the general public agreed with it, so I'd made sure that my staff facilities had a locker room with a shower and the best oil removing soap available.

Liam was my only employee, but the way things were going, I could see myself hiring a couple more people in the next year or so. Especially if it meant I wouldn't need to get anywhere near a car.

I glanced at the corner of the garage where my passion project stood covered up and waiting for me to get my head out of my ass and start working on it.

"All right, boss. I'll see you later," Liam said, coming into the shop area looking fresh as a daisy.

I waved him off.

"Hey, Liam," I said, just as he reached the front door. "I don't suppose you'd want to pick up a few more hours?"

He grinned widely. "You serious, boss?"

I nodded.

"Hell yeah, I'll do it. I'm saving to get Maggie a nice ring. I know we haven't been going out long, but when you know, you know. Right?"

"You can't let a girl like Maggie get away, that's for sure."

He nodded and left with the biggest smile on his face.

My mind went back to the call from Mike. I once thought we had forever too.

Saying life after my parents died wasn't easy was the understatement of the century, so when I met him, he was the ray of sunshine I craved. If he was a flower, I was a bee drunk on his sweet nectar.

Except I carried secrets I had never been able to share and, in the end, that broke us. Yes, he'd cheated, but when you hide who you really are from the person you love, aren't you as much of a cheater?

We normally didn't get many customers in the shop on Saturday mornings, so I busied myself putting things away in the garage and closing it before heading back to close the shop.

I stole another glance at the old Harley and then pulled out the list of parts I needed to order for it. I reckoned I could have it ready by the end of the summer, when I usually closed the shop for a week to get out on the open road.

The thought alone caused my skin to erupt in excited goosebumps. I'd missed out on the trip last year, when I'd come down with an unexpected flu, so I wanted to make this year count.

I pulled out my phone and blocked the number Mike had called me from. I wasn't interested in living in the past.

The man that had saved my life said to me once, *"Slade, son, nothing good comes from looking back. Put the good memories in a safe box and move forward. Only when you're miles away from the past, can you afford to look back inside the box and pick a memory to revisit. Don't do it too early, or you'll be tempted to turn around. Make sure you're far away enough that you can't."*

Those words had carried me from Seattle to Atlanta and then to Chester Falls.

When I'd arrived in the small town six years ago, I thought I'd stepped into a place that wasn't made for people like me. It was too nice, too perfect.

Time showed me that people here were as flawed as anywhere else, and so, a day at a time, I carved out my little spot in the community.

After locking everything up, I went around the building to the outside stairs that lead up to my apartment above the store. I liked that there was a separation. My apartment was my sanctuary. There, I didn't have any secrets. I could open my memory box and bring back the good ones any time I liked.

One scan of my bookshelf reminded me that I'd recently donated some books to Goodwill, so what a perfect day to fill it up with new ones.

Maybe I'd bump into Liam and Maggie at the book fair. Maybe I'd buy her an iced coffee.

Now those were memories I wanted to make.

2

AIDEN

"Aiden, I didn't know you were in town." Ben's smile was as warm as always, but the strain on his arms from carrying a big, heavy box of books was written all over his face.

"Wait, let me help you," I said, taking the box from him. "Where do you want it?"

"Outside, in the square," he said. "You see that gazebo in the middle? That's where we're taking the books."

Bookmarked, Ben's bookstore, was always busy on a Saturday morning, and since the front door had been open when I came in, I didn't even notice the sign was flipped to closed. There was also an unusual number of boxes filled with books by the checkout desk.

"What's going on out there?" I asked.

"It's the Summer Book Fair. We do it every year, but this year is a special one," Ben said, walking past me with another box of books and indicating for me to follow.

"Why is that?"

"It's our twentieth anniversary. My Aunt Jackie started it to offload older books and raise money for town projects."

We crossed the road into the square that always seemed to be the center of the town of Chester Falls.

"That's such an amazing idea," I said.

"Yeah." He put his box down by a few others, and I followed his example. "I still remember the first one she ever organized. It was just a table outside the store with a small sign. The money she raised was enough to pay for catering and some costumes for the school's nativity play. The next year she had more books, and the year after that people asked if they could donate books to raise more money."

"So it's like a big philanthropic book exchange," I said.

Ben grinned. "Precisely."

As we approached the middle of the square, I saw piles of boxes filled with books ready to be displayed on the rows of tables that were already set up under the shade of the gazebo.

It was a warm summer day without a hint of a breeze. Beads of sweat ran down my forehead and I felt them on the small of my back too, but I felt better and more useful than I had in a long time.

"Oh gosh, I didn't mean to put you to work before you even had a chance to say good morning," Ben said, wiping his face with the back of his hand. "Especially not in this heat. We're always lucky with the weather, but this year is definitely warmer. It's a good thing Indy is setting up a stand with cool drinks."

"It's my pleasure to help. You said books and charity in one sentence. If that's not right up my alley, I don't know what is," I said as we walked back to Bookmarked. "Sounds like I picked the right time to visit. Can I help out in any way? Other than helping you carry the rest of the boxes, of course."

We were back inside the store. Ben gave me an assessing gaze that I tried to ignore by bending down to pick up another box.

"Aiden, don't get me wrong, because it's always great to see you, but does anyone know you're here?"

I put the box down and sat on it.

My best friend, Wren, had moved back home to Chester Falls from San Diego eighteen months ago. Since then, I'd visited the small town a number of times and had come to know his extended group of friends, including Ben and his husband, Tristan.

They were the reason I'd come straight to Bookmarked, rather than the store next door, Fabulize, which happened to belong to Wren's fiancé, Tom.

"I...um..." I let out a tired breath, unsure of how much to say.

"For an author, you are strangely out of words," Ben said. He crouched down next to me. While his tone carried a hint of amusement, I could tell he was genuinely concerned, or maybe just curious.

Everyone was used to seeing Aiden, the successful author who had his shit together.

Nothing could be further from the truth.

"I was wondering if Tristan knows anyone who might have an apartment to rent short-term."

Tristan was an interior designer and had moved here from Boston a couple of years ago. I'd heard enough stories from their group of friends to know Tristan worked with a lot of landlords in the local area.

Ben's eyes bugged out. "You want to move here? But how about Rich—"

I shook my head. That was something I really did not want to talk about right now. Outside, the perfect day awaited us, and I was so fucking tired from my own life, I really needed to work on something positive and fun for a change.

"I'm just working on a new book, that's all, and I could do with a change of scenery while I do it."

Ben nodded and stood up, grabbing his phone from the desk.

"Tristan is with a client, but I sent him a message. Do you have anywhere to stay tonight?" he asked.

"I checked a local hotel, and they have plenty of vacancies if I can't get a place."

"You know you can stay with us, right? The couch is quite comfortable. Let's not even mention that Wren and Tom might be upset if they know you're in a hotel and not staying with them."

Yes, I knew that, which was why I wanted to find a place to stay first. Because as much as I loved the generosity of my friends, the last thing I wanted was to be in close proximity to a loved-up couple.

So much for being a romance author. These days I struggled with even the concept of love.

"I'll cross that bridge when the time comes." I stood up. "Should we get back to work?"

Ben squeezed my shoulder and picked up the box next to me.

"That's it," Ben said a few trips later as we stood under the blissful shade of the gazebo. "Each box has a genre label that matches the signs on the table. All you need to do is stack the books neatly so people can read the titles on the spine."

"Got it, boss."

Over the next hour we worked on the book displays. I made sure to stay away from the romance section because it was a surefire way of getting distracted. I'd have time to scan through the titles later.

A small crowd gathered around the square, eager to check out the books on offer.

Indy opened up his cold-drinks stand, which included his new special-blend iced coffee. I'd been to his coffee shop, Spilled Beans, enough times to know I needed to get my hands on one of those coffees.

As soon as we cleared the space from all the empty boxes, Ben declared the fair open, giving a little speech about his aunt and how happy she'd be to see her project still alive after all these years.

My little writer heart jumped for joy seeing everyone happily scanning through the books and buying more than a few.

"Hey, guys, sorry, I'm late. Charlotte wanted to come with me, so Hannah and I had to use some diverting tactics," Ellie, Ben's business partner, said joining us. "Give me another six months, and I'll be ready to graduate from ninja school with honors."

We laughed. I'd met eighteen-month-old Charlotte before, and she was a bundle of energy and unparalleled cuteness.

"Nice to see you, Aiden. I didn't know you were coming to the fair," she said.

I rubbed the back of my neck, a little embarrassed at the reminder that I'd turned up unannounced.

Fortunately, Ben jumped in the conversation. "It was a last-minute thing. I messaged him about the fair, and the next thing I knew... poof, he's here."

"Oh…my…bubblegum-flavored ice cream with a cherry on top."

I put a smile I didn't feel on my face and turned around to face Tom, whose eyes were on my designer shirt. He came closer and started stroking the fabric on the sleeve.

"Holy mother of pearls, this feels beautiful," he said and kissed my cheek. "Nice to see you, Aiden."

"Hi, Tom."

Tom's literal sparkling personality brought a smile to my lips, but it soon died down when I saw Wren's frown.

"Baby, why don't you grab us an iced coffee from Indy?" he said to Tom.

"Coffee for everyone with cream and sprinkles coming right up," Tom said before walking away.

Ben and Ellie both made themselves scarce.

Great. Thanks, guys.

"What's going on?" Wren asked.

"Nothing's going on, what do you mean?"

"You're in Chester Falls."

I looked around and smiled. "Yup."

"Why didn't you say you were coming?" he asked, not bothering to hide the hurt in his voice.

"Surprise!"

"You're staying with us," he declared, crossing his arms in front of his chest.

"Wren—"

"No, something's going on, and if you don't want to talk about it, that's okay. But you're my best friend and I want to be here for you."

Even though I already knew that, his words still meant more than he could possibly imagine.

"Thank you, but I have a place to stay already," I lied.

"How long are you staying?"

"Maybe a few weeks? I'm researching for a new book."

"Weeks?" His frown gave turn to a wide grin that made his light-blue eyes shine even brighter. "Man, this is going to be great. I've gotten my running buddy back."

I laughed.

"Don't laugh. By the time I'm done with you, you'll be moving here permanently."

As much as the idea had some appeal, I wasn't sure I was ready to move away from San Diego. That felt too permanent. Final.

3

———

SLADE

THERE WASN'T MUCH a cold shower on a hot day couldn't fix, in my opinion, so thirty minutes after closing the shop for the weekend, I was feeling refreshed and ready to head out.

I hadn't missed a single book fair since I'd moved to Chester Falls, and as soon as I turned the corner from my street onto the square, I could tell this year's fair was bigger and better.

There was a line for Indy's iced coffee stand, and a separate one spilling from his coffee shop onto the street. The main event of the day was the book fair, but no one in Chester Falls would go without a cold drink and a pastry.

Not that I could blame them, Indy's cakes were the best, even though I didn't indulge in them often. Being in the shop all day didn't leave me much time to work out and, at forty-eight, my body didn't bounce back from a sugar-filled diet in the same way it had when I was younger.

Maybe I'd grab a pastry to take home for later, but I didn't want my hands busy with drinks and food while I scanned through the books.

That was my mission for the afternoon, to fill up my bookshelf with as many romance novels as I could carry home.

As they say, those who can't, teach. With me, it's more a case of those who can't romance, read about it.

I moved through the small crowd, smiling and nodding my greetings to the locals I already knew well. It never ceased to amaze me how welcoming everyone was. If I didn't know better, I would think I'd lived here all my life.

Wren Mason, the high school coach, waved from where he stood with Tom near Indy's stand. His eyes lit up, but I smiled and shook my head at him. He grinned and came over.

"Oh, come on, Slade," he said.

"I'm too old, Wren. The only group sport I'm interested in is the kind I watch on PornHub."

He snorted. Since Wren had moved back to Chester Falls, he'd been on a mission to get the whole town involved in some kind of sport or physical activity. The kids' football team was currently winning their league, and as a former professional player, that was probably not enough winning for him.

He was starting an adult football team, and maybe he hadn't had enough young people join because now he was coming after the old farts, like me, too.

"It's only for fun, Slade. Let out some steam after a day of hard work at the shop. It'll be great."

"My fun after a hard day's work includes a beer and one of the books I'll be buying today." I patted his shoulder and carried on toward the gazebo. He seemed a little deflated by my refusal, and I almost felt bad for not joining him in his excitement, but football had never really been my thing.

As I'd predicted, this year's book assortment was bigger than last year's, and the romance section had doubled in size.

Trying to get to it was a challenge in itself, but at least on this occasion, my six-foot-four height was an advantage. I moved through the tables, peering over people's shoulders to see if I recognized any of my favorite authors.

A glance over the thriller section proved fruitless, but it was useful in biding my time until the crowd moved away from my favorite genre.

I waved at Ben, who was at the other end of the gazebo busy ringing through all the purchases. We were both on the Chester Falls Chamber of Commerce and often discussed our favorite romance novels between meeting breaks.

He'd been a little shy at first. A reaction I often got from people that didn't know me, but once he'd gotten past the height, the beard, and the rough exterior, he didn't stop talking about books until I confessed my love for gay romance. We even shared the same favorite author.

I moved out of the way of a little girl holding a bunch of children's books and an ice cream, just in time to avoid wearing it on my jeans.

As the girl ran to her mother with the ice cream miraculously still attached to the wafer cone, I let out a relieved breath and turned back to the table.

A book I'd been wanting to read for a while caught my eye. It had mixed reviews, but the blurb had caught my attention when I read it online.

I reached out for it just in time to get caught in a tug-of-war with someone else over the book.

"I'm sor—" My gaze followed the soft, pale skin of the hand gripping my book. The guy's shirtsleeves were rolled up, which showed off his slim but defined forearms, though not nearly enough.

I kept looking up until I met with chestnut-brown eyes that even behind the slim dark-metal frames were deep and assessing.

"I'm sorry. You have it, you went for it first," he said, pushing the book in my direction.

"No, no, you have it."

"No, honestly, it's okay."

I took the book, since he didn't seem prepared to relent.

"I'm not even sure I'll like it," I said. "I've read the reviews online."

He smiled. "That's exactly why I wanted to read it too."

"Please, I insist." I gave him the book and, that time, he took it.

His face seemed familiar, but I couldn't place it. We definitely hadn't met before because I knew I'd have remembered. With his sharp jaw and soft eyes, he looked like he could take me out with one look and then hug me to make up for it.

The back of my neck felt hot. Hell, it wasn't just the back of my neck, and I don't think I could blame it entirely on the weather.

Putting it simply, the guy was stunning, even if he was far too young for me. And those eyes... God, they could probably pry the deepest secrets out of me without even trying.

I definitely needed to move my attention back to my book-finding mission.

"Well, enjoy the book," I said, picking up a random novel without checking the title or author name.

"Maybe..." he trailed.

I looked up at him. He tilted his head and bit his lip, and my dick enjoyed the image far too much.

A tiny blush appeared under the collar of his shirt, and I wondered if his skin was as soft and pale all over. He was probably some kind of lawyer or accountant. Someone who spent his life indoors.

Suddenly I felt the urge to invite him for a ride on my bike, just so I could see what he'd look like with his skin flushed from the adrenaline of being on the road.

"I'm staying in town for a little while, maybe you can borrow the book when I'm finished with it?" The question took me by surprise.

"I'm sure Ben has more copies of the book," I said, immediately regretting it when the guy flinched.

"Oh...yeah, of course. Well, um...happy book hunting." He turned around to face another row of books.

"I'm sorry, that came out all wrong," I said.

"It's okay, I know when I'm being dismissed. Just for the record, I wasn't flirting."

He walked away, and I knew I should have gone back to the books, but my legs decided for me by chasing after him.

"Hey," I said, grabbing his wrist. It was such a bad idea because just the feel of his soft skin under my rough hands made all the heat from the earth's core climb up my arm. "For the record, I wasn't dismissing you."

"Right." He pulled his hand back and put it in the pocket of his jeans.

I tried not to stare, but for all the self-restraint I had, I never claimed to be a saint.

"People aren't really my thing," I said.

He looked around us and raised his brows.

I laughed. "I'm fine with crowds. It's single people I'm not as good with."

"What makes you think I'm single?"

I opened my mouth and shut it again.

He laughed. "Relax, I was only joking. Let's start from the beginning."

I nodded, still not trusting anything else out of my mouth while in the presence of this guy that somehow got my gut all twisted.

"Hi, I'm Aiden, and I love books. I think you do too. I'm kinda new in town, so if you're free any time, we could meet up for a coffee and talk about this book we both want to read. Oh, and I'm single but not looking for a relationship. Just putting it out there."

It took me a moment to notice his outstretched hand between us. I met it with mine, ignoring again how nice it felt. I definitely needed another shower when I got home.

"Nice to meet you, Aiden. Maybe I'll see you around."

"Maybe..."

He smiled and left me staring at his ass as he walked away toward the checkout desk Ben had set up for the fair.

It was hard to focus on any books after that, so I picked a few random titles and paid for them before heading back home. I didn't bother seeing Liam and Maggie or buying a pastry from Spilled Beans.

The second shower did a good job of cooling me down before I put my new books away on the shelf. One of my favorites, one I could never give away to Goodwill, caught my attention, so I pulled it out from the shelf and sat on my couch.

The sunlight from the tall window in my living room made my couch the perfect reading nook, so I made myself comfortable and opened the book to the first page.

Some days it was better revisiting old friends than meeting new ones, even when they had deep, brown eyes that sucked you in and promised to keep you warm.

My hands stilled and my heartbeat increased when my eyes stopped on the author photo on the inside of the cover.

Brown eyes, this time without the glasses but unmistakably deep and soft, stared back at me. Aiden was A. Lawton. All that time when I thought I recognized Aiden but couldn't place him.

"I'm such an idiot." I groaned.

Now I definitely couldn't read the book. That's how deep my embarrassment level was.

I just hoped he wasn't staying in town for too long. Maybe if I kept to myself and didn't leave the shop, I'd avoid bumping into him. That seemed like a good idea, and I had my bike restoration to work on, anyway. I'd be plenty busy with that.

I was definitely not going to think about how I'd embarrassed myself in front of the man who was responsible for so many of my lost hours, heartbreaks, and happy-ever-afters.

4

———

AIDEN

I SHOULD HAVE KNOWN I'd be ambushed. I should have recognized the first sign a mile away.

After all, how many times had I written a main character being coerced into facing their issues by well-intentioned friends?

The answer was too many to count, but enough that I should have known when it was happening to me.

"What did you think of the fair?" Wren asked.

I raised a brow. Was that really what he wanted to ask me? Okay, then.

"It was great. I was only recognized a couple of times, and now I have a handful of books to read."

I raised the menu high enough to cover my face and started reading through the options. Indy had been generous enough to offer me one of his amazing pastries earlier, but that had been too many conversations and forced smiles ago.

"I'm torn between having breakfast for dinner or a burger that'll send me to my grave too early. I could do both. I always wondered what my mother would wear to my funeral," I said.

After wrapping up the fair, Wren had cornered me inside Book-marked and more or less given me no choice but to follow him to

29

Benny's Diner. His excuse? We needed to save a table for everyone because it was Saturday and the diner always got busy.

I looked around. He was half right, which also meant he was half wrong. Most people picked one of the booths by the window, so the bigger tables in the middle of the diner were empty, apart from the one we'd claimed.

"Have one today and the other tomorrow. After all, you're staying in town," he said.

I bit my lip to stop from laughing. He was trying so hard to raise the subject without raising it.

"Yeah, I could do that."

"So what are you working on? You said it's a new book."

"Yup."

He let out a frustrated sigh. "You're really not going to tell me what's going on?"

Wren's big heart was what drew me to him when we kept bumping into each other on our daily runs on the beach in San Diego. Even before we'd officially met, he'd already done enough little things that showed me how good he was.

His car was bigger than mine, so when he would get to the beach parking lot before me, he'd pick one spot away from the corner, which made the free space harder to see unless you knew it was already there. If he saw me running without any water, he'd leave a new bottle by the front wheel of my car.

Somehow I'd never felt sexual attraction toward him, and not just because all the time we'd known each other I'd been in a relationship. Wren was gorgeous, but to me he was like the big brother I'd never had. So I'd declared him my friend and introduced myself to him.

"Fine." I gave in. "I don't want to worry you, and I know Tom will cut off my balls if he thinks you're upset because of me."

"You're not wrong there. You really don't want me to be upset." He pursed his lips, which was a ridiculous expression for someone his size, although I'm sure that worked on Tom all the time.

"Richard and I broke up—"

"Thank fuck."

I stared at him.

"Sorry, was that too soon? Oh my god, are you hurting? I mean, he was a douchey dickwaffle, but I know you had feelings for him." He ran his hand through his short hair. "Fuck. I'm sorry, Aid, I am…shit."

"That was a little too quick, I'll admit, but you're not wrong. He is all those things, it just took me a long time to realize it."

"What happened?"

"He proposed."

Wren opened his mouth but was interrupted by the larger-than-life owner and namesake of the diner, Benny.

"Well, look who we have here. If I'd known we were having a celebrity in the house, I would have made a cake."

I laughed. "Word on the street is that you're not allowed in the kitchen."

"Yeah, yeah, the fire department has no sense of humor. Anyway, what can I get you? I'm assuming you're waiting for the gang, so let's start with drinks."

We went for a beer each and Wren asked for a bowl of nachos to snack on until everyone else arrived. I wasn't sure who everyone else was, but I suspected that Ben and Tristan would come and so would Indy and his husband, Tate. And Tom, of course. That he wasn't here already, grilling me, told me exactly how worried Wren really was.

Wren turned to me as soon as Benny left. "What do you mean, he proposed? And don't get me wrong; I think it's good you're not with him, but how do you go from a proposal to a breakup?"

"Easy, he didn't propose to me."

If I had a camera on hand I'd have taken a photo of Wren's face, but my phone was in my pocket, and as soon as I laughed, he changed his confused expression to a scowl.

"He proposed to my mother, assuming I'd say yes. Her monthly calls became weekly and then daily. She was cagey whenever I asked her about it. At some point I wondered if she had a terminal illness. Then one day she let it slip that she'd booked the Plaza in New York."

"Are you joking?"

"I wish I was. I asked Richard about it, and that's when he

31

confessed his plan to take me to New York on our anniversary and get married the same day."

Benny brought our drinks, and I drank half of my beer in one go.

"Hey, don't do anything silly, okay? We don't have to talk about this," Wren said.

"Don't worry, I won't drink myself stupid. After all, I still have no clue where I'm staying tonight. Tristan said he had the keys to an apartment I could use. Apparently the owner is traveling, and her parents are quite happy that someone will keep an eye on it."

The guys all turned up at the same time, which put an end to our conversation. The look Wren threw my way told me it wasn't over.

Somehow just saying what happened aloud made me feel a little better, a little less alone. Even though we hadn't gotten to the best part of the story yet. It was just a shame that, unlike the books I wrote, this one didn't have a happy-ever-after.

The noise level at the diner went up a few decibels with the guys all talking over each other to put their orders in. How Benny kept track of any of it was beyond me. I'd asked for the double cheeseburger with bacon and Momma Ruth's special sauce, but I was hungry enough that I'd eat anything he put in front of me.

With the orders in and the center of the table filled with drinks for everyone, five pairs of eyes stared at me. Wren gave me a break by focusing on Tom instead.

"Don't look at me like that. I basically saved your asses by turning up today. Don't question it," I said.

They all laughed and lifted their drinks for a toast.

"I'm beat, but it was so worth it," Ben said, leaning against Tristan, who put an arm over his shoulder and kissed his head.

"Uh huh," Indy muttered. Tate had his fingers laced through the back of Indy's hair and was massaging the scalp under the dark-blue hair he always wore tied up in a bun.

I studied everyone and wondered how soon I could leave without seeming rude. After all, they were all nice enough, but there was just too much love around the table, and not all of it was contained within couples.

Not to mention that after a week of traveling and staying in random hotels, I was dying for a real bed with bedsheets that hadn't been slept in by thousands of people.

"What I want to know is what kind of book you're writing?"

The question came from Tom, and was so out of the blue, I had to look around to make sure I'd heard correctly.

"Oh, don't be so surprised. I read," he said with indignation.

"Fashion magazines don't count, babe," Wren said.

Tom gave him a pointed stare and then turned to me again. "Okay, I'm being nosy, but I'm also asking what everyone wants to know but doesn't have the sparkles to ask."

He definitely had the sparkles all right. Tom was such an infectiously positive human, I was pretty sure there wasn't a single person who would deny him anything.

"I only have half a plot bunny, but this character won't leave me alone. Thing is, he's a biker, and I have no clue about biker culture or bikes. I've done as much research on the internet as I can, but something tells me I need to find someone who lives that life. I just don't know where to start."

They all looked at each other.

"I know someone you can talk to here in town," Wren said.

"Really? That would be great."

"Slade owns the vintage bike store in town. I'm picking up mom's car from him on Monday, so I can take you there."

I nodded and munched on a couple of nachos.

Slade...good name.

Would he have a beard? Leather jacket? Cloudy blue eyes that hid a secret?

My thoughts ran away from me, until I realized in my head I was describing the sexy, older man I'd met earlier. He'd left without giving me a name.

Maybe it was for the best. He could be the mysterious inspiration for my new character...Slade.

5

SLADE

"Fuck!"

"Slade?"

"Out here," I answered from under the fucking car.

Liam had gone out to Spilled Beans to get us coffee, and in my misplaced sense of teamwork, I decided to change the oil filter in a car we'd had in this morning with an oil leak. Liam was probably going to kill me and ask me to stop helping out and stick to working on the bikes.

I hated working with cars. They were messy, bulky, and had a lot less class than a Harley, in my opinion. No one ever looked sexy driving a car…unless it was an Aston Martin, of course.

Sadly, that was not the kind of car I was unlucky enough to get stuck under while doing the simplest task in the world and still managing to spill oil all over my shirt.

"Oh man, so many jokes, such a small audience," Wren said. I didn't need to see him to recognize his voice.

"Hey, respect your elders. You're here for your mom's car?"

"I was, but now I'm wondering what filming a mechanic coming out from under a car all rugged and oil stained will do to my sex life."

I replaced the drain plug and tightened it. That was the end of the messy job, now I just needed to fit the new filter.

"Put that phone away or I'll charge you double. Besides, with the smooshy-happy face Tom goes around with, I didn't think you had any problems with your sex life."

I heard two sets of chuckles. Considering the way he was joking, I assumed Wren was with someone we both knew. Or at least I hoped he was.

The last thing I needed was for a new customer to hear the exchange and have a bad impression of me and my business.

Not that they'd get a better one once they saw me wearing engine oil on a T-shirt that would never be white again.

I slid out from under the car. "Thanks for waiting, Wren. Let me just change this shirt before I—" The rest of my words became lodged in my throat, as thick as the oil coating my clothes. Because right there next to Wren, was the owner of those brown eyes that had haunted my dirty dreams all weekend.

A. Lawton…Aiden.

He grinned. "We meet again. Did you have a chance to read the book?"

I looked at him and then Wren, who was staring back at me with strange interest.

"You two know each other?" Wren asked.

"Yes, we met on Saturday at the fair, but I was short-changed," he said.

"How so?" I asked, trying to ignore the fact that A. fucking Lawton stood in front of me like an advertisement for fashionable casual clothing while I was a mess.

"I never got your name."

His gaze scanned over me. If this was another place, and he was another man, I'd think he was undressing me with his eyes, but he looked like he was cataloguing me as if he wanted to remember all the details down to the shape of the oil stains on my shirt.

I followed his gaze. He wasn't wearing his glasses today, which I thought was a shame.

He stopped when he noticed my tattooed arms, and I swear I saw a hint of a blush rising up his neck.

"Slade. Slade Warren." I stretched out my hand but pulled it back again when I saw all the oil, turning to grab the nearest rag I could find.

His smile had a hint of shyness now, which I didn't think suited him.

Not that I knew anything about him, but I'd read all his books. He had the skill to draw all the right emotions from a character, to the point that they felt more real to me than actual people. That said a lot to me about him.

"Let me get the keys and the invoice for you, Wren." I walked over to the office, stopping by the sink to wash my hands. I'd need to change my shirt too, but that could wait.

"How's business, Slade?" Wren asked. I handed him the invoice.

"Can't complain," I started, but then saw the smile in his eyes. "It's busy, really busy, so busy I barely even have time to take a break. I definitely don't have time to throw a ball on the football field and risk breaking my back."

He laughed and shook his head. "I'll get you one day, Slade. I'm this close to unleashing Tom on you."

I shivered. My smile turning into absolute fear.

"Please don't. I'll think about it, okay? Just give me some time to figure something out."

He smiled so wide, I threw his mom's car keys at him.

"See you later, Slade. Be gentle with my man, his clothes are very expensive."

Aiden rolled his eyes, and I watched as Wren got in his mom's car and drove off, honking the horn on his way out.

I turned to Aiden and said, "What was that about?" at the same time he said, "What did he mean?"

"You first," he said, tucking his hands in his jeans pockets. Not that I was looking or anything.

I groaned. "Tom has threatened on more than one occasion to give me a makeover. Apparently my exterior is too rough and doesn't match my soul, or some weird shit like that. I wouldn't put it past Wren to release Tom on me if I don't join the team."

"Nothing wrong with your exterior," he said and then closed his lips, catching himself.

I always imagined authors to be the kind of people who would think a lot before they spoke, as if words were so special that they needed the right kind of attention before being used. I never thought Aiden was the kind of man to let his mouth run away from him.

It was cute. Very cute.

"Speaking of exterior, give me a moment to change my shirt, or I'll be wearing this oil for real. Being a mechanic isn't as fun as Billy Joel made it look."

I could tell from the shine in his eyes that he'd stopped himself from making a comment. That, and the way he bit his lips shut.

Aiden had to be too young to know who Billy Joel was, but if he didn't get the reference he didn't show it.

Changing into a clean shirt gave me a moment to gather my thoughts.

What was he doing here? How did he know Wren? Did I make it known that I'd recognized him?

He'd said on Saturday that he was staying in town for a while, maybe his car had broken down or he was interested in buying a bike.

I ran my hands through my beard, which surprisingly had escaped the oil spill, and went back out to the garage.

Aiden was crouched by my Harley. His elbows propped on his knees and his hands supporting his head.

I'd forgotten I'd uncovered it earlier.

"It's a 1983 FXRT."

"What?" He stood and turned away from the bike.

I walked over and ran my hand over the torn leather seat. "It's a 1983 Harley-Davidson FXRT. Long-travel suspension, anti-dive front forks, stiffer frame, enclosed rear chain, and a rubber-mounted, eighty-cubic-inch Shovelhead engine. The best bike there has ever been."

"I have no idea what you just said."

Aiden stared at me with an assessing gaze. Similar to the one Wren had given me earlier, but also not.

"I'm sorry, bikes are my thing. You probably came here asking for help with your car, or something, and here I am with a bike boner the size of Texas."

He stared down at my jeans and smiled. The biting of his lips returned and, despite my inappropriate comment, I wished I could tell what he was thinking.

"Actually, I'm here for your bike knowledge."

"Okay, how can I help?"

He opened his mouth but didn't say anything, at first. In my experience, people always said exactly what they wanted when they wanted, even if they needed a little longer for the words to come out.

"I'm...um...I'm an author, and I...um, I'm doing research and need help. Wren said you could help."

His gaze veered away from me when he said he was an author, as if he were embarrassed about it. That didn't sit well with me.

"I know who you are."

"You do?"

"You seem surprised."

He put his hands in his pockets again, a gesture I was coming to understand was his way of dealing with something he wasn't comfortable with.

"No, I'm not." And then he laughed. "Sorry, actually, I am, but I know I shouldn't be."

"Oh?"

"You don't look like the kind of guy who'd read my books, although that's a terrible and judgy thought to have. Then again we met in the romance section at a book fair, so I shouldn't be surprised at all."

I smiled. "It's always a good day when you can surprise someone in a positive way." He returned my smile with his own, and his eyes were shiny with life again, more like the guy I'd met at the weekend. "So how can I help you with your research?"

6

———

AIDEN

"Are you really offering to help?" I asked.

He laughed. "You haven't yet told me what you need help with."

I pointed at the old Harley in front of us. The way he'd described all the important features of the bike told me he was absolutely the perfect person to help me with my research.

He wasn't just a subject matter expert, he was passionate about it in a way that was so captivating that I'd had to run the list of all my character names in my head to stop myself from getting a boner. And I couldn't exactly explain mine as a bike-related one, it was more a Slade-related one.

"I can tell you anything you want to know about motorcycles in general or Harleys. I've been obsessed with them since I was a kid."

"What's this bike's story?"

Slade went around the Harley, running his hand over the seat and the rusty metal arch at the back. Was that so the person riding behind had something to hold on to? I had so much to learn if I was going to make the biker in my story believable.

"This bike..." He paused, his eyes fixed on the bike and his brows furrowed. "This bike belonged to someone who meant a lot to me a long time ago."

"Does it work?"

"It's hanging by a thread. It was my passion project. I wanted to restore it to original condition, but every time I went to work on it, it didn't feel like the right time."

"And is it the right time now?"

He looked at me. His blue eyes were framed by a few wrinkles, but it only added to the broody, weathered demeanor he had going on.

"I don't know. A bike is meant to be ridden. Keeping it under a cover isn't good," he said.

"I think you should restore it. Maybe in honor of your friend, or maybe just for you, so you can drive it on your days off."

"Ride it."

"What?"

"You ride a bike, not drive it."

I sighed. "See? That's my level of understanding on this topic. I need some serious help."

He laughed, and then glanced toward the open garage door where a guy about the same height as Slade, but slimmer, came in with two coffees and two bags from Spilled Beans.

"You're a lifesaver," Slade said to the guy. "Aiden, this is Liam, he works with me."

Liam gave Slade his coffee and pastry and then shook my hand. "Pleasure to meet you. I'm really just here to do the coffee run and make sure Slade doesn't touch any cars."

I snorted and looked at Slade, who shook his head.

"Sorry, if I'd known the boss had company, I'd have brought enough for you too." Liam gave me an apologetic smile and went over to the other side of a car, where he put his coffee and pastry bag on a worktop.

Slade nodded for me to follow him inside the store. Wren and I had come in from the street straight into the garage space, so I hadn't seen the shop, other than at a glance from the other side of the glass wall.

The first thing that hit me was the smell of leather and wood. It was such a contrast from the garage, but it worked. The shop was like one of those middle-of-nowhere roadside bars. It even had some bar-like features, such as a couch and a high bar table with stools in one corner.

A photo of a bike just like Slade's hung on the wall. It was shiny and red, and I could only imagine Slade's bike would end up the same after it was restored.

"Wow, your shop looks amazing. This isn't at all how I imagined a vintage bike shop would be," I said.

Slade sat on the leather couch that was halfway between the front door and the register.

"I'm very proud of it. The whole unit, including the garage, already had the basic features I needed. The workbenches, power supply, and even the equipment. It was old but working. Where I spent more time and effort was with the shop side. I've dreamed of this space for longer than I care to remember."

He surveyed the space with a big smile on his face.

I tried not to notice the way his lips touched the coffee cup when he finally took a sip, and how his tongue poked out of his mouth a little with each sip, but that was a failed mission from the get-go.

"Is it just you and Liam?"

"Yeah, for now. I think I'm going to hire at least one other person. The car jobs are becoming more frequent, and I'd like to focus more on the bikes. I've had to turn away bike jobs to work on cars."

"Do you cry silently in the shower every time that happens?"

I pinched the bridge of my nose and let out a silent groan. Why did my mouth always run away from me when I was in this man's presence?

"Not so silently. It's more like uncontrollable sobs and very ugly crying. Not a pretty picture."

I looked at him and couldn't help laughing when I saw the teasing in his eyes. It wasn't hard to imagine Slade riding a bike, wearing a leather jacket and mirrored-lens sunglasses, his long beard with the perfect mix of silver strands through it. He'd be the perfect model for a book cover.

"So, how do you want this?"

His question brought me out of my reverie. "What?"

"How do you want to do your research?"

"Oh, um, I don't know. You're busy, so I don't want to take a lot of your time."

He ran his hand down his beard, a little lost in thought as he stared out toward the garage. Liam was surveying the tools they had hanging on the wall. Picking them and inspecting and then putting them back until he found the right one.

"The best way to learn is by doing. That's how I learned," Slade said.

"What do you mean?"

"You help me with the Harley restoration, and I tell you everything you need to know while we do it."

I laughed. "For a moment there I thought you said you wanted me to—" But his face was serious. "No…no. No! Are you insane? I'll break your bike."

He took his pastry out of the paper bag and gave it a big bite. My brain immediately forgot what we were talking about and decided to focus on the small drop of icing on his bottom lip, just where the soft-looking skin met his beard.

"Those are my terms. Come back tomorrow after five and we'll start with lesson one."

He licked his lip, catching the icing with his tongue, and then finishing the cinnamon roll in three bites.

And now I have a boner. Fan-fucking-tastic.

"What's it gonna be?"

"Do you promise I won't hurt your bike?"

Slade laughed again. His deep rumble doing nothing to make my dick get back to a disinterested state. Unlikely to happen any time I was around him. My dick was very, *very* interested.

"Don't laugh, it's a genuine concern. Do you know how many tools I own?"

His brow quirked, and a wave of heat rose up my neck. With my paler-than-vampire skin, he'd no doubt noticed the blush. Damn my parents and their genetic makeup. Couldn't I have been one of those sun-kissed kids? It wasn't for lack of holidays in the sun while growing up. But I'd never been able to tan. I was destined to look like a lobster the moment the sun so much as touched my skin.

"Why don't you tell me?"

"Huh?"

"How many…tools you own."

Go big or go home, right? "Maybe I'll show them to you one day, but I can tell you none will help fix your bike."

This time it was Slade's turn to blush. His slightly tan skin and his beard made it harder to detect any embarrassment, but there was an unmistakable twitch of his lips and shine in his eyes.

"Maybe you should go now before I decide we need lesson number one right this moment."

A shiver went up my back, and not a totally unpleasant one. His words felt like a promise, one I was absolutely certain I didn't want to accept, regardless of how much certain parts of my body wanted to.

On the other hand, my track record with men wasn't the best. Case in point, my ex who left me for another man when he figured out I had no intention of marrying him or using my family money to pay my way in life. And when I say my way, I mean his way.

No. Reading any meaning or intent into Slade's words was not the smart thing to do. I needed to just pretend I didn't see the way he looked at me, or how he seemed almost as confused about my presence as I was with his.

I stood up. "Okay. I guess I'll see you tomorrow."

His smile made the wrinkles in the corner of his eyes appear again.

Fuck my life. This was such a bad idea.

7

———

SLADE

"Hey, boss, I'm all done here, and I've rang Mr. Stevenson to collect his car in the morning. If you have nothing else for me, I'll head home," Liam said as I came out of the staff room.

"Thanks, Liam, that's all for today. Good job with Reed's truck."

"It's a good thing I'm not allergic to bees. I guess this one beats the sex toy catalogue I found last month."

We had a notice board in the staff room where we hung photos of all the weird stuff we found inside cars. The stranger the items were, the higher up they went on the board.

I laughed, thinking of the photo I'd taken with my phone of Liam chasing a bee around the garage and Reed chasing Liam. In the end, we managed to capture all five escaped bees and put them in a box.

Reed had a lavender farm outside town, so I was pretty sure he'd just parked his truck in the wrong spot. Bees were known to feel attracted to cars because of the warmth of the engine. Hopefully, they were now in their more natural habitat.

"I didn't think you were shutting down early today," Liam said.

"I'm not, what makes you say that?"

A smile spread on his lips.

"So you're saying you had a shower and changed into clean clothes so you can get dirty again during your lesson with the hot writer?"

I stared at him. "What? No. I stank from working all day, and I don't expect there to be much to do for the rest of the afternoon. And it's just polite to not smell like an engine when you're around other people."

He snorted. "Sure, boss. Whatever you say."

"Besides, how do you know he's hot?"

"I'm straight, boss. Not blind."

He didn't give me time to reply before he waved goodbye and ran out of the garage, saying he'd see me in the morning.

I looked at my reflection in the glass panel of my office. Did it seem like I'd made an effort?

Despite Liam's teasing, the reason I'd cleaned up before Aiden arrived was because I'd once again spilled oil all over me. Give me a bike and I was a surgeon; give me a car and I was a fucking klutz.

The phone in the office rang, but we had a cordless unit in the garage to stop us from getting our dirty hands all over the paperwork, so I walked over to the workbench and picked it up.

"Warren Automobile and Bike Repair, how can I help you?"

The chuckle from the other side made me straighten my back. "Who is this?"

"Hey, babe, it's just me."

"What do you want, Mike?"

I grabbed a wrench from the wall and squeezed it tight in my hand. The cold, hard metal a good reminder of where I was. " Why are you calling?"

My voice was steady enough, so that was good. I put the wrench back when it felt warm in my hand and picked another one.

"You put the phone down on me the other day." His voice was whiny, and it grated on me. Had he always been like this? Had I been so in love that I'd blocked it out?

"I told you I'm not interested in revisiting the past, and I'm struggling to come up with any kind of valid reason for us to be in touch."

"That's really hurtful, bab—"

"Don't call me that. Use my name and tell me what you want, or I'll hang up."

There was a brief silence on the other side.

"Why don't we speak more often, ba—Slade?"

I chose another wrench, but this time I brought it to my forehead. As ridiculous it was, the tools were actually grounding me. Or at least stopping me from blowing a gasket.

"Walking into our apartment, coming face to face with a naked twink, who looked at me as if I was the one trespassing, and then being told you were a good fuck was not, surprisingly, the highlight of our marriage."

"You said you forgave me."

His outraged tone made my blood boil.

"I took responsibility for the break in our relationship. The betrayal, the cheating, that was all on you." I hung up the call, bracing myself on the workbench.

I stared at the phone, willing it to stay silent because if it rang again, I'd need to go to the general store to buy a new one after I destroyed this one.

Maybe Mike knew it was best to stay away, or maybe having the truth slapped down the phone worked because there was no second call.

"Hey, Slade. Is this a good time? Am I too early?" Aiden asked, coming in from the street.

His smile was enough to change my mood and banish my ex so far out of my mind, I couldn't even remember why I was holding the phone in my hand.

"Perfect timing."

"I brought you a coffee and a cookie from Spilled Beans. Figured it was the least I could do. Indy said this is how you take your coffee. Milk, no sugar."

"He's a good kid," I said, taking the coffee and cookie from Aiden. "Thank you for these. I skipped lunch."

"He's not a kid."

"Who?"

"Indy. We're the same age, and I'm definitely not a kid."

I gazed into his eyes—he'd worn his glasses again— and even from a distance I saw the challenge.

"No," I said, taking a sip of the coffee. "You're not."

"Now we've established that, how do I look?"

I spat out the coffee. Fortunately, not in his direction.

"Why do I feel that it's going to be dangerous having you around?"

He shrugged, looking down at his clothes and back to me.

The black T-shirt he had on was probably new, but his jeans…fuck me, they looked soft as butter and fit him like a glove.

"I've had these jeans since college, so I don't mind if they get ruined. And I figured I'd go for black in case I got any oil on my shirt. I hear that happens a lot here."

I'd have spat out more coffee, but after his last comment, I'd put the coffee down on the bench.

"Those are good, and we'll see how funny you are when you start getting your hands dirty. Follow me."

He chuckled but followed. The size of the garage made it easier to claim a space to work on the bike exclusively. If we were going to do this; I wanted to do it right.

"You see the tape on the floor and the wall?"

Aiden nodded.

"This means nothing that belongs to a car or another bike will ever enter this space. I know it sounds a bit much, but trust me, when you have over one hundred parts laid out on the bench or on the floor, you don't want to be guessing where they came from."

"That makes a lot of sense."

I grabbed my digital camera and handed him a notepad.

"We're going to photograph the bike, so we know exactly the state it was in originally. Everything we do will be photographed."

"Okay, what's my job, boss?"

I didn't mind when Liam called me boss, but coming from Aiden's lips it sounded wrong, unfitting.

"You write what I tell you to. This part is for your benefit. When we print out the photos, you'll be able to match them to your notes. Think of it like building a bike bible."

"Thank you, that's…really helpful. Do you not need to know what each photo is?"

"No," I said, trying but failing to keep the smugness from my voice. "I know the name of each part on this bike, down to the size of the nuts and bolts."

"Wow…" Aiden ran his hands through his hair and looked at the bike. "This is never going to work, is it?"

"What do you mean?"

"Maybe I should pick another profession for my character."

I put my hand on his arm to grab his attention.

"We need to make the most of this lighting before I shut the door. Help me with the photos, and we'll talk about that after, okay?"

Aiden nodded, still looking pensive. Yes, he could pick another profession for his character, but I'd read too many books with doctors, baristas, Navy Seals. Maybe it was stupid, but knowing there would be at least one romance novel out there with a mechanic made my profession feel visible. Like we existed not just to fix people's vehicles, but also as people who could find love. Even if only on paper.

8

AIDEN

I FOLLOWED Slade around while he took hundreds of photos, but I couldn't find the excitement in it anymore.

He told me what each piece was, and I wrote it all down. Then he started removing parts from the bike and placing them neatly on the bench.

"These need to be powder-coated, we need a full engine rebuild, and—" Slade stopped and looked at me.

"Sorry, do you mind repeating that? The powder thing?"

He glanced back at the bike, and said, "You know what, let's finish for the day. We've done enough work."

"No, no, it's okay, we can carry on." I raised my notepad to show him I was ready to make more notes. "What's powder…um…thingy, anyway?"

"Powder-coating is a type of coating you apply to metals such as aluminum extrusions, drum hardware, cars, bikes, and bicycle frames. It creates a hard finish that's tougher than conventional paint."

"Okay…wait…" I wrote everything down quickly before I forgot. "Got it. Thanks."

"Aiden."

"Hmm?"

"Let's finish here. Do you want to go for a walk?"

It wasn't sunny anymore, but it was still light outside. "Sure."

I placed the notebook on the bench and waited while Slade returned the camera to his office and did the necessary checks to close the garage.

Movement from the door to the street caught my eye, but when I went to check, I didn't see anything.

"Ready?" Slade said from behind me.

"Yeah."

We slid the long metal door shut and Slade set the alarm.

"Do you live far from here?" I asked.

"I live above the shop, but there's a separate entrance."

As we walked past it, I noticed for the first time the gate to a small alleyway with a staircase at the end.

"It's nice being so close to the shop, but I miss riding to work. Where are you staying?"

"At the Old Mill."

"Oh yeah? Nice place. If the shop hadn't come with its own place, I'd have definitely considered those apartments."

The road had a curve at the end, so it wasn't until we'd gotten closer that I saw it didn't lead to another street but to a forest. A river ran between the trees and the houses, like a border to separate man from nature.

"This must be the river that runs past my apartment," I said.

We crossed the small bridge toward the forest where there was a path running alongside the river.

"That's right. We can stay on this side almost all the way to the Old Mill, then we cross again," Slade said. "If you talk to me about what was bothering you earlier, I might even buy you dinner at Benny's."

His voice was soft and low, like a caress.

I focused on the rapid flow of the water so I wouldn't have to look at Slade as I spoke.

"It's nothing big, really. My mind just went from zero to a hundred and I was overwhelmed. It happens sometimes when I can't process information in a way that makes sense. My brain is wired for storytelling. And don't get me wrong, I love research, but if I can't fit it into the story in my head, then it's like...I don't know, frustrating."

"Which part overwhelmed you?"

A hollow laugh escaped me. "All the nuts and bolts. You mentioned all the parts and suddenly my brain realized that I'll never know enough to write a credible character."

Slade put his hand on my shoulder.

I stopped and stared at him, happy to see understanding in his blue eyes. He wasn't going to make fun of me.

"That's not true, Aiden. Do you have a medical degree? Because Doctor Misha could give me a physical any time."

I laughed at his reference to a character in one of my books.

"You should see who I used for inspiration."

"Hmm, maybe not, I'd rather imagine him in my own head. But am I right?"

I shrugged. "I guess."

"Why don't you tell me a little about your character and your story? I promise I won't share it with anyone. I don't even have a social media account."

Damn the man and his thoughtfulness.

I needed to remember that it was only acceptable to find him attractive. He was the definition of a hot silver-fox. Books should be written about how soft his beard looked, how blue his eyes were, or how the muscles in his arms moved under his white work T-shirt.

But that was it. Just because he was sweet and thoughtful didn't mean anything other than he was a decent human being. *And* just because my life, until I arrived at Chester Falls, lacked in the decent human being department, it didn't mean I was going to latch on to Slade. And his sexy beard, or his arms, or...fuck.

"It's a second-chance romance between a biker and a teacher. They grow up together, then separate, meet again in their early twenties and have a fling, but something happens and they separate again. They meet ten years later when the biker has lost his husband to heart disease."

"That sounds like a great story. As long as you get the terminology right, no one will care to read the names of the parts. It's all about the love story, and that, I know for a fact, is something you excel at."

We continued walking, and I let his words sink. The path wasn't always close to the river and in some parts it went farther into the forest before winding back to the water's edge. At some point we came across a set of steps leading down to the water.

"Do people swim here in the summer?" The water flowed quite fast, but where the river wasn't as deep the sand bed beneath was visible and it didn't seem too dangerous.

"Yeah. I've seen kids jumping in and messing around, but only on really hot days."

What would it be like to use the world around you as your play-ground growing up? I'd lived in New York all the way until I escaped the claws of my parents' expectations and moved to San Diego. I'd traveled a lot, but I didn't remember ever feeling that free to explore the surroundings.

"You never answered my question yesterday," he said.

We crossed the bridge back to the other side, and I saw the Old Mill building and the bright neon sign for Benny's Diner.

"What question?"

"Did you read the book? I've had sleepless nights wondering."

I welcomed the change of topic as much as the warm breeze in the summer evening.

"I'm halfway. I get the reviews now."

"The ones that wish the author would slay his hands and never think a word again, let alone write it? Or the ones that think he's God's gift to literature?"

Slade wasn't wrong in his assessment of the two review camps. If that book were food, it would be pineapple on pizza.

"Hmm, I think I'll let you judge for yourself. I can give you the book at our next lesson."

Slade's grin revealed a perfect set of teeth that I was absolutely not imagining biting any part of my skin.

"Does that mean you won't give up on your story?"

I shrugged. "What can I say? This biker won't leave my mind alone."

He bumped my shoulder as we walked into Benny's.

Momma Ruth's food was, as always, amazing. How I ever survived in San Diego without this on my doorstep, I didn't know.

"What are you thinking about? You're staring at your steak as if you want to make love to it. I'm a little concerned," Slade said.

He had a crab roll and a salad, which also looked amazing.

"Are you afraid because you're going to walk home alone after dinner?" I took a bite of my steak and smiled as I chewed it.

"I am now," he said, laughing.

"I was thinking, where will I get this amazing food when I go back to San Diego."

"Is that where you're from?"

"No, I'm from New York. I moved to San Diego after college. How about you?"

He sat back and looked out the window toward the garden separating the diner and the Old Mill building. The sun was gone now, so I wondered how he'd get back home in the dark. Maybe there was a way through town.

"You know Wren from San Diego then?" Slade asked.

The avoidance of my question was as clear as if he'd written it on a piece of paper.

I leaned forward, putting my empty plate aside and crossing my arms over the table. The aluminum edge of the table was cold and dug into my arms.

"What's your story, Slade Warren?"

He smiled, but I could see it was forced. We'd only known each other a matter of days, so I had no right to press him for information. It didn't mean I wouldn't let my creative mind make something up.

I raised my hand before he spoke.

"You don't have an accent. My feeling is that this has helped you fit in everywhere you've ever been, and you've been to lots of places."

Slade's gaze cut into me, but there wasn't any anger in his eyes.

Confusion? Wonder? Maybe.

But anger? No.

I could work with that.

9

———

SLADE

I'D MET enough people in my forty-eight years that I was rarely surprised. I'd seen the best and the worst in people.

It was easy to understand people using my language. For instance, Mike was a bike. And if there was one thing I knew well, it was bikes. From the moment I'd laid eyes on him, I'd known all his parts, how each fitted into each other, and how to make the best of it.

Mike had been exactly what I'd needed at twenty-four. He didn't have a past, or anything to hide, so it had been easy to hold on to him and pretend I was like him. That there were not any ghosts chasing me. Our ride had been mostly smooth, at least I thought it had.

Aiden? Aiden was a car. It ran on the road, had an engine, breaks, and accelerator—just like a bike—except with Aiden I was a klutz, who didn't know how anything worked, as if I hadn't been around vehicles all of my life.

Four days after our dinner at Benny's, and I still had a feeling that around Aiden I'd end up with oil on my shirt more often than not.

I thought about the way he'd looked into my eyes, as if he could see past them and locate the soul I'd sold to the devil a long time ago.

There was something about Aiden. In some ways he was a little like Mike had been when we met, but he was also so different.

I was pretty sure Aiden was a four wheels kind of guy. He was safer, had room for more people, and he could go the distance. He was definitely not the guy for me. Or the guy I deserved.

Laughter bubbled from inside me and I couldn't help but let it out. It was a good thing Liam had gone home and Aiden wasn't here yet.

Why the fuck was I thinking about Aiden?

First of all, even though I didn't know exactly how old he was, he looked like he could be my son.

Second, he was in Chester Falls only for his research and to see his friends. I knew absolutely nothing about his life in San Diego. Maybe he even had someone to go back to when he was done with me and Chester Falls.

That particular thought made my stomach churn.

Stop it, Slade.

The only mystery I wanted to solve about Aiden was why he hadn't published anything in the last year, when he was such a talented writer. And if his next book depended on the research he was doing, then I was going to do my best to help him out. End of story.

"Hey, boss, sorry I'm late."

As always, Aiden came in wearing his worn jeans and black T-shirt, except this one had NYU in washed-out writing on the front. Why did he have to be so damned sexy?

The need to get up and kiss the shit out of him to the point his glasses were all foggy and wonky on his face was too strong. I picked up a wrench and went back to the bike. Thank fuck I was sitting on a stool.

"Not your boss. I'm not paying you, remember?" I said.

"Meh, depends on what currency you trade in."

I looked up and caught him staring unashamedly at my ass.

His eyes met mine and our gazes held for a second too long.

"So, where do you want me today?" he asked, breaking the spell.

I coughed. "What?"

"Damn, you're too easy to rile up," he said, leaning against the workbench with his hands holding on to the edge.

I walked over to him, leaving only a couple of inches of separation between us.

"You know," I said, lowering my voice and whispering in his ear. "Before you rile up a biker, you should know we either ride hard or stay home."

"And...um, which one are you?"

"Take a guess..."

When I moved my head back, I saw the bob in his Adam's apple, and I'd be damned if I didn't want to take a bite.

Aiden's eyes were a dark pool, drawing me in and willing me to drown in them.

"Hello? Cover up your tools, boys."

Tom's voice coming from the door made me jump away from Aiden so fast it was as if I'd been electrocuted.

Aiden snorted, but I was already walking toward Tom, hoping the bulge in my pants would go down extra quick.

"Hey, Tom. How can I help? Car trouble?"

Tom narrowed his eyes, surveying the area as if he were trying to find something suspicious. He would have, if he hadn't announced his arrival, because I'd been half a second away from testing Aiden's lips to see if they tasted as good as they looked.

"Nope, no car trouble. I was just...um...checking in on your work."

I crossed my arms over my chest. "Oh really? I didn't know you had an interest in bikes."

He had the decency to blush a little. Tom was a firecracker at the best of times, but I hadn't met anyone more genuine and generous while also being a little, insane ball of energy in a tiny, neat package.

His outfit for the day consisted of grey slacks and a bright-yellow button-down shirt which he had paired with a burgundy fedora. Tom was a one-man runway show, making the streets of Chester Falls brighter every time he walked past. Wren was a lucky guy.

"Me? Bikes? Nah. Not interested. I just wanted to make sure Aiden wasn't wearing anything unsuitable for this kind of messy work. I couldn't live with myself if I witnessed his Tom Ford shirt get ruined and didn't do anything to stop that crime from happening."

Aiden laughed and did a full turn for Tom's benefit. "Happy?"

Tom did a big sigh and ran his hand over his forehead.

"I'm going to pretend you're not wearing university-branded cotton."

I laughed, but it soon died in my throat when Tom approached slowly, circling around me.

"Blink once if you're scared and twice if I should run for my life," Aiden said.

Tom waved a hand, coming even closer. "Pah, you already have enough style, but Slade…he's like a rough diamond. A pearl straight out of the shell. Maybe I could—"

"The only thing Slade needs is a bike between his legs."

My eyes moved to Aiden, who'd covered his mouth with both hands, as shocked with his statement as I was.

Tom grinned. If it were possible for real life sparkles to shine out of someone's eyes, Tom's gaze was the proof.

He tipped his hat before he turned around and walked away muttering, "I hope for Wren's sake there's cupcakes at home."

I was frozen in place for a moment after Tom left, but when I finally turned to Aiden, he had his back to me and was sorting through the multiple boxes where we kept all the different small parts.

The bike engine needed to be removed today because I had someone collecting all the parts that needed painting, including the frame.

We worked in silence for a moment. Me removing as much of the small parts from the engine as I could before taking it all out, and Aiden applying WD40 to all the small pieces he bagged and labeled.

Tom's visit had caused an awkwardness to grow between us, and I didn't like that.

Aiden was usually chatty as he worked. He'd told me that when he's writing, he needed complete silence, but if he was doing something with his hands, he just couldn't keep his mouth shut.

His words had created a back and forth of comments between us. Just one of the many times we'd flirted all week. I couldn't explain it, but we'd found a rhythm of working and teasing each other that made the evenings go fast too quickly.

I found myself wishing every day away so the afternoon would come and it would be time for Aiden. And most evenings this week, we'd ended up having dinner together at Benny's.

"Can you give me a hand?" I asked, hoping I could gauge his mood if he was actually facing me.

"Sure."

I explained where he needed to hold the engine while I worked on the last few bolts.

"That's it…nearly there."

With the engine out of the frame, we packed up for the evening.

"Slade?"

"Yeah?"

Aiden cleaned his hands on a rag and looked at the empty frame of the bike.

"How does it feel? Riding a bike?"

I smiled. Riding a bike was like staring into Aiden's eyes. It was scary and exhilarating, pleasure and anxiety.

"Riding a bike is…life, Aiden. It's the scariest thing you can do, but also the most freeing. When you're on a bike, it's just you, the power between your legs, and the road. There are no expectations, no judgement, no history, no past. Sometimes there's no future, but you always have somewhere to go. The destination rarely matters, it's the journey that makes the difference."

I didn't realize Aiden had come closer until his arms wrapped around my waist and I was enveloped in a pine-scented hug.

My heart beat so fast that I wondered if I was at an age where I needed to see the doctor for it, but I knew it was all Aiden. He was the one bringing out all the feelings I mostly shied away from.

"Thank you," I said.

"What? No, I'm the one who needs to thank you for sharing that with me." He stepped away from my embrace and put his hands in the pockets of his jeans.

It was such an adorably Aiden gesture.

"Are you doing anything on Sunday?" I asked.

"Not particularly. Do you want to work on the engine? I've been reading the manual. You can test me on it."

That was another uniquely Aiden trait. Despite his initial lack of confidence about the challenge of rebuilding the bike, he'd made it his job to learn everything he could.

"Not quite. Meet me outside at ten on Sunday morning."

"Okay, what are we doing?"

"You'll see."

10

———

AIDEN

It didn't matter that I'd had a whole day before my date with Slade.

I ran through all my clothing options and still came up short on what to wear. If it wasn't for the certain inquisition I'd get from Tom about this supposed date, I'd have called for his help.

And I definitely did not need anyone else to blow this out of proportion.

I was doing that very well on my own, considering in my head I'd been calling this a date.

A date.

Just because he said we wouldn't be working on the bike.

Just because it was Sunday didn't mean this was a date.

And just because we nearly kissed before Tom interrupted us, it didn't mean Slade wanted to kiss me. At all. No matter how much I wanted to kiss him.

I'd spent the whole week sneaking peeks at him while we worked. I just couldn't help myself.

Slade was unlike any man I'd met before.

On the outside, he had this bad-boy biker look going on. I'd noticed the tattoos that peeked from under the short sleeves of his

60

work shirts and wondered if he had them only on his arms or else-where on his body.

His hair was a perfect mix of grey and white, shorter on the sides and back and longer on top, and then there was his long beard. Richard had always had a close shave, so I'd never considered how I might enjoy or appreciate facial hair on other men.

Slade was also kind and patient. Even after a whole day at work, he still had time for all my questions. He seemed to be going through the process of breaking the bike into its several parts, with the joy of a child playing with their favorite new toy on Christmas morning.

There was only one topic he'd avoided. Every time I mentioned motorcycle clubs, he changed the subject. He was nice about it, but I could tell it wasn't something he wanted to talk about.

Which, of course, meant I was even more curious about it, and him.

I arrived at his gate with five minutes to spare. My heart was beating so fast I thought I was going to pass out. Dammit, I should have had more than half a bagel for breakfast.

The big metal door to the garage was closed, as was the gate to the alleyway to Slade's place.

I couldn't see a bell either, but since we agreed to meet at ten, I figured he'd be down soon, so I sat on the concrete step outside.

More thoughts of Slade filled my head. Whatever the day brought, I was really excited to be spending more time with him. My new daily routine consisted of writing in the morning followed by research while I tried to not arrive at the garage so early that I'd come across as overly keen.

I was so lost in thought that when I felt a bump against my back, I jumped up from the step.

"What the—"

A kitten was on the other side of the gate, sitting on its back legs and staring at me.

"Hello, you. Was I in your way?"

I crouched to his level, thinking he'd probably scoot off to his home, but he just stood there roaring at me. He had a beautiful ginger coat and green eyes, but he was so small that he couldn't be an adult yet.

"Are you lost?"

He replied with another tiny roar.

"You have quite a big roar for such a little kitten," I said, reaching out to him slowly. "I hope you're not lost, buddy."

He stretched out his neck to meet my hand and bumped his head against my fingers. I turned my hand slowly to pet him, but suddenly he ran back toward the alleyway.

A minute later I saw Slade come down the stairs at the end of the alleyway holding a bunch of stuff.

"Hey. Sorry, I realized too late that you didn't have my number and there's no doorbell. I hope you weren't waiting long."

My brain struggled to form words at the sight of Slade in black jeans, a white T-shirt, and a leather jacket.

"No, not waiting long…um, just got…here. What have you got there?"

"This jacket is for you to wear and this is your helmet," he said.

"My what?"

He chuckled. "Hold these, I'll be right back."

When my brain caught up, I laughed to myself. Surely he didn't mean—

"He fucking did."

Fortunately, he didn't hear me over the noise of the big, badass bike.

I was still staring at him when he parked the bike to close the gate. Was that the right term? Do bikes get parked? Or is it a different term?

Slade appeared in my line of sight.

"You look a little terrified… Okay, a lot. You don't have to do this, but I thought it would be fun for you to experience what it's like to ride on a bike."

"I am…terrified." The bike was big and sturdy. Newer than the one we were working on, but still a Harley. Still only two wheels.

Before I could change my mind, I gave him my helmet so I could put the jacket on. It was surprisingly light. Then I put the helmet on my head but couldn't figure out how to fasten it.

"Here. Let me do it," Slade said, taking over with the expertise of someone who'd done it a million times. I tried to ignore the little sparks I felt when his fingers brushed against my skin.

He put his helmet on and straddled the bike.

"Damn."

"What's up?"

"Do you have a pair of sunglasses?" I asked.

"Yes."

"Put them on."

He raised a brow but did as I asked.

I took my phone out of my pocket and snapped a photo.

"Thank you, god. I'll never ask for anything ever again," I said to myself, pocketing the phone.

"My name's Slade, and those who don't ask, never get."

His teasing smile was what wet dreams were made of.

"I think I need a cold shower," I muttered as I tried to get on the bike behind him in the most gracious way I could. Mission failed.

"Maybe later, if you're good," he said.

"Damn it, Slade, if you're gonna look like my teenage fantasy and talk like it too, you better come through."

He laughed and told me to hold on tight.

I kept my eyes closed to start with because I was terrified that if I opened them, I'd throw up from fear. Especially as Slade navigated the tight streets of Chester Falls.

When it seemed we were on a straight road, I loosened my grip around Slade and opened my eyes.

Everywhere around us was green. Green fields, pastures, hills. It was beautiful. The rumble of the bike was loud, but after a while, I got used to it and it became almost soothing. I didn't realize how smooth it could be to ride a bike.

I didn't know how long or far we traveled because at some point Slade put his hand over mine and left it there. I leaned my head against his back and just enjoyed the ride.

We occasionally traveled through towns, but mostly through the countryside. I stopped trying to make sense of our destination or direction until Slade took a turn to a small track and stopped the bike under the shade of a tree.

My legs were shaking with adrenaline when I came off the bike, so I sat on a patch of grass nearby. We were in some kind of forest, but the trees were spaced enough apart that sunlight still came through the branches.

Slade took my helmet and his and hung them on the handles of the bike. Then he sat next to me.

His eyes had never looked so blue before, his smile so candid. He had never looked so free.

Maybe it was the adrenaline still rushing through my veins, but before I could think too much about it, I straddled Slade and pressed my lips against his.

His hand came up to rest on the back of my neck to keep me exactly where I was. As if I had any intention of going anywhere.

Slade's lips were ridiculously soft and his beard was a little rough against my skin, which only served to make the kiss a thousand percent hotter.

I wanted his mouth everywhere on me; I wanted his beard to scratch me head to toe.

Breathing was so overrated. Who needed to draw a breath when we could live on each other's taste forever?

I deepened the kiss, running my tongue over his lips and sucking them into my mouth, first the top one and then I dragged my teeth over his bottom one, pulling it.

Slade let out what sounded like a growl and flipped us around so he was on top of me.

The squeaky sound of his leather jacket, how he owned my mouth, the way his bigger body was heavy on top of me...I needed more and I needed less. Less clothes, more Slade.

This was getting out of control. Would taking this farther be taking it too far?

When Slade stopped the kiss, leaning his forehead on mine, we were both breathless.

I stared into his eyes and they were no longer blue. They were as dark as night, and I'd be damned if I didn't want a sleepover.

11

SLADE

"AIDEN," I whispered, still trying to control my breathing and my raging hard-on.

He placed his hands on either side of my face. They were soft, and I couldn't help turning to kiss one palm and then the other.

"Don't say we shouldn't." His voice was low. As though if the world around us discovered what we'd done maybe it would start meaning something.

I nodded, but I knew we shouldn't. Aiden was too young, too good for me, and I could never be the person he deserved.

Not that it had stopped me from claiming him like a wild animal.

Once his lips had touched mine and he'd ran his fingers through my hair, pulling it so tight my scalp still hurt, I would have had to be a saint to be able to resist Aiden.

And one thing I knew for sure, I'd never claimed to be a saint. Quite the opposite.

The thought that he'd gotten as lost in the kiss as I had, made me feel like a man half my age. I couldn't remember the last time I'd kissed like that, the last time I had been kissed like that.

"Why did you bring me here?" he asked.

I stared into his big, brown eyes. He'd worn his contacts, so I could see from this close how beautiful his eyes were, so deep, with a dark-blue ring around the iris.

To prove to myself I really wasn't a saint, or maybe that I'd just lost all self-control around Aiden, I kissed him one last time before standing on my knees and bringing him up with me.

Even though this was a fairly unknown spot—something I'd assumed from the lack of seeing anyone else around whenever I came here—I made sure the bike was locked properly.

I took the two helmets from the handle and told Aiden to follow me. We didn't have to walk farther than a hundred yards to get to the spot I wanted to show Aiden.

We were on higher ground, looking into the valley below.

This was my thinking place. It was peaceful and undisturbed.

Coming here served as a reminder of how lucky I'd been. Still was. My fate could have been so different if I'd carried on the destructive path of my youth.

When I was here, I knew I'd made at least one good decision in my life.

"Wow, is that lavender?" Aiden asked as soon as we got to the top of the small incline.

"Yes. That's Reed's farm."

"Reed… Isn't that where Indy and Tate got married?"

"Yeah." Most of the time I'd spent with Aiden was just us, so I'd forgotten he knew the guys due to being friends with Wren.

"I thought we were farther away from Chester Falls. Isn't Reed's farm only half an hour away from town?" he asked.

"Yeah, we're quite close. We went in a big circle to give you the riding experience, but I wanted to bring you here."

Aiden closed his eyes and inhaled the lavender-infused breeze.

I wanted to put my arms around him, inhale his scent, and lick that spot of exposed skin between the collar of his shirt and his hairline.

In the sunlight his skin was even more perfect. So white, smooth, soft. I imagined Aiden wasn't the kind of man to mark his skin with tattoos. Not that there was anything wrong with tattoos. I had plenty and liked them, but the thought of exploring Aiden's unmarked skin made me lightheaded.

"Slade."

"What?"

"You're looking at me like you want to eat me. Should I be worried?"

I scratched my beard and ran my fingers down to straighten it. Aiden's eyes followed my hand as if he wanted to do it himself.

"Only if you have issues being mauled by an old man with very little self-restraint around you."

He turned his back on the view to face me and ran his hands up my chest slowly before grabbing on to the collar of my jacket.

"First of all, you're not old—"

"I'm forty-eight."

"Thank you for telling me, but I don't care about your age. I'm thirty, by the way, so you're not exactly cradle snatching."

I smiled.

"And second, I am very up for being mauled."

"Oh, Aiden…" I let my words hang because I didn't know what else to say. This man was something else. "How about we grab some lunch? There's a place not far from here. They do good food."

"Sounds excellent."

The roadside diner wasn't as busy as I'd seen it before, maybe because it was still a little early for lunch, so instead of sitting at the bar, I led us to a booth.

"Do you do this often?" he asked.

"I try to ride on Sundays. There aren't as many tractors on the roads that I like to take."

"When did you start riding?"

The waitress came to take our order, so I waited until she was gone.

"I was fourteen. The guy living next door to my foster parents had a bike and was always working on it. He'd leave his garage door open. There wasn't much to do outside of school, and my parents couldn't afford to send us to after-school classes or do sports, so I started hanging out with him. When I turned fifteen, I got my learner's permit and he taught me everything he knew."

"I can imagine you as a little kid, hovering over the biker dude, asking a million questions, and dying to ride a bike."

I laughed. "How do you do that?"

"Do what?"

"How do you know...me?"

I wasn't sure I wanted him to answer the question, but it was the second time he'd assessed me correctly, as if he'd been there all my life.

He shrugged. "It's all written in your eyes. You just need to learn how to decode it."

Our food came—putting an effective stop to our conversation—piping hot and looking as delicious as every other meal I'd had on the few occasions I'd stopped there.

"Oh my god, this is amazing. Jesus, between this place and Benny's, I'm seriously considering moving to Chester Falls."

I examined his expression to see if there was any real truth or intention in his statement, but Aiden was focused on dipping chunks of the homemade sourdough into his soup.

Would he really consider moving to Chester Falls? As an author, I guessed he could work anywhere, but since he'd already moved from New York to the west coast, maybe he didn't want to move back east again.

And why was I thinking about it as if it could happen?

The waitress came over to refill our coffee.

"Can I interest you in a slice of pie?" she asked. "Today's special is my great-grandma's cherry pie."

Aiden's face lit up. "Is it really?"

"Nah, I got the recipe off the internet, but I can tell you it's better than my great-grandma's pie. Legend goes that she was a terrible cook."

"Two slices please," I said. "And can you put two more in a box to go?"

"Sure thing, Daddy."

Aiden was struggling to keep a straight face after the waitress left.

"Um...anything you want to share...Daddy?"

There was a glint in his eyes. I liked that. I liked that a lot.

"Look around. The girl can't be older than twenty. Half the men here are old enough to be her dad."

"Uh huh, if you say so…Daddy." The way he said the word as he held my gaze under his spell was enough to get my dick hard again.

I wasn't into Daddy kink, or that kind of role play, but I had a feeling I'd be into anything with Aiden if he ever asked for it.

He chuckled. "You are a lot more transparent than you think, Slade Warren."

"While you are still a mystery to me, Aiden Lawton."

"I'm anything but a mystery. In fact, a few google searches will tell you anything you need to know."

Despite his smile, and how casual he tried to sound, I still detected a hint of unease.

"I can guarantee that what I want to know about you can't be found on an internet search," I said, reaching out for his hand over the table.

He gave it to me, no questions asked. I ran my thumb over his knuckles before drawing circles over the back of his hand.

"Aiden, I need you to know I wouldn't look you up and invade your privacy like that. Not even before I met you." He nodded and a small smile graced his lips. "But if you tell me there's a sex tape out there, then I have a cupboard full of popcorn at home."

A piece of bread flew in my direction, but I was quick enough to catch it midair and stop it from hitting anyone sitting behind me.

I put the bread in my mouth and grinned.

"You're an animal," he said.

I winked at him. "About that sex tape…"

He bit his lip.

Fuck.

12

AIDEN

Of course there was no sex tape. Not that Richard hadn't asked on multiple occasions if we could tape ourselves having sex, but I'd always said no.

It didn't mean I couldn't tease Slade though, but a group of men walking in the diner got my attention.

"Oh my god, Slade, are those real-life bikers?"

He looked behind him to the door where the men wearing leather vests with patches sewn on them had grouped by the bar. The waitress pointed toward a booth on the far side of the diner and they all followed the guy that came in first.

"Do you think they'd be willing to talk to me?"

"No!"

Slade's answer was so abrupt that I turned my gaze from the bikers to him.

"Why?" I frowned and crossed my arms.

So far he'd avoided all my questions about bikers. Anything about motorcycles he'd spell out the equivalent to a ten-page essay for the smallest question. When I wanted to know about bikers, he clammed up.

Well, I had a book to write, and my career was on the line, so if he couldn't help me, then I'd find someone who could.

"You don't want to mess with bikers, Aiden."

His tone was so unyielding it was getting on my nerves. I was tired of half-answers.

"Why? Because they're dangerous?"

"Yes."

"Are you saying that all bikers are dangerous? Because that's incredibly judgmental. I don't want to know what activities they get involved in. I want to know how they function as a unit, how do they find each other, and how they decide who's in and who's out."

He looked behind him again. One of the bikers was back at the bar talking to the waitress. They seemed friendly enough. I tried to read the patch on the back of his vest.

The letters were too close together, but I could make out *The Lost Puppies*, and then under a logo, which looked like a dog, it had *Connecticut*. A motorcycle club named The Lost Puppies couldn't be all that dangerous, could it?

"Aiden," Slade's voice was calm, but I could detect the underlying unease. "Biker clubs *earned* their reputation. Think about that. Can't you find what you need for your book on the internet?"

"No."

"Fine." He got up from the booth and put some money on the table. "Go talk to them and come find me when you're done." Then he turned around and left.

What the fuck?

My blood that had been simmering under the surface came to a boil. I took the money to the bar and gave it to the waitress. She tried to give me the pie slices, but I couldn't think of anything food related right now. I told her to keep the pie money as a tip.

Slade wasn't by his bike, so I walked around and saw a path leading to an empty kids' playground. I found him sitting on the back of a bench on the other side.

"Got what you need?" he asked, standing up and not looking at me.

"Of course not, you dumbass."

He raised his eyes to meet mine.

"Do you think I was going to approach a group of men I don't know to ask them those kinds of questions just like that? Do you think I'm that stupid? Especially after you warned me?"

His shoulders sagged a little, but I wasn't backing down. I needed an explanation.

"I take it they're not that dangerous, considering you walked out knowing there was a possibility I might approach them."

The twitch of his lip told me I was right.

"Dammit, Aiden, what do you want?"

I went over to him and put my hands on his jacket, forcing him to look me in the eye.

"Would they have answered my questions?"

"No."

"Why?"

"Because they have a code of conduct and you're not part of them."

"And how do you know that?"

His eyes left mine briefly before they returned full of pain.

"Because I used to be one of them."

The statement didn't surprise me. The fact he didn't want to talk about it made me wonder how much he really knew about motorcycle clubs and why he didn't seem to be in one.

"You used to be in that club?" I asked.

"No, not that one." He took a deep breath. The wrinkles around his eyes suddenly seemed deeper. "It was a long time ago, Aiden. It's a part of my life that I don't want to remember. I did things I'm not proud of. But it's in the past. I've already shared with you more than I ever shared with anyone else. Doesn't that count for something?"

I went on my tiptoes—because the man was a freaking giant—and kissed him. He relaxed and allowed me to deepen the kiss.

When his arms went around me, I knew we were okay...well, sort of.

"Slade, I don't want you to ever do anything that is painful to you.

I know this might seem like just a book to you, but this is the most important thing I have in my life right now. I need to make it right."

He nodded. "Maybe I can help you." I smiled and was going to thank him when he put his finger over my lips. "I can't promise I'll be able to answer all your questions, but I'll try."

"Okay."

"In return I need you to make me a promise."

"Okay."

"If there is something I can't tell you, it's because it could put your safety in jeopardy. It means you can't go ask anyone else, especially not random bikers you might find at roadside diners."

"I promise," I said.

"Just like that?"

"Just like that."

Whatever was in his past was in his past. Maybe he'd done stupid or dangerous stuff, but I trusted him.

When we got back to the bike, he helped me put my helmet on. I wasn't stupid enough to admit I'd figured out how to do it on my own. Having Slade's hands on me beat not having them on me any day.

He put his own helmet on and then grabbed my hand and placed the keys to the bike in my palm.

A rush of excitement and nerves went up my spine. "Are you serious?"

"A little bit too much sometimes, or so I'm told," he replied.

I went to punch his shoulder, but he anticipated my move and wrapped his arm around my waist. The rush that went up my spine turned into lust when he nuzzled my neck and sucked my exposed skin.

"I bet you're gonna look so hot riding that bike," he said into my ear, just before he sucked my lobe.

"I won't be able to drive if my brain is a puddle of mush by our feet. Keep doing that, and I'll forget how to walk, let alone drive this thing," I said. I didn't move away from his touch though.

It felt so damned good, and I was not a stupid man. Well, not always.

"Ride it, Aiden. You're gonna ride it."

"I fucking hope so," I muttered to myself and forced a separation before I did something that would give the people in the bar a show and us arrested.

He chuckled and pointed to the bike.

I straddled it first and he got on behind me.

"Okay, what do I do?"

"First you need to unlock the bike. Put the key in the fork lock right over there." He pointed to the side of the bike under the handle.

The bike wobbled a little when I unlocked it, but Slade put his hand on the handle to keep it steady. My hands shook from nerves.

"I'm going to crash."

Slade laughed.

"I hope you enjoyed your time on this planet. Did you ever think you'd die at the hands of your favorite author?"

He turned my head around to face him and kissed me senseless.

"I can think of worse ways to go than on a bike with my all-time favorite author, but we're not gonna die. At least not before you have a chance to ride me."

I groaned. "Fuck me, Slade."

"I plan to, baby. Now stop freaking out. I'm here to help you."

"Wait," I said, "Are you saying that to distract me?"

He traced my lips with his thumb, and then groaned when I opened my mouth and licked it. "It's really not in my best interests to have you distracted, Aiden. I can ride if you're too anxious."

I turned around and steadied myself. "Nope, I'm doing this."

"Okay, open the door on the ignition switch, put the key in, and turn it to the right."

I jumped when the bike started and felt Slade laughing behind me. I'd have elbowed him, but I was too scared of what was coming to focus on payback. He'd have that later, with a cherry on top.

And by cherry, I meant me.

Slade's height proved useful because he was tall enough to reach the side of my head and talk to me. He also helped me to get going by showing me how to use the handles and the brakes. It was a little weird at first, but as soon as we got on the road, it was much easier, and I found my own stride.

"Woohoo!" I shouted. "Let's get home and get naked!"

Oops, did I say that aloud?

13

SLADE

Okay, I was officially impressed. Not only had Aiden learned how to ride the bike in no time at all, but he also seemed to be a natural.

Curves were tricky for a beginner, and I'd been ready to help him, but he seemed to have figured it out all on his own.

Not that the road to Chester Falls was particularly challenging, but damn, I was so proud of him.

I was also fucking hard to the point of being painful.

We had to contend with the town traffic, but forty minutes after leaving the roadside bar, we were pulling up at the Old Mill.

Despite having openly flirted with Aiden, I didn't want to make assumptions. Hell, flirting wasn't even it. I'd categorically said I wanted to fuck him.

He'd been partially correct, I was trying to distract him. It just so happened I was also telling the truth. After that first kiss, I knew there was no way I could resist Aiden. If he was up for some fun, I wasn't going to say no.

When Aiden stopped the bike, I helped him turn it off and lock it.

He removed his helmet and ran his hand over his hair before turning his head around. His eyes were filled with anticipation, heat, and uncertainty.

"Um…do you want…would you like…um, do you want to come up for a coffee?"

I smiled and removed my own helmet. "I'd love to."

We walked silently side by side to the main entrance of the building.

Ollie, the town gardener, was on the lawn in front of the building watering the flowers while barefoot.

"Hey, Ollie, how's it going?" I asked when he waved.

"Good, good. Always good when the sun is shining and the flowers are thirsty. Growing takes a lot of effort," he said.

"You're preaching to the choir, Ollie."

He turned his head sideways, his gaze going between me and Aiden. "Mmhmm, I don't know, sometimes growing can be a lot of fun too."

He reached out to a box he had nearby and took out a small bag. "Here you go. Plant these in a pot by your window. They're tough little plants, so even if they don't get lots of attention growing up, they always seem to shine through in the end."

I took the bag from Ollie, unsure of what to say.

He waved us off and we waved back. Ollie was a funny old character. No one was quite sure how old he was because with every conversation he always imparted some bite of wisdom, but he also looked weirdly youthful. Maybe that was what working with nature did to you.

I followed Aiden through the main door of the building and into the elevator. Throughout the ride up, he kept moving his weight from one foot to the other.

Everyone knew coffee didn't really mean coffee, but what if he *really* meant coffee and now he wondered if I thought we were having coffee or having *coffee*?

I hadn't been with someone in such a long time that I'd forgotten all the rules. To be honest, I'd never played by any rules because I'd never played.

With Mike I'd been straight with him from the get-go. I'd told him that if we were working together and fucking, he'd better tell his uncle. I'd expected him to back off before anything started, but my straight forwardness only spurred him on.

After Mike, I'd only been with a handful of men. Not quite hookups, but also not quite relationships. And I'd been as open with them as I'd been with Mike.

I followed Aiden down a long corridor, appreciating the architecture of what had been left from the old textiles mill that gave the building its name.

Aiden stopped so suddenly that I nearly bumped into him.

"I don't want coffee," he blurted out.

"Okay."

His eyes were wide and his breathing was coming in short bursts, as if he couldn't quite believe what he'd just said. He stared straight ahead, which meant he was staring right at my chest.

"So…no caffeinated drinks," I said.

He nodded.

It didn't take more than a small move to have him against the wall. I braced against it with one hand and ran the other gently up his neck, caressing his sharp jaw and tilting his head up.

"Maybe soda?" I teased.

He shook his head.

I didn't know where this shy Aiden had come from all of a sudden, but he was fucking adorable. Still sexy as hell though. But there was no way we'd do anything he didn't want or wasn't ready for.

"Cake?"

He shook his head again. "No cake."

"Damn, I didn't even get pie earlier."

Aiden's brown eyes darkened and a smile teased his lips.

"Where's the Aiden that wanted to ride me?"

"He abandoned me."

"Oh really?" I took his hand in mine and laced our fingers. "Is this the hand that commanded my bike so perfectly? That knew when to brake smoothly or accelerate?"

He nodded.

I kissed his hand, and then using my knee, I coaxed him to spread his feet wider, wedging my thigh between his legs. His hardness gave me the confidence to carry on.

"Are those the thighs that kept us stable on the straight road and made the bike hug each curve?"

He closed his eyes. His mouth parted slightly as he leaned his head back against the wall.

I wanted to suck on that perfect skin, kiss those lips I now knew to be softer than cotton candy and just as sweet.

"Then, *that* Aiden is here. The question is... Does he still want me?"

"All the Aidens want you, Slade," his voice was almost a whisper.

A cough made me jump away from Aiden, although I didn't know why I bothered because there was no way to explain why we were basically eye-fucking against a wall.

"Tristan...hi," Aiden said.

I never thought it was possible for someone to go that red, but Aiden managed it just by looking at Tristan's all-knowing smile.

"So..." Tristan said, pointing at both of us. "I like it. I really like it. Now, I know you don't need the talk about the birds and the bees, so you're off the hook."

He scratched his hair, pretending to think carefully about his next words.

"I'll give you a free full car service if you wait at least twenty-four hours until you tell anyone what you saw here," I said.

"Twenty-four hours?" Aiden screeched.

"Aid, there's a five hundred percent chance he snapped a photo of us and sent it to Ben before he gave his presence away."

Aiden's chin fell, and I wasn't sure if it was because of me openly giving him a nickname or because, from the expression on Tristan's face, I'd been right on the money.

"I guess it's only fair. You're lucky I'm not married to Tom, or you'd have your wedding planned and your children's names picked by now. As you were..."

Tristan walked down the corridor and pressed the elevator button. Since we'd just gotten off of it, the doors opened straight away. He wedged his foot to keep them open and said, "Oh, you might want to accept the invite to come out with the guys on Friday."

"What does he mean?" Aiden asked. "Wait, let's go into the apartment before we have any more weird encounters."

I followed him inside. Aiden had said he was renting the apartment from someone who was away, so that accounted for all the elements that made the place feel really homey, but it was all the papers, notepads, and laptop on the dining table that made the place Aiden's.

"Do you want a drink?" he asked.

"I thought you didn't have any drinks available." I put my hands in my jeans pockets, mirroring him. He was going to have to make the first move if he wanted anything to happen between us, but I'd be damned if I wasn't going to show how much I really wanted him.

He looked at my growing bulge and walked toward me. With one hand he pushed me backward until the backs of my legs touched the couch.

I sat down and was surprised when Aiden straddled me for the second time that day.

If he was going to make a habit of this, I'd need to invest in sweatpants. Easier access and more room to move.

Aiden rested his hands on my chest and sat back on my legs.

"About Tristan…"

"What about him?" I asked.

"Is he really going to tell everyone he saw us?"

I tried to see in Aiden's expression if this was something that worried him. I understood that it could be an issue because he wasn't exactly an unknown person.

"He was mostly teasing, but he won't tell anyone if we ask him," I reassured him.

"Would it bother you if they knew?"

I chuckled. "I'm too old to care about what people think."

"There you go again with the age thing. Do you have a problem with your age? Because I resent that on your behalf."

"How noble of you. My fragile ego thanks you."

His eyes scanned me from my head to my crotch. "There's nothing fragile about you."

"So you don't mind if they know who you're sleeping with?"

Aiden came so close that I felt his breath on my lips. "Who said anything about sleeping?"

He slammed his mouth against mine, which was when I gave myself permission to touch him.

Fucking finally.

"Jesus. Fuck, Aiden. You're going to kill me with how fucking sexy you are," I growled against his lips.

"Shh, no dying. I'm not done riding for the day."

14

———

AIDEN

I FELT like we'd been engaging in the longest foreplay in history since that first kiss this morning, and oh my sweet lord, what a kiss that was.

Slade's mouth was commanding, demanding, sweet, and tender. How did he set my body on fire with just one kiss?

So yeah, I was desperate for more, and I wasn't waiting another second for it.

I pulled away from Slade's mouth— using self-restraint that should earn me some kind of award—and tried to stand up, but he put his hands on my thighs.

"Where are you going?"

"Unless you have a self-lubricating dick, we're gonna need supplies," I chuckled.

He pulled me in for another kiss, biting my tongue gently before letting go. "I love your smart, sassy mouth, Aiden Lawton."

"You better have lost those jeans by the time I'm back...oh, and leave the jacket on."

I ran to the bathroom attached to the bedroom. When I opened my washbag, I realized that my condoms could well be out of date. I'd bought them as an act of rebellion after my relationship with Richard ended but hadn't actually used them.

82

Fuck, fuckity, fucks.

I turned one over, letting out a *fuck yes*, when I saw it was still good, then grabbed the bottle of lube from the bedroom and ran back to the living room.

My throat closed up at the sight of Slade almost fully naked on the couch, wearing just the leather jacket, a pair of red boxer shorts, and tattoos that definitely went beyond what I'd seen on his arms.

"Fuck my life, Slade, you're…fuck."

"I'm naked, that's what I am. And you're not."

I threw the supplies onto the couch next to Slade and started by taking my shoes off, nearly keeling over in the process.

"Slowly, Aid. I want to watch as you reveal your milky white skin to me."

"You mean pasty," I said. I'd always been quite self-conscious that I couldn't get a tan and now, facing a very naked Slade with his tan complexion and tattoos, I realized we couldn't be more different than a car and a bike.

He stood up and pulled me by the hand to come closer. "I've been wanting to see you naked since you stole that book from me—"

"Hey," I tried to argue, but he laughed and took my distraction as an opportunity to lift my shirt over my arms.

"As I suspected, you're perfect."

I traced the tattoos on his chest. There were so many that I'd need a lifetime to explore them all to my satisfaction. The thought gave me butterflies in my stomach. What the hell was I thinking? This was just sex between two people who clearly were extremely attracted to each other.

It was time to take control and stop the mushy thoughts.

I pushed Slade back onto the couch and he landed with a thump. Then I finished undressing until I was fully naked in front of Slade.

His eyes zeroed in on my cock and he wet his lips. I stroked my length, running my thumb over the crown and picking up a bead of precum.

Slade's eyes went impossibly dark when I raised my thumb to my mouth. "You want it?"

"Yes." His voice was breathy.

I kneeled between his legs and fed him my thumb, which he licked and sucked on as if it were my dick. I treated it as a promise, but not for that moment because I needed him inside me, stat.

"I never pinned you for a red underwear man," I said, running my hands up his thighs until the tips of my fingers ghosted over his erection.

He hissed. "Oh yeah? What did you pin me as?"

"Someone who likes to take control, but you'll give it up for the right man. Someone who isn't afraid to be himself. You're dark, sexy leather, but sometimes you're soft, silky satin."

I bent down to kiss his cock over his underwear. My mouth watered at the thought of sucking him and hearing him moan under my touch.

"Aid." His voice was raspy and full of need. Wren was the only person that had ever called me Aid, but the nickname coming from Slade's lips sounded so different. It was like a prayer only I could answer.

I pulled his boxer shorts down and under his ass until they were gone. His cock was thick and long, framed by a trimmed thatch of grey hair. I hoped he didn't mind that other than shaving my balls, I didn't trim my pubic hair.

His cock was heavy in my hand, like a satin-covered rod of steel. I cringed at my own thoughts, but once a romance author, always a romance author. And Slade's cock was very much romance-novel worthy.

"Are you going to suck it or write stories in your head about it?""

I looked up at him.

"I'm not the only one who's easy to read, Aid." He ran his hand over my head, gently. "And I definitely want to know what that dirty little mind of yours was thinking, but I'll get a complex if you don't actually—"

His words got stuck in his throat at the same time his cock went deep into mine. Because, apparently, I'd decided I had no gag reflex and wanted Slade's dick in my mouth so much that I couldn't wait to find out if I could fit it all in.

I couldn't. Of course, I couldn't. His romance-novel-worthy cock was too big, but fuck it felt amazing in my mouth. If only it were possible to have it in my mouth and get fucked by it at the same time.

"Aid, fuck…stop."

As soon as I released him, he pulled me up on his lap so I was straddling him again and kissed me until I failed to remember my name.

"What's wrong?" I asked.

"You were in another world. Jesus, Aid. I nearly blew in your mouth."

"You make it sound like it's a bad thing," I said.

"It is if you still want to…you know. My recovery time isn't what it used to be."

There was no way I'd tell him what I had in mind when I was sucking him, but the thought he nearly lost it made me hot all over.

He took a deep, steadying breath and ran his hands over my chest and down my belly until they reached my cock.

"God, you're so beautiful, Aiden."

"Says the sex-on-legs, hot silver-fox biker."

"You seem to have a thing for bikers," he said.

"I do now."

I rolled the condom down his length and added some lube to it. Then I ran a lubed finger over my hole.

Slade held me up. One of his hands stroked my length, while the other followed my hand as I prepped.

"Need to make sure you're ready," he said.

"I'm ready." I raised myself up on my knees and lined his cock with my hole.

"Aiden, that wasn't enough."

"Trust me, it's enough. I'm already stretched."

I felt my skin heat up even as I said the words, so I replaced the awkwardness of having to admit to using my toys while thinking of him, with something better.

"Fuck, you're so thick. Make me feel so full," I groaned as inch-by-inch Slade filled me. He was so hard and hot inside me that I needed to be careful or I'd come as soon as I moved.

My cock was hard and leaking between us.

I took Slade's mouth and kissed him with all I had while I held on to his hair. Only by distracting myself with his mouth would I be able to move again without setting off my orgasm.

Had it been so long since I'd had sex that my body was ready to explode in just a minute? Or was it because Slade was just so good?

"Jesus Christ, Aid. Ride me. Please, ride me."

As if he had to ask. I was building up to it. Every time I raised my hips and lowered myself down on him, his cock hit my prostate.

There was no description I could find in all my romance books for the sounds coming out of me.

I was desperate to come, afraid that it would end and I wouldn't get more, and amazed that sex could be this good. And then I looked into Slade's eyes. That blue, like the sky on a summer day.

His hair was all tousled from where I'd pulled it, his lips were red and swollen from my kisses.

My sexy silver-fox biker was hanging by a thread.

"I'm so close, Slade."

"Me too, baby. Let go. I'll be here to catch you."

So I did. My thighs burned from exertion, sweat ran down my back. My ass burned and my cock was ready to burst.

I leaned against Slade's chest and wrapped my arms around him, feeling the cool leather jacket under my hands. In that position he was able to fuck into me at the same time as I rode him.

With my cock trapped between us, it didn't take long until the friction set off my orgasm and I spilled all over his chest.

"Aiden." He screamed into my neck as he came.

I wanted to say something, anything to tell him how good it felt, but how could I explain that?

"Best sex of my life. You may have ruined me for other men. When can we do it again?"

"Likewise. Ditto. Anytime you want."

I sat up, wincing when I realized his dick was still inside me. I lifted a little to let him slide out.

"Did I…um…"

"Say that aloud? Yes, you did."

I hid my heating face with my hand.
"Well, I guess now we know," I groaned.
"We certainly do."

15

SLADE

"Morning, boss...whoa...do we need an emergency coffee run?" Liam said from under the hood of a truck.

I grunted. Okay, so I was a little late coming down to the shop this morning, so what?

"Seriously, Slade. You might want to look in the mirror."

"Why?"

"Just do it."

I groaned when I realized I was wearing my shirt inside out. "I was rushing this morning," I said as a way of explanation.

"Of course you were."

I ignored his comment and pulled the shirt over my head to turn it the right way.

"Damn, Slade. I didn't know you were hiding that under your shirt."

I sighed. Just what I needed right now. Wren Mason before coffee. Or should I be relieved I hadn't been caught semi-naked by Tom instead?

"How can I help you, Wren? I haven't made up my mind about the team. To be honest, I don't think I have the time."

He crossed his arms over his chest and smiled. Wren was wearing running shorts, so the scar on his knee that had ended his pro football career was visible.

"How's your knee? I injured my shoulder years ago, and even though I'm fully recovered, it still gives me trouble when the weather changes," I said.

I walked over to the office, where I had a tray with the day's jobs, to look for the right one.

Wren walked over and leaned against the desk.

"I went running with Aiden this morning," he said, ignoring my question.

"That's nice. I didn't know he was a runner too," I replied as casually as I could, even though I was leafing through the jobs without reading any of the information on the forms.

"Yeah. He seemed a little tired today."

When I didn't say anything, Wren continued.

"Maybe you've been working him too hard."

"He's an adult, he'll know when it's too hard."

Wren snorted.

"How's his research going?"

"Don't know. Well, I think. He's a fast learner."

For the love of god, I couldn't do this without coffee. Why did everything out of my mouth sound like an innuendo?

"There's something you should know about Aiden. He doesn't always know when to stop."

What did he mean? Stop what?

I wanted to ask the question, but that would raise more questions from Wren, and I wasn't sure his visit had purely good intentions.

"Thanks for letting me know. I'll make sure to go easy on him."

"Yeah, you do…that."

He patted my shoulder and left.

"Liam, I'm going to Beans. Do you want anything?"

"No, thanks, boss. Maggie's off work today, so we're having lunch on the square."

Since Liam and Maggie had gotten together, he was different. We weren't big talkers. I always thought that was why he had fit in here with me so well from the start, but he'd definitely opened up more recently. He was more relaxed, happy, and the times when I found him staring at a tool lost in thought were fewer and far between.

He'd lost his wife not long after they were married. He hadn't known until after she'd passed, that she was pregnant with their first child. I didn't need to know the circumstances around their passing to understand the severity of the loss.

So seeing Liam find someone to love again made me wonder about things I thought couldn't happen.

I wasn't going to pretend that being with Aiden yesterday was the start of a new happy-ever-after for me. Far from it. But I also couldn't deny how great it had been to ride with someone. Share my secret spot. Talk about bikes and riding. And the sex...

Fuck, the sex had been wonderful. Even that word fell short of describing how it had been.

Spilled Beans was unusually quiet for a Monday morning, with only a few customers sitting inside, no queue, and Indy was humming to himself while writing on a blackboard behind the counter.

"Hey, Indy."

"Oh, hey, Slade. How's it going?"

"Great, thanks. Where are your customers?"

Indy chuckled and leaned on the counter to whisper. "Jake had an appointment, and my part timer is at school, so I'm on my own. I put a sign out front saying we'll have fresh cinnamon buns at eleven. It's been a blissful morning."

I didn't doubt it. Indy's pastries were to die for, so I wouldn't be surprised to see a line forming just before eleven.

"In that case, I'll have my usual coffee and two lemon muffins, please."

"Coming right up."

The bell above the coffee shop door dinged with a new customer. My smile dropped when I saw Ben grinning at me.

"Morning, Indy. Morning, Slade," he said, extra chirpy.

I smiled and nodded.

"Oh, *two* lemon muffins. I see…you're sharing those with some-one?" Ben said in that casual tone that no one ever believes is casual. And of course, Indy raised his head from behind the display cabinet.

I was going to kill Tristan.

"I hear there might be an outing on Friday," I said.

"How do you know?" Indy asked with interest.

"A tall, nosy bird told me yesterday," I said, looking at Ben, who snorted.

Indy was clearly confused but confirmed their group of friends was going out to The Falls. "Are you joining us?"

"Yes, he is," Ben answered.

I took my coffee and muffins from Indy and put my money on the counter.

"Who knew I'd be back in high school at my age?" I asked and waved them goodbye.

Ben laughed.

"What was that about?" Indy asked, but I didn't hear his reply because I was already out the door.

The rest of the day was busy with customers picking up their cars and a couple of new bookings. I even spent an hour going through options for a customer who was interested in buying a Harley.

By the time Aiden walked in later in the afternoon, I was buzzing with energy and happy to have completed a chunk of tasks on my list.

"Hey," I said as he approached the checkout desk and came around the side where I sat on a barstool.

"Hey."

"Come here." I stretched out my hand until he was within reach, then I pulled him closer until he was between my legs, and kissed him.

Aiden tasted of coffee and smelled of pine, and if we weren't in my shop and risking being interrupted, I'd have already pulled his shirt up to touch his skin.

He was breathless by the time I released him.

"I…um…wasn't sure how…um, if we were going to do this again," he said.

"You mean, me staying at your place all night and sneaking out early this morning before being late for work wasn't enough to show you how much we're doing this again?"

He chuckled. "That was very college-like."

"I don't know, I didn't go to college. But it was definitely not very Slade-like."

"So we're...what are we doing? Sorry to sound like a lovesick teenager; it's not that at all."

I ran my hands over his hair. It looked too long for it to be his regular style, but I liked it. He closed his eyes when I pulled on it a little and sighed when I massaged his scalp.

"I know, Aid. Wren was here this morning."

He opened his eyes wide and tensed.

"You know they're gonna be on us like a pack of hungry wolves, right?"

"Oh god." He leaned his head against my chest. We already had a significant height difference, but this position with him between my legs, seeking comfort, made me feel things I hadn't felt in a long time.

"Aid, I know they have good intentions, but ultimately this is our business. We can tell them to back off. You know that, right?"

"Yeah, I know."

"We're two adults who happen to be ridiculously attracted to each other. I'd question your taste in men, but it's working for me, so I'll keep quiet." He slapped my chest, but I grabbed his hand and kissed it. "We're enjoying ourselves. That's it, right?"

"Right," he agreed. Something passed over his eyes, but it was gone too soon for me to see what it was. "I definitely enjoyed myself yesterday...multiple times."

I snorted.

My dick hardened at the thought of him riding me yesterday, and then how he'd taken us to the shower and sucked me until my dick came back to life before demanding I fuck him again.

My growing problem didn't go unnoticed by Aiden, who pressed closer against me and looked me in the eye, as if daring me to do something about it.

"Oh, Aiden, you're gonna be the death of me."

"But what a great way to go, right?"

I kissed his sassy mouth until he was all soft and pliant in my arms, which still didn't help my hard-on at all.

"Shop's still open, but we don't have any work to do on the bike, so what do you want to learn today?" I asked.

"Will you tell me what it's like to be in a motorcycle club?"

Hard-on sufficiently not hard anymore.

16

AIDEN

SLADE TENSED UP, but then he gave me a kiss and led me to the couch in the middle of the shop.

He rarely had any customers later in the afternoon after Liam went home, but I suspected that he just enjoyed being here, catching up with paperwork with few interruptions.

"Okay, what do you want to know?" he asked.

I shrugged. "I want to know so much that I don't even know where to start. How did you get into your club? How old were you?"

"Joining an MC, that's a motorcycle club, isn't easy. You need money and connections. Remember I mentioned my neighbor that taught me how to ride?"

"Yeah."

"I basically hung around his place any time I wasn't at school since I was fourteen. He taught me everything I needed to know about bikes and helped me find a part time job at a garage. My foster parents were so happy that I was able to help them out a little that they didn't ask any questions."

Slade was staring ahead at the bikes on display in front of us while I watched him tell his story. What he was saying sounded so wholesome and good. The story of the foster kid who learned a trade and helped out his foster parents, who were actually good people. But the way he spoke, the pain in his voice was clear.

I had a strong feeling that a lot of the small decisions Slade had made because of his passion for bikes had led him down a path he later regretted. Maybe he wouldn't tell me everything, but I had to remember that he was here with me now, and he was safe.

"When I turned sixteen, I was so excited that I could finally get my license. When I got home from school, I went over to his place and just walked in, as I always did. There were a few guys there all wearing leather jackets with patches. I'd never been so impressed in my life. Even though I had no clue who they were, I wanted to be like them. Eventually my neighbor told me about the motorcycle club. He was their Road Captain. I can give you a breakdown of the ranks, but it means he had an important role, and as such, people usually listened to him. "

"So you tried to join?"

"Yeah, but I was too young. You have to be an adult to join, and you also need money and connections. I had the connections part down because of my neighbor, but I didn't have the money."

Slade went on to explain how he worked over the next two years to save as much money as he could so he could join the club.

"Before you're a fully-fledged member of an MC, there are three stages you have to pass: hang around, prospect, and probation."

"Let me guess, you were already hanging around, so you went straight to the second stage," I joked.

Slade laughed. "Yeah, you're right. The clubhouse was outside of town, but for some reason they liked hanging around my neighborhood. When I turned eighteen, I already had enough money saved to join. I was sponsored by my neighbor and became a prospect."

I didn't miss that with all the information he'd shared so far, Slade hadn't actually said where he came from or the name of his neighbor. My curiosity spiked, but he was giving me the information that would help my story. The details were irrelevant.

"I guess after you became a prospect, everything changed for you."

"Yeah."

Slade went quiet, so I accepted that was as much as I'd get from him.

"Is this hard for you to talk about?" I asked.

"Not as much as I thought. It's mostly bringing back memories… I haven't talked about this in a very long time."

"I understand."

He smiled. "You know how tough everyone thinks bikers are?"

I nodded.

"The president was a neat freak. I mean, all bikers are a bit like that, but mostly with their bikes. This guy wanted everything around him in its place. So, more often than not, I found myself cleaning up after the guys and cleaning the clubhouse. I took such pride in it."

"Do you think that gave you something you didn't get at home?"

Slade looked at me with the same expression he had that first night at Benny's Diner.

"Yes. I didn't know it at the time. I thought I was being a rebel. When I finished high school, I started working full-time at the garage. I'd aged out of the system, so I should have been kicked out of my foster parents' home, but my mom got sick and they couldn't foster anymore. I stayed with them another year to help out around the house before I left."

"Why did you leave?"

"To keep them safe."

I reached out to run my hand through his hair, feeling nothing but relief when Slade leant into my hand. "Maybe we should—"

My words were interrupted by someone walking in the shop.

"Hey, Slade, I think I'm ready," the guy said.

Slade turned to me. "We had a part delivery. It's on the workbench if you want to check it out, this shouldn't take long."

"Okay."

The big metal door to the garage was shut, so I was surprised when I got to the garage and saw a bundle of ginger fur on top of the delivery box.

"Hey, buddy, it's you again."

The kitten raised its head and stared at me with big green eyes. I couldn't tell why, but I had a feeling she was a girl.

"Do you live here?" I asked and got a little meow as an answer.

I raised my hand slowly to see what kind of reaction I got and was surprised to see her bumping her head against my hand. She wasn't as flighty or aggressive as she'd been the other day.

"What's your name, beautiful?"

She meowed again.

"I don't speak cat, so you're going to have to help me out here, okay?"

Another bump to my hand.

"I'm not going to invade your privacy, so meow if you're a boy and purr if you're a girl."

I chuckled to myself. I must be losing my mind, but I glanced behind me to the shop and Slade was deep in conversation with the guy, checking something on his computer.

The kitten stood up on the box and did a turn before sitting on its back legs, purring.

"Okay, you're a girl. Thank you for letting me know. Now your name… Ginger?"

She hissed. "Okay, okay, point taken."

"So you're not…" She hissed again. "The name I'm not going to repeat. Sorry if it's a sensitive topic. I know how you feel, I used to get called magnolia at school because I'm so pasty white." I shrugged.

"Hmm, okay, so you clearly live here, even though Slade never mentioned owning a cat. Do you want to give me a clue?"

She meowed again and then jumped from the box onto the workbench and then the floor. She walked around the frame of the Harley, getting a little too close.

"What are you trying to tell me?"

She jumped onto the bike frame. I gasped and closed my eyes, praying to the god of bikes, if there was one, for the frame of the Harley to stay upright on the stand.

"Oh my god, the Harley."

The cat meowed, so I opened my eyes again to see her perfectly balanced on the frame.

"Harley."

She meowed again.

"Is that your name? Harley?"

It totally made sense now. Only Slade would have a cat and name it after his favorite bike.

"Well, hello, Harley. Nice to meet you," I said.

Harley jumped from the bike frame straight onto the workbench, making my heart skip another three beats.

She sat on the box again. "I guess you're not helping me with this delivery, are you?"

Harley purred and raised her paw as if she wanted to play.

"I think you better scoot before your daddy comes over and tells us both off."

She jumped back on the floor and left the garage through the gap under the metal door.

Slade was still with his customer, so I allowed myself a moment to admire him from afar.

I wondered if he ever noticed how often he stroked his beard. The man was sex on legs and, okay, I'd always had a thing for older men, but Slade was more than his appearance.

The way he'd cared for me yesterday had been unexpected.

With Richard, I'd felt like I was always playing the same part. Even though we were both versatile, it had been rare when he'd let me top him. And if he was extra horny, he could be rough to the point of pain.

I pushed those thoughts aside in favor of memories from yesterday. We hadn't switched, but there was something about Slade that told me we could have. I'd been so desperate to have him that I hadn't given him a chance. He'd only drawn the line at taking me twice so I wouldn't end up too sore.

"I thought I was the only one who got hard staring at bikes."

I snapped up to see Slade leaning against the door separating the shop from the garage, a heated smile on his face.

"Harley kept me company while you were busy, but I was actually just thinking about you," I said, walking over to him until we were only inches apart.

"Oh really? And what were you thinking about that caused that problem in your jeans?"

"Unless you suffer from short-term memory loss, you'll know exactly what I was thinking," I said in my best attempt to sound seductive.

He put his hands on either side of my face and pulled me in for a kiss that ignited the need for Slade that hadn't really gone away since he'd left my apartment very early this morning.

"Hmm…I remember now. You see, us old folks sometimes have a hard time remembering things."

I wanted to make a joke about how hard he was, but he kissed me again, and then I was the one with the memory loss problem.

"How about I take you to dinner? I just sold a new bike, so we can celebrate…and if you're lucky, you can have me for desser—"

"Deal."

17

SLADE

I CLOSED the shop and grabbed the paperwork to lock it in my office.

Aiden had been meticulously buffing the engine case for the Harley, following my instructions, while I'd dealt with another bike purchase inquiry.

Business was good, and I'd been spending all my free time with Aiden. Not all of it with clothes on.

In fact, while initially Aiden had been as shy about being with me as he was upfront about what he wanted, in the last week, he'd let go of all his hang-ups, whatever they might be.

We'd even switched from having dinner at Benny's every night to eating in, or ordering in when we couldn't be bothered to cook. Or to be more exact, when we'd been so tired from having sex that we couldn't be bothered to cook.

"Are you going to stand there and ogle me all day?"

Would the answer to that question ever be no, especially when Aiden had such a perfect ogle-worthy ass?

"Aid, you're bending over my workbench, operating a handheld drill. You have no idea how much self-restraint I need right now to keep my clothes on."

He stopped the drill, which he was using to buff the engine casing of the Harley, and removed his protective face mask.

"Well, don't mind me. All the doors are closed. It's just you, me… and the power drill."

I groaned when he shifted his weight from one foot to the other. His ass was basically saying "come get me."

Fucking tease.

I walked over to him, sparing a glance at the clock on the wall that told me we still had time before we needed to leave to meet the guys at the bar.

"Were you doing that on purpose?" I asked, running my hand over his ass. He bent over a little more to press against my front. The bastard.

"Doing what on purpose?" he said with the least innocent expression I'd ever seen on him.

"Do you know what happens to sassy boys who think they're in charge?"

He trapped his lower lip between his teeth. "No?"

"You're not tricking anyone, baby. So you're going to bend over while I eat your sweet ass. No coming until I say so. Got it?"

He looked at me from under his lashes.

"Yes…boss."

"Don't call me boss. Liam calls me boss. It's just weird."

"Okay…Daddy."

"Please don't," I chuckled.

"Okay, then, what can I call you?"

There was an air of defiance in his eyes. I pulled him so he was straight up against my chest and claimed his mouth without turning him around. It was a difficult position for a kiss because he was twisting his neck, but he didn't seem to mind since he gave as good as he got.

"Yours," I moaned into his mouth. "Call me yours."

"Mine, definitely mine."

I ended the kiss before I came in my pants like a teenager. That's how Aiden made me feel, except there was no denying that I definitely wasn't a young man anymore.

My recovery time was long, which actually suited me fine because I could give Aiden extra orgasms, but my back was giving me trouble.

Aiden had noticed it when I'd had a crippling spasm during sex a few days ago and we'd had to stop. Coming prematurely would have been less embarrassing.

Speaking of which, maybe I shouldn't get on my knees on a hard floor as much as I had a hard-on for eating Aiden's ass.

"Change of plans," I said, pulling Aiden toward the staff area.

"What? No fair," he complained, but still removed his clothes extra fast when he saw we were headed for the shower.

I was definitely thankful to past-Slade for having a wet room with a bench and hooks rather than just a cubicle shower.

Aiden turned the water on and pulled us straight under the shower.

"Fuck, that's cold. Are you actively trying to not get laid right now?" I asked, looking down at my cock with pity.

Aiden got on his knees, taking my cock in the wet heat of his mouth as far as he could manage.

The water warmed up at the same time as fire built inside me.

"Fuck, you have an amazing mouth, baby," I moaned.

"I know," he said, letting go of me with a pop and crawling over to where his jeans were to grab a condom and lube.

His shirt fell off the hook and onto the wet floor, but Aiden was a man on a mission to get me inside him. No need for the five-second, self-destroying warning.

Thirty minutes later, we were on our way to The Falls, a bar on the outskirts of Chester Falls.

The Falls had a good atmosphere. With the dark woods, live music, and friendly staff, it was a great place to come for a drink or two. It didn't hurt that it had a wonderful view of the waterfalls that gave the town its name.

In this summer weather, their deck was perfect to chill with friends. Even if those friends were almost half my age. I ignored my internal self-jab and told Aiden to find the guys while I got us drinks.

"Hey, Daddy, what can I get you?" Brent, the bartender, said.

He was a really friendly guy and, so far, I hadn't seen anyone he didn't flirt with. I wasn't sure if that was just who he was as a person or a requirement of the job. He only ever took it as far as he needed to get a smile out of his customer, so I assumed it was the latter option.

"Do I really give out the Daddy-vibe?"

He was preparing a cocktail but stopped and leaned over the counter a little.

"Let me see…you're tall, hot, a total silver-fox, those eyes could stop butter from melting at your request. So yeah…if it's your thing, then…" he shrugged.

I shook my head. "Not my thing. Wren's group is outside, do they all have drinks?"

"They got a round a while ago, and could probably do with another one."

"Can you sort me out?"

"Sure, Daddy."

I laughed at his sugary sweet but teasing voice. The kid was a good bartender.

Balancing all the drinks on a tray was not easy. That was a strikeout for jobs I could do for fun in my retirement.

"I rode Slade's bike," Aiden said proudly as I placed the tray on the table.

"I bet you did, you bad boy," Tom replied.

"I've never seen anyone riding Slade's bike, so you must be special." Wren said. "Can you get him to join the adult football team too?"

"No." Aiden said so quickly everyone's eyes were on him.

He blushed a very pretty pink, that I now knew went all over when he was worked up.

"What Aiden means is that I hurt my back this week, so I probably shouldn't play any kind of contact sports."

Aiden's face turned to me so fast that I wondered if he'd hurt his neck. "Like, *no* contact sports?"

I heard a snort from the other side of the table. Aiden was *not* as quiet as he thought he was.

"Well, maybe a few select contact sports," I whispered in his ear, kissing the lobe before I pulled back.

Wren stood up and stretched out his hand, wiggling his fingers. "Come on guys, pay up."

"Oh, come on, that's not fair. I had less information to go by," Indy said.

Tate took out a bill from his wallet and gave it to Wren, promising Indy he'd let him win later.

Tristan and Ben followed, with Tristan muttering he should have known better and not trusted horny old men...or something of the kind.

"Can I pay you in blow—" Wren covered up Tom's mouth with his hand and said, "Yes, you can."

"What's going on?" Aiden asked.

Everyone looked around, avoiding eye contact.

"What's going on, if I can take a guess, is that your friends placed a bet on us," I said, finally giving up the pretense and placing my arm over Aiden's chair and around his shoulders.

Tom gave a loud sigh and moved to sit on Wren's lap. "Isn't love wonderful, babe?"

"Wait a minute," Aiden said. "How did you all know? Except for my runs in the morning with Wren, I haven't even seen you."

There was a collective snort, including from me, which got me the side-eye from Aiden.

"Oh, my darling second best friend Aiden," Wren said. Tom was looking at him like a kitten ready to be stroked to sleep.

"First of all, you've really slowed down on our runs, like waaaaay down," he said.

"So what? I've been tired, and it's a forest, *not* the paved ground of the beach walk in San Diego."

"Plus, Benny said you were there every night last week for dinner, but not this week."

"Traitor," Aiden muttered between his teeth.

"And you're literally wearing Slade's shirt."

Aiden stared down at the shirt with the logo of my shop that I'd given him to wear after his had gotten wet earlier, and then looked at me.

I shrugged and pulled him in for a kiss.

He melted into my touch immediately. I knew he'd be beet red by the time we were done with the kiss, but I also wanted him to relax and stop worrying.

From the loud cheers around us, I took it that his friends approved.

18

—————

AIDEN

FUCK MY LIFE. Fuck alcohol and fuck hangovers.

"I hate Wren," I moaned into my pillow.

"That's not what you were saying last night. I would have been jealous if you hadn't gone on a ten-minute speech about how platonic your love is, how Tom should definitely not feel threatened, how you'd totally join them for a threesome, and if I'm not mistaken, you offered me to the whole group, saying everyone should ride my bike. *That* was not a euphemism. Or at least it's not when you stare at my crotch as you say it."

I groaned, which made my head hurt.

"Why are you here? Let me die of mortification or dehydration or something."

"Come here, sweetheart."

I kept my eyes closed because it hurt too much to open them but scooted closer to Slade.

He ran his magical fingers over my head, massaging my temples and then my scalp. "My poor baby."

"Hmmm."

I rarely drank, which was why I felt like death would have been a less harsh sentence to last night's outing. And the worst was that I

106

didn't even suffer from alcohol-induced amnesia. Nope. I remembered every single stupid thing that came out of my mouth.

Oh fuck.

"Slade?"

"Yes, sweetie?"

My belly filled up with butterflies at the term of endearment.

"I have questions."

"Okay?"

"How did I get home last night?"

"You were too drunk to be safe on the bike, even with me riding, so I put you in a cab and followed the cab home. We're at my place, by the way."

"We are?" I tried to open my eyes, but nope, it was too early.

"Yeah, I thought you might be unwell today, and I also needed clean pants. As it turns out, my laundry doesn't do itself when I'm not here." His chuckle made everything move, but it felt nice. Everything he did felt nice.

"Another question. Um...did I really talk about my ex?"

"Richard the Tiny Dick? Yup. At length. It was quite amusing. I mean, I'd totally throat-punch the guy if I saw him, but I'm happy to know my dick is better than his...*even* if everyone in the bar now also knows."

Jesus fucking Christ, I was never ever in my whole life, however long it may be, going to have another drink. Ever.

"I'm sorry," I said into his chest.

A phone rang, louder than it should in my opinion. It wasn't my ringtone, so I covered up my head with the bedsheet.

When it stopped, Slade turned back to me. I know this because he kissed my forehead like a gentleman. I knew he was hard. He normally was in the morning—so much for complaining about his age—but he wasn't pushing me for sex.

I hated that the thought that Richard would have behaved differently was even crossing my mind. He had no place anywhere I happened to be, and certainly not when I was with Slade.

"Open your eyes, baby," he said softly.

I did, and this time it didn't feel so bad.

"Hi," I said.

"Good morning, gorgeous. Do you want coffee?"

I nodded.

"Okay, you stay here, don't do anything wild, and I'll come back in a minute with some coffee, toast, and a painkiller, okay?"

God, I love this man.

I opened my eyes so wide that I felt like I was being stabbed all the way to my brain. What the fuck? What kind of weird thought was that?

Temporary. This was temporary because I'd nearly met all of my objectives when I left San Diego, and I'd be ready to go back shortly.

I even took my fingers out to count them.

One. Take a break to cleanse from Richard because, even after almost a year, his presence somehow still permeated the walls of my apartment.

Two. See Wren and the guys.

Three. Research for my secret release. The one that no one knew about so it didn't create a frenzy of questions, because as far as everyone knew, A. Lawton was on a break.

Four. Four…what the fuck was four? Ah well, those were enough. I'd done those, right? Maybe another week or two and then I'd be back home, and Slade would be just a nice memory. A reminder that I wasn't the broken man Richard had left behind.

God, I hated getting drunk. I was always so fucking emotional.

I looked around to familiarize myself with Slade's place. I wasn't sure what to expect, but the best description I had for Slade's room was a sanctuary. The bed was huge and it was pillow central. I never knew you could fit so many pillows on a bed and still sleep comfortably.

The walls were painted a light grey and there were large photos on the walls. Landscapes, roads, buildings. I wondered what significance, if any, they had to Slade.

"Oh, you're up."

I sat back against the headboard, fluffing at least three pillows.

"There's a ninety-five percent chance I'll never leave this bed again. Just saying."

He smiled, putting two painkillers in my hand and holding the cup of coffee. "What does the missing five percent account for?"

"I'm gonna need to pee soon."

"You're something else, Aid—"

The phone rang again. Slade looked at it as if he wanted to throw it out of the window.

"What's up? Who is it?" I asked.

He silenced the phone and put it back on the bedside table.

"My ex-husband."

Slade had an ex-husband? He'd left a lot of personal stuff out of his conversations, but somehow I had assumed he'd always been single.

"Should you…um, talk to him?" I asked. We weren't in a relationship, were we? We were only two people who enjoyed each other. Surely he should find out what his ex wanted.

"I don't have anything to say to him. Aiden, we divorced six years ago, and I haven't seen or spoken to him since. There's absolutely no reason for us to talk again."

Maybe he was saying it to reassure me, or to reassure himself, but he didn't seem convinced.

"I think you should take the call next time. If he already called a few times today, and from your face it's not just today, then something must be up."

Slade caressed my cheek and leaned over for a kiss. "I'll call him tomorrow. Today is our underwear day."

"Underwear day?"

"Underwear day."

True to his word, we spent the whole day in just our underwear. I had a chance to inspect his book collection, which he was only a little embarrassed about when I pointed out most of his books were mine, and he even had some titles twice that I'd recovered for a new edition.

We cooked together, laughed, and made out…a lot.

"You are a fun guy, Slade," I said when we sat on his couch after dinner. It was still early, so the sun wasn't completely gone yet. In fact, his couch was in the perfect spot to relax with the setting sun shining on us.

Slade had my feet on his lap and was massaging them gently. I was doing the same to him.

"I can't say I've ever been told that I'm a fun guy," he chuckled. "Moody? Quiet? Yes. Fun? Nope."

"Well, maybe people weren't paying attention."

"Can I ask you a question?"

"Sure."

"Why haven't you published in a year?"

I knew he'd ask the question at some point, but it was still hard to talk about it.

"How much do you know about me?" I asked.

"Only what you've told me. I've never looked you up, and I'm not on social media nor do I read gossip news."

"You might be the only person out there that has the chance to hear the version of events from me. It's a first."

Slade held out his hand, so I reached out with mine, and he turned me over so I sat between his legs and against his chest. I leaned my head back, taking comfort from his warmth and the smell of his shower soap.

"I met Richard at an author conference a few years ago. He's an agent, so he was outgoing, talked to everyone, and hard to say no to. We were happy for a while until I started making serious money. My family comes from money and I moved to San Diego to get away from all that, but when my bank account became too much for me to manage, I asked my parents for advice. They thought I was ready to get back to the Manhattan scene, so they traveled to San Diego, and that's when they met Richard."

"Were there problems between them? I mean, your folks aren't homophobic, are they?"

"No, they don't really care about that. Richard charmed the pants off them both, especially my mother. After they left, he wouldn't stop talking about them, and even suggested we move to New York. It took me a long time to realize it was all about the money."

Slade wrapped his arms tighter around me and kissed my hair.

"What happened a year ago that made you stop publishing?"

"He became more insistent about moving near my parents and

even used my mom to set me up for a secret wedding. Of course, my mom thought everything was great and we were madly in love. We weren't. I said no to the proposal, and that I needed a prenup, as it was a condition of my trust fund. Without a prenup, I would never be able to access any of my money."

The image of Richard's shocked face when I'd told him the lie was still vivid in my mind. He was so angry; to the point I was afraid he'd become aggressive.

My neighbors had called the police because of the noise. I'd never been so embarrassed in my whole life. The camel didn't need another straw to break its back, but getting a call from the guy he was fucking behind my back had definitely done it.

"Aiden, we may only be temporary, but I need you to listen to me. You're more than your money. You're the most amazing person I know, and you're beautiful, kind, and special. Do you hear me?"

19

SLADE

His silence broke my heart until I felt him nod against me.

"You know what was the worst? I've always been a private person. I have someone that deals with my social media accounts and they're only about my publishing. But within days of Richard leaving, loads of private information was leaked and I was tagged in all of it. Things I'd only told him about my relationship with my parents and how I wanted to make my own way in life. It was all out there, and it was so embarrassing. My parents stopped talking to me. They blamed me for the breakup. After that, I couldn't write. I was in the middle of a book and I couldn't pick it up. I sat at my desk for days, but all I could see in front of me were those lies on the internet, the stuff that was true but private."

His voice sounded so broken. Had Aiden ever told this to anyone? Wren? I was absolutely sure that if he knew, his friendly warning about Aiden would have carried a lot more weight.

If Aiden only knew how I much understood his pain. How much I still carried it.

"Come with me," I said in his ear and made a move to get up. He followed me to the bedroom and didn't complain when I removed his boxer shorts and asked him to lay down on the bed.

His dick was soft, as was mine. This wasn't time for sex. I just needed to offer him some comfort and be close to him.

"When did you get your idea for your book?" I asked.

"I was in line to get a coffee after my morning run. There was this little girl with her mom outside the coffee shop. The girl had a pink backpack and they looked like they were waiting for someone. After a few minutes I heard the rumble of a bike and this really tough-looking guy wearing full-on leather gear stopped his bike right in front of the little girl. I've never seen someone so happy. When he took his helmet off, my heart just melted. The way he gazed at that girl was as if she was the most priceless thing. I couldn't hear what they said to each other, but it didn't matter. In my head, I was already forming my own story."

I ran my hand over his cheek, feeling the rough scruff of his unshaved beard under my thumb.

"I'm glad you found your inspiration. I've missed your stories, and I just know this one is going to be even better."

He chuckled. "Because it has a biker?"

"No, because you're free now. Because I think the Aiden in front of me at this moment, gloriously naked under my bed sheets, is a different person to the guy in the designer shirt that stole my book at the fair."

"I didn't steal—" I laughed, even as I shut him up with a kiss.

It was tender and sweet, and I had to remind myself of the words I said when we were on the couch. This was temporary.

Waking up with Aiden wrapped around me was good any day, but on a Sunday, when we had nowhere else to be, it was absolute perfection.

Light streamed from the gap between the curtains. I had no idea what time it was, but I had no wish to move out of bed, not when Aiden was still snoring lightly against my chest.

His hand rested over my heart and his fingers twitched every so often, as if he was having a dream. Behind him there was a barrier of pillows nested against his back. It was as if overnight he'd built himself a cozy fort made of me and my pillows.

I ran my hand through his tousled brown hair, glad he didn't even stir. I needed a little more time before he woke up. There were feelings bubbling inside me that I hadn't felt in a long time, and I needed to process them.

Last night I'd continued reminding myself that what Aiden and I had was temporary, but there was a strong voice in my head that kept repeating over and over again "why."

After my divorce, I'd decided I couldn't do to another man what I'd done to Mike. The secrets about my past had eaten me up inside and ultimately damaged our relationship. But the longer I spent with Aiden, the more I wondered if it would be different this time.

I'd met Mike at a crossroads in my life. In order to stay on the right path, I'd needed to keep my secrets, leave them there so I wouldn't be tempted to turn around. In twenty-five years, I'd never even looked at the line, let alone cross it.

Would I have a chance with Aiden if I opened up to him? Would he still want me afterward? I didn't even know if he wanted me now. At least not for more than our current casual arrangement.

"I can hear your thoughts from here and the answer is yes."

I looked down at Aiden, who was clearly no longer asleep, with confusion.

"Oh really? And what was I thinking about?" I asked.

He pulled my nipple into a hard peak and then moved his hand lower until he found my cock. I swallowed when he wrapped around my length and gave it a tight squeeze and a long, slow stroke.

"You were saying: Aiden, I'm dying to feel you inside me, please fuck me before I die."

I snorted. "I never knew you were a mind reader as well as a talented author."

He raised himself on his elbows. "Really?"

"Yeah, your hand is down there, please tell me you can feel how hard I am at the thought of you fucking me."

"Yeah, but…I was joking, you don't have to."

"Aid, I know, but I want to. I told you I like to switch, I just haven't done it in a while."

He climbed on top of me and took my mouth like a starved man. I liked it. No, I loved it.

God, I was so fucked.

"Shit, what's the time?" Aiden asked.

I grabbed my phone from the bedside table and pressed the home button to show him.

"Shit, I have a run with Wren, and he'll never let me live it down if I'm late. Slade, this is going to be dirty and quick," he said.

I licked a path from his neck all the way up his chin and took his mouth, all while wrapping my legs around his waist. I was older, but I still had some moves.

"Baby, make it real dirty, and you can be as quick as you like."

He threw himself over the pillows on his side of the bed to get to the other bedside table, where he already knew I had condoms and lube.

"One of these days I'm going to get oil all over this hot body of yours and I'm going to fuck you right up against that workbench you keep so neat and tidy."

Aiden's dirty talk was enough to rile me up with such need that I barely even flinched when his fingers worked to stretch me.

"More," I growled.

"Oh, you like it like that? Turn around."

Fuck, his commanding voice was going to make me come before he put his cock inside me.

I grabbed two pillows and placed them under me, tucking my hard cock between them. Aiden placed himself between my legs, running his hand up the backs of my thighs as if he had all the time in the world.

"I thought you had somewhere to be."

"It's cute you think you're in charge here," he chuckled.

I was going to retort back when I felt his cock push through the rim of my ass. I rested my head on my forearms and relaxed as much as I could.

The burn was there, unmistakable, but unlike times when I'd bottomed for Mike, my brain went somewhere else. Suddenly I was super-aware of the way Aiden's legs brushed against the back of mine. How his breaths were shallow against my back, as if he were battling with himself.

It wasn't until he was all the way inside me that I let out a full breath. He lay on my back, his head between my shoulder blades, but when he spoke it was as if he was whispering directly in my ear.

"I hope you're ready for it, Slade, because your ass is hugging my cock like a motherfucking tight glove and I'm not gonna last."

"Talk dirty to me like that and I'll be the one who—fuck."

Words left me when he withdrew almost all the way and pushed in again.

"That's it, Slade. Take it all as I drive in and out of you. You feel so tight, so hot. I'm going to fuck you so good you'll remember this every time you move until I'm back and we get to do it all over again."

"Yes, fuck, yes."

My strategic placement of my dick between the pillows and the way he was driving into me was making me fly to heights I never thought possible.

"Aid, I'm so close."

He put his arms under mine and reached for my hands, lacing them together.

"Do you need help?" he asked, but I shook my head. No hands needed, and that was a definite first.

"No, just fuck me hard, I need it."

I was surrounded by Aiden. In me, on me, he was everything. My orgasm came hard and fast. I knew the pillows would be ruined, but I'd buy a million pillows if I needed.

"Slade." Aiden shouted as his orgasm took over him, and there was an unmistakable stinging on my back that I bet had Aiden's teeth marks written all over it.

He withdrew his spent cock from my ass, collapsing on his back next to me with the biggest grin on his face.

"Show off," I teased, even as I pulled him in for a kiss.

A quick shower later and he was walking out to meet Wren, wearing a pair of my shorts and an old T-shirt of mine. Nothing ever felt so right.

My phone rang sometime later, and since I'd promised Aiden I'd hear Mike out, I answered it.

"Hello?"

"Why the fuck haven't you been answering my calls?"

I wanted to say a few choice words, but there was an edge to his voice. I'd known him for far too long to ignore that.

"What's going on, Mike?"

"I need you to come home, Uncle Ted is in the hospital… Slade, it's not good."

20

AIDEN

"So...you and Slade, huh?"

"Don't give yourself a stitch, breathe."

Wren slowed down and laughed.

"I've lost count of the times we've talked through a five-mile run stitch free, and now you're claiming amateur status? No way."

I smiled. When he'd texted asking if we were running, I knew he just wanted some time alone to talk. It didn't mean I was going to make it easy on him.

"I think you're just finding an excuse to cut the run short. Is Tom tiring you more than usual?"

"I could ask the same of you." He looked at his wristwatch. "You do realize in the old days we'd be on the way back, right?"

Yeah, I was aware of that, as much as I was aware of how much my thighs ached from fucking Slade this morning. I'd have asked him to stay in bed until I got back, for a repeat, but I needed to get back to the apartment to pick up my notes and my laptop.

Slade had asked me to spend the night with him again and there was as much a chance of me saying no as there was of me avoiding this conversation with Wren. But I did need my stuff, so we'd agreed I'd get back to his place in time for a late lunch.

"What do you want to know?" I asked.

"Length, width, and thrusting power."

I coughed. "What?"

"Jesus, man, your face just now," he laughed, and I hoped he got a stitch. It would serve him right. "I was joking. I can see by your blissed-out face that there are no issues in that area. Way to go, Aid."

"Um, thanks?"

He slowed his pace down to a fast walk.

"How did you guys go from him helping you out with research to…whatever it is you're doing? I mean, I knew you had a thing for older guys, but since you've been with The Tiny Dick for so long…"

I snorted. Wren had been calling Richard "The Tiny Dick" since I had told him about one of our first arguments. It stuck, but it was just between us. I guessed Richard had been downgraded now.

Wren slowed his pace to a stroll, which meant things were about to get serious.

"I'm going straight to the point, Aid. What's going to happen to you when you go back home?"

"We agreed this is casual while I'm here. That's all. There's no point denying ourselves when we know we're attracted to each other. It's been a while since Richard, so I think I've earned some fun, haven't I?" There was a slight bite to my voice, and I didn't know if it was as a response to Wren's question, or if what I'd said sounded a lot like bull-shit to me.

"That's not what I meant, Aid. What's going to happen to *you* when it's over."

"Why?"

He sighed. "Aid, I've known you a long time, but I've only known you after Tiny Dick. The Aiden I saw two days ago was a different person. You were carefree, happy, and I dare to say, in love."

"Don't be silly." I laughed, but it sounded wrong even to me.

Wren stopped completely and put his hands on my shoulders. "Look at you. You're wearing his clothes for goodness sake. Have you even been home since Friday?"

I shook my head.

"I can see you have feelings for him and, based on his behavior on Friday, he feels the same way."

"I don't know," I confessed. Did I want to believe Wren? Hell yeah. But as much as my confidence had grown since being with Slade, I was still afraid to take such a big risk.

Breaking up with Richard took a toll on me, not because of us, but because of what he did.

If Slade didn't return my feelings and didn't want a relationship with me...I didn't think I'd survive that. Which told me exactly how deep my feelings for him went.

"Hey, come here." Wren hugged me tight. "I wish I could take back all the things Tiny Dick did to you, but since I can't, I'm going to say this, and I hope you're listening to me. You have a family here. Slade or no Slade, if San Diego becomes too lonely you will be welcomed here."

"Thank you. I know that...I do...and I'll think about it."

"Okay, how about we race back? Tom is making brownies, so I need to burn some calories before I spend the rest of the day eating chocolate off him."

"TMI, Wren. TMI."

"Like you don't want to do the same," he snorted before he took off running.

I had a second shower at the apartment, grabbed my stuff and walked back to Slade's place.

Since I'd been in Chester Falls, my car had been thoroughly neglected, and I couldn't bring myself to regret it. It felt good to walk into town along the river path, and whenever Slade and I worked late, he'd sometimes take me home on his bike.

I was avoiding thinking of my return to San Diego, as much as it was also constantly in the back of my mind. There was no question that I needed to get back, but the thought of stepping into my much larger apartment didn't hold any appeal. To think I'd once thought it was the perfect place for me. View of the ocean, lots of light from the floor-to-ceiling windows, it was perfect for someone who worked from home. But was it still?

When Slade opened the door to his place, I knew something wasn't right. I put my bag on the floor by the door and took the box with the apple pies that I'd picked up from Benny's into the kitchen.

Slade sat on his couch facing the window, wearing an expression I couldn't decipher.

I was relieved when I made a gesture for him to scoot over and he did, so I wedged myself between him and the arm of the couch. He didn't complain when I put my arms around him, in fact, as soon as I did, he leaned back and laced our fingers together.

"What happened?"

"Mike called again. His uncle is in the hospital."

"I'm so sorry to hear that, sweetheart. Are you close to him?"

Slade's voice was low and laced with pain. "He saved my life."

I wanted to know the story behind that statement, but it was only another piece of the puzzle that was Slade Warren. Maybe one day I'd see the whole thing complete, or maybe not, but this wasn't about me.

"How serious is it? Should you go see him?"

"I don't know. How serious it is, I mean. Mike just told me to come home."

"Do you think he would say that lightly?"

"No. Mike loves his uncle like a father. Ted…he's…fuck, I don't know what to do. I haven't seen him or talked to him since I left Atlanta. He's an amazing man. He gave me a job at his garage when I had nothing but my bike and the clothes I was wearing."

I kissed the side of his head, and he let out a sigh. "I've never looked back, Aid. Always kept moving. I'm scared that once I go back for one thing, it'll force me to face the rest."

"Revisiting the past isn't always bad. We change as we grow. Sometimes going back means you can bury the past and put it to rest. Which…fuck…that's not what I meant about your uncle. Shit."

How un-fucking-sensitive was I? In trying to make things better for Slade, I was basically saying he was going to Atlanta for a funeral.

Slade chuckled. "You are such a writer, baby. Don't worry. I know what you meant. Maybe you're right. I love Ted. He was part of my life for such a long time, and if he's not well then I need to put my shit to one side and go see him."

"Do you want me to come with you?"

Slade turned around in my arms and I braced myself for the rejection.

"I couldn't ask that of you, Aid. You have your own work to do."

I remembered my conversation with Wren and decided to push it.

"Slade, I care about you. Let me go with you for support. It's what, an eight, nine-hour drive? When we get there, I can be with you as much or as little as you want. We can book a hotel room and I can stay away if you'd rather be with your family."

"I'd really like that. Thank you."

Slade's kisses always took my breath away, but this one felt even more reverent than usual. As though he didn't know how to thank me with words. If only he knew there was nothing to thank me for. I'd be there for him any time.

"Right, now that we have that sorted, who wants a slice of apple pie?" I said, pulling on his beard.

"God you're an amazing man, Aiden Lawton."

21

———

SLADE

"Who's going to keep an eye on Harley?" Aiden asked.

Weird question, but it was early in the day. "Liam will make sure nothing happens to her."

"Okay, that's good. Right, I'm driving, which means you're the deejay. A word of warning. I take my driving music very seriously," Aiden said, giving me a side-look and a smile before focusing back to the road.

The sun was barely up in the sky. Aiden had suggested we travel earlier in the morning rather than set off immediately and need an extra night halfway to Atlanta.

I felt a lot more rested this morning than I thought I would. I had Aiden to thank for that, too, because he'd taken care of me in every sense of the word.

We'd had Momma Ruth's apple pie from Benny's, and then I'd packed my stuff and taken Aiden back to his place so he could grab more clothes. When we got back, he cooked us dinner, keeping me distracted throughout by doing it buck naked.

After dinner he decided we should pick random books from my bookshelf and read the sex scenes aloud. It didn't take long until we

123

broke down in fits of laughter at how silly they all sounded when read out of context.

Laughter gave way to making out, which gave way to making love.

I took the opportunity that Aiden was driving to check him out. He'd given me so much last night. There was no mistake there, we'd made love to each other.

The heat was there, as was his dirty talk. Who knew he had such a dirty mouth when he topped? I'd happily bottom for the rest of my life just to hear him give himself over to the power of his body and the need to chase his orgasm.

"I can feel your eyes on me. And no, no blowjobs while I'm driving."

I laughed aloud.

"What, are you saying I was the only one thinking that? Damn," he said.

I connected my phone to his car and looked for the music streaming app.

"Before you do that, can I ask you a question?"

"Sure." I put the phone on my lap and turned in my seat to face him.

"I've been working through my plot and trying to figure out my character's connection to the motorcycle club, what he did there, but also how he got out. Although I'm not sure I want him out. I don't want him to give up something that is so important to him."

"What kind of business does the MC do?"

"What do you mean?"

"Remember I told you how the MC is like a family business. You have a hierarchy, which dictates what kind of power each member has. MCs also run businesses, and they vary from doing charitable work to illegal stuff and everything in between."

Aiden seemed to think about it for a moment. "I'd like them to do charitable things. The conflict between my characters is the reason they separated, heightened by the time they spent apart. The other guy made assumptions about what kind of stuff bikers do, so I'd like my biker to show the reader that he's not a bad guy."

I liked Aiden's idea. Selfishly, I hadn't wanted his character to be an outlaw.

"And who's your other guy?"

"He's an elementary school teacher. They bump into each other because the husband of the school's principal is in the same MC as my biker. There's an event at school and my biker goes in to give a talk about safety on the road."

"Let me guess, the teacher has all these assumptions about bikers, and at the end of the speech he goes over to his old friend and goes on a rant about how dare he come to his school?"

Aiden laughed. "Yeah, like that."

"Ooh, is there going to be hate sex?" I asked and then lowered my voice. "I love how you write your sex scenes."

I didn't miss Aiden's cock hardening. If there wasn't a chance we'd end up dead on the side of the road, I'd be whipping it out and sucking it like a lollipop.

"Whatever you're thinking about, don't," he warned. "Let's listen to some music before I stop the car and make you blow me."

I debated the merits of that, but decided he was right and looked up a Bon Jovi playlist.

"Good choice. The ultimate silver-fox," he said.

"Hey! You know he's ten years older than me, right?"

He raised one hand off the steering wheel and counted on his fingers. "One, I told you I don't care about age. Two, if he was inclined toward men I'd totally do him. Three, don't worry, I'd still have enough energy to do you after. Or maybe at the same time."

I ran my hands over my face and groaned. He was going to be the death of me.

We caught some heavy traffic on the way into Atlanta, so we went straight to the hotel and ordered room service.

The long drive made us both tired, so after dinner we settled in bed, facing each other and talking about everything and nothing.

Now I knew Aiden hated Ramen as much as he hated designer clothes, which he only wore to annoy his mom who kept on sending them to him in hopes he'd find high-society events to attend.

I also found out he had graduated top of his class, gave his parents his Business degree, and left for San Diego the next day.

Maybe there was more in common between us than I thought, despite our age and background difference.

"Will you tell me about your Uncle Ted? You said he saved your life."

I stared at Aiden. There were so many ways I could tell this story, including the one I'd told Mike when we met. But when I opened my mouth, nothing came out.

Aiden held my hand and took it to his lips, keeping it there.

"Aiden, I…what I'm going to tell you could change the way you see me or feel about me."

"You're wrong. Nothing you can tell me will change how I see the man in front of me, nothing."

He sounded so sure of himself, of me.

A tiny moment in time was all it would take. I took a deep breath.

"I shot a man when I was twenty years old."

"What did he do to deserve it?"

I sat up.

"What? What kind of question is that? No one deserves to die at the hands of another person."

Aiden pulled my arm to lie down again.

"Tell me your story and I will prove you wrong."

"How can you do that? You weren't there?"

"No, but I know you, Slade."

I put my hand on his face, feeling his warm skin. How could I tell him he didn't know me at all?

"Remember when I told you that I left my parents' place to keep them safe?"

"Yes."

"I'd been a member of the club for a year when the president died in an accident. He was succeeded by the vice president. For some reason, that guy didn't like me. I overheard someone say once that the reason I'd been voted in was because the president thought my skills with the bikes would be handy in the club. The vice president disagreed."

"So, when he became president, things got hard for you?"

"Yeah, weird stuff started happening around me. Dead animals were dropped on my foster parents' doorstep. I'd wake up with shit smeared all over my bedroom window. But the worst was when those things happened even when I wasn't at home. I figured it would stop if I moved."

"Did it?"

"Yeah. I rented out a room in a house with some students because it was cheap. Same stuff kept happening, so I had to move again."

"Did you tell anyone about it?"

"I didn't know who to tell. The police wouldn't do anything, and the new president of the club hated my guts for no apparent reason. He did let me stay at the clubhouse until I found a new place."

Aiden scrunched up his eyes. "I'm not gonna like this, am I? I know you're here and you're okay, but I don't like where the story is going."

"I was attacked on my first night. A group of men beat the crap out of me and left me there with broken ribs, a bleeding eye, and lots of bruises. The guys started an investigation, thinking it was a rival club that had come in looking for revenge on some stuff our club did."

"Was it?"

"I thought it was at the time. Weeks later, I was asleep when I heard noise in the house. I'd gotten a gun after the beating because I was too scared of being on my own. When the door to my room opened, I pretended to be asleep. The first thing I saw was a gun pointing at me. Everything happened too fast. I shot my gun and the attacker fell on the floor. It was like everything was silent, then there was this loud noise, and then silence again. I was so terrified of even turning the lights on, I ran out of the room and called my old neighbor. He called an ambulance and told me to get out of the house."

AIDEN

THE STORY out of Slade's lips was the stuff of movies and books, not real life.

"Who was your attacker?" I asked.

"The son of the new president. I shot him in the neck. He's paralyzed for the rest of his life... Aiden, I didn't even aim. I just shot."

Slade's voice had been steady, up to the moment when he finally broke down.

"I have so many regrets," he said as his eyes filled with tears.

"You acted in self-defense. If you hadn't shot, you would be the one who was dead. So how did Ted get to save your life?"

"My neighbor gave me the signal to run because the president was out for revenge. He said I'd killed his son and needed to pay with my life."

"But he didn't die."

"No, but for a biker, being unable to ride is as good as being dead. So many times I wished I'd aimed at a leg or an arm, or that instead of a gun I'd had a baseball bat or something. I don't know. Anything but that fucking gun."

He shook his head. I wanted so much to take that pain away, but I had a feeling that Slade needed to finish the story.

"What happened next?"

"I ran, but every time I got a job and a new place to stay, I'd find myself being followed, getting threats in the mail. They were tracking my social security number."

"If they wanted to kill you they could have done it from afar without warning."

"The bastard wanted me to be scared, to keep running for my life until he was tired of playing. This went on for four years until I went to the police. I promised I'd tell them anything they needed to know about the club if they helped me hide somewhere safe. I was so scared that even if they had put me in jail I would have thanked them. The officer I spoke to lost his brother to gang crime, so he took all the information he could from me and gave me an address in Atlanta."

"Ted?"

For the first time since Slade started his story he smiled, a genuine happy smile.

"I was gathering enough courage to go in and speak to Ted when Mike saw me. His smile was infectious, and if I'm honest, that's what made me cross the road. Someone who smiled like that couldn't have a difficult life, couldn't know what I knew. I craved that. He was like those jam-filled doughnuts. You have one and then another. But by the third you think you're gonna die, so you wait a little longer and then you can eat another one. And when the bag is empty, you go buy more. Because who wouldn't want to live for jam-filled doughnuts?"

My heart filled with hope for the young guy who'd gone through so much and finally found his little piece of heaven.

"There was a cost to all that though. Ted knew about me, but Mike couldn't. Within a few weeks I had a new name and social security number. I was a new person. It took me exactly six months to ask Mike to marry me, even when it wasn't legal to do it. We actually never really got married, even though we used the terms marriage and divorce, we didn't do it officially."

"Why?"

"I don't know. I always held back. The longer I lived my new life, the longer the lie chased me. Mike knew I loved him, but there was something missing."

He didn't need to tell me anything else. The time for talking was over.

I ran my fingers softly down his face, collecting the few tears that left his eyes, stroked his soft beard, and then pressed my lips against his.

"Slade," I whispered.

"Yeah?"

"I'm still here."

"I'm still me."

"You are, as am I."

For the rest of the night, Slade took solace in my body. I was his safe place because he was mine. I'd decided I was going to keep him because anything else just didn't seem like an option to me.

When I opened my eyes the next morning, Slade wasn't in bed. I knew I was a cuddler, so it was a testament to how much he wore me out the night before that I didn't feel him leave.

I got up to use the bathroom, and when I came out, he was coming back into the room with coffee and a bag.

"Morning. I got us some pastries. Figured we should eat something, even though I'm not really hungry."

I walked toward him and smiled when he opened his arms for me instantly.

"Thank you. You're right, we should eat something."

The hospital was a short drive away from the hotel. The closer we got, the more fidgety Slade became. He was clearly anxious to find out more about his uncle's health, and I suspected also nervous to see his ex-husband.

Mike was nothing like what I'd expected. Physically, if Slade was a silver-fox, Mike was a total bear. He had shiny eyes, a thick beard, and a friendly smile.

"Mike this is Aiden, my..."

"Friend," I said, interrupting Slade. "Nice to meet you."

Mike held out his hand. "Likewise."

There was an awkward pause until Slade said, "Can we see Ted?"

"Of course. I'm afraid it's family only," Mike said, looking at me. I couldn't tell if he was apologetic or not.

"That's okay, I expected that. I'll wait for you here."

Slade seemed a little lost, so I stepped into his arms, hugging him tight. I didn't care who Mike thought I was to Slade. Friend was an accurate term and friends supported friends in difficult times.

"You'll be okay. And if you're not, that's okay too. I'll be here. I promise."

He nodded and disappeared into a corridor with Mike.

I took a deep breath. The nurses station was quiet, so I thought I'd chance my luck. Slade had told me last night he took Ted's surname when he got his new ID, so I approached with a smile and fingers crossed.

"Hi, I was wondering if you could help me, please."

"I'm afraid I'm limited in the information I can give out if that's what you're needing."

I smiled at her. "You get that a lot, do you?"

"Yup."

"I don't want any specific information. I just…my friend has gone to see his uncle. They're very close. All I want to know is…is he likely to be very upset when he comes out of there later?"

She gave me a sympathetic smile. "What's the patient's name?"

"Ted Warren."

She tapped on her computer and seemed to be reading some information.

I already knew the news before she even spoke because her eyes spelled it out.

"There's a cafeteria down that hall. Buy a bottle of water. Next door there's a small store that sells essentials. Get a pack of tissues. You might not need them, but…"

"Thank you so much."

A few minutes later I was back in the waiting room. It was hard to guess if Slade staying in the ward too long meant good or bad news.

I nearly jumped out of my skin when my phone buzzed in my pocket.

Richard's name was on the screen.

What the hell?

I declined the call, but a few seconds later, he rang again.

"Hello?

"Aiden… Hi, how are you?"

"Surprised to hear from you if I'm honest."

This was so not the time for this.

"Yeah, I'm sorry. I wanted to get in touch but…well, we didn't part on the best of terms."

Gee, I wonder why.

"Richard, I'm busy at the moment. How can I help you?"

"When are you back in town?"

"What…what do you mean?"

"I stopped by the apartment and you weren't there. I'd love to take you out when you're back."

Something didn't feel right about this. Why was he at the apartment?

Calm down, Aiden. He can't get in. He doesn't live there anymore.

"I don't know when I'm going to be back, and I'm also not available to go out with you."

"Why? Don't tell me you found yourself some loser to fuck around with."

My nerves reached such a high just from hearing his voice that I laughed aloud.

"First of all, Richard, my life is none of your business. When I say I can't see you, take it at face value. Good—"

"Wait."

"What?"

I was losing patience now. Slade had been in the ward for almost three hours and I needed to know if he was okay.

"I'm going to send you a little gift. Just watch it and call me after."

He ended the call, and a moment later I received a message with a video attachment.

I opened the video. As soon as it started playing I turned the volume down. It was footage of my apartment. Someone was taking the camera from the living room through the hall and into my bedroom.

As soon as I saw the next frame I got up from the chair and ran to the nearest bathroom.

I barely had time to close the door behind me before I emptied the contents of my stomach into the toilet.

No, this could not be happening.

23

———

SLADE

THE MAN on the hospital bed wasn't Ted. The man on the hospital bed looked frail, pale, far too slim, and like someone whose life was hanging by a thread.

I'd watched him sleep for the last hour. He hadn't moved, but the machines around him beeped reassuringly. Mike had tried to talk, but I couldn't.

Maybe that was the last time I'd see Ted. Silence was what I needed. Silence and Aiden.

I'd have given anything to have him there with me, but he couldn't be, so I had to focus on the knowledge he was down the corridor waiting for me.

"How long?" I asked when staring at Ted didn't give me the answers I needed.

"The doctors don't know. The cancer spread to his vital organs and he's too weak to have any more treatment."

"Why didn't you tell me?"

"Would you have come? You left as if what I did was the worst thing someone could have done to another person. I didn't kill anyone, Slade. I cheated, and only because our relationship had been

134

dead for years. Did you ever think what your distance was doing to us? To me?"

Anger bubbled inside me.

"Don't you dare make this about us. This has nothing to do with you and me."

"Oh really? Then how many times have you called Uncle Ted since you left? The man gave you his name. He treated you like a son."

"Boys."

Ted's voice was weak, but even now he was able to convey the warning tone he'd used on us so many times when we hadn't been able to agree on something.

"Will you make me rise from the dead to stop your stupid arguments?"

"Hey, Ted." I stepped closer to the bed and took his hand in mine. He squeezed it tight, his hand trembling.

"Hey, son, you lookin' good."

I smiled. "I wish I could say the same about you. You look like shit."

He laughed and then coughed until he got his breathing back again.

"Mike, will you give us a moment?" Ted asked.

Mike frowned at me. I knew he wanted to argue.

"I promise not to die in the next ten minutes," Ted said when Mike didn't move.

"Jesus Christ, Ted. This isn't funny."

"I disagree. Now scoot, I need a word with my boy."

"Why do I feel like I'm going to have my ass handed to me?" I said as Mike stepped out of the room.

Ted smiled, his eyes scanning my face as if he were trying to remember what I looked like.

"I'm sorry I didn't—"

He raised his hand to stop me.

"Son, when time is in short supply there's no need for apologies or regrets. It is what it is."

I nodded.

"Tell me something, son. Did I help you? Did I do the right thing?"

Tears ran down my face, and I didn't even bother to stop them or pretend they weren't there. Sometimes it was okay to think you're too fucking old to care about crying in front of someone else.

"Ted, you gave me a future. You could have said no to your friend, and I'll never understand why you'd put your life at risk for a nobody like me, but there isn't enough gratitude in the world for what you did to me."

"Let me tell you a little story. Before I married my darling Rose, I was a bit of a player. I got my first bike at fifteen, and in those days, you could do what you liked. So I saved up some money to go traveling the country. My mom and dad weren't too pleased, but I promised I'd come back and take over the business. So, at eighteen, I left. Traveled all the way to the west coast and then followed the ocean north. You're staring at a wrinkly old man now, but I tell you, I was quite the catch back then. Never had any problem getting girls or boys."

He stopped to catch his breath.

"You're bi?"

"Don't be so surprised, son. Remember Walter? The army friend who lived with me for a few years?"

I laughed. "He wasn't just your army friend?"

"That man saved me from spending the rest of my life grieving for my Rose."

I couldn't believe it. Walter had lived with Ted for five years and there was never any indication they were more than just friends. Considering Mike and I were together, I didn't think coming out would have been an issue. Then again, Ted had always been quite private with his life.

"Anyway, back to the early days. I met Nico at a party. We hit it off immediately and he came traveling with me. We both knew our relationship was only temporary because I had to come back to Atlanta, and he had to get back to Seattle. We parted on friendly terms and kept writing to each other for years after that. He became my best friend. He knew Rose and I struggled to conceive, and I lost all hope of becoming a father when she was taken from me too young."

Ted told me the story as if he was recounting someone else's life. How could he be so measured when inside my heart was breaking with each word he spoke?

"He gave you a son," I said. My words choked as I said them. "He gave me to you."

"That's right. It wasn't the intention, I guess. He knew I ran a business and could use a hand, and he trusted me to keep your secret and keep you safe. You became my son when you told my horndog of a nephew to take a hike unless you could tell me about you two. That was the kind of respect you showed a parent. That was when you became my son."

I stood up from the chair and hugged Ted. I'd always looked up to him like a son, but I didn't know he'd felt the same way. Why was I losing him now?

He stroked my hair, and we stayed like that for a moment until my tears stopped.

"I know Mike did wrong by you, and I know you had secrets to keep from him, but..."

"Ted, we can't get back together, you know that, right?"

He smiled. "I know. It's too late now. Can I ask you something? Will you keep in touch with him? Since you left he hasn't been with anyone. He's lonely, and I think he's still in love with you. I'm not asking for more than a friendly hand. Don't let him lose himself to work."

"I promise, Ted. I do miss him and his annoying habits and terrible taste in music. Does he still play Britney Spears in the garage while he works?"

"He's graduated to Beyoncé."

I snorted.

"And how about you? Your business doing well? Mike searched for you on the internet and said you have a vintage bike shop and garage?"

"Yeah. Business is doing well, and I love Connecticut."

Ted closed his eyes for a moment, his face looked tired all of a sudden, and I wondered if he was ready to sleep again.

"Let me call Mike back, okay?"

"Just one thing, son. Don't let the past drag behind you like a bad smell. We all have pasts. I know you couldn't have done anything about Mike, but you're still young. If there's another chance out there waiting for you, take it."

I thought about Aiden and the conversation we'd had last night when I'd told him everything. Ted was right.

"Ted, my second chance is on the other side of that door a few yards away, waiting for me. He's wonderful, and you'll get to meet him soon."

He nodded and closed his eyes.

I called Mike back into the room.

"So I guess that's it now. We can't fight and you have to be my friend," he said.

"You got the pep talk too?"

Mike smiled. His brown eyes looked at me with the same love they always held, but also more.

I walked over and hugged him. He hugged me back. We were the same height, but Mike always felt like he was bigger to me.

"You still give the best hugs," I said.

"Remember that."

Ted opened his eyes again and raised both his hands. We stood on either side of his bed, holding his hands, and then reached out for each other too.

"Now that's better," he said, his speech a little slurred. "Rose, honey, I'm on my way. There better be cherry pie."

He closed his eyes, and a minute later, the machines Ted was connected to gave us the warning he was no longer with us.

The nurses ran into the room to silence the beeping noise and do what they needed to do. Mike and I held each other as we said one final goodbye to the man that had been a father to both of us.

24

———

AIDEN

If I was writing my life as it was, I'd have the presence of mind to know I was in shock. But I wasn't writing it, I was living it, and when you're living your life, you don't stop to consider your feelings, your actions, the bigger picture.

So yeah, the moment I saw Slade walk down the corridor hand in hand with Mike, I pocketed my phone and ran toward him.

He opened his arms for me and held me tight. I felt his tears on my neck. There was nothing I could say in that moment, so I let him cry as I ran my hands up and down his back.

When he finally stopped, I cleaned the tears with a tissue and handed him the bottle of water.

Slade smiled and drank most of the water in one go.

"I'm so sorry for your loss, Mike," I said and ran my hand up his arm. He looked very shaken too.

"Would you...would you come home with me? There's a few things Ted said he wanted you to have," Mike said to Slade.

"I'll go back to the hotel and pick you up later when you're ready," I said.

"No. You're coming with us."

Mike nodded. He didn't seem upset that I was tagging along, but I still felt like I was being assessed.

We followed Mike's car in silence, which put me a little on edge. My phone burned in my pocket, buzzing every so often, but I ignored it.

I looked at Slade, who was staring out of the window, lost in thought.

"Hey," I said gently.

"Hey," he replied. I glanced at him when we hit a red traffic light and he was staring at me.

I took his hand and lifted it to my lips, kissing his palm.

"It's been a while, huh?" I said.

"Yeah. These streets are so different now, but they're also the same."

Ted's place was like I'd imagined. The garage was shut, but from the size of the metal gates, it was much bigger than Slade's, though there was no shop attached to it. We followed Mike to a door on the side which led to an indoor staircase. At the top there were two doors, one on either side.

Mike opened the door to the left, but I noticed Slade staring at the door on the right.

It was strange being in the house of a man I hadn't met and that had just passed away.

The place was very tidy and didn't have much inside.

"He started getting rid of stuff when he got the terminal diagnosis," Mike said. "He said there was no point in keeping old crap as he put it."

"He got rid of his chair too?" Slade asked.

"No, that's at our place, um…my place. He moved in with me a few months ago."

Mike picked up a box and took us to his place, which as it turned out was the door opposite Ted's.

I felt like I was intruding in Slade's old life as I followed them into Mike's place. There were photos of them all over the walls.

Two young guys with their arms around each other, clearly so much in love. There were photos of the beach, mountains, viewpoints. It looked like they'd traveled and enjoyed their life together.

"Um, can I make myself useful? I can make coffee or get some water, if you like?" I asked. They were both on the couch with the box on the coffee table in front of them.

"Thank you, Aiden, coffee would be nice, actually. The kitchen is through there, everything is easy to find."

I nodded and walked toward the corridor leading to the kitchen, busying myself with the coffee machine. My phone buzzed again. I took it out just in time to see the screen go dark as the battery died. That was probably for the best.

I needed to keep going, keep focusing on Slade and what he needed. Mike too. What I saw on my phone had to have an explanation, but now wasn't the time to seek it.

As I waited for the coffee to brew, I inspected a notice board next to the fridge. There were cards with medical appointments, takeout menus, and some photos. All of them included Slade.

Was Mike holding on to Slade? Had he not moved on?

We spent the rest of the day with Mike. I mostly watched as they remembered Ted as they went through old photos and memories. I could see how Slade and Mike had been so suited to each other.

Mike was, for the lack of a better term, a big teddy bear of a man, with his sparkly eyes and friendly personality. He really didn't match the actions of a man who'd cheated on his husband.

After dinner I offered to wash up the dishes while they put all the photos away.

I was drying them when Mike came in the kitchen.

"Hey," I said. "All okay out there?"

"Yeah, he's just in the bathroom…um, Aiden…I'm…I don't know how to say this, but I hope you love him as much as he loves you."

"What do you mean, he doesn't…"

My heart raced. Okay, I'd hoped that was the case, but that was before my phone call this morning. Before the video. I still hadn't handled that. How would Slade react when he found out?

"I've known that man half my life. I always knew there was something he wasn't telling me about himself. There was something missing in our relationship. My uncle always defended Slade, so I learned to accept that something happened in his past that I couldn't know about. But I can tell he's told you because he looks at you like you're his lifeline. He leans on you more than he ever leaned on me. So if you know his truth, you know how much that means."

I put the dishcloth on the counter and hugged Mike.

"You're a good man, Mike."

"Eh, I have my moments."

"Will you be okay after he leaves?"

"I'll make do."

We ended up checking out of the hotel and staying with Mike for a few days until the funeral.

The ordeal of putting his uncle to rest was too much for Slade, so whenever he wasn't helping Mike with stuff, he was asleep.

I ended up finding Mike and I had more in common than just Slade, and before we left I made him promise to visit Slade in Chester Falls at some point.

He gave me a pointed stare when it sounded as though I might not be around then, but I deflected.

When Slade had been asleep, and with my phone's battery fully charged, I'd finally seen the whole video. I'd had to hide in the bathroom so I wouldn't disturb Slade.

I'd also read the messages from Richard. *I want to see you. When will you be back? Don't ignore me, dammit. Aiden, we have a history together. Did you like the video we made, sweetie? You loved being a dirty little whore for me, didn't you?*

I stopped being able to read more of the messages through the tears in my eyes.

There was no way out of this. What if he went public with the video? He'd been clever enough so that while I'd been fully exposed, his face wasn't visible. The person on the video could literally be anyone. Which meant he was holding the cards in my life. Again.

The closer we were to Chester Falls, the more anxious I got. I still hadn't decided what I was going to do about Richard. I knew I had to call him, but I was terrified of doing it.

"Hey, you're a million miles away," Slade said, taking my hand and lacing our fingers together over his thigh.

"Just thinking."

"About your book?"

"Um, yeah…"

"Let me know if there's anything else I can help you with for your research. Liam texted me to say the parts that went off to be powder-coated are back."

It seemed that as my anxiety spiked, Slade's seemed to disappear, so I let him believe I'd simply been thinking about my book.

When we arrived at his place, I made excuses that I had stuff to catch up on and told him to spend some time with Harley. He'd looked at me funny but didn't argue, especially since he did have a business to run and had been away for almost a week.

As if Richard could guess I was on my own, his name appeared on the screen of my phone.

I straightened my back, hoping it would give me extra courage, and answered the call.

"What do you want?"

"I told you, baby. I want you to come home. To me. Where you belong."

"What's the point? I don't love you and you don't love me. You know I can't get married without a prenup, so what's your goal?

"Oh, honey, a relationship is much more than loving someone. It's about companionship, it's about the things we can do for each other." His voice grated on me. How had I never noticed how whiny he sounded? Oh yeah, because he'd manipulated me into loving him.

"You mean you want access to my money."

He gasped. "Honey, I'm shocked you'd say that. This is about us taking care of each other. Your mother agrees we should give our relationship another try."

My heart sank. He'd been speaking to my parents?

25

SLADE

AFTER BEING around Aiden for a whole week, it was strange not having him around. My apartment felt empty, and I was at a loss for what to do.

He'd seemed eager to go home on his own, which after the week we'd had didn't surprise me, and that was why I hadn't pressed the matter.

Aiden had gotten along with Mike better than I'd expected. Well, I hadn't expected them to get along at all.

Since my talk with Ted, and then after going to Mike's place, I'd noticed certain things about Mike.

He'd lost a little of his spark and there was no indication in the apartment that he'd had anyone over at all. In fact, visiting the apartment now was more or less like stepping into our old life.

Had Mike been on his own since we split? Maybe I'd been unfair to him when we spoke that first time. It didn't matter, we'd parted on good terms and I had a feeling we'd stay in touch.

If that had been Ted's last wish, then he'd succeeded.

But I couldn't shake the feeling that there was something up with Aiden. I'd noticed he'd been quieter than usual.

Was he having doubts about us? Was coming to Atlanta with me too much? After all, he was young, and guys his age didn't often have to face the mortality of a loved one, even if he didn't know Ted. Or maybe it was all the stuff I'd offloaded on him.

I ran my fingers through my hair, walking up and down my living room. He'd said he was there…here, he'd said he was here for me. But what if he'd said it because he knew we were about to visit a dying man? What if he was trying to make me feel better?

There was a knock on my door. Was Aiden back? I ran to it so fast, I nearly tripped on my feet.

When I opened the door, I was faced with the last person I ever thought I'd see again.

"Hey, Doc, you gonna invite me in?"

The respect for a fellow club member was so ingrained in me, even after all these years, that all I could do was step aside and let him in.

"Nice place. I see you're in shock, so let's clarify some things first. I'm alone. I come in peace, just to see a friend."

I knew he wouldn't harm me, he'd been one of the nicest guys at the club, but the thought that they were still out there and maybe looking for me made my blood run cold.

"Kickstand," I finally said.

"Once a Kickstand, always a Kickstand, right? Although it's President Kickstand now."

He turned around to show me his club patch. *The Lost Puppies.*

"You're not with the club?" I asked.

"Nah, man, the club disbanded after the police got their hands on the president and found out he was involved in a load of illegal shit. Haven't seen any of them for years. Last I heard, half of them had died either from illness or less natural causes, if you know what I mean."

I shook my head. "I can't believe you're here."

"If I'm honest, me neither."

"Let me get us something to drink. You riding?" I asked.

"Yeah. If you have beer, I'll take one and a glass of water."

I grabbed a couple of beers from the fridge and went back to the living room where Kickstand was inspecting my bookshelf.

"Damn. I wanna make fun of you, but I did a stint in prison a few years back and started reading to pass the time. This A. Lawton guy is good."

I smiled. "That he is. So, tell me, Kick…I don't even know what your real name is."

"Travis."

"Travis, how did you find me?"

"I should be offended that you didn't recognize me, but then again you were with a guy that had the tightest ass I've ever seen, so I don't blame you for not noticing."

I ignored the way he spoke about Aiden and tried to think instead about where I'd been with Aiden that Travis would have been too.

"The roadside bar. Was that you…your club?"

"Yeah. I wanted to approach you then, but I didn't know what kind of life you have now, or who you're involved with, so I took your license plate and did some digging around to find you."

I laughed. "Haven't been involved with anything since I escaped that hellhole. I ride solo these days."

"Yeah, I gathered. Your shop looks great, by the way."

"Thanks. So tell me about your club. President? Who did you accidentally kill to become president of anything?"

He raised a brow and took a sip of his beer.

"Fuck you, Doc. No one was hurt in my quest to be president of The Lost Puppies."

I nearly spluttered my beer all over the couch.

"Okay, please call me Slade. Doc died a long time ago, and I'm an independent now, so there's no formality there. What I want to know is…Lost Puppies? Really?"

"I'll spare you my life story, but we're mainly a child support charity. We organize runs to raise money for kids that need help with medical care, education tools, and we run a Big Biker, Little Biker group for kids without a male role model."

I had no words. I always saw my past as something ugly, rotten, evil. Everyone and everything was bad. Even when I knew I'd met good people, such as my foster parents and my neighbor, they were linked to that time in my life and became mixed in with the darkness.

Maybe I wasn't the only one in the darkness. And maybe just like

I'd found something good to hold on to, Ted and Mike, other guys had too.

"How did you get into the club?"

"I married into it."

"Congrats, man."

He shook his head.

"Oh, fuck, I'm sorry."

"Yeah, lost Sam going on ten years ago."

"I'm so sorry, Travis."

He finished his beer and drank the full glass of water straight away.

"I look back sometimes and wonder at how many lifetimes I've lived already, you know? How many life-changing decisions I've made. How cursed I felt and how lucky I was. Still am."

Wasn't that the truth?

"I know how that feels more than you know, brother."

He peeked at his watch and stood up. "I better get going. Sorry to drop on your doorstep unannounced like this. When I saw you, I...I don't know. I don't have great memories of that time, but I always thought you were a good guy, and if life taught me anything, it was to hold on to the good guys."

I stepped into his space and gave him a hug.

"Thank you, Travis. I am glad you came by. Let's keep in touch."

After he left, I had a sudden rush of energy come over me. I was dying to see Aiden, touch him, make love to him, tell him I was so ridiculously in love with him. I wanted to beg him to move to Chester Falls, or hell, I'd move to San Diego.

Was there anything more worthy in life than pursuing this? No.

I'd lost so much in my life already. But I'd also gained so much. It was time to focus on the good stuff. And Aiden was my good stuff.

But after being thrust into my life over the last week, Aiden deserved some time to himself. I'd give him tonight, and then tomorrow I'd sweep him off his feet or kidnap him and tie him to my bed. Potato, potahto.

I spent the rest of the day cleaning the apartment, catching up with my laundry, and even cooked a nice meal for myself, which I ate after I had a long, hot shower and trimmed my beard.

After dinner I settled on the couch with one of the books I'd gotten at the book fair and hadn't read yet. I hadn't even gotten to the end of the first chapter when my phone rang.

I smiled when I saw Aiden's name pop up.

"Hey."

"Hi…Slade. Um, I'm sorry to do this to you last minute, but I have to go back to San Diego. I can't help you finish the bike. I'm so sorry."

What? No. No. No.

"Aiden, what's wrong? You don't sound like yourself. Let me come over there."

"No! I'm fine, honestly. I just have stuff I need to attend to. I haven't been home for nearly a month, so…"

"Can I come with you? You shouldn't drive all the way on your own."

"No, please, Slade, just…" He let out a breath on the other side.

Was this it? Were we done, just like that, with no explanation?

"Aid, please. I know the last week was tough. All the stuff I told you, and then Ted and meeting Mike, but—"

"Slade." He said my name as if it were final. "I'm sorry."

He hung up, which was as good as sticking a knife right through my heart and twisting it.

26

——————

AIDEN

IT TOOK me a whole hour after hanging up on Slade to pull myself off the floor where I'd sat down crying. I'd promised I'd be there for him, and I was breaking that promise.

I needed to get to San Diego and face Richard. Maybe I could convince him to delete the video.

Even as the thought crossed my mind, I knew it was pointless. He probably already had a bunch of copies. He could delete the video, but I'd never trust that there wasn't another copy out there.

Maybe he just wanted money, maybe I could pay him off. If he'd been after me just for the money, surely that would be it, right? I'd pay him off and he'd go away.

Except he could come back over and over again. I would never be free of him.

A new sob of desperation ran through me.

"Come on, Aiden. Pick yourself up. You need to figure this shit out. Do I fly, or do I drive?"

If I took a flight, I'd get there faster, but I'd still need to drive my car to the airport and then I'd have no way to get it. If I drove, it would take me a week to get to the other side of the country.

I picked up my phone and opened the messaging app.

Aiden: I need to drive home. It'll take me a week.

    Richard: A week? Where are you? Timbuktu?

    Aiden: I'm on the East Coast.

    Richard: Oh, visiting your little friends, are you? I suppose since you're coming home to me, I'll wait.

    Aiden: Thank you.

Two hours later I had the car packed up, saving for some last-minute items, and I'd called the parents of the apartment owner to let them know I'd be leaving in the morning.

There was one last thing, I needed to speak to Wren. It wasn't fair to leave without any warning, but it was already too late to drop by his place. I messaged him for a run early in the morning, which was met with a GIF of a cat yawning, but since he didn't flat out say no, I assumed he'd be here.

Going for a run on very little sleep was a bad idea, but since good ideas were in short supply these days, I'd have to suck it up.

"Why are we running so early? Have you killed Slade with your energetic lovemaking?" Wren said, using the steps outside my building to stretch his legs.

"No, I wasn't with him last night."

"Ahh, too horny to sleep. Gotcha."

We started with a slow jog to warm up. We usually picked up our pace once we were on the forest trail.

"Tom and I have some news," he said.

"You finally got him pregnant after all this time trying?"

"Never have I ever been so glad to be with a guy. We can try all we want. And we do try a lot," he said.

"Is it something you want?"

We ran in silence for a moment, picking up the pace a little. It was harder to speak, but we'd been doing this for a long time and needing oxygen had never stopped us from managing a conversation.

"Yeah. We want to have the wedding first, go on a honeymoon, and then when we're back, we'll start looking into surrogacy."

"That's great. Congrats. Was that your news?"

"No, we have a wedding date."

"Wow, when?"

"December twentieth."

"This year?"

"Yeah."

"Okay, I'm sure I can come back for that."

I was so focused on breathing that I didn't realize Wren had stopped completely.

"What do you mean, you'll come back for it?"

"You know I don't live here, right?"

"Yeah, but with Slade being here, I thought..."

I took a deep breath and went for it. Pull it off like a Band-Aid and get it over with.

"I'm leaving today."

"What?"

Wren's voice was so loud that some birds in nearby trees took flight.

"What happened? Why so soon?"

"It's not really that soon, is it? I've been here for three weeks."

"But you went to Atlanta with Slade. I thought you guys were—"

"Having fun. That's what we were doing. Yes, I was there for him at a difficult time, but it doesn't mean that he'll want a relationship with me. And I have things to do in San Diego, so..."

"I don't buy it."

"You don't need to. It is what it is," I said, hoping this would put the conversation to an end.

He resumed the run, so I thought we were done, until he stopped again.

"Are you in love with him?"

Of course I'm fucking in love with him. That's what I wanted to say, but what I said instead was, "He was a good fuck."

Classy, Aiden. Very classy.

Wren pulled my arm with such force that I thought it was going to detach from my body and wrapped his arms around me.

He didn't say anything for a long time, just stayed there, in the middle of the forest, hugging me. And the longer he did it, the bigger the lump in my throat grew.

"Fuck you, Wren, for making me cry. I'm going to miss you, you fucking motherfucker."

"Since when did you develop such a potty mouth, Aiden Lawton?" he joked, but his hold on me didn't let up. "I don't know what's going on, Aid, but I love you and Tom loves you, and so do the rest of the guys. We'll miss you."

All I could do was nod against him.

"And you better throw me a kick-ass bachelor party."

"What?"

"Please don't insult me by being surprised that I'm asking you to be my best man."

I laughed. "I'd be honored."

We finished the run, and I promised to be in touch soon.

I stopped in Ohio for the night. Exhausted and hungry, I grabbed a burger from a local bar and went straight to bed in a roadside motel.

I had another four days of this until I was home. Not that San Diego or my apartment felt like home anymore. It was more like I was heading to a prison sentence.

Throughout the week, Richard kept texting and asking where I was. I ignored as many of them as I could without setting him off. The drive also made me reflect a lot on my relationship with Richard.

I came to terms that it had been an abusive relationship.

How had I not noticed how we only had sex when he wanted? How I always paid for everything? How he'd put me down if my book didn't hit the charts on release day? How he seemed to be purposefully noisy when I needed silence to write, and then berate me for not hitting my word count?

I tried to keep as many of those thoughts at bay because they made me cry, and I couldn't drive if I was crying.

By the third day, anxiety was my constant companion. Were there more videos?

I tried to remember how many times he'd asked to blindfold me during sex, saying we needed to be more adventurous in bed. Our relationship would last longer if we had fun in bed.

I'd never had fun in those times. I wasn't even able to orgasm. But he seemed to enjoy it, so I did it for an easy life. How had I not seen the signs?

When I saw the road sign for San Diego, my mind was in such a state of confusion that I wasn't sure if I was happy, sad, or afraid to have arrived.

At least I could take a long bath and rest in my own bed before I had to face Richard.

I tried not to think of Slade, but that was a failed attempt. Every mile away from him was like a part of my heart was being shredded and left on the side of the road.

I would call him soon and apologize properly. He deserved that much. Maybe Mike would visit him at some point, and they would rekindle their love.

That thought made me feel sick, and not just because thinking of them together made me jealous. I knew deep down Slade and Mike had had their time and it had ended. What made me feel sick was the thought of Slade either settling for a half-love or being alone forever.

By the time I pulled in front of my apartment, I was beyond exhausted. I knew I'd pushed the last few hundred miles. I really should have stopped another night, but I just wanted my own bed.

I didn't bother with anything else in the car other than my laptop bag, which had my wallet and phone inside. I locked the car and dragged my tired legs up the stairs to the front door.

My stomach jumped when I saw a figure standing by the door. My eyes were dry from the contacts, so I rubbed my them and looked up again.

"Slade? What are you doing—"

27

SLADE

"I LOVE YOU. I love you. I love you."

Aiden threw himself at me, saying the words over and over again. I wasn't even sure he was conscious that he was saying it. But damn, even if I lost my hearing, I'd still remember it for the rest of my life. All I could do was hope that I would hear this for the rest of my life.

"Well, that was easier than I thought," I said into his hair, kissing his head as he lowered his voice to a whisper but never stopped saying he loved me.

"Baby, let me take you upstairs," I said. He nodded and leaned into me as he got out the key to the door. I grabbed the handle of my suitcase and let him guide us.

Aiden's apartment was enormous. Most of it seemed open plan with a corridor on the opposite end to the front door.

"Is that the way to your bedroom?"

He nodded.

We dropped the bags by the couch and walked to the bedroom.

Aiden seemed to be in a zombie-like state. He was probably overly tired and had just stayed alert long enough to make it home. The thought that he could have had an accident made my blood run cold, but he was here and unharmed, and that was all that mattered.

When I found the bathroom attached to his room I helped him out of his clothes and turned the shower on. It was quite warm inside the apartment, so I opened a few windows to get a breeze through and some fresh air.

When the water was warm enough, I undressed and pulled Aiden into the shower with me.

"Are you okay?" I asked.

"Yes. Are you really here?"

"I am, baby. And in case you're wondering, I love you too."

He started crying into my chest.

"It's okay, baby. I'll keep repeating it until the words are all you can remember forever."

I grabbed his shampoo and lathered it in my hand before running it over his hair, massaging his scalp. Aiden looked like he was hanging by a thread, but he was still standing up on his own so that was a good thing.

As soon as we were both washed, I helped him get dried and then carried him over to the bedroom.

"I'm not a princess," he slurred.

"No, baby, but I'm going to treat you like one until you're feeling better."

"No pillows..."

"You don't want pillows or you do?"

"More pillows, your pillows."

I chuckled. His closet held two extra, so I grabbed them and placed them behind him before I settled against him, pulling the covers over us.

Aiden was asleep even before I finished tucking him up properly. I wrapped my arms around him, feeling at peace for the first time since he'd left me in my apartment.

Sleep claimed me shortly after.

I woke up to Aiden's barely coherent moans. He was moving, but without enough force that he'd hurt me or himself.

"No, please, don't do it. Please..."

"Shh, baby, it's okay," I whispered, hoping he'd wake up of his own accord.

"No, no, it's not. Don't do it."

I had no clue what he was dreaming about, but it didn't sound pleasant.

"Aiden, sweetheart. Can you wake up for me?" I ran my hands through his hair until he stopped moving and his eyes opened slowly.

"Slade?"

"There you are," I said, smiling. "My beautiful, brown-eyed boy."

"No," he screamed, sitting up in bed. "No, you can't be here. Oh my god, what if he sees you?"

He scrambled off the bed to a chest of drawers, taking out underwear and then a pair of sweatpants and a T-shirt.

I got up and went over to him. When I turned him around, his eyes were full of tears.

"Aiden, what's going on? You're worrying the hell out of me."

I'd known something was wrong with Aiden even before Wren and Tom had turned up at my doorstep with blazing guns and threats of the make-it-right-or-lose-your-balls kind.

So I'd spent a whole night tossing and turning, trying to analyze every conversation we'd had, every time we'd been together, and as a last resort, I'd called Mike.

After all we'd been with him almost a week, so maybe he'd seen something in Aiden, or maybe they'd talked. Mike had not just suggested but pointed right out that we were in love with each other but neither had actually said those words.

And *that* was what I thought was wrong.

But the state Aiden was in meant there had to be more to him rushing to San Diego.

I ran over to the living room to grab some clothes from my suitcase and rushed back to the bedroom.

Aiden was sitting on the edge of his bed with his head down. I sat next to him.

"What happened, Aiden?"

"Richard...Richard called me when we were at the hospital in Atlanta. He wanted to see me, but I told him I wasn't home. He told me to come home because it was important. I refused, so he sent me something."

I ran my hand between his shoulder blades, but it didn't seem to release any of his tension.

"What did he send you?"

"A video. A video of me…and him. Slade, I had no idea he'd done it. It's so embarrassing. He blindfolded me and told me to say certain things. Then he…we had sex. He filmed everything. And he's threatening to release the video on the internet unless we get back together."

So many feelings came over me, with the dominant one being anger at Richard the Fucking Tiny Dick for doing this to Aiden. For abusing his trust. For using it against him. For daring to threaten him.

Aiden had been carrying this anxiety on his own for ten days. No wonder he was at a breaking point.

"When is he expecting you?" I asked.

"I don't know. I was meant to have stopped for the night yesterday, so I guess…tonight? I wanted a few hours to get myself together before I got in touch with him."

"Do you think he'll release the video before he sees you?"

Aiden looked at me. His eyes full of fear, as if he hadn't considered that option, but then he said, "No, I don't think so. He wants money, so if he releases the video that's it, the video is out there."

"So he wants to keep the threat over your head, so you'll do anything he wants. Would he ever follow through on his threat?"

"Yes. If I push him far enough, he'll do it out of spite to ruin my reputation. This would ruin my parents' reputation too. We don't have the best relationship, but this could blacklist them from a lot of stuff they're involved with in New York. They mostly do charity work now, so this could have a bigger effect on the people they help."

I got up and walked around the room, trying to put my feelings aside so I could think straight. There was no way of telling how many copies of the video Dick had, and if there was more than one.

One thing was certain, I wasn't giving up Aiden for anything, so the moment Dick found out about us, he could well go off the rails and release the videos anyway.

"Okay, it's a wild shot, but I think there is someone who could help us," I said.

I grabbed my phone and sent Tom a message asking for his friend

Connor's phone number. Connor's husband, James, had once been the bodyguard to the Prince of Lydovia, who happened to be married to Tom's best friend, Charlie. But my understanding was that before that he'd been some kind of computer whiz in the special forces.

I put the phone down while we waited for Tom's reply and then went over to Aiden, kneeling in front of him.

"Are you okay?"

He shrugged. "How did you get here? How did you know where I live?"

I chuckled. "You know airplanes travel faster than cars, right?"

"I thought you preferred riding."

"I do, but when there's something wrong with the love of my life, I'll fly, swim, run, walk, I'll do anything to get to you when you need me. Even when you don't tell me you need me."

"Wait…love of your…"

He widened his eyes and covered his mouth with his hand as he gasped.

"Oh my god, I totally threw myself at you last night, didn't I?"

"Uh huh." I pulled his hand down and replaced it with mine, tracing his soft lips. "And you told me you love me."

"I did…I mean…I do. I love you, Slade. So much."

I pressed my lips against his, feeling his warm breath on my skin. He put his hands on my face and pulled me closer, running his fingers down my beard. It was a tame kiss by all accounts, but it was by far the best kiss ever because it felt like coming home.

It was right, comforting, and it was Aiden.

"I love you too, Aiden. In case that wasn't clear by flying across the country to meet you or by telling you last night."

He laughed, and it was the best sound ever.

It was followed by my phone dinging with a message I hoped would help us get rid of Tiny Dick from Aiden's life once and for all.

28

AIDEN

I KEPT my eyes on Slade as he made the call to Connor.

My recollection of the night before was hazy at best, but I did remember declaring my love for him as soon as I saw him. I must have been in a state of delirium from overtiredness, but the words and the feelings were real. And he loved me too.

Now I could see how ridiculous it was that I ran away, but at the same time, acknowledging our feelings didn't make Richard's threat go away.

I had no solution for a way out other than give Richard what he wanted, as much as it would destroy me and Slade to do it. But maybe there was something.

Slade seemed to be speaking confidently to Connor, or maybe James. I couldn't get much from his side of the conversation.

"Babe, James wants to ask you some questions."

"Okay."

Slade passed me his phone.

"Hello?"

"Hi, Aiden, this is James. I'm really sorry this is happening to you. I'll do whatever I can to stop Pencil Dick from ruining your life. I just need some details, okay?"

"Sure, anything." I loved how everyone kept giving Richard those ridiculous nicknames. Under any other circumstances, I wouldn't encourage it, but it did make me feel like he had a little less power over me, just by the fact that no one respected him enough to ever use his name.

"I need to know a little about his shopping habits. Like what he buys online, what brands, etc."

"He likes to shop in person, but he will only buy socks from this online store that uses high quality cashmere. You can buy suits cheaper than a pair of those socks."

"That's great. Here's what we're going to do…"

I put James on speakerphone so Slade could hear it too.

The plan seemed fairly easy to execute, but the worst was that, in order for the plan to work, I'd need to have Richard over.

We ended the call after agreeing with James to lay low in the apartment and move my car so Richard wouldn't see it if he thought to come by. As far as he was concerned, I was still on the road, but there was no way to know if he'd checked up on the apartment or not. At least he didn't have a key, so he couldn't come in.

Thirty minutes later, Slade walked back into the apartment after moving the car. He was holding a shopping bag.

"What have you got there?" I asked.

He wiggled his eyebrows, taking a box of pancake mix, a bottle of chocolate sauce, and a squirt can of whipped cream out of the bag.

"No…"

I was still wearing the sweatpants I'd put on in panic earlier, but even my underwear was doing nothing to hide my hardness as Slade walked toward me, slowly removing his shirt.

"We have some time to kill, and you need breakfast," he said.

I walked slowly backward, biting my lip so I wouldn't moan at the sight of Slade removing his pants.

"And what are *you* going to have for breakfast?" I asked, even though I already knew the answer.

He crossed the space between us. "I'm going to have you."

A shiver of anticipation went down my spine. I ran toward the bedroom with Slade on my heels. He caught me by the waist and we both fell on the bed.

My clothes disappeared in a second and then there was only warm skin to warm skin.

He kissed a trail down my neck until he reached my chest. His beard tickled, which only served to heighten the sensation of Slade's teeth biting softly and then licking over my nipples.

I let out a moan and fisted the bedsheets.

"Hold that thought."

A minute later chocolate sauce dripped from the bottle onto my stomach, followed by a squirt of cream.

"You look delicious, baby. I might have to have a bite."

I couldn't even look at him. His eyes were on fire and his tongue worked me into a frenzy, and it wasn't anywhere near my cock.

"Please, Slade. If you love me just a tiny bit, you'll fuck me right now."

"Just a tiny bit? Babe, I love you more than love itself."

I sat up to kiss him and sighed when he followed me back to a lying position with him on top. His weight felt so good on me. His strong thighs against mine, the way his hair tickled me, and even though we were making a mess with the chocolate and cream, I didn't give a shit. I just wanted to feel him.

"Bedside table. Second drawer."

He looked at me. "What's in the top drawer?"

I bit my lips shut and smiled, shrugging innocently.

"Aiden...?"

He opened the top drawer and discovered my secret. Something I'd gotten a while ago but hadn't used.

"Why do you have a make-your-own-dildo kit in your drawer?"

"It was a joke gift from Wren...I never thought I'd get to use it, but now..."

I felt myself blush. Was I really going to confess it? He took a condom and lube from the second drawer and kneeled between my thighs.

"You have until I'm inside you to tell me what's in that sexy, dirty little head of yours."

I laid back down, moaning as Slade opened me with his fingers. How was I supposed to talk when he was doing *that* to me?

"Um…fuck, like that…Jesus, Slade…give me your big, fat cock," I demanded.

"Nuh huh, this isn't how it works."

I groaned. "Fine. First time we fucked, I thought that I'd do anything to have you in my mouth and my ass at the same time. There. Fuck me now."

His dick pressed against my hole, and I moved to bear down on it. I needed him so badly.

"So you're saying you want to make a mold of my cock," he said, pushing in a little farther. "So you can suck me," and a little more, "while I fuck you with the dildo of my cock?"

"Fuck, yeah," I moaned embarrassingly loud when he was all the way inside me. "God, I love your cock, Slade."

"It's a good thing I love your ass, baby. And you."

I couldn't tell how long we were like that for, him sliding in and out of me, slowly building up his speed as if we had all the time in the world.

Every time I was close to coming, he slowed down. I was going to punch him hard next time he referred to himself as old or lacking stamina. My legs were shaking and my body was sore, even though I was doing nothing else but taking him in, welcoming him, and letting him claim me.

I wondered if he'd be up to getting tested soon because I wanted him with no barriers between us. The thought of fucking his ass without a condom was almost enough to bring on my orgasm.

"Fuck, baby, you feel so good."

I couldn't even speak. Nothing intelligible, at least.

"Hook your legs over my shoulders," he said between gritted teeth.

Good. I wasn't the only one struggling to keep going.

In this position we didn't have as much skin contact, but the angle was perfect for him to hit my spot. He wrapped his hand around my dick and stroked me in time with each one of his.

Ropes of cum covered my stomach as I gave in to my orgasm. Sparks danced in my eyes as blood rushed all over my body. Slade came a moment later, biting my calf as he emptied into the condom inside me.

He withdrew from me and then laid down next to me, pulling me in for a slow, languid kiss.

"I think we should take this into the shower," I said. Not that my legs had any will to move, but I was sticky with cum, chocolate, and cream. Debauched was an understatement for how I felt and looked.

Slade gave me a heated gaze full of promise. I just hoped James's plan worked and we could be happy together without any threat from Tiny Dick. And now even I was calling him by his nickname. Maybe having Slade here with me took some power away from Tiny Dick already.

"Hey," I said, scooting out of bed after Slade. "Is Liam still taking care of Harley? How often do you feed her? Last time she ate up the ham I brought her, as if it was going out of fashion."

"Huh?"

He looked puzzled.

"I'm confused that you seem confused."

"That's because I am. You know bikes run on gas, right?"

"Not the bike, dumbass. The cat."

"What cat?"

"Your cat."

He laughed.

"I don't have a cat."

"What?" I grabbed my phone from the bedside table and searched for the photo I'd taken of Harley asleep on top of a toolbox. "Yes, you do. This one."

Slade looked at the photo and laughed aloud.

"Babe, are you telling me that you've been feeding a stray cat all this time?"

"I didn't know she was a stray. She told me her name was Harley."

He laughed again, pulling me toward the bathroom.

"Sounds like you need feeding more urgently than I thought." He sprayed the warm water over me before using my shampoo to wash my hair. "Tell me, how did she tell you her name?"

I rolled my eyes. "I asked her if her name was Ginger, and she seemed offended by it and then she jumped on the bike, so I asked her if her name was Harley, and she meowed."

Okay, now that I said that aloud maybe it sounded a little weird.

He ran the water over my head to wash off the shampoo.

"I guess we're now the proud parents of a cat named Harley, aren't we?"

I shrugged. "I guess we are."

"Oh, Aiden, Aiden, what am I going to do with you?"

I ran my hands over the silver hairs on his chest. "I can give you an idea…or a hundred."

Slade's phone ringing in the bedroom put an end to our shower and brought back some of the anxiety that Slade had successfully banished.

29

SLADE

RELIEF WASHED through me when James told us he'd successfully deleted all the videos from Richard's laptop and cloud. We just needed to execute part two of the plan, which unfortunately involved Aiden calling Richard to come over.

Aiden stilled when the intercom buzzed and looked at me like a deer in headlights.

"Hey, you're gonna be fine. You've got this."

"What if I can't get his phone?"

I'd pressed the buzzer to let Dick in the door downstairs, so we only had a minute. "Then we'll try again another time. It's unlikely he'll notice all the videos on his cloud are gone, so we have time."

I kissed him and went to hide in the spare room, leaving the door open a crack, so I could overhear them.

Moments later Aiden opened the door.

"Hey, beautiful. So glad to see you finally. You really could have made an effort to get home earlier. I missed you so much."

I clenched my fists until my knuckles were white and I felt my nails bite into my palms. Even the guy's voice was annoying.

Calm down, Slade. We have a plan.

"Nice to see you too, Richard. Please come in."

"You don't look pleased to see me, honey."

I couldn't hear anything for a moment until Aiden replied, "I'm just tired from the trip, that's all."

"Anyway, I spoke to your mom yesterday and she's coming to visit soon. I think it's only wise that I move back in, don't you think?"

"Why?"

"You don't want her to think there's problems with our rekindled relationship, do you?"

I heard more movement, and from the small opening of the door, I saw Aiden move to the kitchen island. Perfect.

That's it, baby. You're doing well.

"Richard, we split up over a year ago. Do you think it's believable that we'd go straight back into a blissful relationship?"

Dick came into view. Aiden had shown me a photo of him, but in person he was even more sleazy than I'd imagined. The guy looked okay. Tall, with dark, styled hair, but when you're an ugly person on the inside, it doesn't matter how much you shine on the outside, you're still full of shit.

Aiden placed a glass of water on the island. He was keeping busy as I'd told him to because it would disguise any nerves.

Dick reached out for his hand. Aiden tried to pull back, but Dick held it.

"Baby, you have the perfect incentive, don't you? If you don't want your sick perversions to come out, you'll play nice with Mommy."

"Why are you doing this?" Aiden asked.

"Isn't it obvious?" He ran his finger up Aiden's arm.

He was lucky that they were on opposite sides of the island, or I wouldn't be able to contain myself. Punching him until his nose needed corrective surgery was not part of the plan.

"Not to me, Richard."

"I loved you, Aiden. Even when you were a nobody. But you never listened to me. You could be even more than you are. Reach heights other authors in your genre could only dream to reach. It was as if you were allergic to making money."

Aiden shook his head.

"I made enough money, Richard."

"Only people with money say that, you privileged little brat."

Aiden flinched but held himself. We needed Richard to keep going.

"When you didn't want to follow my advice, I thought maybe we could get married. Have the lifestyle we dreamed of, the lifestyle we deserved. But you had to come out with that lie about your trust fund."

"I didn't—"

"Shut up," Dick said louder, placing his phone on the island. "I have it right here. I recorded a call with your mother in which she told me that wasn't true. In fact, you can access your trust fund any time you want. Isn't that right, Aiden dear?"

Aiden went around the island. "Is that what you want? Money?"

"No, Aiden. I want everything. You, your money, your lifestyle, your connections. I want the life I thought I was going to have when we first met, and I found out who you are."

Aiden's voice was low, but not low enough that I couldn't hear it. "Please forgive me. Please, Richard. You're right. I was selfish, and I was only thinking about myself. When we're in a relationship it's about us, both of us."

Aiden threw himself into Richard's arms and the fucker fell right into it.

"How about we make it right? Let's make it official. We'll ring my parents and set a date for the wedding."

Richard grinned. "Oh yeah?"

"Yeah...but first...how about we make it official in a different way?" Aiden's voice was sultry and low. "It's been a long time since we've been together. I miss you...all of you."

Aiden took Richard's hand and pulled him into the master bedroom. I hid behind the door of the guest room until it was safe to come out. As soon as I heard the hushed voices, I retrieved my phone from where it was recording the whole scene and stopped it. Then I grabbed Dick's phone, deleted all of his videos and photos and did a factory reset on it before I removed the sim card and snapped it in half.

Then I walked into the bedroom to claim my man. It was time to be a super, badass silver-fox biker as Aiden had called me.

As planned, Aiden had made his moves slowly, so he was still fully dressed. Richard had lost his shirt.

"You might want to leave now," I said.

"Who the fuck are you?" he asked. "Aiden, who the fuck is this? Call the police."

Aiden came over and put his arms around me. I felt all of his tension disappear like a cloud of smoke.

"This is my boyfriend. Please leave."

Dick's face went all red.

"Do you know what you're doing? I will come through on my threat. Just watch your precious reputation go down in tatters. Let's not mention Mommy and Daddy. All those poor loser kids they keep throwing money at? All gone at the touch of a button."

I held up his phone.

"You mean this button?"

I threw the phone at him and he scrambled to unlock it.

"Don't bother," I said with a chuckle. Aiden looked at me, and I nodded. It was done. All done, and he was free.

"What the fuck did you do, you asshole?"

Aiden moved so fast I couldn't hold him back. He grabbed Dick's shirt off the floor and threw it at him.

"You leave my house right now and never even think of me again. Since you won't have my number on your phone and your memory is shit, I know you won't call me."

Dick put his shirt on and walked toward the door, but he still wasn't ready to give in.

"Do you think I'm that stupid? I have more than one backup of these videos. This isn't over."

"That's where you're wrong, Dickhead," Aiden spat.

Go, baby. Was this the wrong time to get horny for my boyfriend?

"Buy any new socks today?" He asked.

Dick frowned.

"Thank you for giving us such easy access to everything on your laptop. We found some interesting things there. I'm not one for kink-shaming, but you have some fucked up stuff on there. Don't worry, we didn't delete it, we only made copies for ourselves."

Dick's face was a picture. I just put my hands in my pockets and enjoyed the show my man was delivering.

"Oh, you didn't think I could play the same game? I guess you underestimated the 'silly, overemotional romance author,' to quote your words. All the videos you made of me without my consent are gone. Do you know what will happen if you ever try to contact me?"

"You'll release the videos?"

"No, Richard. Unlike you, I wouldn't take something private and show it to the world. But I do have some interesting information about your work practices, your clients, and your finances, that I also copied from your laptop. If you ever come for me, that information will be handed to someone who will know exactly what to do with it. Somehow, I don't think seventy square feet is your idea of a nice retirement accommodation."

I walked around Aiden, stopping to kiss him on his head, and opened the door for Dick.

He walked away without looking back.

As soon as I closed the door, Aiden was on me. I took him by the backs of his legs until he wrapped them around my waist.

"You were fucking fantastic, baby. I'm so proud of you," I said.

"That was so nerve-racking, but it felt so good. Better would have been to punch him."

I laughed. "Not worth it. Besides, I can think of better things for you to do with your hands."

"Oh yeah?"

"Oh yeah.

30

AIDEN

"BABE?"

"One sec, just need to tuck this corner in," I said, pulling the white sheet tight under the mattress.

"Babe..."

His deep, husky voice was like a caress down my back and a stroke of my cock all in one. It was impossible to resist Slade. I didn't know why I'd even tried, because I'd been doomed to fail that particular objective from the get-go.

I turned around to see Slade wearing nothing but a towel around his waist, his chest hair still wet from his shower.

He ran his fingers through his hair and then down his face. His piercing blue eyes never left me as he stroked his beard before moving his hand farther down his stomach to where the towel was wrapped into a knot.

Fuck, he could put on a show.

"You know Tom and Wren will be here in a couple of hours."

"Uh huh."

He flipped the knot, but held it in a way that it all came undone while still covering his cock.

"Fuck, you're killing me, Slade. We have loads to do before they get here."

"Yeah, I know. You're too tense. I thought you could work some of that off...on me."

And then he dropped the towel onto the floor.

I groaned at the sight of his hard shaft, begging to be touched.

"Fine. But I'm not going to enjoy this."

He laughed. "Liar."

He was right. I was going to enjoy every single second of it.

I followed him out of the guest bedroom, where I'd been making the bed for our guests, and into the master bedroom.

"On your knees," I commanded.

He got up on the bed on all fours.

I was only wearing sweatpants, so I pulled them down and stepped out of them.

The bottle of lube was already on the bed.

In the last week we'd been tested and had received our results, but with putting my place up for sale and dealing with all the admin of moving my business to Chester Falls, we hadn't had energy for more than blowjobs or hand jobs in the shower.

Now it seemed my man needed more than a rushed orgasm. Well, we did have a couple of hours, and God had invented restaurants exactly for these times when we were too busy having sex to cook. True story.

I ran a finger up his thigh, teasing him. "You want me inside you, baby?"

"Fuck, yes."

His hole twitched in anticipation. I loved seeing him all open and ready for me. The trust he'd shown in me was humbling, and not only when it came to sex.

Now we knew everything about each other. There were no secrets, no skeletons, no lies. We knew each other, despite having only met weeks ago.

"Have you been getting yourself ready for me in the shower? Are you all nice and clean?"

"Yes."

Without any warning, I ran my tongue from his taint all the way up his crease.

"Oh, fuck," he moaned.

I used my hands to keep his ass cheeks apart so I could dive in, taste him, and show him how much I loved every single inch of him.

My cock was achingly hard, but I ignored it. I wanted him soft, relaxed, and ready for me.

"Aid. Please…"

His strained voice was music to my ears. I loved how he wasn't afraid to be vulnerable with me, wasn't afraid to love me and let me love him.

I grabbed the lube and ran a generous amount over my cock and onto his hole.

"Are you ready to take me?"

"Yes."

I pulled him back so his knees were on the edge of the bed and slowly eased myself inside him.

"God, you're tight."

"Just for you, baby."

I ran one hand up his back and kept the other on his hip to keep him in place.

"You love it when I take charge, don't you?"

"Yes."

"When I thrust inside you, filling you up and making you mine."

"Yes!"

"And you love it when I talk dirty, don't you?"

"Yes…fuck, yes!"

I held both his hands behind his back as I kept up a steady pace of hard thrusts. The only noises in the room were the slapping of skin against skin and his sharp intakes of breath.

There was no way to see his cock from where I was, but I imagined it was leaking like a tap. The way his moans were more and more broken told me how close he was.

I helped him straighten his back so he was against my chest, knees wide open, and head held back against my shoulder.

"Next time we'll have a mirror so I can watch you as you come apart. I want to see how much your cock leaks with every thrust—"

"Aiden..."

"Look at you, so beautiful, giving yourself to me. I will never take this for granted, Slade. I promise to always cherish every moment we have together."

"I love you so much, Aiden. So much."

He brought his arms around me from behind, so I kept one arm around his waist while I reached out for his cock. I gripped it tight as I drove into him harder until he shouted my name again as spurt after spurt of cum hit his chest and dripped down my hand.

My orgasm followed, hitting me with such force I had to lock my knees to stay upright.

We both collapsed on the bed, breathless and blissed out.

"We're gonna have to change the sheets again," I groaned. "This is all your fault."

He laughed and then stopped my protests with his mouth.

"How about a shower?"

"Yes, please," I agreed.

There was another small hurdle to face, which was to tell my parents about Richard's true intentions. Part of me didn't care if they believed me or not, but a bigger part of me wanted them to support me and be part of my life with Slade.

Freshly showered and with a coffee in my hand, I dialed my parents' number.

"Hello, Aiden, is that you?"

"Hi, Mom."

"What's going on, Aiden? Richard has been calling saying you're getting back together. That is excellent news. I'm so pleased for you—"

"Mom, I'm sorry to interrupt you, but Richard and I aren't back together, we never were and never will be."

"What do you mean?" She sighed. "Oh, Aiden, darling, when are you going to settle down?"

"Mom, I am settled. I am in love with a man that loves me in a way I never thought I deserved. He makes me feel worthy and capable."

"But what about Richard? We were so fond of him."

That was it. I took a deep breath and told her everything, leaving out only the blackmail video part. I'd use it if I needed to, but I was still embarrassed that I'd been put in that situation and wasn't ready to talk about it.

I offered to send her the footage from Slade's phone, but to my surprise, she told me it wasn't necessary.

"Sweetheart, we may not always approve of your choices, but you are our son. We just want to know that you're happy, and I'm sorry that we thought it would be with that man."

"Thank you, Mom. That...that really means a lot."

A lump formed in my throat. It had been a long time since I'd wanted to hug my mom this much.

"Hey, Mom, I don't suppose you and Dad would like to visit me and Slade at some point?"

"That would be wonderful, dear. Let me run it by your dad. You look after yourselves, okay?"

"Thanks, Mom."

Not long after, we were ready to receive our friends, and I was ready to say goodbye to San Diego.

"I hope you understand that us 'helping you move,'" Tom said in air quotes as soon as we opened my apartment door, "means me raiding *your* closet to make sure all the good stuff is transported safely into *my* closet."

Wren shook his head at his fiancé, even though nothing but love shone through. Now I knew why everyone in our group of friends was so keen on pairing me and Slade up. Love really was the best thing ever.

"No." I pulled Harley into my arms. She came happily, nuzzling against my neck.

"But, babe, we can't really claim her as ours unless we know if she's chipped or registered somewhere."

"I don't care. No one's feeding her but us. I haven't seen any notices of people searching for a cat anywhere. She's ours."

Slade stared at Harley and me with raised eyebrows. Okay, so pouting wasn't working. Dammit.

He sat next to us and ran his hand over Harley's fur. She purred and went over to him. She always liked nuzzling under his beard.

Traitor.

I knew Slade was right, but I couldn't bear the thought of giving Harley to someone else.

We'd been back in Chester Falls for two weeks, and she'd become my writing companion. She'd sleep at my feet while I worked on my book, and then she'd follow me down to the garage and watch as Slade and I worked on the bike.

"If she was yours and you lost her, wouldn't you want to have her back?" he asked.

Damn him and his reasonable…reasoning.

"Okay, fine, but if she belongs to someone else, I'm going to buy her off them."

He chuckled and turned my face for a kiss.

Harley wasn't keen on PDAs unless they were directed at her, so she jumped off Slade's arms and went to hide in the bedroom.

With Slade's lap now vacant, I made my move.

"I believe this is how it all started," he said, running his hands over my jean-clad thighs.

I sighed. "I've thought back trying to find the defining moment that led me to being here with you, but I can't find it. It could have been the guy on the bike looking at the little girl that gave me the plot bunny for my book. It could have been the desperation to leave San Diego that brought me to Chester Falls. Maybe it was that split-second decision to help Ben out with the book fair. Or maybe it was the moment I was trapped in the intensity of your blue eyes."

He placed his hands on either side of my face and pulled me in for a gentle kiss. "You really are a writer."

I chuckled.

"Come on, let's take Harley to the V. E. T.," he said.

Tom had recommended Dr. Sawyer's practice, saying he'd been excellent with Coco, his and Wren's cat.

From the number of people in the waiting room with their pets, it looked like Dr. Sawyer was popular, or at least very good at his job.

Slade put his hand on my shaking leg.

"Sorry, I'm nervous for her. What if they hurt her?"

"They won't, baby."

I peered inside the travel box and Harley was happily asleep. To think our first encounter was her jumping on my back. She did have a naughty streak, but she seemed to pick her victims.

Liam often lost his lunch to mysterious events, but despite the warnings, he still made a habit of leaving his lunch on the bench while he answered the phone or saw a new customer in.

"Harley Warren-Lawton?" the girl in reception called.

"That's us."

We followed her to the consultation room.

"You gave the cat a hyphenated surname?" Slade asked.

"Of course. What else would she be called?"

"Hello, I'm Doctor Micah Sawyer, but you can call me Micah. Who do we have here?"

I looked at the doctor and then at Slade, who winked at me.

And now we knew why Tom had recommended this particular vet. Also why there was such a long line of mainly women with their pets outside.

"Hello, Micah. I'm Aiden, this is my boyfriend, Slade, and our daughter, Harley."

Slade coughed to disguise his laugh, but I didn't miss his look of pride when Harley didn't attack the vet. Maybe even she had a crush on him.

I mean tall, blond hair, green eyes. He had eye candy written all over him.

When Micah started his examination, my anxiety increased. Thank goodness Slade was there with me.

"Okay, so she's healthy and seems like a happy kitten. I'd say she's four, maybe five months old, and may have been the runt of the litter, which is why she's quite small. There's no chip on her either. I'm sad to say she may have been abandoned, but it seems like she's found a nice family to adopt."

Slade laughed. "You got that right."

Minutes later we left the practice as the official parents of Miss Harley Warren-Lawton.

I put my arm around Slade's waist while he had Harley in her carrier.

"I can't imagine life being more perfect than it is right now," I said.

"Not going to argue there, sweetheart."

We crossed the town square toward our street. I stopped and glanced around. It was another beautiful summer day. Soon it would be autumn and with it all the beautiful colors of the changing season.

"You know," I said, looking up at my gorgeous boyfriend, "after everything that happened with Richard, my parents, and when I couldn't write, I thought I just couldn't catch a break. But something —chance, fate, whatever—made me get into my car and drive. And look at me now. I caught myself a bunch of friends, a new home, and, more importantly, I caught myself a sexy silver-fox biker."

"Oh, Aiden…you caught my heart and soul when you saw me that first time. You caught me when I was falling, and I know you will for as long as we both shall live."

"You should put that in your vows," I said.

He widened his eyes and pulled me closer. "I hope that's you asking."

"I hope that's you saying yes."

I hope you enjoyed reading How to Catch a Biker.

This is book five in my bestselling small town romance series, Chester Falls. Are you curious about the other guys in the book?

Tom and Wren and the baking competition.

James and Connor's long-lost friendship turned into more when Connor's life is suddenly in danger.

How about the twins, Tate and Tristan and their men?

Check out the complete series, which is also available in audiobook narrated by Nick Hudson.

Chester Falls (readerlinks.com/l/1733751)

Before you read the next age gap novel, would you like a bonus scene?

Follow Slade and Aiden as they celebrate finishing the bike restoration with a road trip.

Click the link below to sign up to my newsletter and receive the scene in your inbox:

Sign up here (anawritesmm.com/sol-signup)

BREAKTHROUGH

Dads of Stillwater

ANA ASHLEY

ABOUT BREAKTHROUGH

A young single dad. An older man. An impossible love story.

Milo
I lost everyone I've ever loved, but there's one person I'm determined
to keep. The baby I was left with when tragedy struck once more.
Now my life is all about surviving. I don't have time to date, or relationships.

That is until Ellis, the sexy, older, and kind primary school teacher
who's currently living rent free in my head with no intention of
moving out, gives me the second job I desperately need.
But why would he want a guy from the wrong side of town, who's
barely paying the bills and comes with a plus one?

Ellis
Moving to Stillwater was the fresh start I needed after having my heart
stomped on and my career practically destroyed.
Despite my family's best efforts, I'm determined that nothing shall
break through the walls I've built around myself. No more relationships.

That is until I meet the much younger grocery store cashier with the warm brown eyes, and accidentally give him a job.

As I get to know Milo, brick by brick that wall is coming down and no matter how much I resist I'm starting to run out of excuses as to why I shouldn't give in.

But why would he want anything with someone much older when he could have anyone else?

Breakthrough *is book 3 in Ana Ashley's series,* Dads of Stillwater. *This story contains an age gap, a sweet nine-month-old baby everyone will coo about, all the feels and Ana Ashley's usual happy ever after.*

TRIGGER WARNING

THIS BOOK CONTAINS on page mentions of drug use, violence, and suicide. No actual drug use, violence or suicide happens on page.

1

———

MILO

My mom always used to say there are three certain things in life. Birth, the shit in between, and death.

"Milo, you just have to find that gap in the shit and break through. Then you'll be free."

Well, shit or clouds, whichever way the wind blew that day. Sometimes I got dreamy, happy mom. Other times, I got sad mom.

Regardless, I've held on to her words for as long as I can remember. It's difficult when shit keeps piling, people keep dying, and there aren't many clouds. At least not the white, fluffy kind.

I push my thoughts aside as I stare into the big brown eyes of the one person who makes all the shit in between worthwhile and makes me think my mom was right about the clouds. Sometimes there is an opening.

Like Sara.

She's the gift life gave me when it took everything else away. The breakthrough in the middle of all the really hard stuff. She's my fluffy white cloud.

"Hello, babydoll," I coo, tickling her tummy. "Shouldn't you be asleep?"

She does a long stretch from her nap and then kicks her arms and legs. I can't resist taking her from the crib and into my arms. I love how she smells and how soft she is.

"Oh, someone needs a diaper change." She blows some bubbles as her agreement, and my practiced moves take care of the rest.

Kissing the top of her head, I walk into the living area. Well, living area is a stretch. It's more like my lounge-slash-bedroom-slash-kitchen, but never mind. It's clean, tidy, and for as long as I can afford rent, it's mine.

"You'll spoil her rotten," Florrie, my neighbor, says. "She needs to get used to waking up without you here."

"I know, I know. I won't do it tomorrow," I say, kissing Sara on her cheek and giving her to Florrie, who'll look after her while I'm at work. Sara doesn't complain.

"You say that every day."

"You also say every day this is your last babysitting day because you have your knitting club, your bingo night, and lord knows what else, and yet, here you are."

She gives me a look that tells me not to sass a retired teacher if I know what's good for me.

"Her dinner is in the fridge," I say, "and I put a set of spare—"

"Clothes on the chair in the nursery. I know, I know. This isn't my first rodeo, my boy. Now, off you go to work. Us girls have some important things to get on with. No boys allowed." She ushers me out the door, and I let out a little sigh.

My heart breaks every time I have to leave my girl, even though I know she's in the best hands.

God bless the day Florrie moved next door to the townhome we live in and needed help with the water pipe in her kitchen sink. Florrie, of course, fell in love with Sara while I fixed her problem. I got soaked in the process but gained a new friend.

She's not from around here. You can tell because there's no way she'd have moved to the south side of Stillwater if she knew better. Then again, on a teacher's retirement salary, I don't know if she could have afforded anything in a nicer part of town.

I look at my flip phone and see I have time to walk to work, so I save the bus money for the journey back.

Saving money is a bonus, but I enjoy the walk when it's a beautiful summer day like today. If I ignore the old houses with the broken window panes and the overgrown grass and broken swings on what used to be our playground, then it's not so bad.

The birds are chirping away, the sun is shining, and I know my girl is safe.

In a few more blocks, I'll be in the rich part of town. During the thirty-minute walk to work, I get to pretend I live in a nice house with two bedrooms, one for me and one for Sara. We'd have a backyard and a living room big enough for a play area.

Yes, we'd definitely have a garden.

I'd plant my mom's flowers there. Her favorite pink roses. And even though we probably wouldn't have the right weather for it, we'd plant tulips. Because she loved tulips and because it would be our house, so we could.

And Florrie would live next door to us like she does now, of course.

Before I know it, I arrive at the grocery store where I work, setting my dreams aside to make way for the real world.

"Milo," Pauline, one of the stockers, pulls me toward the break room when I'm barely through the door. She always knows everything. It's like she has ears everywhere in this place.

"Wow, are you trying to dislocate my arm?"

She looks around as if to check that there's no one nearby.

"Rumor is there's a new supervisor vacancy coming up," she says.

"And by rumor, you mean…"

She shakes her shoulders and straightens her work shirt, which is a hideous brown we all hate. "I was in Gerald's office earlier."

"Ew, are you okay? Do you need a shower? A Lysol spray?"

She laughs. "He didn't get that close. Only close enough to notice the top two buttons on my shirt were undone, so he had a peek at the top of my bra." She shudders. "Fucking pervert. Anyway, when I asked him about any jobs coming up, he sang like a canary. He thinks I want a promotion so I can be in the office with him all day. As if." She rolls her eyes.

I give her a hug. "Thank you. Every time I ask for more hours, his excuses are budget cuts, his hands are tied, blah, always the same."

"Bullshit. I don't know why he's got it in for you, but I'll find out." She looks at her watch. "Oh crap, I gotta go. My boyfriend is picking me up. We'll catch up about this next time, okay?"

"Sure."

Pauline grabs her bag from her locker and runs out the door. I love her for her tenacity. She's moving to Florida in a few months, not that anyone else but me knows it, so she's taking it upon herself to right all the wrongs in the store.

We all know Gerald, the store manager, has a thing for her. And by the looks of it, she's using her powers for the greater good. The girl is crazy, but I'll miss her when she goes.

I don't have much on me. Only a sandwich to eat on my break and my phone, so I put those in my locker and get ready to start my shift.

The late shift is hard because I don't get to read Sara a bedtime story and watch as she falls asleep for the night. But it's the best shift at work.

As everyone finishes their jobs, they come in for their last-minute groceries, so we get busy. And busy means time goes by fast.

It also means there's a chance I'll see one of my favorite customers. Which is the highlight and one of the worst parts of my working day.

Ugh, it's awful having a crush on someone and being so tongue-tied you could literally spit out a scarf.

I settle in at my usual register.

"Psst. Hey, Milo."

I roll my eyes and turn around in my chair to face Jimmy, who should pay attention to the customer he's serving. I point to the customer, and he shrugs, so I shake my head and turn back around. The last thing I need is Jimmy getting us in trouble because he's bored and wants to chat.

Gerald has a way of sniffing out when someone so much as sneezes in the wrong direction, and then he's there, in your face, ready to lord over his menials.

The store gets busy, and I lose track of time as I serve one customer after the next until they all blend into one. Well, almost.

Like my mom said, sometimes there are those breaks, and Ethel is one of them.

She always picks my checkout lane, and I adore her.

"Hey, sunshine," I say as I scan her groceries. I do it slowly and help her bag everything up to ensure nothing falls out of the basket in her walker.

"Hey, gorgeous. Have you found yourself a good man yet?"

"Not yet, Ethel. I might just have to marry you after all."

She gives me the biggest smile and takes out her purse to pay. I make sure she's all set before she goes. I know her son or grandson is waiting for her in the parking lot. Ethel is nearly ninety, but she's fiercely independent and says she can still do her own shopping. *Thank you very much.*

"Oh, I almost forgot," she says.

"What's that?"

She looks for something in her purse. "Oh, there it is. I'm practicing my crochet. I prefer knitting, but you're never too old to learn something new, right, dear? Anyway, I learned how to crochet these little fish." She takes it out and places it in my hand.

"It's for your baby girl. I hope she likes it."

I have to bite my lips to stop myself from laughing as I hold the gift to my chest.

"Thank you so much, Ethel. Sara will love this. She's been really into…fish recently. I'm reading her a book about the ocean."

Ethel nods, and off she goes with a spring on her step.

I jump when I see Jimmy right next to me.

"Christ. Warn a guy."

"Dude, why did Ethel give you a crocheted butt plug?"

I snort as I look down at my hands, and he's right. Okay, so it vaguely resembles a fish…if it was a butt plug going to a dress-up party dressed as a fish.

"Bless her. Her eyesight isn't what it used to be. It's the thought that counts, right?"

I see Gerald coming straight at us, and it's too late for us to return to our respective posts. I only have time to put Ethel's gift in my back pocket.

"What's going on here? Are we on vacation? Is this time out?" he says, and I can smell his horrible tobacco-and-coffee breath.

"Not at all. We were just helping Ethel. You know how she is," I say, pointing toward the parking lot.

"Yeah, she's very stubborn, Gerald," Jimmy says, retreating to his checkout lane.

Gerald narrows his eyes, clearly not believing a word we're saying.

"Well, she's not here anymore. Back to work, and I better not see you two messing around again." He turns around with the air of superiority he likes to display.

He's only the manager of a chain store. He's as much of a nobody as we are. He's just a better-paid nobody. But since he's in charge, he loves to make sure we all know he's the boss.

"Gerald?" I call, trying to gather my wits once again with the newfound information from Pauline. "I know you said you can't give me more hours because of budgets. The thing is, I'm struggling to get by on just three days a week, you know, with trying to raise a baby and all. Are you sure you can't stretch it? Just maybe an extra half-day?"

He puts his pudgy hand on my shoulder, and I almost recoil. "Sorry, Milo. It's the powers above. You understand, right?" he asks, pointing up as if his boss is god herself.

"You'd tell me if there was a new job opening, wouldn't you?" I ask, knowing he'll never tell me what he told Pauline. "I don't mind traveling to another store either."

"Of course," he says in a suddenly sickly-sweet voice without missing a beat.

The fucking bastard.

He leaves me to get back to work, and I struggle to find my usual spark. I like to be in a good mood when I talk to my customers. Sometimes people have bad days at work, and you never know if smiling and talking to them could cheer them up and turn their day around. But right now, I'm as deflated as a three-day-old balloon.

I'm looking down at my hands, lost in thought as I wait for my next customer, when someone clears their throat.

I stand up straight.

"Mr. Bradford…um…good day…well, it's really evening, isn't it?" I say, fumbling with my words like my brain has melted.

"Hi, Milo. You were in a world of your own. And what have I been saying about calling me Ellis?"

"Okay…Ellis."

God, his smile does things to me.

"Yeah…um, I was just thinking about the library."

"The library?"

I scrunch my face. He must think I'm an idiot.

"Yeah, I need to return some books I got for Sara and get some more. She loves them."

He smiles again, and I melt a little inside.

"It's good to get children used to touching books and listening to stories, even when we don't think they can understand. They can take in a lot more than we think."

I nod. I want to say that Sara loves touching her books and turning the pages. Well, mostly trying to chew them, but I'm afraid my brain-to-mouth function has been temporarily disabled.

A few months ago, I was going about my life. No need for relationships. Wasn't thinking about boyfriends—let's face it, Sara had just been born. I didn't need anything else. Until Ellis Bradford moved to Stillwater and started to live rent-free in my brain.

The elementary school teacher with a gentle manner, who always has a smile for everyone and is far too intelligent and refined for someone like me.

But what can I do? It's those kind eyes. The hair that already has a hint of salt and pepper on the sides.

He's older than me. If I was to guess, I'd say he's already forty, which would make him fourteen years older than my twenty-six years, but I don't care. All I know is that my heart beats a little faster when he's around, and that's never happened with all the guys I've messed around with in the past.

He only has a bottle of wine and a box of chocolates today. I wonder if he's going on a date, and my heart sinks a little.

"These aren't your usual purchases," I say before I stop myself. "Crap. I'm sorry. I mean…not that I notice what you usually buy."

Yeah right. Or commit it to memory.

"That would be creepy," I continue because my mouth has a will of its own. "I'm not creepy. I just notice things, and I see everyone's shopping. Not that I remember everyone, although I remember yours because you always smile at me…"

I trap my lips between my teeth to force myself to stop talking before Ellis places a complaint against me to Gerald.

He tilts his head a little like he's simultaneously trying to figure me out and not laugh.

"My sister has invited me for dinner at her place. When I say invited, I mean she threatened to come over to my place and drag me out if I declined," he says, smiling in that way that makes it impossible for me not to smile back.

So he's not going on a date. It's messed up that my stomach does a little happy flip.

Yeah, definitely not a normal reaction to someone I barely know.

"I hope it's a nice dinner, and I'm sure she'll love these chocolates," I say, impressed that all the words come out in the correct order. Maybe it's because I'm scanning his items, so my brain momentarily restarts.

After he pays, he gives me another one of his nice smiles and leaves.

"You *so* have a crush on the elementary school teacher," Jimmy says.

"No I don't. Shut up. I'm going on my break," I say and close my register.

"Hey, Milo," Jimmy calls out. "You know it's pointless, right?"

"What is?"

"Guys like him will never even look twice at guys like us. We don't know enough about fancy stuff. I mean, what would you even talk about on a date? Guys like us should stick together, ya know. We come from the same place. This is as good as it gets for us."

I'm not sure if he means that in the general sense or if this is his weird way of asking me out, which wouldn't be the first time.

As for the assumption that people from different worlds can't be together…maybe so…but all the romance books I get from the library tell me otherwise, so Jimmy can stick to his reality. I reserve the right to my own dreams.

I shrug noncommittally. "Doesn't matter because I don't have a crush on him, and I'm not interested in a relationship. My priority right now is Sara."

I *so* have an impossible crush on the elementary school teacher. Then again, my life is already full of dreams, so what harm can one more do?

2

___

ELLIS

THE DRIVE from the store to my place is filled with thoughts of the young man with the warm brown eyes that seem so out of place at the store.

I could use any other checkout lane, but if Milo is working, I can't go to another one. It's as if my body has a mind of its own, and before I know it, I've already unloaded my cart at his register.

He has these brown eyes that look at you with a mix of innocence and too much of the harsh reality of life. Like they've seen all the darkness there is to see. It's such a contradiction.

And then there's his sweet nine-month-old daughter, whom he seems solely responsible for.

I want to know more, but asking is inappropriate because we're not friends.

The only time I've seen him away from the grocery store was early in the summer at the end of the music festival.

I'd been trying to get the school approved as a GED testing center, and I guess the word got around town.

He approached me about the program while I was with a few friends watching my brother's rock band perform. But I check the school email daily, and I haven't seen his application for the summer preparation classes.

It's not my problem. I need to remind myself of that.

No matter how much I want to know what lies behind those young, sweet brown eyes.

Once home, I shower and get ready to go out again.

This time I walk to my sister's place. It's not far, and the evening breeze is a good reprieve from the warmer day.

I steel myself for the onslaught that is my niece and nephew before I ring the bell. When I moved to Stillwater, I stayed here for a few months, but I eventually found my own place, and I know the lovable little terrors miss me as much as I miss them.

I hug the bottle of wine to my chest in case they decide to climb me, just as the door opens and Alice ushers me inside.

She's wearing a nice dress…and heels. At home?

Are we celebrating something?

"You're early, but I'll forgive you because…" She takes the box of chocolates from my hand. "Yes! And this is why you're my favorite brother."

I roll my eyes. "How am I early? You said eight, right? Where are the kids?" I follow her, and as we pass the hallway toward the kitchen, I look around and see no trace of children.

The house is oddly tidy.

I'm getting a strange feeling about this.

"They're in bed already. Max took them to the park this afternoon, and they exhausted themselves. As soon as they had dinner and their bath, they were down for the count." She smiles like that was a carefully crafted plan.

I don't blame her. If you could produce energy from children running and screaming at a pitch heard by dogs ten miles away, my sister's kids could provide power to this town for weeks.

She goes around the kitchen island, where something is bubbling away on the stove.

"Smells nice. What are you cooking?"

"Italian beef ragu with pasta. I found this recipe online, and it had loads of great reviews, so I hope it turns out good," she says.

The dinner table is fancier than usual, and it's set for four, which means our brother Darius must be coming too.

"Are we celebrating something?" I ask, pointing to the table.

"Oh, that's nothing. You know, it's nice to get out the adult stuff sometimes. Unless you want to eat from Marnie's *Paw Patrol* plate." She raises a brow.

"No, you're okay," I chuckle. "Need help with anything?"

"All under control. Let me pour you a glass of wine. After all, you bought it."

I shake my head. My sister. Scatty. A little crazy. A lot lovable.

I hear the front door open, and a moment later, my brother-in-law, Max, comes into the kitchen holding a cake box from Bittersweet.

"Hey, Ellis."

I raise my glass, and he gives me a sympathetic nod. Sometimes you need a little fortification to handle my sister.

"Babe, I'll put the cheesecake in the fridge until after dinner," Max says to Alice. "Ty—" Alice interrupts Max with a kiss and sends him upstairs to check on the kids.

"Tying loose ends at work. He's been doing that all day, poor thing. One more reason for this nice dinner."

That's…weird, but I don't mention it. I pick up my glass of wine and walk to the window at the front of the house.

My sister lives in a friendly neighborhood. One of those places where you can leave your kids' toys outside and no one will take them. Everyone knows everyone, and they even have monthly barbecues in each other's backyards.

It's sickly nice, and somehow it suits perfectly the girl who, like me, grew so tired of traveling around the world with our parents that she made a life for herself in the small town we spent our summers in with our grandparents.

Sometimes I wish I'd been as courageous as she was and demanded to come back to Stillwater to live here permanently, finish school, and create some roots. But then again, I settled in Boston when I went to college, and I loved it there. I didn't consider not living in the city until…well…

I take a sip of wine. I hope it doesn't go to my head because I'm not in the mood to feel broodier than usual, and it's hard to put up an act in front of my family.

It's dark outside, and I can't even lie to myself. I love my sister, but I'm a creature of habit, and I'd rather be home planning next year's lessons.

A car pulls up to their driveway and someone gets out. A moment later, the doorbell rings and Alice rushes to the door, probably so it doesn't wake the kids.

"Hey, glad you could make it," I hear her say. "Follow me, and I'll get you a glass of wine. Dinner will be ready in a minute. We're just waiting for Max to come down."

Alice comes into the kitchen and behind her is a man who, from the look on his face, is as surprised to see me as I am to see him.

Where's Darius?

"I better do some introductions, right?" Alice asks, pouring a glass of my wine and giving it to the guy. "Tyler, this is my older brother, Ellis. He moved here a few months ago and teaches at the elementary school." Then she turns to me. "Ellis, this is Tyler. He's kind of a transplant from somewhere." She makes a zip motion over her lips. "Don't ask, he'll never confess, but he's lived here for so long I don't think anyone remembers a Tyler-less time."

Tyler holds out his hand, and I shake it.

"Nice to meet you," I say.

"Likewise."

Alice leads us to the dining room and insists on placing Tyler opposite me.

Thank you, sister, for not making this awkward at all.

I take the guy's features in. He's good-looking, but his eyes are weary. I notice we're about the same height, but he carries himself with some reluctant confidence. It's as if he's used to being in charge but doesn't know what to do when he's in unknown territory.

"So, Tyler, what sins did you commit to have to endure my sister's cooking?" I ask.

He runs his hand over his short scruff. "I don't quite know, but if you know your sister, you know there was no way out for me. So here I am."

I laugh. "Yeah, she certainly has a way of making you do things."

Max sits next to me and leans forward on the table with a pleading expression. "Please say the food is good. I have to live here. I'll buy you drinks next week."

Both Tyler and I share a look and chuckle.

I'm not one for stereotypes, but Alice insists on serving everyone herself like she's a fifties stay-at-home parent, which is so not her style. Tyler and I share another look. I hope the food is good because there's so much on the plate I don't think we could fake it if it's not.

It's not that Alice is a terrible cook. She's just very adventurous, and it doesn't always work out.

She raises her wine glass in a toast.

"To finding love in unexpected places."

And that's when Tyler and I stare at each other, realizing Alice has set us up.

"Babe…" Max pleads.

"What?" Alice asks with her most innocent voice. "Come on, let's try the ragu."

The food is superb—*well done, little sis*—and the conversation flows nicely. I always forget that without the kids, my sister is an actual adult sometimes.

Tyler and I share a few smiles, but I think we both know there's no spark.

Alice is delighted that we've cleared our plates and leaves us with the excuse to slice up the cheesecake and make us all some coffee, while poor Max is once again sent upstairs to check on the sleeping kids.

"I'm so sorry," I say to Tyler once we're out of earshot. "She's been trying to get me to start dating from the day I arrived here, but trying to set me up is a new level of crazy, even for Alice."

Tyler raises his hand. "It's okay. I was hoping for dinner with friends, and I can't say it was too bad. I'm sorry, and I don't want to be rude, but…" He shrugs and shakes his head.

"Yeah, me neither."

His relief is instant, and his smile returns to his face.

"She doesn't need to know though," I say.

"Oh, you're evil. I might change my mind after all."

I laugh. "So, tell me more about your work with the soup kitchen. I'm embarrassed to say I didn't know there are people who need that kind of support in such a small town."

"Yeah. There are people in Stillwater who don't want to talk about the poorer areas and even go as far as campaigning so that no funds go toward improving those areas," he says.

I'm shocked to hear it because Stillwater is a fairly small town. How many of my students come from those neighborhoods?

"How often do you run the soup kitchen?" I ask.

"Three days a week. I wish I could do more, but we spend the remaining days sourcing the food and preparing it. We rely on volunteers to help make it all work."

I reach out and touch his hand. "I'd really love to help, Tyler. I don't know if any of my students are from those poorer backgrounds. I want to learn so I can help more."

"All help is welcome. I'll be happy to show you as much as you want to see," he says.

Alice comes with the dessert just as I'm taking my hand back, but she doesn't miss it, and her eyes go comically wide.

Great.

Tyler winks at me, and I relax. At least if Alice thinks we've hit it off, she'll be off both our backs.

"I love you, honey, but if I was gay, I'd marry Julius tomorrow," Max says, tasting the cheesecake he bought from Bittersweet, the coffee shop on Main Street.

"I wouldn't mind being in a threesome with the two of you, babe," Alice says, and I almost snort the coffee I've just drunk.

"How weird is it that the bakery in Stillwater only sells bread and cookies, but the coffee shop sells all the other baked stuff?" I ask.

"That's Stillwater for you. It's the town where The Academy isn't a school but a bar and restaurant. Make it make sense." Tyler says. "But to be fair, Liv from Lovely Buns only sells cookies because even Julius says hers are the best, and it would be a sin to deny the good people of Stillwater."

I look at my watch. "Wow, I'm sorry I didn't realize it was getting so late. I really need to go. I have an early meeting tomorrow for the GED summer classes."

"I'll walk you out," Tyler says. "It's getting a bit late for me too."

We all stand from the table, and Alice is like a bunny on springs from excitement.

"Have you guys exchanged contact details yet?" she asks.

"Subtle, babe," Max deadpans.

"We're covered, you big meddler." I give her a kiss and a hug and then pat Max's back before heading toward the door.

Tyler follows me out.

"Where's your car?" he asks.

"I walked. I only live a few blocks away."

"Want a ride?"

I look behind us and see Alice trying, not very discreetly, to see how we part ways.

"Oh man. If you give me a ride, she'll be planning our winter wedding by the weekend."

Tyler's deep laugh makes me feel something I haven't in a long time. Companionship. Like someone is on the same page.

I go over to the passenger side of his car and jump in.

"Take me home, lover," I say.

"Who calls their lover, lover?"

"Would you prefer mon amant? Amore mio?" I say, laying on my practiced French and Italian accents.

"God, no! And this is why we're so wrong for each other," he says with a hearty laugh. "But I really like you, Ellis."

"I like you too, Tyler."

He drops me off in front of my place. We exchange numbers and he gives me the address of the soup kitchen.

I knew early on that I wanted to teach because I can't help caring about people and helping them get where they want to be. Especially young people. And I've never been afraid of working hard. Grading papers until midnight. Seeing all the little scribbles as the students try to write their first words. I love it all.

But knowing I can now also make a difference in my community makes me feel right and at home for the first time since I arrived in Stillwater.

Somehow the image of the young man that scans my groceries every week returns to me, with his reserved smile and his shy, intelligent eyes that look back at me with so much untapped potential.

3

MILO

I STARE AT THE LETTER, but I'm not even reading it anymore.

A knock on the door forces me to look up.

"It's open."

Florrie walks in.

"You got it too?" she asks.

I nod, resting my head hopelessly on my hands with my elbows on my knees. How will I afford a rent increase? It's not a lot, and it's been a while since the last one, but ten months ago, I had a full-time job. Even without help from my brother's income, I would have easily afforded it and more.

"I don't know what to do, Florrie. I can't afford to put Sara in childcare, so I can get a full-time job. What employer will let me bring her with me?"

She sits next to me, and I feel her hand on my shoulder. "It'll work out. Life has a way of making things work. We just have to believe that if we put good energy out there, we'll get good energy back. In the meantime, I'll help you where I can. You know that."

A lump forms in my throat, and I have to take a deep breath to stop a stray tear from falling because Florrie sounds so much like my mom that it's as if she's here, speaking to me.

God, I miss her. And my dad. And my fucking brother. Even Sara's mom. I miss everyone.

"Look, there's no point sitting here worrying about it. Why don't we get all dolled up and go check out this month's craft fair?" she asks. "I'll drive us into town, and we'll walk the rest of the way. How does that sound?"

She's right. I look at her and smile. "Thank you. Let's do it. And when we're back, I'll make you my mom's tuna casserole for dinner. I promise it's the best."

"Sounds like a plan."

It's a hot day, so I put Sara in a cute little white dress I found at Goodwill. It still had the tag on it and everything. She looks adorable and smiles at me like she knows it.

"Yes, you're so beautiful, aren't you?" She kicks her arms and legs excitedly as I comb her short hair and catch it with a white bow. "You'll be the prettiest girl at the fair. Yes, you will."

Once Sara is ready, I make sure I have her bag with a change of clothes, diapers, snacks, and her bottle. I'm all kitted out like I'm moving to a different country.

"You girls are far too complicated," I say to her, tickling her tummy as I walk past her crib to get her favorite toy. "Gone are the days when I only needed my clothes, wallet, and phone."

She babbles back at me. Her bunny sits next to Ethel's gift. I put it on the shelf since it's pink and can kinda pass as a fish, sideways, of course. I'll draw the line at taking it out with us, so I hope it never becomes Sara's favorite toy.

"Are you ready?" I ask, and she holds out her hands to get picked up.

Florrie finds a lucky parking space in the shade, and we walk the rest of the way to the fair. This is a monthly event in Stillwater, and it's becoming bigger and bigger each year.

Sara falls asleep in the car and wakes up a little cranky when I move her to the stroller, staring at me like I'm not her most favorite person.

I'm just happy looking at all the beautiful things people can create. It seems there are some people a little more talented than Ethel with crochet because we see a stand that sells anything and everything crocheted.

"I never had much patience to sit around doing that sort of thing," Florrie says. "My Tony used to say I had ants in my pants. Couldn't sit around."

I can believe that. When Florrie isn't looking after Sara, she's always walking to stay fit or working in her yard doing something or another.

We continue our way around the fair. Just because I can't buy anything doesn't mean I can't look or appreciate the effort and skill that goes into a lot of these crafts.

I particularly like the stand selling plants growing in recycled stuff. There's a half-dome made from recycled plastic growing a spider plant. It looks pretty and easy to look after. It will look great in someone's home.

"Oh look, Milo. Aren't those precious?"

I turn to see what Florrie is pointing at. "That's Arlo's stand. Come on, I'll introduce you."

We walk over, and as usual, Arlo crouches by the stroller to say hi to Sara.

"Hello, princess. Don't you look stunning." He says.

"Florrie, this is Arlo. He makes the most beautiful wings for children to wear on their back, like butterflies, bees, anything kids want, but he also does other pieces of art."

"Pleasure to meet you, Florrie," he says, taking Florrie farther inside the stand to show her some of his pieces.

We're in the shade, so I take out the water bottle to see if Sara's thirsty. She takes it happily without fuss, drinking until she's had enough. Even though she mostly drinks formula, she's starting to have some water. My baby girl is growing up too fast.

I wave one of her snacks in front of her to see if she's hungry, and she takes it immediately.

"All right, all right, little Miss Impatient," I say to her.

"Is that your baby?"

It doesn't surprise me to see Ava at the fair with Arlo. She's Arlo's boyfriend's eight-year-old daughter, and she's as sweet as she is smart.

She's wearing her ladybug wings Arlo made for her.

"Yes, she is. Her name is Sara."

"That's a pretty name. Do you have a wife or a husband?" she asks.

"Ava," Arlo says from where he's standing with Florrie.

"Sorry, Daddy Arlo," she answers but looks at me expectantly.

I smile and whisper. "No, I don't have a husband or a boyfriend."

Ava's forehead crinkles as if she's thinking about a complicated problem. I notice Sara is about to drop half her now-soggy snack on her dress and catch it just in time.

Look at that, and I was even bad at sports at school. Who'd have thought I'd suddenly get Spiderman reflexes with the birth of a baby?

"I know!" Ava says, pointing her finger up. "My teacher, Mr. Bradford. He doesn't have a husband or a boyfriend. I know because my best friend, Megan, who was in my class, told me. Anyway, I think you and my teacher, Mr. Bradford, should get married."

I stare at her, dumbfounded. As she waves her hand in front of my face.

"Hello? Didn't you hear me? I said you should marry Mr. Brad—" As if by magic, Arlo appears behind Ava, silencing her with his hand, which is just as well because in the stand next to Arlo's, I see Mr. Bradford—Ellis—with his sister and her kids.

"She has a knack for predicting these things," Arlo says, "but…let's maybe allow destiny to do its thing first, shall we?" He winks and then whispers something in Ava's ear. She runs off to the back of the stand.

Arlo leaves me to serve a customer that calls for him, and I don't see Florrie, so she must have moved on to another stall. We agreed to meet back at the car if we got separated, so it's not a big deal, but now I don't know what to do.

Do I acknowledge Ellis? Do I pretend I don't see him? Ugh, stupid fucking crush.

I stare at Sara, but she's just babbling away and playing with her toy. Not that I'd expect a nine-month-old baby to tell me what to do in this situation. Obviously.

By the time I decide to move on, he's already seen me.

"Milo, how nice to see you here," he says.

"Oh…er…hi, Mr.—Ellis." I hold on to the stroller, trying not to fidget. Usually, the checkout counter is my safety buffer, but now I don't know what to do with my hands, and he's close enough that I can smell his cologne.

"Oh my goodness, is that your daughter?" Alice asks.

"Um…yeah." I always forget that I know most people in Stillwater because they see me at the store, but they don't know me. They know nothing about me. At least those from this side of town.

"She's so precious. What's her name?"

"Sara."

"That's a beautiful name," Alice says.

"Thank you."

I look at Ellis, and he's staring at me like he's trying to figure me out. He seems to do that a lot.

"Milo, I'd like to talk to you about something. Would you be okay leaving Sara in my sister's capable hands for a few minutes?"

I waver for a moment. It's not that I don't trust Alice. She's raising two children, and they're a wonderful family. But Sara…

"You know what? Never mind," he says. "Alice, do you mind meeting me by the ice cream cart?"

"Sure." She gives Sara one last goodbye and leaves us, taking her two children with her.

"They're really well behaved," I say.

"That's because they know there's ice cream in their future if they do," Ellis says, laughing. "Come on, let's get a cool drink."

I follow him, pushing the stroller, unsure of what's happening or what he wants to talk about.

There's a cart nearby selling cold drinks. He stops, so I do too, and my stomach sinks, especially when I look at the prices. I wasn't expecting to spend any money today.

"What would you like to drink?" he asks.

"I'm okay, thank you," I say. "I have water in my bag."

He turns around. "I'd like to buy you a drink. Is that okay? Would you like a cool lemonade?" My skin overheats as it becomes clear that he knows I can't afford a simple drink at a fair, but I appreciate him asking away from the cart man's hearing range.

"That would be nice, thank you."

Ellis buys the drinks and then points to a bench under a nearby tree.

The cool lemonade gives me the boost of sugar and hydration I didn't realize I needed after walking in the sun. I check on Sara, and she's fallen asleep, so I change the position of the stroller so she's lying flat.

"Milo, please forgive me if I'm stepping way out of line, but when I saw you at the summer festival, you seemed excited about taking the classes to do the GED exam in the fall."

I look down at the cup in my hands. Why did I have to get overexcited about it?

I should have known it was an impossible achievement and left it at that.

"Talk to me, Milo. Is there anything I can do to help you?"

I shake my head.

"I just can't do it right now, Mr.—Ellis," I say, correcting myself since he keeps insisting I call him Ellis. I'm not at work, so I don't need to be formal.

"You don't need to give me any reasons, but trust me when I say there's often a solution. Even when you don't have it, someone else might."

This would be one of those times when my mom would have something wise to say. She'd probably tell me to trust Ellis. But what can Ellis do?

"Thank you. I'll think about it." That's all I can say because I don't want to lie to him.

He gives me a smile, and I notice the small wrinkles in the corners of his eyes. They're the lines of someone who's smiled a lot in his life, even though I don't see him smiling often.

"I should get back to my sister. I don't want to break my ice cream promise," he says. "The favorite uncle crown is mine to keep."

Sara wakes up and starts getting fussy, so I pick her up and push the stroller with my free hand. The street where Florrie parked her car isn't far and Sara has her hat on, so we make our way.

Before we get there, I see Florrie talking to a friend, so I approach slowly, not wanting to interrupt if it's a private conversation.

"I can't believe it. We need to fight this," the other lady says.

"Count me in, Vera," Florrie says, and the other lady walks away.

"What was that about?" I ask.

"Apparently, some rich woman in town is petitioning the mayor to turn the playground near us into a parking lot. Can you imagine?" She's so incensed you'd think she'd lived in Stillwater all her life.

"Nothing surprises me in Stillwater anymore."

"Something to do with not wanting people to park on residential streets during the craft fair. I mean, hasn't the fair been around for a long time?"

"Yeah, since before I was born."

"Then why now? It doesn't make sense."

Sara starts fussing, so I gesture for us to head to the car.

"Wait, you don't seem bothered about it. Didn't you play there as a child?"

It's hard to explain the complex relationship I have with that playground, even though Florrie knows some of my family's history.

We reach the car and I strap Sara into the car seat.

"It's not that I don't care what happens to it, but the playground hasn't been used in years. At least a parking lot would be something." I get into the passenger seat and put the seat belt on. "I can't remember the last time there was any investment on our side of town."

When Florrie doesn't start the car, I look at her and find her staring at me.

"What?"

"Nothing..." she says unconvincingly. "Anyway, I bought these tiny angel wings from Arlo's stand for Sara's room. They're so precious. He made them himself by hand. Can you believe it?"

"Thank you, Florrie, you didn't have to buy anything for Sara. You already help me so much."

She puts her hand on mine and squeezes it. "I know, dear, but I don't have anyone else to spoil, so entertain the old lady here. Let's get home. I believe you promised me a tuna casserole," she says, letting go to turn the keys in the ignition.

"I did indeed."

4

———

ELLIS

Tyler's soup kitchen isn't hard to find.

I park by the church he mentioned and walk around to the back. It's late afternoon, but unlike the Stillwater I've come to know, this part of town looks sad, unattended, and forgotten in the dusky colors of the sunset.

There are few trees, no flowers, no life. I'm pretty sure the grass is dead, and people must have walked on it so often they've created their own clear paths because you can see the dry soil underneath.

I've seen worse, much worse. But I didn't think I'd see this in what seems like such a close-knit community and small town like Stillwater.

The way everyone supported the kids' Spring Fair after a fire in one of the school buildings destroyed everything we'd been working on was the kind of stuff you see in Hallmark movies.

That Stillwater doesn't match this one. Why aren't people getting together to improve this area?

"Ellis, hey, glad you could make it."

I see Tyler coming from behind a rusty white van that looks like the last time it saw better days was a few decades ago.

"Hey, I'm happy to help. Where do you want me?"

"Can you grab those two boxes from the back? They're big but light. Just rolls."

I do as he says and then follow him inside the building. We go straight into a kitchen, where there's a group of people busy around three stoves, chatting animatedly.

They don't notice as we walk behind them. Tyler puts his box down and then sets mine on top of his.

"Ready for intros?" he whispers as if I'm about to be induced into a super-secret society.

"Feed me to the wolves," I joke.

"Not quite, but," he says, looking me up and down, "you're easy on the eye, so I'd stay away from Emy. She's a flirt, but she keeps her hands to herself."

"So why do I need to stay away from her?"

"Do you have a particular interest in earthworms, fig wasps, or Star Wars fan fic?"

"No?"

"That's why."

Okay…

He turns to the group, and I take a second to process what he just said before Tyler makes the introductions.

"Hey, team, this is Ellis. He's a teacher at the elementary school, and he's helping us today. Be gentle," he warns, and they all laugh. "From left to right, that's Anne, Bob, Cathy, Dave, and Emy."

I smile and raise my hand in a collective hi.

"He likes to keep us in alphabetical order so he doesn't forget our names," Bob says. They all laugh again and return to the stoves where they're preparing the food.

"He's not wrong," Tyler says. "Come with me."

We walk through a set of double doors that leads straight to a hall with faded parquet flooring.

"This used to be a sports facility?" I ask.

"Yeah, a long time ago. Since they built the new high school years ago, this building became too far away and impractical. The kids didn't have enough time to walk back to school between PE and the other classes."

Tyler shrugs as though that's just the accepted way of things, like a weathered man who's seen it all and is doing the best with the little he has.

There are a bunch of tables and chairs stacked up by the wall, so we line them until the hall fills up with rows upon rows, and it looks more like a school cafeteria than an empty space.

"We have a volunteer who comes in at night and cleans the floor, so we always stack the tables and chairs on the side to make it easy for him," he says. "Let's get back to the kitchen and see how they're doing. I think we have bean chili with rice, vegetable soup, some good old fried chicken, and mashed potatoes."

I'm impressed. And I won't voice it, but I also feel stupid that I assumed a soup kitchen would only serve soup.

Tyler sets up the serving table in the hall by the double doors for easy access from the kitchen. I'm given the task of putting rolls in baskets and then taking stuff out when it's ready.

It's organized chaos. Everyone works around everyone else like they can predict each other's moves. I feel like I'm mostly in the way, but everyone seems too nice to say anything.

While we're preparing the serving station, the hall fills with people. There's animated chatting and some heckling at Tyler, who taunts back without missing a beat.

It's almost easy to forget that these people are here because they're struggling financially. This might be the only meal they get today. Or the most nutritious one they get until the next time the kitchen is open.

When the food is ready, Anne, Bob, Cathy, Dave, Emy, and Tyler all line up, each in front of a station. Tyler rings a bell and people form an orderly line.

They pick up trays from one end and make their way along, choosing what they want.

I'm at the very end next to Tyler, just making sure they have cutlery and a roll and reminding them to pick up a plastic cup if they want water from the dispenser.

My job is totally superfluous, but it's giving me exactly what I want.

An opportunity to get to know these people.

And they're not people without housing wearing ragged clothes, looking dirty. These are the hardworking people who, for some reason or another, cannot afford to put food on the table, the system failed them, or they've had to make some really difficult choices.

As they come around, I recognize a face, and as soon as she sees me, she looks down and gets closer to the person in front of her as if to blend in. She doesn't even pick up a roll before she goes to a table on the far end and sits with her back to us.

"Tyler, is it okay if I go speak to that lady over there?" I ask.

"Do you know her?"

"She's the mother of one of my students."

He gives me a knowing look and nods.

I grab a roll and head over to her table. She looks up when she notices someone sitting in front of her, and her face is full of panic when she realizes it's me.

"Mrs. Salvador, you forgot your roll."

She stares at me and then the roll. Her hands shake as she takes it and places it on her tray.

"Do you mind if I talk to you for a moment?"

"Are you going to call child services?"

I'm taken aback by her question. "Why would I do that?"

She shrugs. "Isn't that what you people do when you think the kids are in a bad situation?"

"I'm not going to do that."

"Why not?"

"Because I'm not worried about your son. He's a smart boy. He always did his homework, made friends easily, and never thought twice about helping one of his classmates. He's a credit to you and your husband. I'm sure he'll do just as well next year."

She smiles, and I see the pride shining from her eyes before her expression darkens again.

"Then why are you here?"

"I'm here because I would like to volunteer, which means you may see me more often. I am not here to judge. If you ever want to talk, I'm an excellent listener, but please don't be afraid when you see me."

She nods, and I'm not entirely certain she trusts my words, but hopefully, we can build that over time.

On my way back to the serving station, a guy shouts, "Hey, new guy, next time, give us a proper portion. We ain't kids here."

"I wasn't the one that served you, Geoff. Go complain to management."

He looks a little shocked by my reply, and his friends are making fun of him, so I go over and give him a pat on the back. "I'm a teacher, Geoff. I'm good at remembering names and faces, and I know Cathy gave you a little extra rice under that chili."

"You're funny, Mr. Teacher. You can come back again," another guy, Bill, I think, says.

"I intend to. And now I should get back to work before I'm fired on my first day, right?"

"Tyler runs a tight ship round here," Geoff says.

On my return to the station, Tyler is arguing with someone.

"Joseph, don't be greedy. You know the rule. One roll per person until everyone's had a portion. If there are leftovers, you can have more."

Joseph goes off mumbling something or another that I can't understand.

I lean closer to Tyler. "I saw Kay take two rolls earlier."

"I let her because she takes one for her friend, Brian, who's too damned proud to come here and get a meal. Usually, if there're leftovers, I'll give her a box to take away too."

I gesture at the room around us. "Tyler, this is an amaz—"

"Hey, Ty, sorry I'm—"

If my heart could beat any faster, I'd have a coronary because the last person I expected to see in Tyler's soup kitchen was Milo, in well-worn, slightly torn jeans and a faded T-shirt that might have once been red, but it's hard to tell now.

Milo's gaze shifts between Tyler, me, and the floor.

"Hi, Milo, nice to see you again," I say to break the silence because a glance at Tyler shows he's confused by Milo's reaction.

"Hi," he replies. "Um…Tyler, sorry I'm a little late. I'll go out back and start now, okay?"

"Sure thing. Anne left your favorite for you."

"Thank you."

Milo practically runs toward the kitchen without glancing back.

I look at Tyler, who's grinning. "Well, well. Looks like *he* is the one Alice should have invited over for dinner the other day." And then he leaves me to go clear the tables.

What does he mean?

Cathy and Dave clear tables too, so I help Bob and Anne make up some leftover boxes. Kay is the first to come up to get one for her friend, thanking us.

The double doors have round glass windows you can see through into the kitchen, so with the pretense of getting some napkins, I go to the other side of the station and try to look through them.

I see Milo leaning against the kitchen counter, joyfully eating a portion of rice and chili like it's the first meal he's had today.

My memory goes back to the day I bought him the lemonade at the fair.

It suddenly dawns on me. He didn't want to get a drink, not because he was shy or unsure. It was because he couldn't afford it.

I'm not sure if I want to be sick, run inside the kitchen and hold Milo in my arms, or scream.

"Sorry, guys, I need a breath of fresh air. I'll be back in a moment."

Emy nods and carries on with her work while I basically run to the door.

It's dark outside now. It's one of those mild summer nights that would be perfect with a breeze but feels sticky and stifling without one.

I lean my back against the wall and close my eyes.

Maybe I stay outside a little too long because I hear the door open, and when I open my eyes, Tyler's standing next to me.

"Are you okay?" he asks.

"Honestly? I'm not sure." I stare into his eyes. "What is Milo doing here?"

"He volunteers, just the rest of the gang."

"But it's not just that, is it?"

Tyler puts his hand on my shoulder and squeezes tight. "That's a conversation you need to have with him."

I nod.

"I'm going to give a piece of advice because I've been doing this too long on my own."

"Okay."

"You can't help everybody. I've seen you talk to people today. It's good to be familiar with them. But you can't rescue them. We're here to make today a little better than yesterday. Some people don't want to be rescued. Some people can't."

I nod, even though every cell in my body wants to fight it.

"But Milo. He's different."

Tyler smiles. "Milo is a special person. He's very guarded and has good reason to be. If you want to help him…gain his trust."

"I don't know how. He seems…flighty."

"Then catch him before he takes off."

5

MILO

I NEED to stop running into him. I need to stop running into him.

That's the mantra I keep repeating as I prepare to wash the large pots and pans the team used to make the meals.

I'm not sure how I can make it happen when he seems to be wherever I go.

I've been volunteering with Ty practically since he started the soup kitchen. I'm not that great a cook, but I can certainly do the dishes, which means the rest of the crew gets to go home early.

This is my community. Where I grew up. So I want to help.

Most of them knew my family, which is why I stay behind the closed kitchen doors, but it won't stop me from helping out.

I don't want to hear the stories or see the pity in their eyes. Or worse, the hatred at my brother for being part of what makes this area of town what it is now. Even if he paid for it with his life.

No. I just want to help. Doesn't hurt getting a free meal out of it too.

Anne's chili is the best, but since I've been on my own with Sara, I've noticed Tyler keeping food behind for me more frequently.

"We saved your favorite before it ran out," he always says. "Or there was too much because fewer people turned up today."

It's a silly game we play with each other. He pretends he doesn't know I need the free food, and I pretend I eat it just to make him happy.

The truth is, I do need it. Desperately.

I don't get paid till Friday, and the last of my money went toward today's groceries, which only covers the vegetables I need to make Sara's meals. I cook them in a batch and freeze them in little pots, so I know she'll have food for the next two weeks.

Anne's chili is the only thing I've had to eat today, apart from a piece of toast for breakfast.

I debated whether I should keep half of it to take home for tomorrow, but my gluttony won and I ate it all. Damn Anne's cooking skills.

With renewed energy from my meal, I tackle the pile of dishes. I start with the big pans because they dry quickly, and I can put them away to make space for the smaller stuff.

The problem with this job is that it doesn't require much thought. At the store, I need to pay attention to what I'm doing. I don't want to overcharge someone because I accidentally scan an item twice.

But washing pans requires no brain work. Which means my mind is totally switched to the man on the other side of the double doors.

Ugh, even casually dressed, as he is today, he still looks so good.

Did anyone notice how he usually wears dressier clothes but today he's wearing jeans and an untucked shirt? I bet not.

That's the kind of thing I notice because I have a stupid crush on him. He's not wearing cologne. His shoes aren't polished. He's not trying to blend in. He wants people to be at ease around him.

I don't know him that well, but even I know that's what he does.

It must be a teacher thing.

Except when it comes to me. There's no easing or relaxing around Ellis. Just lots of blood flow, feelings, breathlessness, lightheadedness— I should probably see a doctor.

At least he was outside when I had my dinner. I'd be mortified if he knew that chili was my only meal today.

It's stupid, I know. It's obvious we come from different worlds.

Maybe Jimmy is right.

Ellis is older, educated, well spoken, while I'm…just Milo.

But even just Milo still has a little pride left.

"I think that pot is as washed as it's ever going to be."

I jump at the sound of his voice, sending a big splatter of water everywhere.

"Oh my god. I'm sorry," I say, grabbing a dish towel and trying to pat his shirt dry.

He laughs. "It's okay. It's only water. I've been under the rain before and lived."

I stop, unsure of what to do. "I'm still sorry."

"I'm the one who should apologize. I shouldn't have come from behind you like that."

My cheeks heat at the thought of Ellis coming from behind me for a totally different reason, and I have to try really hard to push away the butterflies in my belly and send signals to my dick, who's starting to have ideas.

I rinse the pan before putting it on a table to dry and grabbing another pot.

"Have you been volunteering here long?" he asks.

"Yes, since Tyler started it."

"That's nice of you, especially when you're already busy with work and raising a baby."

I stop scrubbing the pan for a moment and look at him. "I live right around the corner, so it's no big deal."

"You'd be surprised how many people can help and don't or won't, so don't sell yourself short," he says.

"Why are you here?"

Ellis is as taken aback by my question as I am. What the hell has gotten into me? I almost want to take it back, but I'm curious. What brings him to this side of Stillwater? How did he come to know Tyler in the first place, anyway?

He folds his shirt sleeves and starts washing the cutlery in the smaller sink next to mine.

"I'm embarrassed to say I didn't know there was such a class divide in Stillwater." He laughs to himself. "Even saying that sounds so wrong."

"It's the truth though. A lot of folks from here, especially the older ones, used to work at the old mill factory in Chester Falls. When it closed down, everyone lost their jobs."

A pang of sadness hits me as I still remember the day it happened.

It's one of my earliest memories.

"A small town like Stillwater would never have enough jobs for everyone," Ellis says.

I rinse the pan and grab the last one.

"Some retired. Some went on disability. There were…a lot of men who took their lives thinking their insurance would provide for their families." I can hear my voice break as it all comes back to me.

My mom crying while cradling her pregnant belly. Me holding my favorite teddy and asking her why she was crying. My dad was home during the day. He was never home during the day.

I clear my throat.

"Anyway. How did you meet Tyler? He's not usually the sociable kind, and he doesn't have kids, so it can't have been at school," I say, changing the subject.

When the hell did I get so chatty around Ellis? Where's tongue-tied Milo who doesn't ask inappropriate questions?

Ellis lets out a laugh that makes me forget everything and reawakens the butterflies in my belly. The small lines in the corner of his eyes return, even as he's rolling them.

"Believe it or not, my sister tried to set us up on a date."

"Oh." That's the butterflies all gone. Puff. No more.

Thankfully, he's still washing the cutlery and doesn't see my reaction, so he carries on. "I don't know what even possessed her to think Tyler and I would be a good match."

I look at him. A flicker of hope—well, more like keeping my little dream alive—rises in my chest, but he's still distracted.

"He's a great guy, though, and I'm so glad I met him. I think we could become good friends. And I would never know about the support he's giving the community. I mean, how many of my students come from this part of town, and I don't even know it?"

"There's a lot of good people in this part of town," I say.

He turns to me and his eyes are on mine, capturing them, holding them hostage because I can't look away.

"From what I can see, there's at least one good person in this part of town."

He slowly removes his gaze from mine, which is just as well so he doesn't see me blushing or my infatuated smile.

The rest of the team comes back after a while, having gotten the hall ready for the cleaner, and with Ellis's help, the dishes are done in half the time.

"Good effort, team. Thank you all for coming again. See you for more fun and games in a few days," Tyler says. "Now, skedaddle off home. I'll lock up."

"Yes, boss," we all say and spill out of the building through the kitchen door.

I wave everyone goodbye, but I'm not sure what to do with Ellis.

"Um…I guess I'll see you when you're next shopping…or maybe here?" I ask, putting my hands in my jean pockets.

He smiles. "Do you want a ride home?"

I point at the street behind me. "I really do live just around the corner. It would take you longer to drive me there."

"Oh."

He half-turns to go but doesn't, and I'm not sure what to make of it. It's like he's disappointed.

Nah, the chili must be going to my head. Or maybe it's spending time with Ellis and managing several complete sentences without breaking down in a pile of goo that has clearly messed with my brain.

"Well, as you say, I'll see you around," he says and then walks away.

I wasn't lying when I said I live nearby because, in just a short walk, I'm turning onto my street.

I hear Sara crying and screaming, and I run toward the house.

Florrie is holding her, and I see her go-bag is ready.

"We need to get to the hospital. Sara's temperature is too high, and I can't get it down."

"Have you given her anything?" I ask, knowing it's a stupid question because Florrie looks after Sara well.

"I've given her Tylenol and used some cold compresses, but her temperature hasn't gone down."

My hands shake as I hold Sara in my arms.

She's burning even through her clothes. Thankfully, Florrie thought to change her into something lighter and easier to remove than her one-piece pajamas. I strap her into the car seat while Florrie goes to the driver's side. I get in on the other side of the car next to Sara.

"It's okay, baby. We're going to the doctor, and they'll make you all nice and better, okay?" I know she's probably not listening to or understanding what I'm saying, but I say it for my sanity because right now, I'm close to losing it.

Florrie is driving as fast as she can. We're not talking. I know she's as worried as I am. We can talk as soon as we see a doctor.

She drops us outside the hospital, which I'm not even sure is allowed, but I don't care. I grab the car seat and run to the reception desk.

"Hi, my baby is running a really high fever. I need to see a doctor or a nurse. Please, can you help?"

My hands shake as I expect the woman behind the desk to tell me I have to wait a long time to see someone. Sara is crying so hard her face is red and streaked with tears.

"I'm no doctor, hun," she says as she types on her computer. "Hold up."

She's looking at her screen and then at sheets of paper. Behind me, the waiting room is full of people. Babies have priority, right?

Please, god. Let babies have priority.

The receptionist looks up, "Hey, Darius, be a sweetheart and help this gentleman over here." I turn and see a tall guy approaching. He's wearing scrubs, so he must be a doctor or a nurse.

He looks straight at Sara and touches her forehead. "Hey, gorgeous. Wanna be my date for the night?" He has a deep, calming voice that seems to have an effect on Sara. Then he looks at me. "I'm Darius. I'm a nurse practitioner, and I'll be looking after your baby. Follow me."

"Um…my friend, she's my babysitter. She's been with Sara all night, so she might know more about when the fever started. She's parking the car."

"What's her name, hun?" the receptionist asks.

"Florrie."

"Leave it with me."

Darius takes us into a room.

"How old is she?"

"Nine months. She's just started eating solids but still takes formula," I say.

"Eating well?"

"Yeah, she likes her food. Drinks some water too."

Sara's been a healthy baby, and we've never had to come to the emergency room before. I really hope this isn't something serious. The thought is too painful, so I push it out of my head.

Darius removes Sara's clothes until she's in only her diaper and starts checking her over while having an adult conversation with her about how hard it is to find cheap vegetables these days and how criminal it is that they still haven't invented a bubble gum-flavored twinkie.

She seems completely fascinated by his deep voice, and I feel calmer now that she doesn't look so distressed.

He turns to me. "Her lungs are clear. It looks like it might be an ear infection. I'm going to give her an antibiotic and connect her to an IV to give her some fluids for dehydration."

His voice seems to have the same magical effect on me because all I can do is stare at him. He looks familiar, but I can't place him, and I know for sure I've never met him before.

"Will she be okay?" I ask.

"I'm sure she will. She wouldn't be doing her job right if she didn't give you a few white hairs before she's one. I'm still going to take a blood sample and send it for analysis to make sure the cause of the fever is just the ear infection and nothing else. It could take a couple of hours for the results to come through."

I nod. "Thank you so much for helping us."

He puts his stethoscope around his neck and smiles. "I love my job, and it's not a hardship when the patients are this adorable." He tickles Sara's tummy, starting another one of their conversations as he connects the IV line.

"See ya later, alligator." He says when he's finished, and then turns to me again. "I'll be back in a while to check on her fever, okay? If you need anything, just press that buzzer on the wall."

He leaves us, and a moment later, Florrie comes in with the receptionist.

I explain what the nurse did, and we finally take a moment to breathe.

"She was fine all evening. When I put her to bed, she didn't even complain," Florrie says. "Then she suddenly started crying, so I checked on her, and she was burning. I tried to get her temperature down with the Tylenol and a wet cloth, but it wasn't working."

"Thank you, Florrie. I don't know what I'd do without you."

She gives me a hug, and we wait. I hate seeing my baby girl with the needle attached to her tiny hand, even though I know it's making her better. Sara's fever goes down and her bloodwork comes back clear, so Darius is happy to send us home a few hours later.

By the time I get to bed, I'm so exhausted that I put Sara's baby monitor on the loudest setting to make sure I can hear her if she wakes up again.

I look at a photo of my mom that was taken when she and my dad got married. She looks happy and carefree. Like she has her whole life ahead of her.

"I miss you, Mom. Keep an eye on her for me. She's all I have left. Love you."

6

ELLIS

I DON'T KNOW what possessed me to say yes to meeting up with a couple of my students' parents for Thursday night drinks at The Academy a couple months ago. I knew it had bad idea written all over it.

Okay, so after Harrison and Fletcher helped me with the school's Spring Fair, we kinda became friends. When I say friends, it's more that they decided I need to be taken under a wing as a single gay newbie in town.

No amount of insisting that I spent plenty of summers in Stillwater convinced them I wasn't much of a newbie. And it didn't help that my sister—God rest her soul when I eventually kill her—sided with them.

Apparently, I need to have a social life.

Apparently, Thursday is the new Friday.

Thank god the summer break came soon after their "new" tradition because teaching a classroom of energetic seven-year-olds after a late night is definitely not on my list of favorite things to do.

Each Thursday seems to bring out a different set of parents and friends, so my need for predictability and stability goes well out of the water every week.

When I arrive at The Academy, Fletcher and Harrison are in a booth at the far end of the bar, sitting as close together as two humans possibly can without risking being arrested for indecent behavior.

They're drinking their usual, so I head up to the bar and order a glass of wine for me and a new round of drinks for them before joining them in the booth.

It turns out Levi isn't working behind the bar this evening. His daughter, Ava, is having a sleepover with Fletcher's and Harrison's kids at Harrison's ex's place, so he and Arlo squeeze into our booth shortly after I arrive.

"First round of shots is on me," Levi says and then waves at his best friend and fellow server, Penny, as she walks past with a tray of empty glasses. "Hey, Pen, can you bring us a round of Spiky Roses?"

"Sure can, gorgeous."

"Not wanting to state the obvious here," Harrison says, pointing to all the drinks in front of us, "but that's not our first round."

"What's a Spiky Rose?" I dare ask.

"It smells nice but stings like a motherfucker on the way down," all but Levi say in unison.

Levi waves them off. "It's a little something I've been working on to update the drinks menu...it may need a few tweaks."

Arlo gives him a side look. "That thing should be illegal."

"I suppose I could make it smoother, but some people like it a little rough sometimes."

Fletcher snorts as Arlo tries to hide his reddening cheeks behind his hands.

"Here you go, boys." Penny sets down a tray with five small shot glasses containing a pinkish drink.

"I'm not sure about this," I say, already feeling tomorrow's regret.

"Come on, Ellis, it's summer break. It's like spring break, but without boobs or dick. You know I was an equal opportunity kind of guy." Fletcher says, raising his glass and then downing his shot before sounding like he's about to cough up a lung.

"Good save, baby," Harrison says before taking his shot, and Fletcher laughs.

"Yup, no boobs for me now," he grins. "Just your big, fat—" Harrison shuts him up with a kiss, which we're all thankful for.

Levi looks at me expectantly.

I groan and close my eyes as I take the shot. I'm not sure what hits me first, the sting as the drink goes past my throat or the overwhelming smell of roses. "How much...alcohol"—I cough—"is in this?"

My question remains unanswered as Fletcher calls Penny and asks for another round.

At some point, I start questioning my life choices or my choice of friends before remembering I didn't choose them. They picked me, so for their sins, I get them a couple of rounds.

Of course, with my not-quite-drunk-yet state of poor judgment, I forget the rounds include me. At least the last time I drank wine was a while ago, so I'm not mixing drinks...I think. There are so many glasses on the table, I'm not sure anymore.

"How do you do it?" Harrison asks, staring at me.

I shrug. "It's easy. You hold it like this, and then you raise the glass up to your mouth and drink the poison inside. You've been doing well so far. Four out of five because you spilled a little on your shirt earlier." I give him a pat on the head.

"No, you dumbass," he says before covering his mouth with his hands in the same way his daughter does in class when she says something she's not supposed to. "The kids."

I point at his chest. "I don't have no...any kids. You have two."

"Nah, dude, you have like..."—Arlo stares at the ceiling—"fifty, sixty kids in your class?"

"Feels like that sometimes, but it's twenty. Why are we talking about my work? You,"—I point at all of them—"said I need to chill. No work talk. Besides, it's bummer seak...summer break."

"Fletch is feeling broody," Harrison says.

"Broody as in..." I prompt.

"He wants a baby because we bumped into Milo last week at the craft fair and he got to hold his baby daughter for a millisecond."

Fletcher nods fiercely.

"How did he get his baby, anyway?" Fletcher asks. "As far as I know, he's single, and he didn't have a baby, and then boom…baby."

"You do know how babies are made, right?" Levi asks.

Fletcher holds out his hands, arguing back, "Yeah, but he's gay."

I'm staying in my corner and away from the conversation between them because Milo's personal life isn't my business. What does it matter if he's single or gay or how he got to have a baby? That's surely his business.

"Hello," Levi waves. "I'm also totally one hundred percent gay."

"I can vouch for him," Arlo interrupts.

Levi gives him a kiss and continues, "And I have a kid. All I'm saying is…I don't know, I need another frink…drink…"

"And all I'm saying is, we've been together for two months, Fletch," Harrison argues. "I'm not ready to be interrupted by a crying baby when…you know…every five minutes."

"You have sex every five minutes?" Arlo asks and then whispers, "Do you take like…medication?"

"What? Fuck no."

I laugh at Harrison's shocked expression that his manhood might be questioned even if what's at stake is an impossible five-minute refractory period.

"Aw, the baby phase is the best," Levi says, leaning against Arlo, who's giving him a weird side look. "That's when they're all cute and smell nice."

"And puke all over you when you're about to go into a meeting to ask your boss for a raise," Harrison interjects.

Levi waves him off. "Pfft, it's when they learn words and use them to ask you for a tartant…turt…tarantula." He punches the air when he gets it right. "It's when they ask you for vemonous pets that you have to worry."

Arlo rolls his eyes. "Ava didn't ask for a *venomous* pet. She asked for a brother because Megan now has George."

Penny brings more drinks I don't remember anyone ordering, but they look different from the Spiky Roses.

Fletcher downs a shot of something that looks vile and then kisses Harrison to the point he has to not-so-discreetly adjust himself in his seat, probably far too gone to remember he's sitting right next to me, and then points at Levi. "My son is not a vemo…nous pet."

"He does have a new sister though," Harrison adds, and the way Fletcher looks at him could melt the most frozen of hearts.

Not my heart though. Mine has been signed, sealed, and delivered to the ice caps. Lost forever. At least as far as love is concerned. And I'm not drunk enough to consider admitting to myself that I may be a tiny bit jealous of them and their perfect relationships.

"This is all your fault," Levi says.

"Who? Me?" I ask since he's pointing in our general direction and it's hard to tell.

I raise my hand to get Penny's attention and ask for a new round for the table. If I'm going to be blamed for poisonous pets and extra children, I need more alcohol. In for a dime, in for a dollar.

"No. Them," Arlo says. "They had to go and get together, and now Megan and George have each other."

"So, are you having a baby?" Fletcher asks.

"We said we'd get married first," Arlo says pointedly.

Levi gasps and brings his hand up to his mouth. "Are you asking me to marry you?"

"I guess I am," Arlo says.

Penny rolls her eyes as she sets the tray with the new round.

"Are they proposing to each other again?"

"Yup," Fletcher says.

Harrison adds, "At least they're not proposing to anyone else this time."

"This is true." Penny puts a cocktail in front of me and gives me a sympathetic look.

When did we switch to cocktails?

"Penny, bring me some water, please. Someone needs to sober up enough to stop them from heading over to the town hall to get married in the nude," I say. "They've all mentioned it before, and at this rate, I'm not even sure they're sober enough to marry the right person."

She laughs. "Meh, worse things happen at sea. Let your hair down, honey."

"Yeah, Ellis, let your hair down," Fletcher says, imitating Penny's voice.

I take a sip from the cocktail Penny just brought.

Let my hair down. *Isn't that what I've been doing tonight?*

"How about Milo? I bet he'd help you let your hair down," Fletcher says, leaning over Harrison to get closer to me. "He'd mess it all up and then mess it all up again."

"That makes no sense."

He stares at me, but whatever he's looking for seems lost, so he leans against Harrison, who puts one of his muscly arms around him and kisses his hair.

"Yeah, what happened between you and Milo?"

Levi and Arlo look at each other and then at me. "Something happened between you and Milo?" Levi asks.

Arlo adds, "I knew I thought I saw you two together at the fair after Milo's neighbor left."

I feel my skin warm up.

Fuck. The wine, those Spiky Roses, and whatever else I've had are going to my head.

Correction: have gone to my head.

"No. I don't know what they're even talking about," I say.

"Oh come on, Ellis," Fletcher says, wiggling his eyebrows, "You can tell us. You like Milo, don't you? Who wouldn't? He's so adorable and smiley and cute."

"No point denying it. We all saw it," Harrison adds.

Huh? Saw it?

"Yeah. Why are they wasting their time?" Fletcher asks the group, totally ignoring my presence or state of confusion.

"I'm sorry. What are you talking about?" I ask.

Fletcher gesticulates like it's supposed to mean something. "You know, at the summer festival. That thing between you two when he came to ask you about something, and he was all shy, and you went all red."

I stare at him.

"Oh come on, you said, 'How many times do I have to ask you to call me Ellis?' And then he goes, 'At least one more time.' Come on,

Ellis. That's so romantic that I could have painted you on canvas right there and then."

Fuck, maybe Fletcher isn't as drunk as I thought.

I look at Harrison for help.

"He's not entirely wrong," he says, being no help at all.

The change to this topic is enough to sober me up a little.

I shake my head. "No, that's ridiculous. Yes, he's a nice young man, and he needed help with his…stuff. That's all. Nothing else. That's it. Besides, I'm forty-two, and he's all of twenty-something. What a ridiculous idea that something would happen between us."

"So you admit you like him. Ha!" Fletcher says, a little too loud. People from a few tables down look at us, and I pray to god no one knows Milo.

"How come we missed that?" Arlo asks.

Levi thinks for a moment. "I think we were working real hard on that brother for Ava."

"Ahhh, that time. Wasn't it the time when you did that thing where—"

"Please don't finish that sentence," I plead. "I'd like to keep all the drinks I've had inside my stomach…at least until I get home."

He raises his hands as a form of apology.

"I'm tapping out, guys," I say.

Getting out of the booth when I'm in the middle of two couples presents a challenge, but when I offer to pay for another round of drinks and their cabs home, they let me out.

I drink two full glasses of water and take two Advil as soon as I get home, hoping it'll make tomorrow a little less painful.

With any luck, everyone's memories of tonight will be erased, and there will be no further questions about the nothing that is happening between Milo and me.

Because there isn't and never will be.

7

ELLIS

Focusing on next year's lesson plans when my brain is pounding from last night's hangout is a challenge.

Now I know two Advil and water before bed no longer works. And I shouldn't trust Levi when it comes to trying out new drinks.

The teacher has learned the lesson.

I'm definitely sitting out next Thursday. They can pick a new victim.

I close my eyes and rub my temples, taking a deep breath, willing my headache away.

I'm also willing away the recall of all conversations involving Milo.

Where the hell did they get those ideas? I'm only trying to help him.

Okay, yes, Milo is an attractive young man, but what does that have to do with anything? Can't someone find another person attractive and still keep a friendly relationship?

That's probably what Milo needs more right now. A friend.

He has a daughter to raise, and from what I saw in the soup kitchen, he may have other problems too. If getting his GED helps him get to where he needs to be, I'll be there for him.

My phone dings with a notification, and I don't need to read it to know what it is.

I groan, which makes my headache worse.

Picking up my phone, I pull up the teacher's group and type a message before getting up from my desk to get ready.

Ellis: I'm on my way. Not feeling a hundred percent.

Jan: Oh dear. We'll order your coffee.

Ellis: I love you.

Jan: Of course you do. I'm awesome.

Fifteen minutes later, I arrive at Bittersweet, where a few of the teachers arranged to meet up for a midsummer-break catch-up over lunch. Except I haven't even had breakfast.

Jan's curious gaze peers at me from the top of her pink-framed glasses as I sit across from her on the empty chair with the full cup of coffee in front of it. The secretary is the most lovable person in the school, but also the nosiest and sharpest. I better keep my mouth shut until I have more caffeine in me.

"Hey, Ellis, partying hard this summer?" someone teases.

"You know it. Me and my wild ways." I take a sip of the coffee and lean back on the chair, closing my eyes and waiting for the caffeine to reach my bloodstream. "Thank you to the angel who brewed this coffee," I mutter.

"Anytime, Ellis." I open my eyes and see Julius, the owner of Bittersweet, clearing a nearby table. "You look like you need a couple of painkillers to go with that." He laughs.

I raise the cup. "I'm good on painkillers, but I'd murder for one of your lemon muffins."

"Coming right up."

Julius goes inside, so I turn to the faces around the table. "Sorry I'm late. What did I miss?"

"Looks like we're the ones missing something. Our summer has clearly been a lot less interesting than yours," Sonya, the PE teacher, says, raising a brow.

"If you want to subject yourself to liver failure"—*and years of therapy*—"I can tell you where to be next Thursday evening."

"I hear you're volunteering at the soup kitchen," Jan says.

A change of topic. *Thank you, Jan.* "Yeah. It's been a real eye-opener, but I'm enjoying supporting that community."

"There's a rumor going around that Mrs. Martin is pushing the mayor to turn the playground by the church on the south side of town into a parking lot to stop the tourists that come to the craft fair from parking on the residential streets on the north side of town."

"Hold up," someone else says. "Sonya, doesn't your girlfriend work closely with the town council?"

"Yes, she does."

A lot of eyes meet in a silent conversation.

"I'm a little lost here, people. Does anyone care to fill in the newbie?" I ask.

Sonya looks at everyone. "At the moment, this is just a *rumor.*" The way she emphasizes the word makes me wonder if this is more than a rumor. "But yes, it seems Mrs. Martin has moved on from crafts into town planning."

"I'm even more lost now," I say.

"Mrs. Martin is basically Stillwater's Wicked Witch of the West, or whatever they call it. If you want to know more, ask Arlo and Levi. You taught their kid, Ava, right?"

"Yeah, she was in my class last year."

"One thing is for sure. If Mrs. Martin's really got it in for that playground, it'll take the town or a very strong-willed mind to change the course of action."

If I was already struggling to get Milo and yesterday's conversation off my mind, it's even worse now that I know there's a chance the playground he may have played on growing up could be destroyed.

There's not much I can do right now, so I park the information I've just learned to one side and join the conversation as we start talking about classes for next year, activity plans, and teaching schedules.

When I go back home, I realize lesson planning isn't going to happen, but there are a few other jobs that need to be done around the house. Or maybe I could stop by Birchcraft, the craft store where Arlo works, and ask when he might be free to talk. Or willing.

If this Mrs. Martin woman is as bad as Sonya made her out to be, Arlo may not want to talk about her. It's worth a try anyway.

The rest of the day goes by quicker, and Julius' lemon muffin must have magical powers because my headache subsides considerably afterward. At home, I look at the new posters I ordered to put up on the classroom walls and go through my school supplies to see what will make it into the new year and what will go in the spares box.

By the time I look at the clock again, it's too late to go to Birchcraft and speak to Arlo, but I still head out because I need to stop at the grocery store to get a few things for dinner.

It's funny how my shopping habits have changed. When I lived in the city, I did one weekly trip, and it was rare that I needed to supplement it with anything extra.

In Stillwater, I enjoy buying fresh food more often. It's nice having better meal options and changing my mind because I don't have to stick to the ingredients I bought a week ago.

It's also because you like seeing Milo.

Yes, fine. It's because I like seeing Milo. So what? I'm only human. When you connect with someone, you should hold on to it, right? I might ask him how Sara is.

That's what friends do, right?

As if by luck, the first person I see in the vegetable section isn't Arlo, but his boyfriend, Levi. He's adding a few items to his cart when he sees me.

"Hey, Ellis. How are you feeling after last night?"

"A lot worse than you look. Have you got some kind of special medicine, or is just age on your side?"

He laughs. "It just takes practice, my friend."

"Somehow I doubt that."

"At least it's summer break so you didn't have a class full of kids to teach today."

I laugh. "There's that, but I do miss them. I've been to the school for a couple of meetings, and the classroom feels too empty."

"Maybe next year I'll take photos of them to stick in their chairs so you can still look at their faces. It'll be my contribution to your summer break wellbeing."

I laugh. "Photos aren't quite as noisy. But I like the idea. How's your photography business going, anyway?"

Levi is a photographer, but when he returned to Stillwater after years away, he took a job as a bartender at The Academy bar and restaurant while he started up his business.

"It's good, thanks. I'm still working up to what I really want to photograph, but in the meantime, just getting people from Stillwater to come to me is…well, quite a miracle, considering."

I scratch my day-old stubble, unsure how to approach it.

"Actually, Levi. I…um…I'm looking for some information, and I was told you and Arlo might be able to help."

"Sure."

"Who's Mrs. Martin?"

Levi's expression changes immediately. He's holding a tomato in his hand and places it carefully in his cart.

"She's the person responsible for the lies that took me away from my family for twelve years. She was also on the craft fair committee until earlier this year when she refused to give Arlo a stand at the fair."

"What? Why? He's super talented and everyone loves his stand."

Levi smiles proudly. "He is. Which is why the town stood by him when her lies came out. The craft committee stepped down, so at the moment, there's nothing in place, but Arlo is working with the other stand holders to come up with a solution." He adds more things to his cart. "Why are you asking about her?"

"I hate gossip, but I heard there's a chance she may be involved in plans to transform the playground by the church on the south side of town into a parking lot. Does she really have that much influence with the mayor?"

He looks around as if to ensure there's no one listening.

"Stillwater is one of those funny places. On the surface, it's very accepting, open, the perfect place to live. But underneath it all, there's still some old money trying to influence where they can bring back the 'old values,'" he says with speech quotes. "Sometimes they get their way, sometimes they don't."

I pick up a couple of peppers and roll them in my hand. Maybe this is all a hearsay and nothing will actually happen.

"Thank you for the information, Levi. I'm sure she's not the most pleasant topic of discussion for you, so I apologize but appreciate the information."

"Don't worry about it. If there's anything Arlo and I can do to help, let us know. Now I gotta go before Arlo and Ava destroy our kitchen. They're making dinner together, and Ava is the chef." He looks at the contents of his cart. "I should probably grab some frozen pizzas just in case."

I wave him off and continue shopping. The peppers go in my basket, along with a couple of onions, tomatoes, and a few more vegetables before I check out the fruit section.

"That's quite a healthy basket you have there."

I turn around and see Fletcher and Harrison, who also look as fresh as two daisies in the spring. I really must find out what their secret is.

"Hi, guys. How's it going?"

Harrison just nods, but it's Fletcher's smile as he stares at my basket that scares me a little.

"We're good. Shopping for movie night with the kids," Fletcher says. "And you? Just…buying extremely healthy food?"

"Fletch…" Harrison warns, but it goes totally ignored, so he rolls his eyes.

"Or maybe…" Fletcher continues. "Is it because this is the best vantage point to watch a certain cashier?"

I feel my skin warm even though I didn't see Milo when I came in, but he's not wrong when it comes to my other shopping trips. My fruit and vegetable consumption has increased. Which is a good thing for a man my age. It's healthy.

"Not this again."

"All Fletcher is saying, in a very bad and totally roundabout way, is that if you're attracted to Milo, it may not be totally unreciprocated. We all see it. But you do what you want with that. Also, add some protein to that basket if you don't want to be too obvious about your shopping…habits."

"And ice cream," Fletcher adds before Harrison pulls him away to do their shopping.

Ice cream might be an excellent idea since it means staying in the frozen aisle long enough for my body temperature to self-regulate.

I still need to handle looking into Milo's eyes while trying not to wonder if Harrison and Fletcher are right.

8

—————

MILO

"Hey, Milo, wait up."

I stop and turn around. "What's up, Jimmy? Did I forget something at work?"

It would be unusual since I never carry much on me. I pat my pocket, feeling for my phone. My sandwich is long gone since I had it for lunch, and I also have my keys.

"No, um…I just thought we could go home together. I finished my shift."

"Oh, okay, sure."

I wait for him to catch up before I resume walking past the cars in the store parking lot.

"Where are you going? The bus stop is that way." He points in the opposite direction.

"I only take the bus if there's bad weather or it's too late in the day. It's three o'clock in the afternoon on a nice day. No point wasting money on the bus fare."

He stares at me like what I'm saying is ridiculous, but then I see understanding dawn in his eyes and he walks beside me.

We grew up in the same neighborhood, but Jimmy was one of my brother's school friends. One of the few that got out of the bad life early enough to change.

"You have a lot on your shoulders, don't you?" he asks.

"Everyone has, Jimmy. Last time I heard, your mom's health hasn't miraculously improved." I catch him from the corner of my eye as we walk.

He's not a bad guy, but we're not close enough to be considered friends. I'm not even sure we have anything in common other than being gay.

"She has her good days," he sighs. "But it's different, man. Mom can call me if she needs help. She doesn't need a sitter. I know Gerald has been giving you a hard time lately. He's a dick."

I shrug. What can I say? It's true. Gerald is a dick, but talking about him in my free time is something I don't want to do.

We're walking past some of the most expensive houses in Stillwater. Some have high surrounding walls like they're hiding some super-secret mansion. Others have lower walls, showing the beautifully manicured front yards with green lawns and carefully curated flowers.

What Florrie told me about the playground has been playing in my mind, which annoys me because it's not like I even care about it. But now, instead of thinking about my dream house when I walk by, I wonder which of these big houses belongs to the person responsible for wanting to change the playground.

For the past twenty years, no one's looked twice or cared about the south side of Stillwater. Why now?

And why am I giving it brain space? Maybe it's just some kind of morbid curiosity.

"What do you think it looks like inside those big houses?" Jimmy asks.

I shrug. "Who knows? Probably lots of expensive things. Maybe old furniture that is so ancient you can't touch it because you'll ruin it, uncomfortable couches that make you sit straight and give you a back-ache. I don't know."

He laughs. "I'm not sure what I'd do with so much space. Would you spend your day going from one room to another, just sitting there and thinking, 'I fancy spending some time in my third bedroom today,'" he says in a posh voice. "And now I'm going to the living room with my extremely large television because I need to compensate for the small size of my dick."

We see an old lady on the other side of the road staring at us like she clearly heard Jimmy. He crouches next to a parked car, laughing so hard he's holding his belly.

"I think she's gone now. You're safe," I say a moment later after waving at the lady in the form of an apology.

When he stands, I see his green eyes are watery from laughing.

He stares at me, and for a moment, all I see is the innocence of a young man. His freckles are more pronounced, and I remember Mikey used to make fun of them. I think they're quite adorable.

"You're staring at me," he says. His voice is breathy, and I realize we're standing too close.

I take a step back. "I'm sorry. It's just…" I look down at the ground, searching for my words. "You just reminded me a little of Mikey, you know, from before…but also after he came back."

Jimmy puts his hand on my shoulder. "He really was trying to turn his life around, wasn't he?"

"In his own way, yeah, I think he was."

I want to believe that because it's the only way I can carry on day after day. Pretending what happened to my brother wasn't meant to happen. He was in the wrong place at the wrong time, and that single moment changed my world forever.

We walk in silence until the houses become more working class. Closer together. Smaller. Familiar.

"Do you think they'll really turn the playground into a parking lot?" Jimmy asks, breaking our silence.

"Don't know."

"We should do something about it. Florrie was visiting with my mom the other day and talking about starting a petition to stop it."

I snort. "Like that's ever worked."

"Why are you so cynical about it? If the entire neighborhood gets behind this, we can make a difference, Milo. Come on, this is where we grew up. Don't you want Sara to have somewhere to play when she's old enough?"

The intensity of his feelings about the playground takes me by surprise. As does the anger that suddenly comes over me.

"Since when did you start caring about all this? When was the last time you were there, Jimmy? Answer that question, and then tell me why you want the playground to be saved. Because all I have is bad memories, and if the place burns down or sinks into a hole, it's not a day too soon."

I don't realize I've sped up my pace until Jimmy grabs my arm.

"I'm sorry." I can see it in his eyes. He's been here for all of it. He feels it.

But those two words aren't enough.

All the sorry in the world won't go back in time and stop Jimmy, Mikey, and their friends from using the playground as their personal drug playpen.

All the sorry in the world won't bring my brother back from the dead just as he'd turned his life around.

"Look, I just want to get home to Sara so Florrie can go to her knitting club," I say, trying to find some calm inside the storm swirling in my heart.

He nods, and we walk the rest of the way in silence.

His place is a few houses down from mine, so I'm opening the front gate I share with Florrie when he says, "I guess you'd probably say no if I asked you out now, wouldn't you?"

I smile. "I would, but not for the reasons you're thinking, Jimmy."

He shakes his head. "How do you know what I'm thinking?"

"We work together, which is a bad idea from the start. We have nothing in common, and I'm too busy with Sara to even consider dating right now."

"Not to mention you already have a crush on a certain elementary school teacher." He puts his hands in his pockets and stares at me. I see the defiance in his eyes.

"I need to go inside, Jimmy. I'll see you at work."

"That wasn't a denial," he says, walking away.

No, it wasn't, but I don't owe Jimmy or anyone an explanation about my feelings for Ellis. As long as Jimmy doesn't say anything inappropriate at work, I don't give a crap if he thinks I have a crush on Ellis.

When I walk inside my small house, Sara is standing on Florrie's lap.

"Look, Daddy, we're doing our exercises so we're good and strong for when we start walking," Florrie says, holding Sara's hands. "Isn't that right?"

Sara calls out Dada as she's been doing more and more. It breaks my heart as much as it fills it with joy and love.

"Hello, beautiful. Did you have a good day?"

I take her from Florrie and relish in her baby smell as she grabs hold of the neck of my shirt and continues babbling.

"Oh, that busy, huh?" I joke. "Sounds like I'm missing out on all the fun."

"You definitely missed out." Florrie laughs.

"What happened?" I squint my eyes, almost afraid of what's coming.

"Oh, nothing much, just Little Miss Independent wanting to wear her snacks rather than eating them."

I give Florrie an apologetic look, but we both know this comes with the territory.

"Righty-o, I better get ready for my club," she says, getting up. "Oh, by the way, I saw something in today's newspaper that you might be interested in and made a phone call to inquire."

She points at the paper on the table as she leaves.

I look at Sara and poke her tummy. "What trouble is Florrie getting us into this time, sweetie?" But when I see the paper, I know it's far from it.

It could be the solution, even if temporary, to my problems.

9

ELLIS

I STAND in the middle of my backyard and stare at the mess, struggling to see its potential.

The grass, or what I think is grass, is dead. Well, everything that looks like it may have once been a living plant is dead. Or at least looks dead.

There's a shed at the far end of the backyard, but it's got so many parts missing that I'm not sure I can call it a shed anymore. It's more like an assembly of wooden planks, precariously joined by rusty nails and a collapsing roof.

I don't dare approach it and see if there's anything useful inside.

Even though I have a sizable backyard, there are properties on all three sides divided by tall wooden fences.

I like that it offers privacy, but I can't imagine how much work it will take to make this into a semi-decent backyard I'll actually want to spend time in.

Not that it's a priority for me right now. I've been working on the inside of the house since I moved in because I'd rather spend the summer focusing on the part I use. But my meddling sister had to go and place an ad in the local paper to hire someone to fix the backyard for me.

The doorbell rings, so I go back into the house. All Alice said was that the guy she spoke to would be here at some point in the morning, so that might be him.

I open the door, and I'm wrong. So wrong.

"Wow, you could be happier to see me," Alice says, following me inside.

"Yay, how nice to see you," I say sarcastically.

She goes straight to my coffee maker, which was her house-warming present for me. I'm sure she only ever comes to visit so she can use it.

"You're cranky. Things aren't going well with Tyler?" she asks. "You seemed to really hit it off."

"Like a hammer on a nail."

She scrunches her face. "I don't need the details, thank you very much. I just want to know if you've had any dates. If he's...the one...?"

I laugh. "Christ, Alice. I met the guy a week ago. Even if we hit it off in the way you're hoping, don't you think it's a little too early to be talking about 'the one?'" I ask, making quote signs.

She scoffs, adding cream to her coffee. "Max was my one straight away."

"That's because you're slightly deranged, and he was way too slow on the uptake. He's been plotting his escape since."

She throws her stirring spoon at me after licking it and hits me even as I try to dodge it. "Damn you."

She grins at her victorious throw, but then her expression changes. "So, what did you mean? You didn't hit it off with Tyler? You seemed to get along so well."

"We did...do." I walk over and give her a one-armed hug because no one gets in the way of her coffee. "Tyler and I hit it off as friends. We both agreed during dinner that we didn't feel right for each other."

"Why not?"

I shrug. "Sometimes, you just know these things. But you did something really amazing, little sister."

"I did?"

"Yes. I helped Tyler in the soup kitchen this week, and it was a really enlightening. I've wanted to help the community here for a while. I didn't know how, but I guess volunteering with Tyler is a start."

She smiles. "He's a really good guy. Does so much for others, but I don't think anyone ever does anything for him."

"Alice…" I warn.

"No, I'm not playing Cupid again. I'm just saying."

The doorbell rings again.

"You expecting someone?" She waggles her eyebrows as if she doesn't know and doesn't totally intend to interfere with the plans for the backyard.

"Yes. Santa," I say and give her what she calls my teacher look. "Please be…just, you know."

"Yeah, yeah…"

I open the door, and for the second time this morning, I'm faced with an even more unexpected visitor.

"I see the face, but I know inside you're smiling, right?" Darius, my younger brother, says, enveloping me in a bear hug that almost lifts me off the floor.

He's wearing a T-shirt that shows his tattoo sleeves. The collar has been stretched enough you can see more tattoos underneath, and he's wearing jeans I would have thrown out years ago. But this is my brother. One coin. Two very different faces.

"I'm ecstatic."

He ignores me and, like my sister, goes straight to the coffee maker.

"What's up? Is Bittersweet closed today or what?" I ask.

"Yes," they say in unison.

I cross my arms. "You're both here because the coffee shop in town is closed. Nothing to do with Alice having a big mouth and you being nosy?"

"Uh-huh. Do you have any of those French sweet buns you always buy?" Darius asks.

"In case you didn't notice the lack of signage outside, this isn't a coffee shop."

He ignores me and starts going through my pantry.

"Bingo. Want one, sis?"

"Is it those brioches with the cream inside? Hell yeah."

Darius grabs two and throws one at Alice, who catches it expertly. I was never the sporty sibling in this family.

"Hold up. What happened at Bittersweet for Julius to be closed on a Saturday?" I ask.

Bittersweet is the best—well, only—coffee shop in town, and everyone adores the gentle giant owner, Julius. He's also a super-talented baker, but he can't catch a break with trying to find someone to help him out.

"Has one of his new baristas tried setting his kitchen on fire again?" I ask.

"No, I think it might be a family thing this time," Darius says. "And before you panic, don't worry. I've already checked with the hospital, and he's not there, nor is anyone from his family."

There's a collective sigh.

"Well, this has been great. Thank you for drinking my coffee and raiding my pantry, but you probably have a load of stuff to do, and as you know, I'm expecting someone," I say, trying to not so subtly get them out of my place before the guy turns up.

"D, is he kicking us out?" Alice asks Darius.

"I think he is, Al. Question is…why?"

I put my hands in the pant pockets and calmly stroll toward my siblings. I even whistle a little tune for good measure.

"Is it almost August already? Oh my, it'll be Christmas soon…let me think…whose turn is it to have Mom and Dad over for Christmas this year…"

Alice and Darius say each other's names, followed by a semi-heated discussion about Christmas being for the children and Alice having the bigger house…I tune out after a while.

If I'm right, they'll argue for another three minutes and then go their separate ways.

"Wait up," Alice says, raising her hand and narrowing her eyes.

Dammit.

"Good try, bro," Darius says. "Three out of five on the distraction tactic. Why don't you want us to be here for your gardener, helper, whatever he is? Or are you expecting someone else?" He winks and then elbows Alice.

"Ugh, I tried to set him up with Tyler, but now they're just friends." She sulks.

Darius laughs. "Tyler? Seriously? Anyone could tell from a mile away those two would never work."

"Anyway. It doesn't matter. You know I'm expecting this guy Alice apparently contacted, and I want you both out before he comes."

"Why?" Alice asks.

"Yeah, why?" Darius repeats.

"Oh for the love of god. I know you'll both butt in with your… ideas, and even though I didn't start it, this is something I'd like to do on my own."

"How boring. That's all you had to say. But I want a fire pit," Darius says.

"And fairy lights," Alice adds.

They both start walking to the door when the doorbell rings.

To give them credit, I can see how restrained they both are when they want to open the door to see who the guy is. I roll my eyes as I get past them.

As they say, third time's a charm. But the last person I expect to see when I open my front door is Milo.

"Ellis," he says, clearly as surprised to see me.

He looks around and then down at a piece of paper in his hand.

"Um, I think I'm in the wrong place. I'm sorry," he says, looking a little flustered, probably because of the additional sets of eyes on him. I elbow my siblings.

"I'm looking for 10 Rosebush Drive. Maybe I wrote it down wrong. There was a Rose Street a few streets ago."

He's pushing Sara's stroller back and forth.

"You're in the right place. Come on in. Let me help you with the stroller and get you out of the sun," I say.

I practically have to push Alice and Darius out of the way to let Milo in.

"Hey, this is my girlfriend from the other night," Darius says.

"How has she been? Fever went down, okay? She's eating and drinking well?"

Milo looks confused.

Darius looks down at his clothes and laughs. "Sorry, I'm the nurse you saw at the hospital. I don't usually wear scrubs outside of work." He winks, and Milo smiles.

"Ah, of course. Sorry, that night was a bit of a blur. I didn't recognize you. Thank you. Sara has been a lot better. The antibiotics must be working because she hasn't shown any signs of pain or discomfort."

"Sara was sick?" I ask. "When?"

"That night after the soup kitchen. When I got home, she was running a high fever."

I look at Sara in the stroller, and she's alert and smiling at the attention she's getting from Darius.

"Anyway, Darius and I were just leaving. Weren't we?" Alice says, poking our younger brother in the ribs.

"Ouch. Yeah, yeah, we were leaving."

"By the way. Bittersweet is closed, so make sure you get coffee and a brioche out of this one." Alice points at me, and then they're both out, closing the door behind them.

I let out a deep breath.

"Siblings, eh? I'm sure they were born to terrorize me. Do you have any?"

Milo looks at Sara and runs his hand over the pretty yellow dress she's wearing today. "No."

The way he says it makes me wonder if there was ever a brother or sister in Milo's life that is no longer around.

"So, are you really the person from the advertisement? You need someone to do your backyard?"

I smile. "I really am the person from the advertisement, although calling that jungle-slash-junkyard a backyard is a bit of a stretch."

"Can I see it?" he asks.

"Let's go, but I won't blame you if you run without looking back."

He laughs, and dammit, I want to hear more of that sound coming from Milo.

"I hear there's coffee and some other thing I can't pronounce but might be delicious, so I'm not running anywhere. I can easily pretend your junkyard is the most beautiful backyard in town for coffee."

His smile is infectious and is doing things to me that a smile from a twenty-something-year-old man shouldn't do.

Keep your walls up, Ellis.

10

MILO

I FOLLOW BEHIND ELLIS, still trying to process that one, I've kinda just flirted with him. I mean, that was flirting. Could be construed as flirting, right?

Ugh, stupid crush.

And two, that he is the ad person and might become my future boss, which means I'll see more of him, which is going to be awful for my delicate heart but so good for my greedy eyes that are checking out the way his ass fits perfectly in the pants he's wearing.

Or how even though it's the weekend, he's not wearing jeans or sweats. He's still dressed like he could be going out at a moment's notice, like someone who has places to go, like meeting with friends, a brunch, a drive in the country…I don't know, just things people like me don't do.

"Is it okay for Sara to stay here?"

"Huh?" I look up at his face, and I'm sure he's caught me staring at his ass.

"It's hot outside. Besides, I'm not sure the yard is totally safe. If you're happy for her to stay inside, you can leave her in the stroller or maybe set a blanket on the floor."

The job. You're here for the job you desperately need. Focus, Milo.
"She'll be okay in the stroller."

Ellis turns the TV in his living room onto the baby channel and faces the stroller toward it. Sara makes a face like she doesn't like it at first, but then, as they play a song, she smiles and shakes her arms and legs.

We don't have a TV because I had to sell my old one to pay some bills. Maybe one day, when I can save enough money, I can buy another.

I want to tell Ellis that he's just witnessed one of Sara's rare life experiences since she only watches TV when Florrie takes her to her place, but I'm too embarrassed, so I turn to him instead. "The yard?"

"Right. This way."

Ellis wasn't lying when he described his backyard. It's not in great condition, but it has so much potential.

First of all, it's huge. He can have flower beds, grass, a deck for barbeques, and a chill-out area with some outdoor furniture.

"This is amazing, Ellis."

"Are you running a fever? This is chaos."

I laugh. "You have to see past that. Pretend none of that is there and replace it with what you want to see."

He puts his hands in his pockets and takes two steps away from me, walking in a semicircle. "I've never been much of a dreamer. I can read books and imagine what something looks like from the description on the page, but I'm not talented enough to make it up myself."

He's standing in the middle of the yard. And yes, there are broken pots and piles of god knows what. It's a mess...a mess with potential.

"Close your eyes."

"What?" He stares at me.

"Just go along with it."

He narrows his eyes. A frown line appears in between his eyes, and I want to touch it so bad that I scrunch my hands into fists so I don't give in to temptation and make this a lot more awkward.

"Okay. Fine," he says, taking a breath and closing his eyes.

I flick a bug off his shoulder, which landed after he closed his eyes. I have a feeling Ellis would barricade himself in the house if he saw it.

"Why did you buy this house?" I ask.

He sighs. "Um…because it's close to Alice's place, and it was a good price because it needs some work. I've done some on the inside. Haven't finished yet, which is why the outside, as you can see…"

"That's the practical stuff. I want to know *why* this house. There are many other similar houses in the neighborhood." I walk around him, wanting to touch his hair and see if it's soft, feel his shoulders to see if they're strong.

Stop it, Milo.

I have to remember this is about him. My financial future depends on this, however much I want to throw myself at him.

Christ, if only he knew the thoughts I have about him. He'd have a restraining order in place before the end of the day.

"This was the only house that felt like a home to me," he says. "I've always wanted a family, and even though…um…it just felt right."

He opens his eyes, and I wonder if I've accidentally touched on a sensitive subject.

"Nuh-uh. Close your eyes."

He smiles but obeys.

"And in your dream home, what do you want to do in the backyard?" I ask.

"I want a space to relax. Somewhere I can sit and maybe do some work if the weather is nice. Have my family over." He shrugs. "I don't know."

"It's a start."

He opens his eyes again. We're face to face, on the verge of something.

My mom used to call these *life-defining moments*. When nothing would be the same again because whatever happens will change you as a result, and you can't stop it from happening.

Ellis's gaze is warm but firm. He's someone who knows what he wants, and just like the time at the soup kitchen, my eyes are held captive.

A shiver runs up my spine, and I know this is one of those moments. Inconsequential but irreversible.

"When can you start?"

"What?"

"When can you start?"

I stare at him, dumbfounded. "But...you haven't asked me any questions. How do you know I can do the job?"

"You answered the advertisement. I'm assuming you have at least a better understanding of this mess than I do."

He walks inside, and it takes me a moment to catch up to him. "But—"

"Let's talk about the details inside. I have it on good account that my coffee is second best to Bittersweet's." Then he puts his hand on his chin. "Or maybe that's because it's free. I'll let you be the judge of that."

"I'll just check in on Sara." I head to the living room and crouch by the stroller. She's still happily awake and babbling to the music on the TV. "One of these days we'll get you one, I promise. Until then, I guess you'll have to live with my terrible voices when I read your books." I kiss her head and return to the kitchen, where Ellis has a cup of coffee and a delicious-looking cake thing on a plate.

"Is this for me?"

"It is indeed," he says. "I'm addicted to these cream-filled brioches, so it's probably a good thing I'm three down today. If you see me with a new pack at the checkout this week, you'll have to promise you'll take it out for me."

I take a bite, and it's so not what I was expecting. The bread is soft and sweet, and the filling Ellis mentioned isn't *cream* but more a custard. It's like nothing I've had before.

I shake my head. "Sorry, but this is too good. I can only encourage you to buy more. It's French, right? It sounds French. It has to be healthy."

Ellis laughs. "It's a French sweet bread, yes. I guess in a health war between a croissant and a brioche, the brioche would probably win."

"I rest my case," I say, eating the rest of the small brioche and then taking a sip of the coffee. "And this is good too."

Ellis rests his elbows on the kitchen island. "So, Mr....actually, I don't know your last name."

"Allen. Milo Allen."

"Mr. Allen. Tell me, how can you transform my backyard into the peaceful retreat of my dreams?"

I smile. "Do you have a piece of paper and a pen or pencil?"

He rolls his eyes. Of course, he's a teacher, so he opens a drawer and presents me with a notepad and a pencil.

I bite my lip to keep from laughing at his smug face.

"I'm not great at drawing, so this is just a rough sketch of my first thoughts. Feel free to tell me you don't like it."

I draw the outline of the fences first and the ideas I had when I first saw the backyard. Basically, I'm drawing what I'd do if this was my place. Not that I'll tell Ellis that. I just think it'll look nice.

He scrunches his face, trying to understand what I'm doing.

"Okay, so I'm thinking you can get rid of the shed and replace it with a deck for lounging. Some couches, beanbags, lamps, that kind of thing." I point to the opposite corner to the lounge area. "Your neighbors don't have trees, so in the summer, you might want to find a way to create some shade. There are a lot of different options for that. I suggest something solid and permanent that can sustain through the winter or something lighter you can store and take out when you want."

I point to the line of the fences. "If you want more texture and life, the easiest place to plant anything will be by the fences. You can keep them on the ground or build raised beds. There are some flowers and plants that don't require much upkeep."

I look up, and Ellis is staring at me.

"What?"

"Nothing. Please, continue."

"Um, so the rest can be grass, which, you know, grows, so it'll need to be cut. And then I was thinking that by having the lounge area where you have the shed, you won't need to extend the porch. You can just repaint and add a grill. Maybe a chair or something."

I stare at the drawing and try to think if there's anything I can add. The backyard is big enough that if Ellis ever had kids, he could still separate an area for an outdoor playset.

"This is perfect, Milo. It's…simple, minimalistic. I have very little free time outside of work during the school year, and now that I want to volunteer with Tyler, that's some more of my time taken up. This looks perfect for me. I love it."

I don't know at what point Ellis put his hand on mine. I'm sure he's not thinking too much of it. Hell, I've done it a million times without thinking.

But this is Ellis. The man I somehow feel so unexplainably attracted to, and his hand feels heavy and warm. The kind of heavy that makes you feel safe and grounded.

The warmth from his hand is spreading up my arm, and I feel my face heat.

The way he's gazing into my eyes, it's as if he knows my secret.

Oh my god, he knows I'm attracted to him.

Sara cries from the living room, breaking the spell between us, and his hand is gone.

I go over to the living room and know immediately what's happened. Ah, the lovely smell of baby poop.

"Ellis, I'm sorry. Could I use your bathroom to change her diaper?"

"Of course, it's through that door. The main bathroom has a surface big enough. Do you need anything?"

"No, I'm good."

As soon as I close the door behind us and take her clothes off, my heart resumes its normal tempo.

"Thank you, baby girl, for saving me from whatever that was," I say to her. "Embarrassment. That's what it was. If you were older, I'd give you ice cream or something. Even if Florrie disapproves. But since you're not, I'll just give you extra raspberries in your tummy and some cuddles later. Ew, girl, those raspberries will have to wait until you've had your bath."

She giggles like she's proud of the sheer amount of poop she's made.

With nine months of practice, I've changed her diaper so many times that we're done within a few minutes, but I need longer before I can face Ellis. I stand her on the bathroom counter and make her face the mirror.

"What do we do with ourselves, princess? Keep dreaming? Or come back down to reality and accept the hand that life has dealt us?"

She repeats the *dada* sounds she's been making recently, and I stare at both of us in the mirror. "I wish your dada was here too, baby."

When I can no longer hide in the bathroom, I come out with a chatty Sara, who refuses to get back in the stroller, so I hold her as Ellis and I discuss the work in the backyard.

"There's an access gate on the side of the house. This is the key," he says. "I know you work at the store, so you can work around that. I'm in no rush, and apart from unwanted visits from my siblings when they want free food or to annoy me, I don't have any other visitors, so you can come on the weekend too."

Sara bounces in my arms. I need to ask the most important question, so I steel myself for the make-or-break answer.

"My main issue is childcare. My neighbor, Florrie, isn't always available. That's why I liked your advertisement. I was wondering if you'd be okay if I brought Sara with me. She'd just be in the stroller, and if I feed her, she usually sleeps for a couple of hours. Not even a hurricane will wake her up."

"Of course."

Ellis stands and starts opening and closing drawers.

"Found it. I knew I had it here somewhere."

I'm not sure what he means.

He places another key next to the gate key.

"This key opens the back door. Feel free to bring Sara any time, but please don't leave her outside. I'd feel awful knowing she's out in the heat. Bring her inside. You can use the bathroom to change her, the microwave if you need to heat up her bottle, or you can get water."

A lump is forming in my throat, and I need to not say anything right now because I will cry.

Ellis holds his arms out, and Sara stretches hers, so I pass her to him.

"Of course, that's if you come and I'm not here. With the summer break, I'm home most of the time, and I'm more than happy to keep an eye on her."

I look up at the sky, well, the ceiling, and curse my mother for passing her super-sensitive and emotional genes on to me because I simultaneously want to cry and also run.

If Ellis Bradford keeps being nice to me, I can't be held accountable for what my hopelessly romantic heart will want. And that is not a good thing.

Not a good thing at all.

11

———

ELLIS

A week later, I find myself fidgeting as I wait for Milo to arrive for his first day.

I move the coffee table in the living room and lay a couple of blankets and extra pillows on the carpet. If Sara is crawling as much as Marnie was at her age, I don't want her to get hurt.

Everything else is tidy and clean. I'm on my third cup of coffee and resisting having any of the cream-filled brioches because that's a slippery slope when I'm already this nervous.

Why am I even this nervous?

Because you're about to have a hot young guy working in your backyard. That's why.

The last person I expected to answer my sister's ad in the paper was Milo, but after the walk through the backyard and hearing his ideas, I know I made the right decision.

Not only did he seem to get my hopelessness when it comes to gardening or looking after a backyard, but he also had some fantastic ideas to keep it simple and manageable.

As an added benefit, I know I'm helping him too. If I ever see Milo eat a meal like he did at the soup kitchen, I want to know it's because he's enjoying it, not because it's the only one he's had that day.

When we discussed pay rates, he asked for such a paltry amount I had to check with Alice if that's really how much a landscape gardener —or whatever they're called—gets paid.

After that call and some research, I decided on my own pay rate. Thankfully, Milo agreed when I asked if I could just transfer the money directly into his bank account.

I'm not stupid enough to think he won't notice or question the amount, but I'll deal with that when it comes.

There's a knock on the back door. I jump in place and let out a squeaky noise I hope goes unheard.

"Sorry," Milo says as I open the door. "Didn't mean to scare you. Just wanted you to know I'm here, and if it's okay, I'll leave my assistant inside."

I peek into the stroller. "I'm not sure she'll be assisting much."

Sara is asleep, and from her cute little snores, it sounds like she's down for the count.

"Yeah. She had a rough night. She's teething, so we were up quite a bit. After I gave her some formula, she settled a bit and then fell asleep during the walk here."

I help Milo get the stroller inside without disturbing Sara.

"Are you sure it's okay for her to stay here? I don't want to give you any work. I'm the one who's supposed to work here," he says.

"You kidding? Like staring at her adorable face is any work."

He snorts. "Just wait till she wakes up."

"That's when it'll mysteriously be your break time," I say, winking.

He chuckles. "Right, let me get started. I don't think you need to rent a dumpster because a few large bags might be enough for the trash you have here." He rubs his hands together and smiles before taking a pair of gloves from the back pocket of his jeans. "Let me see what treasures you have in that shed."

Milo has an old baseball cap in his pocket that he puts on backward as soon as he's outside.

Fuck my life.

Okay, I may be in my forties, but a guy in ripped jeans, an old T-shirt, and a broken-in baseball cap worn backward will never not be sexy.

"Sara, your dad is going to be the death of me." And as I say it, she lets out this tiny sound like she's dreaming and her lips form a tiny *O*. Her hands ball into fists, and I think she's going to wake up, but she settles again.

Ignoring the paperwork I was working on at the kitchen island last night, I take the stroller farther into the kitchen. I stop by the table, pull up a chair, and sit down, staring at Sara.

"He's the same age as you now. Nine months. I didn't even get to see him."

How can a person grieve the absence of someone they never met? Someone who was never theirs to start with?

The weight in my chest threatens to take me down. I stand and walk to the back door.

Milo has already created several piles of things, and he's whistling a tune.

I focus on the way he moves. How his shirt rides up, showing a bit of skin every time he pulls something from the shed.

Milo is beautiful. Not just good-looking. There's something special about him.

And yes, right now, he's the sexiest thing I've seen in a long time.

I don't understand why, but looking at him is the only time I ever find a glimpse of the peace I've been searching for since I came to Stillwater.

He looks my way and waves.

I go still, unsure of what to do. Will he think I'm spying on him? Or that I doubted he could do a good job?

He comes over.

"Hey, can you make a sign or something that says *free treasure to a good home* and then underneath *no takebacks*?"

"Sure, why?"

"Do you have any use for an extra sink or a set of red dining plates?"

I smile. "I'll make up the sign."

"There are some wonderful treasures for keeps too." He runs the back of his hand over his forehead to wipe the sweat. "But I'll show you those at the end. You might not think they're treasures." He laughs.

He goes back to work, and I check on Sara before following his instructions. I go to my office and print out a sign. I stick it to a piece of cardboard I cut out of a box from something I recently ordered.

Then, in a role reversal, I'm ordered to take the "treasures" to the front lawn and stick the sign next to them.

Can't even say it's not hot being bossed by backward-cap Milo. Nope.

With those jeans riding low on his hips, the fucking cap, and his easy smile to match the soft brown eyes, Milo can boss me around all day.

Get a grip, Ellis.

Milo comes in at lunchtime, removing his dusty boots and leaving them outside. He asks if he can use my bathroom, and a moment later, he comes back wearing a different T-shirt.

"I don't want to pick Sara up in my dusty clothes," he says as justification.

"Do you want to use the microwave for her food?"

I offered before, but if I know anything of Milo by now, it's that he doesn't take anything for granted, and I can see he appreciates me offering again so he doesn't have to ask.

"Why is she wearing different clothes? Did she have an accident?" he asks, looking mortified.

I raise my hands. "No, no, no. It was all my fault. She warned me, but I didn't take her seriously enough. My mistake. I cleaned her and changed her diaper. Hope that's okay. I also put her clothes in the washing machine."

"Oh god, I'm so sorry. I've come here to work, and now you're having to...I'm really sorry. I'll check with Florrie to see if she's free tomorrow."

The microwave pings, indicating Sara's food is ready, so I take it out. As if she knows it's for her, she starts jumping excitedly in Milo's arms.

"Milo, please. Don't do that. I honestly enjoy looking after Sara. Dirty diapers and all. Let's face it, you couldn't have picked a boss with more experience. Alice made sure of it. She's even trained Darius, and *he's* a nurse."

I finally draw a smile out of a worried Milo.

With her full belly, Sara is as chatty as she can be, pulling on Milo's arms as he's eating.

"No way, you greedy girl. This is my sandwich. You didn't see me try to eat your yummy veggie sludge, did you?" Milo says to her.

I've prepared my sandwich, which I'm eating as I observe the interaction between the two people in front of me.

I'm caught staring when Milo suddenly looks up. "What? Do I have anything on my face? Please tell me none of her orange food is on my face because that stuff is worse than fake tan. Who'd have known carrots and tomatoes were so fierce?"

"You say that from experience?"

"Nope, I'm happy being pasty white. But I see my fair share of fake tan fails at the store. Anyway, time to get back to work. What do you say, princess?" He pokes Sara's tummy, and she holds on to his hand.

"No, don't go. I want to play," he says in a jokey voice.

"Okay, you be my sugar mama, huh?"

Sara stares at him like she understands.

"Yeah, didn't think so."

I laugh and hold out my arms. Without hesitation, Milo places Sara on my lap, then goes to the bathroom again and returns wearing the dirty T-shirt.

Sara and I watch as Milo works for a while.

"Your daddy is quite something, isn't he?"

She makes a dada sound. "That's right, he's your dada."

I'm not sure how long we stay there, but Sara seems happy to watch the activity outside, so we remain as we are.

Milo keeps ripping planks of wood out of the shed and putting them to one side. The collapsed roof of the shed comes apart, creating a cloud of dust.

I know Milo isn't near it, so I'm not worried for him, but I realize I'm the one who may need medical attention when I see that he's removed his shirt in order to protect his face from the dust.

"Christ, why didn't you warn me, girl? You could have said *that* is what your dad looks like under his clothes."

Great, and now I'm talking like a pervert to a baby.

But fuck. Milo is slim but strong. Not muscly, but with definition, although I'd love to see him fill out a little more. Even though his hair is brown, he has a lighter, almost blond trail of hair below his belly button that disappears under the waist of his jeans.

He's determined, and as I've observed, he's also capable of anything he sets his mind to.

What would it be like if he set his mind on me?

What would it be like being held by him?

Taken by him?

Why do I feel like the one man I can't have is the one that could give me everything I've ever wanted, including the treasure in my arms?

I step away from the door.

My thoughts are too much to bear.

12

MILO

THE GREAT THING about working for Ellis, even these few hours over the weekend and some here and there in the week, is that now I will have enough money to cover my rent and bills when I get paid.

I don't want to think about when the job is over. I'm still trying to save as much as I can. I don't know what I'll do then. How long I'll be able to pay the increased rent if I don't get another job. But it's not something I want to think about right now.

The problem with taking the job working for Ellis is that I didn't consider how often he'd be home.

It's summer break, so it makes sense that he doesn't have to go to the school. I'm just the dumb person who forgot that tiny detail.

I shouldn't complain because he's so generous looking after Sara, which he says he really enjoys. In fact, I suspect he stays home on purpose when he knows I'm coming in to work.

The problem is that spending so much time around Ellis means I'm getting to know him better.

The devotion he has for his students when he talks about his plans for his classes. The way he moans about his brother and sister, but I can tell he'd do anything for them. How he's building relationships with people in the soup kitchen. Even from my side of the double doors, I hear it. He's popular with people in my neighborhood.

They all think he's funny for going all Mr. Teacher on a bunch of people that are much older than him, and the other day I heard Emy say he was bribing some of the guys with extra rolls to get them to convince Brian to come over and have a proper meal.

Once upon a time, I wondered what it'd be like to face my dad's best friend again. Especially after everything he did. But I doubt the cantankerous old man will ever come to the soup kitchen.

Regardless, I don't think Ellis will give up easily.

He's a solid person. The kind that would never let you down.

My silly little gay heart keeps beating a little faster every time he's around.

I can't stop it, and that's a bad, bad thing.

Because once all this is over, I'll go back to being the three-day-a-week cashier struggling to pay the bills, except I'll be doing it with a sad heart that wants Ellis more than ever before.

Why is life so unfair?

"Hey, Milo. Do you want a drink?" Ellis calls from the porch.

"Sure."

I don't even know what the time is. I've gotten so lost in my thoughts as I work on flattening the ground before I prepare the foundation for his deck.

As usual, I shake off as much dirt as possible before I go inside without my work boots. I grab my clean shirt and then go to his bathroom.

I wash my face and under my arms and use the dirty T-shirt to dry off. It's so hot outside that I know it'll be dry again by the time I put it back on.

After using water to make my hair somewhat straight-ish and with the clean T-shirt on, I go to see how my girl has been.

"Hey, baby-boo. What exciting and wonderful things have you been up to?"

She raises her arms from the high chair that recently appeared in Ellis's kitchen, so I pick her up.

"Well, let's see, she's started out by helping me with my banking, then she pointed out that I had my autumn lesson plans back to front and that Christmas isn't indeed in September, and then we agreed to disagree on whether whole peas are better than mushy peas."

I laugh. "Sounds like a very productive morning."

"Don't know about her, but I could use a nap," Ellis says, going to the fridge and taking out a bottle of lemonade.

"I'm sure there's enough formula in her bag to put you both to sleep if you want. I'll even throw in a bedtime story." As I say it, Ellis hands me the lemonade, and our fingers brush just a little, but it's enough to send sparks all the way through my body.

I don't miss how Ellis tenses too.

"I was joking," I say.

"Huh?"

"About…um, the bedtime story and…um, never mind." I open the bottle and gulp a fair amount.

Fuck, I've just made things weird. *Well done, Milo.*

"Are you hungry? I've made too much salad for my lunch, so if you like tuna, you're welcome to the rest," Ellis says.

"I brought my sandwich." I take it out of Sara's bag, and even I know it's a sad-looking lunch.

"Please, I insist. The lettuce will be all soggy by tomorrow, and I hate having it go to waste. Besides, after all the work you've done outside, I bet you can manage the salad and your sandwich."

He's not wrong, so I gratefully accept.

His tuna salad is delicious, and it's not a huge amount, so I supplement it with my sandwich, but I'm not convinced Ellis *accidentally* made too much.

When you're a single man who doesn't like waste, you don't *accidentally* make too much of anything. I would know.

Since it seems to make him happy, I don't say anything.

I'm too full to go back out in the sun and work, so it's a good opportunity to broach the subject I've been avoiding for a while.

"Ellis, you said I could ask you anything about the GED exam."

He straightens and smiles, almost like he's been expecting me to bring it up. "Yes, anything."

"I've, um…been going to the library to study in my free time. I did almost all of high school, so I didn't miss all that much, but I don't know what to do to actually take the test. Do I still need to attend the classes?" I sigh. "It's probably pointless anyway because I'm struggling with a few things, so I'm sure I'd fail."

"You've been studying on your own?"

I nod. It's hard to read him as he gazes at me with his lips slightly parted as though he wants to say something but doesn't know what.

Ellis's expression changes as he places his hands on the table.

This one I know. It's his teacher face.

"Okay, first, you need to register on the GED portal so you can access the resources and book your exam."

I stare at him. "How do I do that?"

"I'll take a guess you don't own a computer," he says, and I nod. "I'm happy to help you register using my laptop. We can do it now if you like. It doesn't take long."

"Okay."

Ellis leaves the table and returns a moment later with his laptop.

"What made you change your mind?" he asks.

I look at Sara, happily chewing on her toy. "I need a better job desperately. At work, all the supervisor jobs require a GED." I let out a tired sigh. "Not that it matters. The store manager doesn't like me, so he'll probably never promote me, but maybe I could get another job somewhere else."

Ellis turns on the laptop and searches for the website.

It doesn't take long to register me on the portal. I write down my access details so I can go back and explore the area better from the computer in the library. After all, I do have to get to work.

"Thank you for your help with this. I should probably get out there. I want to finish what I started today so I can dig for the deck foundation next time."

Ellis shuts down his laptop. "I'm glad to help."

I'm almost by the door when he calls me.

"Milo, I just want you to know that GED or no GED, you're an amazing person. You're raising a child on your own and you're a hard worker. You're smart, and clearly, you have initiative. I know the job market out there won't see all of that. They'll just see three letters from an exam taken at a moment in time that show you have some education. So anyway, you know those things you said you were struggling with? I'm happy to tutor you after work if you like."

My words are stuck in my throat. Between feeling like Ellis can see the person I am and his generous offer, I might actually cry.

"I...I don't know what to say."

Ellis comes closer. I see it in his eyes. The raw need to help someone. This is what he needs to do. I can't let my pride get in the way and end up disappointing him.

"Okay."

He smiles, and in the sun reflecting from the glass door, his eyes are a deep dark blue with a brown rim and golden flecks inside.

His gaze travels to my lips. My heart is beating so fast I'm sure he can hear it.

"Um..." I point to the yard behind me.

"Oh, yes...yes..." he says, taking a step back. "Are you at the soup kitchen this week?"

"I'm doing the first day only."

"Meet me in the playground beforehand. I'll collate a list of resources to help you."

"Okay," I say.

It's not until I step outside that I realize I haven't changed into my dirty T-shirt, but I can't go back now. I'm feeling too many things and my body is all over the place.

If I get close to Ellis and see him look at my lips like he did, I may actually do something stupid.

Something really, really good. But still stupid.

13

MILO

"Wow, so that's what your happy smile looks like."

I look up from the workbook I borrowed from the library. Pauline is sitting opposite me at the large table in the break room, but I must have been so focused on studying that I didn't see her come in.

Correction. I was too distracted thinking about Ellis to see her come in.

"What do you mean? I smile plenty."

She crosses her arms and gives me a pointed stare.

"You smile at customers. I'll give you that. But not *that* smile. What gives?"

I shrug. "I guess I'm just less stressed. I picked up a second job that I'm really enjoying."

"That's great, hun. I'm so happy for you. Tell me about your new job."

I look at the clock on the wall and bite my lip.

"I think my break is finishing soon. We can talk about it another time, maybe?"

She laughs. "Nice try. I know you still have at least ten minutes left." She leans over the table and narrows her eyes. "Come on. Spill."

"Fine. I'm working for Ell—Mr. Bradford, renovating his backyard a few hours a week. And since Gerald is still not giving me any extra shifts, this job is a lifesaver for now."

She snorts but covers her mouth with her hands as Jimmy enters the break room.

It's clear he heard what I said because he pauses for a brief moment. Then he goes straight to his locker, puts his stuff away, and slams it shut before walking out.

"That was weird," Pauline says. "Anyway, you were telling me how you're working in Mr. Bradford's *backyard* a few hours a week."

I laugh at how she says backyard like it means something else.

"Take your mind out of the gutter. I really do mean his backyard. It's actually a fun project, and it'll help pay my bills. Ell-Mr. Bradford is even helping look after Sara, so I don't need to bother Florrie or hire a sitter."

She sucks her cheeks in, and I can tell she's trying to contain a smile. "How generous of Mr. Bradford."

"He's very kind, yes," I say, rolling my eyes.

She squeals and then drags her chair next to mine. "So tell Aunty Pauline. How long is it going to take you to work your way from his backyard to his in-yard?"

"Shut up. That's not going to happen."

"Why not?"

"Pauline, why would he even take a second look at me when he can do so much better? He probably knows dozens of more sophisticated and educated men. I wouldn't stand a chance even if I wanted to."

She turns me around in my chair with strength I never knew she had and puts her hands on either side of my face.

"You listen to me, Milo, and listen to me good."

"Okay…" I say with my cheeks all squished.

"Mr. Bradford would be lucky to have you. It's never about how educated or sophisticated someone is. It's about what's in their heart. You know that. Don't come to me with that kind of bullshit because you're lying only to yourself."

I manage a nod, and she releases me.

"Good. I'm not saying to jump the man's bones, for crying out loud. But have you noticed how he only ever goes to your register?"

"I'm sure that's not—"

She stares, daring me to challenge her. Thinking about it, she might be right. I don't remember seeing Ellis use another checkout whenever I've seen him in the store.

"It doesn't mean anything. Besides, I'm working for him, and I don't want to mess things up. I have responsibilities, Pauline."

"I know you do, hun. But you're also human. Now go out there before Gerald comes to get you with his slimy, greasy hands."

"Ew."

I put my book away and go back to work, but Gerald catches me before I make it to my register.

"Milo, have you finished your break?" he asks, looking at his wristwatch.

I'm sure I'm not late back. "Yes, I was just on my way back out. I'm not late."

"I know everything that happens in this store, including when someone is half a minute late." His smug smile makes me want to hurl.

"Then is there anything I can do for you?" I ask, already dreading the answer.

"It's more what *I* can do for you."

"I'm not following."

"I wanted to catch you about the job opportunities you've been asking for."

Color me speechless. "Really? That's great, Gerald. I'm currently studying to take the GED exams at the end of the summer, so that should help, right?"

He stares at me blankly.

"I'm not sure how you'll have time to study when you'll be working nights."

"I'm sorry, Gerald. Did you say nights? You know I can't work nights. I have Sara."

He places his pudgy hands on his hips and lets out a frustrated sigh. "I don't know what else I can do for you, Milo. You tell me you want more hours. I'm helping you out, offering you an additional job that pays better, and now you say you can't do it?"

I don't know what to say to save the situation. I need the security of this job, but I can't work nights. There's no way I can ask Florrie to look after Sara during the night. And how would I take care of Sara during the day? When would I rest?

When I don't answer, Gerald continues, "Word on the street is you have a second job working somewhere else."

My blood goes cold. I know Pauline couldn't have told him, especially since she's still on her break.

Jimmy. It has to have been him.

"That's right, Gerald. I am doing a few hours here and there, but I promise it's not affecting my work here. I just needed the money, and you said you didn't have hours to give me."

"Well, I do now. Starting today. Jimmy was feeling unwell, so he went home. You're doing his shift."

"But—"

Gerald raises his hand. "Think carefully about what you're going to say next, young man. Remember the chain of command in this place. If you still want a job to return to tomorrow, you're staying to cover Jimmy's shift. As for the night job. Take it or don't take it, but don't come crying to me asking for more hours because there won't be any."

I nod. "I'll stay tonight, and I'll let you know about the other job."

He turns around and heads toward his office, where he'll no doubt sit doing nothing for the rest of the afternoon, as usual, or thinking about how he can make someone else's life miserable.

No matter how much I try, I can't muster my usual cheerfulness. Even Ethel notices, and I have to convince her I have a headache and will be fine as soon as I have my break.

When I have a break, I grab my phone to call Tyler to tell him I can't make the soup kitchen shift and ask him to apologize to Ellis for me for standing him up, but the battery is dead.

Next to my phone, there's a chocolate bar with a note. I recognize Pauline's handwriting.

Sorry the dick made you stay late. Hope this cheers you up. See you tomorrow.

Her message makes me feel better, and I praise the day I gave her my locker combination when she forgot hers because this chocolate bar is the only thing I'll have to eat until I get home tonight.

The chocolate gives me some energy, but it also settles in my stomach like a heavy rock. Or maybe it's just the weight of the decisions I have to make.

I can't afford to lose my job at the store and could use the security of another permanent job.

The work I'm doing for Ellis is only temporary, even if it's the most fulfilling thing I've done in years, apart from raising Sara.

I feel like I'm stuck at a crossroads, and no matter which way I go, I still lose.

14

———

ELLIS

THE MEETING with Principal Lewis drags a little longer than I expected, but I'm glad she agrees on the updated after-school program I've been working on at home in my spare time.

She then surprises me by encouraging me to apply for the assistant principal job that will come up in the middle of the next school year when the current assistant principal announces his retirement.

When I moved to Stillwater, I expected a lot of challenges. After all, I transferred in the middle of the last school year and hadn't been here a month before she discussed the after-school program with me. Something I expected to be handed over to a more established teacher.

I didn't need to be afraid because I felt part of the team from the first day. To be encouraged to apply for the new vacancy is something I need to process.

Being a principal is one of my professional goals, and god knows I've been knocked down enough to want to hold on to this opportunity with everything I have. But I also don't want to jeopardize the great relationship I have with the other teachers in the school.

I feel bad for clock-watching, but I want to make sure I have time to stop by my place to pick up the stuff I've gathered for Milo.

Principal Lewis closes her notebook. "I think we've covered everything. I'm sorry for keeping you so long. I'm meeting the gang at The Academy for a few drinks. Want to join us, Ellis?"

"I would, honestly, but I'm volunteering at the soup kitchen this evening and have an errand to run before. I really should be going."

She nods. "If there's an opportunity for the school to be involved, please let me know. The success of the Spring Fair taught me how the community can really pull together in times of need." She stands. "I'm sure I'll run into you in town at some point, but whatever you're doing, enjoy the rest of your time off. And think about what we discussed today. We make a good team, and most of the teachers have expressed their desire to get involved in other projects or prefer focusing on teaching."

"Thank you, Principal Lewis. I will consider it and let you know at the start of the new school year."

I have little time to stop at home, especially since I still want to look up a few things, but I can do that another day. I'm sure Milo will already have plenty of resources with what I have for him.

When I arrive at the playground, it's as deserted as the last time I saw it. There are a few wooden picnic tables that seem relatively clean, so I step on a bench and sit on one.

From here, I have a definite vantage point of the surrounding area. It looks as if all the streets were built to lead to or from the playground and the church, which is an interesting layout I haven't noticed before. I wonder if it was intentional planning.

The few houses that front the square have their shutters closed even though it's not dark yet. There's a feeling of sadness around here. This part of town never recovered from the closure of the mill, and it's affected not just that generation but their children too.

I look at my phone. It's almost time for Tyler and the soup kitchen crew to arrive, but there's no sign of Milo.

He said he's working but finishing early today. I regret not taking his phone number now.

"Hey, Ellis."

I turn and see Tyler approaching.

"Hey, man. You heard from Milo by any chance?"

He shakes his head but takes his phone out. "Should I have?"

"Nah. We were supposed to meet here early but he didn't show. Stupid me, I forgot to ask for his number."

Tyler puts his phone to his ear and waits. "Going to voicemail. He's probably stuck at work. His boss is kind of a douche."

I've seen the man walk around the store once or twice but never paid much attention to him. Milo must be sad to miss his time in the kitchen today, especially since he said this was the only one he could do this week.

I get down from the table. "I guess I'm on pan duty then."

Tyler laughs. "Thankfully for you, this is a soup kitchen and not a retirement home."

"Oh man." I shudder.

I follow Tyler inside, and we get busy with the preparation. Now that I've been a few times and know my way around, I feel like I'm no longer a hindrance, having to ask where things are or what to do next.

Bob and Dave take the food outside while I help Anne and Emy with the rest.

Without Milo helping, I've been trying to keep up with the dishes as we go, so I haven't seen people as they arrive like I usually do.

The chatter today is different. It sounds more animated at some tables, while at others, it's more subdued.

Anne sighs. "This thing about the parking lot is affecting everyone. Even those who don't live anywhere near the square or the church."

"Does anyone know for sure it's happening?" I ask.

"I heard there was a planning notice on a board in the town hall. If it's not disputed, it can go ahead."

"What's the deadline?"

She shrugs. "That I don't know."

We ring the bell to start serving. The line forms quickly, but the chatter doesn't stop. As people come closer, I overhear some comments.

"What's the point? They'll fit in what, twenty cars?"

"Not if they build one of those, whatchacallit, multilevel parking garages."

Some people within earshot gasped.

A parking garage right by the church, crowding all the surrounding houses, would be horrendous. Who'd want to live here?

"Why in hell would this town need one of them big parking garages?" someone else asks.

"The craft fair brings a lot of folks from all over. They gotta park somewhere, and I bet those rich people don't want them on their streets."

I try to tune out the chatter and focus on serving the food before I go into the kitchen to start washing the pots.

Before I moved to Stillwater, Alice used to say there was never a dull moment here, and now I can see it.

Between worrying about the possibility of a parking lot being built right by the church next door and Milo doing a double shift, I don't notice the time passing.

I hear the squeak of the double doors and look behind me. Tyler comes in holding a takeaway box.

"Hey, Cathy saved some jambalaya for Milo. He'll be finishing his shift soon, so if you still want to catch him, you can head off now. We'll take over from here."

I turn the water off and dry my hands. There's no doubt I'm not the only one worried about Milo, so I'm taking the offer and making sure he gets a proper dinner and gets home safe.

"Thanks, Tyler."

His nod says everything. The man has a heart of gold.

Tyler is everything I've ever wanted in a partner. Head screwed on, caring, funny, and okay, he's a little older, but four of five years is an appropriate age gap.

Why can't I be attracted to him?

I arrive at the grocery store just after closing, but all the lights are still on inside. I get out of the car and lean against the hood.

A few people come from the side of the building, so I keep my eyes peeled for Milo. The last thing I want is to miss him.

Ten minutes later, I see him come from the side of the building with another group of people. Among everyone, he's the first one I see.

It's like my eyes have a Milo detector that even if he was wearing the darkest of clothes in the dead of night, I'd still see him.

He gives a girl a quick hug and they go their separate ways. The girl goes toward a parked car, and I see Milo walk to the edge of the store corner and then stop.

I'm parked so he'd see me on the way to the bus stop, but the way he's wavering and looking at the alleyway on the side of the store, I'm wondering if he's considering walking home. He mentioned before he does that sometimes, but not when he finishes late.

Except he wasn't expecting to finish late today.

I breathe a sigh of relief when he makes the right choice and walks toward the bus stop. His shoulders are low like they hold the weight of the world, and he must be lost in thought because he doesn't see me until he walks past my car.

He looks up and stops when he spots me.

"Ellis."

An advantage of my parents' work and travels around the world is that I've learned to read people well. They always told us to trust people's first reactions to anything.

Whether it's trying caviar or meeting someone for the first time, they always told us to look at people and not the surrounding things.

I always find Milo to be a little guarded, even if he's been opening up a little more when working at my place.

But he wasn't expecting me, so with his guard down, in that split second before he called my name, I saw it in his eyes. The kind of happiness you get when the person in front of you is exactly the person you want to see in that moment or forever.

I've seen that look before, and then I lost it. I was so blind that I didn't even see when it stopped.

"What...um...what are you doing here?" he asks, and I see his guard go up again.

I swallow, trying to push my thoughts away, and then smile. "I have it on good account that Cathy's jambalaya is the best outside of Louisiana, and since it's best eaten warm, I figured you might want it now."

He gasps. "You came all this way to bring me jambalaya?"

"And a ride home, which, by the way, is nonnegotiable," I say when I see he's about to argue.

I grab the box from the passenger seat of the car and point to a bench on the side of the parking lot.

Milo follows me to the bench but stops for a moment before opening the box. "Did Tyler send you?"

"He couldn't get ahold of you, so he figured you'd be on a last-minute double shift."

He takes the plastic fork and starts eating. "Oh my god. I love Cathy. This is so good," he says between mouthfuls.

It's a pleasure to watch him eat and enjoy the meal.

"Tyler says your boss isn't the nicest."

Milo snorts. "That's an understatement."

His hair falls onto his face as he tries to keep his food from falling out of the box while he eats. I feel a compulsion to push it behind his ears and wonder if his hair is always like this or if he's due for a haircut.

I like it like this. It's a little wavy and perfect to run my hands through.

Once again, I curse myself. Why am I not attracted to Tyler?

Why does it have to be this much younger man?

"Do I have food on my face?"

"What?"

"You're staring."

"Oh, no, I'm sorry. I was just lost in thought," I say. "Did you enjoy your dinner?"

"It was perfect. Thank you so much for bringing it to me. I wasn't expecting to stay at work. All I had today was my lunch sandwich, so I was a little hungry," he says apologetically.

I put my hand on his arm. "Never apologize for something out of your control. Come on, let me get you home."

15

MILO

My mom was right about many things all the time. Or so she made us believe.

But this time, she was wrong. Working hard in the backyard, digging up soil, and breaking into a sweat isn't helping me figure out any of my problems.

I can't figure out how to approach the topic of my pay with Ellis. Money keeps appearing in my bank account, and it's far too much. Definitely more than the hourly rate we agreed on.

And I can't figure out how to stop wanting Ellis so much.

If the money is a problem, then wanting Ellis is a catastrophe.

He's been more than generous with his time, tutoring me after work and answering all the questions I've had. Especially with science, which is my weakest topic.

Two weeks ago, he suggested I bring a spare change of clothes, so I could use his shower and change after work to feel comfortable and clean while we study together.

I should have said no.

That had bad idea written all over it.

But did I say no?

Has hell frozen over?

So every time I come over to work in the backyard, I shower in Ellis's spare bathroom, then eat the dinner he insists on cooking for me before we do an hour or two of studying. I go home feeling sated, happy, and smelling like Ellis's shower soap.

Even my sheets smell like Ellis.

Trying to sleep with an erection is not fun. I draw the line at rubbing one out in his shower, but when I get home, it's like my dick knows that once Sara is asleep, it's adult time.

It's the lonely nights when I wish for nothing else but to be held by another human that I give in.

I close my eyes and see Ellis staring at me like he always does. Full of wonder, like I'm something special.

His touch is always timid, like he wants to ask for something but is too afraid to do it. And when I feel as if I'm the only one who can give him what he needs, that's when my desire and my mind take over.

I wrap my hand around my hard cock and show him exactly how I like it as I whisper in his ear how much I want him, how amazing it'll be to feel him stretch around me.

My breath catches with every stroke as the intensity builds and the world around me narrows to only Ellis. I moan his name as I grip my cock tighter, pulling my foreskin back and teasing the head with my other hand.

His scent is everywhere. Every time I inhale, I smell his essence and my mouth waters. I want to taste him, feel his hard cock heavy on my tongue as I suck him deep and hear him moan my name.

The thought that I may have the same effect on Ellis that he has on me is as powerful as the electric current that runs through my body.

It never takes long for my orgasm to hit, and I fall asleep surrounded by remnants of his soap smell and my silly dreams.

Ellis is now such a familiar figure to Sara that as soon as we get to his place, all she wants is to get onto his lap.

I'd argue against it, but Ellis seems to relish it. I don't know why, but it's like he looks forward to seeing Sara almost as much as I look forward to seeing him.

Between my lust for him and his behavior with Sara, how am I supposed to keep my poor heart in check?

How am I supposed to stop myself from falling for this man I'm already stupidly attracted to if even my kid can't resist him?

Ugh.

The sun is high and there isn't a cloud in the sky. I clean the sweat off my forehead with my shirt.

Fortunately, I'm not digging holes today.

The soil beneath the shed had a little surprise waiting for me, so when I started digging the foundation for the deck, I came across a lot of rocks. That led to more digging.

I used the rocks with the concrete to strengthen the structure of the deck's base, but by the end of that day, my back was totally fucked.

Now, while the concrete is drying, I'm working on the raised beds.

Ellis wants a natural look like the deck, so I'm building the raised beds with reclaimed wood from a local supplier.

He hasn't decided what he'll plant in them, but I have some ideas. If he asks for my opinion, of course.

I hear the double doors open and look toward the house. Ellis comes out with Sara in his arms, as usual.

"If she gets used to being carried everywhere, I'm giving her to you. No take-backsies," I joke.

He mock gasps. "Did you hear that, princess? Your daddy says you can stay with me forever and ever. How about that?"

Sara giggles because Ellis tickles her tummy.

"I think we have a deal," he says.

"Well, in that case, how may I help you further, Mr. Bradford?" I stand and stretch my back, which feels good after bending down for so long.

He gives me a regretful look. "I'm afraid we've been summoned."

"We've…what?"

"My sister just called. *Apparently,*" he says, using quote marks, "my brother-in-law got the grocery order wrong, and they have far too much food at home, so they're having a barbeque and invited us over."

I laugh. "Your sister has heard of freezers, right?"

He rolls his eyes. "I also asked that question, and *apparently*," he says, using quote marks again, "both her freezers are full."

"Then why did she need more food?"

He sighs. "She doesn't. It's totally an excuse to be nosy and ask you questions about what you've been up to in my backyard."

"Hasn't she seen the progress?"

"No. I've red-taped Alice and Darius from coming over until the backyard is ready. I'd like to get everyone together when it's finished so they can see your amazing work, but I don't want them in your way."

"Oh." I feel my cheeks heat. "It's not that great."

"You can't be serious. This already looks a hundred times better." He turns to look around the backyard, where there's no more trash or broken things. Everything here now will be used for the deck or raised beds.

When he turns back to me, my heart skips a beat. God, his smile is disarming. Maybe the sun is going to my head, but us standing in his backyard with him holding a happy Sara in his arms feels too good.

"So what do you say?" he asks.

"Huh?"

"Shall we go eat all of my sister's food?"

"I don't want to impose, and I still have a lot of work to do here."

Ellis laughs. "Are you kidding me? The invite was for you and Sara. I'm being invited only by extension."

I don't know what to say. Why is Ellis's sister inviting us to her house?

"Um…okay? I'll need to take a shower, though, if that's okay."

"Sure. Do you want me to give Sara her lunch before we go?" he asks.

"I can do it after my shower, unless we're late for your sister's thing."

Ellis smiles again. "Not at all. I'm just trying to help, and I think she's getting hungry. She had a bottle a little while ago."

"Okay, then. If you're sure."

I try to be quick in the shower but can't help taking a moment to enjoy how refreshing it feels after working up a sweat in the backyard.

My thoughts rapidly veer toward Ellis. Does he use this shower at all? I assume he has one in his bedroom upstairs, or there's at least a separate bathroom with a shower.

My dick hardens as I'm cleaning myself. It's not unusual since I can't remember the last time I had sex with anything that wasn't my hand. But the scent of Ellis's soap and knowing he's on the other side of the door at the end of the short hallway is enough to drive me crazy with lust for the man.

One of these days, I'm going to lose it, throw myself at him, get fired, and get a bad reputation all in one go. All because I can't stop thinking about Ellis.

Maybe I should take Jimmy up on his offer. I've still not forgiven him for telling Gerald about my work for Ellis and leaving me to cover his shift, but desperate times call for desperate measures.

Could I fuck my frustrations out on Jimmy? The thought alone is enough to kill my boner, so I turn off the water and dry myself with the towel Ellis left for me.

I go to grab my clothes when I realize I didn't bring them to the bathroom with me.

"Fuck."

I pace the bathroom, but there's only one solution. I need to go out and grab my clean clothes.

Wrapping the towel around my waist as tight as possible, I open the bathroom door and almost bump into Ellis.

A shirtless Ellis.

"I'm...um..."

I'm not sure which of us is mumbling, but we both stare at each other for what seems like forever until he breaks the silence.

"Sara decided she didn't like her lunch today. It's totally my fault. She was waving her arms, and I wasn't paying attention, so when she knocked my hand, it all went flying," he mumbles as he lifts his hand, holding the shirt dirty with Sara's food.

"Oh, Ellis, I'm so sorry. I'll buy you a new one if that one's ruined."

"I'm sure it's not. I was just going to change. You should too," he says, going to the end of the hallway and disappearing into a room I've never been in.

I look down and remember I'm almost naked. My dick is noticeably half-hard, and I think I'm going to die of embarrassment. It's clear I made Ellis uncomfortable.

Well, at least that clears any chance of my dreams coming true.

I grab my clothes and get dressed, not bothering to go back to the bathroom since there's no sign of Ellis.

Sara's plastic bib is surprisingly clean, as are her clothes, so it seems Ellis's shirt took the brunt of Sara's mood.

"What's up with your lunch today?" I ask her.

She cries, so I pick her up to calm her down a little.

"It's okay, baby. Sometimes, I don't like my lunch either. And I always feel like throwing it at Gerald. But we don't do it to Ellis, okay? Because he's nice to us."

I always carry formula and extra food for Sara, so I take a fruit jar from her bag and feed it to her. She eats it all without fuss, which is a relief, and I give her one of her favorite cookies to chew on.

When Ellis comes back, he's wearing a pair of jeans and a shirt with the sleeves rolled up to his elbows. The shirt is untucked, just like the first time I saw him at the soup kitchen.

It looks great on him.

"Ready?" he asks.

"Yeah." I strap Sara into the stroller and quickly wash her jar and cutlery before placing them back in her bag.

Ellis says Alice's house isn't far, so we can walk.

This isn't a part of town I've walked in before because it's not on my way to work.

The houses are all really nice and have beautiful front yards. It's like everyone is proud of their neighborhood.

"This is a really nice area," I say.

"Alice lives in our grandparents' old house, so everyone kind of knows everyone around here. But yes, it is. It's why I tried to get a place as close to her as possible."

We arrive at a white colonial-style house with a double garage on the side and a beautiful front yard with peonies planted all around it instead of a fence. There's a large rose bush in the middle that looks like it's been there for generations.

"This is it. Are you ready?" Ellis says.

"If this is your sister's place, and she likes peonies, then yes, I'm more than ready."

Ellis laughs.

"Well, I'm only here for the food, so let's go in."

16

ELLIS

As soon as we're through the door, it's clear Alice's impromptu barbeque is anything but a last-minute, unplanned event.

She ushers us to the backyard, where she's set up her pop-up shelter to provide shade to the seating area. The kids' playset is pulled closer to the tree so it's in the shade.

"Take a seat over there. Max has started on the food. I'll bring the drinks out in a minute," she says before leaving us in the middle of the backyard.

I gesture to the shade tent so we can get out of the sun.

Milo keeps Sara in the stroller, and since she's in a sitting position, she can see everything around her.

"Where's my girl? She here yet?" Darius steps out of the kitchen into the backyard and comes straight to us. He looks at Milo for permission, which he gives with a nod, and Sara is happily giggling in Darius's arms in no time.

"Should I be worried about the age gap in this relationship?" Milo asks. "What are your intentions toward my girl?"

Darius laughs. "Don't worry, Pops. My intentions are pure. She's my new best friend. Isn't that right, sweetie?" he says to Sara. "Want to play with Uncle Darius on the grass?"

Darius takes Sara's socks off and goes to the play area, where there's a bunch of the kids' toys. He sits on the grass cross-legged, and we watch as he places Sara barefoot on the cool grass.

She doesn't like it initially. Pulling her legs up as soon as they touch the grass. But after a little while, she seems to get used to the feeling and stands, holding on to Darius's hands.

From the corner of my eye, I see Milo smiling. "He seems great around kids."

"My brother is the type of person who does nothing by half-measure. He plays in a hard rock band. When he's with his friends, it's all about partying, drinking, being tough, getting new tattoos, and getting laid. His words, not mine," I explain. "But then there's his other side that only our family and very close friends get to see. The gentle guy who's happy sitting in the grass playing with a baby."

We sit back and watch Sara as Darius helps her walk a few steps.

Alice brings us drinks and some snacks. While Milo is distracted looking at Sara, I catch Alice giving me a look but don't understand what she's trying to say.

She keeps looking from Milo to me and back.

I shake my head and shrug. She rolls her eyes and purses her lips in a silent kiss.

"What? No."

By the time I realize I voiced my reply, it's too late.

Milo looks at us, and Alice smiles. "I was pointing at the chips. Ellis usually can't decide if he wants the ones I bought specially for him or the ones he brings himself."

I know it's illegal to kill your own sibling, but would it be frowned upon if I tripped her the next time she walks by with a bowl of something that stains, say, barbecue sauce?

"Your sister is funny."

"Or extremely irritating. It's such a fine line."

He laughs, and I'm so glad we got past the awkwardness of earlier.

If he knew the effect that seeing him in just a towel around his waist had on me, he'd run out of my place and never look back.

My only regret was not having more time to take my fill of him, but I didn't miss the bulge under the towel. Not when he came out of the bathroom, or as it thickened the longer we stood there.

A part of me still wants to feel desired by a man. To think his body reacted to me. The reality is he's a young guy who probably doesn't need much to get an erection, and any shirtless man will do.

"Uncle Ellis!" Marnie comes running toward me with Benji on her tail.

"Hey, kiddos. How's it going?"

"Benji said a bad word yesterday," Marnie whispers. "But I didn't tell Mommy because I don't want him to get in trouble."

At only two years old, Benji rarely says much that makes sense, so I seriously doubt he said any kind of swear word.

"Did you tell him he shouldn't repeat the word?" I ask her.

She nods, taking her big-sister duties far too seriously for her age.

"Come on, Benji. Let's go play with Uncle Darius and the baby."

A moment later, Darius is attacked by the two, and I watch closely to see if he needs rescuing, but in typical chill-Darius mode, he manages the situation perfectly.

The kids sit next to him as he tells him some kind of story, and even Sara stares at him as if she understands what he's saying.

"Wow. Those are some superpowers right there," Milo says.

"Speaking of superpowers," I say, leaning back on the chair to face Milo slightly. "How come you know so much about landscaping? Not just the building part, but what you've suggested about flowers and plants for my yard?"

A wide smile spreads across his face as he tucks his right leg under his left to face me.

"My mom. She loved flowers. Pink roses were her favorite. I used to listen to her talk about flowers for hours when I was a kid. We didn't have a TV, and my brother was more the type to play outside. After she got sick, I used to go to the library and borrow books for her. We'd spend entire afternoons reading about how to look after different flowers. Annuals, perennials, what to plant for what weather."

"How long has she been gone?"

Milo looks down to where his fingers play with the hem of his shirt. "She died when I was eighteen, just before I finished high school."

"Is that why you didn't graduate?"

He nods. "My brother was fifteen, so social services wanted to take him away, especially because…well, anyway, I got a job at the grocery store, and they let us stay together as long as Mikey went to school."

The brightness in Milo's eyes dissipates and is replaced with pain. He glances at Sara. Some of his smile returns but not completely.

"My mom used to talk about this place. A little village tucked away in a corner of the White Mountains. Every year in June, the lupines bloom for a short time, and the entire village and the surrounding fields look magical."

"Lupines?"

"They're these kind of tall cone-shaped flowers. They're hard to describe, but you can look them up on your computer. I don't even know where this village is, but I've always wanted to find it so I can take Sara one day."

The vulnerability in Milo's voice makes me reach out to him. I touch his shoulder, and he looks at me.

"I hope you can make your dream come true for Sara."

"It's just a silly dream. The place probably doesn't even exist. My mom made up a lot of things to pass the time, especially after my dad died. She used to tell all these stories about things they'd done when they were young. It never occurred to me at the time that some of them might not be true."

I squeeze his arm. "It's okay to have dreams. Without them, what's the point of living? How do we continue getting up each day if we don't have something to look forward to?"

"What's your dream?"

I look at the surrounding setup.

Max is at the grill, wearing his *Kiss the Chef* apron my sister gave him for Christmas last year. Alice keeps bringing bowls of food covered with foil, assisting Max, and never for a second taking her eyes off her kids, even though they're in the safest hands.

And then there's my tough-as-nails on the outside and marshmallow on the inside little brother. We're all so different, but in a way, we're all the same.

"You're looking at it," I say, answering Milo's question.

"You want a free barbeque?"

I turn to him, and his teasing smile makes me happy.

Only a month ago, Milo was really shy around me. Rarely made eye contact and his words always seemed to get stuck before coming out together all at once. It was adorable, but I never understood why he reacted to me that way.

I guess now that I know him a little better, I can see he was shy with someone he didn't know very well.

"A family. Our parents always traveled a lot for work. Sometimes out of need, but I think it's just how they are. Free and adventurous spirits who are curious about the world. Naturally, they'd produce three children who'd be the polar opposite."

Milo smiles.

"Darius was the least exposed to all the moving around, and Alice put her foot down when she was in high school and demanded to stay here with our grandparents. I was the only one who followed them, maybe out of obligation. I didn't want them to think they were being abandoned by their children. But when I finished college, I settled in Boston, and things changed for me."

"You wanted to settle down and start a family?"

17

MILO

SOME KIND of emotion goes through Ellis before he smiles and picks up a chip.

"Yeah, I mean, isn't that what most people want? Come home to the person you love, a couple of kids, that kind of thing?" He plays with the chip before putting it in his mouth.

I tilt my head and rest my chin on the arm I have over the back of the chair.

"Generally, yeah. A lot of people want that. But you're dedicating your life to educating our next generation. You light up when you see Sara, but you also look at her like you're afraid to get too attached."

"What are you trying to say?"

"That it's okay to want more. That it's okay to say you want it."

Ellis licks his lips and takes a sip from his drink. "Still won't make it come true."

"No, but sometimes the best things that happen to us are the most unexpected, so you never know." I shrug and smile encouragingly.

I don't even know why I'm trying to get Ellis to open up about this. It's not my business anyway.

He sighs. "You're right. I've only ever wanted two things in my life. To teach and to have a family. Not just to have children, but to have the kind of relationship Alice does." He looks over at his sister, who's by the grill, kissing Max like they're a couple of teenagers.

"No matter how crazy my sister is, Max loves every single part of her and she loves him, and together they have these two amazing little humans who will grow up to be happy people with great role models."

Ellis stares at his drink. "It's a silly dream, quite boring when you think of it. Just wanting to come home, kiss your husband silly, and tuck your kids into bed. But that's all I ever wanted."

"You don't want that anymore?"

He shrugs. "I don't know. Maybe. It may be too late now. I'm too old."

I don't understand why. Ellis isn't old by any means, so why wouldn't he still be able to have what he wants?

"Every time I was sad, my mom always tried to find the positive. If it was raining, she told me to stand by the window and wait until I saw the break in the clouds. When I saw it, it would stop raining, and I could go out and play," I say. "A lot of the things she said when I was young didn't make sense. At least not until Sara was born. Before her, there was nothing… No, that's not fair. Before her, life was different. But she was my break in the clouds. My rainbow gift from the world to let me know I'm not alone."

Ellis's gaze burns into mine. "She's an amazing baby. I see so much of you in her."

My throat closes up, and I have to look away.

"She's not mine," I confess, but it's more like a whisper I'm not sure Ellis even hears. This isn't something I tell many people. There aren't many people to tell. Those who know, also know why she's with me. "I mean, she's my daughter on paper." I finally look at Ellis and see nothing but compassion. "I'm her uncle."

"Boys, my man's meat is almost ready," Alice says, laughing at her own joke. "Ellis, do you mind if I borrow Milo for a moment?"

"Sure."

I follow Alice, grateful for the interruption.

Was I about to tell Ellis my story? It's not a secret, but the only people who really know it are my neighbors who knew my brother.

Most just assume I had a drunken experimental night with some girl and Sara magically happened.

We go through the kitchen to the garage.

"Milo, please feel free to refuse or tell me to fuck off, but the thing is, you'd be doing me a favor," Alice says, stopping beside their car.

"I don't understand. Why would I do that?"

She grabs a box from a small stack and opens it. Inside is a bunch of baby clothes.

"These were Marnie's clothes. I held on to all of them in case we had another girl. I kept anything that I could for Benji, except things like dresses or clothes that didn't fit. He was always a little bigger than Marnie was when she was born."

I stare at her as she pulls out some beautiful, colorful dresses and pretty shoes that look expensive and of good quality.

"They're adorable, right? I went a little over the top. First child and all." She laughs. "I'd like you to have them for Sara."

For the second time in a short time span, I'm speechless and on the verge of tears.

"I don't know what to say. You should give these to your friends, or you can probably sell them online," I say.

She takes my hand. "From one mother to another"—she winks—"I'd rather know the clothes I picked so carefully for my first baby are with someone who deserves them. I know you're only working in my brother's backyard, but I haven't seen him smile or relax in months. Maybe years. I think you're a good person to have around. There's no one else I'd rather see wearing these clothes than your daughter."

I take a step forward and give her a tight hug. "Thank you so much. I am grateful and honored that you've picked Sara to wear Marnie's clothes. We'll look after them."

When we part, she reaches for my face and wipes the tears I didn't realize were falling.

"I'm sorry. I didn't mean to cry on you."

"It's okay, honey. I was hoping you wouldn't take offense at me being so forward or think of it as charity."

I smile. "Thank you for taking my feelings into consideration. I'm not offended. I'm grateful I can use my paycheck for other important things for Sara and not worry about the clothes she grows out of so quickly. And I'm so grateful you invited us today. Sara is having a great time."

I take some clothes from the box to admire how cute they are.

"You'll have a hard time prying her from Darius's hands. He acts all tough, but he's dying to have a family. He just doesn't have the time between work and his band."

"Sounds like he's not the only Bradford brother to want a family." I gasp. "Crap, I'm sorry, that was out of line. I was distracted looking at the clothes and wasn't thinking. Please—"

"Hey, don't worry. I know my brothers. Both of them," Alice says. "And you're right." Her face falls. "Ellis was seriously hurt before, so he says he's written off love and having a family. I hope the right person comes along to show him it's never too late."

"He's not even old at all," I say.

"He's forty-two. You're right. Not old at all." She smiles, and a glint in her eyes tells me this little conversation between us means more than the words we've just exchanged. "Come on. Let's get some food."

By the time we get back out, Sara is on Ellis's lap, sucking on a piece of fruit.

"She keeps yawning," he says. "I think Darius wore her out."

I hold my arms out, and she stretches to come to me. I get a lovely piece of sticky, partly chewed apple on my neck as she holds on to my shirt.

"She might need a drink. It's quite hot."

"I've already given her some from your bag."

I pause before reaching for the bag. "Thank you." I take the cleaning wipes and get most of the stickiness off her mouth and hands, as well as my neck. Then I place her in the stroller and lean it back a little.

"Well, she's not complaining, so she must be really ready for a nap," I say. "Look at that. I get to eat my food warm today."

Ellis laughs. "I bet it doesn't happen often when you're on your own with her."

"Try never."

It's cooler in the house, so Alice suggests placing Sara in Benji's bed when she falls asleep and then brings out her baby monitor.

Max cuts up all the meat, so it's easy to pick out different bits. From chicken to steak, Ellis wasn't wrong. They really have a lot of meat. Alice made so many sides that it's hard to choose what to have.

I wait for the family to serve themselves before I take some, but Ellis grabs my plate. "Do you want potato salad? Alice's couscous is always superb. And the roasted peppers. Steak? Chicken? Oh, there's some barbecue sauce here. Max, can you pass the ribs, please?"

He puts the plate in front of me, and I struggle not to laugh because at no point did he stop to let me answer his questions.

"I guess those were rhetorical questions," I say, looking at the pile of food.

He grins. "Sorry. I guess I'm a little hungry and assumed you are too. Especially since you've been working since early today."

"Then you better make sure you have as much food on your plate as you put on mine."

He laughs. "Challenge accepted."

The food is delicious. I want to stop eating to tell Max and Alice, but I can't. My moans and nods will have to do.

"Did you hear about the next town meeting?" Max says.

"What about it?" Ellis asks between mouthfuls of potato salad.

"They're discussing the planning permission of that parking lot on the south side by the church, but they're closing the meeting to the public."

Ellis coughs. "It's a closed meeting? How is anyone supposed to challenge it?"

"I think that's the point," Alice says. "Do you think Tyler might know something? After all, he's close to Father O'Reilly, and there's no way they'd do anything without consulting the church."

From the way Max snorts as he takes a bite of his steak, it sounds like he's not so sure about that. I'm inclined to agree, but I don't want to weigh in on this particular conversation.

"I can ask him this week," Ellis says, and I'm glad the conversation ends there and moves on to other topics.

I particularly enjoy watching the siblings bicker over Christmas and whose turn it is to host their parents this year.

I'm not used to eating this much in one meal, though, so I'm full before I finish all the food Ellis put on my plate.

"This was amazing and by far the best food I've ever had. Sorry, I can't finish it. I'm not used to such large portions." I give Ellis a look.

"You mean my expertly reheated leftovers aren't cutting it anymore? That hurts my feelings so deep," he says, putting a hand to his heart.

"What can I say?" I shrug. "Good effort. Must try harder?"

"Damn, bro, you're being roasted better than this chicken," Darius says.

Max throws a bunched-up napkin at him.

"Mommy, is Uncle Ellis being roasted for real?" Marnie asks, scrunching her nose.

Alice laughs. "It's just an expression, honey. It means someone is making a little bit of fun at his expense."

"Ah okay." She seems happy with the explanation.

"Hey, Darius, you know that favorite uncle title you're going for?" Ellis asks. "Now is your chance." He points at Benji, who's falling asleep while trying to eat a chip.

"I fail to see how putting him to bed would give me cool uncle points," Darius says, grabbing a chicken wing with his hands and eating without any care for the mess on his face.

Ellis rolls his eyes and stands.

"Is it okay if I go with you? I'd like to check on Sara," I say.

"Sure."

Alice smiles at me in the same way she did earlier, but now I get it. She's hoping for something between Ellis and me.

Yeah, me too, my friend. Me too. But given the way he reacted to me earlier, it's not happening, so…

Since Sara is occupying Benji's bed, we take him to Marnie's room. I help Ellis clean the remnants of Benji's lunch from his hands, but he definitely needs new clothes, so Ellis points at the drawer where I can get some.

We work together to make sure Benji doesn't wake up. At some point, we stop, look at each other, and smile.

He whispers, "I hope you understand Alice is currently looking at the baby cam and watching us work together, probably picking the colors of our bridesmaids' dresses as we speak."

"Personally, I've always been a sucker for teal," I joke, but then I see the look on his face, and I can't tell if he's terrified because I'm joking, or worse, that I might be serious. Either way, it's not a positive look. "I'm only joking. Don't worry. No misunderstandings here, whatever Alice may or not be hoping for. I think you can do the rest on your own. I'll go check on Sara." I walk all the way to the door before I turn back. "By the way, you were wrong earlier. You're not too old."

I keep my expression as neutral as I can until I open the door to Benji's room and I'm safely inside.

Sara is awake, holding on to her blankie with one hand while the other reaches for one of Benji's stuffed animals.

"Hey, baby girl, ready to go home?"

When she sees me, her smile is so big that it fills up all the empty spaces in my heart.

I pick her up, and she calls out Dada. "That's right. I'm your dada. And one day, when you're a little older, I'll tell you all about your real dada and momma, and your grandma too. She was the best, you know?"

When I return to join Ellis's family, the table has been cleared of all the food. Marnie is asleep on an inflatable toy under the tree and the adults are all in the lounge area.

I approach them. "This little lady was awake. I guess it's time to take her home."

"Already?" Alice asks, sounding disappointed.

"It's been a long day for her. I really appreciate the lunch and the clothes. I'll borrow my neighbor's car this week to get the box if that's okay. I'm walking home, so I can't take it."

She gives Ellis a stare.

"I can borrow their car and drop you off," he says.

"That's okay. After all the food, it will be nice to walk."

"Please, I insist," he says.

There's nothing worse than feeling like someone is doing something nice out of obligation, but I know there's no point arguing, so I agree.

Alice fills the trunk of her car with three boxes of clothes for Sara, and I thank her again for her generosity.

The drive to my place is silent.

"Did I say something wrong? You seem awfully quiet," Ellis says.

"What? No. I'm just a little tired. After work and the big lunch, I just want to see how my neighbor is doing, and then I'll do a couple of hours of studying."

He narrows his eyes as if he's assessing me.

"Okay. I guess I'll see you at the store, the soup kitchen, or next weekend."

"Yeah."

I take Sara inside before coming back out for the boxes.

Ellis helps me bring them to the door and then goes back to the car.

He turns around like he wants to say something but instead just leaves.

"The first time that nice man dropped you off, you were smiling. This time, not so much." Florrie stands from behind a bush.

"Jesus, Florrie. You want to give me a heart attack?"

She laughs. "Sorry, my dear, I thought you saw me here deadheading the roses. Anyway, what happened between last time and today?"

I give her a smile I don't feel. "Nothing, Florrie. We're just friends."

"Hmm...I was just friends with my late Freddie until we weren't just friends anymore."

"We're just friends," I repeat, and I'm sure it's more to remind myself of that than for Florrie's benefit.

If I'm honest, I don't even know if we're friends, but I'd like to think we are. Especially after all the time we've spent together having lunch and Ellis tutoring me. And today, we shared more personal stuff.

Maybe that's just another one of those things that only exists in Milo's world, like love and happy endings.

"I'll let you get inside because I have to get ready for the bowling club, but this conversation isn't over."

"How many clubs do you belong to?"

"A girl's gotta try everything once. Even other girls."

"Florrie!"

She goes off giggling to herself, leaving me slightly shocked on my doorstep.

18

ELLIS

The Academy is noisier than usual. Probably because it's Friday night.

Tonight is the town meeting about the parking lot. Arlo got an invitation to sit in because of his association with the craft fair.

Levi is working the bar tonight, and Fletcher is babysitting all the kids, so Arlo agreed to join us later to give us an update on the meeting before picking up Ava from Fletcher and Harrison's place.

"You're very quiet tonight," Harrison says, leaning closer so I can hear him. "That's usually my job."

"It's noisy here. I can't even hear myself think."

"It'll die down in a bit. Usually, people either stay for dinner or go home after happy hour. Wanna step outside?"

"Sure."

We pick up a couple of beers from the bar and go outside, where there's a cordoned-off area with some tables and benches. Despite the warm summer night, the outside space is practically empty.

"What makes people want to pack like sardines into a hot bar instead of sitting outside where they can breathe fresh air instead of body odor?" I ask.

Harrison chuckles. "Bars and clubs were never my thing unless my best friend dragged me out, but if I remember correctly, it was the whole smelling someone else's scent and rubbing against each other. In the right place, at the right time, it can be a really…enjoyable experience." He elbows me playfully.

"Yes, yes, I remember. I just don't want to relive it."

"Fair enough."

He takes a swig of his beer.

The night is warm, and there's no breeze. It's like the world is still. Not even the leaves on Main Street move an inch.

"Hey, sorry about Fletcher teasing you last time about Milo. He can be like a dog with a bone sometimes and doesn't know when to quit."

I cross my legs and balance the bottle on my knee. "Yeah, I know. It's fine. He's not entirely wrong."

"Wait…he's not?"

"No, of course not. I mean, he's such an amazing guy, but he's still so—"

Harrison puts his hand on my shaking leg and stares at me.

"If you're going to end that with young, then stop right there. What does it matter if there's an age gap between a couple? If you agree on the things that matter, what else is there to worry about?"

I sigh. "Yeah, I know you're right, but it's just that…I don't know. I feel too much like a fool."

Harrison looks at his watch. "Look, this stays between us. If you just want to talk about it, I can listen."

"Thanks."

"Do you actually have feelings for Milo?"

Do I? *Feelings* is such a loaded word. So heavy.

"I…ugh…I am definitely one hundred percent attracted to him. How can I not be? He's so strong, sweet, kind, smart. He's just…I don't know. There's just something about him that pulls me. But I have nothing to offer him. He's raising a child on his own." I run my hands through my hair. "Even if we ignore the age gap, he deserves more than what I can give him."

"Is it the kid thing?" he asks.

"What? No. I love Sara. I just…I have some baggage I don't think is fair to unload on Milo."

"Sometimes that's not our choice to make, Ellis. If Milo has feelings for you, you can't stop that from happening any more than you can stop your feelings from happening."

"He doesn't have feelings for me. Come on, let's be real here."

Harrison laughs. "Okay, let's be real. Ellis, you're a good-looking man. You're the type that'll only get better with age when the rest of us look like overgrown, old teenagers. But yeah, you're hot."

I stare at him.

"What? Just because I'm in love with Fletcher doesn't mean I can't find other people attractive. We compare notes." He shrugs.

"God, please, save me from this," I beg.

"Now, let's look at what matters. What's here"—he points to my head—"and what's here." He lays his hand on my chest. "You care about the kids you teach. When there was a challenge with the Spring Fair last year, you picked the most unlikely pair to run it. Thanks for that, by the way. I still owe you for pushing me toward Fletcher."

"It wasn't intentional. You just had less knowledge of the parent politics, so I knew you'd do a good job. Also, having more LGBTQ+ representation in the school mattered to me too."

"See?" he says, opening his arms as if to prove a point. "You're a good man. I can't think of anything you couldn't offer Milo."

I take a deep breath. "It's complicated. I don't want to hurt Milo in the long run, even though I think I may already have."

Harrison stares at me with disbelief, so I tell him what happened over the weekend, from our tense encounter outside the bathroom to the moment in Marnie's room.

I skip the part where Milo and I talked about our dreams and the things that mattered to us because that's too personal.

Listening to Milo talk about his mom was both sad and riveting. All I wanted at that moment was to take him to that village in the White Mountains so he could see his lupines and connect with his mom.

"Ellis, let me ask you this. What do you want from Milo?"

I finish my beer and set the bottle on the table.

What do I want from Milo? That's a good question.

I know what I want for him. I want to protect him, to make sure he doesn't hurt. I don't want to see him go hungry again. I want him to follow his dreams, and I want to encourage him to look for something in landscaping since he seems to have such a passion for it.

But what do I want from him?

I stare at Harrison, lost for words, and since I don't answer his question, he continues. "Milo reminds me a lot of my younger self," he says. "Almost too mature. Especially after my first relationship ended. I was nursing a broken heart because I had so much love to give and no one to give it to. All I wanted was to love."

"How did you get past the hurt and move on? I mean, you eventually did because you married Megan's mom," I say.

"Let me ask you this. If all Milo wanted was to love you, would you let him?"

"I don't understand."

Harrison stands. "I need more beer for this." He goes back inside, leaving me alone with my thoughts.

If Milo wanted to love me, would I let him? The answer should be yes. Right?

But what would happen when he tired of our life together? What about when I became too boring for him?

Harrison comes back with two more beers and sits in front of me.

"When I met Stella, I didn't think I was worthy of being loved. I thought I had to be the one to do all the love. Otherwise, she wouldn't want me. I worked so hard at being the perfect husband that, along the way, I lost myself. I lost us. It's different with Fletcher. I love him just as much, but I'm not afraid anymore. We are both important to each other."

I see Arlo a few yards away, and Harrison sees him too.

"All I'm saying is that you probably want to take care of Milo. Just remember, he's not a porcelain doll. He's, as you said, a strong man. If he likes you, let him show you. If you like him, show him you do."

I nod. "Thank you."

He nods back, and that marks the end of the conversation.

"Hey, boys. What are you doing out here? Too crowded inside?" Arlo asks.

"Yeah, I like going home smelling like my own aftershave, thank you," Harrison says.

Arlo laughs. "Let me say hi to my man and grab a beer. I'll catch you up with the meeting. Tyler is on his way too."

When Arlo is out of earshot, I turn to Harrison. "Thank you for the talk. I guess I have some stuff to figure out, but I'd appreciate if this stays between us."

"From what I hear, Milo is working in your backyard, so you have plenty of opportunities to figure it out." He raises his beer and winks at me before taking a swig. "And your secret is safe with me."

Arlo comes back with a couple of beers a few minutes later, and then, as he said, Tyler arrives.

"Get straight to it, man. What happened at the meeting?" Tyler asks.

Arlo makes eye contact with each of us. "The vote was unanimous to give the go-ahead for the parking lot."

"What?" I ask. "How can they do that?"

Arlo raises his hands. "Hold your horses. The vote was unanimous because the only ones allowed to vote were those who want the parking lot to happen. A load of people in the audience questioned the ethics of the voting system and the lack of representation from residents from the area."

"Damn right. How can they do something without even asking the people it's going to affect?" Tyler asks.

"The problem is that the playground has been largely abandoned for years. The opinion of the community doesn't hold much weight when the other side is saying the investment in the area is a good thing," Arlo explains.

"They have a point," Harrison says.

"What if we clean it up?" I ask. "We get rid of the weeds. Restore the play structures."

Tyler is playing with the label on his bottle.

"It's not that easy. Do you know how many times that playground has been cleaned up? Too many to count. It doesn't get used by children to play because the parents are too scared."

What?

"Why?"

"A few years ago, there was a surge of drug dealing and drug-related crime. Most of it is gone now because those who caused it"—he looks at me—"are dead. But that won't magically bring life back into the playground."

"Then we make it. We have to start somewhere. Cleaning it up is the start. Then we'll figure the rest out." I turn to Arlo. "What was the outcome of the meeting?"

"They've postponed the meeting until a committee of residents can be formed to represent their opinion. We basically have a few weeks until they demand a meeting or go ahead without one."

"We'll make it happen." I stand.

"Where are you going?" Harrison asks.

"Home. There's a bunch of stuff to plan and not a lot of time to do it. I'll see you guys next week."

I walk a few yards until Tyler catches up to me.

"Hey, walking this way?" I ask.

"I am now."

I chuckle. "Don't worry. I told my sister there's nothing between us, so you don't need to walk me home."

Tyler doesn't laugh at my joke, so I look at him and see his worried frown. "You seem to have a special interest in the playground."

"Of course. I've grown attached to the community, and I think the parking lot would be the end of whatever small thread is holding that community together."

He hums. "Is that it?"

"What do you mean?"

"I'm not going to bullshit you, Ellis. Is this because of Milo?"

I roll the sleeves of my shirt again because, despite the time, the temperature hasn't gone down. Or maybe I'm just feeling too hot all of a sudden.

"Well, it's his community, so yeah. You know I respect Milo. We're friends, and I adore Sara. I'd love to know that she can grow up playing there."

He nods. "From one friend to another, I've said this before and I'll say it again. Milo is a special person. If you care about him, show it. Don't keep it to yourself."

He pats me on the back and turns to go back in the direction we came from.

"Where are you going?"

"I forgot I drove here. I guess it's that old age setting in and all."

I shake my head. "You're a bastard."

"Yeah, but with good intentions, which makes me a fucking fairy godmother."

I pick up a small rock and throw it in his direction. I miss, of course, which was the expected outcome and my intention.

Tyler laughs until I no longer see him.

I walk home thinking about how I can ask Milo out without sounding like I've been thinking about him every day for the past few months.

Harrison's words come back to me too.

Maybe it's time to give Milo some credit and respect him for the man he is.

And also prepare myself for rejection.

19

MILO

THWAT.

"Ugh. Stupid nail." I pull the bent nail from the wooden slabs and try again.

Thwat.

Okay, this one's going in.

Thwat. Thwat.

"Fucking ugh." It bends just as it looks like it's going through.

I stand and stretch my back. The small pile of bent nails is making me angry.

Well, angrier.

I've been in Ellis's backyard since just after sunrise, measuring the slabs to outline the deck's base and ensure I'm using the right ones. Ellis bought them cut to size, so I don't need to do any cutting, but I want to ensure they all fit together correctly. Hence using smaller nails before I use the nail gun I rented.

None of this would be a problem if I wasn't so worked up about talking to Ellis about what he did.

When I get worked up, I get nervous. I shouldn't even be handling a hammer, let alone trying to nail anything in place.

I look toward the house. There's still no movement from inside.

Okay, so that was my intention. To do some work, and by the time Ellis noticed I was here, I'd have gathered my courage to confront him.

"Okay. Deep breaths and focus, Milo."

I kneel again. This time the nail goes in, and it's a small victory. If I can repeat this a few more times to get the basic frame in place, I'll have the confidence to use the nail gun, and it'll all be much easier and quicker.

Hopefully, by the time I leave—if I don't get fired first—I'll have the deck's base finished. My anxiety level spikes at the thought that Ellis may actually fire me. I had to decline Gerald's offer of the extra night shifts, so I need the landscaping job more than ever.

He knew I'd never be able to take the shifts, but now he'll hold my decision against me forever, which means I should really start looking for a new job.

I put those thoughts aside and let my mind focus on the job at hand. And as I see progress with the deck, I have a renewed energy to keep going.

Within an hour or so, the base is in place, and I can start nailing the actual floorboards.

I stop to take a sip of the coffee I brought with me in a to-go mug when I hear the kitchen door open.

Ellis comes out holding a cup of coffee in his hand. He's barefoot and wearing pajama pants and an old T-shirt.

I don't want to look but, fuck me, I look, and even his hair is a little out of place like he's just gotten up. No one should look so...like that in the morning.

It annoys me even more because I want to kill him as much as I want to just pull him down on the newly laid grass and kiss him stupid.

"You shouldn't be out here barefoot," I say, collecting the nails I bent earlier and placing them in a box.

He looks at his feet and goes back inside, coming out wearing a pair of old sneakers.

"How long have you been here? It's barely morning," he says.

"It's past ten, and I came earlier to make sure I can finish this part today."

He narrows his eyes. "Where's Sara?"

"With Florrie."

I resume nailing the boards together.

"Oh, if you'd said you were coming earlier, I could have gotten up earlier to look after her."

Stop being so fucking nice.

"Florrie misses spending time with Sara. Besides, you're usually up early anyway, so it wouldn't have made a difference."

He sits on the grass and crosses his legs, resting his hands on his thighs as he holds the coffee.

"I was thinking about a lot of stuff last night and couldn't sleep."

"Thinking about what?"

"You...mainly."

The nail gun slips from my hand, and I avoid an accident only because I'm holding it with both hands.

"What do you mean?" I ask, putting the nail gun down to face him.

He looks at me. "I...it's hard to explain...because...I have so much respect for you, Milo, and I don't want to—"

I interrupt him because of all the things he could have said, I don't expect him to use words that trigger my anger.

"Respect. Really? Then explain this to me. How come there's more money paid into my account than what we agreed for my hourly rate?"

He looks down and places his coffee on the grass.

"If you respected me, you would discuss what you were doing instead of going behind my back."

"Milo—"

I get closer to him, and now that I'm getting started, I feel the blood pumping through my veins, and it's all going to come out. "I went to study at the library yesterday. I signed into my GED account and saw the fee for my exams was paid. I looked for the payment receipt, and it had your name on it. Were you planning on telling me?"

"I..." He runs his hands through his hair and then looks at me.

We're practically face to face. Him sitting on the grass and me kneeling next to him, standing a little taller.

"You offered me a ride home. You brought me dinner when I was stuck at work. You gave me a job when I needed one. At no point did I feel like I was a charity case to you. But you treated me like one by going behind my back and paying for stuff for me."

I point a finger at his chest. "I may not have much, but I work damn hard for it. I'm not proud. I can accept help. But I deserve to be respect—"

Before I can finish, Ellis yanks me by the front of my shirt with one hand and with the other, grabs the back of my neck and slams his lips against mine.

The move is so unexpected that I lose balance and fall sideways.

Our lips part for a split second. My brain hasn't even caught up before Ellis is there again.

Ellis Bradford is kissing me. I'm not dreaming. His lips are touching mine.

This is one of those moments that I know I will never remember exactly how it happened because it's over so soon.

I can smell the coffee on his breath when he pulls away, resting his forehead against mine.

At some point, I must have closed my eyes because when I open them, I'm staring at Ellis's dark-blue ones.

"Why did you do that?" I ask. My voice is trembling and my body is tense. Trying to hold in what I really want to do.

There's a layer of vulnerability in the way he's looking at me. Like he doesn't quite believe he did what he just did.

That makes two of us.

"It seemed like a good way to shut you up." He smiles. "Milo, I'm so sorry. I didn't mean to make you feel the way you do. Honestly, I paid the fee because I realized the deadline was coming up soon, and I didn't want you to miss it. I should have asked you first."

"You should."

He runs a finger over my cheek. "I don't see you as a charity case at all. And once again, I know I should have consulted you, but I've done some research. You asked for too little, and at the time, I didn't know better, so I agreed. I'm simply paying you what you deserve to be paid. Your exam fees can come out of your pay if you want."

His gaze moves away from mine, but his hand is still on my face. We're still lying beside each other.

"I…um…probably shouldn't have kissed you either. I'm sorry for that."

The heat spreading through my body, threatening to turn my veins into lava, suddenly becomes ice cold.

"Why?"

"Because I want us to be friends. Because we have a working relationship. Because I'm so much older than you."

Wait…what?

My quick thinking gives me an advantage over Ellis, so I roll him onto his back and straddle him.

I keep my hands on either side of his head because if I don't, I might start undressing him.

"What are…you doing?" His voice is thick with want, and now I can see it.

I slide down on him so our faces are closer together. There's no way what I feel against my thigh isn't his erection.

"Those are bullshit reasons, Ellis."

He swallows and looks at my lips.

"Tell me one thing. Did you want to kiss me?"

He nods.

"For how long?"

He closes his eyes like he's in pain. When he opens them, there's nothing but resolution. "Since the first time you said my name out loud."

"When we met at the store?" I ask.

"No. When you called me Ellis."

I run my nose over his. My open mouth catches his lip, and the sexiest, breathiest moan I've ever heard fills me with the confidence I need to know this is okay.

"Ellis," I whisper, rubbing my cheek on his.

I pull his earlobe with my teeth and whisper his name again.

His hands come up to hold my wrists.

"Milo."

"May I kiss you?"

"Please."

This time, when our lips touch, it's not a stolen moment. I will never forget this. It's the culmination of months of wanting, pining, desiring, and hoping. The soft and tender kisses become laced with more need. Our bodies line up until I'm practically fully on top of him.

Ellis's hands move up my arms until he's cradling my face. He opens his mouth, and as our tongues touch, I know I'll never want to kiss anyone ever again.

I push for more because I've wanted to taste Ellis since the moment I first saw him, and he lets me. He gives in like he's meant to be mine.

Each one of his moans is swallowed until I have to come up for air, but even then, I don't stop. I kiss his neck and suck his Adam's apple.

The thought that we have to stop and talk about what's happening terrifies me. But he wants it. He said he wanted to kiss me. So I do.

I kiss him until my dick is so painfully hard that unless we stop, we're at risk of doing something really inappropriate in his backyard.

"Ellis, dear?"

We both freeze when we hear the voice on the other side of the fence.

"Is everything okay over there? I keep hearing moaning and wheezing. I hope Milo hasn't hurt himself."

I rest my head on his chest, trying not to laugh. He brings his hand to rest on the back of my neck.

"It's okay, Mrs. Fisher. All under control."

"You make sure he doesn't put himself under too much stress. He works far too hard."

Ellis's chest rumbles with barely contained laughter.

"I will, Mrs. Fisher. Don't worry."

We stay still until we hear the sliding doors to her home close.

Ellis flips us so he's on top of me. "No undue stress. Mrs. Fisher's orders."

I cant my hips, knowing he'll feel my erection through his thin pajama pants.

"This is your fault," I say.

We smile at each other.

"I guess I'm forgiven for my transgressions?" Ellis asks.

"Hmm, I'm not sure. I haven't had breakfast yet."

He laughs, and I feel it all over. I love it.

"Why don't you get back to work, and I'll prepare something for us."

"Yes, boss." I give him a quick kiss and move him off me to stand.

I'm not made of steel, so I look at the nice tent in his pants.

My mouth waters at the thought of finishing later what we started now. It's with a lot less frustration toward Ellis, but a lot more of the sexual kind, that I grab the nail gun and go back to work.

I pretend not to watch Ellis through the kitchen doors as he puts together something for breakfast—or brunch since it's close to eleven.

The way his pajama pants cling to his ass. The way he moves around the kitchen. The way he felt under me, on top of me. How he tasted.

I look up at the blue sky.

Am I dreaming, or is this really happening?

20

ELLIS

I CRACK the eggs into the bowl and set the whisk next to it. Next, I chop some mushrooms, peppers, and ham.

It's a good thing my hands can work independently from my brain because it's having a meltdown.

I kissed Milo.

Milo kissed me.

I put the knife down before a cut a finger off while remembering every second of that absolutely perfect kiss.

The way we fit together. The way Milo took charge was such an unexpected relief. How did he know that, more than anything, him taking control is the fast lane to me giving it all up?

My control, my sanity, my…fuck.

If I was confused yesterday about how I felt about Milo and if I should tell him or not. If I was afraid of being rejected by him…now it's worse.

I look behind me toward the backyard and see he's working with his usual focus. The base for the deck is almost done, but from where I stand, it's like nothing happened. It's like any other Saturday.

But there's a stark difference now.

He hasn't had the coffee and brunch I usually make for him yet.

Sara isn't here today.

There are no more layers of protection between us.

We broke the seal on that grass, and now I don't know if the lid will ever close again.

I'm too wired to think straight. To remember Harrison's words or Tyler's warnings.

My dick is so painfully hard. Telling me it's been too long since I've used it properly and now it wants to feel more of Milo. Preferably without clothes.

"Fuck. I need clothes." I look down at the tent in my loose pajama pants. "I definitely need clothes."

Milo always lets me know when he arrives. Even if he doesn't want to bother me, he places Sara on the play mat that is now permanently in my living room. The coffee table hasn't gone back to its usual position in weeks.

So when I got up and came down to make myself a cup of coffee, I wasn't expecting to see Milo already here and working. I completely forgot about what I was wearing or that I was barefoot.

I add more coffee to the filter and turn the coffee maker on before going up to my bedroom to put on more appropriate clothing, but when I get there, I don't know what to do.

Do I go for the safe option? Jeans will keep my dick from starring in its own show.

I open the closet and take out a clean pair.

But we kissed. What if he wants more? Will the jeans be in the way?

I throw the jeans on the bed and go to the chest of drawers to grab a pair of joggers.

"Fuck. These are only mildly better than the pajama pants."

But they provide easier access.

Why the fuck am I having such a freak-out over what to wear? I'm not fifteen, for the love of everything sacred.

I'm an adult, and as such, I should behave like one.

Before I change my mind, I put on the jeans and a clean T-shirt.

Ignoring the desire to go outside and pull Milo in here with me, I start making the omelet. I'm almost done when he comes through the door into the kitchen.

"The base—" His gaze runs up my body until it meets my eyes. "You got dressed."

"Would you rather I hadn't?"

He comes forward, and I step aside so I don't accidentally burn myself on the stove.

Milo's usually soft gaze burns through my skin. "Yes, actually," he says, coming even closer. "Your other clothes provided better access."

He runs his nose over my neck, and I feel him suck a patch of skin.

I close my eyes and moan as my dick reacts. "I knew I should have picked the joggers."

"Can I take a shower?"

All I can do is nod.

He grabs his bag and disappears into the guest bathroom.

I take the time he's in the shower to get a modicum of self-control and finish the brunch.

Since I discovered that Milo likes the French brioches, I always have some whenever he comes over. I set the oven to a low temperature and add a couple in. They'll be warm and slightly toasty by the time we finish the omelet.

The coffee maker splutters out the last few drops, so I turn it off and bring the pot to the table.

I'm plating the omelets when Milo joins me. His hair is messy and wet. He must have rushed drying off because there are a couple of damp patches where his T-shirt clings to his body.

The scent of my soap follows him. It wasn't a conscious decision to get the same brand I use for the spare bathroom. More like a desire to not have to think too much about it. But from the day Milo started showering here, I've thanked my past self.

The thought that Milo goes home smelling like my soap makes me strangely possessive of him. Like he belongs to me and no one else.

"Food smells nice," he says, taking his usual seat across from me.

"Thanks. Coffee?"

"Please."

We eat in silence, but if we were in a busy nightclub, it couldn't be noisier than it is right now because of this thing between us.

This thing that has been bubbling inside me for months? It's loud.

We keep stealing glances and smiling at eat other.

He looks so relaxed. Why is he so relaxed? Was he prepared for this to happen?

I don't know how since even I didn't know I would make the first move.

"Freak-outs are my specialty," he says. "And it seems to me you're freaking the hell out."

"That obvious?"

He points to the brioche on my plate that I've turned into crumbs. I clean my hands.

"Sorry."

He drinks the last of his coffee. "Have you finished?"

"Yeah."

Usually, he goes back to work after brunch while I play with Sara, but if he's taken his shower, he must be done for the day. I don't want to feel disappointed that he might go soon, but I am.

He stands, grabs our plates, and takes them to the sink. Then he comes back for our empty coffee cups. A quick wipe of the table to ensure there are no crumbs, and then he washes the dishes.

I just stare as he looks so completely at home in my kitchen.

When he's finished, he wipes his hands on a dry cloth and comes over to me.

I take his hand when he holds it out for me and follow him to the couch. He pulls me down with him. We're sitting so close together that I'm practically on his lap.

His fingers trace the palms of my hands like we've got all the time in the world. I do the same to him, and I'm surprised that his hands are soft despite the hard manual labor he's been doing the last few weeks.

"I feel like I should say something. Do something," I say.

"As long as it's not an apology, what do you want to say?"

"I don't know."

"What do you want to do?"

I look at where our fingers are laced together.

"I want to get out of my head. I want to stop wondering if kissing you was wrong. It felt so good, and I don't know if I could survive not doing it again. And if I…we never kiss again, will I still remember how good it was ten years from now?"

Milo takes one hand back and brings it to my face.

"You can catalog all of our kisses, but if it depends on me, you will never have to wonder if it'll happen again."

He comes forward, and I welcome the touch of his lips on mine.

"I love how you don't know what to do with yourself when I touch you, Ellis."

I want to laugh because he's right, but he keeps sucking my lips into his mouth, and I feel when his tongue runs over them, soft and warm. All I can do is let it happen. Let myself be consumed by Milo.

"Why," I rasp. "Why do you like it?"

He stops kissing me and nuzzles me until I'm lying on the couch with him between my legs.

"Because it gives us an even playing field." He kisses my jaw. "Can I?" He pulls on the hem of my T-shirt, and I help him take it off.

"When I'm around you, I can't think. You're always so composed, so in control," he says. "I like knowing that I can do this to you."

He sucks my nipple into a peak. I cant my hips to meet his, and we both hiss.

"I'm never in control, Milo. Especially when it comes to you."

He treats the other nipple the same way before moving down my chest.

I instinctively put my hand on my chest. He looks up.

"I'm sorry," I say.

"What are you sorry for?"

"I'm not…my hair is…I'm…"

"You're stunning, Ellis. I like your hair, all of it. The dark brown, the white ones on the sides of your head." He kisses my hand and pushes it away. "And I particularly like that your chest hair has even more gray. Fuck, I never imagined you'd be this sexy."

"I'm getting old." Fuck, I hate that my insecurities are getting the best of me when it's clear Milo likes what he sees.

"I'm aware of that and don't give a shit. I bet you a blowjob that I'm growing old at the same rate."

I laugh. "Deal."

He unbuttons my jeans.

"What are you doing?" I ask.

"I won the bet. Or do you need to consult your science books?"

"But I…"

He laughs. "Oh no, no, no. You said you want to get out of your head, and I want to get your head. It's a fair trade."

I laugh, but it turns into a moan when Milo opens the remaining buttons on my jeans and my erection springs free.

"No underwear. I like it." He sits on his heels and pulls my jeans until they're completely off.

He stares at me in what looks like awe, but I have to close my eyes because I'm too naked and he's too dressed. If he doesn't do anything, I might just bolt.

"Milo," I beg.

His hands run up my calves, massaging my muscles and relaxing me. Well, part of me because the other part is anything but relaxed.

With his hands on the back of my knees, Milo pulls my legs up until I'm totally exposed to him.

"What are you—" I open my eyes and gawk as Milo removes his T-shirt with one hand while the other keeps me in place. Then he does what I least expect.

He lowers his face and licks a path from the rim of my hole to my balls, where he sucks them into his mouth one at a time. When I think I'm about to die, he carries on his path until his mouth opens to take my crown.

"Fuck…oh fuck."

I don't know what he's doing with his tongue, but it feels so good together with the suction.

"Ugh, Milo. Christ…fucking…"

"Mr. Bradford, I hope you don't take that potty mouth into the classroom."

I moan as he takes me deeper until my cock fills his mouth.

No, I don't take this language into the classroom, but right now, there are no other words to express what he's doing to me, so fuck will have to do.

His hands explore my legs, my stomach, and around my back, where he squeezes the globes of my ass, but his mouth never stops.

"Fuck, Milo, I'm so close."

He brings up one hand to jerk me. "I'm ready for you." And then he goes back to sucking and licking.

My body is a volcano, and I'm surprised I haven't melted the couch. The tell-tale tingle of an orgasm rises slowly up my spine. It's right there, under the surface.

As if he's been studying my body for an exam he's more than ready to excel at, Milo runs his thumb over my hole, not really pushing in, just applying a hint of pressure, while he increases the suction on my head.

"Milo…fuck…I'm coming…" It's the only warning I can give before my body convulses in an orgasm strong enough to destroy all memories of previous orgasms.

And he hasn't even fucked me yet.

Yet.

What?

Milo catches every single drop of my release until there's nothing left.

I'm still catching my breath, totally boneless and practically brain dead, but my dick still has the energy to stir when Milo drops his jeans and jerks off until he's coming all over me.

I've never felt so owned, and it's never felt so right.

Everything about my life so far has been either one great big lie or an opening act. A prologue to the real thing.

Milo falls on top of me. "That was the most amazing thing ever." He cradles my face and kisses me. "I've wanted you for such a long time, Ellis. I can't even believe this just happened."

"I guess my omelet was really that good, huh?"

His laughter is the best sound ever. I think it's the first time I've heard it.

"It was the best omelet ever. I will definitely want seconds." He kisses me. "And thirds."

He chuckles. "Maybe we should wash up before we…um…cook again. I think the stove is out of service for now."

He stands and pulls me with him, chucking his jeans off. He stops by the guest bathroom, but I squeeze his hand and pull him toward my room.

He blushes, and it's the first time today that I see the Milo I thought I knew. It reminds me that we're both still people with things to overcome and room to grow.

We take a slow shower, during which his cock becomes ready to go again.

My mouth waters at the sight.

He tells me we don't need to do anything, but I'm on my knees with his cock in my mouth before he finishes talking, and since I have a few tricks of my own, I draw another orgasm out of him in record time.

We dry off and then lie naked on my bed, facing each other.

He's the first to talk. "We probably have more questions now than ever before. But I liked this. I like you, Ellis. At the risk of sounding sad and desperate…can we just enjoy ourselves and see where it leads?"

I caress his face and gaze into his warm brown eyes. The heat has been pushed back and I see the soft Milo that's captured my attention for months.

"I mean, we don't have to tell anyone or anything." He tries to push away, but I pull him closer and kiss him.

"I will never be embarrassed to be with you or to have people know I'm with you, Milo. I don't know if further down the line I can give you what you need, and that worries me because I don't want to hurt you. Our age gap worries me, but I can't resist you. And I don't have the strength to push you away."

He nods. "Okay." And then he brings his hand up to my face, caressing my temple. "Ellis, whatever happens between us, I'll make you believe you're not too old for me or anyone. You're perfect."

I pull him closer, and he comes willingly, resting his face against my neck.

Every time he breathes out, it tickles, and it's fucking perfect.

"Are you doing anything tomorrow?" I ask.

"No."

"Do you want to bring Sara and spend the day at the lake with me?"

He looks up to meet my eyes and smiles.

"I'd love to. I might have to ask her personal assistant though. Her schedule is quite busy, you know?"

I slap his ass, and he groans.

"I probably should go," he says. "Florrie will wonder why I'm so late."

"Just tell her you were busy blowing your boss."

I like Milo's carefree smile and the fact I put it there. I like it a lot.

If I'm not careful, he's going to melt the ice around my heart and make me question the decision I made when I moved away from Boston.

21

MILO

WALKING ON AIR, floating on a cloud, being carried by hundreds of butterflies.

That's how I feel on the way home, yet somehow, none of those words are good enough to describe it.

Ellis drives me because we ended up falling asleep together after I finally got confirmation that the shower soap he's given me to use in the shower downstairs is the same brand he uses. A small inconsequential fact, but I like it even more now that I know the smell I've been using to fantasize about Ellis is the one he uses for himself.

We didn't wake up until his sister called to ask about his plans for tomorrow.

I had to put my finger over my lips and point to his phone to remind him she couldn't see us. Once his face returned to a healthier color, it was nice to watch him speak to his sister, who apparently also had a multitude of other things to talk about.

After convincing her that he genuinely had other plans for his Sunday, Alice let him go, so we got dressed and left his place.

"What are you smiling about?" he asks, giving me a quick look when we stop at a light.

"Just the way you and your siblings are with each other. It's…"

"Weird?"

I laugh. "No. It's endearing." And then it's his turn to laugh.

"That wouldn't be my choice of word," he says.

He parks in front of my gate. "Can I come say hi to Sara?" he asks.

"Of course."

Be still my beating heart.

I take a deep breath and get out of the car. Florrie is outside in her front garden with Sara, so it takes approximately three seconds for Sara to see me and call Dada.

"Hello, baby girl. Did you have a good day?" I hold out my arms, and Florrie hands Sara over to me.

"She did indeed. Lots of walking practice, and we read a few books. Then she cleaned the house while I took a nap," Florrie says. "Oh wait, that was the other way around, and then one of us pooped all over our clean clothes."

"You didn't have time to run to the bathroom?" I joke.

Ellis snorts, which is when Florrie seems to notice his presence.

"Well, hello, young man. I think it's about time we were introduced, considering you've dropped my boy home twice now, and I want to know your intentions."

"Florrie!" I admonish.

Sara fidgets in my arms, asking to go to Ellis. I oblige since he's practically taking her off me.

His face goes a cute shade of pink, a slightly lighter color than the red when his sister called. Then again, we were naked, so I guess the embarrassment level goes down a little.

"Florrie, you haven't been formally introduced, but Ellis is the person you spoke to about the backyard job. He's my boss," I say.

"Oh really?" she asks. "Well, I'm sure you're happy with the work Milo is doing in your backyard, or you wouldn't be giving him so many rides home."

Ellis coughs, but as I try to save the situation, he stretches his hand out to Florrie. "Really nice to finally meet you. Milo talks a lot about you. Thank you for connecting us. Milo's work is absolutely the best I've ever had."

It's my turn to choke.

"I'm sure it is," Florrie says, meeting Ellis's unwavering gaze.

"Well, this is…um…not awkward," I say. "But I'm sure Ellis has to get back home."

Ellis looks at me with a warm smile. "Pick you up at ten tomorrow?"

"Yes," I reply, taking Sara back from him.

"Tomorrow? I thought you had the day off," Florrie says.

Ellis places a hand on Florrie's arm, and it's amazing to watch how she reacts to him. Like she wants to trust him, but she's not too sure. "He does. We're taking Sara to the lake tomorrow."

"Oh." Florrie looks from Ellis to me and back to Ellis. The challenge in her eyes is clear as day. "I've never been to the lake. I'm new to the area, you see?"

"Would you like to join us?" Ellis asks.

"I would love to. How very nice of you to ask."

I roll my eyes. "Okay then, now that's sorted, we should all probably…" I gesture vaguely with my hands.

Florrie gives me a surreptitious wink before disappearing into her house.

I give Ellis a nod to follow me into my place. "Do you guys learn poker face or how to be politely awkward at teacher school or something?" I ask as we go inside. I place Sara in her bouncing chair.

"What do you mean?"

"Florrie is a retired teacher."

Ellis laughs. "It all makes sense now."

When I turn back to him, he's looking at the photos I have on the wall, and I realize it's the first time he's been inside my place.

"Is this your family?" he asks.

"Yeah. I think I was five and Mikey was two. That was the year before…anyway…that's my mom and dad."

Ellis pulls me closer and wraps his arm around me, kissing my forehead.

"You all look so happy."

"Dad had just gotten a new job, so he took us all to the pier in Bridgeport. We got to go on the rides and have Slush Puppies."

He points to another photo.

"Is that your brother?"

"Yeah."

"You look very alike."

"People used to say that if it wasn't for the age difference, we'd be twins. There are photos of us as kids that even my mom struggled to tell which of us was in it because she kept all my clothes for him."

Ellis turns me to face him. I wrap my arms instinctively around his waist.

He runs his hands through my hair, resting them on my nape. I close my eyes and let myself relax under his touch.

Talking about my family is always hard for me, no matter how much I remember them daily. Somehow Ellis seems to know it.

He pulls me closer until we're hugging and kisses the side of my neck.

"I'm really looking forward to tomorrow," he says.

"Florrie and all?" I tease.

"Florrie and all."

I pull back to give him a kiss. The knowledge that he'll let me kiss him just how I want is the permission I need to believe that there may be something real between us. Small, but real.

22

ELLIS

FLORRIE IS A HOOT. I can only imagine what it would have been like to have her as a teacher.

As soon as we start the drive to the lake, she peppers me with all kinds of questions. She does it in such a sneaky way that I don't even feel like I'm being interrogated or assessed until Milo intervenes and asks her to stop pestering me.

Fortunately, she's still on the right side of appropriate, but there's no tricking her. She knows something's going on between Milo and me.

I stop pretending halfway through the journey and hold Milo's hand while I drive us through the country roads. That seems to put a stop to Florrie's questions.

The lake isn't far from Stillwater at all, but the place I want to take them is.

When we get there, I find a parking spot in a shaded area. There are a few family cars around, but not as many as I expected, considering it's a warm summer day and kids are on vacation.

"Florrie, do you want to take Sara while Milo helps me with the rest of the stuff?" I ask.

She takes Sara from the car seat as Milo stares at me. "Rest of the stuff?"

He follows me to the trunk and laughs when he sees everything inside.

"Are we spending the day or moving here?" he asks. "Just so you know, I'm good with bugs but not…general wildlife. You know, the kind that bites."

I pull him close and give him a kiss on the lips. "I'll protect you." When we pull back, he's blushing adorably. "Come on, you'll thank me later when it's hot."

We're on a fairly wide stretch of beach with a mix of sand and wild grass. We pick a spot, and Milo helps me build the small beach cabana that will provide us with shade as the sun moves across the sky.

After dropping Milo off yesterday, I went to my sister's and borrowed a few things from her, like the small inflatable boat that makes a perfect bed to keep Sara comfortable and safe when she falls asleep.

I had to confess to my plans and beg her not to crash our day out. Having Florrie with us is already putting a big spotlight on whatever this is between Milo and me. My sister would totally blow it out of proportion before we even figure it out ourselves.

Florrie stays in the shade with Sara while we do the last trip to grab a chair for Florrie and the cooler with the drinks and food.

I close the trunk and lock the car. "I think—" When I turn around, Milo is in my personal space, looking at me like he wants to eat me for brunch.

"You think…" he says, placing his hands on the car on either side of me.

I swallow. "That we have everything we need."

"Not quite." He presses me against the car and kisses me. My body instantly lights up, and I want more of him. I put my hands on his ass to keep him close and feel his body's reaction to our closeness, the meeting of our lips, the dueling of our tongues.

There seems to be no rush on his part to end the kiss, which is something I am easily on board with. As the intensity of our kissing subsides, so do our erections, thankfully.

"Now we have everything we need," he says.

"Maybe another pair of beach shorts on top of these would come in handy. I wasn't prepared."

He looks down at the bulge in my shorts.

"Maybe we can take care of that later."

"You can count on it."

We finally grab all the stuff and walk to our spot, where Florrie gives us a look before telling Sara, "I think your daddy's boss might have been looking for the ice chest at the back of your daddy's throat."

Milo groans, but I laugh because Florrie isn't wrong.

"How about we go check out the lake water, sweetpea?" Milo says to Sara.

He removes her clothes and dresses her in the cute navy swimsuit with white bows that I remember Marnie wearing when she was the same age.

I remove my shirt and put on sunscreen. Milo does the same, and we do each other's backs before putting a hat on Sara and lathering her with a protective layer of children's high-SPF sunscreen.

"Are you joining us, Florrie?" I ask.

"Nah, I'm happy sitting here watching people and reading my book. You go on ahead."

The water is cool but not as cold as I expected. It still takes my breath away as we go in slowly.

Sara's holding on to Milo. Her little hand closed in a fist around a clump of his hair.

We stop when we're short of waist deep.

"What do you say, sweetpea? Want to try out the water for size?" Milo asks.

He holds her out, and as soon as her toes touch the water, she pulls her legs up as far as she can.

"It's a bit cold, isn't it?" I ask.

Milo wets his hand and then touches Sara's feet. The more her feet get acclimatized to the temperature, the more she kicks, and before long, we're waist deep and she's kicking her legs in the water.

"Thank you for bringing us here, Ellis. I can't even remember the last time I came to the lake, and I certainly didn't know about this beach."

I straighten Sara's hat. "It's my pleasure. I admit I don't take days off like this often enough. It's nice."

"Why not?"

I shrug. "During the weekends, if I'm not seeing my family, I end up working and preparing my lessons for the week. And this summer, I've been busy with a few school projects I want to complete before the start of the year."

"It must be hard being a teacher. So much responsibility," he says.

"No more than being a parent, but I get to give them back," I joke. "I like it. Despite my parents' lifestyle, working and traveling all over the world, they never pressured us to do anything we didn't want. When I said I wanted to be a teacher, they were supportive. Just like when Darius said he wanted to be a nurse. For me, being a teacher gives me the opportunity to help all those young minds open themselves up for the future. I don't want to shape them. I want them to question the world, to be brave, and not be afraid to find out who they are."

Milo smiles. "I think I understand it. It's important for kids to have good role models, and I know it sometimes doesn't happen at home. My mom always encouraged us to follow our dreams."

"She sounds like she was an amazing woman."

Milo looks at Sara. "She was. I miss her a lot. She never batted an eyelid when I told her I was gay. She never once told me I couldn't be what I wanted to be."

"What did you want to be?"

"At the time? A cowboy. I was obsessed with old western movies."

I tilt my head and narrow my eyes. "I can see that. You'd make a great cowboy. Riding your horse, wearing your cowboy hat."

I reach for his hand under the water, and he laces his fingers with mine.

"Don't forget the boots. It's all about the boots," he says.

Sara reaches for me, so I take her from Milo's arms. "Hello, gorgeous." She's so beautiful. Her nose is just like Milo's, her eyes too. Probably because of the similarity between the brothers.

She looks at me and babbles like she's trying to make conversation.

"Well, I don't know about that. It's a little early for boys or girls, but you'll need to ask your daddy," I say, booping her nose. She giggles.

"Hell no. No boys, no girls, no nothing until you're at least… forty," Milo says.

"How did that turn out for you?"

He blushes and bites his lip.

I laugh. "You can't have a rule for her that you didn't follow yourself."

"Fine. Thirty then."

"Twenty."

"Twenty-five."

"Deal!" I hold out my hand to Sara for a high five, and she pulls it to her, holding two of my fingers in her little hands. "See? That's called negotiating."

"We should probably get in the shade for a while," he says.

"I have a better idea. Stay here."

I take Sara to the cabana and strap her into the inflatable chair I borrowed from my sister so Sara can see us.

"You two seemed deep in conversation out there," Florrie says, putting her book to one side.

"Milo is easy to talk to. It's easy to forget there's such an age gap between us."

"Does it bother you?"

"I don't know. Sometimes I think we should be into different things. We should find it harder to talk because we grew up in different times."

Florrie nods. "Should is such a powerful word, isn't it? My late husband should have married the girl he was engaged to. He should have followed in his father's footsteps. Instead, he ran away. One night, in the middle of a storm, he knocked on the door of an old farmhouse. He told me that as soon as I opened the door that night, he knew I was the girl he was going to marry." She looks out into the distance. "Sometimes we can be so stuck on what life should be that we forget what it could be."

A tear falls down her cheek and she swiftly wipes it clean. "Don't listen to the rambles of an old woman. What do I know, hey?"

"You care about Milo a lot, don't you?"

She looks at me. "We couldn't have children. In those days, it was different, especially where we lived. Medicine may have advanced in the city, but our doctor was still the one that helped my mom give birth to me. In any case, we were happy. Very happy. Milo is a gentle soul, a good man with a big heart. If I could ever ask for a son, I wouldn't mind if it was him. And he lets me indulge in pretending to be a granny to this precious little girl."

"Florrie…"

"Oh shush, enough of the emotional. Go out there and play with my boy in the water. I'll look after the little one."

I stand and lean over to give Florrie a kiss on her cheek, then I run to the water, diving in and bringing Milo down with me.

"Freaking fudgesickles, warn a man. I was not ready for that," he says, splashing water in my direction.

I grab his arm and pull him to me. "Are you ready for this?" I kiss him on the lips and then down his neck to his shoulder.

"Thank fuck the water is cold," he says, and I laugh.

We mess around in the water until our fingers look like prunes before joining the girls.

We share a towel to dry ourselves and then sit next to each other on another one.

Florrie takes her phone out from her pocket when it dings.

"Now that's what I'm talking about."

"What's that?" Milo asks, grabbing the cool bag to get Sara's lunch.

"The girls from the knitting club have recruited some helpers, and we're going to protest against that damned parking lot they want to build. Vera is getting supplies from Birchcraft to make signs and everything."

"Not that again," Milo says.

"Just because you don't want to get involved doesn't mean the rest of us want to watch as they destroy our community," Florrie says.

Milo looks at her like he wants to say something but then stops himself. He peels off the lid from Sara's yogurt and grabs her spoon from the bag.

Florrie makes eye contact with me.

There's definitely tension between them about the parking lot issue, but it's not something Milo and I have ever discussed.

"I heard Tyler is talking about a cleanup operation at the playground to convince the council to drop the application," Florrie says. "You know about that, don't you, Ellis?"

Milo looks at me.

"I…yeah, I met up with him and a couple of friends after the town council meeting."

Milo frowns and goes back to feeding Sara.

"Anyway, what's this knitting club about, Florrie? Can anyone join?" I change the subject to avoid any more tension.

It takes Milo a while to come out of his head and be more himself while Florrie tells us how the knitting club is the best place to be for all the gossip because everyone there is either related or knows someone who works in the various businesses in town, including the mayor's office.

The rest of the day goes by peacefully, and we even manage to get Florrie to the water's edge to get her feet wet.

By the time we're pulling up at Milo's and Florrie's homes, Sara is fast asleep in the car seat. She had a great day and exhausted herself by trying to stand on her own while holding on to Milo.

She even loved when we sat on the water's edge and the small waves kept coming in and getting her wet while she grabbed clumps of sand that we tried very hard to make sure didn't go in her mouth.

Florrie retreats into her place, and I follow Milo into his.

Sara wakes up while he's giving her a bath, but after a bottle of formula, she's out again, so he takes her to her bedroom.

"Where's your bedroom?" I ask. When I was here yesterday, it didn't occur to me that I'd only seen two additional doors in the small house. One of them I now know is the bathroom and the other is Sara's nursery.

"Why? Want to take advantage of me, Mr. Bradford?" Milo asks, taking my hand and pulling me closer. He nuzzles my neck and inhales, causing all my hairs to stand to attention and my dick to react.

"I might."

"Then you're standing in it." He runs his hands up until they're behind my neck, keeping me in place while he kisses me with as much heat as he did this morning against the car.

"Where do you want me?" I gasp when he releases my lips.

23

MILO

WHERE DO YOU WANT ME?

Is Ellis really asking what I think he's asking?

"Maybe here." I push him to face the nearest wall. "Arms up."

He does as I command, and I remove his shirt. I kiss the middle of his back between the shoulder blades. He moans, pushing his ass back.

"Or maybe…here…" I take his hand and turn him so his back is to the kitchen sink. I fall to my knees, pulling his shorts down with me.

He's hard and needy. I never thought I'd love having this kind of power over someone, but hearing Ellis moan as I stroke his dick and nuzzle against his balls is an addicting sound.

I take his shoes off and then stand to meet him face to face.

"You're a little overdressed," he says.

"It seems we have a habit of ending up in this predicament, Mr. Bradford."

He laughs.

"Tell me. Do you usually lose your clothes this quickly?"

He looks straight into my eyes. "I never lose anything, Milo. My clothes, my mind, or my willpower. Except when I'm with you."

I have to take a deep, steady breath to keep from turning him around and fucking him until we've both forgotten our names.

No, I have a bed, and I intend to use it.

"If this is your room, do you sleep standing up?"

I shrug. "I've been known to do it, especially just after Sara was born and I was practically a zombie."

"Hmm…" He puts a finger to his lips. "If there's no bed…where are you going to fuck me?"

I growl. Fuck me. I growl.

"Just remember, my old bones might not enjoy the floor as much as a comfortable bed or couch," he says.

I look down at his erection. "You don't have a problem with your boners, from what I see."

"And you still have too many clothes on. Like, all of them," he moans.

I pull down the Murphy bed from the cabinet in the wall.

"Space saver," I say before I throw him on the bed. He pulls me with him, and his hands get busy trying to undress me while we kiss again.

"God, I love your body," he says.

"Ditto."

We wrestle to get me out of my clothes because we can't stop touching and kissing. It's as if a switch has flipped in both of us and it's a race to heaven.

"Fuck." I knee him in his thigh, trying to get out of my shorts. "Sorry. At least it wasn't your balls."

"No, but you can apologize to them too."

"My pleasure."

I travel down his body but don't spend much time in any particular area. My goal is to suck his dick and eat his ass before I prep him.

"God, your cock is beautiful." I take his head into my mouth and suck.

He cants his hips, asking for more, and I oblige.

"Turn around," he says.

"What?"

"Turn around and let me suck you."

I let go of his dick with a pop.

"Can't. If you do, I'll come in three seconds flat," I say.

"Milo," he says with the calmest of voices. "Let me make you come to take the edge off. I promise to help you recover so you can fuck me."

I fall on the mattress, partly across from him. "Fuck, you drive a hard bargain."

He covers my body with his and kisses me. I open my legs to give him space, and he lines up our cocks.

I don't even know if we're the right way up on the bed or across it. All I know is that Ellis's cock rubbing against mine will be enough to make me come if he doesn't stop it.

"Ellis…" I moan.

He wraps his hand around my cock and strokes it slowly, twisting his wrist and tightening his grip. The more I beg, the less he gives me.

I grab a pillow and put it over my face because I can't risk waking Sara. This is going to be one motherfucker of an orgasm. I can already feel it building.

He releases my cock and replaces his hand with his mouth. My ears ring and my breathing is labored. Who knew Ellis Bradford, the teacher with the gentle manner, could be such a surprise in bed?

I open my legs wider to give him a hint, and he takes it because the pad of his finger massages my rim. It's too much sensation with his mouth bobbing up and down on my cock, the sucking, the wet warmth, the fact that it's Ellis.

Before I can warn him, my balls draw up tight and my orgasm takes over. My body makes so many involuntary jerks that, for a brief second, his finger breaches the ring of muscle in my ass. That just draws out the pleasure even more.

I feel like I've just run a marathon. My heart is racing, my dick is extra sensitive, and I'm still hard.

There's movement on the bed, but I'm too dead to check what he's doing.

A second later, something wet cleans my dick, and then I feel him line his body next to mine. He lifts a corner of the pillow.

"Are you alive?"

"Barely, you motherfucker," I say. "What kind of fucking special ninja blowjob skills are those?"

He chuckles and removes the pillow from my face, placing it under my head.

"I didn't do anything you wouldn't in my place."

"Yeah, fair enough. I can't move now though. I want to. But you deceased me."

He rests his head on his forearm and faces me. I put my arm around him, and he cuddles against me, placing one leg over mine.

"You didn't come," I say.

"I wasn't supposed to. I'm saving it for later. Us old guys can't get it up as often as you."

"Don't say that."

"What?"

"Don't refer to yourself like you're some kind of old grandpa. Especially because I'm not into grandpas, but I'm very much into you." I turn my face to him. "I really don't care about our age difference, Ellis."

He goes silent, and I think I've lost him to his thoughts. "You say that now, but you can't deny that there's a significant age gap, Milo. You're in the prime of your life. This is all great fun, but you'll want to find someone you can grow old with."

I tilt his head so he has to not only hear what I'm saying but see it in my eyes too.

"My parents never grew old together. My brother will forever be young. We only have now, and now? All I want is you."

I kiss him before he can argue and don't stop until he's mush in my arms and his dick is hard again. Mine shows signs of recovery but not enough for a full hard-on.

"Tell me more about your family. Where's Sara's mom?"

I close my eyes and try to remember Sienna's beautiful face as I saw her for the last time.

"Is this a painful thing to talk about? I'm sorry. I didn't mean—"

"It's okay. I don't talk about her enough, and I should so I don't forget her." One day, I'll want to tell Sara about her mom. The good parts, at least. I want her to know she was wanted and loved.

"There was a period of about two, almost three years where my brother disappeared. We had this massive argument where I tried to convince him to straighten up, get a job, and we'd support each other. He left that night and didn't come back for two years."

"I'm so sorry, Milo."

I caress his cheek. I know he's telling the truth and not just doing what everyone else does. There's no pity. No poor Milo. Just understanding.

"Shh, this is my story. Anyway, one night, there's a knock on the door, and he's there. He looks good, healthy, happy. With him was this girl he met at some point during the time he was away. Her name was Sienna. She was beautiful, funny, caring. I knew it was because of her that my brother got his act together. We hit it off straight away, and she became like a little sister to me."

My throat chokes, so I reach for Ellis's hand and lace our fingers together.

"They moved in with me because they didn't have anywhere to go. I gave them my room and started using this bed. Shortly after, they found out Sienna was pregnant. I've never seen my brother so happy. I thought I was finally going to have another chance at being a real family."

"What happened then?"

"It was hard for him to get a job in a town where he was the catalyst for most of the stuff that turned this neighborhood into what it is now. He was getting more stressed the closer it came to Sienna giving birth. I should have seen it coming, but I was so happy that I became blind to him defaulting to his old behaviors. Coming home late. Mentioning some of his old friends."

I take a breath. Ellis holds me tighter as if trying to remind me where I am.

"The night Sienna's water broke, I couldn't reach Mikey. I left loads of messages on his phone, but he never called back. I was there when Sara was born. I held Sienna's hand as she brought the most precious gift into the world and, at that moment, I forgot about my brother. In the morning, two police officers came in asking for me. They told me my brother had been shot during a drug deal gone wrong. He died trying to protect a police officer his friend shot at."

"Oh, Milo."

"The change in Sienna was immediate. When she had to register the baby, she put my name on the birth certificate. I tried to argue that Mikey should be the named father. He was Sara's father. But she just looked at me and said he'd made a decision that night and didn't get to be anyone's father. Once again, I was blind to what was happening around me. We were both grieving, so I didn't notice when Sienna started changing her language. She spoke like there was no future. She said I was going to look after Sara so well. That she was so lucky to have me as her dad.

"Sara was five weeks old when Sienna took her life. She left a letter for me and a for Sara to read when she's older. My letter just contained an apology and said she knew I'd look after Sara like she never could."

"Once again, it was only you, but now you had this tiny baby to look after," Ellis says.

"Believe it or not, it helped. The steep learning curve into parenthood made me put aside my pain to focus on Sara. Then Florrie moved in next door. We've been a family of sorts ever since. It's been almost ten months since Mikey died and eight since Sienna. Some days it all feels so far away, like it never happened. Other days, the pain is so alive like it's happening right now."

"I'm really sorry that happened to you. I can't even comprehend the pain you must have felt and the strength you needed to move on. Now that I know your story, all the gentle, shy smiles you always had for me whenever I went shopping mean so much more. I wish I had an ounce of your strength."

The way Ellis says it makes me wonder if there's something behind the statement, but I'm tired of the heavy stuff. I want to go back to feeling light and happy because I have my absolute crush and all-time-sexiest man in my arms.

I flip us so I'm on top of him.

"I believe I owe you an orgasm, and you promised me I could have this." I run my hand down his side until I reach his ass and squeeze his butt cheek. "I wouldn't want to break a promise, would I?"

"I hope not."

I reach over to the bedside table to get supplies, and then I remember I'm out of condoms.

"Fuck."

"What's up?"

"I don't have any condoms. I haven't been with anyone in a long time. I've been tested since, and I'm negative, but I can't afford PrEP, even with my insurance," I say.

"My last relationship was exclusive, but I got tested when it ended. Haven't been with anyone since."

I look into his eyes.

"Are we good?"

He smiles. "We're good. But I'll be even better once you get your dick inside me."

24

ELLIS

"I NEVER PEGGED you as a demanding bottom," Milo says, grabbing the small bottle of lube. "Always so calm and collected every time I saw you."

He places the bottle on my stomach. "If this bottle moves an inch…"

I laugh, and he gives me a serious look, placing the bottle back after it slides onto the bedsheets.

"And I never pegged you for a teasing top," I bite back. "Always so shy and couldn't put one word in front of the other."

"I was only shy because I had a massive crush on you and didn't want to make a fool of myself. Now…like I was saying, if the bottle moves, I get to pick where I come."

"And if the bottle doesn't move?"

"I still get to pick where I come, but you will also come."

I drop my head on the pillow. "Fuck."

"We'll get to that. Now open up."

I raise my legs, careful to mind the bottle. This would be so much easier if I had abs, but I've never in my life had any definition in my stomach other than flat, which it no longer is. I put that wish aside and focus on breathing through my chest.

Milo runs his blunt nails over the back of my legs. I feel goosebumps rise on my skin. My cock is impossibly hard, but he's not getting anywhere near it.

"You look so good like this," he says. "Your ass fills out a pair of pants like nothing I've ever seen, but I like it better when it's filling my hand." He kneads both globes of my ass and lowers his head.

I prepare myself for the feeling of his tongue on my hole and hope I'll last longer than last time, but he kisses and teases me everywhere except where I need him.

"Are you trying to kill—ugh…fuck, yes," I cry when I finally feel his warm tongue in the right place.

"Shh, be quiet, or it'll be game over for both of us."

"Sorry, but Christ, Milo. Do that again, please." I'm not beneath begging or indulging in something that feels so good. Which is the reason I keep buying those damn brioches and my stomach is no longer flat.

"You taste so good. I could be here forever," he says against my hole. More goosebumps, and then he's seeking entry with his tongue.

I reach for my dick because it all feels so good and I need more. I also discreetly reposition the bottle so it's in a better position.

I'm not cheating myself out of an orgasm.

"I saw that," he says, grabbing the bottle and squirting a good amount of lube on his fingers and some directly on my hole.

"Shit."

He comes up to kiss me, but his hand stays put, with his finger gently massaging my rim.

"Afraid I won't let you come?" he asks, kissing my jaw.

His finger presses harder on my hole, and I relax to let it in. Once it's in, he crooks it, finding my prostate straight away. My body convulses, and I have to hold on to Milo and think of rotten food, sports, or something to stop myself from coming too soon.

"Not anymore. You keep doing that, and I'll come before your dick is in me."

I turn my face to kiss him, and he swallows every moan I let out while he's opening me.

"Are you okay?" he asks.

I nod. "Please, Milo."

He sits back, and I watch his face as he lines up his cock with my hole. The look of concentration and self-restraint tells me we're so much on the same page.

Milo has a decent-size cock, so it takes a few tries until he's able to release his hand and just use his hips to push through.

"God, you feel so big," I say.

"You can take me, Ellis. Just relax a little, baby."

Our eyes meet when he uses the term of endearment, and for a split second, I see the old Milo back. Unsure if what he said was okay or afraid of how I might react. I just kiss him and wrap my legs around his waist.

He responds to my kiss, pushing forward and settling more of his body weight on me.

Before long, he's fully seated inside me.

"Fuck, you're tight. Tell me when I can move," he says.

His balls are resting against my ass. My cock is hard and trapped between us. Sweat runs down his brow, and I know we're both hanging by a thread.

"Move, Milo. Give me everything you have. Show me how much you want me. Make me forget everything else."

"Fuuuck." He pulls back a little and pushes in.

I gasp, and he does it again and again until he's practically fully withdrawing his cock before slamming into me again.

Every other time he does it, he changes the angle so he's hitting my prostate.

"I'm close, baby," he says without stopping. I take my cock and stroke it until I'm on edge.

My orgasm builds until it's right on the crest. I know I don't need anything else other than Milo.

"I'm ready, Milo. Do it."

He rests his face in the crook of my neck and his moves become jerkier, less refined and controlled. I feel his moans against my skin and have to pull the other pillow onto my face.

We're practically glued to one another. The only part of him that moves are his hips as he nails me faster and harder, seeking his relief.

I come without needing to touch myself. An orgasm so strong that I bite the pillow.

The aftershocks are still reeling through my body when I feel the warmth of Milo's release inside me. He's panting against my neck.

I put the pillow to one side now that I no longer need it.

Neither of us moves. His cock is still hard inside me, but I feel it slowly softening.

He pulls back, and with energy I certainly don't feel, kneels and watches as his release leaves my body.

Our eyes meet, and then he looks down again.

"I wish I could be inside you longer," he says.

I smile. "I'm sure there will be some of you left behind, even after I clean up."

He pulls me into a sitting position, and I scrunch my face at the thought of the mess on his sheets.

"Let's have a shower. Then you can help me change the sheets."

"Yes, boss," I say teasingly. He slaps my ass.

We have to take turns in the shower because his doesn't fit both of us. Milo lets me go first, for obvious reasons, while he grabs the towels and then disappears for a while.

Unlike him, I'm happy checking him out while he has his shower.

"You're a pervert," he says but puts on a show for me, sensually stroking his cock with one soap-covered hand while thoroughly cleaning his balls and ass with the other.

"How can you even get half-hard after two orgasms?"

He comes out of the shower dripping wet, so I throw him a towel. I have mine wrapped around my waist as I lean against the sink.

"That's not me," he says, wrapping his towel around his waist, water still dripping from his hair onto his chest. "That's all you."

He kisses me, and I'm tempted to see if he can go a third round, but it's getting late.

"I'd love if you could stay the night, but I'm working tomorrow, and you might not want to be here when Florrie comes over to babysit Sara."

"That's okay." I grab a small towel and dry his hair. "I'll see you in the soup kitchen on Tuesday?"

"Definitely."

"We could grab some food after or before, whichever works better for you."

He smiles. "Pick me up from the store at four. There's a place on the road to Windsor that sells the best and cheapest crab rolls in the world."

"Is that your expert opinion?"

"Sure is."

"Okay then, it's a date."

We get dressed, and I see he's made the bed with fresh sheets.

I get back in my car to drive home.

This is definitely the right decision, but I wonder if there will ever be an opportunity to spend a night with Milo or if we'll just have these brief moments together.

I berate myself for even thinking about it. Am I not the only one worried about the sixteen-year age gap between us?

Besides, we've just spent a whole day together, not to mention had the best sex I've ever had. I need to just enjoy this while it lasts.

25

ELLIS

"Okay, you were right. Those were the best crab rolls I've ever had," I say, wiping my mouth with a napkin and finishing my drink.

"Told you so."

We're sitting outside the small dive. There's a bench with a view of the valley below, which is filled with rows upon rows of purple.

"This place is stunning," I say.

"I used to bring my mom here. We'd spend hours looking at the view. That's Reed Knox's lavender farm down below."

"Really? I know Reed. He helped out in the spring with the fair. I didn't realize his farm was this huge."

"Yeah, and apparently, Aiden Lawton and his husband live around here too."

"No way, *the* A. Lawton? The author?"

"Yup."

"Can't say I blame them. Can you imagine waking up every morning to a view like this?"

Milo smiles. "It's a nice dream to have."

"Come on, let's get back to town before we're late and Tyler fires us," I joke.

Milo calls Florrie to check on Sara while I drive us back. I find my usual parking spot by the church and we walk into the hall together.

Tyler looks at me and then at Milo.

"Everything okay?" I ask.

"Sure. Milo, Emy, is sick today. She picked up some bug her kid brought home from kindergarten. I'm going to need you out front if that's okay."

Milo tenses. "Um…are you sure?"

Tyler comes over to Milo and puts a hand on his shoulder. "I need you there. If there are any issues, we'll deal with it, okay?"

Milo nods.

We prepare the hall together while the others work on the food.

"What did Tyler mean?"

"Nothing, it's not important."

We're carrying a table over to the center of the hall.

"Milo, I saw your reaction to Tyler's request. It's not nothing."

He ignores me and lines up the table with the others, then goes back to the stack of chairs.

"Milo—"

"Just leave it, okay? It's really nothing."

He clearly doesn't want to talk about it, and I doubt Tyler will say anything, but it doesn't mean I'll take my eyes off Milo until the end of the shift.

People spill in at the usual time, gathering in their groups.

I notice a few looks in Milo's direction.

Milo himself is trying everything not to look up. He's filled the cutlery baskets and brought the bread out, but every time he finishes something, he doesn't make eye contact with anyone.

Tyler rings the bell and the line builds.

Milo is between Dave and me, serving soup.

The usual whispers get louder as people approach our stations. I start to make out what they're saying.

"I can't believe it. If I didn't need this food so much, I'd stop coming here."

"That family." The words are said with such venom that I see Milo recoil a little.

One by one people pass us, but no one picks the soup.

"I heard rumors he worked in the back but never saw him."

"That poor little girl. Would be better off with a foster family."

That does it for me. Whatever the hell they're talking about, I'm not letting anyone question Milo's parenting.

I step onto a chair and ring the bell.

"Can I have your attention, please?" Close to a hundred faces stare at me. "I'm new here, as you know, but I've attempted to get to know you, and I'd like to think we can talk when things get tough. I don't know what's happening, but I've been hearing a lot of words directed at Milo that no one should have to hear. Especially not when they're working, giving up their time to make sure you have a good meal every night you come here. The reason you're here is because you all know you can't take anything in life for granted, but slapping the hand that feeds you is not right. That's all. Please resume your meal."

I step down from the chair and see the team staring at me.

Tyler looks furious, and Milo is no longer there.

I walk over to Tyler. "I'm sorry. I couldn't listen to it anymore."

"He's gone out back," he bites out, but I ignore him.

I go through the double doors, but Milo isn't in the kitchen. There are a few other rooms through a hallway, so I try every single one until I find him sitting in a corner with his knees pulled up to hide his face.

"Milo." I go over and kneel beside him.

"You had no right," he says without looking up.

"I couldn't stand there listening to what they were saying."

He looks up, and his face is covered in tears. "It wasn't your place to defend me. I could have finished the shift, and next time I'd be back in the kitchen, and everyone would forget they ever saw me here."

I wipe the tears from his face. "Milo, I thought you were the most unforgettable person I've ever seen, and that was even before you spoke to me. I'm so sorry I did something that's hurting you. Please tell me what's wrong, what I did wrong, so I don't do it again."

"They all hate me and my family."

"Why?"

"My dad worked at the mill in Chester Falls. He had just been promoted when there were rumors about the factory closing down.

The neighborhood was like a family, so they all went to him, hoping he could convince his bosses to keep the factory open. When they didn't, they blamed my dad. Said he didn't try hard enough. Said that because he was a manager, he probably got a settlement while everyone else got nothing. It was all a lie. My mom told me they promoted him to use him as the go-between for the factory workers and higher management. He did the dirty work while they kept their hands clean, and he never got one cent, just like everyone else."

I sit on the floor and pull Milo into my arms.

"You must have been a child. How can any of this be your fault?"

"I was six, Mikey was three, and my mom was pregnant. My dad tried to find another job, but it was hard. Dad traveled for hours every day because he could only get a job somewhere that no one knew about the factory or him. My dad started drinking, and there were a lot of arguments about how they could afford another child. My dad took out a life insurance policy, and then one night, he drove into a tree to make it look like an accident. He thought that when he died, we'd all be taken care of, but the coroner said there wasn't enough alcohol in his blood to make him lose control of the car. The police investigation concluded from the weather conditions and lack of any tire marks on the road that it wasn't an accident. Mom never got any insurance money, and then she lost the baby because of the stress and grief. She was going to have a girl."

"Oh, Milo." I kiss the top of his head. "You know this is still not your fault, and people shouldn't talk to you like it was."

"That's not the worse part."

26

MILO

FOR THE SECOND time in less than a week, I'm reliving the wounds of my past. The history that follows me everywhere in this town because I can't afford to escape.

For a hair's breadth of a moment, I thought I had a chance with Ellis, but who would stay with someone with so much baggage?

"Tell me, Milo."

His voice is soft, almost soothing. I don't hear any judgment, so I tell him the rest. At least he'll know, and then he can decide for himself.

"Most people stopped talking to my mom. Things were hard, but we managed, except Mikey was too young to remember when people were nice to us. All he ever saw was the nastiness, so he rebelled. Petty theft. Threatening people for no reason. Doing drugs. Mom didn't know what to do to help him. He was so angry all the time, and she worked two jobs to keep our heads above water. As he grew older, the crime and drugs got worse. The neighborhood became a hell to live in. Some of his friends died of an overdose, and some ended up in juvie, but he always got out of trouble. We couldn't afford to move away, then Mom got sick. I dropped out of high school to work to help her out. After Mom died, I tried to keep us together, but that only lasted three years. As soon as Mikey turned eighteen, he left."

"When people hurt, it's harder to forgive those that hurt them. Even when the truth is staring them in the face. They know it's not your fault, but you're the only one they can aim their anger at."

"It wouldn't be so bad if they were just angry with me. But Sara is a baby. This isn't her fault. She never asked to be born. If I could, I would take her away from here, from Stillwater. We'd start all over again in a new place where no one knows us."

Ellis holds me tighter. "Where would that leave me? Who'd scan my groceries? Who would I lust over when I stare at my backyard?"

"What? You...still want me?"

Ellis cleans my tears and cradles my face so I have to look at him.

"I don't *still* want you. I want you, Milo. My want isn't conditional. Hell, it's not even up to me. It's just there, like a living thing I can't control."

He leans over and kisses me. It's gentle and caring, and I'm half a heartbeat away from falling all the way in love with Ellis.

I miss his lips when he breaks our kiss.

"Can I ask you something?" he asks.

"Sure."

"The way you reacted when Florrie mentioned the playground at the lake. Does it have anything to do with this?"

I look down at my hands, but he takes them in his, making me look at him again.

"She wants me to fight for the playground. Fight for the good memories."

"And you don't want to?"

"Many times when I was playing there, kids used to repeat to me the stuff their parents would say at home. It hurts when I think about all those memories. When I think about it becoming a parking lot, I'm ashamed to feel relief that I won't have to face those memories. The good ones, like Mom pushing me on the swing or Mikey hanging from the monkey bars pretending to be a real-life monkey...they almost feel like they're not real memories. Detaching myself from the playground issue is the coward's way out, I know."

"I can understand that, and you're anything but a coward. You're the bravest person I know, Milo."

I take a deep breath and try to get up. I won't go out into the hall, but I can still do the dishes. Ellis stops me.

"Why do you volunteer here?" he asks.

"Because I want to help those who are less fortunate. I don't have much, but so far, I've managed…well, mostly…to keep food on the table."

Ellis tells me about the first time he saw me here. I feel my face heat from embarrassment.

"Hey, you don't need to be ashamed. You work so hard and never complain about it. You appreciate when people do nice things for you. You don't take anything for granted."

I lean on him so much that I'm practically in his lap and rest my head against his.

"I think I've been in survival mode for so long that I don't know how else to be."

He kisses my lips gently. "You have Florrie, me, my family. We're all here for you. The question is, can you let go of the past so you can heal and move on?"

"You think I should fight for the playground?"

"No. I think you should do whatever feels right for you. You don't need to be involved with anything unless it serves you."

I try to stand, and this time, Ellis doesn't stop me.

He follows me out of the room.

Dave is in the kitchen doing the pans when we walk in. He doesn't say anything but gives me an encouraging smile as I head toward the double doors.

I take a deep breath and go through.

Most people are still in the hall, so I take the bell and stand on the same chair Ellis did.

"Can I have your attention, please? Most of you know me, and most of you think you know the truth about what happened with my family. I don't owe anyone my story, but all I ask is that you look at what's in front of you. I've lost my whole family apart from the one gift my brother left me. You see me at the grocery store. You see me raising a child I love more than anyone can imagine. I was one of you when I was six and barely understood what was happening, and I'm still one of you now. I will continue to volunteer here like I've done since the first day. I hope, whatever your opinion of me is, that you either speak to me, get to know me, or move on. Life is already hard enough in this neighborhood for us to turn on each other."

I step down from the chair and stand behind the soup I was supposed to serve earlier.

My hands are shaking from adrenaline, and I half expect everyone to boo me out of the hall.

Instead, something else happens. One by one, everyone stands and starts lining up in front of my post.

"Can I have a small portion, please?" someone asks.

I take a bowl from the stack and serve her the soup. Within minutes, the soup is gone.

"As far as olive branches go, that was kind of awesome," Anne says. "Thank you."

I look at Ellis, and his proud smile warms me and gives me strength. He would have supported me if I hadn't done this, I know that. But I did it for Sara and for me. We both have a place in the community and deserve to be treated kindly.

At the end of the evening, Ellis walks me home.

Sara is asleep and Florrie is reading her book when we come in.

"Oh, my lovely boy," she says, almost in tears. "I'm so proud of you."

"That knitting club gossip mill sure does run overtime," Ellis says.

Florrie waves him off and goes to her place.

Ellis follows me to the nursery when I go to check in on Sara.

"She's so precious," he says.

"She's my whole heart."

Sara never stirs as we talk. Ellis gives me a good-night kiss and leaves.

It takes a couple of seconds for my brain to catch up. I run outside.

"Ellis."

He turns around. "Yeah?"

"I'm working a late shift tomorrow. Do you want to stay over?"

He smiles and walks back in my direction. When he's close enough, I pull him to me and give him the kind of kiss that promises more.

"I thought you'd never ask."

27

ELLIS

"PLEASE DON'T BE WEIRD," I beg.

"Pfft, who me?" Fletcher says. "Like I would ever. But I called it first, so whoever gets the next round, I'm getting a bubble…double."

Harrison rolls his eyes. "You're getting a double glass of water. That's what you're getting."

Fletcher pouts. "This isn't fair. What's my reward then?"

Harrison whispers something into Fletcher's ear that makes his entire face go bright red, which is always more visible when he wears his long blond hair in a bun, like today.

"Okay, I can be on board with that."

Levi comes in with the drinks. I slip out of the booth so he can sit next to Arlo.

"Can someone explain to me why I'm the last one to know? Where are my bartender privileges? You're supposed to pour your heart out, then I make you *the* best cocktail in the world, and we're friends happily ever after."

"That's it. I'm going if you're all going to be weird about it." I stand.

"Where are you going?"

Four big grins face me as the voice behind me puts a smile on my face.

I turn around, and Milo has his hands in his jeans pockets. His smile is shy and uncertain. A reminder of the person I met all those months ago, but now I know he has depth, confidence, and a sense of humor.

"Hi," I say.

"Hi."

"Awwww, they're so cute together," Fletcher says behind me.

I roll my eyes, and Milo smiles.

"Where's Tyler?" I ask.

"He's parking the car."

"Can I talk to you outside?"

He frowns. "Sure." And then he follows me.

Before we get to the front door of The Academy, I pull Milo into the hallway that leads to the restrooms.

"I thought—" he starts, but I stop him with a kiss. His hands come up to hold my shirt as I press him against the wall.

He tastes like strawberry, which is Sara's new favorite fruit. He must have had some too. It's delicious and refreshing, or maybe that's just how Milo always tastes.

"Wow." He puts his fingers to his mouth, and I love that his lips are already swollen from my kiss.

Since when am I so possessive?

"I missed you," I say, and he melts into my arms.

"I missed you too. Sorry I couldn't work at your place this weekend. Gerald is being a dick again."

A big part of me wants to go to the store and put Gerald in his place, but I know that's wrong. I can't interfere with Milo's primary job, no matter how much I want to punch his manager.

"Come on, let's join the group, or they'll come to find us."

"Did you want anything? Why are we here?"

"I did, and I got it," I say, giving him a peck on the lips. "I would have done it in front of the guys, but as you can tell from their stupid grins, they're ridiculously and unexplainably invested in our relationship."

Milo smiles. "So we're in a relationship then?"

"Are you seeing anyone else?"

"Nope," he says, shaking his head with an even bigger smile.

"Me neither."

He pulls my hips against his, and I feel the tell-tale sign of his arousal.

"In that case, if you're not busy later, maybe you can take me to your place and…" Someone walks past us to the bathroom.

"And…?"

"Take me to your place, and I'll fill the blanks later," he says.

"Can you stay the night?"

He nods. "Florrie has Sara. It was actually her idea." He bites his lip. "Apparently, we're not as quiet as we think, and the walls are paper thin. Florrie said her friend Vera introduced her to gay romance novels. They're quite…descriptive. She says she doesn't want to think about what we might be doing on the other side of the wall now that she's read about what…might be happening on the other side of the wall."

"I guess I can understand that. And as a bonus, I get to keep you all night." I take his hand and we walk back to the group.

Tyler has arrived and already has a drink, so I grab one from the bar for Milo and join them.

"There's never a dull moment in this town," Arlo says. "First, we saved the craft fair from the claws of that woman, then we saved the school Spring Fair, and now we're trying to save a playground. For a place called Stillwater, not much stands still."

"Sorry I'm late." Sage pulls out a chair and sits at the end of the booth. "Hi, all…Milo…"

He says Milo's name like he's more than pleasantly surprised.

"Hey," Milo answers back.

"It's been a while," Sage says.

From the corner of my eye, I catch the guys looking at each other, but my eyes are on Milo.

"Yeah, it has," he says.

"If you want to catch up, just give me a call anytime."

What the fuck?

"Is it me, or do we need to start saving a bigger table? These booths are cozy and all, but in case no one noticed, it's summer," Harrison says.

"Quite true," Levi says. "I suggested to the owners we should invest in bigger ones for larger groups of friends. The glass partitions help keep the noise down."

"Anyway," Tyler says. "You guys up for helping clean up the playground or what?"

It's a yes all around, but I can't take my eyes off Milo. He's not exactly uncomfortable with Sage's presence. I've been to his store, Birchcraft, and Sage helped a lot with the Spring Fair. Is there something between them? Or maybe there was in the past?

I put my hand on Milo's thigh under the table, and he looks at me and smiles. Then he laces our fingers together.

"The knitting club ladies are fierce," Sage says. "They're ready to burn their bras in front of town hall, but they've had an idea to do a silent protest."

"Shoot," Tyler says.

"We go around the neighborhood and ask people if they have old photos of kids playing at the park before it was overgrown. We blow up the photos and put them on an exhibition wall in the middle of the playground. It shows people the history of the playground and community."

Is it normal for me to dislike Sage a little for bringing forward such a great idea?

It's definitely not normal for me, or for any sane adult.

"I love that," Fletcher says. "Arlo and I could paint around the photos. Some frames or something artier."

We spend an hour making plans for the photograph exhibit before we move on to the more important part. The cleanup, which will require some expertise.

"I can't really do weekends," Milo says. "I can start with the grounds. Pulling weeds and turning the soil to prepare the areas that will eventually have grass. But I need to do it around my grocery job."

"Why's that?" Sage asks.

"Um...because during the weekend, I'm usually at Ellis's place."

Sage looks at me, and then it's like something clicks. "Oh my god. I'm really sorry about earlier. I didn't know you two were a thing. Not that I have a habit of hitting on just anyone."

Arlo coughs, and Sage gives him the finger. "But Milo and I have been…we've known each other a long time. I'm sorry, Ellis."

I smile. "No harm done. What Milo means is that he's been working in my backyard during the weekends."

"I'll bet," Fletcher says, wiggling his eyebrows.

Everyone looks at Harrison. He raises both hands in apology. "Hey, I didn't break him. He came to me like this. You knew him first. I just love his crazy."

"Awww, baby. I love you too."

They're kind of adorable to watch.

"Hold on, so does that mean you're not…" Sage says.

"No, they totally are," Levi replies.

"Ugh, the best ones are always taken."

"Can we focus on the job at hand?" Levi asks. "We need to pick up Ava from my sister's place, or she'll want to stay the night."

Tyler raises his hand. "I know some guys who might help restore the swings and the slides. I'll get back to you on that."

"Okay, sounds like everyone has a job," I say. "Look at the time. It's getting late."

I get up and pull Milo with me.

"Yeah, nine o'clock is totally the new midnight," Fletcher says.

Milo leans against me, and I put my arm around his back.

"Nice to see you all," he says. "You too, Sage."

We walk out to my car.

"I guess that went well," Milo says.

"The guys behaved."

"What do you mean?"

I unlock the car, and he gets into the passenger seat.

"They've been teasing me about you since the summer festival."

Milo's expression is one of shock before he hides his face in his hands.

"God, I'm such a loser. I saw you there, and I was so nervous. I don't know if I wanted to ask you about the GED for the GED or just talk to you somewhere outside the store. It clearly didn't go that well because I could barely string together a sentence."

I pull him closer to give him a kiss. "You were so adorably dorky. I just wanted to take you home and look after you."

He bites his lip again. "Well then, what are you waiting for?"

28

MILO

THE DRIVE to Ellis's place is filled with tension…the sexual kind.

I haven't seen him in days, and we haven't had any time together since last week. I'm so desperate for him. I palm my erection through my jeans.

"That meeting took far too long," I say.

We stop at a red light and Ellis sees what I'm up to. He almost growls and places his hand over mine, applying pressure. My cock fills to an uncomfortable level.

"In case you didn't notice, that wasn't a meeting. That was the guys making sure you passed their assessment."

I laugh. "I know what cereal they prefer for breakfast. If I'd known it was a test, I would have made my own presentation beforehand." I place my hand over Ellis's, encouraging him to rub my cock.

The light turns green, but he doesn't take his hand away. Instead, he unbuttons my jeans and puts his hand inside, stroking me through my underwear.

"Fuck…Ellis. That feels so good…" I let my head fall back against the headrest and close my eyes.

"They can assess all they want, but it doesn't change the outcome," he says.

I'm not sure how he expects me to keep up with an actual conversation when he pulls my boxer shorts down just enough so he can tease my cockhead.

"Hmm…" I bite my lip. "What's the…outcome?"

He pulls into his driveway and turns the car off before tucking my dick back into my jeans and pulling me in for a kiss.

"The outcome is that you're going to fuck me against the wall as soon as we get inside."

He puts a small packet of lube in my hand and gets out of the car.

I scramble to get out after him, almost getting stuck in the seatbelt in the rush.

"Shit."

He locks the car from the front door of the house just as I catch up to him.

We stumble into the hallway, kissing and groping each other. Locking the front door is almost an afterthought when he presses me against it and pushes the lock in place without even stopping his assault on my mouth.

"God, I missed these lips," he says.

"Me too…yours, not mine."

His hands go under my shirt until they find my nipples. He teases them into peaks and then helps me out of the shirt, which is when he lets go of my mouth.

He goes down on his knees and pulls my jeans down just enough to release my cock. The relief of having it in his mouth is quickly replaced by the need for more.

Looking down at him almost undoes me. He looks so good with his lips around my cock. His hair has grown since the early summer, and I see more of the salt and pepper hairs on the sides. They curl up a little, making him look younger.

With his mouth on my cock and moaning like he's enjoying it more than I am, he really looks like a kid in a candy store.

He releases my cock and stands.

"I hope you're ready because I'm more than ready for you, Milo."

He turns around and leans against me. I help him out of his shirt, kissing his neck as it goes over his head.

He pushes his ass against my dick, and we both groan.

"You wanted the wall," I rasp.

He steps forward to face the wall and pulls his pants down to his knees, taking down his underwear.

"Lube," he says.

I appreciate his perfect ass for a moment, running my hands over it, giving it a slap and loving how it jiggles slightly. He moans.

"You like that?"

"Uh-huh."

I caress his skin and give him a few more slaps until it's pink and warm under my touch. With every slap, he moans more, which turns me on to no end.

"Lube up, please," he says.

That's a strange request, considering I haven't prepped him.

I kneel, ignoring his pleas, and then I discover two things. Why each of my slaps sounded so pleasurable to him and why we only need a small packet of lube.

I stand and rub my cock along his crease.

"Were you that desperate for me?" I kiss the back of his neck.

"You have no idea."

I coat my cock with lube and throw the packet on top of the discarded clothes.

"I think I have an idea."

I pull out the butt plug he's been wearing since god knows when and immediately replace it with my cock.

"Oh fuck, fuck...nghhh."

He's still so tight even after wearing the plug. My dick feels like it's trapped in heaven.

"Was this what you wanted? For me to fuck you hard and fast against the wall?"

"Yes."

I pull out a little, and his ass follows my dick.

"Nuh-uh. I'm in charge here. You made the request, so you're going to get what I'm giving you."

"Fuck yes, Milo. Please."

I wrap my arm around his waist to keep him steady, and he presses his hands against the wall.

This is the most desperate, animalistic sex of my life. Anyone passing by his house will probably hear us through the door, but I don't care.

I fuck him as hard and fast as I can until I'm on the crest of my own orgasm. Our breathing is labored like we're running a marathon neither of us trained for.

When Ellis pushes his ass back at the same time as I thrust farther inside him, I can tell he's getting close.

I'm about to reach for his cock when he shouts my name, and I feel warm cum hit my hand. This is the fucking train ride of my life, and I'm about to crash right now.

A few more thrusts into him, and I'm coming, pushing him until he's flush against the wall.

I can't move. I don't want to. My forehead rests against the back of his neck.

He's silent. Too silent.

"Did I hurt you?" I ask.

He hisses when I withdraw my deflating cock and then pulls his pants up before turning around.

My chest is pounding, and I'm scared I've done something wrong. That I was too much, too rough.

He turns around slowly. When his eyes meet mine, I'm already in too much panic to be able to read him.

"No," he says, almost as a whisper. "You didn't hurt me."

"Talk to me, Ellis."

His eyes turn shiny and a tear falls.

"This is my fault," he says.

"I don't understand, baby. Please tell me what's wrong." I cradle his face and clean the stray tears with my thumbs.

"I went and did what I promised myself I wouldn't do again."

"What's that?"

"I've fallen for you, Milo. I'm sorry. I didn't mean to."

I hold him in my arms as more tears fall.

There may be a reason he's breaking down over this, but he doesn't realize he's just saved me. He's done what no other man I've been with has done before. He's made me feel like I'm worth loving.

I don't think he's ready to hear it back, even though it's on the tip of my tongue. Somehow, I don't think he'd believe it.

"Come on. Let's have a shower and go to bed. I can still stay the night, can't I?"

He nods.

I grab the clothes from the floor and take him upstairs.

Once in his bathroom, I help him get fully undressed and turn the water on in the shower.

He's no longer crying, but he's retreated inside his mind. I can give him time to figure out his feelings, but there's nothing in the rule book that says I can't take care of him, so I wash his hair and clean his body.

Somehow, Ellis Bradford wants to love me but thinks he can't. Does he realize he probably loved me before tonight?

All the small things he's done for my daughter and me. That's his love language. Taking care of people. From his students to his family and now me, Sara, and to an extent, Florrie.

I dry myself quickly, use the same towel on him, and then take him to bed.

There's no point bothering with clothes. I want to feel him against me all night.

My first full night with the man I love.

"I love you," he says, whispering in the dark.

"You won't believe me if I tell you I love you too, will you?"

He lets out a choked laugh. "Probably not."

"Then I'll just have to show you."

"Okay."

"Sleep, my love."

I hold him close and wait until he's asleep to let my own emotions out.

I look up at the ceiling. "Thank you, Mom."

I wake to the sound of my phone ringing, and it takes me a moment to realize where I am.

Ellis's arm is around me, and he's sleeping so soundly that I don't want to wake him up, but it could be Florrie. I carefully move his arm and grab the phone from my jeans pocket.

The ringing stops by the time I get to it. I don't have a chance to see who was calling before I'm grabbed from behind and carried back to bed.

"Who said you could get up?" Ellis asks, yawning and cuddling up to me again.

I chuckle. "You were sleeping."

"I fail to see your point."

He kisses me, and I forget about everything until the phone rings again.

"It's Florrie."

He smiles and runs his hand over my chest as I answer the call.

"Hey, Florrie. Is everything okay?"

"Good morning, sweetie. I hope I didn't wake you up. I waited as long as I could."

I sit up.

"What's up? Is Sara okay?"

"Yes, yes, she's okay. She slept all night and just had breakfast."

I look around for a clock and see it on the other side table. It's after nine in the morning. I must have been a kid the last time I slept this late.

"Okay, then what's up? You've got me worried."

"Yesterday evening, this woman knocked on the door asking for you. She was dressed all nice in expensive clothes. I asked her what she wanted, and she said she wants to talk to you because she's Sienna's mother."

I feel all the blood drain from my body. Ellis tenses next to me as if he can feel my anxiety.

"What...what did you tell her?"

"I told her you were working and you'd be back tomorrow. She didn't argue with me, just asked if she could leave her phone number.

She said she's in town for a few days and staying at the B&B on Main Street… Milo, I don't think she knows about Sara."

"Okay, I'm on my way home."

I end the call, and for a moment, I can't move, trying to process what Florrie said and the implications.

"Are you okay? You're shaking," Ellis says.

I look at him. "Florrie said Sienna's mom came to my place last night."

"Do you know what she wants?" he asks, holding me tight.

"No. Sienna always made it out like she didn't have any family. Florrie said the woman wants to speak to me." I run my hands through my hair. "She can't take Sara from me. She can't. She's my only family."

"She won't. It'll be okay. Do you want me to be there with you?"

"Will you?"

He kisses me. "Of course, baby."

We get dressed quickly, forgoing breakfast because I need to see Sara with my own eyes and know she's at home.

Florrie comes over to hug me as soon as we're through the door.

"I'm so sorry. I shouldn't have opened the door, but Sara had just gone to sleep, and I didn't want her to wake up with the noise."

"That's okay, Florrie. You had no way to know. Hell, I didn't know Sienna had any living family. The way she spoke about them, which was rarely, it sounded like they were all dead."

She gives me a piece of paper with the woman's number.

"I'll be next door. Let me know if you need anything from me, okay?"

"Thanks, Florrie."

Sara is in her high chair, so I pick her up, inhaling the comforting scent of her baby shampoo. I almost break down when she calls me Dada.

"I have to call her, don't I?" It's a rhetorical question, but I want Ellis to say that I don't have to do anything I don't want and that Sara is mine.

My hands shake as I dial the number.

Why does it feel as though life always wants to take something from me just as I gained something else? What is it about me that indicates I can't have it all?

29

ELLIS

I can't begin to unpack everything that's happened in the last twelve hours because right now, I need to be strong for Milo.

He doesn't know how much I feel his pain, and it's not the right time to tell him.

No. Now is the time to put on a brave face and fight for him and his family.

He hands Sara over to me and dials the number. I know when someone picks up because he tenses and grabs my hand so tight it almost hurts.

"Hi, I'm um…Milo Allen. You came to my place yesterday."

He goes quiet while he listens to her. His Adam's apple bobs up and down as he tries to remain calm.

I take my phone out, type out a note, and then show him the screen.

Suggest meeting at Bittersweet.

He looks at me and nods.

It's so painful to watch him hurt, not knowing this woman's intentions or if Florrie's instinct is correct and she doesn't know about Sara.

"Yes, okay…um, I'll see you later."

He ends the call and looks at me with red-rimmed eyes.

"She's looking for Sienna. Oh my god, Ellis. How can I tell her the truth?"

"One step at a time, baby. Let's meet her first and go from there."

I place Sara in her high chair and pull Milo onto my lap.

"What I said yesterday…I'm here, Milo. And if you need to fight for Sara, I will be here. Always. Okay?"

He holds on tight, and we stay like that for a few minutes until we have to go.

We leave Sara with Florrie, agreeing that if Milo feels it's the right thing to do, we'll introduce her to Sienna's mom.

We arrive at Bittersweet early, so I get us a drink while we wait. The sun shines like this summer will last forever. Only we know the storm that could be brewing.

I see the woman before Milo does. It must be her. Dressed like someone who comes from money and holding herself straight.

"Milo?"

He turns and stands.

"Hi, I'm Gloria Seymour. Thank you so much for agreeing to meet me."

"Hi. This is…" He looks at me.

"I'm his boyfriend, Ellis. Would you like something to drink?" I ask.

She smiles. "I'd love an iced coffee, please. It's such a warm day, isn't it?"

I leave them to place the order with Julius. When I return, Gloria has sat down, but it doesn't look like they've exchanged any words. One looks as unsure as the other.

"Milo, I'm so sorry to appear out of the blue like this. I've only recently found your details."

Julius brings out Gloria's drink. She takes a sip and then a deep breath.

"Sienna is my only child. We've always had a complicated relationship. I guess we are just too different, and I haven't always understood her choices. One day, out of the blue, she tells me she wants to marry this boy she met in rehab, Mikey. I couldn't agree with it. She was too young, and I hadn't even met him. We had an argument and then compromised. Mikey would move in with us so I could get to know him, and then we'd talk about marriage at a later date."

Milo reaches for my hand, and I hold it.

"It was clear Mikey needed help, but also that he cared for my daughter a lot. They lived with me for a year. Mikey found a job, and they were taking the right steps. I felt that, for the first time, Sienna and I were getting closer. On her twenty-second birthday, they both went out, and when they came home, it was clear they'd been drinking. Sienna knew this was a step back in recovery for both her and Mikey. We had an argument about it, and the next day when I got up, they'd left. I tried to track her phone and credit cards, put a search alert to the police, but nothing came back."

The more Gloria tells her story, the more I feel Milo is upset and anxious. He seems to be holding it together, but I can tell he's hanging on by a thread.

"The police told me to give up. Sienna is an adult, so she probably decided to move on with her life. I've been searching ever since. Some days I feel her presence near me, and others, I feel like I'm too late. It was Sienna's birthday a week ago, and I finally gained enough courage to go into her room. I saw a note in Mikey's handwriting. It said: *step one, reach out to Milo.* And there was an address. I went to the address yesterday, but the person in the house said you lived in a different place on the same street."

"I moved after my mom died and Mikey left. I couldn't afford the rent."

Gloria looks down at her hands.

"I was wondering if they made contact with you. If they came to see you." She takes a tissue from her handbag and wipes a tear. "I'm already expecting the worse, but I just want to know something. Anything that gives me hope or closure."

Milo's hand is shaking under the table. He looks at me, and I hope he can see that I know how strong he is.

He moves to the chair next to Gloria's.

"I'm so sorry."

As soon as Milo says the words, it's clear Gloria understands their meaning.

"Yes, Mikey came home and brought with him this really amazing girl who became a little sister to me," Milo continues.

I watch in awe of Milo's courage, once again sharing the story he told me only a couple of weeks ago. He just leaves out a baby-sized detail, which I can't blame him for.

Gloria cries, holding on to Milo.

"Thank you for telling me. I can go home now and move on with my life." She takes a deep breath and stills herself. "At least I know she was happy and loved until the end, right?"

Milo looks at me, and I nod, hoping to convey how much I am here for him.

"Gloria, there's someone I'd like you to meet, but first, would you like to see Sienna?"

Gloria nods, still holding Milo's hands. "My car is at the B&B."

"We can take you in my car," I offer.

The drive to the cemetery is silent. Milo is so tense next to me that I'm afraid to touch him, even though I want nothing else but to offer him some comfort. I know he isn't going to relax until he sees Gloria's reaction to Sara.

I give them space as they visit the grave, but I remain within earshot.

It's so painful to see Milo go through the emotions he's had to deal with all on his own for the last nine months, and it's hard to tell if Gloria's presence is a good or a bad one.

"Before I leave, I'll come back with some flowers. Your favorite," Gloria says, touching the stone with Sienna's name. "Thank you for bringing me here, Milo. I'm sure you know how much it means to me to see where she's laid to rest."

"This isn't our last stop," Milo says. "Remember I said there was someone I wanted you to meet?"

Gloria follows us to the car again.

When we get to Milo's place, it's clear he's nervous.

"Gloria, would you give us a moment?" I ask.

"Of course."

I walk outside with him. "Baby, you've got this. It's the right thing to do."

He nods. "I know. She seems like a nice person."

"She does. And remember, I'm here for you." I give him a kiss of encouragement. "Go get your daughter."

I walk back inside, where Gloria is sitting at the kitchen table.

Milo comes in a minute later with Sara.

"Gloria, this is Sara. She's your granddaughter."

30

MILO

"Oh my god." Gloria's hand goes to her mouth, and I can almost feel the shock, the disbelief, the full range of emotions. I'm feeling them too. "How is it possible?"

"Sienna found out she was pregnant shortly after they came here. Sara was born the night my brother died. When we got the news, Sienna was in shock. She…she made me sign the birth certificate to say I'm Sara's father. I'm sorry. I didn't know about you. She always said she had no family."

Gloria's eyes are on Sara. "Can I hold her?"

"Of course."

My heart will be in my hands every moment from now until she utters the words I need her to say.

"She's so beautiful. She has Sienna's eyes, but I can see so much of Mikey too." She straightens Sara's dress in that way grandmothers do. I've seen Florrie do the same thing so many times. "You've been looking after her all this time on your own?"

"She's my daughter. Maybe not biologically, but I held Sienna's hand as she pushed. I heard Sara's first cry. This girl has been my world since the day she was born."

I'm the one crying now, but I don't care. I need Gloria to know I haven't just been looking after Sara. She's my only family.

"We don't have much, but Sara has her own nursery. She has her favorite toys, and I've spent so many nights watching her sleep and wondering how it's possible for someone to sleep with her hands tucked under her chest and her butt sticking up."

Gloria looks at me and smiles. "Sienna used to sleep like that. My late husband wouldn't come to bed until she moved to a better position on her own. I think in her first year, he slept less than I did."

She places a kiss on Sara's head and gives her back to me.

"She's really the most precious thing," she says.

I sit at the table with Sara on my lap. "Will you tell us more about Sienna?"

"I'll make some coffee," Ellis says and starts looking around my cabinets.

Gloria spends the next two hours talking about Sienna. From when she was a little girl to a rebellious teenager. I tell her what I learned about her when she came here with my brother.

By the end of the afternoon, I feel lighter because this meeting with Gloria has been unexpectedly enlightening, but I'm still on edge.

Neither of us has mentioned what happens to Sara now that she has another living relative, and I'm too scared to bring it up.

"Thank you so much for today. I think I need to go back to my hotel, cry some more, and make a few phone calls," Gloria says. "Could I visit with Sara again tomorrow?"

"Um...it's not...I'm working."

"That's okay. I understand. When will you be free?"

"Wednesday?"

She nods. "I guess that gives me a couple of days to get some shopping done. I have a new granddaughter to spoil."

"Would you like me to take you back to your hotel?" Ellis asks.

"Thank you. That would be really nice of you."

Ellis gives me a kiss on the lips and leaves, promising to come back straight after.

As soon as they leave, Florrie comes over.

"I've been worried sick since you told me that the woman is Sara's grandmother. What happened? She's not threatening to take her away, is she?"

I sigh. "Not yet. I don't know if she will. I don't know what rights I have. I don't know anything."

She wraps her motherly arms around me, and I let myself be comforted by the closest thing I have to a mother.

"I grew up on a farm, honey. I may be old, but I can still throw a punch. No one's gonna take this baby girl from you. I promise."

I stand and shake myself. "Right. No point worrying about what I can't control right now. I'm going to feed my daughter and then play with her because that's what we do on Sunday nights. Isn't that right, sunshine?"

Sara waves her arms like she understands what I'm saying.

"I'll leave you to it then. Goodnight, my dears."

I prepare Sara's food since Florrie gave her a bottle of formula earlier, and even when she decides it looks better on me than in her belly, I can't stop laughing.

"You're a little terror, you know that?" I point to her full belly. "I need better reflexes because you throw a mean punch."

She starts one of her long conversations that makes her giggle a lot, so I reply, making jokes about her coming home before ten when she's a teenager and how I'll veto every person she might be interested in… but only when she's twenty-five.

I give her a bath and read her a book before putting her to bed.

It's not until I consider having a shower that I realize Ellis hasn't returned.

I check my phone, and there are no messages, so I grab my shower. When I get out, I check it again, and there's a message waiting.

Ellis: Sorry, baby. I got caught up doing something. I'll see you on Tuesday before the soup kitchen. I'll meet you at home.

I reply *okay* and pull down my bed. It's probably a good time to do some studying for my exams. They're just around the corner, and I don't want to fail.

Hopefully, it'll also keep me distracted from other thoughts.

Like Gloria taking Sara away from me.

Like Ellis getting cold feet on our relationship because there's just too much drama with me.

Even though he said he loved me, and love is unconditional, right?

"Ugh. Stop thinking so much," I say to myself.

"Hey, hun," Pauline says when I arrive at work on Tuesday morning.

"Morning."

"You look tired. Is everything okay?"

"Yeah, just a few things going on at home."

She looks to the door. "Does this have anything to do with the rich woman that was buying a bunch of toys and talking about Sara?"

"What?" I turn to her, closing my locker so quickly that I almost get my fingers stuck.

"Yeah. A woman was asking about the best place to buy toys and baby stuff yesterday. When I asked if she had someone in mind, she said she has a new granddaughter, Sara. I didn't think too much of it until just now. Who is she?"

"She's Sara's grandmother. Fuck." I rub my hands over my face. "Don't worry, it's nothing really. It'll sort itself out."

She looks at me like she has some doubts, but my shift is starting, so I have to go open my register.

Jimmy waves at me and smiles while he's serving a customer. I wave back but ignore him, thanking the gods that customers are waiting so I can get straight to work.

"Gerald is off today," Jimmy says when his line subsides.

"That's great for him."

I smile when I see my next customer.

"Ethel, you're a sight for sore eyes."

She waves me off. "You're a charmer."

"But I don't lie. What have we got today?"

"Just a few essentials."

I ring up her stuff and take the payment.

"How's your new hobby going?" I ask.

"It's great. I gave some of my fish to the vet out in Chester Falls, and he's going to put them up for sale there. Can you believe it? He's such a sweetheart too. I wouldn't want anyone else looking after my cats but Doctor Micah Sawyer."

I try to keep my laughter in. I wonder what the poor vet thinks of Ethel's *crocheted* fish. "That's very entrepreneurial of you, Ethel."

"Just goes to show it's never too late to do something you care about. You remember that."

"I will, Ethel. Do you want help to the car?"

"No, I'll be fine, dear." She leans over the counter and whispers, "My son thinks I can't see what he's doing, parked out there spying on me. I'm not du-lah-lah yet. And I can still do everything myself."

I smile. "Ethel, I want to be just like you when I grow up."

She blows me a kiss and off she goes, holding on to her walker with her groceries in the basket.

"So, is it true? You and the school teacher are a thing?"

I bite my tongue and put on a fake smile before I turn around.

"Who wants to know, Jimmy?"

He puts his elbows on the counter and leans forward.

"Maybe *I* want to know."

"Why?"

"Because maybe I think you and me together would make more sense? If that woman who's going around saying she's Sara's grandma takes her away to look after her, you'd be free from that responsibility. Maybe you could start acting like you're twenty-six instead of sixty-six."

I stare at him in disbelief. He couldn't have just said what I think he did.

"So what do you think? Ditch the old teacher and come out with me?"

I leave my register and head toward his. He smiles, thinking he's won me over, but I see the moment he realizes that couldn't be further from the truth.

I grab him by the collar of his shirt. "Don't you ever talk about me or my daughter in that way, or any way, for that matter."

"She's not your daughter," he bites between gritted teeth.

Red boiling rage builds inside me. I've never wanted to punch someone so much, and I'm so close to doing it. Jimmy sees it in my eyes because he tries to get out of my hold.

"Milo. Leave him. He's not worth it." I listen to Pauline's words and release him. The last thing I want is to do anything that could jeopardize my custody of Sara.

"You wouldn't be so precious about your little perfect teacher if you knew why he came to live in Stillwater," Jimmy says.

"Jimmy, you shut your face, or I'll shut it for you," Pauline threatens.

"What are you talking about?"

Jimmy sniggers. "Your teacher was fired from his last job because he had an affair with a married teacher at his school. The guy had a wife and a kid on the way, and he tried to destroy their lives with lies about the kid. Saying the kid was his. So maybe he's not that gay after all. Or maybe he's with you to get his hands on Sara."

Pauline punches Jimmy so fiercely that he falls to his knees. He stands back up as if he's ready for a fight, but then he sees the customers looking at him and thinks better of it.

I close my register and run to the break room.

Pauline comes in straight after me.

"Why did you do that? You're going to get yourself fired."

She shrugs. "He deserved it. He's been deserving of it for a long time, but you guys seemed friendly, so I kept it to myself. I don't like how he's been talking about you behind your back, especially to Gerald. He can fire me all he wants. I'm going anyway."

I give her a hug. "You're a good friend, Pauline."

"You forgot gorgeous."

I chuckle. "You're a good, gorgeous friend."

"Yuck, no, you can't fake it enough to make it sound right."

"You're certifiable, but I love you," I say.

"I know. I'm pretty awesome. Why don't you go? Gerald isn't here. I'll cover for you. Jimmy won't say a word, or I'll put a complaint against him."

"Thank you."

I kiss her cheek and leave the store, running home as fast as I can.

First, I need to see Sara and then speak to Ellis.

31

ELLIS

ALICE's squeal is so loud is almost makes my ears bleed.

"God, woman, get a hold of yourself."

"I can't help it. You know I'm a hopeless romantic, and this is beyond romantic."

She spins around her living room.

"My big brother is in love again."

She throws herself on her couch with a long, happy sigh.

I roll my eyes.

"Look, I didn't come here to tell you so you can go all heart eyes and forget about the serious stuff."

"What serious stuff?"

I give her a look.

"Oh…"

"Yeah."

"It's not a deal breaker, is it? Everyone has a past. Didn't you say Sara isn't his biological daughter? So he has a past too. What's the big deal?"

I lean back in the armchair.

"When…Boston happened, I was broken and lost. I promised myself that I wasn't going to fall in love again."

"Well, that's a stupid thing to promise yourself because it's obvious you were going to break that promise," she says.

"What do you mean?"

"Ellis, you're the most loving person I know. Do you know how often you randomly mentioned Milo in conversation before you even got to know him?"

I frown. "I did?"

She rolls her eyes.

"Constantly. '*I went to the store, and Milo was talking about this book he read. Did you know Milo has a daughter? I don't know why Milo is so shy when he's the nicest person,*'" she says, imitating my voice.

I want to argue with her, but thinking about it now, it's obvious there was always something about him.

"Don't you think the age gap between us is too big? He's twenty-six. God, when I was twenty-six, he was a child."

"Yeah, and when he's forty-two, you'll be fifty-eight. Congratulations, we can both do math," she says. "Don't be silly. Milo isn't like any other guy his age. He's mature, responsible. He's absolutely perfect for you."

"But what about when he wants to do fun stuff and I don't because I'm old and set in my ways?"

She leans forward and rests her elbows on her knees. "In the time you've been together, has he ever given you the impression he's bored or not having fun?"

"No. Quite the opposite. He's great to talk to, and we don't need to do anything extravagant in order to have fun."

My memories take me back to the crab rolls we shared. Milo insisted on paying for them, and I let him because it was his idea to go there and they were cheap enough.

We sat looking at the amazing view, and nothing in my life ever felt so right.

"That look on your face," Alice says.

"What about it?"

"I've never seen it before. I know how much you loved…you know who. But the kind of love you feel for Milo? That's a completely different kind. It's the forever kind. Can I be honest?"

I chuckle. "When have you ever not been?"

She throws one of her decorative couch pillows at me. "When you told me about the surrogacy, I thought you were joking."

What?

"Why?"

"Because I felt you were the only one who wanted it. Being a parent when you're part of a couple is a two-person job, even when you disagree. I don't think he ever wanted it as much as you did."

Her words make sense, but they're also a dagger to my heart because I was the one who lost everything in the end.

"I know what you're thinking, but trust me, all the pain you went through will feel like it was worth it when one day you get to walk down the aisle and marry Milo. Or when you take Sara for her first day of school."

A lump forms in my throat.

"Oh, Ellis."

I could never hide anything from my sister, so it's no surprise that she knows how much those things matter to me. How much and how long I've wanted them.

"I'm going to tell him, but I don't know if this is the right time. He's got all this stuff going on with Sara's grandmother turning up, and he's scared of losing her."

"Will you tell him you spoke to Harrison?" she asks.

"Of course. I'm meeting him at his place before we go to the soup kitchen, so I'll tell him then."

"Okay then. Deal with one thing at a time. Put him first if you think that's what he needs, but don't forget, you're also important."

I nod. "Milo would never make me disappear. If anything, he lifts me up every time he so much as looks at me."

"Fuck, I'm going to cry. I need a glass of wine now."

She gives me a hug and ushers me out the door to go be a knight in shiny armor, as she puts it.

When Milo opens the door, he throws himself at me, holding tight.

"Hey, what's the matter?"

"Just…hold me. Only for a moment, okay?"

His voice sounds broken.

"Baby, I'll hold you forever if that's what you need."

I see Sara playing with her musical animals on her high chair.

"Do you want to sit or lie down and talk?" I ask.

He nods.

"Gloria has been going around town to all the stores, buying things for Sara and telling people she's her grandmother. I don't know if she wants to have Sara or if she expects me to give her up. She's coming tomorrow, and I'm terrified, Ellis."

I run my hand through his hair. He leans his head against my palm when it touches his cheek.

"I hope you forgive me for this, but I spoke to Harrison on Sunday. That's why I didn't come back here. It was too late by the time I left their place."

"Okay. What did you speak to him about?"

I cross my fingers mentally, hoping he won't get mad.

"I asked him what your rights were as the named father on Sara's birth certificate."

He gasps. "Really? I totally forgot he's an attorney. Thank you for doing that for me."

"He says that as the named parent on the birth certificate, you have all the rights of a biological parent because it's assumed you are the biological parent. Gloria can, of course, challenge it and request a DNA test. Chances are that if the mother willingly named you as the father, and you've been caring for the child and providing all their needs like a father, then you'll continue as the parent. She can take you to court, but it may be easier to appeal to her heart and work out visitation rights."

Milo lets out a breath that sounds like it's been held since he met Gloria.

"I guess I might find out tomorrow what her intentions are."

I nod. "We can fight this together. Hopefully, Gloria will decide to work with us rather than against us, but I'll be there every step of the way."

"I love you, Ellis."

I gasp.

"I promised myself I'd wait longer to tell you, but I don't know why. What's the point? Everything we have can be taken away from us at any moment, with no warning. Why shouldn't I be true to you? Please believe me when I say it. I've never said it to anyone before. The word always felt too big to express what I felt at the time. But not with you. With you, it's the easiest thing. And before you stop me, I'm not too young. I know what I want, and I—"

As much as I love to hear him ramble, I want to kiss him more, so I do. I relish in the way Milo melts into the kiss, allowing me to protect him, keep him safe, love him.

"Are you sure?" I ask, still afraid to believe this can be true. "In a few years, I'll be in my fifties, and you'll still be in the prime of your life. I don't want to drag you down, Milo. I want you to experience life and everything you deserve."

He looks at me and frowns. "Do you think I don't deserve you?"

"I think you deserve better."

Milo shakes his head. "Ellis, *you* are my better. No one else will ever match up to you or how I feel about you. If you've changed your mind about us, that's one thing, but if you love me like you say you do, then let me love you back."

"I do. More than I ever thought I would love someone again."

His lips meet mine with passion and love that cannot be denied. Because it was always bound to happen and because it's hopeless to fight it.

Sara giggles and lets out a few squeaks.

"Not until you're twenty-five," we say simultaneously. We laugh, and she claps her hands.

Milo turns to me. "I don't know how to bring this up because I don't believe one word of it, but I feel that you should know."

"Know what?"

"Someone I work with, who, by the way, got the best punch in the face from a girl today, said something about you and the reason you left Boston and moved here."

I frown. "How would he know? Only my family knows."

Milo shrugs. "I don't know. Maybe he overheard Alice? Probably he made it up. Hold on, you're saying only your family knows, so Jimmy was right…there is something."

I hold his hand. "I spoke to Alice about it earlier because I want to tell you. It may explain some of my insecurities or strange behavior."

"Ellis, I already loved you before I knew there was anything else to know. Nothing you tell me will change that. Unless you bring up the age gap again. I'll have you know I'm one punching opportunity short today, so I might take it on you."

I laugh. "I know. You're an incredible man, Milo. I know you wouldn't lie, and I believe you when you say you love me, but I don't want any secrets between us, and if anyone starts any rumors, then I want you to be the first to know the truth."

"Okay."

"I was in a long-term relationship with another teacher at the school I worked with in Boston. We didn't live together, but we talked a lot about moving in. We basically had two sets of everything in each other's apartments. I've always wanted to be a father, so I discussed it with him, and he seemed happy to start a family too. We moved in together and started looking at surrogacy options. The first two attempts using my sperm didn't work. We used a considerable amount of my savings, and after two years, we were exhausted, losing hope, and it started affecting our relationship. We even had counseling to talk about it and work through it together.

"One day, he said his best friend was willing to carry a baby for us, but she would only do it with his sperm. At the time, we had some unexpected bills, so I couldn't afford another round of IVF. He offered to pay for it since they were using his sperm.

"He never wanted me to go to any appointments with him, which was disappointing because I felt like I was missing out on part of the process, but I didn't say anything because I felt like our relationship was getting back to how it used to be before.

"About a month later, we got the news that his friend was preg-nant. We were so happy. The first scan was okay, and then we found out we were having a boy. We picked names and talked about what school he would go to. I'd never been so happy. Then, when she was six months pregnant, she started acting weird. She'd be really clingy with him and talk about the baby as if it was theirs and not mine.

"One day, she came over before my ex was home from work, and I mentioned to her that we needed to deal with the adoption paperwork. She looked at me like I'd grown a second head. Then she told me they'd conceived the baby the normal way. Basically, they had sex."

"Wait, your ex is bi? Did you know?"

"No, I didn't know. And his best friend wasn't just his best friend. She was his ex. She used the opportunity to get closer to him. It worked. Before she was due to give birth, he broke up with me and said they were going to raise the child as their own since they were the biological parents."

Milo holds on to me. "You lost your baby."

"Yes. Word got out at the school about what happened. Some people were supportive, but then the word spread to the parents, and there were complaints."

"What reason did the parents have to complain? That was your private life."

"Our conduct. How we couldn't be trusted with their kids if we weren't responsible adults. No homophobia, just misinformation about who did what to whom. In the end, my ex said I should quit and find a job in another school. Even though he was younger than me by a few years, he held a more senior position. I had no choice. So that's when I moved to Stillwater to start fresh."

Milo looks into my eyes and says, "I was wrong. What you told me changes something."

My heart sinks, and I brace myself for the worse.

"If I was already in love with you, I'm even more now. I have no doubt you are the person I want to spend the rest of my life with, but now I know you will always be there for me and Sara because you want it as much as I do."

We hold on to each other tight.

"You better let me spend the night here with you because there's no way I'm sleeping on my own when all I want to do is hold you all night," I say.

"Cook breakfast for me in the morning, and you have yourself a deal."

I kiss him with all the love I have for him.

When the time comes for us to head out to the soup kitchen, I want to go but also not because staying at home with Milo and Sara is my absolute favorite thing to do.

"Don't pout," he says as we walk to the hall together. "I promise I'll eat your ass like a starved anteater approaching a termite's nest."

"I'm not sure if I'm turned on or not."

"Oh, you will be. I bet I can make you come twice just by teasing your ass with my mouth," he says.

"Are you sure you want to volunteer tonight? We can still go back."

His laugh fills my heart, and I make a new promise to myself.

I'll make Milo laugh like that at least once a day for the rest of our lives.

32

MILO

"Milo, baby, come have some food," Ellis calls from the kitchen door.

"In a minute."

I'm planting all the flowers Ellis had delivered from a local garden center. The deck is finished, and the furniture will be delivered this week. The only thing that's left to do is the porch.

Max has a pressure washer, so tomorrow, I'm going to wash the porch so it has time to dry before I paint.

And that will be the end of my work for Ellis, which is why I'm at war with myself.

Part of me wants to see it all done. Ellis goes back to work in three weeks, so he'll have less time to enjoy his new backyard.

But at the same time, once I finish, there's no easy excuse to be with him for the whole weekend.

I mean, he introduced himself to Gloria as my boyfriend, but even though we've declared our feelings for each other, we haven't spent any time together except at the soup kitchen or when I'm working in his backyard.

We haven't had any dates since the crab-roll lunch, but we've spent a few nights together, and the sex…fuck me, it's the best sex I've ever had.

It's like we can read each other's needs so well that we barely need to exchange words. But it's hot, fast, and even though we always cuddle and talk afterward, I'm still left feeling a little empty.

When did I become so needy for affection and attention?

I plant the last flowers in the row and go inside.

Since the work I'm doing is less physical, I wash my hands and return to the kitchen.

Sara is chewing on a piece of apple, sucking all the juice out. It looks sticky, but she seems happy with it.

Ellis fills my cup with coffee and gives me a plate with pancakes and some fruit.

"You really don't have to go to so much trouble to feed me. I'm happy with my sandwich," I say.

He comes around the table and turns me so I'm facing him. He sits on my lap and tilts my head up.

"What if I want to feed you and make sure you're eating properly when you're working so hard outside?"

"I can look after myself."

His brows narrow. "I know you can, but I like looking after you too. What's up, baby?"

I lean my forehead against his chest.

"I haven't heard anything from Gloria since she sent all those toys. I don't know if that means she's out of our lives, which would be sad because I think it would be great for Sara to have a grandmother, or if I should be scared that she's gone away to start proceedings to take her away from me."

Plus all the other stuff about us.

"You have her phone number, right? Why don't you call her?"

"Because I'm too scared of what she might say. It's a little weird, right? She seemed nice, but instead of visiting like she wanted, she got someone to drop off all those gifts for Sara, and it's been radio silence since."

He doesn't need to say it. It's all over his face. He's worried too because he also thinks this isn't normal behavior.

"She also just found out she never got to say goodbye to her only daughter. Maybe she's grieving," he says.

"Or maybe she's realizing that Sara can replace the daughter she lost."

"Shh," he says, resting his forehead against mine. "There's little point in worrying before you need to. Eat something, and then maybe we can go for a drive out of town. Stop somewhere for dinner. What do you say?"

"Okay…that sounds like a good idea. Thank you."

He kisses me gently and then gets up to go back to his chair.

See, Milo? You're going on another date. Stop being stupid and needy.

After I eat, I finish planting the rest of the flowers, which doesn't take long, and then I grab a shower while Ellis feeds Sara lunch.

I avoid thinking about how domestic it all feels. Ellis no longer needs to ask me questions about Sara's food or how she alternates solids with her formula. He knows what to do from the moment we arrive in the morning. He's the one that puts her stuff away, makes sure she drinks some water, plays with her, reads her books, and knows when to feed her without asking if it's time.

We get in his car, and I focus on the outside landscape. Ever since I sold my car to pay for Sienna's funeral, I haven't left town much. I forget how beautiful everything around Stillwater is, not just the lake area.

"Have you thought about what you want to do after you get your GED?" Ellis asks.

We haven't talked much about my exams. I'm starting to get a little anxious about them because there are so many distractions. Thinking about what comes after feels so far away when all I can think about is Sara, Gloria, and what happens when my only source of income is the three days at the store.

"Not much. After what happened with Jimmy, I doubt I'll ever get a promotion or a better job at the store. Gerald offered me a night-shift job, but I declined because I can't leave Sara with Florrie every night, and I doubt he'll ever give me the job if I go back on my word. Right now, the GED feels pretty redundant."

He turns onto a small road, and I see a metal gate that reads: Knox Farm.

"I thought you might want to show Sara the lavender fields. I looked up their website. There's also a large garden we can walk around and a kids' play area."

"She's a little too young for that, isn't she?" I look to the car seat in the back, and Sara's fallen asleep with the car's motion.

"Oh no, that's for me," he says, and I give him a playful punch on the arm.

We park and carefully transfer the sleeping baby from the car seat to the stroller.

The lavender fields are even more beautiful up close, with their bright-purple color and neat rows.

"I thought you might like it here," Ellis says.

"It's...I have no words. It's so calm."

"Do you hear the buzzing sound?"

I close my eyes, and I do. It's faint, but it's there.

"That's Reed's bees. I read on their website that he keeps the beehives in the middle of the fields so the bees pollinate the lavender. His honey is amazing."

"I've seen it in the farmers' market but couldn't afford it. I hear people ask about it at the store all the time, but we don't stock it."

He kisses my hair. "How about we check out the gardens?"

"Okay."

I didn't think the lavender fields could be topped, but the gardens on the side of the main building are even better.

"Wow. My mom would have loved it here," I say. "You see those roses over there? They're her favorite."

Ellis looks at me. "They look like the ones you planted in my backyard."

I feel my cheeks warm, and not from the sun. "Yeah...I wanted to leave something of myself behind. Like a kind of personal touch."

He frowns. "Are you planning on going anywhere?"

"No. No, of course not...never mind."

"Good."

We hear footsteps on the gravel path, and then a tall guy with dark hair and a lumberjack-type shirt comes from between two hedges. He's on the phone shouting at someone but then stops when he sees us. "Don't bother coming back." He pockets his phone and holds out his hand to Ellis.

"Hey, Teacher. How's it going?" he asks Ellis.

"Hi, Callan. We've come to visit the lavender fields and your gardens. This is Milo, and this is Sara," he says, then turns to me. "Callan is Reed's farm manager."

"Hi, nice to meet you. I'm so in love with your gardens. Whoever looks after them does a great job."

Callan wipes the sweat off his forehead. "Not any longer he doesn't. What you just witnessed was him getting fired. Why is it so hard to get good workers these days? Anyway, I don't want to disturb your visit. Come by the farm restaurant when you're done. I'll set up a honey tasting menu for you on the house."

He takes his phone out and waves us off as he heads to the main building.

"I guess you're going to try Reed's honey after all," Ellis says.

I laugh. "Are you saying you brought me all the way here, and you weren't going to treat me?"

Ellis pulls me closer until his lips touch my ear. He nibbles my earlobe, and his warm breath makes me shiver in the best way. "If you wanted to try Reed's honey, you could have told me. I have some at home. I propose I accidentally spill some of it on me so you can help me clean it up."

I swallow. "That's a…yes, please."

For the rest of the day, it's easy to forget everything else happening in my life. The honey tasting is wonderful, and I spend the whole time wondering how it'll taste when I eat it off Ellis.

He squirms in his seat and keeps giving me heated looks, so I know he knows exactly what I'm thinking.

Since we're quite full from honey and bread, we decide to buy three crab rolls and take them home in time to give Sara her dinner. I wasn't prepared for us to be out, so I have snacks but no actual food and no extra formula.

Ellis invites Florrie to join us while I get Sara's dinner ready, and it's the end of a perfect day.

That is until my phone rings and I see Gloria's name pop up on the screen.

I answer, and for a moment, there's just silence.

"Hello?"

"Hi…Milo. This is Gloria. I'm calling to apologize for missing my visit with Sara. I hope she likes the things I bought for her."

Her voice has an edge to it that I can't read. All I want to say is that Sara will be ten months in a few days. She doesn't know or care about gifts, but I bite my tongue.

"Thank you for your generosity, Gloria. I hope you're able to return to visit Sara soon." I don't mean the words. At least, I don't think I do. I want Sara to have a grandmother. I'm just too afraid of her right now.

"I'm sure I will. I've been thinking a lot about Sara and her future. You've been doing a great job raising her so far, but I can imagine it's not easy for a young man your age to raise a child on his own."

"Sara is my daughter. My age is irrelevant. I love her and will always put her first." Now I'm the one on edge. What is she getting at?

"I know, Milo. I'm not disputing that, and I could see how much you care for her. I just want to tell you I'm looking into some options."

My knees give way, but Ellis is there to catch me.

"Options?" I ask. My voice is as shaky as my hands holding the phone.

"Nothing for you to worry about. I just want to know my rights as Sara's grandmother. You must understand this all came as a surprise and a blessing to me too."

"I…understand."

"Splendid. I'll be in touch soon. I'm looking forward to seeing you and Sara again."

I'm left holding my phone and staring at it as though it could self-destruct any moment now. Or maybe that's just my life crumbling right beneath my fingers.

Today I can't bear looking at the sky because for the first time since my mom died, I feel hopeless, numb, and alone.

33

ELLIS

The playground is a hub of activity. I've never seen so many people in or around it at the same time.

Tyler set up a pop-up shelter that works as the coordination center, which Florrie is managing. Who knew she'd thrive so much on bossing people around?

"Once a teacher, always a teacher," she says, justifying her whip-cracking.

I approach her to check in on things. "Ellis, dear, can you see that we have enough bags for the landscaping waste? Dave is almost finished pulling the weeds."

"Of course."

I check Tyler's van and find some extra compost bags, so I take those to where several residents are helping out by collecting the waste.

Fletcher and Arlo are working together using chemicals to remove the old paint from the swings. There's a cordoned-off area around them to ensure no one gets hurt.

For the first day of the playground cleanup, it seems we're on target.

"Hey, Ty, have you seen Milo?"

He points to the hall, so I run over there.

I find him in the kitchen making sandwiches and muttering to himself. There's a small radio playing music in the background.

He smiles when he sees me even though the smile doesn't reach his eyes. "Hey, has Alice called? Is Sara okay?"

"Alice hasn't called, and I'm sure Sara is okay. I just came to check on you."

"Why? I'm okay. The sandwiches will be ready by lunchtime, and Julius called just a minute ago to say he's closed Bittersweet, and he'll be getting here within the hour to serve coffee and cold drinks."

I lean against the counter and cross my arms. "Yes, that's good, but I'm still checking on you."

"I don't understand."

"Milo, you've been avoiding talking about Gloria's call last weekend. You've practically been avoiding me too."

He fills up the bread and pushes both sides together with such force that he's practically flattening the sandwiches into pancakes.

"Milo, baby."

"No, Ellis. I don't want to talk about it, okay? Can I forget this is happening? You wanted me to help out the playground, so I'm helping out the playground. You wanted me to take the GED exams. I'm taking them next week. I don't know what else you want from me."

He's practically shouting. I know it's not directed at me, but it still stings.

"Do you want me to leave you alone?" I ask.

He puts the knife down. "No."

"Tell me how I can help you, baby."

"I don't know, Ellis. That's the problem. I don't know how to solve anything anymore."

I wish he would lean on me, but I feel like he's slipping through my fingers, too lost in his pain to see how many people he has around him, ready to stand up and help.

A knock on the door stops our conversation. An older man comes into the kitchen, stopping when he spots Milo.

"Brian."

"Hey, son."

Brian?

Milo looks like he's seeing a ghost.

Brian, who I assume is *the* Brian that keeps refusing to come to the soup kitchen, is rooted in place, his hands together in front of him, but I can see them shaking.

"It's been a long time, hasn't it?" Brian asks.

"It has."

"I just wanted to say that your old man would have been very proud of you. I know I'm a cantankerous old bastard. I do all the things I shouldn't and very few of the ones I should. But I just wanted to tell you that I'm sorry for what happened. I wish I'd seen it coming, but I was too blinded by my anger. Your father was my best friend, and I let him down. I let you all down."

Milo gets closer to Brian and places his hands on Brian's shoulders. "Someone very wise keeps telling me that when we spend too much time thinking about the things we should do, we forget about those we can do."

"Wise words indeed."

"I'll introduce you to her later. Do you want to help me with the sandwiches?"

Brian smiles and rolls up his sleeves.

"I've always done a mean sandwich. Your dad used to barter for them when we had lunch together at the mill."

"Really? I didn't know," Milo says.

"Let me tell you a few more things about your dad. Not many people knew him like I did."

I leave the kitchen silently so as not to disturb their conversation. I have a feeling that after this, Tyler won't need anyone to convince Brian to come to the soup kitchen.

It takes almost two hours to remove all the compost and load it into the van someone managed to borrow from a friend.

With it all gone, the playground already looks like a completely different place.

Florrie rings a bell. "Lunchtime, troops."

"I hope that's not how you used to call your students," I say.

She chuckled. "No, I called them little bastards, but in those days, we got away with a lot more. Nowadays, they're all angels who can do no wrong."

My phone rings, and I see Harrison's name pop up. "Hey, Harrison."

"Hey, Ellis. I know you're busy with the playground stuff, but since I've got all the kids here, I was wondering if you could stop by. I wanted to talk to you."

"Sure, give me twenty."

I get in the car and drive to Harrison and Fletcher's place. There's a lot of noise coming from the back, so instead of ringing the bell, I go through the side and into the backyard.

There's an inflatable pool on the grass, and the kids are all playing and splashing around.

I see Harrison sitting with a bottle of pop in the shade, overseeing the activities.

"On lifeguard duty?" I ask.

"Oh man, I'm not fit enough for this. How do they get so much energy? We're used to Megan, George, and their friend, Ava, but with everyone helping at the playground, this is like a living hell. How you do this for a job, I don't know."

I laugh.

"They're expected to behave at school, so I have that advantage. Plus, there are no wading pools there either."

He raises his bottle. "True. Anyway, take a seat. Can I get you a soda or something?"

"I'm good, thanks. What did you want to talk about?"

"What I'm about to do is beyond unprofessional, but I'm doing it as a friend. Since Milo brought you with him after he received the call from Sara's grandmother, I feel it's not totally unethical to discuss this with you."

"Okay. Should Milo be here?"

He sighs. "That's the problem. I've tried to contact him to discuss options, but he's avoiding me. Hasn't answered any of my calls. Without his permission, I can't represent him or start any proceedings on his behalf."

I lean forward and rest my elbows on my knees. "I know. I've been trying to get him out of his head ever since, and I'm failing too."

Harrison takes out his phone and taps something. Seconds later, my phone dings.

"I've just sent you Gloria's address. It wasn't hard to find her, especially since Sienna's driver's license on record still had her home address. Milo may want to avoid the situation, hoping it'll go away, but Gloria is a grieving mother. If she's ignored, it could backfire and push her over the edge. If I were you and Milo, I'd get on the nearest flight to Chicago and talk to her personally. Appeal to her mother's heart. I have no doubt that Milo has a good chance of winning a case against her, but it will be costly and emotionally draining."

"Yeah, I get it. Thank you, Harrison. I appreciate this."

34

MILO

I NEEDED one small victory to balance the scales back in the right direction. Brian not only coming to help out with the playground cleanup but specifically coming to me feels like that victory.

After twenty years of false accusations, being almost ostracized in my own community, and seeing the effect it had on my mother and brother, I feel grateful Brian has reached out.

He was my dad's best friend, and he knew, more than anyone, how much my dad fought for everyone, but in the end, he's only human.

Having lost his young wife to cancer shortly after losing his job would have anyone hurting to the point they're not thinking clearly.

I listen as Brian tells me story after story about my dad. The stuff that even my mom didn't know. How he fought for the right things, how funny he was at work. It seems he liked to play small pranks on his friends to lighten the mood.

The time when their work bus got stuck in the snow, and instead of going back home, they pushed the bus all the way to Chester Falls. They were in the factory for three days during the blizzard, but when they came home, they all had a small bonus because being in the factory all hours meant they produced more.

I swallow it like a thirsty child, needing to know everything my parents can't tell me themselves.

Before we take the sandwiches out for everyone, I invite Brian to have dinner with me, Ellis, and Florrie later.

Surprisingly, he doesn't decline the offer.

We set up a table under the pop-up shelter with sandwiches, chips, and other finger foods. It seems enough to feed a battalion, but we've had so many people turn up to help that I grab a sandwich for myself before they're all gone.

I look around for Ellis but don't see him anywhere.

Vera, Florrie's friend, tells me the truck with the flowers has turned up, so I go over and ask them to unload them next to the church in the shade.

After watering them to make sure they survive the heat, I go over my basic drawing for where each flower bed will go.

Tomorrow, once the soil has been turned over and additional nutrients added, I'll be able to plant the flowers. We already have volunteers to take turns maintaining the flower beds and pulling the weeds as they try to grow back.

If the mayor doesn't decide to keep the playground after all this effort from the community, there will be collective heartbreak.

The gate to the cemetery is open, so I go inside and look for my mother's grave.

The rosebush I keep for her in a stone pot needs deadheading, so I sit next to it and remove the dead rose heads to promote fresh growth.

"Hey, Mom. Sorry I haven't been here in a while. It's been a little crazy, but I guess you know that already, right? Sara is so grown up. Well, as grown up as a ten-month-old baby can be. She can walk when she's holding on to things now. I'm sure it won't take long until she's walking all on her own."

I put all the deadheads in a small pile to drop in the trash outside.

"I have so many questions and doubts, Mom. I wish you were here so I could talk to you. Brian spoke to me today. For a while, it was like Dad was back. Even the way Brian talks is how I remember Dad talking."

I sigh. "Anyway, I was nearby, so I wanted to see you, but I have to go. Keep an eye on us as always, okay? Love you."

I place a kiss on my palm and run my hand over the stone.

By the time I'm back, Ellis is still nowhere I can see, but with Florrie in charge of task giving, who knows what she's got him doing.

By late afternoon, when everyone is packing up to go home, I'm exhausted but also excited to plant the flowers tomorrow.

"Hey, Tyler, have you seen Ellis? I haven't seen him all afternoon."

"He got a call earlier and left. I thought he'd be back, but I haven't seen him."

"Okay, thanks."

I wash my hands under the water fountain Anne's husband managed to bring back to life and reach out for my phone. There are no missed calls or messages. I dial his number, but it goes straight to his voicemail.

Florrie has finished packing her *mission control desk*, as she calls it. A lot of stuff will remain here overnight, such as the pop-up shelter.

"Florrie, can I borrow your car to pick up Sara from Alice's place? I can't get hold of Ellis."

"Sure, honey. I'll get home and start dinner. Brian said he wanted to grab some old photos for you, so he'll come over later."

"Okay. I'll see you soon then."

I park in Alice's driveway, half expecting to see Ellis's car there, but it's not.

My gut tells me he's okay, but my brain is worried.

I rush up to ring the bell. Max answers the door.

"Hey, Milo, come on in. Alice is just changing Sara's diaper."

"Thank you."

I wait in their living room. "Hey, Uncle Milo," Marnie says.

"Oh, hi, Marnie."

"Can Sara come play with us another time? She's really cute."

I nod, trying to process that Marnie just called me uncle. I guess it kind of makes sense for her to think of me that way after seeing Ellis and me together over the summer.

Benji comes running over into my arms. I pick him up and sit him on my lap.

"Hello, Benji."

"Hi, Miwo."

"Can I just say your daughter is the best babysitter in the world? I put her in Benji's high chair, and these two spent the afternoon staring at her with fascination. Can she come over every day?" Alice says, holding Sara.

"Hello, princess. Did you have a good day?"

She mumbles her usual words, but the ones I always recognize and fill my heart every time are Dada and a new one: Papa.

"Hey, Alice, I don't suppose you've heard from Ellis. He was at the playground this morning. Tyler said he got a call and then left. I'm a little worried."

Her smile is a little contrived. "Oh, it's nothing to worry about. He had to make a short trip, but he'll be back tomorrow."

"Okay."

I take Sara and walk to the door.

"Milo? My brother has a big heart, so everything he does is because he always wants the best for everyone around him."

I smile. "Yeah, I know."

The drive home isn't long, but I can't stop thinking about what Alice said.

He went on a trip? Where? If he's back tomorrow, he couldn't have gone far, right?

Boston?

He lived there, so maybe he had some outstanding things to tie up from the move.

His ex…

Someone beeps their horn behind me, and I see the traffic light has turned green. I'm not quick enough and the light turns red again.

"Hey, asshole!" the man behind me shouts.

I roll the window up and focus on the lights so I don't miss them next time.

Florrie knows something's wrong as soon as I arrive to give her the keys.

"Hey, Florrie, do you mind if I don't join you for dinner? I'm not feeling great, so I'm going to give Sara her bath, and then I'm going to bed."

She reaches over and puts her hand on my forehead.

"You're not especially hot."

"What do you mean? I'm smokin'," I joke. "Sorry, Florrie. Maybe you and Brian can still have a nice time."

She crosses her arms. "Are you trying to set me up, Milo Allen?"

I gasp. "Moi? I would never."

She gives me a kiss on the cheek and one on Sara's hair.

"I can see you're not yourself, despite your awful sense of humor. Don't worry, I'll entertain Brian."

"I'll bet. Just keep it down. The walls are paper thin."

I manage to get away from her swat just in time.

"I know just how paper thin the walls are. I wish I didn't," she says.

The rest of the evening is carried out on autopilot. Bathing Sara. Giving her formula. Reading her a story. Putting her to bed.

And when it's just me alone with my thoughts, I start to panic.

What if Ellis got a call from his ex, who wants to get back together? It sounds so ridiculous when I think about it, especially when I know how hurt he was. But just like I can't bear the thought of losing Sara, I can't imagine what it would be like to think of a baby as mine and then have it taken away before I could even meet him.

I must fall asleep at some point during the night because I wake up to a knock on the door.

Rushing to it, I forget I'm in only my underwear.

"Jesus Christ, son. And they wonder why I don't like leaving my house," Brian says, covering his eyes.

I hide behind the door. "Sorry, Brian, I thought you were someone else."

"Clearly." He snorts.

"Florrie asked me to come get you because there's a bunch of people at the playground trying to stop the work. We need all the help we can get."

"Okay, I'll be there as soon as I can."

I open the curtains in Sara's room to let her wake up while I jump in the shower.

Thank god she always wakes up in a good mood. I get dressed in record time and prepare Sara's breakfast while also checking for any messages from Ellis.

Still nothing.

With Sara in the stroller, I walk to the playground as fast as I can.

I want to cry when I see all the people standing on the freshly prepared soil. At least I didn't plant the flowers because they would be destroyed.

As I approach, I see there's a clear standoff.

On one side are all the community members who've spent the last few weeks gathering materials, begging, donating, and doing everything possible to ensure we could carry out the work over just one weekend.

Tyler is in the middle, facing a woman, and behind the woman is a group of people. Some of which I recognize from the store.

I don't want to get too close to people in case things get messy. I need to keep Sara safe first and foremost. Florrie sees me and comes over.

"What's going on?"

"That Martin woman has brought her rich friends, and they're protesting against the playground. Tyler is trying to keep them away, but they're pushing."

"Florrie, can you take Sara and stay as far away from the crowd as possible? I'm going to see if I can help Tyler."

She does as I ask, and I navigate the crowd to get to Tyler.

"What kind of person wants to destroy a children's playground to build a parking lot?" Tyler asks.

The woman sticks up her nose. "The parking lot is essential to the development of our town. Everything is growing, and there isn't enough space for all the cars."

"Then build it elsewhere. What makes you think people will want to park this far from the town center, anyway?" he argues back.

"Hello, Mrs. Martin. It's me, from the grocery store, remember?" I ask, trying to keep my voice calm. The woman is a homophobic bitch, but her gaydar must be broken because she's always nice to me at the grocery store.

"Milo, what are you doing here with these people?"

"Mrs. Martin, I live here. This is where I grew up, and this playground is where I used to play. I have a baby daughter who I hope will one day play here too."

She wavers for a moment but stands her ground. "We need a parking lot. This land belongs to the town, and the project must go forward. Isn't it true that, until recently, this playground was abandoned?"

"Mrs. Martin, families fight, but they always come back together. That's what's happened to this community through no fault of their own. Society and people with money ruined these people's lives. It's taken a long time, but we're coming together now. You are a mother. Surely you must understand."

Something passes through her eyes and her whole demeanor changes.

"Family can also lie and betray you and doesn't always deserve forgiveness."

"Are you describing yourself, Mrs. Martin?" Levi says, coming from behind me. "You've lied and betrayed your family. You've ruined people's lives, but that's not enough. Now you also want to ruin the lives of people who have never done you harm?"

She sniggers. "I should have known you'd be involved in this."

A police siren silences everyone. The car stops, and right behind it, there's another car.

Both a police officer and the mayor get out.

Everyone speaks simultaneously until the police officer uses a megaphone to tell everyone to keep quiet.

The mayor comes over to where we're standing.

"May I speak to Mr. Tyler David?"

Tyler comes forward. "That's me, Mr. Mayor."

"Mr. David, here's some paperwork for you to keep. It's redacted to protect the identity of the person who has completed the purchase of the land on behalf of the community."

"What does that mean?" Tyler asks.

"It means, Mr. David, that the land where the playground sits is now yours, with the condition that it remains a playground for the children of this community."

"I'm sorry. What now?" Tyler takes the envelope from the mayor. He looks as confused as everyone else around.

"Read the paperwork, Mr. David. It's all in there."

"Hold on, Mr. Mayor," Mrs. Martin says. "At the last meeting, the purchase of the land for the parking lot was a done deal."

"Mrs. Martin, I'm not at liberty to discuss details, but the buyer has made a generous offer the town could not refuse. I am sure we can find other locations within our town to build the parking lot."

The mayor returns to his car, and the police give a disperse order.

Slowly, people either leave or return to working on the playground.

Florrie comes over and tells me I should go home. Someone's waiting for me. Sara's at home too.

Ellis.

35

ELLIS

AFTER THE RUSH of the last sixteen hours, I'm afraid I've made a huge mistake by getting involved.

I pace the small living room in Milo's house.

He comes rushing in and jumps straight into my arms.

"Ellis."

He holds me so tight I can barely breathe. Then he releases me and pushes me away.

"Where were you? I was worried sick. Why didn't you call me or leave a message?"

"I couldn't. If I told you where I was going, you would have tried to stop me."

He drops down on a chair and covers his face with his hands. "You're leaving, aren't you? You lied. You said you loved me, but you're going back to him."

"What? What are you talking about?"

He looks at me, so heartbroken. "Alice said you had to take a trip. You always follow your heart. You wanted your son more than anything."

I have no idea what he's talking about, but I kneel in front of him. "Baby, that boy was never my son. He was a dream I had, and I wanted it so much that I forgot everything else. What you and I have is more important than anything. If there's a child I ever want to be mine, that's your daughter. I want to be able to love her like a father and for her to recognize me as such. And I want to do that with you. I don't know why you'd think I don't want you or that I'd go back to my ex—"

"Where's Sara?"

"In the nursery."

He stands.

"Milo…"

I follow him. Sara is on Gloria's lap, playing with one of her favorite books.

She calls Dada, but Milo is frozen.

He looks at me. His eyes filled with tears.

"What did you do?"

"Milo, please listen."

He walks out of the bedroom.

"I can't believe you'd betray me like this. You went to get her? Is she going to take Sara away?"

He walks to the door. "I can't watch it happen."

I manage to stop him before he opens the door. "Milo, listen to me, please. No one is taking Sara away. Sara is yours. Please listen to Gloria."

He cleans his tears with his shirt and sits at the table.

Gloria comes out of the room with Sara, handing her over to me.

"Milo, we need to talk," she says. "But first, I need to apologize to you."

He looks up at her.

"Finding out my daughter died at her own hand and then finding out the same day that she left a baby behind was too much for me to handle. I think I was on a happiness and adrenaline train when I bought all the toys. Then I got to my hotel room, and I realized that I hadn't processed any of the information properly. That's why I left and sent the toys through someone else. When I arrived in Chicago, there was this emptiness. I didn't need to search for my daughter anymore. I had no purpose. So I thought my purpose was to raise Sara. I spoke to my attorney, who, by the way, gave me some bad advice, so he is no longer my attorney. That was when I called you.

"That was a misguided attempt at something I wasn't sure how to handle because I was still grieving. I tried to get back in touch, but you wouldn't take my calls. I didn't know what to do until Ellis turned up on my doorstep last night."

Milo stares at me. "You flew to Chicago?"

I nod and smile at Gloria.

"Ellis told me he'd spoken to an attorney that suggested we come to an agreement. I've thought about it and don't want to take Sara away from you. If Sienna named you as her parent, it was because she wanted you to raise Sara. All I'd like to ask is to be her grandmother. I'd like to be able to visit her here, and maybe when she grows up, she can come visit me on her vacation. Who knows, maybe I'll move closer. It's not like I have anyone else in Chicago."

Milo looks like he's in shock. "Are you serious? Do you really mean that?"

"Every word. I can't bring Sienna or Mikey back, but I'm sure we can sew up a new family between us, can't we?"

Milo breaks down again, and I want to hold him so badly. He stands and hugs Gloria. "I think we can do that. I'd like very much for Sara to have a real grandmother."

Like a real mother, Gloria reaches over to a box of tissues on the table and cleans Milo's tears. "Now, I'm going to finish reading my granddaughter a story while you two talk."

Gloria takes Sara and goes back into the nursery, closing the door behind her.

Milo looks at me, shaking his head. "I'm so—"

"No." I break the space between us and kneel in front of him. "You don't get to apologize because you've done nothing wrong."

"I doubted you. I doubted your love."

"I went to Gloria behind your back, not knowing if she was going to accept my proposal or not. If anyone should apologize, it's me."

"How about no apologies?"

I nod. "Milo, I love you so much. Now I know why it's taken me so long to find the kind of forever love I've wanted all my life. I was waiting for you. And you come in a beautiful, heartfelt, complete package that includes the best plus one in the world."

"I love you too, Ellis."

He pulls me closer, and I submit to his kiss, letting him own me, heart and soul. Our friends think they called it before we did, but there was always something about Milo.

In a stormy sky, Milo is the rainbow breaking through the clouds, lighting up my heart, and making me feel like I am enough. I can be loved. There's nothing boring about me. He's not settling with me. If that's not the most powerful and humbling feeling in the world, I don't know what is.

Our lips part, and we stare at each other, communicating without words.

"You missed the showdown at the playground," he says. "It turns out Tyler now owns the land and the playground will remain a playground forever."

"Then I guess there's a lot of work to be done."

Milo goes into the nursery. "Gloria, do you mind watching over Sara while we go help out at the playground? There's a free lunch at one o'clock, so you can come over if you want. Sara's food is in the fridge. She'll let you know when she's hungry."

"Just like my Sienna," Gloria says, caressing Sara's hair with all the love of a grandmother. "I'll see you later. I may have money, but I'm not stupid enough to decline a free meal."

"You sure you're okay leaving Sara with Gloria?" I ask after we leave the house.

"Yes. I looked into Gloria's eyes. I know what's in them."

My man has an unmatchable heart.

I wonder if he saw something in my eyes too. If he always knew I was his, even when I didn't.

36

MILO

"Sir, would you please put your hands on the fence…that's it…now stick your butt out…yup, just like that. Perfect."

I hear the sound of a camera.

"Am I being arrested, officer?" I ask.

"I ask the questions here. Now turn around slowly."

I do and try to keep a straight face when I see Ellis wearing Benji's police officer hat and toy badge. I keep my hands raised.

"Now, what's going on here?" he asks.

I look around and bite my lip, knowing how turned on he gets when I do my whole innocent look.

"It seems, Officer, that I am looking after your…backyard. Is there a problem?"

Sara reaches out to hold the toy badge.

"I'm afraid we'll have to take you in. My deputy here will be doing the interrogation. Do you have the right permit to carry out this type of work?"

I look down and pat the nonexistent pockets of my shorts.

"It's here somewhere, Officer. Maybe you'd like to carry out a search?"

He comes forward and takes my mouth in a kiss. He keeps it baby-rated, but it doesn't have any less of an effect on me.

"Ah, of course, that's where I keep my permit sometimes," I say. "Maybe when your deputy is off duty, you can do a more thorough search?"

He kisses me again and then murmurs against my lips. "You bet."

I follow him inside. "Did you really take a photo of my ass?"

"I did."

I'm not surprised to see a stack of pancakes and a fresh pot of coffee waiting for me.

"It's a good thing I'm doing so much physical work these days because your brunches are going straight to my ass," I moan while adding three pancakes to my plate.

"In that case, there's a free daily brunch available. Just stop by, and it's yours. Come to think of it, maybe you should just move in, and then I'll make sure you have all the brunches you need to keep your ass in top shape."

He looks up, just realizing what he said.

I laugh. "If you didn't mean to say it, that's okay. I still love you. If you meant it and you're scared I'm going to say no, then don't worry because I'll say yes."

He twists his lips. "Wait…what question did I ask?"

"Doesn't matter. The answer will still be yes."

"So…say I suggest we drop Sara with Florrie, go out to The Academy for a light meal, then come back here to celebrate you passing your GED exams…naked…will that be a yes?"

"Did you buy a new pot of Reed's honey?"

"Yes."

"Then I reserve the right to change my answer to hell yes," I say, stuffing my mouth with pancakes, chocolate syrup, and strawberries.

It feels like a lifetime ago, but it's only been two weeks since we completed the work on the playground.

Arlo and Fletcher are still working on the photography exhibit because they had the idea of making it into a permanent installation. Each new generation will know the history of the playground and how it was saved by the community.

Plus the anonymous donator, of course.

I've also completed Ellis's backyard and already have a bunch of his neighbors asking when I'm free to help them redo theirs, which will be challenging since I'm about to start a new job working with Callan at Reed's farm.

Gerald's face when I resigned from the store will forever be framed in my memory as an unforgettable and totally satisfying moment.

After passing my GED exams, I decided I want to go to college and study landscape design, starting off with becoming a landscaper.

I guess all those books my mom read with me gave me the knowledge to do the job, but now I want to take it further and eventually start my own company.

I'm not afraid to dream and even less afraid of my dreams not coming true. The best one has, so the sky is the limit.

"I can't believe this is your last weekend before school starts again," I say.

"I know. I missed the kids though. It'll be nice going back into the classroom. Although now I'll be looking forward to my vacation time a lot more," he says.

"Did you see the letter from Gloria's new attorney?" I ask.

He nods, eating a bite of his pancake. "It's very generous of her to transfer Sienna's trust fund to Sara."

"Sienna never said anything about coming from money, and she never behaved like she cared about it that much. I guess what she and my brother had really was as true as love can be."

"Hmm, it'll be a nice story to tell Sara one day," he says.

We clean up from brunch and then take Sara back home to Florrie, who's pretending she's not dating Brian, even though he comes over for dinner almost every night.

The Academy has an early happy hour, so we head up to the bar for a drink before dinner. I see Tyler sitting alone, nursing a drink.

"Hey, Tyler, you okay?"

"Yeah, why, do I not look okay?"

Ellis raises a brow.

"No, you look fine, just…never seen you here on your own."

He shrugs and downs the drink in front of him before waving to the bartender.

When he comes over, Ellis orders our drinks too.

"Ty, you helped me when I really needed it. Friendship goes both ways, you know?" I say.

He scoffs. "I don't need a friend. I need an ax murderer."

"Okaaay," I mouth to Ellis,

"Does this have anything to do with the playground land?" Ellis asks.

Tyler scoffs again.

"The mayor said the name of the buyer was redacted. Are you trying to find out who it is? Is that it?"

Tyler stares at his drink.

"I know who it is. They didn't redact the signature. Not that I needed to see it to know who the bastard is."

"Oh. So, you know," I say.

"Yeah, I know. Anyway, don't let me be a downer on your date. I'll go take my murderous thoughts all the way home. I have next week's soup kitchen menu to plan."

I turn to Ellis after Tyles leaves. "That was a little strange, right?"

"Yeah. From what I've heard, Tyler's past is this big black hole of nothing. Do you think this buyer is someone from his past?"

I get closer to Ellis. "I don't know, but thinking of past…and more appropriately of the future…"

"Yes?"

"How about we order our dinner to go, finish our drinks while we wait, and then have a private date night at your place?"

He kisses me, lingering just a little too long, making the kiss dirtier than suitable for public consumption. "I think you're very smart. No wonder you passed your GED with flying colors."

I punch his gut, and he coughs. "I prefer it when you slap my ass."

"Based on your current behavior, I'd say that'll be a given. You continue like that and I'll fuck you against your front door, then on the staircase, and once again in the bedroom. I won't let you come until I've had my fill of you, and when I'm done, I'm going to lather your cock with honey and suck you until you come or pass out, whichever happens first. But I know what it'll be."

He holds me closer, and I feel his thickening erection against my thigh.

"Those sweet brown eyes and those full delightful lips hide the dirtiest mind."

I grin.

"I think I'm not hungry anymore. I have a pack of your favorite brioches and more pancake mix if we're hungry after."

"I love it when you talk dirty to me."

He laughs. "Move in with me and I can do anything and everything you want for the rest of our lives."

I look in his eyes, wondering how I got to be so lucky, but now I know that with my mom as my guardian angel it was bound to happen.

"Then take me home," I say, injecting my voice with all the promise of a lifetime of worshiping the man who saw Milo, just Milo, and still fell in love with him.

He drops a few bills on the bar for the drinks, drags me out of the building toward his car and a night full of everything dreams are made of.

***

Dear reader, I hope you've enjoyed Ellis and Milo's story. How adorable was baby Sara?

Breakthrough is part of my Dads of Stillwater series. If single dads is your jam then this series is for you. The series is also available on audiobook narrated by John Solo.

Check out Dads of Stillwater here (readerlinks.com/l/3027183)

FINDING YOU THREE
LOVE
Again
ANA ASHLEY

ABOUT LOVE AGAIN

Can you get more than one true love in a lifetime?

Three years after his husband's death, Vitor is still grieving. Too young to be alone and too old to start again, he feels stuck. Accepting a new job in Lisbon is just what he needs, but it also means going back to the city that sealed his fate nearly thirty years ago.

Between looking for his missing brother and running an LGBTQ Youth Center, Tiago doesn't have time for dating or commitment. When his best friend asks him to find a family member that ran away years ago, Tiago welcomes the distraction.

A past full of secrets.
An anonymous kiss that turns their world upside down.

When past and present clash, will the two men put everything aside and give themselves a chance at happiness? Or are the things keeping them apart stronger than the feelings keeping them together?

Love Again is May-December MM romance with hurt/comfort and second chance themes, lots of steam and a HEA.

1

VÍTOR

THE SCENT COMING from the oven told me dinner was nearly ready —roast pork marinated with my secret mix of herbs, accompanied by roast potatoes and salad. This was the Sunday meal I'd had for as long as I could remember.

As a kid, I remembered coming home from Sunday mass with my brother Mário and smelling it all the way down the street.

The first stop was the bathroom to wash our hands before sitting at the dining room table where my father and the neighbors would be waiting for us to get home from church.

I don't remember having a Sunday meal with just the four of us from my earliest memory until the day I left home.

After that, Sunday meals were very different. After an initial period of rebellion where I refused to have any kind of formal meal on Sunday, my upbringing had a stronger influence than I wanted to admit, and I craved the companionship of others on that one meal a week.

It had started with getting some college friends together on Sundays, and we'd each bring something to share. They'd realized very quickly that not only did I cook well, but I also enjoyed it, so they started helping with the grocery shopping as long as I did the cooking, which I was more than happy to do.

It was a tradition that had carried on throughout the years, even when money was no object to those of us who still remained in touch after college. They still insisted on paying for the food, but it was more a symbolic gesture than anything else. In the last three years, I'd started donating the money they'd give to a cancer research charity.

I put a hand on my chest, thinking of the man who came into my life a long time ago and who was taken away too soon because of cancer. We'd thought we'd have a lifetime together.

In some ways, we had. We'd traveled, built a home, raised a child, and loved each other with all we had. But it wasn't enough, and three years after his death, I was still waiting for him to walk through the door complaining that a client wanted him to design a boring house and couldn't see his vision and then how he could design the house of their dreams if only they listened.

A laugh escaped my lips at the thought. He'd always loved the Sunday lunches, and when we'd been away on vacation, he'd always found a way to make up for the lost meals.

The oven timer dinged, bringing me back to the present. I'd come into the bedroom to pick up a shirt after my shower, and hadn't realized that I'd ended up looking through Rodrigo's side of the wardrobe instead.

Maybe that was what brought the memories on. Not that I didn't normally think about him. He was a constant presence in my mind, but the sight of his shirts all lined up and color coordinated was a reminder that I needed to do something with them.

I'd had no problem giving away his suits and other clothes, but there was something about his shirts. Maybe it was because they were the last things left that were truly his.

We were different sizes, so I would never be able to wear them myself. Rodrigo had been taller and bigger than me. I didn't quite have the presence he'd had when he'd walked into a room wearing a tailored shirt with the sleeves rolled up to show his strong forearms.

"I miss you so much, Dri," I said as I closed the wardrobe door to go and check on the food. Today was a smaller dinner than usual.

Luís was the only one of our friends who wasn't an architect, which was why on the weekend of the biggest industry conference, he insisted on coming over for Sunday lunch when he found out I wasn't attending again.

The doorbell rang right on time.

"Hey, sweets, how are you doing?" Luís asked before enveloping me in one of his big bear hugs. I allowed myself to melt into it before I answered.

"I'm okay."

I'd met Luís on the same night I'd met Rodrigo at a student party. I'd been talking to Luís and had thought he was cute, but Rodrigo stole my heart from the first moment our eyes met. When Dri had stolen me away at the party, I'd thought I'd never see Luís again, but when we'd bumped into each other at the university campus a few days later, we went out for coffee and ended up becoming good friends.

"Are you really okay?" He put a hand on my chin to tilt my head up so I could look him in the eye.

"I was going through Dri's shirts earlier and it brought back some memories. Hey, I don't suppose you want his shirts? You're the same size." Despite asking the question, I was relieved when Luís said he didn't feel right taking them, and besides, he didn't have any use for them since he was an artist and spent more time covered in paint than in nice clothes.

"So, where's this dinner then? I haven't eaten since breakfast in anticipation. And since the others aren't here, I expect a mega-sized portion," Luís said, patting his flat stomach.

I smiled and guided him to the kitchen.

This house was Rodrigo's indulgence. When he'd asked me to marry him, even before it was legal for two men to marry in Portugal, he'd promised he'd design the best house in the country. I never needed anything so large, but the kitchen was the one part of the house I was grateful I'd allowed him to indulge in the design.

The food was perfect as always. Then again, after cooking this meal most Sundays for nearly thirty years, I could almost do it blindfolded.

We ate mostly in silence, which was welcome because I was feeling out of sorts. I also wondered what was in Luís' mind. In the nearly thirty years I'd known him, I'd never seen him go longer than a few minutes without talking. Even when we were younger, he'd always been the one who would bring someone into the conversation by asking the right questions and making them feel like they were the only person in the room.

That was how he'd got me talking that night in the bar until a single look from Rodrigo had made me feel like he and I were the only people on the planet.

The thought made me shiver. Luís looked at me but didn't say anything.

Since it was just the two of us, I hadn't bothered making dessert, but I had made an effort to get Luís' favorite pastries.

"Have I ever told you how much I love you?" Luís said before stealing one of the mini palmiers that had been partially dipped in chocolate with a sprinkle of coconut.

"Several times."

We took our coffees and a plate with the tiny pastries and sat in the living room facing the garden.

"What's going on?" Luís asked before I had a chance to take a sip from my coffee.

"What do you mean?"

"Something's not right."

I took a deep breath and let out a sigh. What could I tell him? That I felt like part of me had died with my husband and the other part was slowly dying because my son wouldn't talk to me? That I hated going to work because the desk next to mine was empty? Was three years too long to still be missing him? Or not long enough?

"Talk to me, sweets," Luís said, putting his hand on my cheek and rubbing his thumb gently over my skin. I always loved how tactile Luís was, almost as if touching people was part of his language.

"I don't know what to say. I feel lost without Dri and Mateus won't talk to me. I don't know how to handle it all on my own."

"Do I need to go kick Mateus' ass?"

"No, he's not the one to blame. I'm hurt and angry because Dri should have told us the truth about Mateus' mom. He should have trusted me." I got up and walked to the patio doors.

"Do you think he didn't trust you?"

"I don't know. All I know is that he's gone, Mateus won't speak to me, and this house is suddenly feeling too big."

"Maybe you need a fresh start somewhere else."

I looked out to the garden where the fairy lights were now lighting up a few trees, giving the garden a magical feel. We'd spent so many summer nights under those lights, waiting for Mateus to fall asleep before we took a precious moment to ourselves and made out like teenagers under the stars.

"I'm too old and cranky for that."

"Sweets, you are most definitely cranky," he said, coming over and giving me a playful punch to the stomach, "but not too old."

I considered his words, but at nearly fifty years old, the thought of starting from scratch somewhere else filled me with dread. Besides, I wasn't sure I could leave this house despite the growing loneliness. This house was Dri's dream; he was in every wall, every detail. I could only ever leave if Mateus decided he wanted to raise his family here, which didn't seem likely considering none of his girlfriends ever lasted very long.

"Vítor, you can't leave your life on standby for Mateus. Try to reach out and rebuild your relationship, but don't let that stop you from living. You are too young to give life up."

Luís was far too perceptive for his own good.

"Thanks, Lulu. And how about you? You've been quieter than normal. Is everything okay with you?"

"Yeah." He sighed and then chuckled. "No change. Maybe one day I'll be able to take my own advice."

I loved Luís but always struggled with his choice to stay in the closet for the sake of his parents.

"Why do you do it, Lulu?"

"You know why. They gave everything up for me. I was the child they never thought they'd have. From the moment I was born, they worked to give me everything they could. I know they are too conservative and their beliefs on homosexuality are wrong, but I respect them too much to hurt them. Besides, you know I'm not a relationship kind of guy, so what's the point of rocking the boat?"

"I get it, but are you in the closet because you're not a relationship guy, or are you not a relationship guy because you're in the closet?"

He tapped his nose and smiled, but there was sadness in his eyes that even he couldn't disguise.

After Luís left, I settled in my office. I turned my computer on to look at my schedule for the week, but my mind was still going through the conversation we'd had earlier.

Despite Luís' earlier encouragement to make a change, I didn't want to admit that I'd been getting calls from an architect partnership in Lisbon for close to a year now.

Even though I was reluctant to admit it, I couldn't deny that lately I found myself more and more tempted to go down to Lisbon and meet with the partners.

I just wasn't sure I could ever go back to Lisbon after making a life for myself in Porto. That city had too many bad memories for me, and while they were in the past, I couldn't deny the sliver of fear I felt every time I thought about the events that happened on my twenty-first birthday and the last time I was there.

Then there was Mateus. Even though he wasn't talking to me, he still lived and worked in Porto. Would my leaving the city be the last nail in the coffin of my relationship with my son?

After doing some work I decided to send Mateus an email. He wasn't responding to my calls or text messages, so maybe he would read an email. I could only hope.

From:vitor.alves@alvesfamily.pt
   To:mat-alves@gmail.com
   Subject: Your papa was an ass

Hey son,
   I hope this email finds you well. You haven't replied to any of my texts, and my calls have all gone unanswered.

Mateus, I can't begin to imagine how much you're hurting right now, but I need you to know that, just like you, I didn't know.

I never thought there were any secrets between your papa and I. Yes, there were little things, which I'm sure weren't secret at all, but I never thought there would be something this big.

You became my son the day Dri introduced you to me, and I've loved you ever since. Please don't let this get in the way of our relationship.

I already lost my husband. Please don't make it so I've lost my son, too. It's more than my heart can bear.

With all my love,

Dad V

2

TIAGO

"Hey, mate, are you calling to say you're finally going to take on the running of the center?"

The hopeful voice of my best friend, Isaac, was almost enough to break my resolve.

"I already run the center." I chuckled.

"My point precisely, and that's why I want your name on the foundation letterhead."

I sighed. "You know I can't do it."

We'd had this conversation many times. I'd met Isaac at university when he'd started a student network to provide support and a safe place for LGBTQ students to talk and access support services.

When he'd graduated, Isaac was able to secure some key funding to open Lisbon's first youth-dedicated LGBTQ center, *Fundação Arco-Íris*. Despite being three years older, I'd taken a break in my studies, so I'd joined Isaac as soon as I'd graduated a year later. It was a partnership that worked well for us. We ran the foundation together, but he was the name and the face behind it all, while I looked after the daily running of the center.

It was as much as I could offer. There was no question about my commitment to it, which was the reason Isaac had been pushing for me to take over running the entire center since he now lived in Manhattan with his husband, Max.

Isaac knew why I didn't want to take on any more responsibility. For the last nine years, any time I'd not been at college or working, I'd been looking for my missing younger brother, Afonso.

"Tiago?" Isaac called from the other end of the line.

"I'll think about it, okay?"

"Okay," he said with a mix of hope and resignation. "Was there anything in particular you were calling for?"

"Yes. Is your apartment still on the market?"

"Yeah, why?"

"Would you mind if I rent it for the next two months? My landlord is finally going to do some work to my place, and I need somewhere to stay. I'll pay you, of course."

"Don't be silly. You don't need to pay. I'll tell the agency to take the apartment off the rentals list until you don't need it anymore."

"Thanks, Isaac. I really appreciate that. How's Max?"

"He's starting school for his specialization in pediatric nursing, so he's a bit stressed, but nothing we can't handle."

I couldn't help being a little envious of Isaac and the relationship he had with Max. In another lifetime, I'd have loved to have been in a committed relationship with someone I could share my life with, the challenges and the victories.

Unfortunately, my experience was that my burden was too much for guys to handle, and after a string of failed attempts at dating, I'd decided to stop trying. Waking up to someone whose first smile of the day was for me was, at the moment, just a pipe dream.

"You're happy in New York, right?" I asked before I realized how the question might sound.

"Of course, why do you ask?"

"Never mind, sorry, I don't know why I asked."

I heard a shuffle on the other side of the line before Isaac said, "I gotta go. Lucy's home from school, but we'll speak again soon."

"Okay, thanks again for letting me stay at the apartment."

"Sure, no problem. There's a spare key in the office safe at the center. Bye, Tiago."

"Bye, Isaac."

It was a relief knowing I had a temporary place to live, and if Isaac didn't want me to pay rent, I could save some money to use toward the search for my brother.

Now that was something I should be focusing on rather than my lack of a love life. Maybe I needed to go out dancing soon to get the need out of my system. That always helped when I hit a slump in my search.

I spent the rest of the evening packing my stuff in boxes to take to storage. No point in moving everything over to Isaac's apartment. For the sake of two months, I could live out of a suitcase. Besides, Isaac's apartment was fully furnished and very nice. I was already looking forward to sitting on his balcony and enjoying the views over the river Tagus.

When Monday didn't start in the best way, I knew there wouldn't be much hope for the rest of the week. It began with a local furniture company withdrawing their offer so they could help furnish a homeless shelter. They'd originally promised us their old display bedrooms so we could finish furnishing the last few rooms we had left in the center. .

I couldn't even argue because it was also a good cause, but I was starting to get more and more fed up with the LGBTQ center's help being withdrawn to support other causes that weren't as *controversial*, because somehow, helping young people in need became controversial from the moment their sexuality or gender preference came into play.

The rest of the week didn't fare any better. While we already had a few rooms furnished so we could offer emergency accommodation to LGBTQ youth, the fact was the building we were in was old and the running costs were increasing, as were the number of repairs that were needed. A meeting with the Lisbon Council representative was the final nail in the coffin. There were no additional funds for us this year, and since we already had the building, furnished accommodations, and all the facilities of a day youth center, there was no way they'd relocate us to better facilities elsewhere.

By the time I met my friend, police detective Fred, on Friday night, I was ready to forget the week.

"Hey, T, you look like you need to get drunk, laid, or both."

I laughed. I'd met Fred around four years ago when he came to the center to introduce himself as the detective in charge of missing persons. As a gay man himself, he took particular interest in cases that involved LGBTQ people. Not surprisingly, he hadn't been aware of my own ongoing case since his predecessor hadn't briefed him. That was something else that didn't surprise me. The man had been nothing short of a homophobe who kept insisting that my brother was likely dead because that's what happens to the majority of LGBTQ homeless kids.

I hadn't been too sure the young detective had enough experience to do any more than the last two detectives had done, but he'd proved me wrong.

In the last three years, Fred had used all the technology that was available to him to find Afonso. He seemed almost as invested in finding my brother as I was, which was something I couldn't quite understand but appreciated nonetheless.

"Freddie, sweet cheeks, have you got anything for me?"

That was the first question I asked every single time I saw Fred, and nine times out of ten the answer was no, but man did I live for the one time he said yes, even when it had turned out to be a dead end.

"Not today, babe."

The words were expected, but there was something behind them. Reticence? Did he know more than he could tell? Despite our friendship, I knew sometimes Fred couldn't tell me what he knew. I still trusted him to share what he had as soon as he could, so I decided to not give it too much thought.

"Well then, let's get drunk." I grabbed his hand and pulled him toward the bar and ordered two shots and two beers.

As the alcohol settled in my stomach, I started feeling more and more relaxed. Most of the time, I was in control, always prepared in case I heard any news that meant I'd need to go get my brother. The times when I let go were few and far between, especially since Isaac got all loved up and then moved to New York, which increased my workload at the center.

The beat of the music was inviting, and I found myself wanting to let loose on the dance floor.

I took Fred's hand and pulled him toward the mass of bodies grinding and moving with the song.

Fred was taller and bigger than me, so I placed myself with my back to his front and wrapped his hands around my waist. We moved together to the rhythm of the song. Maybe it was the alcohol or the funky mood I was in, but suddenly I felt I needed more than the innocent grinding that we always defaulted to when we came out dancing.

When Fred first came to the center, he'd crushed hard on Isaac, who was at first totally unaware and then unavailable. Since then, I hadn't seen Fred with anyone, which wasn't to say he didn't date.

We had this unspoken agreement that we wouldn't take things any further than the drunken kiss we'd shared a few months ago. We both knew it wouldn't lead anywhere and could ruin our friendship.

Today, however, with his hardness grinding against my ass and his hands roaming my chest, I was ready to let go of that agreement and ask him to fuck me five ways into Sunday.

Fred was totally my type: taller than me, bigger and stronger, someone who lives to care for others. Maybe for tonight, I could pretend that we were into each other and I could chase the loneliness away. Just for tonight.

"What's going on in that pretty head of yours?" he said in my ear. It was loud enough to be heard over the *thump thump* of the music, but quiet enough that his low voice and his breath on my ear made me shiver and my jeans tighten.

I turned around, and as he took in a breath when our hips lined up, Fred's eyes went dark and searching.

"Been a while for you, too?" I asked.

"Yeah," he said, running a hand through his short beard. "You know we shouldn't."

"I know. Don't you sometimes just want to forget about all the shouldn'ts?"

"More often than I care to admit."

"Do you ever give in?"

"No," he said. No further explanation needed.

I placed a light kiss on his lips and rested my head on his shoulder as we swayed along with the music.

We stayed a little longer in the club and then Fred drove me home since he'd had nothing else to drink after the first two, and that had been hours ago. Despite my initial plan for the evening, I wasn't half as drunk as I thought I would have been, considering the amount of shots and beer I'd downed earlier in the evening.

"Thanks for watching out for me, sweet cheeks," I said, taking the house keys from my pocket.

"Anytime, babe."

Fred paused, like he was considering what to say next.

"Tiago, you know I'd tell you if I could, right?"

I nodded. That was all he needed to say. I had to be patient and soon he'd be able to let me in on what he was working on, especially if there was a chance of it leading to the location of my brother.

Fred kissed me on the cheek and left.

I hated going to bed without a shower, especially if I'd been out dancing. It was nice getting clean of the club smells, the sweat, beer, and bitter disappointment of coming home alone.

The hot water felt like heaven on my skin.

While my dick was all up for playing earlier, now it was truly out for the night. Maybe the alcohol did have an effect on me after all. Still, I had a weekend of packing and moving ahead of me, so I went to bed hoping for a peaceful night without the usual nightmares that consisted of all the horrible things that may have happened to my little brother in the last eight years.

3

VÍTOR

"Mr. Alves, can I call you Vítor?"

"Of course."

He nodded. "And please call me Bernardo. Don't take my question in the wrong way, I am very pleased that you agreed to meet with me. My question is, why now?"

I couldn't say I was caught off guard, after all, I'd been asking myself the same question from the moment I'd decided to accept one of the many requests for a meeting from one of the partners at Lopes Dias Gomes Architects.

I was expecting the question. After all, Bernardo had been trying to meet up with me for the last year, and even when I'd repeatedly said I was happy in my current partnership, they'd always kept the door open for me.

Answering it was the harder part. I knew I was meant to keep my cards close to my chest to get the best deal, but that had been a role best suited for Dri. He'd always said that no matter how much I tried, I was like glass, totally see-through. He'd also said it was one of the things he loved about me.

A pang of sadness and unease came over me. Was I betraying him by being here in Lisbon meeting with another firm? We'd worked so damned hard to be taken on as joint partners, especially because we'd had to keep our relationship a secret initially.

I decided to be honest.

"Bernardo, I want to say that this is a great opportunity for me and I would welcome the change. I've followed the projects your partnership has been involved with, and I've been impressed with how you manage to bring history and tradition into the current times." I let out a long breath. "If you want to know the truth, I don't know why I'm here."

"We've also been keeping an eye on your work, Vítor. We've wanted you with us for a long time, but we didn't think you would ever consider a partnership that didn't include Rodrigo. We are a smaller firm of three with a few junior and senior architects. Over the years, we've wanted to bring you in as a senior architect, but then our hopes were crushed when you became a partner in your current firm. Now that my good friend and partner João Dias is retiring, we thought it would be a good opportunity to bring you on as a partner to Lopes Gomes Alves." He took a sip of his espresso and smiled. "It has a nice ring to it, don't you think?"

I laughed. "You're a good salesman, Bernardo."

"I'm not selling, Vítor. The job is yours. We are ready for you. the question is, are you ready for a move?"

Part of me was ready for a move. Professionally, it was a great move. Recently I'd felt that, while I had a certain degree of influence in my current partnership, the fact that there were six partners in total made it challenging to get the right projects through the door. They were all about chasing the next big contract to design shopping centers, government buildings, and celebrity homes. Dri and I wanted to design people's dreams, not chase the next big paycheck.

I got that it was important for our reputation to do a certain amount of work that put our name out there, but since Dri's place in the partnership had been replaced by a senior architect who was more interested in being in celebrity gossip magazines, I felt the partnership had lost its way.

"Bernardo, I really appreciate your offer. You are right, I'm not sure I'm ready for such a big move. Professionally, it makes sense, and if there were no other factors, I'd be jumping in with both feet. Personally, there are a few things I need to work through before I can accept your offer and we start working through the details. I'm in Lisbon until tomorrow. I can come to your office before I drive up to Porto. I'll have your answer for you then."

I needed to think about Bernardo's offer, and since I'd spent the morning in the car and then sat down for lunch with Bernardo, I felt like walking it out.

Maybe taking in the sounds, the smells, and the people of Lisbon would give me some clarity.

A long time ago, this city was my escape. The place I used to go to when I was trying to figure myself out. That was before the events that changed my life forever happened right here.

I couldn't blame the city, of course, but the feelings that were being churned up were still hard to face.

When I'd moved to Porto, I found my real escape. I was lucky that I found someone that helped me when I needed it the most. I met Dri shortly afterward and hadn't looked back since.

Well, that wasn't totally true. While I didn't think of the past, I wondered if my brother still lived in the same place with his wife and kids, if they were happy. Despite everything, they were the ones I hoped I'd saved when I'd made the decision to leave.

He'd always been my protector. Whenever my father had decided I wasn't man enough to be his son, it was my brother that put himself between us, almost always ending up on the receiving end of our father's fists.

I wondered about Paula. My best friend and keeper of my secrets. Would she hate me too because I didn't tell her I was running away? Maybe it was too much to hope that she'd understand why I'd had to do it.

She'd been the only person I'd confided in when I was struggling with my sexuality and myself.

Despite my father's jibes about me being girly, weak, a sissy, I'd always thought I was just an introvert. I'd focused on my drawings and dreams of designing buildings. I guess I was a late bloomer, or maybe it was because under the watchful eye of my father, I naturally stopped thinking of myself in the context of sexuality or sexual identity.

It wasn't until I saw an actor on a popular telenovela that I wondered for the first time if I was interested in boys. I was only sixteen. He was so beautiful that I couldn't take my eyes off the TV. I became obsessed to the point I would never miss an episode and had to watch it with a cushion on my lap to hide my erection.

Sharing a bedroom with my brother then didn't allow me much privacy, so I became an expert at bringing myself to climax in the bathroom in record time. Of course, that only brought on more guilt and fear of my father because he was actually right.

As I grew older, my dad's physical abuse decreased slightly, but the emotional and verbal abuse became so bad that I started denying to both Paula and myself that I was gay.

I took on a job on a building site, much to the disappointment of my brother who wanted me to go to university and even offered to help me with the costs.

No, I needed to do a man's job because I was strong and straight, and one day I would marry Paula because she was my best friend.

I laughed. So much for taking in the feel of Lisbon when I'd been walking for around two hours lost in thought. I found myself in downtown Lisbon near a famous café known for its custard tarts. Dri had been addicted to custard tarts so he'd buy them anywhere he could, although more often than not they were from a store. It had been a while since I'd had one in a café, especially one that made them on site.

Before I could go in something pulled at my coat sleeve. I turned to see an older Gypsy woman looking at me and thrusting a small bouquet of dried flowers in my direction. Her clothes were well-worn, but the scarf on her head was full of bright colors in a traditional pattern of gold and red flowers.

"Oh, no, thank you." I tried to decline the offer. She was probably trying to get some money from me.

"For the love of your life," she said. Her eyes were bright green and didn't go with the dark color of her skin and the wrinkles that adorned her face.

Maybe it was the mood I was in, or maybe it was the piercing look she gave me. I couldn't dismiss her.

"I'm afraid the love of my life is no longer with us."

She took my hand and turned it over so my palm was facing up before looking closer and tracing some of the lines in my hand.

"My son, we can have more than one great love in our lifetime." She placed the small bouquet in my palm and wrapped my fingers around it. Then she smiled at me and left.

I stared at her as she disappeared around the corner. I considered chasing after her to tell her she was wrong and to return the flowers, but decided against it and went into the café instead. What I needed was a custard tart and a coffee. Putting the small bouquet in my pocket, I approached the counter to place my order.

After an afternoon of reflection, I was considering accepting Bernardo's offer. I decided I would attempt reaching out to Mateus once again and then make up my mind.

The call was about to go to voicemail when I heard the voice on the other side.

"Hi, Dad."

Those two little words nearly brought tears to my eyes.

"Mateus, son. I'm so—"

"Wait, Dad. Let me speak."

"Okay."

"Look, I trust that you didn't know, and I think Dad probably thought he was doing what he thought was best, as always."

I let out a choked laugh, he was so right. Dri did think he always knew best. He'd done everything with the best intentions, and he'd had the biggest heart of anyone I'd ever met, but man, did he think he knew it all.

"Thing is, Dad, I don't know who I am now. Everything I knew to be true about where I come from isn't, and I need some space to come to terms with it and figure out what I'm going to do. I just need some space, okay?"

If it meant I wasn't going to lose my son I was willing to give him all the time in the world.

"I'll be here when you're ready, Mateus."

I paused, considering how to tell him about Lisbon.

"I'll speak to you soon, Dad."

"Wait, please. There's something I need to tell you. I've been offered a partnership in a different company. I'm considering it."

"That's great. I think you should take it."

"They're based in Lisbon."

"Are you going to move there?"

I really wished I could tell from his voice how he felt about this.

"Temporarily, yes, if I take the job. I may be able to negotiate working from a satellite office in Porto."

"Go for it. It would be good for you to have some change."

"Thanks. I'd like to see you before I move."

"I'll think about it."

"Okay, son. I love you, Mateus."

"Love you, too, Dad."

When I ended the call, I felt a need to move, do something, so I left the café and resumed my walk.

I don't know how I didn't realize the direction I'd been walking in, and then didn't have to wonder for very long if the bar was still there, because as soon as I turned a corner, what I saw had me stop in my tracks.

After twenty-seven years I'd expected the entrance to have had an upgrade, but the "Bar Livre" sign was still the same. One thing was strikingly different, and that was the big rainbow flag flying proudly above the door.

Two guys walked out of the bar hand in hand. The music coming from inside was inviting. Maybe it was morbid curiosity, but suddenly I needed to revisit the place that had sealed the fate of my life.

4

TIAGO

"Hey, gorgeous, what can I get you?"

"A glass of Apothic Red, please."

After two weeks of busy work at the center and moving to Isaac's apartment, I was in the mood to feel the warmth of the alcohol in my stomach and the relaxed feeling that came with it. The Californian wine was the perfect aid.

I looked at my phone. Fred should have arrived by now. We'd arranged to meet in one of our favorite bars, which was conveniently located only a few blocks from Isaac's, so I'd even walked here.

The waiter placed the glass of wine in front of me, giving me a long stare before he let go of the tall stem of the glass.

"You waiting for someone, gorgeous?"

If he batted his eyelashes any more they'd fall out any minute now. I was feeling flirty and wouldn't normally have minded the attention, but I was meeting Fred, and the waiter wasn't my type.

"I am, yes."

"Shame," he said as he turned back to the other side of the bar, but not without giving me a smile that told me he'd be game for some fun any time.

I took a sip of the wine, tasting the sweet fruitiness. I only drank wine when I was in the mood, and it had to be a sweet variety with good legs. This Californian wine was definitely my favorite.

Fred would no doubt tell me off for my choice of wine, since he preferred Portuguese brands, but I always found them too dry.

I took another sip and looked toward the door once again. Someone was coming in, and from the body type, it looked like it could be Fred, but as soon as the man came through the second set of doors, I realized it wasn't.

Rather than getting back to my drink and texting Fred, I kept looking at the man because my eyes refused to shift. He looked to be in his mid-forties, tall, slim, and with dark hair that turned a salt-and-pepper shade on the sides. I couldn't see his eyes from this distance, but I noticed the tension radiating from him.

He looked around like he was trying to take in his surroundings.

Most of the tables were taken up by couples, which was why I'd sat at the bar while I waited for Fred.

Usually, there were less tables to allow for a bigger, standing crowd when they played live music, but throughout the week, this was a pretty chill bar to hang out in.

I saw my phone light up from the corner of my eye, so I turned my attention from the striking stranger.

Fred: Hey T. Sorry to let you down, I'm stuck at work.

Me: You owe me one.

Fred: Maybe, maybe not ;)

My heart skipped a beat at Fred's text. Did this mean that whatever he was working on could give us some answers on my younger brother's location?

In all the years I'd been searching for him, I'd tried to not spend much time thinking about what had really happened to him. I'd decided I'd focus on finding him first and then deal with the rest later.

The only thing I knew was the reason he'd left home the day he went missing, and I'd never forgive myself for it.

I texted a smiley face back to Fred. We were always careful not to have text conversations that had any meaning in relation to how much he shared with me. After everything he'd done, the last thing I wanted was to get him in trouble.

"Hey, sweetie, can I get you anything?"

I hadn't realized the silver fox I was ogling earlier had sat down on the empty stool next to me and was now under the scrutiny of the waiter.

He looked at my glass of wine and then asked, "Is that red any good?"

When his eyes locked onto mine, I lost my breath for a second. The man wasn't just beautiful, his eyes were the most striking shade of dark blue I'd ever seen, and he had the sexiest chin dimple. My jeans felt tighter as I thought of my tongue running through that dimple.

I shook my head, trying to find words to answer his question, but he was looking at me like he recognized me, which I knew was impossible since I was pretty sure I'd recognize those eyes anywhere.

"If you like sweet with a hint of fruit, then yes, it's a great one," I said, finally finding my words.

He turned to the waiter and paused before saying, "I'll have what he's having."

I laughed at the movie line and saw a smile tease his lips, but it was the way he kept twisting the watch on his wrist that gave his nerves away.

He looked away and kept silent after that. I wanted to take in the lines of his face, the blue in his eyes, that fucking dimple, and I'd be damned if I wasn't curious about what was making him so tense when he'd walked in the bar.

Yep, there was no denying it, I was attracted to my bar neighbor, and for the first time in a while, I wanted to do something about it.

I was thinking about how to best strike a conversation with the somber man when the waiter came over with his drink.

"Is there anything else I can get you, Daddy?"

"Er what? Oh, er no, thank you. Just the wine. Thank you."

I wanted to roll my eyes at the waiter's obvious and unabashed flirting. Maybe it was just part of his act or what he thought was expected of a waiter in a gay bar. Regardless, he wasn't reading the cue that he was making the guy uncomfortable, and that got my hackles up just a little.

"Are you here on your own, or are you meeting someone, Daddy?"

What. The. Fuck.

I'd tried to keep my eyes on my drink up until then.

"He's with me," I blurted.

Both the man and the waiter looked at me, and I waited for either to challenge my obvious lie, but the waiter simply turned and went on to flirt with another customer.

My drinking neighbor looked more relaxed.

"Thanks," he said.

"I'm sorry to have stepped in, but you didn't look like you were enjoying the attention."

"Yeah, it's been a long time since someone was that forthcoming." He laughed, but then something passed over his eyes that I couldn't decipher. I almost didn't hear when he said to himself, "The last time that happened I ended up marrying the guy."

Damn it, why were the good ones always taken? Not that I knew if this guy was one of the good ones or not. There was something about him I couldn't put my finger on, but I felt this compulsion to find out.

He exuded a quiet strength with an underlying layer of vulnerability. How could I even see that when we'd barely exchanged any words?

Maybe I should've left before I did anything I would regret. I was single, but the guy was clearly not.

"He died three years ago," he said, still more to himself.

I realized then that I hadn't acknowledged anything he'd said. His dark blue eyes were fixed on mine, and I wondered if even through my glasses my eyes would give away my attraction.

"I'm sorry."

He smiled and nodded.

"This wine is really nice," he said. "I'm not really a wine person, but sometimes I'm in the mood for it, you know?"

"I'm the same."

"What do you normally drink?"

"Beer, Sagres. You?"

"Same, but the beer of choice in Porto is Super Bock. I never used to like it as much but acquired the taste for it."

"Is that where you're from?" I asked.

"Kind of. I was born there but moved to Caparica when I was a kid. I moved back to Porto in my twenties and have stayed since."

"What brings you to Lisbon?"

"Job opportunity."

"I take it if you're here drinking that you're not too sure about it?"

Talking to this gorgeous man was as easy as breathing. The wine kept coming, and I felt more relaxed than I had in goodness knows how long.

I found out about his job as an architect, and despite my mild state of drunkenness, I got the feeling that in his career, he'd mostly stayed in the shadow of his husband. I didn't get the idea that this was something that bothered him, more like it was a role he'd comfortably settled into.

He was also curious about me and my job. As it turned out, he'd helped design a youth shelter in Porto and was working toward getting vital funding from the city council to design a center for LGBTQ victims of domestic violence.

He was talking about his designs so excitedly that he didn't notice he was leaning toward me. To be fair, neither did I until he stopped talking, his eyes moving between my eyes and my lips. I didn't think it was possible for his eyes to get any darker, but I was wrong.

It would only have taken a small move forward and my lips could've been on his and then I could've found out what I'd been dying to know all night, how soft his lips really were. My mind conjured an image of him lying on top of me, his eyes burning with pleasure, and desperate moans escaping my lips as he consumed me like the last drop of water during a drought.

The only thing that was stopping me was that we'd both drunk more than a few glasses, and something was telling me he would regret it afterward. That damned vulnerability I saw in him was still there, and I didn't want to take advantage of how easily I'd been able to read him.

As soon as I leaned away from him, his expression changed from desire to disappointment. I excused myself to go to the bathroom before I gave in to the kiss he so clearly wanted.

I sagged against the bathroom sink and looked at myself in the mirror as I washed my hands. My skin looked pale thanks to the amount of time I spent indoors. My dark-rimmed glasses did nothing to disguise the bags under my eyes, a side effect from never having enough sleep.

The bathroom door opened with enough force that the loud noise caused me to look in that direction. I didn't have enough time to react to the presence of the sexy man I'd been talking to all night before he took a few steps in my direction, put a hand on my neck, and crashed his lips into mine.

When our lips met, I jolted with the spark that went through me. He stopped for a quarter of a second before he took everything from me with that kiss. His hand tightened around my neck while the other went around my back to pull me closer. I had no choice but to let him take, borrow, steal anything he wanted from me. No, that's not correct. I had a choice, and I chose to give in. I'd never been one to submit to someone before, and I also couldn't understand how I knew this was what both he and I needed. I just did.

My hands were on the sink behind me, so I used them as leverage to grind against him. His body was a fireworks display of emotion as he pressed against me. I wanted to put my hands around him, touch him like he was touching me, but I was too afraid any sudden movement could pierce the thin bubble we were in.

"Fuck, you guys are hot together."

As soon as I heard the voice coming from the door, I knew the bubble hadn't just been pierced. It had evaporated.

My passionate and vulnerable silver fox took a few rapid steps back until he hit one of the stalls. His chest was heaving, and he was struggling to breathe. He looked from me to the guy at the door.

I thought he was going to have a panic attack, so I dared to move forward toward him.

"I'm sorry. I'm sorry." Was all he said before he ran out of the bathroom. I wanted to go after him, but I was sure he'd left the bar, too, and my self-preservation instinct kicked in to stop me. I'd already given too much to a man I hadn't even got a name from.

5

VÍTOR

THE GUILT alone was enough to almost make me skip the visit, but I knew I'd hate myself for it afterward, so I picked up a bouquet of daisies, his favorite flowers, and went over to the cemetery.

The sunny and warm spring day helped calm my nerves. I'd be able to sit on the grass by the grave and talk to him. Some people might have found it strange to sit next to a grave and talk to someone who couldn't answer back, but I always found it strange to stare at a grave and say nothing.

Dri was my best friend, my lover, my everything. Maybe it was crazy, but I would always talk to him, and I would always know in my heart what he'd say back.

The cemetery was on a hill with beautiful views of Porto and the river Douro. The caretaker was a dedicated old man who'd worked at the cemetery since his wife had died years ago. He'd told me he'd applied for the job when he saw it advertised because he wanted to be close to her every day.

When he saw me there for the first time, he'd offered his condolences on the death of my wife. I'd clarified that I'd lost my husband, which he looked surprised about but didn't say anything. As I kept my weekly visits, I got to know Sebastião better. He became the calm presence that soothed my soul on those days when the grief was too much to take on my own.

"Hey, sweetheart," I said as I sat down and placed the flowers on the grave, "I brought you your favorite."

Everything was immaculately clean, but I still felt the compulsion to pass my hands over the stone and his engraved name, removing the invisible dirt.

I could tell that Sebastião had noticed my absence the week before because there was a single rose on the grave that matched the roses on his wife's grave.

My heart swelled at the thoughtfulness of the man who'd lived for his wife, and now that he'd outlived her, spent his days making sure no one was forgotten.

"I'm sorry I didn't come to see you last week." I felt tears burning in the back of my eyes.

If he was here, he'd have had his arms around me and asked me what was up. He'd have said that nothing could be that bad, and if it was, he'd solve it for me. My very own hero.

"I accepted the offer from Bernardo, so I'm going to be in Lisbon for a little while." I picked one of the daisies from the bunch and traced the shape of the petals with my fingers.

"I guess you already knew that, with you being up there watching over me like you promised and all."

When I'd run out of the bar that night, I'd grabbed my overnight case from the hotel, stuffed it all in the car, and driven straight back to Porto. Despite the two glasses of wine and the happy buzz in my belly, I hadn't even been tipsy. I'd been bewitched.

I'd cried all the way home, and it was a minor miracle I hadn't had an accident. The guilt was so crippling that at some point I'd had to pull up at a service station to empty the contents of my stomach.

Bernardo had left a worried message on my phone the next morning. I'd been so exhausted when I'd got home that I'd slept for a day straight. Once I'd showered and felt more human, I'd called him, apologizing for missing the meeting in the morning.

There had been no doubt I'd accept the job when Bernardo was more concerned about my wellbeing than a missed meeting.

As a married man with three children and a few young grandchildren, he'd told me worrying was part of his job description.

I didn't want to say that at nearly fifty, I was far too old to sit in the children category; I also didn't want to say how it had warmed my heart that he'd put me in there regardless.

It was this kind of family-oriented business I wanted to be part of. I didn't need to make money anymore. My career from now on was about the projects I wanted to work on and the revenue came second.

"I feel guilty for giving up my place in the partnership we worked so hard to be part of, but before your diagnosis, you talked about us opening our own office so we could pick which projects we wanted without any politics or agendas. I think this is the closest I'll get, sweetheart."

Dri would have agreed with me. We'd had many conversations over dinner about the direction of the partnership and how some of the senior partners were reluctant to change things because they liked the money coming in hard and fast, especially only a few years away from their retirement. Dri didn't think there would be anything to save from the old partnership.

"You were such a great architect. You never compromised on your vision even when we were still a little wet behind the ears." I chuckled. "And when you walked into a boardroom, fuck, it made me so hard. Every time you set your eyes on mine, I could tell you knew I was hard for you, and I knew you'd be on me as soon as we'd walk through the door at home."

We had so many great memories together, but how could I remember them without also feeling so sad and angry that he was gone and I wouldn't have that again?

"This Gypsy woman stopped me in Lisbon and told me about having more than one love in our lifetime. Do you think that's true? I don't think so. You were it, Dri. You were my once in a lifetime love."

I shook my head as though I was shaking off the feelings and thoughts provoked by the woman's words. Dri would have asked me what I'd want him to do if I'd been the one dying. As much as I couldn't bear the thought of seeing him with anyone else, I'd have wanted him to have a life with a new chance at being happy.

If he was really watching out for me, he'd know what I did, but I needed to be the one to confess.

"I kissed another man, Dri. No, scrap that, I kissed a kid. Fuck, Dri, he can't even have been thirty. I feel so fucking guilty for betraying you." I was looking at the gravestone like I was looking at Dri himself, but everything was blurry from the tears.

"I went into that bar from my twenty-first birthday. I was confused and raw from being there. The kid looked so much like the guy from all those years ago, I think I kissed him to prove to myself that I could do it without consequence, like I was daring the world to tell on me again. Stupid, right? The worst thing is, I don't think it was only that. He was so beautiful and smart, and before I knew it, I'd run into the bathroom after him and kissed him senseless. I took everything I could with no mercy or permission." I didn't stop to breathe until I'd finished my confession. "Why the fuck am I even telling you this?" I choked.

Dri's voice in my head told me I couldn't betray a dead person. I knew he was right. If anything, I'd betrayed the young man by taking advantage of him.

"I love you, so much, that some days I can't even breathe because of how much I miss you. I can't stand being in the house knowing you're never going to come through the door again, and at the same time, I'm terrified of leaving because that would mean putting you behind me. I'm so scared."

I jumped when a hand touched my shoulder.

"It's only me, son." I looked up to see a concerned Sebastião.

"I didn't mean to overhear, but I was walking past to see my Margarida and saw you crying. Do you want to talk?"

I got up from the ground, placing the daisy I had in my hand next to the rest of the bouquet.

"Come on, let's go for a walk," he said.

I followed Sebastião as he led me out of the cemetery toward the Luís I bridge over the river Douro. I smiled as he stopped in the middle. On one side we had the colorful houses on the Porto riverfront and on the other side scattered across the hill of Gaia we could see the many Port wine caves with their big signs.

"You're smiling. I see the walk has already done you good."

"This is where Rodrigo proposed to me. He said that on one side we had the city that was our forever home and on the other, we had the Port caves, meaning our love, like Port wine, would only get better with age. He was right. Every day with him was better than the day before."

"That's not true, is it?"

There was no malice in his voice as he questioned my statement.

"No. Some days he was downright difficult to be around. He thought he was always right and couldn't stand when he was challenged. Not even when that came from me. But damn, I loved how he stuck to his beliefs regardless of what anyone thought. He had such presence, and man did he ever fill out a suit nicely."

"Margarida was very intelligent, but she was a terrible cook. She wanted to be a teacher, but her parents thought the place of a woman was in the kitchen. When we were married, she went back to school, and whenever our parents came over for dinner, I did all the cooking. Till the day the last one of them died, no one ever found out that it wasn't my Margarida cooking dinner."

The glittery water of the river framed by the buildings around it was mesmerizing. I'd never get tired of this view.

"I thought we still had a long time together," I confessed. "He was my first boyfriend, my best friend. How do I carry on without him? I accepted a job in Lisbon, and I'm not sure I can do it now."

"I can't tell you how to grieve, Vítor. God only knows, some days I think I can hear the sewing machine in the spare room where she used to make the costumes for the student plays. But I can tell you that keeping still is no life for anyone. If you carry on and cross the bridge, you might just find that things from the other side look just as nice. Sometimes there's enough time in our life to live on both sides of the bridge."

Sebastião patted my back and smiled.

"I will look after him until you can visit again. And that young man that visits him every day. Leave him to me."

I was speechless as Sebastião walked away from me in the direction we had come from. Had Mateus visited his dad's grave? Was he doing it on a daily basis? Maybe there was still hope that he'd one day forgive his dad for what he'd done.

The other side of the bridge was calling for me, so with Sebastião's words in my head, I decided to go for a walk. Maybe things wouldn't be so bad after all.

6

TIAGO

I HADN'T HEARD from Fred in a week, two if I was to count the week before when he stood me up at the bar, and I was becoming more and more worried with each day that passed. I didn't want to text him or call if he was in the middle of a case, but the silence was driving me nuts, especially because of his last cryptic text.

Living in a constant seesaw of hopefulness and hopelessness was exhausting. I had to believe my brother was out there somewhere. He would be twenty-one now, so he was no longer the little boy that ran away all those years ago. I'd kept all my social media channels open in case he ever wanted to reach out. I didn't engage much, but my name and photo were available for anyone to see. Equally, I spent hours each day looking through photographs, profiles, and names, anything that could lead me to him.

Some days I woke up in fear that I would walk past him in the street and not recognize my brother as the young man he now was. Today was one of those days, and when I felt like this, I couldn't be at the center. It hurt too much to see the young kids who spent time there because I wanted all of them to be my brother, and none were.

I decided to get in the car and drive south of the Tagus river to Caparica to see David, one of my best friends.

Until last year, David was out only to a few very close friends; that was until his childhood best friend and love of his life came back to Portugal from America and they fell in love. It was beautiful seeing David and Joel together. Much like Isaac and Max, they had the kind of love that happens once in a lifetime, and when it does, it changes everything forever.

David was also a top baker and volunteered his time at the center, running baking workshops. The kids loved it so much that some went as far as enrolling in college to become chefs. It made me so proud to see that life could knock these kids down fiercely but they were still strong enough to stand on their own feet and fight back.

As entrepreneurial as he was charitable, David had taken Bruno, one of the kids we helped at the center, under his wing and given him a job at Café Lima, the business he owned with his aunt and uncle, Teresa and Mário.

They'd worked hard over the years to build up the business David's mom, Paula, had started up, and now that David's talent as a baker was becoming more widely known, they were always featured in some kind of best-kept-secret list.

Every time he added a new video to his blog, it went viral because David was not only very talented and came across as passionate about his craft, he was also very kind and extremely easy on the eye.

The scene I walked into in the café made me want to get my phone out and take a photo. Teresa and Mário were huddled behind the counter working on some kind of paperwork, and Joel was sitting at one of the tables with Filipe, Bruno's five-year-old little brother.

While Teresa and Mário looked up and smiled when I came in, neither Joel nor Filipe saw me, such was their focus on the picture they were coloring in. My guess was that both Bruno and David were in the kitchen working.

"No, you're doing it wrong, Uncle Joel." Filipe huffed. "Let me show you." His tiny hands took hold of Joel's big hand and pen as he *helped* Joel color in properly.

"Tiago, how are you doing, dear?"

Teresa's greeting turned Filipe's attention toward me, and in no time at all, both Joel and the coloring pens were discarded as he ran toward me.

"Uncle Tiago"

"Hey, Pip, shouldn't you be at school?" I asked as I picked him up.

He rolled his eyes, which made me smile. "No, silly. It's Easter break. Do you want to color with us?"

"I'm not sure I'm very good at coloring."

"I'll teach you. I'm teaching Uncle Joel, too." He leaned closer and put his little hands around my ear. "He's not very good at coloring."

I wanted to laugh at his not-very-whispery whisper but managed to keep a straight face.

"I need to speak to Uncle David, but I'll come back after, okay?"

"Okay," he said as he wormed his way down to the floor and back to Joel.

I put my hand out over the counter to shake Mário's hand, but Teresa came around to give me a hug. Considering Teresa didn't have any children of her own, she was the most motherly person I knew.

"Is he in the kitchen?"

"Yes, they're working on an order. Go right in. Do you want a coffee and a custard tart?"

"Is the Pope Catholic?" I replied as I kissed her on the cheek.

David and Bruno were mumbling the words of the song that was playing on the radio as they worked around each other. Bruno was covering the smaller of two cakes with white fondant while David applied small decorations to the larger cake.

"Hey, guys."

I got a collective "Hey" but only David looked my way since Bruno was focusing on rolling the fondant on the cake. The guy really had a lot of talent. Although, to be fair, since I was barely able to put a basic meal together, anyone that could put eggs, flour, and butter together and produce a cake was a genius to my eyes.

"What brings you south of the river? Did you want to go through the workshop schedule for the next couple of months?" David asked.

"Yes, that would be good, but that's not why I came. I was wondering if we could talk more about Mário's brother."

Before Christmas, David had asked Isaac for help finding Vítor, Mário's younger brother who'd run away when he was only twenty-one. The event had been a family secret until Mário had confessed to David that the reason he'd reacted so badly to the idea of David being gay was because he was afraid of losing him like he'd lost his brother.

The relationship between uncle and nephew had been very rocky for a long time, but fortunately they'd been working on it since the summer and seemed to be in a good place.

Since then, Café Lima had gone from being the place where David worked to the place we all hung out and felt welcomed by both Teresa and Mário.

With Isaac in Manhattan, there was a lot of work I'd needed to pick up, so while searching for Vítor was on my radar, it hadn't been a priority. Now, with Fred going silent and the workload stabilizing, I needed something new to focus on. Especially since my head was flickering between thinking about my brother and the hot older man I'd kissed in the bar a week ago.

"I'm sorry it's taken so long," I said, taking a seat at a small table on the other side of the kitchen so I wasn't in their way.

"Don't worry, I'm in the center all the time, remember? I know how busy you are, especially now without Isaac there. So, what do you need to know about Vítor?"

"Start at the beginning. What happened before he disappeared?"

"On his twenty-first birthday, he went to a gay bar in Lisbon. I don't know which one. He was seen kissing a guy by someone who knew his dad." David looked at me then, his expression one of anger.

"Never mind that in order to see Vítor there, this person had to be in a gay bar, too. I don't know if they lied about where they saw the kiss happen or what. I just know that this person told Vítor's father who then beat him up so badly he ended up in the hospital."

"Jesus." I'd heard this story so many times before, and each time it made me want to be sick. For all the stuff my stepfather had done to me, he'd never hit me. Although now I wondered if he had whether I'd have tried to protect my brother from a violent man rather than assuming his abuse was solely directed at me.

"What happened in the hospital?" I asked.

"I don't know. Uncle Mário wanted to visit Vítor, but their father was against it. At the time they were quite interdependent and Aunt Teresa was pregnant."

That stopped me in my tracks. "Teresa had a baby?"

"It was a high-risk pregnancy. Sadly, she lost the baby shortly after." There was a little sadness in David's voice as he shared his aunt and uncle's story.

"They didn't try for babies again?"

"They did, but it never happened."

"Okay, so Vítor was in hospital and Mário couldn't visit. When did he run?"

"I think Vítor had quite severe injuries but nothing life threatening. He was in hospital a few days and then one day, he was gone. Uncle Mário was devastated. He started looking for his brother, severed ties with his dad, and rented a little property just for the three of them, but then Aunt Teresa lost the baby."

In a short time, the young couple had cut ties with their family and lost their brother and their child. The story hit me harder than I had expected. I'd already been feeling on edge when I'd decided to come to the café.

"Excuse me for a moment." I looked for the door I knew led out the back of the building. My hands shook as I struggled to open the door. The sunlight outside was too bright, but it didn't matter because my eyes were closed and all I could see was the image inside my head that was causing my panic. The image of the last time I'd seen my brother, not knowing it would be the last.

"Tiago! Are you okay?"

A pair of small arms came around me and a calm voice told me to take in a breath and hold it, then let it out. I kept doing it until the buzzing went and I could breathe better. That's when I realized Teresa was standing in front of me. Her hands went from rubbing circles on my back to wiping my tear-covered face.

"I'm so sorry," was all I could say. "I'm so sorry."

"What are you sorry for, my dear?" Her voice was calm and soothing, much like my mother's had once been. I shook my head to stop myself from talking because if I let out all the pain in my heart, I was absolutely certain I would crumble into a million pieces.

"Come on, dear. Let's go inside."

I got up and followed Teresa to the table where she'd placed the coffee and custard tart I'd asked for earlier.

"I'm sorry about that. I guess I wasn't expecting Vítor's story to hit me so hard," I confessed.

"You will find your brother, my dear," Teresa said, squeezing my hands reassuringly. There was a part of me that doubted it. Sadly, that part was getting louder with each month that passed and I didn't find Afonso.

"Tell me about Vítor. What was he like?"

Teresa smiled. "He was a gentle person, so kind and honest. You could read him like a book. He would try so hard to show a brave face when he was upset, but we could see through it." Her eyes saddened. "I think that's why he became such an easy target for his father. When Mário wanted to be friendly with me at school, Vítor got close to Paula to help his big brother. They became best friends. I always wondered if they'd eventually get married because they were inseparable, especially after Joel's mom left to live in America."

"What kind of things did he like?"

"He always carried a drawing pad with him. He liked to draw things that caught his eye, people, buildings, the world around him. He was so excited to become an uncle."

Teresa's voice left her and tears ran down her face. It was my turn to put my arms around her.

"Aren't we a pair?" I said, trying to inject some humor. "Let me have this coffee before it gets cold, and there's no amount of tears that will stop me eating that custard tart."

She wiped her tears and smiled.

I didn't know what I'd expected when I came to the café to talk to David about Vítor, but I definitely hadn't expected to have my core shaken to the ground.

After twenty-eight years, it would be very difficult to find Vítor, but I'd be damned if I wasn't going to give it my best try.

Coloring with Filipe was the therapy I'd needed after the day I'd had, and I promised I'd take him to the zoo in the next week or so before he went back to school. His excitement was one of the highlights of my week, the other being the man that had starred in all my dreams in the last week, even though he ran away after giving me the best kiss of my life.

7

VÍTOR

THE HOT WATER was hitting all the right spots on my sore back, helping me to finally relax.

I hadn't been able to sleep last night and had ended up giving the house a last-minute clean at three in the morning, even though it wasn't necessary because my cleaner had kindly agreed to come in every few weeks to air the house and keep the dust out.

I knew my lack of sleep and restlessness had been caused by the mixed feelings today's move brought. My head had refused to settle and let me have the rest I'd needed to drive down to Lisbon and unpack before my first day.

As it was, I'd managed to do it all, and even with the heavy traffic on the approach to my new city, I'd managed to arrive at the apartment at a decent time. I was grateful the agency had thought to courier the keys with the lease paperwork. I suspected Bernardo's faithful secretary had had much to do with it. The petite white-haired lady had been nothing short of superhuman each time we'd discussed the arrangements for both my move and the transfer to the new partnership.

Interestingly enough, I'd thought it would have been harder to terminate my connection to my old partnership. As I'd suspected for a while, the partners had been hoping I'd move on after Dri died and had been grooming one of the senior architects to take over. It wasn't so much a surprise for the partners when I announced I was moving on, but a surprise for me when on the same day they announced my replacement.

I couldn't deny my disappointment. Both Dri and I had given most of our careers to that partnership, we'd delivered plenty of successful projects, and Dri in particular had given them the media exposure they'd needed to be one of the most sought-after architect partnerships in Porto.

A little self-doubt had crept up. Maybe Dri had been the talented one, the one who could charm the right people to bring in the projects we'd needed. What if I couldn't do it without him? I couldn't deny that in the last three years I'd basically completed only our outstanding projects and had taken very little new on.

I'd convinced myself that, despite Dri not being around, I could give our clients what they needed to complete their projects. What if I couldn't do it on my own?

Dri's voice in my head was telling me to stop those insecure thoughts and trust myself.

"You are a talented architect, baby. I can go out there and be a showman because I have you beside me, not behind me." He'd told me those words so many times they'd stuck, but without him to repeat them, in my head I was letting an older, darker voice come through. The voice that told me I wasn't man enough, smart enough, or strong enough to amount to anything in life. My father's voice.

I turned the water off and grabbed my towel before I stood in front of the mirror to stare at my reflection.

"Get a grip, Vítor. You are forty-nine years old for goodness sake."

What I needed was some food and a coffee to line my stomach before I read through some information Bernardo had sent me ahead of my first day.

I would have to buy Bernardo's assistant some flowers to thank her for making sure I was comfortable in the apartment because somehow, the agency had even stocked the fridge with some basic foods and there was fresh bread, too.

Wrapping the towel around my hips, I walked out of the bedroom and down the corridor leading to the living room and kitchen.

My intention was to get the coffee going while I got dressed. The apartment had a stunning view of the river, and I hoped it wasn't too chilly outside for me to enjoy my snack on the balcony. I hadn't explored the two-bedroom apartment properly in my haste to unpack and shower after my trip, but one thing was unmissable, the stunning view. I could already see myself enjoying many evenings out there on the balcony with a beer in my hand.

I heard the noise of a key at the door as I was turning the corner from the corridor and stopped in my tracks in the middle of the living room when the door opened.

Big brown eyes stared at me from behind dark-rimmed glasses. We were locked in position for minutes or hours, I wasn't sure.

As those deep eyes left mine and started drifting down my body, I remembered I was only wearing a towel and blood had started rushing south. No wonder I'd lost the ability to think, let alone question why I was facing the beautiful young man I'd kissed at the bar just over a week ago.

"What are *you* doing here?"

There was a hint of anger in his voice. What the hell?

"Do you work for the agency?" I asked.

"What?"

He reached for the phone in his pocket.

"Who are you calling?" I asked.

"My friend, the owner of this apartment. Who do you think I'm calling?"

He looked like he was about to lose it, and I was only wearing a towel.

The ding coming from the elevator made us both jump and realize the front door was still open behind him.

He turned to close the door but didn't shut it all the way, as though it would be a bad thing to have us both together within the four walls of the apartment.

"Look, I'm not sure what's happening, but I'm feeling a little underdressed. Do you mind if I go put some clothes on and then we can figure this out?"

"Fine." He huffed as I turned back toward the master bedroom.

When I returned to the living room, he wasn't there and the front door was closed properly. I followed the noise of the coffee machine. He didn't hear me approach, so I was able to take him in as he moved around the kitchen like he was at home.

His jeans clung to his ass like they were made to measure, and he'd changed from a shirt to a long-sleeve T-shirt that fit his slim form perfectly.

When we'd met at the bar, he'd been sitting down, and then when I'd kissed him, my brain had been all but short-circuiting. All I remembered about him, apart from the feel of his body against mine and his soft sweet lips, were his eyes. That shade of dark chocolate I'd wanted nothing more than to indulge in.

I forced myself to look away and get my lust under control. The guy was too young, and I was definitely not on the market. For goodness sake, I loved my husband.

He went to the fridge and took the plates of ham and cheese, and I saw he had a few slices of bread ready to make a sandwich. Shit, maybe the guy lived here and this had been a mistake by the agency. To think, I actually thought the agency had been extra efficient by giving me some welcome groceries. Unfortunately, it was too late to call them and clarify, so we'd have to agree on some kind of arrangement for tonight.

"I'm sorry, I may have overreacted a little earlier," he said, "but I thought you were a burglar."

"Oh yes, the semi-naked burglar gang. I've recently been initiated." I chuckled and saw the tips of his ears go pink.

He didn't turn from his sandwich preparation. "I'm starving and assumed you might need something to eat, too. Is a sandwich okay?"

"Yes, thank you. You're right, you caught me just as I was on my way to prepare something to eat. I want to help, but I haven't been here long enough to locate the cups and cutlery."

"That cupboard, first door, bottom shelf, and the spoons are in that drawer." He pointed to the cupboard on his left-hand side.

Once I located the cups and filled them with fresh coffee, we sat at the table with our food.

"So," we both said at the same time.

"What's your name?" he asked.

"Vítor, yours?"

He stopped what he was doing and stared at me for a few seconds before he shook his head like he was shaking an errant thought and put his hand out in my direction.

"I'm Tiago. Nice to meet you, Vítor."

We both laughed. We were introducing ourselves like we'd never met before when only days ago we'd had our tongues down each other's throats. Somehow, the moment dissipated some of the tension between us.

"This is my friend's apartment," he said. "Isaac lives in New York now. I'm staying here for the next two months while my place is remodeled. How is it that you had a key to get in?"

"I have a new job here in Lisbon. My partner's assistant arranged the rental. I had a few options for apartments and picked this one because of the view of the river. The agency sent me the contract and the keys, so I know I'm not in the wrong place."

Tiago's face dropped, and he put his sandwich down.

"I guess you have more right to be here than I do. Isaac was going to remove the apartment from the market, but my guess is this all happened too quickly." He paused like he was steeling himself to ask a very difficult question.

"Can I ask a favor? I can find somewhere else for tomorrow, but could I stay for tonight?"

Part of me was angry that he'd think I'd kick him out on the street just like that, but I also saw the vulnerability in his eyes.

"I've only been here long enough to unpack and take a shower, but I know there's a second room, probably the one you've been staying in since there were no personal belongings in the master bedroom."

"That used to be Isaac's room. I felt odd sleeping there, so I took the guest bedroom."

"Why don't you stay here as you planned."

He nodded, but he didn't look any happier with my offer.

"Oh, er, I'm not sure that's a good idea," Tiago said. "I mean, it's for two months."

"Why?"

"Because… well, er…" His cheeks went a delectable shade of pink. "The bar. Umm, what happened the other week."

I knew we'd have to talk about it eventually, so I guessed this was as good a time as any.

"Look, Tiago, I'm sorry I kissed you like that and then just ran out. I was going through some stuff that day, and I have a history with that bar. I wasn't thinking. If you can forgive the momentary lapse of an old man, then I could use the company."

Tiago stilled and got up. I thought he might walk out on me, which I would have deserved considering what I did to him, but he only went to grab a glass of water.

"You're not an old man, and thank you, I would love to stay if you're sure I won't be in your way. Two months is a long time."

"Yes, I'm sure. Two months will fly by, and as I said, I'd love the company," I said.

We ate the rest of our sandwiches while we made light conversation.

"So, you did take the job you mentioned at the bar."

"Yeah, I guess I did."

"You're still not sure about it."

That wasn't a question. I looked at him and he smiled. I hadn't noticed he'd placed his glasses on the table while he ate. His eyes, without the glass barrier, were deeper and even more piercing than ever.

"Has anyone ever told you how see-through you are?"

"Yes. Yes, someone has," I struggled to say.

"Shit, I put my foot in it. I'm sorry, I shouldn't have said that."

"No, it's okay. You were right. I always struggled to keep my emotions to myself. It has landed me in trouble more than a few times."

Tiago looked like he wanted to say something, but it never came. Instead, he got up to clean up the dishes.

"Nope, it's my turn. You prepared the food."

"Thanks. I had a long day, so I'm going to grab a shower and go to bed," he said.

"Tiago," I called before he left the kitchen. "I should do some grocery shopping. The fridge is rather empty. Is there anything I can get you tomorrow?"

"No, thanks. I don't do a lot of cooking, especially not in Isaac's nice kitchen. Let's say fire and I don't get on very well." He laughed.

I smiled back. "Okay."

And as he turned back toward his bedroom, I decided what I was going to do with the food situation in the apartment. I was also not going to think of Tiago naked in the shower only a few rooms away.

I realized then that I hadn't thought of Dri in all the time I'd been in Tiago's presence. A heavy weight settled on my heart, and my hand rubbed my chest almost instinctively. The apology wanted to leave my lips, but I knew wherever Dri was he knew how I felt.

As soon as I finished in the kitchen, I went over to my room and opened my laptop to do some work. Tomorrow was a new beginning. Whatever that meant.

8

TIAGO

"Morning!"

I looked up from my computer to see David and Joel coming into the center. I normally didn't have any visitors this early, which meant they were concerned about me.

I got up to greet them. "Guys, shouldn't you be in bed?"

They exchanged a look and a smile that managed to warm me even though it wasn't directed at me.

"I'm going to work on the wall," Joel said before he gave David a kiss and went out through the door behind my desk.

The secluded back garden was by far the favorite hangout for the majority of the kids that came to the center after school. When we remodeled it last year, we'd asked for some suggestions, and they'd wanted a wall they could paint over and over again. The idea was that a group would paint something on the wall and we would keep it for some time before we painted over it and started again. So far, we'd had six awesome pieces of temporary art.

The art didn't get completely lost once it was painted over. Apart from the group photos we took after each piece was complete, we also took photos we could use for marketing purposes and to raise money. Some of our benefactors loved the idea so much that they were now collecting each photo every time we had a new painting. Thankfully, that also came with a much-needed donation, so I was glad to see we were about to get a new piece.

"The kids asked Joel to help them with some quotes for the wall. He wouldn't stop talking about it," David said.

"Is that why you're here?" I raised a brow, and David smiled shyly.

"I have custard tarts. Want to get some coffee going?" he said, placing a small box on my desk.

"Like I'd say no. Keep an eye out here."

I left and headed for the kitchen. The garden was out back through the kitchen, so I expected to see Joel getting ready to paint the wall white again, but I was surprised to see him sitting at one of the kitchen tables looking at his phone.

"Why do I feel this is a trap?"

He smiled and pointed at the chair across from his, motioning for me to sit. I noticed the coffee machine was already going.

"Sorry, it wasn't our intention," he said. "David was really worried about you yesterday. He wanted to follow you home to make sure you were okay."

"Thank you. I am okay, honestly."

He played with the phone and then took a big breath. "I know we haven't talked much about it, but if you ever need to, you know you can talk to me, right? After yesterday, I realized what an unfair thing it was to ask you to find Vítor. David had a hard time growing up with such a strained relationship with Mário. Now that things are back on track, I know he's desperately trying to do this for his uncle, knowing how much he still misses his brother."

"If anyone gets it, it's me." I put my hand on Joel's restless one.

"I want him to be happy."

"He is happy. This is the happiest I've seen him since I've met him. He was always good at pretending he was okay, but now that I've seen how his face lights up even when he just says your name, I can tell the difference. That is true happiness. He may want to find Vítor so badly that it consumes him, but it doesn't mean he's not happy."

"Thank you," Joel said, and I got up to pour the freshly brewed coffee into our mugs so I could return to the front of the center.

David looked more worried than before as I placed the coffee mug in front of him and reached out for the custard tart box.

"Come to daddy," I said, inhaling the scent of the pastries and taking one out. "If Joel doesn't come out, I'm having his, too."

"They're all for you."

"Man, you keep this up and *I'll* marry you." And as if he was listening behind the door, Joel came back, planted a toe-curling kiss on David's mouth, stole a tart, and left again. I couldn't help laughing.

"Now that he's marked his territory, shall we talk about what's on your mind?"

He put an envelope on the desk and pushed it toward me.

"What's this?"

"Aunt Teresa said they don't have any photos of Vítor because his dad destroyed them all. Last night, Joel had the idea to go through my mom's old photos. I found a few that I'm pretty sure have Vítor in them."

I opened the envelope and took out the three photos. On one of them, two young guys and two girls sat on the beach. My guess was they were eighteen or nineteen when the photo was taken.

"That's my aunt and uncle," David said, pointing to the couple on the right, "and that's my mom, so I guess Vítor is the other guy, but he could also be the one taking the photo. If you look at the other photo, he's there again with my mom next to the car she owned with Joel's mom."

"How about the third one? I can't see him." The third photo was a large group photo taken at Mário and Teresa's wedding. The age and resolution of the photograph made it difficult to distinguish faces, but after a minute I spotted him.

"Oh yes, he's here next to Mário. He looks really happy, and look, your mom is next to Teresa."

"I showed these to my aunt. She told me Vítor and Mom were their maid of honor and best man. They joked that day that Mom and Vítor would be the next ones down the aisle."

I looked at David. "Do you think they were together?"

"They were best friends, for sure."

I looked at the beach photo again. They all looked happy and relaxed. I noticed that Vítor had blue eyes unlike his brother but still had the same dark hair. The photo was old, but I could tell he'd been a very handsome young man. Paula and Teresa could have been twins with their long wavy dark brown hair and brown eyes.

"Can I keep these? I want to study them further."

"Sure. Thanks, T, I really appreciate what you're doing. I know it's not easy for you. So, what else is going on with you? I haven't seen Fred around in a while."

"Well, if that's not the million-euro question. I haven't heard from him, either, and it's worrying me, but I know sometimes he can be away for long periods of time."

"And how about you?"

I sighed.

"Believe it or not, there is more than one Vítor in my head at the moment." I chuckled.

David perked up. "Do tell."

I told him about the evening Fred couldn't meet me at the bar and how I met Vítor, the kiss, and then last night when he turned out to be the new tenant from the agency.

"He didn't have to do that, you know. He could have kicked me out right there and then."

"What's he like, then?"

"He's a little taller than me, well-built but not overly muscly, and he has this little dimple on his chin and salt-and-pepper hair—"

"Oh my god, you want to get in his pants."

"I don't think he heard you all the way from wherever he works now."

"Wait. How old is this guy?"

"Forty-five? A little older? Don't think he'd be fifty, though."

David stared back at me.

"What? I don't care about shit like age. The man is unarguably beautiful. It doesn't matter, anyway, because nothing is going to happen between us."

"Why not?"

"Because he lost his husband a while ago, and I'm not sure he's ready for anything."

"Not even some no-strings-attached fun?"

I shook my head.

David insisted that I could stay with them in their apartment in Caparica, but I didn't want to be in their space. After thirteen years apart, they deserved all the alone time they needed.

"Pass, I'd get diabetes in three days flat from pastries and your sickly-sweet love."

When Joel joined us, we'd already done the baking workshop schedule and a shopping list, so they went back to Caparica and left me to my work and thoughts of the man I wanted to jump but couldn't. They'd also left behind the box that still contained two custard tarts, one of which I was going to save for Vítor.

While the day started well with my friends' visit, it went downhill very quickly. I was starting to think this was now my life.

The water company sent us a bill that was more than double our normal amount. After hours on the phone with numerous customer care assistants and going through all the bureaucracy that came with having to explain why it was me on the phone and not Isaac, I managed to speak to someone who still had both halves of their brain talking to each other.

"To be honest, Tiago, I can't see an error in the system. I was hoping there was one because if the charges are correct, then it means you have a leak somewhere in the building."

"Fuck my life. I don't need this," I muttered to myself but clearly not quietly enough because the guy on the other end of the phone laughed.

"You need to call the maintenance helpline. They'll arrange for a certified plumber to inspect the property. If it turns out you have a water leak, they can help fix it. If not, then you'll need to come back to us so we can have another look at the bill."

The only thing that was keeping me from having a mental breakdown was the stress ball I was holding in my hand. It was bound to burst any time now from being overworked, and it wouldn't even be the first time that had happened, or the second.

By three in the afternoon, I'd spent a total of four hours on the phone, mostly on hold, and had explained the problem to at least five people. By six, I still didn't have a plumber willing to come to inspect the potential leak.

"Can I speak to Oliveira, please? Tell him it's Tiago from Fundação Arco-Íris." Oliveira worked for Lisbon city council and was one of the few people I knew there who used their power and influence to help people.

"He's not available, sir. Can I book an appointment for another time?"

"He's never available. Please tell him it's me. He will pick up my call."

For all the challenges I faced and the damned homophobic bastards that put walls in my way, there were still a few places I could go to. Oliveira always listened without judgment and then decided if he could help or influence a decision. He was also a straight-as-an-arrow married man with two children. He was the personification of an ally if there ever was one.

"Tiago, my man, what's up?"

"Oli, I'm having the day from hell and I need some strings pulled if you can help."

"Any time, man, you know I've got your back. Tell me what's going on."

I explained what was happening and the risk to the building and neighboring buildings if there was a leak. Delays with the inspection could put not only me and the kids at risk but also the businesses and residences right next to us. In recent years there had been far too many buildings collapsing in the center of Lisbon for me to afford to take this lightly.

Oli, as always, was fully supportive and promised to do what he could to help, and I had no doubt that help would come. Just like he was the string I could pull, he also had his own strings in the form of his dad, the former president of the city council and one of the most respected retired politicians in the city.

By the time I pulled up at the apartment, my head was banging and I wasn't even sure I could be bothered preparing a sandwich to eat.

Unfortunately, my tummy rumbled as soon as I got out of the

elevator and smelled whatever the neighbor was cooking, so I knew I definitely couldn't get away with going to bed on an empty stomach.

The smell was somehow stronger when I opened the door to the apartment, and I realized that in all the stress of the afternoon, I'd forgotten I now had a roommate. One that seemed to be an excellent cook.

Perfect, just what I needed. Food envy for the next two months.

9

VÍTOR

I HEARD the key in the door and moments later Tiago stood by the archway entrance of the kitchen.

"Hey, I hope you like risotto because I'm sure there's enough here for us and the neighbors."

Tiago's face lit up like it was Christmas morning. He also looked exhausted.

"Hey, are you okay?"

"Yes, just tired. You made enough food for me?" he said, coming closer and looking at the pot.

"Of course. It would be silly to go to all this trouble just for me." I'd been doing it for the last three years and hated it every single time. "Not to mention you left enough coffee for me this morning and that made my day."

He snorted. "That's as much as I can do in the kitchen without needing to call the fire service."

"I'll happily wake up to a fresh cup of coffee every day, even if I do have to make my own toast." I winked.

Tiago chuckled. He was so close to me the hairs on my arms were standing up. I could smell the remnants of his aftershave together with his natural scent. I looked at his lips and my mind went straight back to the night at the bar and the way his body had molded to mine, how pliable he'd been in my arms.

"I should take a shower before dinner," he said, stepping back, his voice deeper than earlier.

I turned my attention to the food, not daring to look into his eyes in case I saw something I didn't want to see, or even worse, something I did want to see.

"Yes, of course, there's enough time until dinner is ready."

He walked out of the kitchen but came back seconds later with a small box.

"I have dessert," he said, placing the box on the table before leaving again.

It was only when I heard the shower going in his en suite that I took a deep breath and gave myself a pep talk. I'd never been attracted to younger men before. Why was I struggling so much with this particular young man? For goodness sakes, I was pretty sure I could be his dad.

I stirred the risotto and then got working on setting the table.

When Tiago came back into the kitchen, he was wearing some old jogging bottoms and a University of Lisbon T-shirt and looked a lot more relaxed. His hair was still wet from the shower, and it appeared as if he'd only run his hands through it.

He took two beers from the fridge and joined me as I served our dinner.

"Oh my god, this is really good," he said with a mouthful of risotto. "Sorry, I'm behaving like a pig, but man, where did you learn how to cook like this?"

"I always enjoyed cooking, so I guess it's the many years of practice from doing it at home for us and when friends come over for our usual Sunday lunch. It wasn't always this good, though. One time we'd gone out to a party on a Saturday night and we overslept. Dri had the worst hangover and couldn't even help me with the preparation. Since our friends had all been drunk the night before, they weren't very discerning with the food, so no one realized I hadn't cooked something properly until two of the guys were sick."

Tiago was staring at me with a big smile.

"What?"

"You got so animated talking about your friends. Was Dri your husband?"

I stared back at him.

"Your face lit up when you said his name," he said as if he could tell what I was thinking.

"Yeah, he was. His name was Rodrigo."

"Well, I'm glad you practiced your cooking skills on them. I expect only top-quality food in this establishment."

I couldn't be more relieved that he'd lightened the mood with a joke instead of asking me questions about Dri. As it was, my mind and my body were already confused whenever in Tiago's presence.

"You got it," I said. "Just make sure there's always coffee in the morning for me."

"It's the least I could do."

His smile did nothing to stop a few butterflies from making themselves known in my stomach and my cock to stir in my jeans. I was so glad I'd changed from my suit trousers when I'd got home because those were unforgiving at keeping my indiscreet thoughts discreet.

"And I know people." He pushed the small white box toward me.

I opened it to find two delicious-looking custard tarts.

"Man, you know the right kind of people. I knew it was a good idea to let you stay."

I reached out for one of the pastries and gave Tiago the other one. I moaned at my first bite into the smooth custard and flaky pastry. I couldn't remember when I'd last had a custard tart that was this good.

"You're supposed to eat it, not make love to it," he said as he took his first bite and let out his own moan.

I looked at him with a raised brow, and we both started laughing.

We cleaned the kitchen together, going around each other like we'd been doing it for years. A pang of sadness and longing for Dri came over me, but this time it didn't hit me as hard as before. I remembered the time Dri decided to cook a surprise meal for my birthday, and when I got home, the kitchen looked like it had been hit by a tornado. He'd been so pleased with his effort; I could have lived with a messy kitchen for the rest of my life just to see that smile every day.

"What are you smiling about?" Tiago asked.

"Nothing, just a nice memory of Dri."

"Hold on to those, Vítor. They're the most precious treasure you'll ever have."

He looked at me with such earnest eyes, I just knew he was also living with his own loss. I wanted to ask him about it but decided to go with a safer topic.

"So, are you going to tell me more about your center and how I can volunteer?"

I didn't think it was possible to see an even bigger smile on his face. I was wrong.

We settled into a comfortable routine for the rest of the week. Tiago would always leave freshly brewed coffee for me in the morning before he left, and I cooked dinner for us. Two days this week he even left a sandwich I took to work for lunch. Our conversations over dinner were easy, like we'd known each other for years rather than days. We kept to safe topics like how much we both disliked football, how much we both liked custard tarts, and the differences between living in Lisbon and Porto.

Our conversations never went into personal territory. Tiago was like a locked diary, and I hadn't yet discovered where he kept the key.

This normally wouldn't bother me, but Tiago had come home looking more exhausted with each day that passed. Yesterday he'd fallen asleep on the sofa a few minutes into the movie we were watching after dinner. He'd leaned into me and I'd shifted my position to make him more comfortable. It had been both a delight and torture to have him so close to me, especially when he'd moved in his sleep and ended up with his head on my chest and his arm around my waist.

I wanted to know what was causing his tiredness. Was he having problems at the center, or was it something else? The longer I spent with him the more I could see the pain he carried, even with his eyes hiding behind the dark-rimmed glasses he wore all the time.

I'd allowed us to stay in the same position for a while, but when there was no sign that Tiago was going to wake up, I'd lifted him off the sofa and carried him into his bedroom. As I'd pulled the bed covers on top of him, he'd called out a name I couldn't understand under his breath and that he was sorry.

He'd calmed down after I'd whispered a few words to him and had tried to erase the creases in his forehead with my thumb.

"Can I borrow the key, Tiago? I promise to look after it. Let me take the pain away, my dear."

Like all the mornings since I'd moved in, Tiago was gone by the time I got up, and like all the mornings before, there had been fresh coffee waiting for me.

How long would he carry on like this before he burned out? Part of me wanted to fix whatever it was that was making him so tired and sad, and then there was part of me that reminded me he wasn't my responsibility. I was only someone he shared an apartment with, and even that was temporary, so why did I feel so strongly about the well-being of this young man?

I was surprised to see him home earlier than normal, and despite the bags under his eyes, he looked happy.

"Hey," he said.

"Hey, you're home early. I haven't even got dinner started."

"I was hoping to return the favor tonight."

"I thought you couldn't cook for shit."

"I can't, but there's a great restaurant a block away, and I assure you the chef can most definitely cook."

"Great, let me grab my sweater and we can go."

It was nice being able to walk to the restaurant. In Porto, I'd walked to most places and only driven when it was necessary. With the slight spring chill in the air, it was a perfect evening for a stroll.

The restaurant was on the riverside, so we followed the pedestrian path between the buildings toward the river. I hadn't had a chance to explore the surroundings yet and look at the architecture of this newly developed part of the city.

"This area has changed so much. I still remember when it was an old shipyard, and look at it now, full of homes and green areas. The Expo '98 was the best thing that happened to Lisbon."

"I agree. I remember seeing it on TV. The first time I visited this area was just after I moved to Lisbon."

"You're not from here?"

"No."

The question flew out of my mouth before I had a chance to censor myself, but now I had no doubt that whatever put all the sadness in Tiago's eyes had to do with his family, and fuck if I couldn't relate to that.

He stayed silent as we walked by the river, and it wasn't until we arrived at the restaurant that some light returned to his eyes.

"You're going to love this place."

"I know."

He looked at me, surprise written all over his face.

"I'm here for the company," I said.

A small blush appeared under the collar of his shirt. I wanted nothing more than to kiss that neck and see how far down the shade of pink went.

It was becoming harder and harder to deny my attraction to Tiago, and it would only be a matter of time until I did something about it.

The Vasco Da Gama Bridge in my line of sight reminded me of the wise words Sebastião left me with. There was nothing stopping me from visiting the old side of the bridge while I figured out why I was so attracted to the new side.

Tiago's voice interrupted my thoughts.

"Vítor?"

"Yes?"

"When was the last time you went to the zoo?"

10

______

TIAGO

As I crossed the bridge over the river Tagus on the way to pick up Filipe for our day out at the zoo, the only thing on my mind was what I'd been thinking when I'd asked Vítor about the zoo yesterday over dinner.

"God, I think my last time there was on a school trip. Amélia Sousa pulled me into the spider house and tried to kiss me," he'd replied.

"What happened?"

"I threw up on her."

"I take it you weren't into girls even then."

"Girls were fine. It was the spiders I didn't like."

I couldn't help my laughter. "So, you're saying Amélia would have been lucky if she'd taken you to the butterfly house instead?"

"She never had a chance to find out." He'd winked.

"I promise I won't make you go into the spider house."

"How about the butterfly house?"

"What?" I'd choked. He'd had his elbows on the table and his chin resting on his hands, and all I could think was how much I'd wanted to lick that fucking dimple.

"Will you take me into the butterfly house?"

"Oh, er, yes… if you want." And that had been when I'd tripped over myself explaining it was a day out with Filipe, but yes, if he wanted, we could go into all the houses, including the reptiles. Vítor simply smiled and said he would love to join us on our adventure to the zoo.

Before I rang the bell for Bruno's apartment, I saw Filipe running down the stairs with his little backpack on and his Superman doll in his hand. He struggled to open the front door to the building, but Bruno was right behind him to help.

"Uncle Tiago, I'm ready to go."

"He's been up since six," Bruno said. "Wouldn't even sit down long enough to eat his cereal."

"Come on," Filipe said, taking my hand and dragging me toward the car.

I laughed and followed him. Bruno was working this morning, but he was going to join us at the zoo after lunch.

Vítor was waiting for us by the entrance to the zoo. His smile as we approached did funny things to my tummy.

Filipe had been chatting non-stop in the car about all the animals he wanted to meet, but when he saw Vítor, he went a little shy and tightened his grip on my hand. Despite what had happened to him, he was comfortable around adults once he got to know them, which was demonstrated by the number of uncles and aunts he'd adopted.

Vítor noticed and crouched down to Filipe's level and stretched out his hand.

"Hi, you must be Filipe. I'm Vítor, and I'm Tiago's friend."

Filipe looked up to me for confirmation, so when I smiled and nodded, he smiled back and held out his little hand to shake Vítor's.

"Hello, I'm going to see the animals today. Are you coming with us?" he asked.

"If you don't mind me joining you, I would love to see the animals, too."

"Okay. This is Superman. He's coming, too."

I chuckled when Filipe pushed the doll into Vítor's face, causing him to pull back at the risk of being punched by Superman's extended arm. Vítor's expression changed for a moment when he looked at the doll, but he recovered too quickly for the little boy to notice.

"What's your favorite animal?" Filipe asked.

Vítor pretended to think for a long time and then said, "The lion."

"Is it because they roar really, really loud?"

I heard Vítor mutter under his breath, "It's because they sleep all day," but then he said to Filipe, "because they live in a big family."

Vítor's joke made me laugh, but the last statement cut through to my heart.

"I have a big family, too," Filipe said, holding on to Vítor's hand on his other side and leading us toward the entrance gate. "I don't have a mummy and daddy. Well, I have Aunt Tee and Uncle Rio. They're like my mummy and daddy because they look after Bruno, too. Bruno is my big brother, and I have Uncle David and Uncle Joel, and Uncle Max and Uncle Isaac." Filipe carried on naming all the adults in his life, including all the extended family that had adopted him and Bruno into their lives.

He was so excited we had to look for the lion enclosure first, which of course was at the other end of the zoo. Not that Filipe minded because he didn't stop chatting to Vítor for a single moment. I couldn't even remember when I last heard Vítor speak. He was simply smiling and nodding at everything Filipe was saying.

I wondered if Vítor had any children. Many times, I'd caught my friends totally engaged in Filipe's conversations and could see the longing in their eyes to have children of their own. The way Vítor was looking at Filipe was different; it was the look of a parent who wanted to protect their child from the bad stuff around them.

Vítor would have questions about Filipe. Everyone always did once they got to know him. How did a little boy that had gone through so much in his short life have so much happiness, love, and trust within him?

Part of me wondered if the reason we hadn't veered into personal territory during our many conversations was because we were both afraid to get too involved. I could tell we were already both struggling with our attraction to each other, because too often we'd caught ourselves flirting as we'd worked around each other in the apartment. Our text message conversations when we were both at work had been my lifeline all week when I was dealing with the leak the plumber finally found in the kitchen.

"Uncle Tiago, why are they sleeping?"

"What? Oh, the lions." I'd been so lost in my own thoughts that I'd forgotten to listen. "That's because lions sleep sometimes twenty hours in the day."

"They sleep all day?" His wide-open eyes and mouth made me laugh.

"Did you know lions like to play at night and that's why they sleep during the day?"

"Wow."

He pressed his hands and face to the glass separating us from the animals. Filipe was so enraptured by the lions, Vítor and I decided to sit on a nearby bench and wait for our sign to move on to other animals.

"He's a very special young boy, isn't he?" Vítor said, resting his arm behind me on the back of the bench.

"He is."

"Do you do stuff like this with him often?"

"As often as I can. Bruno is raising him on his own, and he works a lot. David doesn't mind him being in the café after school, but during the vacations, it's a little boring for him. I try to do educational stuff with him or take him to the beach. Bruno is a great guy, so I'm just doing my bit to help out."

He looked at me like he was trying to read my soul.

"Is that the only reason?"

No, it wasn't, but I didn't want to talk about it, so I got up and asked Filipe which animals he wanted to see next. After taking a few photos of Filipe with the sleeping lions in the background, we went to see the elephants.

I saw Vítor's gaze on me throughout the day. He didn't touch on the subject again, but I could tell my reaction had bothered him. Part of me wanted to tell him about Afonso, and part of me was reluctant. For as long as Vítor didn't know about Afonso, I had a little part of my life where I could be myself rather than the person on an endless search for his younger brother. The problem was that I wasn't sure how good I was at being myself any more.

When Bruno joined us in the afternoon, we'd had to wait for Filipe to catch him up on everything he'd seen before I could introduce him to Vítor.

We saw the dolphin show and went into the farm animals' enclosure where Filipe was able to pet some of the animals. I thought he was going to explode from excitement.

"Can I go on the rides, Bruno?" Filipe asked as we approached the small amusement park inside the zoo.

"You guys have a rest. I'll keep him busy for a bit," Bruno said.

There was a small coffee shop nearby, so we grabbed a coffee and sat on the metal chairs outside.

"So, what do you think of Lisbon Zoo? Is it everything you imagined?" I teased. "I bet you've never had this much fun in your life."

"It's been great, but I'm a little disappointed." His blue eyes looked anything but disappointed.

"Why are you disappointed?"

We were sitting next to each other so when Vítor turned to face me and put his hand around the back of my chair all air left my lungs.

"This zoo doesn't have a butterfly house."

It took me a while to understand what he meant because my brain was trying to cope with how close he was to me and how soft his lips looked. When I did, I looked up to his eyes. They were looking for answers I wasn't sure I could give.

"Vítor."

My voice was a whisper. Vítor stared at my mouth, his eyes hungry. I licked my lips, ready to throw caution to the wind and give in when I heard a little voice calling.

"Uncle Vítor, look at me!" Filipe called from the carousel. "I'm going fast like the cheetahs."

An unexpected sob tore through me, and I had to cover my face with my hands and press my fingers to my eyes to try to stop the tears from coming out. It was all too much. The emotions from spending the day with Bruno's younger brother when I didn't have mine with me, trying to fight the attraction to Vítor, and then witnessing Filipe "adopting" yet another uncle. It all had to come out.

"Hey, what's the matter?"

Vítor's voice was so worried it made me feel even worse. I didn't want this to happen here, didn't want Vítor to see me like this, and, more than anything, I didn't want Filipe to pick up on my emotions. Vítor's arms came around me, and I found myself pressed against his strong chest.

"Do you want to go home?"

I nodded as I tried to compose myself. Once my eyes were no longer red from crying, we went into the amusement park to tell Bruno we were going home. I wasn't sure he bought my excuse that I'd got a headache, but he didn't say anything.

"I think we'll head home, too. He's fighting his tiredness something fierce, but I know as soon as we're in the car he'll fall asleep. Thank you so much for spending the day with him. He's going to be talking about the zoo for the next month."

"Don't worry, I'll think of something else for him to chew your ear off about next time."

"Thanks." He laughed.

It took a while to get Filipe away from the rides, even though we could all see how tired he was, but in the end, Vítor came to the rescue with a small scoop of ice cream in a cup.

The car ride back to the apartment was silent. Vítor had taken the bus to meet us at the zoo, so I drove us back home.

When we arrived at the apartment, I went straight to my room. I'd taken my shoes off at the entrance but didn't bother getting undressed before I lay face down on my bed. Moments later, I heard the bedroom door open gently. I thought Vítor was checking on me and would leave me alone until I felt a dip in the bed next to me and strong arms maneuvering me so I was lying facing him with my head on the crook of his neck.

"You don't have to tell me anything, but please let me hold you."

The tears I'd been working so hard to keep away started running again. Vítor worked one of his hands up and down my back, soothing me, and the other gently cleared the tears from my closed eyes.

"I don't know where my brother is."

11

VÍTOR

THE SOUL-WRENCHING sobs coming from Tiago broke my heart. It was like he'd been building up to say those words aloud for years, and now that he had, they came with a vengeance, bringing all the emotions he was struggling to contain and nothing could stop it.

All I could do was hold him tight in my arms and wish I knew how I could take some of the pain away because it was clearly too much for him. It probably had been for a very long time.

Tiago cried until he was so exhausted he fell asleep in my arms. If I'd thought sleep would bring him some peace, I was wrong. His sleep was fitful, and, like a few days ago, he was calling out a name that I now understood to be Afonso. Was Afonso his lost brother?

I wasn't sure how long Tiago had been asleep in my arms. I was about to drift off myself when I felt him stir. Wondering if he wanted to be on his own, I started moving to release him, but he tightened his grip around my waist.

"My mom married my stepfather when I was five," Tiago said. "When he told me I could call him dad, it was the best day of my life. I was ten when he took me on our first fishing trip. I'd been so excited. He taught me how to set up the rod and the bait. I never caught anything that weekend, but I'd come home beaming. For weeks I asked him when we would go again. My brother was two, so he couldn't come, but I wanted to learn so one day I could teach him."

He took a deep breath, and I wasn't sure he was going to continue with his story. I was about to reassure him he didn't have to relive memories that were clearly painful to him when he resumed.

"I think we had a few trips that were really good. It was just the two of us messing around and not catching anything. Sometimes, when it was really hot, he'd let me swim in the river. Things changed months later when, during the summer vacation, he suggested we go fishing for the whole weekend and camp by the river. I'd never camped before, so I was really excited. We lit a fire to keep warm and had sandwiches and cake my mom had made us.

"That night was cold, so he said we should sleep in the same sleeping bag so we could keep warm and use the other bag as a blanket. We were both dressed, my back was to his front, and he had his arms around me. He didn't touch me, but I felt him move against me. It was slow at first, his breathing was heavy in my ear, and he kept whispering."

Tiago stopped, and I could tell he was crying again.

"That's okay, baby. You don't need to tell me."

I continued moving my hand around his back in a circular pattern to soothe him.

"No. I… I need to do this."

"Okay, but please know you can stop any time. I'll hold you for as long as you need until you don't need me anymore."

He sighed. "That could be a long, long time."

I kissed his head. "I'm not going anywhere."

He was quiet for a while, so I thought he'd fallen asleep when he continued his story.

"He said I was a good boy for helping to keep him warm, and my mom would be really proud of me."

"*Meu menino, tão bom, meu menino.* My boy, so good, my boy."

"I still have nightmares where I hear the sounds he made."

"Did you ever tell anyone?"

"No, I was embarrassed for him because at the time I thought he'd accidentally wet himself, so I didn't mention it. Nothing happened on the next trip, so I thought it had been a one-time thing."

"It wasn't, was it?"

I felt him shake his head against my chest.

"He wouldn't do it all the time, but I started noticing when he was going to do it because during the week, he'd be all over my mom with little touches and kisses. It was two years until he took the next step. I never wanted him to touch me, but my body reacted."

My shirt was soaked from his tears and the pillow was soaked from mine. My heart broke for the little boy who thought he'd gained a new dad and instead, got a sexual predator.

"It's okay, baby. You were a teenager, even if you didn't want it, your body didn't know what was happening."

"He thought I liked it and started doing it more often. He never went all the way, but he did everything else, and he made me—"

"Shhh, it's okay, you don't need to say it."

I held him tighter, kissed his hair, his forehead, and then tilted his head so he was facing me and I could kiss his tears away. It was the only way I could try to give him some comfort and express the pain I was feeling for him, because I wanted to go out and find the monster that did those things to my beautiful young man and beat the shit out of him.

"Vítor."

"Yes, baby."

"I haven't finished telling the story."

"Shall I stop kissing your face?"

"No."

I was going to lose my heart to this man. When I didn't think I had it in me to love someone else other than my husband, I was finding that maybe my heart still had some room for more.

"I asked him to stop, but he wouldn't. He said he was in love with me and couldn't stop thinking about me. I knew it was wrong, and I didn't want it, but he said if I said anything to anyone that my mom would be the one to suffer. I knew she loved him, and in a way, he loved her, too, but he was also a sick bastard.

"When I realized I couldn't make him stop, I did everything I could to leave. I'd been helping some elderly neighbors with gardening and shopping since I was thirteen to earn some pocket money, but as soon as I turned sixteen, I got a job and started saving money. I studied so hard I got a scholarship to go to university. When the letter came through, it was like I was finally free."

"Did it stop when you went to university?"

"It did for me."

Fuck. I knew what he was saying. The abuse stopped for him because the monster found a new victim.

"I didn't come home for the whole of the first year. I used work as an excuse because even with the scholarship, I still had to pay my living expenses, so I got a part-time job during term time and worked full-time during the breaks. When I finally came home after almost a year, Afonso was different. He'd always been such a chatterbox and used to follow me everywhere. Even when I was doing my homework, he was in my room with me. That summer, he was quiet. I tried to do things with him, but he didn't want to do anything. He was eleven then. I never thought my stepfather would do the same to his own son. I thought he did it to me because I wasn't his."

Tiago's hands clenched around the fabric of my shirt.

"You have to believe me, Vítor. I didn't know. That bastard was doing it to his own son, and I let it happen for three years until he'd had enough and ran away from home. He didn't even try to call me. I would have come for him; I would have brought him to the city and kept him with me. I would have told the truth."

"I know you would have. Your brother was scared and probably felt as alone as you had in all those years. Maybe he saw running as the only option to keep you safe, too."

Tiago looked up and locked eyes with me. I saw the questions there, but this moment was about him letting go and sharing his pain.

"Tell me what I can do to take the pain away, baby."

I knew if I did this, there would be no going back. Dri had been the first and only man I'd ever been with, and here I was contemplating intimacy with another man. But even as doubt crossed my mind, it wasn't that I thought I'd be cheating on Dri or that I didn't have enough experience, but that I knew deep down being with Tiago would change my life.

"It'll never go away," he said.

"Then how about we put it in a box and seal it away just for a little bit?"

His nod was so slight I could have missed it if I wasn't so focused on giving him the respite he needed. His hand came up from my chest to reach behind my neck and pulled me into a kiss.

His kiss was gentle, not more than a peck, but it was enough to set my body on fire, and I had to fight hard to keep my hands where they were, resting on his waist. I didn't want to deepen the kiss before he was ready for it. Not that I had to wait long because when Tiago reached under my shirt and touched my skin, I gasped, which gave him the right opening to explore my mouth with his tongue.

Tiago was everywhere, while his mouth hadn't left mine, he'd positioned himself on top of me and was using his hands to touch any part of me he could reach, and even though they hadn't been anywhere near my cock, his hip movements were enough to get me close to coming.

There was a desperation in his touch. I wanted to believe that desperation was for me, but I suspected in that moment, he just wanted to feel so he could forget.

"Baby," I whispered when he left my mouth to kiss all around my chin and down my neck, "fuck... Tiago, baby."

He stopped and looked at me. I could see he was about to apologize and stop, which hadn't been my intention, so I pulled him into a stupor-inducing kiss, and then said, "Let me look after you."

He nodded and followed my direction when I asked him to lie down on his back. His glasses had been on the bedside table all this time, and I was in two minds to ask him to put them on because I'd been fantasizing about him in nothing else but those damned glasses since the night we'd met.

I didn't bother taking off his T-shirt because the sounds he was making as my hands roamed his body told me he was already on the edge, so I went for the buttons of his jeans.

"One day I'm going to chart the miles of your skin and make a map of all the places I'll want to come back to."

"Vítor, please..." His voice was demanding and desperate.

I chuckled.

"Trust me?" I asked.

"Yes. Yes..."

I removed his jeans and underwear in one go, freeing his cock with it. The man was beautiful with clothes on, but with clothes off, he was a work of art, and he'd been hiding the most perfect, thick cock I'd ever seen. My hole clenched in hope of one day feeling the thickness filling me and hitting all the right spots.

"I'm not very big." His self-doubt had no place on this bed, and I wanted to kick whoever it was that had made him feel he was less than perfect. Instead, I took my own pants off and set him straight.

"You are perfect, all of you, and I can't wait to feel your beautiful, thick cock inside me. Got it?" I asked as I kissed him again and pressed my hips against his, allowing our cocks to rub against each other, trapped between us.

I'd planned to unravel him with my mouth, but now that I was face-to-face with him, I had this inexplicable need to see his face when he came. In all my years, I'd never had such an intense need to protect and care for someone like I did with Tiago. I put the thought aside and focused again on the man under me.

He lifted his hips up to meet mine in an attempt to get his relief, and our cocks leaked between us, which gave us some lubrication. I opened my legs slightly and moved so I could create a tight cocoon around his cock. Tiago gasped when he realized he was now sliding his cock between my legs and close to my desperate hole.

Our mouths met again; our kiss desperate like we were trying to draw a breath from the other. His cock slid against my balls and teased my hole, making me perilously close to coming, so I clenched my thighs and increased the speed of my movements.

Tiago's expression as he came was one of wonder. He only closed his eyes for a short moment before he opened them again and locked his gaze with mine. That was enough for my orgasm to tear through me like a freight train.

I lost my ability to speak, to think, to do anything other than feel. When my brain function returned, I moved so I wasn't on top of Tiago. He didn't let go of his hold on me but whispered, "thank you," before he fell asleep in my arms.

I waited until I was sure he wouldn't wake up and went to the bathroom to grab a washcloth to clean us both and then settled next to him in bed. My last coherent thought before I fell asleep was that I hoped he wouldn't freak out in the morning, or worse, regret what happened, because as much as I thought I should, I couldn't regret a single second I'd spent in Tiago's company.

12

TIAGO

IT HAD BEEN a while since I'd felt like I'd actually slept during my sleep. I wondered if it had anything to do with the man currently lying in my bed with his arms around me. I opened my eyes to see Vítor's face. Even in his sleep, he was the sexiest person I'd ever seen.

I'd never intended on telling anyone about what my stepfather did to me. Many times I'd considered seeking support from a counselor, but I didn't think I suffered from PTSD, so I hadn't felt it was necessary to open the wound.

All I'd needed was to find my brother and everything in my life would be perfect. What I hadn't realized was that I was a pressure cooker ready to explode.

I tried to find the embarrassment or the regret about everything I'd shared last night and what we'd done after my confession. It wasn't there. That was a surprise I wasn't expecting, and I couldn't stop letting out a small laugh because I'd never felt more lighthearted in my life. It was almost like I could float away if it wasn't for the heavy arm around me keeping me grounded.

Vítor's dark blue eyes looked at me and he smiled. I smiled back.

"Morning," he said in a low, sleepy voice I felt all the way down my spine.

"Morning."

He brought his hand to my face and caressed my cheek, using his thumb to trace my lips. I kissed his thumb, and his morning wood twitched against my stomach. I guessed he could feel mine, too, since neither of us were wearing any underwear. I still had my T-shirt on, but Vítor was fully naked.

My hand rested on the soft salt-and-pepper hairs of his chest.

I thought he was going to kiss me, but he kept his touch light, like he was memorizing every line of my face.

"You have a beautiful smile," he said. "How do you feel?"

"Lighter than I've felt. Maybe ever."

I touched the dimple on his chin, feeling the rough hair underneath, and couldn't resist replacing my fingers with my lips. Vítor let out a breath and at the same time pressed harder against me. His eyes were closed, and I took that as a sign he was enjoying my touch and wanted more.

"I've been wanting to lick this damn dimple since I saw you walk into that bar," I said before I did just that and moved my hips so our erections were sliding against each other for good measure.

In three seconds flat, I found myself under his strong, heavy body and looking into his eyes; my absolute favorite place to be.

"I like you under me."

"I like me under you."

He placed open-mouthed kisses below my ear, his rough scruff causing me to shiver as it touched the sensitive skin on his way down to my chest. I cried out when he licked and sucked on one of my nipples and then the other. I was desperately grinding against him, trying to find some friction, but he moved so he was no longer on top of me.

"Vítor, please."

"What do you want."

"Your mouth on—"

I didn't have a chance to finish before heat surrounded the head of my cock. I looked down to see it. Vítor had his eyes on me as he worked his way down to take more of me. My dick wasn't long by any means, but I could see he was struggling with my thickness, not that it looked like it was slowing him down in any way.

Turning my eyes from his was the only way to keep from coming too soon, and when I noticed he was grinding against the bed sheets, I angled his hips toward me and took his cock in my mouth. He only stopped sucking me long enough to take a breath and let out a curse when he realized what I was doing.

Vítor had been blessed in the anatomy department because not only was he long but was also fairly thick and had the same salt-and-pepper hair at the base of his cock as he had all over his body.

Why it turned me on so much, I didn't know, but I didn't care, either. All I cared about was feeling this man unraveling under my touch. It would be a competition to see who could hold out the longest because I knew I was too close and his jerky movements as he tried to pump into my mouth told me he was, too.

Using my hand to aid the movements of my mouth, I sped up and sucked him hard. When I brushed a finger from my free hand over his hole, it was game over. He put his hand on my head to keep me in place as he came hard inside my mouth, and fuck me if that wasn't all it took for me to let go, too.

We both laughed as we came down from the high of our shared orgasms. Vítor changed position to face me again and planted a hard kiss on my mouth, no doubt tasting himself on me just like I could taste myself on his tongue.

"I win," I said breathlessly.

He looked down toward our softening cocks. "I think we both won."

We lay in bed in silence after that. I noticed that, despite having a good night's sleep and the second-best orgasm of my life, it was still only just after eight in the morning, so I was in no rush to get up. Vítor's hand was stroking my back lazily and was dangerously close to sending me to sleep.

"Do you have to go to work on Monday?" he asked.

"No, we have a water leak, so the center is closed next week while the plumbers fix it."

"Do you have to be there?"

"No."

"I need to go to Porto to deal with a couple of things. I'm back on Monday afternoon. I was wondering if you'd like to come with me."

The question caught me by surprise. I sat up in bed, facing him, unsure of how to answer because I didn't know what any of what happened in the last twenty-four hours meant.

"Hey." He sat up and put his hands on either side of my face. I couldn't resist leaning into his touch. "After what happened yesterday, I don't want to leave you on your own. Besides, the weather is meant to be good and there's a place I'd love to show you."

"Okay."

His eyes lit up and he kissed me in such a way that my body was getting ready for round two, until my tummy rumbled.

"Right, we need a shower and breakfast. In that order."

I laughed. "Are you saying I smell?"

He tackled me so I fell on my back, pinned my arms above my head, and he buried his face in my armpits.

"Hmm, you smell divine."

I giggled when he planted soft kisses that revealed how ticklish I was under my arms and all down the sides.

"Unless you're ready for round two, old man, I say we follow your suggestion," I said, pushing him away and running toward the bathroom. He was behind me not a second later, showing me that being older also meant he had a trick or two up his sleeve.

On our way to Porto, we decided to stop for lunch in Aveiro. I'd never been to the aptly named Venice of Portugal, but it didn't disappoint. After lunch, we walked along the canals and admired the colorful boats and houses that gave Aveiro its nickname.

Despite not being directly on the seafront, there was still a small breeze that kept us cool as we walked along the canal. I admired the colorful paintings on the sterns and bows of the gondola-style boats, which depicted scenes from old times.

The seaweed trade had died a long time ago, so the boats were mainly used for tourists to enjoy riding along the canal, and for a moment, I wished we had enough time for a ride.

"I want to help you look for him."

I stopped at Vítor's words, not just because they were unexpected since we hadn't talked about anything personal all day, but also because of the underlying assumption.

"Tiago, I haven't known you long, but I don't believe for a second that you haven't been looking for your brother since the day he ran away."

Once I recovered from his words, I told him about my failed attempts and the struggle with keeping the authorities on my side, especially after they found out I worked at a LGBTQ center.

"Until then, I'd been just one of many people looking for a loved one. Their lack of interest came from the slim chances of actually finding my brother. I made the mistake of asking a detective to meet me at work. We'd had this kid come in. He was in such a bad state, Isaac took him to hospital. I tried to rearrange my meeting with the detective, but he insisted it had to be that day, so I asked if he could stop by the center. After that, they were even less interested in helping me until Fred came along."

"Fred?"

"Frederico Mendes. I met him a few years ago. He actually came by the center to introduce himself. He didn't have a problem with me because he's gay himself. I don't know why, but he took a special interest in my brother's case, and he's been helping me since."

Vítor's face dropped, and I had to think for a moment what the reason could be for the sudden mood drop.

"We're just friends. He was really into Isaac before Max came along and hasn't had anyone since. Besides, he's not my type."

He pulled me into a small walkway between two buildings and pushed my back against the wall, caging me in with his arms.

"What is your type, Tiago?"

"Tall, older men with eyes as deep as the ocean and who can go for two rounds of sex before breakfast."

His laugh reached all the way inside my heart, and I pulled him closer so we were nose-to-nose, well, as much as we could be considering our height difference. He got the message and kissed me, a bone-melting kiss.

After that, we spent the rest of the car journey talking about Afonso and all the good memories I had of our childhood.

"This is us," he said as he approached a tall gate that opened as soon as we were close enough.

Inside the gate, there were trees on either side of the short driveway up to the house.

"It's weird, isn't it? The house is kind of back to front. The best parts are inside and the back. Dri designed it, and he always thought it was a waste to have the front of a house looking so grand and beautiful if no one ever enjoyed it."

"I am inclined to agree with him, but I'll reserve my judgment once I see the rest," I teased.

I grabbed my overnight bag and followed Vítor to the front door. He paused before he put the key in the lock and looked at me. There was uncertainty in his eyes. He looked so fragile in that split moment that I didn't want to make things any worse, so I spoke without touching him, even though I wanted nothing more than to offer some comfort or reassurance. Whatever he needed.

"Hey, I know we haven't talked about it, but I get it. If nothing else, we are at least friends, right? I'm not expecting anything, okay?"

He nodded and smiled. He'd given me more in the last twenty-four hours than I'd ever gotten from anyone else in my entire life. I felt such a connection with him that I wanted to crawl into his arms and live there forever. The reality was that even if the feeling was mutual, Vítor was clearly still grieving the loss of his husband, and I would never put myself in a position where I may end up hurting him.

Let's face it, how many other guys had been hurt because they tried to give me something and I couldn't give anything back? Maybe coming to Porto with Vítor was the reminder I needed to be careful with both our hearts.

If Vítor had frozen at the thought of bringing me to the home he'd shared with the love of his life, I froze as soon as I walked in behind him for a totally different reason. Because in the hallway hung a pencil drawing that was the carbon copy of the photo David had given me of his aunt and uncle, his mom, and Vítor.

13

VÍTOR

As soon as I opened the door, I excused myself to the bathroom, making a joke about old men's bladders and a long car journey. It hadn't been that long a drive from Aveiro, but I hoped Tiago wouldn't call me on my white lie.

There were too many thoughts and feelings warring for attention, and I needed to make sense of it, with the biggest one being the feeling that I was betraying Dri somehow by bringing Tiago here.

I splashed some water on my face and looked at myself in the mirror.

Nothing had changed in the last few weeks since I left for Lisbon.

I looked closer, my nose nearly touching the cold surface. There was a small difference, and it was one I couldn't see but could definitely feel. It was the splinter of a future that wasn't just made of dinners for one, of attending conferences on my own—or even worse, avoiding them altogether. A future that still held some excitement because it was unknown but full of possibilities.

I'd never considered I'd have any kind of relationship after Dri was gone. When he was in hospital after his surgery, he'd asked me to not forget to live after he was gone. I'd laughed it off because at the time, I'd still had hope that the surgery and the following course of chemo would kill the cancer. It didn't, and I'd wondered if he'd known even then that his life wasn't going to be as long as we'd hoped.

It was one of my many conversations with Sebastião, the closest thing I had to a father figure, that once again put things in perspective for me. "You don't need to figure things out straight away, Vítor. Life is rarely long enough for that, so you may as well buckle up and pull the window down. Enjoy the wind on your face."

I looked for Tiago when I came out of the bathroom and was surprised to see he was still by the front door. His eyes were on the pencil portrait I'd done years ago.

"This is beautiful, it looks so real, who are they?" he asked.

Even though the portrait had been hanging on the wall for years, I'd got used to walking past it without paying any notice. "Er, it's me, my best friend, my brother, and his wife."

The portrait was the only thing I had from my old life, and even that had only been drawn once I'd escaped.

"You made this?"

"Yeah."

"How old were you in the picture?"

"Twenty. Shall I give you a tour of the house? We can stop by the guest bedroom so you can drop your bag."

He looked disappointed, but I didn't want to answer any questions about the portrait or the people in it.

After I showed Tiago where the guest room was, I took him around the house, finishing in the kitchen where my cleaner had left a homemade cake knowing I'd be back this weekend.

"I can see it now," Tiago said as we sat on the swing in the garden, facing the house. "You can appreciate the design of the house from here, but you'd never sit at the front and do the same. I also love the way you have the glass doors going across the whole house."

I nodded. All the living areas had been designed to be part of the garden so when the glass doors were open, it was hard to see where the building ended and the garden started, making that part of the house open plan. It also meant we could go from the kitchen right through to the living room and my office.

"Do you mind if I disappear into my office to deal with a few things? Feel free to explore or take a dip in the pool. You can see me from here." I pointed to the far side of the building where we could see my desk through the glass.

"You have a swimming pool?" His mouth was wide open as he stared at me. "Man, you married well."

I smiled and kissed his head before I got up from the swing, leaving him with his coffee and a giant slice of cake.

The pile of unopened letters sat in front of me for a whole ten minutes before I was able to divert my attention from the young man sitting on the swing with one leg under him and using the other to keep the swing in motion. His coffee was on the little table at the side and he was paying full attention to the cake on his plate.

Tiago looked a lot more relaxed now, and despite my doubts, I was glad I was able to give him some time to just be himself. He put the empty plate away and sipped his coffee, leaning back on the seat and enjoying the mild weather.

Tomorrow was going to be another nice day, so I knew exactly what we were going to do. Now I just needed to stop staring at him and deal with these bills.

I looked at the clock on the bedside table. It hadn't moved much since I last checked it just after midnight.

Once I'd dealt with the bills and outstanding correspondence earlier, I'd asked Tiago if he wanted to go for a swim. He'd been like a kid in a candy store. When I'd left him, I'd thought he'd get curious and look for the swimming pool and the secret garden beyond, but he'd stayed where he was until I'd joined him again.

After the swim, we'd ordered takeout for dinner and watched a movie. He'd been leaning against me throughout the movie, so I'd not even noticed he'd fallen asleep. Like a few nights ago, I'd lifted him off the sofa and taken him to the guest bedroom. The difference was this time, he called my name instead of his brother's.

It had taken willpower I didn't know I had to stop myself from slipping under the covers and wrapping myself around him. Once he'd settled in, I'd left him and gone to my own bedroom, the one I'd shared with Dri and where we'd made love, laughed, and cried more times than I could count.

Feeling frustrated with myself, I decided to get up and do some work if I wasn't going to sleep. On my way to the office, I noticed the guest bedroom door was open and Tiago wasn't in bed.

I found him curled up on the living room sofa facing the garden. The lights were off but the moon was shining a bright light on his lonely figure.

"Hey," I called in a whisper so I wouldn't spook him as I sat down next to him.

"Hey."

I pulled him into my arms and was glad when he settled with his back against my chest and put his hands over mine.

"What are you doing here in the dark?"

"Just thinking. Couldn't sleep."

"Thinking about what?"

"You. Me." He took a deep sigh.

"I know. I'm sorry I was a bit off after we got here."

He tightened his grip on my hand. "No, don't apologize. I can see you're still grieving, and that's okay. You don't stop loving someone just because they're gone. Besides, I wasn't expecting anything more, and you've given me so much already."

"You're right, I still love Dri and always will. I don't know how to navigate this, Tiago. What I feel for you is unexpected." I sighed. "You know why I'm here?"

"No."

"I couldn't sleep, and you know why? Because I couldn't stop thinking about you, and even though part of me felt guilty for it, there's a bigger part of me that craves having you in my arms. I don't know how to stop it."

He turned around to face me.

"Then don't."

His kiss was light, barely a touch of our lips, but its result was devastating because I realized then I was on a fast track to falling in love for the second time in my life, and like the first time, I wasn't sure I could do anything to stop it... or wanted to.

Tiago turned again and settled against my chest, pulling my arms around him. I kissed his temple, and he let out a contented sigh.

"Do you want to go to bed?" I asked.

He shook his head. I sensed some hesitation from him.

"Vítor, will you tell me about the picture by the door?"

"Why?"

"Because it's important to you."

I took a deep breath and considered if I wanted to open that wound. I didn't want my relationship with Tiago to be about all the hurt we'd had in the past. At the same time, he'd been so open with me, so I felt I owed him my story, especially since we'd actually met in the place that had sealed my future.

"Mário is older than me only by a few years, so we were always very close. My father wasn't a nice man, and Mário made it his life mission to protect me from our father's fists. We met Teresa and Paula at school shortly after we moved to Caparica. It was love at first sight for Mário and Teresa, and in a way, for Paula and I, too.

"I thought I was in love with Paula because she was my best friend. We hadn't even ever kissed, but I was determined I was going to marry her because she was a girl, and I liked her."

"When did you realize you were gay?"

"I was sixteen. Things were different in those days. There were no role models, no one to look up to, so the first time I found myself attracted to a guy, it confused the hell out of me. I hid it and tried to pretend I wasn't like that.

"The drawing was based on a photo we took on my brother's birthday. We'd had a great day at the beach and then a bigger group of friends joined us in the evening. We made a fire and drank beer. This guy who was friends with my brother came to sit next to me and started leaning into me, and he put his hand on my knee. I panicked because I thought he knew my secret, so I took Paula by the hand and the two of us went for a walk.

"We'd both been drinking quite a bit and maybe we were both in need of something. We lost our virginity to each other that night. It was great because she was my best friend, she was soft, beautiful, but..."

"She wasn't a man."

"No, she wasn't. Afterward, I think we both felt embarrassed but relieved. Also happy that we'd been each other's firsts."

"Did she know you're gay?"

"Yes, I'd told her when we were eighteen. Of course, I'd also told her I was still going to marry her."

Tiago laughed. "What did she say?"

"She said that if by the time we were both twenty-five if we hadn't found anyone, she would marry me. That day at the beach was the last happy day I remember from my old life."

"What do you mean?"

"I turned twenty-one a month later. I guess what happened at the beach got to me and I felt this need to explore my sexuality. Pride bar had been in the news as the new place for the gay community in Lisbon. I was curious and went there on my birthday." I let out a choked laugh as I remembered the moment I'd been approached by another guy. I hadn't been able to string two sentences together. Now I was sure that had been part of my appeal to him.

"My first kiss ever with a guy was caught by someone who knew my father. To this day, I still don't know who it is, not that it matters."

"What happened?"

"My father was waiting for me when I got home. I'd been on such a high from my experience that I didn't even find it strange that my dad was awake in the middle of the night. He took me out into the back garden and beat me with one of the wood planks he was saving to cut up for the fireplace. At some point, I must have blacked out because the next time I woke up, I was in the hospital.

"He was sitting next to the hospital bed. The look in his eyes scared me like nothing else had in my life. When the nurse came to see me, she mentioned something about the attackers, and I realized he'd lied to them. He'd said he found me on the street and that I'd been attacked.

"When she was gone, he turned to me and gave me a choice. He said he'd rather have a dead son than a gay one, but he drew the line at killing me himself.

"He told me to think about my mom, my brother, and his wife

and baby, and then he was gone. I'd been so badly injured I'd had to stay in hospital for a few days. All the time I was hoping my brother would come to see me. He'd been my protector, my big brother who was always there for me. When he didn't come, I left the hospital. I never went back and haven't seen anyone for nearly thirty years."

Remembering the past churned back all the hurt. If it wasn't for Tiago's weight on me keeping me grounded, I was sure I'd be retching in the bathroom already. I felt wetness on my hands and realized Tiago was crying silent tears.

I turned him to me and held him tight. "Don't cry for me. It's all in the past, and I've had a happy life since. I wouldn't have met Dri otherwise, and I can't imagine what my life would have been like without him."

"When did you draw the picture?"

"Dri asked me to draw a good memory from my old life so I wouldn't forget where I came from and the people I loved."

"Vítor?"

"Yes, baby?"

"Will you come to bed with me?"

"Absolutely."

14

____

TIAGO

I WAS DISAPPOINTED when I opened my eyes to see the other side of
the bed was empty, even more so when I realized the sheets were cold.
That could only mean that while Vítor had come to bed with me last
night and comfortably fallen asleep with me in his arms, maybe he was
still not entirely comfortable being with another man in the house his
husband had built for them.

The shower gave me a chance to think about everything Vítor had
shared with me last night. When I'd seen the drawing by the door, I'd
known straightaway Vítor, my Vítor, was Mário's brother. What were
the fucking chances?

When Vítor had excused himself to the bathroom after we'd
arrived, I'd quickly taken out the photo David had given me and
compared it to the hand-drawn picture on the wall. There was no
doubt about who he was, and then he'd confirmed it by identifying
everyone in the picture.

What the fuck was I going to do now? I'd been asked to find him,
and now I had. I should be on the phone to David right now to say
that I'd found Vítor, but everything was much more complex now.
While I knew Mário wanted to find Vítor, I wasn't sure the feeling was

mutual. Despite the pain I'd heard in Vítor's voice last night, what if he didn't want to revisit the past and meet his family?

I knew it wasn't my decision to make, so I would have to come clean with him and give him the option, except I was too afraid of opening that Pandora's box and risking losing both Vítor and the friends who were the only family I had.

My thoughts were interrupted by strong arms that wrapped around me from behind.

"Breakfast and lunch are ready," he said, planting a kiss on the back of my neck.

"Jumping into my shower naked is not the way to get me out of it."

He turned me around and caged me against the tiled wall.

"Who said I wanted to get out of the shower?"

Vítor's kiss was possessive, demanding, and everything I needed in that moment.

"Come on, we need to make a move if we want to get there early," he said, even though he'd just completely stupefied me with that kiss.

"Where are we going?"

"We're going to one of my favorite places in Gerês."

"Oh my god, I've never been to Gerês. Please tell me we're going to a waterfall."

"We're going to a waterfall."

That was all it took for me to jump him and kiss the hell out of his face. It was a good thing the shower had actual glass walls because if we'd been in mine, we'd both have been on the floor with the shower curtain around us by now. As it was, Vítor caught me and kept me up by holding me against the wall with his bigger body and his hands strategically placed on the globes of my ass.

My cock went from sixty to one hundred in a heartbeat, and I tried to get some friction by rubbing against him, but in the position I was in, it was almost impossible to move.

"Do you want to come, baby?" he asked between kissing and sucking any skin he could reach.

"Fuck, yes, so badly. Vítor…"

"Yes, baby."

"I need you inside me."

At this point, I was begging him because his hard cock brushing against my hole was driving me insane with need.

"Open your mouth," he commanded. I took one and then two of his fingers in my mouth, and he cursed when I showed him just what I'd do if I had another part of his body in my mouth.

He replaced the fingers with his mouth and within seconds his hand was right where I needed it, with a finger teasing my hole and demanding entry.

"I don't have any supplies here, so I'm afraid this will have to do." The words were apologetic, but his voice was anything but, especially when his lips smiled against mine at the same time as his finger hit my prostate and my whole body jerked in pleasure.

"Shit, fuck, fuck," I cried as he increased his pace and kept hitting my special spot. I couldn't believe he was controlling my whole body with just one finger. When he added the second finger, my balls tightened and I was helpless to stop my orgasm from erupting through me.

It was a good thing he was holding me up because my whole body felt like jelly. When my brain regained its proper function a minute later, I tried to get on my feet so I could give Vítor his orgasm.

"No need," he said with a chuckle and held me in place.

I put my hands on his face and turned it to me.

"You came?"

"Baby, watching you come is the most beautifully erotic experience, so the answer is yes. I didn't even need to touch myself to come as soon as you did."

Fuck my heart. He was going to make me fall in love with him, and I was going to hurt him.

"Come on, let's get dried and eat so we can go to the waterfalls."

The trip to Gerês went beyond my expectation. I'd seen plenty of photos of the many places in the mountain range that had natural water springs, and some even had waterfalls, but I'd never had a chance to take an actual vacation.

Once we arrived at our destination, we still had to trek for around twenty minutes to get to the waterfall. I was expecting it to be busy with people, but it was completely deserted.

Vítor told me that only a few minutes away in a different direction there was a much bigger waterfall that attracted more people, especially tourists, so a lot of the time when he visited, he was the only one there.

The place was stunning. We were surrounded by mountains and forest, but it wasn't closed in, so we still had a view of other mountains in the distance. The waterfall wasn't quite what I expected, because it was more a trickle of water coming down the mountain between the rock formations, but it ended up in a natural pool with the clearest water I'd ever seen.

The water was freezing, but after the trek under the sun, it was so inviting I couldn't resist going for a swim. Vítor joined me, so we fooled around for a bit before we sat on a boulder in the sun with the packed lunch he'd prepared earlier.

After the cold spring water, the warmth of the sun felt glorious on my skin.

"Can I ask you a question?"

"Sure," he said.

"You ran away, so I'm assuming you didn't have much money. How did you manage to go to university?"

Vítor turned to me from where he was sunbathing and leaned on his elbow.

"With some hard work and a lot of luck. I had some money because I'd been working for a while. That allowed me to travel to Porto and stay in a cheap motel. As soon as I got there, I looked for jobs, but there weren't many. I met Julia at the supermarket. She was in her eighties at the time. I helped her with her shopping and she asked me lots of questions about myself. By the time I'd walked her home, I had a job and a place to stay.

"Julia didn't have any children and had been widowed for a long time, so there was no one to help her with some of the repairs in her house. I helped her in exchange for a place to stay, and she still insisted on paying me a wage. She was a great woman. She insisted I go back to school and threatened to fire me if I didn't.

"She was there on the day of my graduation, and even after I moved out of her house and in with Dri, I still saw her a few times a week. She passed away when she was ninety."

I leaned in to kiss him. It was meant to be chaste to thank him for telling me about Julia, but he deepened the kiss. I had no choice but to straddle him, which gave me a slight height advantage I took full advantage of.

"I'm going to need another dip in the water to cool down," he said.

"Your own fault. I was going for an innocent kiss. You're the one that turned it into a porn scene."

He pulled me down so I was lying on top of him, our erections brushing deliciously under our shorts, and whispered in my ear, "If it wasn't for the chance of someone walking past, I'd give you the best porn scene ever."

"Fuuuck." I got up and threw myself in the water to cool down while he sat on the boulder laughing and teasing me by touching his hard cock over his shorts. I was in two minds about caring if anyone walked past and saw us.

By the time we arrived back at his place in Porto, my body was aching, but I hadn't felt this relaxed in years. Vítor also looked content, and on the drive back, we'd talked a lot about some of the work he'd done in Porto for LGBT charities and some of the buildings he'd designed. I couldn't have asked for a more perfect day.

"Dinner is in the oven and will be ready in half an hour."

I'd been staring at the various plants, flowers, and trees in the garden, mesmerized by the color effect as the sun set. Vítor placed his hands on my neck and massaged gently. My hands instinctively went to his waist, and I let my forehead rest on his chest as he continued to massage down my back.

"Thanks for taking me to Gerês. I always wanted to go."

"You're welcome. It has been a while since I was there. I forgot how calming it was."

Time stopped as we stood still, staring at each other with the sun warming us through the glass panels. I wished I knew what was on his mind. There was so much I wanted to talk about, but I was so afraid of breaking the spell we were under.

"Dad?"

Vítor stepped back like he was electrocuted by the sound of the voice that came from the hallway. A guy that looked to be in his late twenties was staring at us, his face a mix of anger and confusion.

"Mateus."

Vítor started walking in the guy's direction, but he put his hands up to stop him.

The guy, Mateus, looked from me to Vítor, like he didn't know what to do.

"What's going on?" he asked.

"Mateus, this is Tiago, he's my roommate in Lisbon. I had to come back for some paperwork and invited him to come along." Vítor's voice was unsure as he attempted to introduce me without giving too much away.

"Tiago, this is my son, Mateus." I stared back at Vítor. He had a son. A son who not only looked to be a couple of years younger than me but was also a split hair away from jumping to the right conclusion.

"What are you doing here?" Vítor finally asked when Mateus didn't react.

"I came back to pick up some of my stuff."

"Do you want to stay for dinner?" Vítor asked. "It's nearly ready and there's enough."

I heard the plea in Vítor's voice and wondered what had happened between them.

"Are you serious? I guess lying runs in the family, then, if you think I'm stupid enough to think there's nothing going on between you and him."

"I think I should go and leave you alone to talk," I said as I left toward the bedroom. When I got there, I picked up my overnight bag and started packing the few things I'd brought with me. I could take a taxi to the station and get on the next train to Lisbon.

The raised voices I'd heard when I was packing had calmed down by the time I turned into the corridor leading to the living room. I knew it was wrong, but I couldn't stop myself from listening.

"I saw how you looked at him, Dad."

"What do you mean?"

"You had the same look."

There was a silent moment, and I wondered if they knew I was listening to their conversation.

"When you looked at Papa, it was like the world around you kept moving while you remained at your own pace. No one could touch you or come between you."

"No, Mateus, it's not like that."

Suddenly I felt like I couldn't breathe.

"Dad, don't be the second liar in the family. It'll only hurt those that love you. Lying to yourself is still lying."

"You know he was doing what he thought was best, right?"

"I know, but it hurts that I didn't have a chance to talk to him about it when he was alive. He made a selfish decision, and we're the ones paying for it."

I heard movement but wasn't fast enough to move. When Vítor's eyes connected with mine, he looked hurt and confused.

I looked down and tried to walk past them toward the door, but Mateus stopped me.

"If you break his heart it'll be the last heart you break."

He turned to Vítor and hugged him. I saw Vítor was surprised by the gesture, but he recovered quickly and hugged his son back.

"I love you, Dad."

"I love you, too, son. Don't ever forget that."

Vítor waited until Mateus had left before he turned and walked to me, his expression completely unreadable.

A shiver went through my spine as he stood as close as he could without touching me. His eyes pinned me in place with their strength, kindness, and determination, a bewitching combination I was powerless to resist.

15

VÍTOR

IN ANY OTHER SITUATION, I would have wanted some time to get my head around what had just happened, but from Tiago's expression and the fact he was holding his overnight bag, I knew I had to make this count. There was no room for misunderstandings or deliberations.

"How much did you hear?" I'd suspected he'd heard most of it. Even when he'd been packing in the bedroom, we hadn't exactly been quiet. In fact, Mateus had been quite vocal initially about what he thought he saw.

I couldn't exactly blame him for his reaction, but I was still his father, so he heard me out and allowed me to set the record straight. That was when he'd turned the earth on its axis by calling out the feelings I had for Tiago.

"Er..." Tiago stuttered, "Mateus said..."

I smiled because I suspected he couldn't get the words out because he was scared they were the truth.

"Tiago, I am falling for you."

He exhaled like he was releasing all the tension in his body. The tears making his eyes shiny fell down his cheeks.

I removed his glasses and put them in the pocket of my sweats. He shook his head lightly like he didn't quite believe what I was saying.

"You can't, Vítor. Not me."

"Why, baby?"

"Because I'm going to hurt you."

I finally pulled him into my arms and felt him sob against my chest. I rubbed my hand up and down his back to calm him.

"Tiago, I never thought I'd feel this way about anyone again, and I'm still trying to figure it out because it's so much of the same I felt for Dri but also so different. I knew I was falling for you, but I didn't know how deep in I already was until my son pointed it out to me. I'm tired of denying it."

His hold around my waist tightened. I put my hand on his chin to make him look at me again.

"If you feel for me even a fraction of what I feel for you, please let's work this out together. Don't go."

"I feel it, Vítor. I feel it."

I didn't need to keep looking at his beautiful face, because I'd already mapped it during the few times I'd had him asleep in my arms, or when he didn't realize I was looking at him. I closed my eyes and placed kisses all over his face, licking the tears clean and using my lips to feel my way around the curves of his face.

"Vítor," he whispered.

"Yes, baby."

"Will you take me to see Rodrigo?"

The request came as a surprise, and for a moment, I wasn't sure how to reply, but Tiago had been nothing short of considerate and attentive whenever I mentioned Dri. Whatever his reasons were to want to see him, I realized I was happy to let him.

"I would love to."

When the oven dinged, I went over to the kitchen to finish up dinner while Tiago took his stuff back to the room. He wouldn't need to unpack as such since we were going back tomorrow.

The rest of the evening was quiet. I could tell Tiago was trying to fit all the pieces of the puzzle in his head, and I was patient enough to give him the time. I suspected he hadn't had many relationships in the past. Considering much of his focus was on his work and finding his brother, I would be surprised if there were many guys out there willing to take second or third place in his life. I would take whatever place he was willing to put me in.

After dinner, we settled on the sofa with him nestled against my chest, watching some reality show on TV about people's tattoo regrets. The longer we stayed in that position, the more relaxed he became until he was crying from laughing so much.

"Oh my god, that's horrendous. I'm not sure if he should sue the tattoo artist or if he deserves it for asking for that tattoo in the first place."

I tightened my arms around him and placed a kiss on his head. He looked up and smiled.

"What?" he asked.

"I like you like this."

"Like what?"

"Relaxed. Laughing. In my arms."

He turned around and pushed me so I was lying flat on the sofa. He rested his head on his hands on top of my chest.

"I like me in your arms, too."

I ran my hands through his hair, and he leaned into my touch. I wanted him like this all the time, and I wanted the underlying sadness caused by his missing brother to be gone.

"Can I ask you something?" he said. "This is probably really weird."

I smiled. As if I could deny him anything at this stage.

"I want to speak to Rodrigo before we take things further. I know it's weird because you can't really ask for permission from a dead person, but I just... I feel like I need to speak to him."

I kissed Tiago to show my feelings because if I dared to speak in that moment, I would cry, and not from sadness or happiness but from the honesty and respect he showed for my husband.

As soon as I showed Tiago which one was Dri's grave, he asked if I could leave him alone for a few minutes. Since I'd seen Sebastião's car parked outside the cemetery, I thought I'd go look for him.

"Vítor, son, how are you doing? Back so soon?" he asked.

"I had a few things to deal with. I was only here for the weekend; we're going back this afternoon."

"We?"

I looked at the spot where I'd left Tiago. He was sitting cross-legged on the grass facing the headstone. He looked like he was engrossed in an animated one-way conversation.

"Sebastião, my friend, when you suggested I try out the other side of the bridge, you never said I might find love."

His eyes went wide as they went from me to the young man by Dri's gravestone, and he laughed.

"Well I'll be damned."

I laughed. "I met Tiago during a trip to Lisbon before moving there was on the cards. The day you saw me here, I was telling Dri about it, but I was also scared about moving and leaving him behind. You gave me the perspective I needed to move on with my life, and only a few days later he waltzed into my life. He even had the right key."

I remembered the moment when I'd come out of the shower to find Tiago coming into the apartment. Even despite the confusion, my first thought had been that I wanted him.

"He will always be here. Just like my Margarida. I will keep an eye on them both, but you promise me you'll visit."

"I promise. Do you want to meet him?"

"It would be my pleasure."

I wasn't surprised that Sebastião and Tiago got along straight away. We decided to treat Sebastião to an early lunch, and as a local man born and bred in Porto, he declared that Tiago needed to try the *francesinha*.

It was clear that the traditional steak sandwich dish covered with melted cheese and a tomato and beer sauce wasn't Tiago's favorite, but he ate it all and then invited Sebastião to visit Lisbon so he could try his friend's food.

The three-hour drive to Lisbon was an exercise in self-control. Tiago wouldn't stop touching me every few minutes. He rested his hand on the back of my neck, ran his fingers through my hair, and the absolute worst, he put his hand on my thigh, stroking it so each time it went closer and closer to my cock.

When one of his fingers brushed past the now fully hard cock, I had to send him a warning look. He simply shrugged.

Keeping the car under the speed limit was a supernatural feat considering I was dying to get to the apartment so I could reciprocate the torture he was bestowing upon me.

Whatever he'd told Dri at the cemetery had clearly put his mind at rest, and he'd given himself permission to have free rein over my body.

When we arrived, I picked up both our bags from the car, so the first thing I did when Tiago opened the apartment door was to throw them on the floor and pin him against the door, claiming his lips. All the pent-up frustration from three hours of teasing was released in that kiss.

Tiago moaned under my touch, and I swallowed every single one of them. If I could merge with him, I would, just to keep bringing him this much pleasure every second of the day.

He tried to pull me even closer by wrapping his arms around me, but I had better ideas on what to do with him.

"Have you ever heard that revenge is a dish best served cold?" I asked, pulling his shirt off and latching onto his left nipple and then the right one.

"I think we've established you're the chef in this relationsh—fuck..." He bucked against me, trying to get some friction through his jeans. I pressed my palm against his erection and heard him exhale in pleasure just before I removed it again.

"Fuck you."

I took his wrists and held them over his head, my body finally covering his from head to toe. I angled my head so I could whisper in his ear, "Yes, please."

His sharp intake of breath made me release his hands and stand back to look at him. He wasn't the only one surprised at my words, but now they were out, I wanted nothing more. Dri and I had enjoyed switching, but more often than not, he'd wanted to bottom.

I hadn't missed Tiago's previous references to wanting to feel me inside him, and to a certain degree, I'd assumed that would be the case for our first time together in that way, but I needed to make sure it was what he wanted, too.

"Are you sure?" His eyes were searching. I could tell he wanted it but also wanted to give me the option to change my mind.

"There are very few things I've wanted this much, baby." I took his hand so he'd follow me to the bedroom. "Unless you're afraid you can't give an old man the time of his life."

He jumped on my back and wrapped his legs around my waist, his mouth latching onto the muscles on the side of my neck, sucking hard until he said in my ear, "You may have experience on your side, but I have stamina."

I let out a curse because I was already on edge. Being around him put me in a constant state of arousal, and I knew it would never take much for him to draw an orgasm out of me. I just hoped I could last long enough to make this good for him, too.

As though he could read my mind and feel my insecurities, he jumped down from my back and led me to the bathroom, turned the water on in the shower, and pulled me in with him. It was only after we'd washed each other's bodies that he spoke softly into my lips.

"It's going to be perfect, Vítor. I know it."

Tiago picked two towels from the cupboard and gave me one. Once we were both dry, he took me to bed and asked me to lie down. I was expecting him to lie down with me, but he left the bedroom, coming back shortly with lube and condoms.

I hadn't had sex with anyone other than Dri, so once we were tested after we'd met, we hadn't needed to do it again, and we hadn't used condoms, either.

It was a good thing at least one of us had supplies and a thinking brain because I was already too far gone and couldn't wait to feel him inside me.

"Next time I'm going to lick every single inch of your skin, but not today. I don't think I can hold very long once I'm inside you." We'd both been hard throughout the shower, even though we'd ignored our erections, apart from when they'd touched and we'd allowed ourselves a moment of pleasure as they'd rubbed against each other between our bodies.

"Fuck, please do it," I begged as he kneeled down on the bed.

I took in a breath when I felt the cold lube at my entrance. His fingers were gentle as he massaged around my rim as though they were seeking permission.

Even though I knew what to expect, it still felt like the first time, and I couldn't deny that it hurt when Tiago was able to get his first finger all the way inside me.

Our eyes were locked on each other when he finally moved the finger so it touched my prostate. My cock was leaking even though he hadn't even got near it. I closed my eyes and fisted the sheets on either side of me as Tiago continued to draw his finger in and out. I didn't even notice he'd added another finger until he whispered in my ear.

"Look at you, taking my fingers in your tight heat. You're so ready for me, baby."

"Nhnn, Tiago, please..."

He removed his fingers, leaving me empty and on the verge of something, but I didn't know what it was. For all I knew, I was on the brink of dying from pleasure. I just needed more, more of him, more of us, until I felt the pressure of his thickness and stopped breathing.

Tiago kissed me like he was worshiping the ground I walked on. He didn't push any farther than I could take until I was ready. Once the initial burn was gone, I started moving under him to get more of his thick cock inside me.

He got the message and soon he was allowing himself to give in to the need to move in and out of me. I ran my hands down his back, settling them on his ass as though I could push him farther inside than he already was.

My cock was aching from the need to come. I tried to get my hand between us so I could stroke myself and find the sweet relief I needed, but Tiago slapped my hand away. Instead, he lifted one of my legs over his shoulder and increased the speed of his movements. That caused him to rub against my prostate with every single thrust.

I was sure I wouldn't survive this and told him as much.

"Oh Vítor. Vítor." He kept repeating my name as he found his release inside me.

My orgasm followed his. I didn't even touch myself because, between his thrusts against my prostate and the friction I got from having my cock trapped between us, I had all I needed for the most intense orgasm of my life.

Tiago kissed me and whispered in my ear. "Didn't I say it was going to be perfect?"

"So perfect."

16

TIAGO

THE MORNING SUN warmed my face, but it was the body half on top of mine that kept me all warm inside. I was in two minds about asking Vítor to take the rest of the week off so we could spend it in bed, especially as he was grinding his morning wood against my hip. I really, *really*, never wanted to leave this bed. Ever.

"I can't take the week off," he said into the side of my neck.

Shit, did I say that out loud? I turned to face him.

"Why not? I think it's a great idea. The best idea ever had by someone."

His laugh turned into a moan when I moved to straddle him and took his nipple in my mouth.

"Fuck, baby, there's no time. I need to get ready for work."

I let out a frustrated breath and lay against his chest.

"Fine, I'll go make you some coffee to go while you get ready."

He came into the kitchen looking like the poster boy for suit porn. I didn't even try to hide my appreciation of how nicely he filled out those suit pants and shirt. His blue eyes stood out like shiny beacons trained on me, which in turn made me so hard I knew the first thing I'd be doing when I got in the shower. I couldn't even hide it since I was still only in boxer shorts and a T-shirt.

"You need to leave right now because I'm not going to take responsibility for what I may do to you."

"Oh really?" He came close enough that I could smell his aftershave but not so close that we were touching. Fuck, I wanted to rip his clothes off and lick him all over, starting with that damned sexy chin dimple.

I couldn't help tugging on my hard cock to find some measure of relief.

"What are you up to today?" he asked as he leaned closer, kissed my cheek, and picked up the travel mug from the counter behind me.

It took me a moment to think about the answer because my brain function had flatlined. When it did start to work, it was like I had a bucket of cold water spilled on my head, and my cock deflated immediately.

"What's up? You look like you've been punched."

"No, I just remembered I have to check in on the center and hope the plumber is managing to fix the leak without creating the need for other building work." I put my arms around his shoulders and pulled him down for a kiss. "I'll see you later. Have a good day at work."

"Thanks, sweetheart. I'll pick up some shopping on the way home, too."

It didn't take me long to grab a shower and drive over to the center. I didn't even bother with a coffee because I knew I could grab one later.

The center was a hub of activity. Mr. Pereira, the plumber, had two young guys working with him, and he was pleased to tell me he was ahead of schedule. He introduced the young guys as his sons. The youngest one looked like he'd rather be elsewhere. He was probably roped in to help while he was on his school break, but the older one seemed happy to carry on working as his dad came with me to my desk so we could catch up.

"Mr. Pereira, thank you so much for coming at such short notice."

"It's my pleasure. I've seen the work that you do here, and I'm impressed."

I must have shown my surprise because he smiled and told me that as it turned out, one of the volunteers that had come in over the last few days went to school with his older son.

"I'm very supportive of my son, and I couldn't care less who he wants to be with other than whether they're a good person. But we've met with our own share of challenges. Being openly gay in a business like ours leaves you vulnerable to all sorts of discrimination, and sometimes worse." I could understand Mr. Pereira's fear as he told me one day his son would take over the business.

"Now the little one over there will chase anything with a skirt. I can only hope I won't become a granddad before he's able to grow a full beard." The pride in his voice as he spoke about his sons was heartwarming. We spent another half hour going through the outstanding work and some suggestions he had, and then, as if he hadn't already done enough for the center, volunteered his and his son's services anytime we needed anything done.

I tried to focus on the high from my meeting with Mr. Pereira as I drove south to Caparica so my nerves wouldn't get the best of me. I'd asked David to meet me at Pedro's little snack bar on the beach instead of the café because I wanted a neutral place for our conversation.

When I'd asked Vítor to take me to see Rodrigo, it was because I felt I needed to somehow tell him about what I felt for Vítor, that I wasn't trying to replace him, and that I was shit scared I'd do something wrong and end up hurting him.

It was like Rodrigo himself was asking me the questions.

How can you care for someone so deeply after only a few weeks?

What is it about Vítor you like?

I'd answered the questions. That was the easy part. The hard part was confessing I could end up hurting him when I told him about his family. That had been the reason for wanting to see David because I needed to give Vítor a choice.

"Hey, man," Pedro said, coming from behind the counter to shake my hand, "haven't seen you for a while."

"Yeah, things have been busy with Isaac gone, you know."

"Yeah, yeah, you kids are always busy these days."

We chatted while I waited for David. Pedro had gone to school with David and Joel's moms, and his snack bar by the beach had been their hangout since they were kids.

"Don't let him give you grief," David said as he pulled up a chair to sit next to me. "We come by all the time. He's getting needy in his old age."

Pedro gave David a playful punch before he went back behind the counter.

"So, why the mystery meeting?" he asked.

"I've been thinking… what if Vítor doesn't want to be found?"

David stared at me like I was crazy, but not a moment later, his gaze dropped.

"I hadn't thought of that. I know how much Uncle Mário would love to have his brother back in his life. That's all I was thinking. Do you think we shouldn't search for him?"

He looked like I'd taken the wind out of his sails.

"No, I just think you have to be prepared for the fact that Vítor may not want to have contact with his family."

"Surely once he knows that his parents aren't alive anymore he'd want to see his brother."

That was a possibility, one that I could test out on Vítor, but there were still no guarantees.

"Maybe, but think about it. He was in the hospital for how many days without a visitor, without anyone showing any support or checking if he was okay? He may think that Mário took their father's side."

David exhaled. "You're right, but what does it mean? We stop looking? Continue? What if he's out there and he wants to reconnect, but he's not sure about reaching out?"

I couldn't look my friend in the eye. I hated lies, and I hated secrets. I'd kept many of those for such a long time, thinking I was protecting my family when all it did was destroy it.

My legs were itching to move, so I got up and went to the edge of the pedestrian walkway where it met the sand. David followed me and stopped by my side.

"I used to come to the beach when I was young and look at all the families. Growing up, Joel was like a brother to me, but it wasn't the same, you know? I wanted a brother that was just a brother, someone I could confide in, especially when he started becoming more than my best friend."

He started walking along the pavement, so I followed.

I knew exactly what he meant because I'd been the same kid, asking my mom when I could have a brother to play with and when I would get a dad.

"I can't imagine a life without Joel," he continued. "I think it's pretty perfect that the one person I've known all my life will always be there with me, and I'm ready to move on from the hurt of the past, but I can't, because there's this unfinished chapter."

"You have no idea how much I get it. I really want to do this for you and your family."

I sensed David's gaze on me but kept mine ahead on the people walking, cycling, and running along the paved road by the beach.

"Wait." He pulled on my elbow to turn me around to face him. "You found him, haven't you? You've been talking about what would happen when you find him, but you never said that not finding him was a possibility."

"David." I didn't know what to say. I couldn't lie to him. He was one of my best friends, and this was going to hurt him. I couldn't do it.

"Tiago, please tell me. Have you found him?"

I nodded and found myself wrapped in David's arms.

"Is he okay?"

"Yes."

"How did you find him?"

We continued walking. I felt like there was a frog stuck down my throat. As soon as the words were out in the world, I wouldn't be able to take them back.

"He found me."

"How?"

"I didn't know, David. Please believe me, I didn't know. The guy I told you about."

"The sexy silver fo—oh my god." He stopped mid-stride. "You've been living with him for a few weeks."

"I didn't know he was Mário's brother." My eyes were a blink away from shedding the tears I felt were coming.

"When did you find out?"

"This weekend. He took me to his house in Porto. He had a drawing on the wall of one of the photos you showed me. I asked him about it, and he named Mário, Teresa, and your mom."

"Does he know you know who he is?"

I shook my head.

"Fuck, Tiago, this is a whole new level of complicated."

"You don't even know the half of it."

We sat on one of the benches facing the beach. There were already a number of people enjoying the warm spring weather on the beach, and even a few brave ones that had taken to the water. I couldn't remember the last time I'd spent a day on the beach. I wondered if Vítor would want to do that.

David's phone dinged with a message.

"Joel finished his tutoring session. I've got to go, but can we talk about this? I understand that we can't just barge into his life, but he should know his brother's side of the story." He paused before he got up to go. "Can I see you at the center before my next class?"

"Of course. Go meet your sexy man and we'll talk about it then."

"Tiago, I can't keep this from Joel."

"I wouldn't expect you to."

He gave me a hug and left.

I stared at the glistening water in the distance and tried to understand the whirlpool of emotions going on inside me.

Vítor had heard about my childhood—he'd been the first person I'd ever told the whole story—but I couldn't tell him about his family's wishes to see him again. In Isaac's absence, David was the friend I wanted to tell about the amazing man I'd fallen for. I wanted to share the excitement with my friend and also ask for his advice and tell him how scared I was I'd do all the wrong things and push him away. Except I couldn't do that because of who Vítor was to David.

There was only one person I could reach out to, and even though I was worried and angry about his silence, I knew he'd be there for me. Pulling out my phone, I sent Fred a text.

Hey. Do I need to fill out a missing person's report? I need my friend back. T

17

VÍTOR

"VÍTOR, do you have a few minutes before you go home?"

I looked up from the plans I was working on.

"Of course, Bernardo, how can I help?"

"Just wanted to check in on you. You seem to have settled in the partnership as though you've been here since day one. How are you finding it?"

"João has been very patient with me, showing me the ropes. It's a shame he's retiring because I'd have enjoyed working with him."

"This is more than a partnership, Vítor, we're a family. João is going to dedicate more time to his family and his charity work, but I'm sure he'll still be up for mentoring. In fact, I'd bet the commission of your next project that for the next year he'll be here at least twice a week just to catch up on gossip."

I laughed. The experience I'd had in this partnership so far had been the polar opposite to what I'd had in Porto. While I wouldn't deny loving my old partnership and the great opportunities it had given us, I felt that at this stage in my life I needed a change. I wondered if Dri would ever have considered it if he was here now.

"Vítor, if you permit the boldness of an old man. You seem

different than when we first met. I'd even go as far as saying you're happy in a way that you can only be when you're in love."

Bernardo was a very perceptive man, and at only fifteen years older than me, I wouldn't exactly call him old.

I shrugged. "I'm not going to lie to you. I am falling for someone. It was as unexpected as my move to Lisbon but here we are."

"Well, what are you doing here then? Go home to your man."

I looked at the clock on the wall. Tiago had texted earlier to say he was going to see a friend, so I was hoping to grab some groceries and still get home before he did. He'd looked worried this morning when he'd mentioned the work at the center, so I wanted to cook him a nice meal and make sure he relaxed this evening.

Fortunately, the supermarket wasn't too busy, so I got everything I needed to cook a stir fry for dinner and a few more things for the rest of the week so I could go straight home from work and make the best of Tiago's time off.

Tiago's car was parked outside the building, so I knew he was home already. I heard the shower as soon as I got in and hoped he hadn't been there long, because I wanted nothing more than to join him.

I took care of any groceries that needed to be in the fridge and left the rest on the kitchen table, removing my clothes as I almost ran to the bathroom.

Tiago let out a cute little squeak when I opened the shower door to let myself in.

"Hey, baby," I said, pulling him close to me for a wet, hot kiss. My day hadn't been particularly stressful, but fuck if I didn't feel like I'd been waiting all day for this kiss.

"Fuck, I think I need to go to the doctor."

"Why?" I asked, taking a step back to look at him and check his temperature.

He chuckled.

"Because you fucking kiss like a god and one of these days I swear I'm going to die from it."

"Like a god, huh? Maybe I should stay clear of your mouth then."

I turned him around, pushed him against the tiled wall, and got on my knees. He let out a moan when he realized what I was going to do and pushed his ass out to give me better access.

"I bet your ass tastes as good as it looks."

There was no point trying to go slow, so I put a hand on the globes of his ass and pulled them apart to display the pink, tight hole I was going to eat like the best dessert ever. I licked all the way from his taint to the top of his crease, stopping only to swirl my tongue around his rim. He pushed his ass back as though he wanted more of it amid a string of curses, which I was more than happy to do.

"Hmm, I was right, delicious." I stood up and turned him around to kiss him. He kissed and sucked on my lips as though he was returning the favor. I took both our cocks in my hand. Fortunately, we were both leaking enough to use our precum as a lubricant.

"Vítor." He groaned against my neck when I sped up. I was already so close, and the way he was fucking my hand, he wasn't far behind.

I laced my fingers through his hair and pulled it down. I needed to see his face and look into his eyes when he finally gave in to the pleasure I was bringing us.

"So beautiful," I whispered into his mouth. "Mine, you're mine."

His eyes locked on mine, and I could read all his emotions like a book. His big, beautiful, brown eyes that were almost always hidden behind his glasses, and I was the only one who had access to the real Tiago. All of him.

His hands were digging in my shoulders, and I hoped they'd leave a bruise. I wanted him to mark me and make me his, too. He was close but refusing to let go as though he wanted to be like this forever.

"Please, baby, come for me. I need it, too," I said as I added a twist motion with my wrist as I jerked us both off. I released his hair but gave him a look that asked him to keep his eyes on mine. My free hand roamed down his back toward his ass. When my finger found his hole, I applied some pressure. I could feel him trying to open up for me as he kept fucking my hand until neither he nor I could hold any longer.

We didn't hurry to finish our shower, but when I heard his tummy rumbling, I declared the fun was over and we needed to get dressed so I could make us dinner.

Unfortunately, the warm spring weather was exclusive to when the sun was out, which meant we still couldn't make use of the balcony, but we could definitely cuddle on the sofa and enjoy the view as the sun came down on the horizon.

After dinner, we settled on watching a series of documentaries about different cities around the world. We'd found that we both enjoyed the kind of documentaries where you learned interesting facts about things without going too deep on the history.

We managed a whole documentary without touching each other, which I think was a personal win because with Tiago plastered against me on the sofa, it had been near enough impossible to keep my hands off him. When the second documentary started, he turned over and kissed me. We were in the middle of our slow and fairly PG-rated make-out session when the doorbell rang.

I got up from the sofa, taking time to adjust my erection in my underwear, and went to open the door.

The guy on the other side looked to be in his early thirties, almost my height and build but with blond hair and brown eyes. He looked like he hadn't slept in months.

"Can I help you?"

"Hi, is Tiago in?"

"Fred!" At the guy's words, Tiago jumped from the sofa, ran toward him, and enveloped him in a hug.

I tried to squash the little tinge of jealousy that sprang up. I'd never been a jealous person, but our relationship had a much different dynamic than what I'd grown used to with Dri. Not to mention that this other guy, apart from being physically very attractive, was also Tiago's good friend.

Tiago pulled Fred into the apartment and guided him to the sofa. I thought I'd give them some space, so I went to the kitchen, thinking I could plan what we were going to have for dinner tomorrow.

I was surprised when Tiago came in a minute later straight into my arms.

"He doesn't look well."

He ran his fingers through his hair, and I kicked myself for letting my doubts and lack of confidence get to me earlier.

"He's here now, so you can look after him, see what he needs. Let me make you guys a coffee and then I'll leave you alone to talk."

"No, please, I need you. Will you join us with the coffee? Can you also make him a sandwich? He looks like he hasn't eaten in days."

"Anything, baby. I'll be out there in ten minutes."

I wasn't sure what to make of the feeling of relief that Tiago needed to lean on me so he could help his friend. It was a feeling I hadn't had for a long time. Even Mateus had been fiercely independent since he was a child. I knew he'd have moved out of home after he finished university if it hadn't been for Dri getting sick.

While I waited for the coffee to finish, I dropped Mateus a text.

Hey son. Thanks for the words of wisdom over the weekend. I thought that was my job, but you've clearly got the touch. I'd love to introduce you properly to my boyfriend soon. Love, Dad xx

When I came back to the living room, Tiago and Fred were on the sofa facing each other. I wasn't listening to their conversation, but I caught a few words and knew Tiago had told Fred about our relationship.

I put the tray on the coffee table.

"Hi, Fred, I'm Vítor." I put my hand out and was glad when he shook it back.

"Hi, nice to meet you."

Tiago looked at me and smiled. I placed a kiss on his head before I sat on the other side of him. When he leaned back on my chest, I gladly put my arms around his waist.

Fred inhaled the sandwich and drank his coffee like a starved man. "Thanks, guys, this really hit the spot. I haven't had much to eat since... well, I can't even remember."

"What's going on, Fred? I've been worried sick."

Fred looked guilty, but before he answered Tiago's question, he looked at me and paused as though he was making an assessment.

"First," he said to Tiago, "you're going to explain to me how you went from poster boy for the gay single life to loved up in three-point-five seconds." He turned to me. "And you, you're going to promise me that you won't break his heart or I'm going to forget I'm an officer of the law and kick your ass so hard you're going to end up in France with no pit stops in Spain."

I held my hands up and away from Tiago who took them and wrapped them around him again.

"Don't worry, babe, I'll protect you," he said, looking at me and placing a chaste kiss on my lips.

"Ugh, another loved-up couple. Am I the only one left now?" Fred groaned.

Tiago leaned forward and put his hands on Fred's. "He's out there, Fred."

Fred looked into Tiago's eyes but then looked away. I saw regret and something else I couldn't name. Was he in love with Tiago?

I didn't have time to think about it because Fred decided to change the subject to talk about the real reason he'd stopped by.

"I'm sorry I've been missing. I know I normally tell you when I go undercover, but things happened so quickly, and I didn't have time to warn you."

"That's okay, you're here now, but you don't look well. Did anything bad happen this time?"

Fred took a moment to choose his words.

"A few years ago, when I was still new in the force, I heard of this pedophile network that had come to an end when they were reported by someone. They were running a massive underground network that provided images and videos to another organization that posted them online. They were difficult to catch because they weren't the ones with the digital print. What they didn't count on was being reported by the son of one of the top guys when he found out what his father was up to.

"When I joined the special missing children's unit, I suggested we create a safe space online where anyone can report any activity where they believe children are being abused. We made it super safe so we couldn't identify the people sending the messages. We wanted to tell the public that they could report things anonymously and we would investigate."

"Did you get a lot of fake reports?" I asked.

"We did, but we also received a few that helped us put some criminals in jail. We hoped that making this public would encourage anyone who was afraid for their safety or the safety of their loved ones to report the activity because we wouldn't know who they were.

"With advances in technology, that website became more or less obsolete. We wouldn't ever shut it down because some people may still have the link and use it, but we didn't get any new reports. That was until about a year ago. There was so little on it, I thought it was a joke, but I still replied to the message. It took two months until I had another message from the same guy using a different name.

"How do you know it was the same guy?" Tiago asked.

"I didn't at the time. It took four messages over six months for the guy to realize that I really couldn't know who he was. That's when he said he was the one sending those messages. I spent some time building his trust. Something told me that he was reporting something big, but also that he was afraid of what would happen not just to him but to others if the information came into the wrong hands.

"I've established that he has access to a number of children that have been groomed and kidnapped. In the last few weeks, I've been working with a network of special agents to coordinate the rescue. What we were missing was the location."

He paused, and my gut feeling told me he was about to pull the rug from under Tiago's feet. I tightened my hold around him and his movement to burrow farther into my chest told me he felt the same.

"I need a halfway house for the kids once they're out. The center is the ideal place because you already have support people in place, and if the press gets wind of this, the first places they'll look are the police stations and hospitals."

"Yes, of course," Tiago said. "The center is closed at the moment because we have some plumbing issues, so no one will be coming in. I'll do anything I can to help."

"There's one more thing."

"Anything."

"I convinced the guy to meet up with me so we could go through the rescue plan. I met him a week ago. Tiago. It's Afonso."

18

TIAGO

"Wha... what?" I wasn't sure I'd heard Fred properly. My mind had been running at a thousand miles an hour, already planning the help we could provide to those kids. We had two nurses who had access to further medical support if we needed and a few social workers who were always available to us. I'd assumed that as a halfway house, our job was to keep the kids safe so they could be assessed and then be taken to a medical facility or back to their families.

Tears started running down my cheeks, and Vítor's arms tightened around me. It was almost painful, but I needed that to stop me from crumbling completely.

"Baby, take deep breaths." I heard Vítor, but he sounded far away. I tried to focus on his voice and count with him in my head as I took a breath and then let it out, but my brain was resisting because it was focused on those words, "It's Afonso."

When I was able to breathe again on my own, I noticed Fred was holding my hands fiercely, and Vítor had moved me so I was on his lap. There was a glass of water on the coffee table. When had all that happened?

I looked at Vítor, unsure of what to say.

"Fred knows where he is, baby, and we're going to bring him home safe, you hear me?"

I was unable to do anything else but nod.

"You met him a week ago. Why didn't you say something?" I asked Fred.

"I couldn't, Tiago. Apart from working on the investigation practically every hour of the day, I'd have been in serious trouble if I was caught sharing any information at the time."

"You said he had access to the kids. What does that mean?" I asked.

"He works for the organization. I couldn't get much out of him, but he said there are too many kids this time round."

"He works for them?"

"I don't think it's out of choice, Tiago."

"How did you recognize him?"

"Babe, I've been looking at your face for years, and I've been studying his photo for just as long. I'd have recognized him if he'd colored his hair or was in women's clothes. Besides, apart from the glasses, he looks like he could be your twin."

"What do we do? I want him home with me. I don't want him to have to do whatever he does."

Fred took a deep breath, and I knew what was coming.

"Tiago, he's an adult now. It has to be his choice."

I got up and paced the length of the living room with both Vítor and Fred's eyes on me.

"He's going to want to come home, right, Vítor? He'll want to come with me, won't he? When I tell him how long I've been looking for him?"

Vítor got up and put his arms around me. I couldn't stop more sobs from coming out.

"What if he thinks I gave up on him? What if he blames me for whatever happened to him? Oh my god, Vítor, maybe he hates me." I wasn't sure he could even hear me with my head buried in his chest, but it didn't matter because I was too scared to hear the answers to those questions.

"Baby, look at me."

I did as he asked. He removed my glasses, cleaned my tears, and pushed my hair back so he could look into my eyes.

"We have a lot of questions that can only be answered by Afonso. The priority is to get the kids out of there. My feeling is that whatever position he's in, he's relatively safe as long as we don't put him in danger by making the wrong move."

He was right. I rested my head on his chest again, trying to take in some of his strength for myself as he ran his hands in circles on my back, calming me.

I couldn't believe it. My brother had been found. I needed to be patient and have a plan, but I could see him again. Suddenly, I had the urge to laugh, so I did. It was probably not the best reaction to the situation, but I couldn't help myself. I laughed until I was crying again, but this time, with happy tears. God help me when I'd actually get my arms around my brother.

"Fred." I looked at him and saw how much his job had taken out of him. He looked exhausted. "Do you want to stay here tonight? We can talk some more tomorrow. I promise I'll do whatever you tell me to do. I want those kids safe."

"Thanks, I'd love to stay if that's okay with you, too, Vítor."

"Goodness, Fred, you found Afonso. I'll sing you lullabies and bring you breakfast in bed in the morning if you want."

I struggled to contain my laugh when Fred's eyes opened wide.

"That, er... won't be necessary. A bed will do. I mean, I'll sleep in the spare bedroom. Or the sofa, whatever."

I addressed Fred while I kept my eyes on Vítor. "You can stay in the spare bedroom, that's where my stuff is. Feel free to use the shower and look for anything you need. I'm sleeping with my silver fox here."

"You bet your cute little ass you are," Vítor whispered before he gave me a kiss that turned from chaste to full-on heated in two seconds. I heard a groan from Fred as he walked over to my bedroom.

"If I hear any sex noises, I'm going to tell Vítor about that time in—"

"Night, Fred," I shouted back.

"What was he going to say?" Vítor asked, tilting his head and narrowing his eyes at me.

"Nothing, nothing at all. Maybe you're hearing things. Do we need to get you a hearing aid?"

He lifted me up and over his shoulder and slapped my ass.

"I'm going to make you eat those words."

"Babe, we have a guest. We can't make noise."

"Don't you worry about that. Your mouth is going to be too full of my cock by the time you come that you won't be making any noises that will be heard from the other room."

"Fuuuck."

I knew what he was trying to do and loved him even more for it. He knew the moment I let my body give in to the orgasm, I'd fall asleep and find the peace I was craving because tomorrow was a big day and I needed all the sleep I could get.

My skin tingled all over, probably from the sun that was also warming my face and causing me to squint in a poor attempt to open my eyes. I was so comfortable, maybe I didn't need to open my eyes at all. This had to be the comfiest beach in the world, so comfortable that I didn't care that I was humping the beach towel under me because I was horny as hell and it felt too good. Maybe I needed to move because the tingling feeling was getting stronger. I didn't remember putting on any sun cream. Thinking about it, I didn't remember coming to the beach at all.

"Time to wake up, baby," the voice whispered in my ear. Vítor.

"Hmm, I am awake."

He chuckled next to me.

"Oh really? Then why are you asking if we can stay on this beach?"

I turned my face to where his voice was coming from and opened my eyes since they were no longer in the sun. His hand caressed my face, and I returned his smile. The last thing I remembered was kissing Vítor after he'd brought me to an earth-shattering orgasm that had left me unable to do anything else but drift off into the clouds.

"We need to go to the beach soon," I said, still feeling sleepy.

"We will, but first you need to get up, and since you didn't wake up with the five million kisses I placed all over your body, I guess you missed out on sexy times."

He pinched my butt, which caused me to rub my already very hard cock onto the bed sheets. I groaned but then lifted my ass up, which earned me a slap.

"If you're going to be a tease, then come to the bathroom. You're far too loud for bedroom activities when we have a guest," he said.

That brought me back to the situation I was going to face as soon as I stepped out of the bedroom this morning. I wasn't quite ready for it, so I followed Vítor into the shower.

After Vítor left for work, Fred and I talked through his plans.

"I'd like to have a look at the center so I can map out the security needs. More than anything, I don't want the press to get wind of what's going on, but if they do, I need to know how we can keep the kids and their families away from that."

"Okay, the plumbers are finishing their work today. The center is going to be closed for the rest of the week."

Fred made a note and sent a text on his phone.

"We've put the house under surveillance. It's an old, colonial-style mansion surrounded by nice gardens. There's a wall around it, but it's the only security measure they have. This means we already have footage of Afonso and some of the kids. We've been able to link them to the database of missing children. Some of them have been missing for a few years, but some have only disappeared weeks ago."

"Fred, I know what you're going to say, but I'll ask you anyway. Will I be able to see the footage?"

He looked at me but didn't make eye contact for long.

"Tiago, I'm sorry," he said, shaking his head.

I was expecting it, but it still didn't stop me from being disappointed. I was dying to see my brother's face and see for myself that he was alive and well.

It didn't take long to check out the center because Fred already knew it so well. He was less familiar with the rooms upstairs, but he was happy we had enough space to keep everyone in this location.

"How about the kids that are staying here?" he asked.

"They're all in accommodations at different hostels this week. We can arrange for them to stay longer if we need to."

"I don't know how quickly we can arrange the rescue operation. This involves several authorities, which means working on someone else's timeline. It could take a few weeks to get it all in place."

"Don't worry, I'll work things out with the kids at the center."

Fred made a move to leave, but I held his arm to stop him. I knew the risk he'd be taking, but the big brother in me would never give up asking.

"Fred, is there any way at all I could see just a picture of his face? The thought that he's out there in some house having to do god knows what is crushing me. I can't wait weeks. I need to see he's okay."

Fred took a deep sigh and then looked at his watch. "Okay, but you have to promise to do what I say."

I nodded.

My anxiety spiked as we drove to Fred's office. The prospect of seeing my brother was exciting, but I was also afraid of my reaction to it.

We parked in an allocated space by the front entrance.

The building that housed Fred's unit was not what I expected. It looked like a regular office building. In fact, it looked like they shared facilities with accountants, lawyers, and even a marketing company.

"We have to be discreet because of what we do. It's better to blend in with the rest. As far as everyone knows, we're an IT company specializing in web security. I need you to stay in the car and wait for me here."

I did as I was told, and fifteen minutes later, Fred left the building and got back in the car, driving us away immediately. He didn't stop until we were a few blocks away.

He took a laptop out of a case and turned it on. A few minutes later, once he'd gone through a lengthy logging in process, I saw the screen fill up with the images of a house.

The house where my brother lived, goodness knew for how long. The gardens looked very well kept. Anyone looking at the footage would be shocked to know what went on inside.

"Is that a live feed?" I asked.

"Yes, we've got the gardens that surround the property covered. Some of the cameras have been able to catch images of the inside through the windows, but when the sun shifts, the reflection makes it difficult."

Fred showed me the angle from each of the cameras. I didn't see anyone until we got to the last one. The camera was pointed at the back of the house where there was a large set of stairs from the top floor leading down to the lawn. Halfway down the stairs, I saw a figure sat down with his elbows on his knees and his head resting on his hands.

"Is that him?" I wasn't sure why I asked, because I knew it was. Even though I hadn't seen my brother in eight years, I knew it was him.

I may as well have been punched in the gut or have had my heart ripped out for how painful it was to see him through the screen and not be able to touch him.

"Look up," I whispered. Fred's arms came around my shoulders, and I leaned in to take the comfort he was offering.

After a few minutes, I saw a kid come down the stairs and sit next to Afonso. He wasn't older than fourteen or fifteen.

When my brother looked up at the kid, my heart stopped. Fred had been right; he looked exactly like me, but he also looked a lot younger than his twenty-one years.

"Can you zoom in?" I asked.

Fred nodded, and within seconds, I had a closer view. Afonso said something I couldn't decipher to the kid and then hugged him before the kid left him again. He looked ahead, and it was like we were staring into each other's eyes.

"Does he know about the cameras?"

"No," Fred said. "They were placed a few days ago. Like I said, the place doesn't have any security, so it was easy to jump the surrounding wall in the dark of night and place the cameras."

I took a guess that it hadn't been as easy as Fred made it out to be.

Fred's eyes were glued to the screen. I could swear there were unshed tears trying to escape.

"He's a victim, too, Fred. We need to rescue him."

"Yes, we do."

When Vítor arrived home that night, I couldn't contain my excitement. He hadn't even closed the front door when I blurted out, "I saw him. He's alive. Oh my god, I saw him. He's so grown up. And Fred was right; he looks just like me but without the glasses."

"Baby, breathe." He put his hands on my face and gave me a kiss that nearly made me forget what I was talking about. "What happened?" he asked.

"I saw my brother. Fred showed me the surveillance cameras on his laptop."

I couldn't ever thank Fred enough for keeping me so involved. Even with the center being part of the post-rescue efforts, I knew he didn't have to share as much as he did. It was risky for everyone, but Fred knew just how much I needed this. He'd been right there with me for all the times when information had led to a dead end and the subsequent disappointment. After today, I was exhausted but also felt lighter than I remember feeling in a long time.

"Oh baby, that's great news."

I burrowed into his strong chest and nodded. His arms went around me instantly. When I was with Vítor, I felt invincible, like I was soaring.

After a few days, the excitement of knowing where Afonso was and that he was okay was quickly replaced with the frustration of not having him with me already.

I ran to my phone as soon as I heard the ringtone I used for Fred.

"Fred, any news?"

"Hi, Tiago. Some, but not the kind you'll like. Afonso was in touch. Apparently, there's going to be a party at the house, so they're moving the kids. We haven't had enough notice to intercept, but I managed to get an invite to the party because one of their big players is out of the country on business."

"How did you manage to get the invite?"

There was silence on the other side.

"Tiago, I…"

"That's okay, I know you can't tell me. Please, Fred, be safe."

If I was already anxious, after Fred's call I was close to panic, so it was a good thing Vítor had arrived home early from work. I went to the kitchen where Vítor was cooking dinner, turned off all the burners on the stove, and pulled him toward the bedroom.

"Vítor, I need you," I said, pushing him onto the bed and trying to get rid of his shirt at the same time.

"What's up, baby?"

"I'll tell you later. Please, Vítor."

19

____

VÍTOR

As much as I was happy to let Tiago lose himself in me, it also worried me that whatever news he'd got from Fred was bad enough to put him in this state.

Unfortunately, I'd had to wait until the next day to hear it since Tiago had exhausted us both to such an extent that we'd fallen asleep straight after finding our joint release.

As Fred and his team worked on the new intelligence they'd gathered at the party, Tiago was getting more and more impatient. He wasn't eating properly, and he wouldn't sleep in the hope Fred might call with news that they were ready to carry out the rescue.

It all came to a head when Tiago had been called by Fred's team to talk about the plans for the center and to make sure now that the center was open, they could still go ahead as planned. He'd ended up watching some of the surveillance with them. I'd been called to pick him up because he was too distressed to drive after seeing Afonso's bruised face on the screen. Fred went mad at the team because he hadn't been there and wasn't able to either warn Tiago or to stop him from seeing his brother after he'd clearly been beaten to a pulp.

I couldn't stand seeing him suffer like that, so I'd spoken to the partners at work and arranged to take a few days off to take Tiago to

Porto for a break. I knew it would take a lot of convincing to get him away, but Fred had agreed it would do him good, and he reassured me that nothing was happening until we came back.

The first part of the plan was to catch him by surprise, so I left work early and headed to the center to take him out to lunch. My workload had grown considerably in the last few weeks, so despite discussing with Tiago about volunteer opportunities, I hadn't actually been to the center.

There was a guy working at one of the desks when I walked in. The other desk, which I assumed was Tiago's, was empty. The guy told me Tiago had gone out for a meeting with the city council, but if I wanted to wait, I could go to the back garden. I'd heard great things about this garden from Tiago, so I decided to check it out.

I was directed to follow the corridor leading to the kitchen. I wasn't expecting to find anyone in the kitchen, so I stopped in my tracks when I saw a guy standing by a kitchen island surrounded by bags of flour, sugar, and various other ingredients.

"Hey, sorry, I didn't know there was anyone here. I'm just on my way to the garden."

"Hi, no problem. Sorry if I scared you. The garden is through that door." He pointed at the double doors behind him. "Are you one of the new volunteers? I haven't seen you around here before."

"Oh no, I'm not a volunteer yet. My name's Vítor." I extended my hand, but the guy stilled and stared at me like I was a ghost. I was about to take my hand back when he recovered from his strange moment and shook it back.

"You're Tiago's boyfriend."

"I am. I bet I'm not what you expected."

He shook his head. "You're exactly what I expected. Hi, I'm David. I'm Tiago's friend."

"Oh yeah, the chef. He's brought home some of your custard tarts. They're the best I've ever had."

There was something familiar about him, but I couldn't place it. He looked younger than Tiago, but not by much, so I wondered if it was my age and the fact I was dating his friend that was weird for him.

"Er... thanks. They're a special recipe I developed with my mom."

He rubbed the back of his neck and then went back to what he was doing, so I moved to go around the island toward the door.

"I could use some help," he said. Well, he almost shouted. I was truly puzzled as to why the kid wanted me around when he was clearly uncomfortable with me for some unknown reason.

"I'd love to help. What do you need me to do?"

"Just weigh the ingredients on that list. I can prepare the baking tins while you do that. Can I get you a coffee?"

"That would be great, thanks."

I looked at the list. It seemed like a simple set of instructions for a marble cake.

David seemed to relax as we worked side by side. Tiago had told me about the workshops David ran, so when I asked him about it, he opened up immediately and our conversation flowed a lot better after that.

Tiago hadn't come back by the time David started his workshop, so he invited me to join in with the kids. I didn't need help learning how to make a cake I'd made hundreds of times, but something got me agreeing to it. The class was fun. And because I already knew what I was doing, I was able to chat to the kids and find out more about them.

They all played out like they only did the class because they were bored, but what I saw as David guided them through the recipe was something totally different.

David was very engaging and inspirational, and the kids hung onto every word he said. When the cakes were in the oven, we worked on the filling and then washed up while the cakes cooled down.

"Why are you making them wash up when there's a dishwasher there?" I asked David so the kids didn't hear me.

"It's about discipline and pride. Before my mom taught me how to bake, all I was allowed to do was watch her. It wasn't until I started asking more questions about what she was doing that she finally allowed me to bake with her."

"How old were you?"

"Ten."

There was sadness in his eyes as he talked about baking with his mom, and I wondered if there was a story there but didn't want to pry, especially as he was finally more relaxed around me.

"What do you do for a living?" he asked.

"I'm an architect."

"That's great. Have you designed anything I'd recognize?"

"Probably not since I've only recently moved here from Porto, so all of my work is there."

There was that look again. Curious, searching, and something else I couldn't put my finger on.

"They're finished, so it's time to ice the cakes and then the best part."

"What's that?"

"We get to try a little bit of each and give feedback."

"I can totally get behind that."

I was having a great time at the center, so much so that I almost forgot the reason I'd come. After David and the kids were gone, I left my boxed cake on the kitchen island and went out to the gardens to wait for Tiago.

The place was as magical as he'd described. I walked around and spent some time looking at the latest painting on the wall before I settled on the cushioned seats under an arch. I'd heard about the ever-changing piece of art created by the kids and loved it. Every time I looked at something in this place, my heart swelled further with pride for Tiago.

I knew he sold himself short when it came to his involvement with the center, but I was pretty sure if I spoke with Isaac, he'd tell me exactly how much work my gorgeous young man had put into it.

In the weeks since we'd lived together, I'd heard the one-sided calls from Isaac, and on one occasion, I'd even joined in a Skype video call when Isaac asked to meet me. He'd apologized for the confusion from the rental agency, but I'd shut him down immediately when I said I'd happily send the agency some flowers or a thank you card for their role in Tiago and I meeting again.

I saw movement from the direction of the kitchen door and looked to see Tiago leaning against the frame with my cake box in his hand. I smiled and crooked my finger to call him to me. He obliged and walked over, straddling me and placing the box next to us.

He was going to say something, but I was missing him too much for words, so I put my hand behind his neck and pulled him down for a kiss. He took advantage of his increased height in that position and took over the kiss, licking my lower lip before demanding entry. As if I'd ever say no to anything he wanted from me.

"Mmm… you taste delicious," he moaned into my lips.

I opened the box, and using the plastic fork I'd left inside, took a piece of the cake and fed it to him. The sounds he made as he took each of the bites I fed him made me so hard I wasn't sure how I'd be able to walk out of there.

"If I knew all it took was cake, I'd have baked you one ages ago," I said, pushing my hips up and showing him the effect his sounds had on me.

"You can bake, too?"

I chuckled and pulled him in for another kiss, tasting the chocolate filling from the cake on his lips.

"I baked this one."

He leaned back to look at me.

"When?"

"I was hoping to meet you earlier, but you weren't here, so I met your friend David and helped him with the workshop. This is the result of my effort." I grinned.

His mouth fell open. "You met David?"

"Yes, he's a nice guy but a little odd."

"How so?"

"He seemed apprehensive around me at first, but once we started talking about his workshops, he relaxed. It was like he was trying to find something in me, but I'm not sure what. Does that make sense?"

"David's a good guy. He's been through a lot. Anyway, what are you doing here? You didn't tell me you were meeting me here."

"I was hoping to whisk you away for a few days to Porto."

His face fell.

"Baby, you're on the brink of a breakdown. Fred has everything under control here, and there's nothing else you can do. Please let me take you away."

He got up and ran his hands through his hair fiercely, like he was trying to hold on to his sanity.

"No. Don't you get it? I can't leave. I can't take any chances. I'm too close, Vítor. Too close."

The last two words were cries into my chest as I got up and put my arms around him.

"Shh, that's okay, baby, we don't have to go. I just wanted to do something for you. I'm so worried about you, and I feel that there's nothing I can do to help you."

"I'm sorry. I haven't been the best person to be around. This wait is killing me, and after seeing him all beat up, I just can't take it anymore. I need to see him, touch him, and promise him that everything is going to be okay."

"You'll have a chance to do that. Just be strong for a little longer."

"I'm so tired."

"I know, baby. Let's take you home."

20

TIAGO

In the eight years of searching for my brother, I'd very rarely lost it, but it was becoming a regular occurrence and I didn't like, especially because of the strain it put on Vítor. I knew it was because we were so close, but the wait made the last eight years feel like five minutes and the last three weeks feel like ten years.

After I'd left my meeting that afternoon, I'd received a text from Fred to meet in a local café. He'd told me they were going to coordinate the arrests of more than twenty people involved in the grooming ring at the same time as they rescued the kids. Some of them were people in positions of power in politics, so they'd needed to gather all the evidence to make sure that once they were arrested, they wouldn't be able to make bail.

I hadn't seen my brother through the surveillance cameras in a few days, but Fred reassured me he was okay and his bruises seemed to be fading.

Fred had also looked like he was ready for this whole thing to be over. The black circles around his eyes were a testament to the hours he was putting in, likely going through the plans and monitoring the surveillance cameras and bugs he'd planted in the house.

Vítor drove us home from the center since I'd taken the bus to work. I looked at the moving city outside the car. So many people, so many lives. Like them, I'd had to keep moving, hold a job, pay bills, be an adult even when all I'd wanted was to curl up in a ball and ask god or whoever was in fucking charge to bring my brother back to me.

At least now I wasn't on my own. I'd never realized how alone I'd felt before. Not only had Vítor given me a safe space to open up and talk about what I'd gone through, he also didn't judge me for any of my decisions. If anything, I was starting to realize I couldn't have done anything else but move away at the earliest opportunity. I'd been a child when my stepdad abused me, and I couldn't have guessed that he'd do the same to his own son, and I still didn't know the extent of it.

Vítor was the sturdy pillar I could lean on and hold on to when things got tough, but he wasn't made of stone. I could tell that watching me go through this was hurting him, too, so I decided I'd wait until tomorrow to tell him about the text I'd received from Fred just after we'd left the center.

48 hours.

It was enough time to call on everyone who was on standby to help.

Tonight, it was just about Vítor and me.

The center was a hub of quiet activity. Everyone was ready to go as soon as the first children came in. We knew the childrens' ages ranged from ten to fifteen and that there were eight of them in total, so even though they would probably be scared to death, they could also understand that we were trying to help.

Our largest meeting room was filled with food and drinks for all the people supporting the rescue as well as the children, although we'd also left food in each of the accommodation rooms. Those would be used to interview the children. Fred had explained that since they hadn't been able to confirm the children's identities, they would have to stay at the center until the families were contacted.

"How are you holding up, sweetheart?" Vítor asked as he rubbed my arms. I was shaking like a leaf.

"My head is struggling to choose what to focus on, the kids, Afonso, or the possibility that he may not be with any of the officers that come in today."

As scheduled, the first child arrived at eight in the morning. He was holding on to the officer that had brought him in and tried to hide behind her when I greeted them. There was no one else around because we didn't want to overwhelm the kids.

I guided the officer to the first room upstairs. That was my only job, to show the officers where to take the kids. Everyone else then played their part in turns.

One by one, the kids arrived, each with an accompanying officer. By eleven, all eight kids were in the rooms. I'd caught up with two of the nurses that had assessed them for injuries, and they told me that none of them needed further medical care but would all need extensive therapy.

The fact that these children would likely carry this with them for the rest of their lives broke my heart. No one knew what the real impact would be on them as adults, and we could only hope therapy helped.

There was some consolation in the fact that all the kids were aware they had been rescued by the authorities and were asking for their families already.

Vítor had been my shadow all morning, so I didn't question that he'd been right behind me when I needed to escape to the garden for a moment to myself. In fact, I was sure he wasn't going to let me out of sight any time soon.

I heard him sit on the stool in front of the sofa where I sat down.

"Today is the day that eight families around the country will always remember as the day their children were found," I said as tears ran down my face. They were the only release I had available to me. I could cry for the families and the children that had survived god knew what and now had a chance of a new life.

"They're happy tears, I promise. I just needed a moment to myself."

"Okay, baby. Can I hold you, though?"

I nodded and felt the sofa dip on my side and then I was being pulled into Vítor's arms. We stayed that way for I don't know how long.

By midafternoon, a few of the parents had arrived and been reunited with their children. That brought on another wave of emotions, but I had to keep focused because those parents had left their homes in a rush and had nowhere to stay. I spent another couple of hours booking accommodations, which was a good distraction from wondering where Fred was because I hadn't heard anything from him since that last text almost two days ago.

"Sweetheart, we should go home," Vítor said.

"No. Fred isn't here. I have to wait for him."

"Tiago." He came closer and put his hands on either side of my face, stealing a kiss.

My phone dinged, so I took it out and saw a text from Fred.

"Fred is meeting us at the apartment," I said.

I hugged Vítor and took a deep breath to gather strength for whatever was coming next.

"Let's go then."

I tried to quell my disappointment when we arrived at the apartment and Fred wasn't there waiting for us.

"Let's grab a shower before he gets here okay? You'll feel better for it," Vítor said.

"You only want to get me naked," I teased, more to convince myself everything was okay than any desire to have sex.

"Baby, I always want to get you naked, but this time, we're only having a shower, okay?"

I took his hand and followed him to the bedroom where he undressed me and led me to the shower. He hadn't exactly kept his hands off me, or his lips, but he'd kept them so tame I wanted to cry for feeling so loved.

Vítor left me a little longer in the shower to go and prepare something for us to eat. I stood there under the spray, thinking about what might happen tonight and how I felt about it. I wanted to see and hold my brother in my arms so badly it was like a living thing bubbling under my skin, but I also needed to consider that eight years was a long time. I had no idea what he'd gone through in that time. He'd had to somehow find his place in that horrid world so he could help other kids.

That took strength. Even if he wasn't ready to see me, I was still so proud of him. Maybe Fred could tell him that for me.

I turned the water off and grabbed a towel to dry myself. I noticed I'd lost weight, and I'd seen the bags under my eyes, but I knew I was strong. I smiled at my reflection in the mirror and then went back to the bedroom to get dressed.

When I turned into the living room, I didn't get a chance to think about the voices I heard before a body slammed into me and tightened his arms around my waist.

Both Vítor and Fred were too tall and bulky, which could only mean one thing.

"Afonso," I cried as I tightened my arms around him. My eyes were shut tight as I processed the feeling of his small body against mine. He was warm, breathing, hugging back. He was here.

Vítor's touch on my arm made me finally open my eyes and look up. I had no idea how long I'd been locked in the embrace with my brother, but clearly, it had been long enough that Vítor thought we might be more comfortable on the sofa.

I nodded but didn't move because Afonso hadn't either. I ran my hands through his short hair and over his back. Afonso had always been a small child, so I wasn't surprised to see he hadn't grown as tall as me. He was also very slight, but I didn't know if that was his natural constitution or if he was undernourished.

"Hey, Flea."

He chuckled at the old nickname I used to call him when we were young.

"Let's sit on the sofa," I said.

He stood straight, and I had the chance to look at his face properly for the first time in eight years. There was a little bit of bruising still, but it was nearly gone. Fred was right, Afonso looked so much like me we could pass for twins if it wasn't for the clear age difference.

I put my arm around his shoulders and guided him to the sofa. We both sat sideways so we could face each other, and I had to hold his hand because I still didn't believe this was real. I felt Vítor's hand on my back, soothing me and reminding me he was here. I looked at Vítor, and his eyes were slightly red, as were Fred's, who was sitting next to my brother looking like he wanted to be closer but was holding himself back.

"Are you okay?" I asked Afonso.

"Yes, I think I am." He looked behind himself to Fred who smiled and nodded as though he was guaranteeing Afonso's safety.

"I don't know where to start," I admitted. "I have so many questions… so much to tell you."

"Me too," he said.

"Fred, what happened today? Is Afonso really safe?" That was my first and most important question. The answer would dictate what we did next.

"He's safe. Everything went according to plan, and we made the necessary arrests. The reason we weren't able to get to you earlier was because we had to take Afonso's statement. He's our best witness, but he was living at the property, so I needed to make sure he wasn't going to be arrested."

"Will anyone come for him now?"

"It's unlikely because the man who owned the house Afonso lived in was very good at keeping him a secret, and when we orchestrated the rescue, we made it look like he was coming against his will. They also know him by another name."

"How about the press?"

"At the moment, the press doesn't know anything, but considering some of the men are in the public eye, it'll only be a matter of time until either the families raise the alarm or the press starts asking where they are."

Knowing Afonso was finally safe and there wouldn't be anyone looking for him was the biggest relief of my lifetime. Now that he was here, I'd do anything to keep him safe.

I mainly stared at Afonso as he ate the food Vítor had prepared for us. The conversation over dinner revolved around the children in the center and their families. Despite the tight balance in the accounts, I'd spoken to Isaac and he'd agreed we needed to support them and figure out later how to raise more money.

Afonso looked as tired as I felt after dinner. Tomorrow I'd have to get back to the center, but we'd have time to catch up properly. I didn't miss that Afonso didn't have anything on him other than his clothes.

"You can stay in the spare room. Feel free to use the shower and look in the drawers to see if any of my clothes fit you. We'll go shopping tomorrow, okay?"

He nodded, then looked at Fred and then back at me.

"Where is Fred staying?" His voice was small and unsure.

I hadn't missed how Afonso had seemed to drift toward Fred all evening, or that Fred always made sure he was there for him. Considering the relationship they'd built over the last few months, I wasn't surprised by the connection.

"Fred, do you want to stay over?" I asked.

"Oh, er yes, that would be nice, thanks. I'm too beat to drive. I'll sleep on the sofa. Do you have a spare blanket?"

Once we had the sleeping arrangements sorted and had let Fred use our shower, I hugged my little brother goodnight and reassured him we were just a room away if he needed anything. He'd been quite shy around Vítor, but he didn't look afraid of him, so I took it that he was just overwhelmed with being around new people.

When we got under the covers, I reached out for Vítor and wrapped myself around him. He chuckled and accepted his place as my big man pillow.

"Today was a big day. I'm so proud of you," he said, kissing the top of my head.

"Thank you for being there. I know how busy you are at work, but it meant everything having you with me today."

"Anytime, baby," was the last thing I heard as I drifted into the most peaceful sleep I'd ever had.

The next morning, I was awake earlier than normal. It was clear that I was too fidgety in bed because Vítor put his arms around me and pulled me closer.

"Let him rest, baby. You can both talk after Fred and I go."

I huffed but let myself settle against his chest.

The next time I woke up, I was alone in bed. I got up and hurried to get dressed.

My chest expanded when I saw my brother, Vítor, and Fred around the kitchen table with coffees in front of them. It didn't feel real that my brother was really here.

"Morning," I said.

When they saw me, both Vítor and Fred got up.

"We're going to leave you two to talk," Vítor said. "Call me if you need me to come back, okay? Otherwise, I'll see you tonight." He placed a kiss on my lips and left with Fred on his heels.

Afonso looked around and gripped the cup in front of him so hard his fingers were white. I struggled to find the right words to start, so I went to the coffee machine and filled a cup for myself.

"Do you want some toast?" I asked.

"No, thank you."

His voice was small. Whatever had happened to him since he'd disappeared, we could deal with. The first step would be to gain his trust. I put my hands over his on top of the table and squeezed them hard.

"Afonso, we have a lot to catch up on, but first, I need you to know that finding you wasn't an accident. I've been looking for you ever since you disappeared."

His eyes went wide.

"Really?"

"Of course, you're my little brother. I'd move heaven and earth to find you a million times over."

A small tear escaped down his face.

The backs of my eyes stung. I knew it would be hard to keep it together while we had this conversation, but I had to try. I went over to him and gave him a hug, feeling his body sag slightly against mine.

"Let's take this to the living room," I said.

Afonso followed, and I was relieved that he sat right next to me.

"Do you want to tell me what happened?" I asked.

He shook his head. "I'm not the same person I was then. A lot of things happened."

I ran my hands through his short hair, and he looked into my eyes.

"I'm not the same person either, Afonso. I promise we can work through this together, and you'll never need to run again, okay?"

He nodded. His eyes were still shiny, but he wasn't crying any more. I steeled myself for what came next. Confessing what our father had done to me.

When I finished, Afonso was gripping my hands so hard, I could tell he was struggling to keep it together.

"Afonso, he did the same to you, didn't he?"

He looked down and more tears ran down his face.

"Yes. I wanted to tell you, but you were always working and then you went away to school and never came back. After you left, it was worse. He started calling me by your name whenever Mom wasn't around. I knew then he'd done the same to you."

"It started when I was still at home?"

My throat went dry, and I wished our father was still alive so I could kill him myself.

I could tell Afonso was struggling with the memories, and I wanted to give him some reprieve, but I remembered how I'd felt after I'd told Vítor and decided to let Afonso make the choice to continue.

"You were so brave. You got a job and studied. You were able to escape. I wanted to be like you, but I was too young to get a job. One day, Mom saw me crying and asked me what was wrong. I told her that dad sometimes touched me. She didn't believe me, so I couldn't tell her he did more than that.

"On my thirteenth birthday, I asked if I could come to see you on the bus. Mom didn't want to let me, but I promised I'd be careful. I packed a bag with a few things. When I got there, I saw you were so happy. You were free."

"I didn't know you came."

"After I saw you, I thought you'd be happier without the burden of caring for me. I went home and ran away a month later."

Our coffees were forgotten as we hugged each other and cried until there were no more tears left from our shared past.

"Afonso, do you want to tell me what happened after you ran?"

"Can we do that later? I'm tired now."

I ran my hands down his head and back. I'd hold him for as long as he needed, and I'd do it for the rest of our lives because I was determined to do everything in my power to take his pain away. My little brother was back. The rest was white noise.

"Sleep, Flea. I've got you."

21

VÍTOR

I loved nothing more than to unravel the amazing man under me, especially when all it took was a cleverly placed finger.

"What do you want, baby?"

"You, Vítor, I want you inside me." His eyes burned with need, and his words were begging to the point of demanding. His hands roamed gently over my body to whichever part he could reach when I was like this, pinning his body to the bed with my own.

He was sufficiently stretched for me, so I wiped my hands clean on my discarded shirt and guided my already-lubed cock toward his hole, knowing we were both on the brink.

So much had changed in the month since we'd got Afonso back, I sometimes had to pinch myself just to check this was really my life.

Things had been hard for Tiago and his brother at first. After the initial relief of finding his brother, he kept panicking that he'd disappear again, and no amount of reassuring him that Afonso didn't have a reason to run would work.

Once the two brothers had had time to catch up and talk properly, Tiago's worry that Afonso would run was replaced with guilt for what he went through in the last eight years.

I could tell Afonso wasn't faring any better in that respect, so I'd suggested they see a counselor separately to deal with their trauma.

Tiago had resisted initially, but he'd known both he and his brother needed help so they could move forward and rebuild their relationship.

Afonso had been more or less a prisoner for the last eight years, even though he truly believed it had been his choice to stay in the mansion and work for the man we now knew was responsible for thousands of illegal images containing minors. In reality, he'd been a vulnerable teenager who'd escaped one abuser to go straight into the hands of another, more perverse one.

It had been a shock when we went out after he came back home and he'd had a panic attack. As much as we could be there for him, a therapist was better placed to help him deal with what happened to him.

They'd had a few sessions separately and then their counselor had suggested they have a joint session.

I'd driven them and had waited outside because I'd known it was going to be a tough one, but even I'd underestimated how much it would have taken out of the brothers. I'd felt powerless to do anything to alleviate Tiago's heartache. I'd hoped it would get better, but in the meantime, all I could do was give him whatever he'd needed, when he'd needed it, whether it was what he'd asked for or not.

And that's what I was doing now.

"Jesus, baby, you feel so good. So tight," I said through gritted teeth.

"More, faster."

Fuck if I didn't want to pound his ass from here to Porto, but I was holding on by a thread and the tight warmth of his channel was too good.

My lack of response must have tested his patience because he pushed me away so hard I landed on my back with my head to the foot of the bed. Before I could react, he straddled me and impaled himself on my cock.

We both groaned. I felt that I was buried so deep inside him I'd need a map to find my way out. Not that I ever wanted to stop this feeling or be more than an inch apart from Tiago.

He leaned down to kiss me, increasing the speed of his thrusts, which I was powerless to slow down because what he was doing felt so good, I couldn't muster the words or the actions to do anything about it. When he massaged my balls and ran a finger down toward my hole, I came so hard the movement of my hips raised him up. That was enough to start off his orgasm. Rope after rope of cum spilled from his cock, landing on my chest. Tiago was a work of art when he came. It was probably one of the few times he really let go and showed me exactly who he was.

Before he could come down from his high, and while I was still inside him, I pulled him down for a kiss and asked him the question I'd been meaning to ask for a few weeks now.

"Move in with me."

He chuckled. "I already live with you."

"I mean permanently. Don't go back to your apartment."

His landlord had recently been in touch to say that the work to the building would be complete on time and they were only doing a few final maintenance repairs. Tiago would be able to move back within two weeks, which wasn't something I was looking forward to.

"How about Afonso?"

"How about him?"

"I can't ask him to move out."

"I'm not asking you to do that. Afonso is a great young man, and I enjoy having him around."

I saw the relief on his face as he lay down next to me. I jumped off the bed to clean myself and grabbed a washcloth to clean him up before I cuddled up to him again.

"Although… we may need to look for a bigger apartment, baby," I said.

"Why? I thought you liked Isaac's apartment," he said with a yawn.

"I love it, but the rooms are too close together, and you're fucking loud during sex."

He chuckled and shrugged.

"Okay," was all he said before he fell asleep.

I smiled and put my lips on his forehead, letting them rest there. Whichever decision he was okay with, moving in, getting a bigger place, or both, I was going to make it happen. Anything for the man that had revived my heart when I'd believed it had been buried alongside my husband three years ago.

I was grateful for the air conditioning in the car because the early summer temperatures were already too high, and the last thing I wanted was to get to the center and smell like I needed a shower. Tiago had been working on the fundraiser for the center for the last few weeks, and today it was all hands on deck for the final touches before the big event tomorrow.

The kids had created art to sell in addition to photographs of the new wall painting they were going to unveil tomorrow. David had worked with the baking group and Bruno to offer catering, and some of the other volunteers were doing crafts to sell, such as bracelets, greetings cards, and other things.

My job was to help out where needed and make sure Tiago didn't work himself up into a state of nerves. Even Afonso, who'd started spending a lot of time at the center, was coming along.

"Don't move," I said as I took out my phone from my pocket to snap a photo.

Tiago's head came out from under the table. He smiled and arched his back.

"You have a great ass, baby."

He chuckled and pulled his T-shirt up, giving me a tease of the jockstrap he was wearing.

"Yours isn't too bad, either," he said as he got up and greeted me with a hot kiss. I had to stop his hands from roaming south of my back because I didn't want to spend the rest of the afternoon with a hard-on, especially now that I knew what he was wearing under his jeans.

"Where do you want me?" I asked.

He quirked a brow, and I could tell what he was thinking but got a straight answer instead.

"See those tables in the corner? They're for the crafts. I need them set up in rows over there." He pointed to where I was going to work and then asked, "Do you want a coffee? David's at the back."

"Sure, I'll come with you. Haven't seen him for a few weeks."

The kitchen was a hub of activity, and I found myself snapping a few photos of everyone dressed in their chef whites before we were spotted. David was coordinating everyone and supervising the making of what looked like hundreds of really fancy mini desserts.

"Why can't I work in the kitchen?" I pouted. "This is where all the good stuff is."

"You're more than welcome to, babe, but David will work you into the ground. Why do you think I'm at the front doing the dirty jobs?" He snorted.

I offered to supply everyone with coffee and started to fill up the water container when I saw Filipe running excitedly toward David who caught him and lifted him up in the air.

"Hey, whatcha doing here? Have you come to help?" David asked.

Filipe rolled his eyes. "No, silly. I'm too small to reach the table, but I can be the boss and tell everyone what to do."

I laughed and high-fived Filipe.

Bruno came in holding a large, clear box with baking supplies, and I stepped in to help him as he was balancing a few smaller boxes on top of the large one.

"Thanks. Mário and Teresa are just behind me with the rest."

The familiar names didn't reach my brain in time to process the information, but I didn't need to, because only a moment later, I saw the two people I never thought I'd see again in my life. My brother Mário and my sister-in-law, Teresa.

I froze, my memories going back to the last time I saw them. It was the dinner on my twenty-first birthday before I went out to the club. We'd been joking about baby names and that if their baby was a boy, he should be named after me.

Everything seemed like it was happening in slow motion. They dropped their boxes on one of the worktops and went over to David. David's eyes nearly shot out of his face when he saw them.

"Uncle, Aunt, what are you doing here?"

Uncle? Aunt?

I felt a hand squeeze mine, but I didn't need to look to know it was Tiago's.

"We've come to help, of course," Teresa said.

My lungs felt like they were being squeezed in a vice, and suddenly, it was too hot in the kitchen. Fortunately, the garden door was behind me. I made a move to escape, but I was too slow because before I could turn, I heard two simultaneous gasps as both my brother and Teresa's eyes were on me.

"Oh my god, Vítor, is that you?" Teresa cried, her hands clasped together.

I couldn't react, couldn't think. I needed to breathe, but it was too hot. I turned to the garden, stopping only when I reached the far wall, damning it for not having an exit to the street. I took deep breaths and leaned on the wall, the cool stone against my forehead.

"Vítor." Tiago's voice was a balm. I turned around and hugged him like my life depended on it. My throat was too tight to speak. What was my brother doing here? Why would he be in an LGBTQ center?

"Vítor, please don't run again," my brother said, coming out of the kitchen and closer to where we were stood.

His words hit a spot in my mind that I hadn't revisited in years. Being in the hospital bed, wondering if my father would carry out his threats as soon as the nurse turned her back. His lies about the causes of my injuries, and his cold stare daring me to report him. And the absolute worst, when he was gone, waiting for my big brother to come for me.

I'd waited four days in which I'd been too unwell to move. Four days I'd spent gathering the courage to tell my brother everything, that I was gay, that my dad had done this to me, and that I was still the same little brother he'd protected all our lives. I'd gathered courage to apologize for keeping something so big from him. But there had been nothing. No visits, no phone calls to the hospital.

The nurse who didn't know who I was, who'd had no interest in my wellbeing other than me making it out of the hospital healthier than I went in, she was the one who'd cared. She'd given me some clothes that belonged to her son and had asked me if I needed money to go to a safe place. That was the one thing I hadn't needed.

As soon as I'd been able to walk out of hospital unaided, I'd walked away from my old life and into my new one. On my own.

"What are you doing here?" I couldn't hide my anger. "Why did David call you Uncle and Aunt?"

"Vítor, David is Paula's son," Mário said.

I looked at David who was just behind Mário looking at me with regret.

"You knew who I was that day we met, didn't you?" I asked.

He nodded.

"Why did you lie?"

He didn't reply or look me in the eye. Behind him, I noticed the kitchen had cleared, and I saw my escape.

I grabbed Tiago's hand and pulled him toward the door.

"Vítor, please listen to them."

I stopped in my tracks and turned around to look at Tiago. I no longer saw the man I'd fallen for. All I saw was the lies, and I was fucking tired of lies. I dropped his hand and left, not caring about the calls from the people behind me or the gut-wrenching sob I heard coming out of Tiago.

22

TIAGO

I could have been punched, shot, stabbed, or all of them at the same time. It still wouldn't hurt as much as seeing the look on Vítor's face when he realized I'd lied to him. I'd known the consequences of holding on to that particular hand grenade, but I still hadn't done anything to disarm it.

My legs failed to keep me upright, and I fell on the hard ground. I couldn't even make sense of the conversations happening around me because all I could hear were the words Vítor had said to David. They may as well have been for me.

Why did you lie? Why did you lie? Why did you lie?

My lungs were struggling to draw a complete breath, and it was as though my body was locked in shock. I tried to calm myself down. I tried to conjure Vítor's soothing voice as he'd calmed me down from one of the many panic attacks I'd had on the run up to rescuing Afonso.

Breathe in. Hold. Breathe out. Repeat.

He said he was falling for me, didn't he? Would he listen to me if I tried to explain?

I had to try. I'd spent eight years looking for my brother and had gotten him back. I could be accused of being a liar and a coward, but I was no goddamned quitter.

"David, I need to go after him. Can you coordinate things here for me?"

Teresa and Mário both looked like they were in shock. I'd forgotten that Mário wasn't even aware that I was looking for his brother. I owed them both an apology, but I couldn't do it now because any time spent here was time Vítor could be at home packing his bags to go back to Porto.

"I'll look after everything, Tiago. Please go."

So I did.

I ran out of the taxi after dropping more money than I owed for the trip. Traffic had been a nightmare, and I could only hope that if I had been stuck in it, so had Vítor.

The apartment was silent as I walked in, but I didn't want to give in to the feelings inside me. If I let them take over, I'd crumble on the floor and never get up again, so I hurried to the room to pack a bag. If Vítor had gone back to Porto, I'd be right on his heels.

I stopped when I saw him sitting on the other side of the bed with a bag by his feet. He was hunched over, and his head was down. He looked broken.

"Why?" was the only word he said.

I walked over and kneeled in front of him. I stopped myself from touching him like I wanted.

"David asked Isaac to look for you last year, but with Isaac moving to New York and me taking over the running of the center, I couldn't do it until a few months ago."

"Did you know who I was when we met at the bar?"

"No. I was there to meet Fred, but he cancelled on me. Vítor, you have to believe me, I didn't know who you were that night. God, I didn't even have your name."

He still hadn't made any eye contact, but he hadn't moved, either, so I saw it as an opportunity to tell him what had happened.

"Afterwards, Fred wasn't around and I needed something to focus on, so I went to see David. That's when he told me what had happened to you. I was trying to build a picture of who you were. That same night was when I came to the apartment and you were here.

"At the time, you were only the guy I'd had a great evening with at the bar and who kissed like a god."

He let out a laugh but still didn't look up.

"Then you were there for me and you listened without judgment. We hadn't known each other long, and you were already taking small pieces of my heart and restoring them for me. David gave me some old photos he believed had you in them. I didn't make the connection until I saw the drawing on your wall."

I pulled my wallet from my pocket and took the small photo out. Vítor looked pained as he took the photo and let his fingers stroke the faces of the younger version of himself and then Paula.

"I didn't know how to handle it. I should have said something right then."

"Why didn't you?"

"Because I was a coward who had needed you too much. I was self-ish. I took all the comfort you were giving me, and I was afraid that if I told you the truth, you'd never want anything to do with me. I was afraid you didn't want to be found."

"You lied. You asked me about the photo after you already knew who I was and heard me talk about everything I went through." His voice was so quiet and broken.

"I'm so sorry."

Vítor got up and picked up the bag.

"Please, don't go." My eyes were burning from all the tears.

"I could have handled anything, Tiago. Anything, except the lies."

"I was going to tell you everything. Please believe me. I was just wai—" He held his hand up to stop me.

"That's the problem. People only admit to lying when they're found out, and sometimes, it's just too late to do anything about it."

"Vítor."

He stared out of the window and spoke so quietly I wasn't sure if it was for me, him, or someone else.

"It was my life, too. I had the right to know and then you fucking died, leaving behind the lies and the hurt. How could you think we would never find out? How could you, Rodrigo?"

His shiny blue eyes that were once full of life, desire, and love were now only puddles of grief.

Before he walked out of my life for good, I went into the guest bedroom. It didn't take me long to find what I was looking for.

I couldn't go after him because his words had sealed our fate, but I could give him something else. Taking his hand, I placed on his palm the small bunch of dried flowers he'd left behind on the night we'd met.

He let out a small gasp and held my gaze for a moment before he closed his eyes and shook his head.

"I'm sorry, I can't do this. I can't do it a second time."

As I walked up the stairs to the second floor of the center, I was relieved that none of the activities of the fundraiser extended to this floor. Apart from a tour of the facilities we'd done earlier for a few select donors who wanted to see what their support had paid for, the floor wasn't being used.

I opened the door to the nearest room and went straight to the enclosed bathroom to empty the contents of my stomach down the toilet. Not that there was much to bring up since I hadn't been able to eat anything since Vítor walked out of the apartment and my life less than twenty-four hours ago.

If I'd had a choice, I'd be hiding in my bedroom and drowning my sorrows in some form of alcohol, except I'd never been a big drinker and I had responsibilities I couldn't hide from. Instead, I did now what I'd done when my brother had gone missing.

I'd buried my emotions deep down inside and carried on with what needed to be done.

I'd arrived at the center earlier than I needed to, and I'd been on automatic pilot since.

Making sure everything was ready for the fundraiser, check.

Greeting volunteers and helpers, check.

Greeting guests and doing tours of the center, check.

Unveiling the new wall art with the kids, check.

Smiling for photographs, check.

Talking to the press, check.

Finally, being able to escape and give myself some time to give in to the pain was my own reward for keeping it together so well all night. I only needed a few minutes alone and then I'd be able to get back downstairs for the rest of the evening.

I wanted to cry at the unfairness of it all. Vítor and I had met by chance at the bar, and his lease of the apartment was another coincidence like the universe was trying hard to bring us together.

I wanted to lash out at David for asking me to look for Vítor, and I wanted to lash out at Mário for not standing up to their father earlier, but most of all, I wanted to lash out at myself for keeping it all a secret.

If I'd told Vítor the truth when I'd realized who he was, the choice to see his family would have been his. We may even have had a chance of staying together, and if we hadn't, at least it would have happened before I'd gone and fallen for him.

The door to the room opened. David had put on his professional mask, but I knew him well enough to tell he was struggling with what had happened.

He sat next to me on the single bed and put his hand on my shoulder.

"How are you holding up?"

I shook my head because I was afraid of what I might say if I tried to form words to explain how I was feeling.

"Is he gone for good?"

"Yes."

David put his arms around me and pulled me into a hug.

"I was stupid and selfish," I said.

"No, you weren't. He's so easy to be around, isn't he?"

I nodded into his chest. That was exactly it; Vítor had such a calming presence. He'd made it so easy to forget everything else when it was just us.

"I think you should go after him."

"He doesn't want anything to do with me. He said as much."

"He may be hurt, but he cares for you. I've seen you together over the last two months."

I was going to interrupt, but David put his hand over my mouth.

"If you're going to say what I think you are, then you can shut it. You were as good for him as he was for you. Let's take that show downstairs home so you can have a good night's sleep before you go get your man tomorrow."

Tomorrow ended up being the weekend because the fundraiser had been such a success that in the last two days, I'd only managed to go home to shower and put my head down for a few hours.

The truth was, the longer I put off going to Porto, the less likely it would be that I'd do it, and I knew it. Afonso called me on it and I tried to use him as an excuse, but he called me on that, too.

My little brother, who wasn't so little anymore, told me I didn't have to worry about him because he was going to spend the weekend hanging out with Bruno. They'd become friends after meeting at the center, and Afonso often took the train to Caparica on his own to see Bruno. If that wasn't proof that he was doing well, I wasn't sure what would be, and I was so damned proud of him.

My hands felt cold and clammy the whole drive to Porto. I'd left early enough so I could see Vítor and still be able to drive back the same day if I had to.

Managing my expectations was my only way to somehow protect myself from what could happen. I had to be prepared to knock on a door that would remain closed.

My first stop was at the cemetery. There was a fresh bunch of daisies on Rodrigo's grave, so I placed the bunch I'd brought with me next to it and sat on the grass.

Unlike the last time I was here, I didn't talk. I didn't know what to say to Rodrigo. I'd promised him that I'd tell Vítor the truth, but I'd failed to do that, so the only thing I could do was apologize. I also asked him to keep an eye on Vítor. That had been another broken promise from my part.

It took me a good thirty minutes to build myself up for ringing the bell at Vítor's house. When there was no answer, I went back to my parked car and waited. I had a clear view of the gate so I'd see when Vítor arrived.

An hour later, a car approached the gate. Vítor came out of the passenger side and went around to the driver. He said something and then the driver came out of the car. The guy was a statue, tall and built; if he were made of marble, he'd be in a museum.

My heart dropped when they embraced and then the big guy put his hands on Vítor's face and placed a small kiss on his lips. They exchanged a few more words and then the guy got in his car and drove off, leaving Vítor to go through the smaller gate into the property.

The kiss hadn't been a lover's kiss, which made it worse because now I knew there was someone in Vítor's life that could give him the comfort he hadn't been able to get from me in that moment when he was face-to-face with his brother for the first time in years.

The guy looked to be closer in age to Vítor, and from a few photos Vítor had shared of Rodrigo, this guy was a similar build. Maybe this was the person Vítor needed to be with. Someone he was close to who would never hurt him in the same way I did.

I was numb as I made my drive back to Lisbon, and my only good thoughts were that Vítor wasn't alone and I had my brother with me now.

By walking away now, I'd be keeping my promise to Rodrigo that Vítor wouldn't be alone.

I'd just have to keep reminding myself that all I'd ever wanted was my brother back. Nothing else.

As tears ran from my eyes, I knew this was just another lie, except this time, I was lying to myself.

23

TIAGO

I loved Mateus and Luís, but if they turned up at the house one more time with the excuse that they wanted a recipe, use the pool, pick up some books, or any such random reasons, I was going to murder them.

Mateus had found me asleep on the sofa three days after I'd been back. He'd thought I'd been drinking and had passed out. I couldn't really blame him for thinking that because I'd still been in the same clothes I'd arrived in and the coffee table was full of cups, plates full of toast crumbs, and a few beer and wine bottles.

He'd made me get up and have a shower, then he'd cooked me a proper meal and made me tell him what had happened.

As a child, Mateus had asked why he didn't have any grandparents like the other kids at school. We hadn't kept it a secret that Dri's parents had died before he was born, and I didn't have a relationship with mine.

When he was questioning his bisexuality as a teenager, we always talked openly about the challenges of being LGBT, but also expressed that we would always support him no matter what. At the time, I didn't tell him what had happened to me because I thought he was too young to hear it, and I didn't want him to think bad things happened to all LGBT people.

He was an adult now, so I had told him everything, and then I'd told him about Tiago. He hadn't asked any questions or tried to convince me I was wrong or too hasty leaving Lisbon. There was no need because I was already doing that to myself.

Two days later, Luís had asked if he could come over for dinner, which was unusual because no one could ever get him out of his studio on a school night. I realized very shortly that Mateus had spoken to him when he hadn't even questioned my strong feelings for Tiago.

"Vítor, you were always very easy to love and loved very easily," he'd said, "that's why we became friends even after Rodrigo stole you from me that night."

"And look what that got me. A dead husband and a whole load of heartache."

"That's because you're focusing on the hurt of the past instead of fighting for the future."

"Aren't you full of wisdom tonight," I'd said.

Despite the jokes, what Luís had said stuck with me, but two weeks later, I was still working from home and considering what to do. Bernardo had been extremely supportive when I'd told him I had a family emergency and needed to be in Porto, but I did have meetings I needed to attend, so I'd gone as far as packing my bags and dropping them by the door.

The apartment in Lisbon was still technically mine, although I didn't know if Tiago had gone back to his old place. Part of me wished he was still there and part of me wished he wasn't. I'd come to the realization that I was irrevocably in love with Tiago, which made it all the harder because as hurt as I was with what he'd done, my heart was starting to understand the reasons behind it. I would have to come to a decision about the future soon.

The postman had already been by, so I was surprised when the bell rang since Mateus had a key and Luís was out of town this weekend. When I looked at the screen that was connected to the small camera by the gate, I was surprised to see David's face. I pressed the remote control to open the gate and then opened the front door.

David came barreling in, walking past me toward the living room. I didn't have a chance to speak before he went off.

"I know what happened to you was terrible and shouldn't have happened, but you don't know the other side of the story. You don't know how much my uncle hurt when you ran away. You don't know what it did to him, to our family. Not to mention Tiago. Do you know when he was last in a relationship? Never. You know why? No, I guess you don't know that, either. Do you think he gives his heart up for just anyone?"

He let out an angry cry and sat on the sofa with his head in his hands, then he was quiet until I heard his quiet sobs.

"David," I said, sitting on the other side of the sofa.

He wiped the tears from his face. "I'm sorry, I shouldn't have done that. It was unfair, and I just…"

"Why are you here?"

"Because they're all hurting, and I don't know how to help them. It's like they went back to how it was before, except it's worse."

I took a deep breath. It was time for me to start acting like the older adult I was. If I ended up being the one that got hurt, so be it. I still had my son and my best friend.

"David, let's start from the beginning."

I repeated the same story I'd shared with Tiago and Mateus, and I had to admit that the more I told it, the easier it was to remember that it was all in the past. Had my injuries not required hospital treatment, I would have had to endure years of abuse from my father, I wouldn't have met Julia and Dri, and I wouldn't have my son. As I retold the story to David, it was the first time in my life that I saw the positives that came from such an ugly event.

"No," David said, "Uncle Mário went to see you in hospital, but you were gone. He searched for you everywhere he could think, but he never found you. They cut ties with your father after that. I think he died not long after, and your mom a couple of years later. I don't remember her."

I was in shock. My brother had done the right thing after all. Even though I wasn't around, he'd still stuck up for me against our father.

"Where's your cousin?"

"I don't have any cousins."

"Teresa was pregnant when it all happened. I was going to be an uncle."

David stared at me; his eyes red from crying. I remembered Mário saying he was Paula's son, and I could see it because he looked so much like her.

"They lost the baby. Aunt Teresa had a miscarriage."

"No." I shook my head. "No, that couldn't have happened to them. They were so happy about becoming parents."

"They were never able to get pregnant again. I guess that's why they kept me."

"What do you mean?"

"Mom died when I was fifteen. She had cancer. Aunt Teresa and Uncle Mário looked after me until I was old enough to live on my own."

I got up and ran to the bathroom, making it just in time to throw up what I'd had for lunch earlier.

When I ran away from the hospital all those years ago, I knew I'd never get a chance to see my family and friends again. I'd spent years thinking my brother had taken our father's side, but I'd always regretted not getting in touch with Paula. She would have kept one more secret for me, even if that secret was that she knew where I was. She would have told me about my brother.

Whenever Dri had asked me if I regretted not going back to see my family or Paula, I'd always said no, and now it was all I had, regret.

I washed my face and brushed my teeth before going back out to the living room.

David stood by the open glass panels. It was a warm day, and with the small breeze, the scent of the flowers came into the house.

I walked up to him and gave him a heartfelt hug. "I'm so sorry, David. I loved her so much. She was my best friend. I'm so sorry."

He tensed up but then gave in and hugged me back.

"It must have been hard on your dad, raising a teenage boy by himself. Is that why you're so close to Teresa and Mário?"

"I don't have a dad. My mom raised me on her own."

"What do you mean?"

"I don't know who my dad is. No one knows. Mom never talked about him." He looked at me and his cheeks went a little pink. "Er, that was one of the reasons I wanted to find you. It wasn't just because of Uncle Mário."

I wasn't sure what he meant, so I nodded for him to carry on.

"Uncle Mário and I didn't have a great relationship for a long time. He suspected I was gay when I was thirteen, and I didn't know this at the time, but he was afraid that I'd run away like you did. It wasn't until last year when Joel was back that I came out to them. That's when they mentioned you. I didn't even know you existed. They said you were Mom's best friend, especially after Joel's mom and dad left for America. I thought… I thought you'd know if she had a boyfriend."

"I'm sorry, David, I don't know. She didn't have a boyfriend before I left."

Looking into his brown eyes that were so much like his mom's, it suddenly dawned on me.

"David, how old are you?"

"I'm going to be twenty-eight at the end of the summer."

I stared at him, unable to talk, and then I laughed. I laughed so hard I started to cry and then I pulled him into my arms.

"I have a son. I have a son."

He looked confused. "I know. Tiago said you have a son called Mateus, right?"

"Yes, Mateus is my son, but he isn't my biological son. But, David, you are."

"What?"

"We can do a DNA test to verify, but I know it, David. You're my son."

"How do you know?" His voice broke, and I could hear the hope and the fear in it.

"Paula and I were together once. It was only a month before every-thing happened. She wouldn't have known she was pregnant then. She was too dedicated to her work and her baking to date; she'd never even been with anyone before."

"But you're gay."

"Yeah, well, it was complicated back then. I was confused, inexperienced, and on that one night, I was also drunk. We both were. Also, David is my middle name."

"She named me after you."

We stood there staring at each other with the sounds of the birds in the background. It was so clear now, yes David had a lot of Paula's features in him, but he also looked so much like me. How had they all missed the similarity? He must have looked so much like me when he was a child.

More regret washed over me. I'd missed so much from David's life: his first steps, first words, first day of school, the first time he'd baked something with his mom.

"David, I want you to know that whatever my father did to me, if I'd known Paula was pregnant, I wouldn't have run. I thought I was protecting everyone that cared about me from my father."

"I believe that. The actions and beliefs of one man shaped the lives of so many people around him, people it was his job to love and protect." He paused before shaking his head and saying, "Oh my god, I have a father."

My chest expanded, and I couldn't stop more tears from falling. "Yes, you do. Nothing would make me happier than to get to know you. I hope soon you can meet Mateus, too."

"Holy shit, I have a brother." He was beaming. "I always wanted a brother."

We hugged again.

"Er, Vítor." We both smiled and then he pointed at the bags by the door. "Are you going somewhere?"

"I have to go back to Lisbon because of work."

"Does that mean you'll go back to Tiago?" He looked hopeful.

I wasn't sure what to say. Despite everything I'd just found out—we'd just found out—I knew David still very much had Tiago's back, and the truth was, I didn't know how to handle any of this.

"Don't stay stuck in the past," David said. "The only past we should remember is the good one. When Mom died, I was so angry because I was left on my own. Yes, I still had family, but I didn't have a dad and Joel was in America. He didn't come back for a long time. I held on to that hurt and hid myself away. We can all live with regret, but I think it would be better if we lived with hope."

I laughed because it was like I was listening to Paula all over again: "*Vítor, you are who you are. What if you get to be ninety years old and you look back and all you can show for it is a life that wasn't yours?*"

"You sound just like your mother," I said.

He rubbed the back of his neck. "I've been told that before."

"Do you think Tiago will forgive me?"

"I'd say he's asking himself the same question. Did you know he came here?"

"What? When?"

"Just after you left Lisbon. He came to speak to you, but when he got here, he said he saw you with another man."

"That would have been Luís. He's my best friend; we've known each other for years. There's absolutely nothing between us."

"Then Tiago needs to know that because he's mopey as shit and my cakes come out all wrong when he's in the center."

I laughed. I didn't believe in a world where David's cakes came out wrong. I'd had some of them, and my boy was talented.

"David, do you have a way to get me in the center while Tiago isn't there?"

"Yes, I have keys."

"How did you get here?"

"By train. It was quicker and I was too angry at you to drive."

"Well then, let's go get my man. I'm going to take the advice of my wise-beyond-his-years son and live for the hope."

He smiled and took one of the bags while I closed up the glass panels and made sure the house was secure before we left.

"I'm going to ask Joel to marry me this summer."

The way he said it, I knew it was the first time he'd said the words aloud. My heart grew in size at the realization that my son, one of them, had just had a first with me. And what a first it was.

"I'd like you to be there."

"I wouldn't miss it for the world."

As I drove us back to Lisbon, we spent the next three hours getting to know each other better and planning how I was going to win my family and the second love of my life back. The small bunch of dried flowers was in my jacket pocket.

Sebastião was right, the Gypsy woman was right, and now it was my turn to do what was right.

24

TIAGO

"Why don't you take some time off and come to New York? I'd love to show you around."

"I can't," I said for the hundredth time, but Isaac wasn't letting up. "Since the fundraiser, things have been crazy around here. There's an art gallery interested in showcasing art made by the kids. I agreed to meet the gallery manager this week. So I can't just pack my bags and go."

"Maybe we can fly out there and you can take some time off? We could do a road trip and show Max the north of Portugal. How about the waterfalls in Gerês? And I'd love to meet Afonso."

My heart skipped a beat and I coughed involuntarily to get it to go back to its regular beat.

"Er, sure, if you're up for it."

"Okay, I'll speak to Max, and I'll let you know."

There was a silence, and I wondered if Isaac was trying to find yet another reason for me to take time off work. Before he did that, I decided to talk about the reason I'd called him.

"Isaac, you know how you've been pestering me to take over the center properly?"

"Yes?"

"I'm ready for it now. Afonso is here and he's safe, so I feel like I can give the center my all."

"Tiago."

"I have some ideas for improvements, and I even have a few people in mind to help me around here."

"Tiago."

"Of course, I'd love you to still be involved, even if we only discuss ideas and work more on the student exchange stuff together. Just because you're there doesn't mean you have to let go completely. This is your baby as much as mine."

"TIAGO!" He shouted so loud I jumped in my chair.

"What?"

"For goodness' sake, man, take a breather and listen for a second."

"Okay…"

I heard his sigh as though he was right next to me.

"I know what you're doing. Do you think that by being busier at work you'll suddenly forget Vítor or stop having feelings for him?"

"No, that's not—"

"Tiago, how did that pan out for me?"

It hadn't. I'd been there for Isaac after he came back from New York talking about this guy he'd met there, Max. And then again when something went down between them in the summer. Isaac had buried himself in work, and we'd spent most of the summer doing various jobs around the center and coming up with initiatives to raise the profile of the center and boost the money we needed to support the LGBTQ kids that came to us. It hadn't been until Max had returned to Lisbon a second time that they'd gotten together.

"What would you want me to do? Unlike your story, mine isn't going to have a happy ending."

"Even so, get out there and enjoy yourself. You've already lost so much of yourself in the search for your brother, if I asked you what your favorite color was, you wouldn't know what to answer."

"It's blue."

"Tiago"—he sighed—"just… look after yourself for once, okay?"

"I miss you here."

"I miss the center, too."

"Say hi to Max and Lucy for me."

"Will do. Speak soon."

I put the phone down and fell back on the bed. Staring at the ceiling, I considered Isaac's words. He was right. I knew I'd lost myself along the way in the search for my brother. When Vítor had come along, I'd leaned on him because it was easy and he was so good at looking after me.

This was the time to think about who I wanted to be.

I already had the best job in the world, check.

My brother was safe and with me, check.

I tried to come up with more but kept falling short. I really didn't have anything else going on in my life. How did someone get to be nearly thirty and not have a hobby or an interest?

I was pulled out of my thoughts by a knock on the door. It would only be Afonso, so I told him to come in.

"Hey, are you okay?" he asked.

"I love you, Flea, but you need to stop asking me that every five minutes. What's up?"

He came over to the bed and lay down next to me.

"I wanted to ask you something."

"Okay."

"Well, it was more your opinion. Dr. Vasco said I need to work on asking for an opinion rather than permission because I have a choice even if you don't agree with it."

I turned sideways to face him and leaned my head on my elbow. He turned to face me.

"That's right. What do you want my opinion for?"

"Do you remember when we talked about what I wanted to do and I didn't know? I think I do, at least for now."

"That's great. You know I'll support you with whatever you want to do."

"Pedro asked if I wanted to work at his beach snack bar. I wasn't sure at first, but I've thought about it."

"What weren't you sure about?"

"I was afraid of all the people. I still get anxious when there are lots of people around."

He was doing much better now, but I could understand his reluctance to work in a place full of people all the time.

"And now?"

"Pedro will be there with me. He said if I struggle, to let him know and I can always go over to Bruno's apartment and hide away until the anxiety goes."

"Sounds good."

"I know it's not a job that will bring in lots of money, but I don't think I'm ready to go back to school just yet."

That had been something else we'd talked about. Afonso had missed all of his schooling from the age of thirteen. He'd had access to books and enjoyed reading, but we still needed to assess how far behind he was and how he could catch up.

"It sounds like an excellent idea to me. I hope I get a friends and family discount." I winked and pulled him in for a hug, ruffling his hair.

This was good. Talking to my brother and finding our new normal was good.

"What if I take tomorrow off and we go over to Estoril to watch the surfers?"

His face went beet red, and he lay back on the bed.

"Fred is taking me to the beach to teach me how to surf tomorrow."

I knew Afonso worshiped the ground Fred walked on, so I wasn't surprised I'd get ditched so easily.

"Can I come watch?"

"No," he said quickly. "Er, what I mean is that it's going to be embarrassing, and I'll probably fall a lot. You should go to work."

"Okay," I said, ruffling his hair again and then laughed when he groaned. It would take me a while to remember he was twenty-one now. My grown-up little brother.

Since Fred had picked Afonso up from the apartment at the crack of dawn for their surf lesson, I decided to get up and go to work. Maybe

I could finish early today and see if Fred and Afonso were up for a movie and dinner.

When I arrived at the center, I was surprised to see the fairy lights in the garden were on. I didn't remember leaving them on, so I hoped it had been one of the resident kids that had forgotten to turn them off last night rather than them being on all weekend. I made a mental note to remind the kids of the fire hazard of leaving the lights on, not to mention the electric bill.

I filled the water container in the coffee machine, added the ground coffee, and turned it on. I knew I'd easily go through the whole pot before lunchtime.

I turned the lights off at the main switch, but they turned back on again. *What the hell?*

When I turned them off again, they turned back on.

"Fuck me if I have to add finding an electrician to today's list," I muttered to myself.

As I stepped out into the garden, a lot more lights came on. It was early summer. The sun was already rising at this time, so the lights didn't have the same effect that they did at night, but it was still stunning. There were also a lot more lights than usual.

I looked around and didn't see anyone until my eyes zeroed in on the wall next to the sofa.

Someone had painted what looked like the plans for a house. The whole thing was black and white, but it was done with such detail I could already imagine what the house would look like if it was actually built.

The house was shaped like an L. At the bottom of the plan, which was the front of the house, there were four bedrooms, and at the back of the house there was a big lounge that was as wide as the whole house. On the other side, I could see there was a kitchen. People living in the house would always see each other whether they were in the kitchen, lounge, or office area, and everything led to the landscaped garden at the back. The front of the house looked plain; there was no garden or much outdoor space. The front didn't matter because no one would spend time...

"Do you like it?"

I spun around so quickly that I lost my footing and nearly fell on my ass. I didn't only because Vítor took a step forward and put his arms around me to stop me from falling.

When I regained my balance, Vítor released me but only took a half step back.

"What… what are you doing here?" I asked.

"I owe you an apology, an explanation, and I have a proposal."

I was confused. He was standing too close for my brain to register what he was saying.

"You don't owe me anything. I'm the one that owes you an apology. I'm so sor—"

He put a finger on my lips to shut me up. It worked, but it also had the annoying side effect of making my dick hard. Why was the man so irresistible? I could only hope he would say whatever he had to say fast so he could leave.

"I know why you did what you did. I get it, and I don't hold it against you."

I narrowed my eyes in confusion.

"Will you let me speak without interrupting or apologizing?" he asked.

He still hadn't removed his finger from my lips, so I nodded.

"Since I moved to Lisbon, I've been wondering about my family. I never expected to see my brother again, but then again, I never expected to be back in Lisbon, either, so seeing him was a shock. I won't deny that.

"There is something I haven't told you that explains my reaction. It's no excuse, because I should have listened to you."

Vítor put both his hands on my face and ran his thumbs up and down my cheeks. I wanted to lean into his touch so badly, but I was too afraid.

"When I met Dri, he told me he had a son. He introduced me to Mateus when we'd been together a couple of months and he knew we were serious about each other. It was love at first babble for me because Mateus was the most adorable child I'd ever seen. That was the day I became a dad.

"When Dri died, Mateus helped me sort out the paperwork in the office. It was something we did together to be closer to each other and Dri. Mateus came across a birth certificate. His birth certificate. There was a name for the mother, but no name for the father.

"We were both in shock because we didn't know what it all meant. We went to the registry office, and after going through all the hoops, we found out that the name on the birth certificate was of Dri's sister. I didn't know much about her, only that she'd committed suicide. She suffered from depression. I only knew this because Dri told me once when he got drunk after Mateus' fifth birthday. He never mentioned it again, so I figured it was a painful memory he wanted to forget.

"Mateus didn't believe me when I said I'd had no idea. I still don't know why Dri didn't tell me he was raising his nephew as his son. You see, Dri was bisexual, something he told me when we met. He'd been with women before, so I'd assumed Mateus was the fruit of a previous relationship."

"I understand that's why you couldn't forgive me for keeping from you that I knew who you were. I lied, too."

"Tiago, why did you go to Porto?"

I gasped. How did he know I'd been to Porto?

25

VÍTOR

"I didn't know you'd been to Porto at first, if that's what you're wondering. I thought it was strange that Dri had two bouquets of daisies, but I thought Mateus had stopped by and left them."

"How do you know then?"

"My son told me."

"Mateus?"

"David."

Tiago's eyebrows shot up in confusion.

"David came to see me in Porto, and we had a long conversation. That's when I realized he was my son. Trust me, it took me by surprise as much as it did him. But we can get to that later. I want to know why you went to Porto."

He looked down, almost defeated, so I angled his head up so his eyes met mine, and I kept my hands where they were.

"I went to fight for us and for your family. I realized there were a lot of things about them you didn't know, so while I did lie to you, I didn't want you to live the rest of your life without knowing how they felt."

"And us?"

He tried to look away again, but he was unable to, so he closed his eyes instead. A small tear escaped his eyes.

I placed my lips on his gently, and he let out a cry but thankfully didn't try to stop me. I deepened the kiss when his hands came around my waist and gripped my shirt. He tasted like warmth and sunshine, and it was just what I wanted to wake up to every day for the rest of my life, so I reluctantly stopped the kiss so I could tell him.

His cheeks were flushed and the fear he had in his eyes was now replaced with lust. Good.

"Baby, I am tired of living in the past. There are many wonderful things in the past I want to remember, cherish even, but I don't want to dwell on the sad times or the missed opportunities."

I took the small bouquet of dried flowers from my jacket pocket and placed it back in Tiago's hands. He looked at me inquisitively.

"This bouquet was given to me by an old Gypsy woman. When she stopped me on the street, I thought she wanted some money, but all she did was give me these dried flowers and an insight into my future, which at the time I chose to ignore. She told me that I can have more than one great love in my lifetime. Later that day, I met you. I don't know if there is more significance to the bouquet or if we were always meant to meet, but I don't care. I love you, and all I want is to spend the rest of my life loving you and letting you love me, if you feel the same way."

"But the kiss… I saw you with a guy. You two looked so comfortable with each other like you belonged together."

"Luís has seen me drunk more times than I care to remember, he babysat Mateus whenever we needed some time off, he's been there through my grief more than any of my friends, and even when I was determined that what me and you had wasn't that strong, he still told me I needed to see you. He's my best friend and a brother. What you saw was a comforting kiss. We've done it so many times I don't even think anything of it, but I can stop it and ask him to not do it anymore."

"No, don't do that." Tiago's hands rested on my chest, and he got on his tiptoes to match my height.

"He can kiss you like this." He placed a small kiss on my lips. "But he can't kiss you like this because I love you, and you're mine."

His arms came around my neck and the rest of the world disappeared when his lips touched mine again. This time, he had a different intention. I opened my mouth to let his tongue in so I could taste him again. Our tongues dueled for dominance, danced together, and spoke louder than any words we could have exchanged.

"Okay, okay, that's enough tongue. One of you is going to get pregnant at this rate if you don't stop."

I stopped the kiss reluctantly to face David who was standing by the door holding a box.

"How long have you been standing there?" I asked.

"Oh, you know, a minute or ten. Enough to need to bleach my ears when I get home or ask Joel to replace the mental image with a better one." He winked.

Tiago buried his face on my chest, and I could see the reddened tips of his ears. David ignored my subtle sign to leave us and came even closer.

He put his arms around both of us and said, "This is great, my dad and one of my best friends. Can I be a page boy at your wedding?"

"Aren't you a little old to be a page boy?"

"Fine, I'll make the cake then. I guess Luís beat me for the best man spot already," he said.

"I could have three best men."

"Wait a second." Tiago put his hands up, his eyes flicking between David and I. "What are you talking about?"

"Our wedding, baby. I'm not asking you yet, but I will, and I hope when the time comes, you'll say yes." I placed a kiss on his nose and felt him melt even further into me.

"Right, that's my cue to go. This box is full of pastries. You might need the energy. Now go home to get the sex out of the way so you can meet the family at dinner later, and I'll keep an eye on the center," David said and then turned to me. "See you both later." And then he gave me a hug.

When David left, I noticed Tiago staring at me.

"What?"

"You are an amazing person; did you know that?"

"I know. I have good taste in men, too," I said, kissing him and then lowering my voice in his ear. "Shall we go home and do the sex?"

He nodded fiercely, his lips trapped between his teeth. This man was going to be the death of me, and what a death it would be.

"Wait," he said, "what's that on the wall? Did you make it?"

"That, baby, is the house I designed for us. Do you like it?"

"I love it. And I love you, Vítor."

"Love you, too, baby. Now let's get home."

The short drive home wasn't dissimilar to the time when we'd traveled back from Porto. Tiago had spent the whole time teasing me over my clothes, and after nearly a month away from him, I was just about to combust or come in my pants.

"Baby, you're forgetting I'm not thirty anymore."

He giggled from the passenger seat.

"I'm counting on you coming very shortly after we get home so I can spend the rest of the day working you up."

"I'm so fucked with you, aren't I?"

I looked at him briefly and saw his grin. This was the real Tiago; the funny, sexy, wonderful man I'd fallen in love with. There would be no more tears in his life, not unless they were happy ones.

As soon as he'd unlocked the door, he pulled me into the bedroom, placed the dried flowers on the chest of drawers, and took us into the bathroom.

He pushed me against the sink and placed my hands behind me. His eyes told me to keep them there, so I did. His gaze burned my skin as he undid the buttons of my shirt one by one, placing kisses and little bites as he moved south.

"Shall I undo your pants, too, or shall I touch you like this until you come?" His hand roamed the front of my pants, gripping my cock and rubbing up and down my length. I groaned in frustration.

"Can we get naked, please?"

"Since you ask nicely..." Instead of reaching out for my pants, Tiago took a step back and started undressing himself. Shirt first, then jeans, socks, and underwear. His cock stood hard and thick, pointing in my direction. I didn't realize I'd licked my lips while I was staring at him until I saw his eyes dark with lust looking back at me.

He tugged on his cock and said with a gravelly voice, "On your knees."

I did as he said, and he stepped forward. His cock was at the perfect height, so I took his head in my mouth, tasting his sweet flavor as I teased the slit with my tongue.

"Fuck, Vítor. That feels so good."

I wrapped one hand around his cock and placed the other on his back to urge him to fuck my mouth as I tried to take in as much as I could. The sounds he made were like a song to me, and I cursed that I still had my pants on. I could already feel my underwear wet where I was leaking just from being on my knees for my man.

He put a hand on my shoulder to stop. I let him go with a pop, and he came down on his knees to kiss me.

The tiles were cold on my heated skin as he pushed me back to lie on the floor and finally took pity on my trapped cock. Everything came off at once, my pants, underwear, and my sanity when Tiago put his mouth on my cock and deepthroated me until his nose touched the hairs at the base of my cock.

My orgasm came without any warning. I shouted Tiago's name as he swallowed every last drop of cum before he lay on top of me to kiss me, allowing me to taste myself in his hot mouth.

"Fuck me, that was hot," he said into my mouth.

"Mmm, it sure was." I placed kisses all along his neck, feeling goose bumps appear on his skin. He moaned and flexed his hips against mine. My cock needed a rest before I could take another orgasm, if I was lucky, but his hardness between us still felt amazing.

"I think the one of us that is still hard should get to fuck the one of us that isn't hard," he said, and fuck me if my cock didn't twitch at his words.

"The one of us that is now growing hard wants that very much, but if we're not making it into the shower, can we take this to the bed?"

His laugh was like a balm to my heart. He got up and took my hand in his, pulling me back to the bedroom.

"We can have a shower later. Let's get dirty first," he said.

I laid down on the bed and pulled him on top of me. Tiago rested his head on my chest and took a deep sigh.

"Is everything okay?" I asked.

"Is this really happening? I mean, have you thought it through? Moving to Lisbon permanently, and how about Mateus?"

"Hey, where is this coming from?" I stroked his hair gently, feeling his chest rise with each breath.

"I don't know. I think I'm just afraid to believe I'm getting you as well. It feels like too much luck for one person, and I'm scared something will go wrong."

"Baby, you had me that night at the bar. I just didn't know it then. When I went back to Porto, I was shattered. I confessed everything to Dri at the cemetery like I was confessing to having committed a felony. It wasn't because I'd kissed another man. I confessed because of what that kiss meant to me."

He lifted his head to look at me.

"Vítor, I want to make love to you."

I smiled and nodded.

When I finally felt him inside, it was as though we were getting to know each other for the very first time. This was the Tiago I should have seen all along. Not that he'd been faking his feelings before. I knew he hadn't, but now he'd freed himself from the self-imposed chains around his heart, and he was finally allowing me to go in and make myself at home.

His cock felt amazing inside me, and every time he withdrew, I pulled him back in because the thought of not having him there was too hard to bear. He managed to draw another orgasm out of me with his slow, steady movements followed by rapid thrusts. I shouted his name for the second time in less than an hour, except this time, I heard him shout mine back as I felt his hot release deep inside me.

We lay in the same position with him on top of me for what felt like hours. His warm skin against mine was bliss.

His words brought me back to reality.

"Are you nervous about seeing Mário again?"

"Yes," I confessed, "but I'm also excited."

"Let's grab a shower, then. From what David said, we're in for a family dinner tonight."

"Sounds like perfection to me."

"I love you, Vítor."

"Love you, too, sweetheart."

Even though it had all been planned with David, I was still a bundle of nerves as we drove south to Caparica to meet my brother and sister-in-law.

A lot had changed in the area in the last twenty-eight years. More buildings, shops, better roads, but in a way, it didn't feel that different because the same old buildings were still there; the bakery my mom used to get the daily bread from, the pharmacy where we went to get our vaccinations, and the small supermarket that always had a large display of fruit outside the bead curtain-covered door.

Tiago touched my hand. I saw his worried expression and smiled to reassure him. I hadn't even noticed we were parked.

"I'm okay, just reminiscing."

I realized once we got out of the car that I had no idea where we needed to go, so I linked my hand with Tiago's and let him take the lead toward David's Café Lima.

David had told me all about the business Paula had started up and how he'd carried on working there with Teresa and Mário. I was so proud of him and what he'd achieved. I couldn't wait to see it.

As we walked down the street, Tiago pointed out where David and Joel lived, as well as Bruno and Filipe, in the apartment opposite theirs.

My pulse raced as we walked into the café, and I came face-to-face with my brother for the second time in twenty-eight years.

"Mário," was all I had a chance to say before my brother pulled me into his arms in a tight grip. My throat was tight with emotion, and I didn't fight the tears when they came. Neither did my brother.

"I never thought I'd see you again," he said.

I pulled away to take a good look at him. He was older, his skin gathered in the corners of his eyes, and his hair, like mine, was more gray than black, but he had the same expression I remembered. Had we bumped into each other anywhere in the last twenty-eight years, there was no doubt I'd have recognized him.

"Vítor, my dear." I heard the voice of my sister-in-law as she approached us from a door on the other side of the café.

I hugged her tight, smelling her flowery perfume, the same she'd worn all those years ago.

"Oh my beautiful Teresa. You haven't aged a day. I thought you'd have upgraded him for a younger model by now," I joked, winking at my brother.

"Nah, I'm too old to train another one. You look really good, too."

She pulled back and told us the rest of the family would arrive shortly, but we had time to go for a walk.

I took it as my prompt for some alone time with my brother. Tiago offered to help out setting the table so Mário and I walked out of the café in the direction of the beach.

"Where do we start? It's been so long," he said, and I smiled because I felt exactly the same way.

"I don't want to focus on the past anymore, but I know we still need to put it to rest."

He agreed, so we each told our version of the events of my twenty-first birthday and subsequent days.

By the time we finished, we were at the beach. We stopped before we got to the sand.

"Do you remember when we all used to come here at the weekend?" Mário asked.

"Oh yeah. Do you remember Paula's picnic meals?"

"Man, I lived for her marble cake," he said.

"What happened to her after I left?"

My heart broke as my brother recounted how Paula had built her business and had looked after our son with the help of her family, and then her fight with cancer, one she'd eventually lost, but not before she'd made sure David would be okay without her.

"I have a great debt to you and Teresa for raising David. He told me things haven't always been easy between you, but you were there for all his important moments, and that matters more than anything."

"It was a privilege seeing him follow his and his mother's dreams. I still can't believe he's your son. He told me your story. It made so much sense then. How Paula would never have a bad word to say about you, or her baby's father whenever. David also said you're an architect."

We walked back to the café, catching up with more recent events.

"So, you and Tiago, huh?"

"I don't know what he sees in me, but I love him, and if he'll have me, I will love him for the rest of my life."

When I was young, I'd always dreamed of being able to talk to my brother like this, and I had to pinch myself because I still wasn't sure this was real.

Everybody was seated at the long table in the café by the time we got back. The teasing grumbles about having to wait for dinner made my heart soar with happiness. I looked for Tiago and sat next to him, stealing a kiss that left him with the cutest blush.

26

TIAGO

"Can you see them?" Vítor asked.

"No, not yet."

"For goodness' sake, how long does it take to ask a question?" Vítor's frustration was so cute I had to turn around in his arms and kiss him. It also served as a good distraction. His excited tension disappeared as he melted against me.

"Thanks, Tiago," Mário said from his place under the gazebo, "I was just about to throw an orange at his head."

I gave Mário the thumbs up without needing to stop kissing Vítor, because if I had my way, I'd never stop kissing him.

Mário chuckled and Teresa told him off.

Considering how long the brothers had been apart and how much hurt had been caused by their father, I was surprised at how they'd settled back into their roles of younger and older brother.

In the last two months since Vítor had come back to me and they'd reunited, Vítor had spent a lot of time with his family. It took more than one family dinner to catch up on twenty-eight years, of course. Sometimes I'd join them, others I'd stay at home reconnecting with my own brother.

We'd also spent many nights wrapped around each other with Vítor asking me questions about David and telling me everything he'd learned from his brother.

Despite everything, Mário had been the closest thing to a father figure to David growing up, which was why on the day he was asking Joel to marry him on the beach they used to frequent as children, Mário was the one in charge.

Vítor's role as his real father was to walk him down the aisle on his wedding day, so he'd been happy to leave his brother to care for the son he raised as his own. Thinking about the day Vítor had told me that David had asked him the question still got to me. Vítor had been beyond happy and proud.

It was a hot afternoon and the cloudless sky was making it almost unbearable, but Mário had managed to source a gazebo to keep all the food for the celebration under the shade, and Joel's family had brought enough umbrellas.

Afonso was helping Mário, and I was so proud of him for playing his part in the celebration and also because he looked comfortable around such a large crowd of people. He'd been working in Pedro's snack bar all summer, and he loved it. Sometimes he came home exhausted, but he'd grown more confident. I'd seen some mail at home for online courses, but he hadn't mentioned anything, so I was waiting for him to come to me and let me know what was on his mind. I wasn't worried, because I knew he would.

"Hey!"

I jumped up from the beach towel where I was sitting against Vítor's chest and ran toward the voice. I hadn't seen Isaac in months, so I only stopped when we were hugging.

"I missed you, man."

"Missed you, too," I said.

I heard two sets of coughs, and we both chuckled as Max pulled Isaac into his chest and I was pulled back into Vítor's.

"Vítor, this is Isaac and his husband, Max. Max, this is my boyfriend, Vítor."

They shook hands and Isaac winked at me and mouthed *hot silver fox*.

I couldn't agree more.

"So, has he done it yet? We were afraid we were late because someone, cough, Max, was too sleepy after the flight."

"If you hadn't—"

Isaac put his hand on Max's mouth to stop him from ending his thought and then replaced it with his own mouth for a quick kiss.

"I see the honeymoon period isn't over yet," I teased.

"Never," they said at the same time.

I laughed and grabbed Vítor's hand and walked him toward the water.

"Come on, let's go in the water because David and Joel are going to take forever and I've got a hard-on for you."

"I'm not going to give you a hand job in the water in front of the family," he said.

I laughed. "It wasn't my intention. I only wanted to cool down, but now that you mentioned it..."

I squeaked when he picked me up, ran to the water, and dropped me in.

"Fuck, that's cold," I said, brushing water out of my eyes and running my hands through my wet hair. "Erection successfully extinct."

Vítor chuckled and pulled me closer, so I wrapped my legs around him. The weightlessness provided by the water gave me additional flexibility to grind against Vítor.

"Baby."

"What?" I said innocently.

"You know what."

I kissed him but didn't pursue my teasing any further; after all, I could have more fun with him and his giant cock later.

"Look, Fred is here, let's go say hi," he said. I reluctantly unwrapped my legs from his hips and followed him back to where our towels were.

Fred went straight over to Afonso. I saw them hug and then Afonso gave him a cold drink before he came over to us. Afonso's eyes never left Fred until someone else's drink request forced him to look away. I wasn't so concerned over my brother's crush on Fred, more that I was afraid it wasn't returned.

"Hey, Fred."

"Sweet cheeks."

He'd stopped calling me that since I'd got together with Vítor unless Vítor was around to hear it.

"If I didn't respect you so much, I'd have you in a headlock, Fred." Vítor growled behind me.

Fred winked at me. I knew exactly what he was up to. He wanted to rile Vítor up so he'd go all Animal Planet on me in bed later. What I wouldn't tell him was that Vítor didn't need riling up to go at me every chance he could grab.

"Hey, Dad." I heard Mateus calling as he came over to join us. Since I'd been officially introduced to Mateus, Vítor and I had spent a few weekends in Porto so I'd had the chance to get to know Mateus better. He was surprisingly receptive to our relationship, which I'd taken to be a very positive thing, considering they'd gone through a rough patch when they'd discovered Rodrigo wasn't Mateus' biological father but his uncle.

"Oh hey, son."

Mateus approached, and I didn't miss Fred's look of interest.

"Son, this is Fred. He's the detective I told you about that helped find Afonso. Fred, this is my son, Mateus."

They shook hands, and I saw something pass between them. I looked at Vítor discreetly and noticed he saw it, too.

From the gazebo, Afonso was staring in our direction, looking confused.

"Hey, Flea. Come over here," I called. "There's someone I want you to meet."

He walked up to us slowly, like he was afraid to approach. His eyes locked on Mateus, but then he looked at Fred and dropped his gaze like he was feeling guilty. Vítor tightened his arms around me, which told me he hadn't missed that, either.

"Afonso, this is Mateus, Vítor's son. Mateus, this is my brother, Afonso.

Mateus gave my brother a hug. Afonso froze in Mateus' arms for a moment before he returned the hug with a "pleased to meet you."

"Er, I have to go help Mário. See you around. Well, I guess when you come to get food. We have drinks, too. Whatever you want." Afonso ran to the gazebo without looking back once.

Fred excused himself, too, to go see Isaac and Max.

"So, where are the grooms to be?" Mateus asked.

"We haven't seen them yet," I said.

"This is such a cool idea. And Joel doesn't have any idea that his family is here?"

"Yup, he doesn't know Max is here, either. They grew up together in America."

"Great, I might go introduce myself to them, but I'm going to say hi to Teresa first. She'll never forgive me if I don't go straight to her."

Vítor turned me to face him and ran his hands through my wet hair.

"I don't know how this is my life now, but I'm not going to complain."

I saw Mateus engulfed in one of Teresa's mom hugs and smiled.

"It never ceases to amaze me how easily he makes friendships," Vítor said as I leaned on his chest, his still-cool skin against mine.

"He was raised well by his dads."

"Oh look, there they come."

David and Joel were beaming as they approached the party. The first ones to get to them were Filipe and Joel's little cousins who were only eight, ten, and eleven. After the rest of the family joined them with hugs and congratulations, the happy couple came over to where we were.

"Congratulations guys. I'm so happy for you," I said as I gave each a hug.

David looked at Joel as if for reassurance and then said, "Vítor, I er… I was wondering if I could call you dad."

Vítor's hand trembled in mine. He'd mentioned not long ago how much he hoped that David would one day be ready to call him dad instead of using his first name.

Emotion caught in my throat. I could only imagine how my man was feeling.

"Of course you can, son," Vítor said. "Nothing would make me happier."

"Does that mean that Tiago is your stepdad?" Joel joked.

"He's going to be our daddy," Mateus said, giving David a congratulatory pat on the back. "Come on, food is ready."

Mário already had the food ready to go and buckets of drinks on ice. Afonso looked busy and eager to do his job.

"I'm so happy for them. David has changed so much since Joel came back. He's so much happier now," I said.

Vítor kissed my forehead.

"What would you say if I asked you to marry me soon?"

I turned and gave him a soft kiss with a promise of more later.

"I would say yes," I said, "but I'm not going to be anyone's daddy unless we have our own child."

Vítor's laugh reached all the corners of my heart.

"How did I get so lucky?"

"A Gypsy, a bunch of dried flowers, and a chin dimple."

I hope you enjoyed reading the love story between Vítor and Tiago. This is book three in the Finding You series and I loved every second I spent writing this story. Giving Vítor his HEA and giving his family all the answers really made my heart sing.

You can check out the full series here (readerlinks.com/l/3147563)

Before you read the next age gap novel, would you like a bonus scene?

Tiago and Vítor are ready to move into the new house. How about a sexy sneak peek of what they get up to?

Click the link below to sign up to my newsletter and receive the scene in your inbox:

Sign up here (anawritesmm.com/sol-signup)
(if you signed up after How to Catch a Biker you don't need to do it again,
just check your inbox for you welcome email with the download link for all
the bonus scenes!)

Christmas
BUBBLE
ANA ASHLEY

ABOUT CHRISTMAS BUBBLE

A Christmas snowstorm.
Two opposites that most definitely attract.
Only one bed.

When the man of your absolute dreams slams their mouth into yours, there is only one course of action. Yours truly–that's me–has broken it down into four easy steps for your convenience.
You're welcome.
Step one: make sure he really is attached to you. Lips to lips. You're a clam. Do not let go.
Step two: climb him like a tree.
Step three: thank your past self for all the squats that gave you those thunder thighs.
Step four: enjoy every second of that kiss before said (maybe-not-so-straight) man realizes what he's doing and has a freakout.

Christmas Bubble is a low angst, standalone, Christmas novel featuring a petite but larger-than-life cheerleader, an older demi-sexual football coach and a winter cabin by the lake with only one bed.

Will this be the season when all their wishes will come true?

1

COACH

Do one thing that scares you each day.
Start a conversation with a stranger.
Wear your team's uniform and sit with the other team.
Blow Bubble.
The only one stopping you is yourself.

"THAT'S NOT RIGHT. It should be *blow bubbles*. Because you know, you don't just blow one bubble, right? You blow lots of bubbles."

I swivel my chair to see one of my star players staring at the motivational poster on the wall behind my desk. A poster I didn't hang, but I one hundred percent know who did.

"Jackson, how can I help?"

The kid seems uncharacteristically lost for words as he takes his eyes off the wall and looks at me, fidgeting with his hands.

"My um…mom said that if you don't have anywhere to go for Thanksgiving next week, you could come to our place since you're kinda new in town and all."

I rub the bridge of my nose, closing my eyes.

"I appreciate the invite. Thank your mom for me, but I have other plans already."

"But the guys said—"

I raise my brow, and he gets the message. I don't care what anyone says. Unless they have access to my personal diary, they don't know a thing. Such as, I really have no other plans but to put a frozen pizza in the oven and drink a few beers as I watch football on TV.

Jackson looks like he's about to say something else but thinks better of it and goes back into the locker room. I catch one of the gym teachers staring at me and give him the finger.

He laughs. "Dude, this is the third invite for Thanksgiving that you've declined. Are you wearing some special cologne or something?"

"It's the fourth, and no, no cologne," I reply, hoping he'll leave me alone to work on the lineup for the Thanksgiving Day game.

"I'm just sayin', all these invites. What's all that about?"

I groan. "How should I know? I'm new around here, remember?"

He gets up to leave our shared office. "Ah, of course, the welcome committee. Man, those were the good times. I remember someone dropping off a casserole or a homemade cake almost daily when I moved here. You should make the most of it before you're the new old news. Although you're like a movie star here. The former Marinos coach here in Windsor coaching our kids? You can milk it for all you got."

"Not really interested."

He closes the door behind him, leaving me on my own. I share the office with the gym teachers and the other coaches, which makes for much tighter quarters than the office I was used to at the Marinos.

Not that I mind my colleagues. It's just an adjustment I wasn't ready for when I upended my whole life and said goodbye to my career in San Diego to start over in Windsor, a small town in middle-of-nowhere Connecticut.

It was your choice, Riley. Live with it.

I stare at my phone and the piling notifications I'm ignoring from my parents. Who'd have thought that at the grand old age of forty-six, I'd still be playing hide and seek with them like a teenager in trouble?

The problem is I know exactly why they're calling. They want to know if I'm going back to the West Coast for Thanksgiving, and especially if I'm going to try to save my twenty-three-year marriage.

They don't know why Mel and I divorced, and there's no reason to destroy yet another relationship just because mine failed.

Mel has always been close to my parents, especially since she lost hers. Despite what happened with us, I can't bring myself to take that away from her.

I put thoughts of Mel, my parents, and my old life aside and grab my heavy coat.

Winter in Connecticut is much less kind than in California. Something else that's changed.

What made you think this was a good idea, Riley? I ask myself for the millionth time as I walk past the team in the locker room. We still practice most days, even though there are no official games until the new year, apart from the Thanksgiving Day friendly, of course.

It keeps the kids focused and out of trouble. Or maybe it's just good for my sanity to focus on something else rather than the fuck-up that is my life.

"Hey, Coach, have you seen this?" one kid calls as I reach the other end of the locker room.

"Seen what?" Even as I ask, I see what they're talking about. All over the walls are sheets of paper covered in googly eyes, and right above them, it says *Earthquake Detection Kit.*

The kids are all jumping around, trying to make the eyes move.

"Get back to your showers and get dressed. It stinks like a locker room in here," I say to get them moving.

"This *is* a locker room, Coach," another kid points out.

"It doesn't need to smell like one. Now stop messing around before I get those things taken down."

They all scramble, and I smile as I walk out the door. I miss the Marinos' locker-room antics, but these kids can give the twenty-something-year-olds a run for their money.

They are more focused and hardworking than my generation ever was. One good reason I am happy to have made this move.

There's only one person who could be responsible for the posters. The same person I try to avoid like the plague. A fruitless exercise since he seems to have taken it upon himself to be up in my business any time he wants.

Case in point, right now…

Even though there's a fresh layer of snow on the ground, the coach of the cheerleading team, Bubble—whose real name I don't know—leans against my car.

He looks like a human burrito, wrapped to his eyeballs in layers of coats, multiple scarves, and two knitted beanies, one of which has Christmas trees all over it.

"How may I help you…?" I say, just like I do every time I speak to him.

"Bubble. Just Bubble," he says, giving the *B* a more pronounced sound and scanning me from head to toe.

His green eyes are so big and deep. They're the color of the rainforest. Weirdly, I've never before given anyone's eye color a second thought.

"I'm sorry. I can't call you that."

"Why not? Everyone else does."

I see the challenge in his eyes, but I refuse to take the bait.

"I'm not everyone else, and I prefer to call people by their names."

He narrows his eyes. "Anyway, did you like it?" he asks, changing the subject.

"Like what?"

"The present I left for you, of course." He frowns and crosses his arms as if he's annoyed that I don't immediately know what he's talking about. Which, of course, is bullshit.

"It's hard to say which one because two weeks ago, the wall behind my desk was bare, and now I'm hard-pressed to remember the color of the paint beneath all those posters."

"If we can't find our own inspiration, it's okay to find it in others."

I chuckle. "What makes you think I need inspiration?"

"We all need a little inspiration every once in a while." I don't know what to make of the way he smiles at me. He seems to genuinely want me to believe all the words he's stuck on the wall behind my desk. He takes a box out of his gym bag. "Here. I made this for you."

"Why?"

He huffs and mumbles under his breath as he holds out the box, "*You didn't need to bake the most delicious cream-filled Shaabiyat just for me, Bubble. But I'll take it anyway and devour every bite of your specially-made gastronomical orgy."*

I stare at him and then burst into laughter. "Did you just say *gastronomical orgy?*"

"Open the box, and you'll find out."

I do, and I'm immediately teased with the scent of orange, rose, and buttery, flakey pastry.

"What is this?"

"I told you. It's Shaabiyat. I saw the recipe on a blog."

"Shay-what?"

"Never mind. Have a bite and tell me if it doesn't taste like the swinging sixties are making a return in your mouth."

I raise a brow. "What do you know about the sixties? You're a kid."

He shakes his head, kissing his teeth. "Oh, Coach, Coach, Coach…I could show you aaall the ways in which I'm definitely not a kid. Just say the word, and I'll give you a free ticket to the Bubble's Privates Member Club."

I snort. "You're barking up the wrong tree."

His gaze runs again from my eyes to the tips of my shoes. My winter coat suddenly feels too hot as Bubble's eyes travel to mine again. I feel exposed in ways I can't explain or understand.

"Am I?" he asks in a sultry voice, and I swear my dick reacts.

What the fuck?

Maybe it's the cold. It's getting to my head.

"I should get home," I say, pointing at my car.

He moves around me, leaving a waft of strawberry scent in the air.

"Think of me when you're licking the cream off…" He nods to the box in my hand. He walks toward the building for his cheerleading practice with strangely compelling confidence.

The kid can't even be thirty yet, but he walks and talks like he's sussed out the world and found it ripe for his taking.

2

———

BUBBLE

I CLAP my hands to get everyone's attention. "Okay, my supple cupcakes, let's nail this pyramid like you're a soft-serve ice cream."

"Melting in the sun, leaving your hands all creamy and sticky?" one kid says.

The entire team laughs. Even Justin, the assistant coach. I elbow him, and he snorts.

"No, we want a good sturdy base, a nice swirl, and those perfect cherries on top. Girls, are you ready?"

They get into formation, and I press play on the stereo. Music with a steady beat fills the large room. This routine isn't new, but I tweaked the ending. I know it'll push them a little out of their comfort zone, but I have faith. We're focusing on pyramid lifts today, which will be tough on them.

It takes the full practice to get it right, but they do it. Not that I had any doubt.

A year ago, this high school didn't even have a cheerleading team. And now they're well on their way to reaching the level needed to compete at the cheerleading high school nationals if they want to.

"Gather round my little muffins of amazingness," I call out to them as I turn the music off.

618

They all sit on the mat, slouching against each other, gathering their breath. Every single one of them looks exhausted and exhilarated. The best feeling in the whole world. After good sex, of course. But I can't tell them that, or I'd be fired.

"Okay, can you tell me what you need to work on?"

"We're still a bit wobbly," Terry says.

I nod. "How do we fix that?"

Everyone looks around as if the person next to them holds the answer, which they do.

"You're a team, and you need to trust your teammates one hundred percent. Mary, Selina, Hannah, and Petra, the guys will hold you up, and they'll catch you if you fall. But if you don't trust them, then you won't fall right, which means you might do something that'll hurt them. If they stop trusting you, they'll be afraid of what you might do when you're up there. You all see how wrong it can go?"

The team nods.

"One team. One hundred percent trust. Now tell me what went well," I say. "Can anyone tell me what went well?"

"No one fell and broke their neck," Sasha says.

"True, but let's go for something a little less dramatic."

"I didn't have to call the nurse," Justin mutters next to me.

"Come on, people. A year ago, you couldn't do a cartwheel, and look at you nailing a twenty-person pyramid. Now, can *I* have a cheer for that?" I shout and jump on the spot.

They all stand and cheer, and the energy is electric. I soak it up like my own personal sunshine.

"Okay, okay, we'll keep working sections this week and building for a full run on Friday. You all up for that?"

"Yes, Coach!" they all shout.

"What was that?" I ask, putting my hand to my ear.

"Yes, Bubble!"

"That's better. I'll see you all tomorrow."

As the kids all spill into the locker room, Justin shows me the footage he captured with his tablet.

"I think Taylor needs to take a rest. Look at his face there. He's clearly in pain but doesn't want to let the team down," he says, rewinding the clip to the moment Petra is flying down from the pyramid. You'd never notice Taylor's pain unless you're looking for it.

"Can you have a word with him?" I ask.

"I sure can. I reviewed some earlier clips during the practice and saw nothing else wrong. I think they just need more time on the mat."

"Can you send me what you have?" I ask.

"Sure."

We walk together to the coaches' office via the locker room.

"Your earthquake detection kit still makes me laugh every time I walk past," he says.

"I have my moments."

He bumps my shoulder.

"You more than have your moments, Bubble. Since you got here, it's like this place has lit up with happiness and joy. I know it sounds sappy as shit, but it's true. The kids are focused, and they work hard. Even the teachers. All they talk about is you."

I laugh. "That's because I bake them cake. Everyone loves cake."

"This is true."

I think about the sullen football coach who only appears to smile when he's coaching his team.

Not that I've been watching or anything. Okay, there was this one time when I forgot my lucky Sailor Moon keychain in the office, so I had to drive back to the school to get it.

I should have known when some douchewaffle tried to run a red light right in front of me that I was missing my lucky charm. It wasn't until I reached to touch the keychain out of habit that I realized it was gone.

After running to the office to grab the keychain, I was on my way back to the car when I heard cheering and saw the coach running across the football field with the players. He was wearing these tight shorts that showed off his thick, muscular thighs, and I basically died on the spot.

That Sailor Moon keychain proved once again to be my all-time luckiest possession because *that* had to be one of the best man-drooling moments of my entire life. Considering I spend a lot of my time ogling men, that says a lot about the quality of Coach's goods.

Justin heads off while I spend some time looking through the footage he sent me. Even though I only work at the school part-time, I still have my own desk, conveniently positioned opposite Coach Dempsey's.

Okay, so maybe I moved my desk a little. But no one said I couldn't, so I guess it's okay.

I contemplate adding another inspirational quote to his collection, but I think he might kill me, so I better wait until Christmas. Who knows, maybe he's a Christmas person.

Everybody loves Christmas, right?

I reach out to pick up my phone when I hear the Lady Gaga ringtone I picked for my best friend.

"Juju, my beautiful doll, don't tell me how hot it is out there because I'm close to turning into a human strawberry-flavored popsicle. No one ever told me Connecticut was in the Arctic Circle."

She laughs, and the sound warms me from the inside out.

"I don't need to tell you, honey. You grew up here, and you know the way back too."

"Don't start…"

"I didn't. You did. Anyway…I was wondering if you're coming for Thanksgiving this year since you missed last year."

I pull the hem of my pink top. It's fraying a little, and with my picking, it frays a little more. "I can't, Juju. We have a game."

The sigh coming from the other side of the line makes me feel super guilty.

"Bubble, last year you'd just taken that job at the coffee shop, Spilled Beans. This year you're also coaching on top of that. Are you ever going to come home?"

No?

"Of course, silly. I'm just having such a great time here." I gasp. "I have an excellent, no, scrap that, a superlative idea. Why don't *you* come over for Thanksgiving? You can watch the game, and then we can spend the weekend eating our weight in cake and watching movies. Yes?"

"I can't, hunni. We're training for a competition. I could try to make it for Christmas."

I try not to show my disappointment through my voice. I miss her so much.

Since my grandmother died, Juju has been my only family. We're not blood-related, but we may as well be with how close we are.

"I'll hold you to that. How's everything else?" I ask, even though I'm not sure I want to know.

"We're going to nationals, as expected."

I hear the excitement in her voice and try hard not to feel jealous that I can't be part of that world anymore.

"Of course, and I bet you're going to win. Again."

She giggles but then stops and lets out a long sigh. "You should be here with us, Bubble."

"Yeah, but I'm not, and there's no point in crying over spilled glitter because that shit's a bitch to clean."

"How can you be so positive after everything that happened? After what that two-timing liar snake did?"

"Because I'm genuinely happy here, Juju. You know I always loved baking with my grandmother, so the job at Spilled Beans in Chester Falls is perfect. My boss, Indy, gives me free rein in the kitchen, especially now that he and his husband have a kid and he wants to spend more time at home. And I love coaching the cheer team too. I'm doing the two things I love the most. Why wouldn't I be happy?"

The award for Best Liar goes to…Bubble! And the crowd cheers…

"I suppose you're right," she says.

"So get your perky ass out here for Christmas, or else," I warn. "But bring extra layers on top of your extra layers because seriously, sister, this place in the winter is an icicle on steroids."

When we end the call, I find myself in that weird state where I'm not sad but also not happy. Sappy?

Every day I walk into the school to coach the cheerleading team, my focus is on them. I want to teach them all the lessons I learned as a cheerleader.

Even when my trust was broken, and even when I was broken, I still learned something. Sometimes the lessons were painful, but the most genuine smiles come from those who have lived to appreciate the moments that made them smile.

And if there's anything Bubble can do, it's smile.

I grab my three scarves and wrap them around my neck before I put my coat on to leave.

Past Bubble was a super-genius for saving a Shaabiyat to have later, and Present Bubble is going to run home to have a warm bath before indulging in the sweet Lebanese dessert.

Thank god for sugar and baking blogs.

Once again, thoughts of Coach fill my mind. I wonder if he's tried the Shaabiyat and what he thought of it.

I'd bet my Sailor Moon keychain he's a cream man. Licking it all clean before eating the pastry.

And just like that, I have an erection.

Great.

3

COACH

THE OVEN DINGS as I turn the TV to the sports channel.

Pizza, beer, and watching football on TV after winning the Thanksgiving game with my team this morning. It can't get any better than this.

I put a pizza slice on a plate and head back to the living room, hoping to catch the rest of the Bears vs. Lions game.

I turn the heat up a bit and sit on the couch, resting my feet on the coffee table.

The pizza is adequate. Not the best I've had, but considering I can't cook for shit and didn't set the kitchen on fire, it does the job.

I can't help laughing at myself because I'm hitting all the bachelor stereotypes in a single afternoon. Then again, I never had the chance to be a bachelor or do whatever the hell I wanted.

I take a swig of the beer and finish the slice of pizza, reaching out for another one.

The doorbell rings, and I do a double-take. I'm not friendly enough with anyone in Windsor that they'd stop by my place. I don't think anyone at the school knows where I live.

I mute the TV and go to the front door. Even before I have a chance to react to the presence of my unexpected visitors, I'm enveloped by my mom's slim but strong arms and familiar floral perfume fills my senses.

"Mom. Dad. What are you doing here?"

I kiss the top of her head and let her go. My dad gives me a one-arm hug and a pat on the back as he comes inside before I close the door to keep the cold out. He's not a touchy-feely person. My mom has always done all the hugging and cuddling for both of them.

"Well, we couldn't let you spend Thanksgiving on your own, could we?" mom says, walking in front of me as if she's been to this place before.

She gasps at the sight of my pizza—minus one slice—and beer on the coffee table.

"Riley John Dempsey, don't tell me this is your Thanksgiving dinner."

Oh, how she loves to full-name me. I look at my dad for help, but he's conveniently distracted by the plain walls of my mostly bare house.

"Mom, I had a game this morning, and I live alone. Besides, you know I can't cook."

"Jeff, go get the stuff we got. I told you we were going to need it," she says to my dad, who knows the drill ingrained by almost fifty years of marriage.

She takes her coat off and drapes it over the couch.

"Where's your kitchen?"

She walks to the hallway leading to the bedroom, and that's a room I really don't want her to see. If she's disappointed with my choice of dinner, I'll never hear the end of it when she sees my bedroom has nothing but a bed and a dresser. Not to mention a pile of laundry on the floor that I was supposed to work through this weekend.

"Mom. Stop."

She comes to a halt.

"What the hell is going on? You don't exactly live around the corner, so you can just drop by. Why didn't you say you were coming?" I ask, guiding her toward the kitchen.

The sadness on her face gets to me, and I pull her into my arms.

"I'm sorry, Mom. I don't mean it that way. I'm glad you're here. It's just a surprise, you know? I didn't even get a turkey or anything."

Dad comes back, holding a few shopping bags.

"We didn't get turkey either, but at least we can have a proper meal," Mom says. "Now take me to your kitchen so I can prepare our dinner while we catch up."

I give up on watching any football and give a passing glance at my now sad-looking pizza, but despite the shock of having my parents turn up unannounced, I'm glad they're here.

Dad follows us to the kitchen with the bags and grabs a beer from the fridge before going out to the living room, leaving me with my mom. At least one of us gets to watch the game.

"This is a nice kitchen, Riley. Mel would have liked it."

"Mom…"

"Sorry, honey. Force of habit."

I try not to take it to heart and leave her to find everything she needs to prepare whatever dinner she's cooking for us. I stand on the side, waiting to be told what to do.

"She still drops by every week and asks about you," Mom says.

"I'm glad you're still getting along, Mom. You've always been close, and I'd hate for her to lose you, but there's no way back for us. You need to know that."

Mom hands me the chopping board, the knife, and a bunch of vegetables. No need for instructions. We've done this plenty of times before.

"I know, honey. I just think that after all these years, it's such a shame. You were so good together. Did you really fall out of love?"

"I love you for asking that, but it was a lot of things, not just that we grew apart."

She puts the knife she's using to cut the chicken on the chopping board and faces me.

"You know you're not an only child out of choice, don't you?"

I nod. We've had this conversation before when my and Mel's struggle to conceive came up. They shared how they tried to give me a sibling, but it never happened.

"I know how hard it is to want that child so much, and it becomes everything. Sometimes you can lose yourself a little," she says. "I could see it in Mel's eyes."

I take a deep, steady breath. "Mom, can we not talk about this? Nothing is going to change things. Mel and I are divorced."

"I just...I never saw it coming. You two were always so happy together."

"We were, Mom, but it didn't work out. Let's leave it at that."

She lets out a resigned sigh. "Okay, sweetheart. I just want you to be happy."

"I know, Mom."

We work in silence until the smell of my mom's cooking reawakens my stomach. The slice of pizza I had before feels like a million years ago.

I set the table as she puts the dishes with vegetables and mashed potatoes on the table and takes the casserole out of the oven.

"Who'd have thought my Thanksgiving meal would be a real meal? Now, this is something to be thankful for," I joke.

"Riley?" Mom asks as I grab the drinks. "I promise I'll put it to rest now, but I just want to know. Are you happy?"

I look at my mom in her white cashmere sweater and jeans, her short blonde bob haircut and her nice soft skin. She doesn't look her seventy years by any stretch.

We've always been very close, and considering I've spent my life on a football field surrounded by alpha male-type guys, I enjoy talking to my mom. She has a way of making me feel balanced.

"Am I happy? I'm working on it. For the first time in my life, I'm putting myself first, which feels good. I just don't know what happy looks like yet."

She comes up to me and gives me a kiss on the cheek.

"You'll know when it happens."

There's a cynical part of me that thinks it'll never happen, but another part of me hopes my mom is right. After all, I've already spent most of my life in a relationship based on a lie. I'd love the chance to find out how it feels to be with someone who is with me for me. No lies.

"Is dinner ready yet? Or are we waiting for next Thanksgiving?"

Mom and I laugh at Dad's yearly line.

"It's ready," we both say.

The food is wonderful, which is to be expected. My mom has always been a wonderful cook. We catch up about all the things happening back home on the West Coast, and I tell them about my new life here in Windsor.

"I know you love me, and I'm your favorite son and all, but coming all the way from San Diego for a meal is a bit much. Who's gonna fess up?" I ask.

Mom smiles wide and looks at Dad.

"Your mom has been pestering me to go on one of those floating bathtubs since I retired, so I guess we're giving that a try," he says.

"Mom, care to translate?"

"We're going on a month-long Christmas cruise. We're setting off from New York next week, and we'll end up in the Caribbean for Christmas. We were hoping that you'd join us in St. Barts. You have vacation days over Christmas, don't you?"

I stare at each of my parents in turn. Two people who've barely traveled out of state because they claimed there was no need to go anywhere else when they had the beach on their doorstep are now going on a month-long cruise.

"I…don't know what to say…this doesn't really sound like the kind of thing you'd do," I say. "I mean, is it safe? Do you have good travel insurance?"

"Riley John Dempsey, don't make me show you how strong my hand still is," my mom threatens.

I stand from the table, collecting all the plates. "Sorry, Mom. That was out of line. I think it's a good idea and you'll have loads of fun. I can't join you though. I'd planned to go to the cabin I bought by the lake in Stillwater."

"You mean that old rackety place in those photos you showed us months ago?" my mom asks with concern. "Is it even heated?"

"Yes, Mom. It has a fireplace, and I have enough wood. Thank you for acknowledging that I'm a grownup and can take care of myself."

She raises a brow. "Was that pizza on your coffee table your Thanksgiving dinner?"

"She shoots. She scores," my dad says, settling the argument the same way he's done since I was a child. Mom is always right.

"Fair enough. But I just want to go out there, do some work on it, and chill."

I grab the dessert plates and the pie I was saving for later.

"Oh, what is this marvelous-looking pie? I know you didn't do this yourself, and this is most definitely not from a store," mom says.

"Someone from work made it for me. It's pumpkin pie."

"Whoever she is, she's going to an awful lot of trouble for you, dear."

"He."

"What's that?"

"He. The pie was made by the cheerleading coach." They keep staring at me, and I realize I was no clearer than before. "He's a guy."

"Oh."

They share a look I don't understand.

"What's wrong? Loads of men can bake. I think Bubble works in a coffee shop owned by a guy who's also a baker." I don't know why I feel the need to defend him, especially considering how much he gets on my nerves with his inspirational quotes and strawberry scent.

"Nothing wrong, sweetie. We just wondered why your friend isn't here having his pie with you."

I shrug. "He just left the pie on my desk. I think he's on a mission to fatten me up or something because he keeps giving me stuff to eat. I don't even know the guy that well."

Mom and Dad share another look and dig their forks into their pie slices.

As with all the other baked goods Bubble has given me, the pumpkin pie is divine.

I really must ask him why he does this. But then, what if he stops?

Or worse. What if I have to confront this weird feeling in the pit of my stomach every time he's around?

Better just eat the pie. Yeah.

4

BUBBLE

"One dark-soul espresso and a sad chocolate-chip cupcake coming right up," I say to one of our regulars at Spilled Beans.

The customer stares at me, her eyes blinking.

"Would you like anything else?"

"Can I have a *happy* chocolate-chip cupcake?" she asks, tilting her head and making a cute face to get a smile out of me. Not happening today.

I look at the display in front of me. All the cakes and pastries created by my boss are impeccable, but I don't see anything happy.

"No, sorry, sweetie. But they're freshly baked and super delicious."

"Let me think about it," she says.

I'm finishing the drink as Indy, my boss, comes from the kitchen with a tray of freshly baked Dutch pepernoten cookies. The delicious scents of nutmeg, cloves, cinnamon, and ginger follow him.

This year we have a few themed days leading up to Christmas, so we're baking specialty cookies and cakes from around the world. It was my idea—a fantastic one, even if I say so myself. But Indy said it too, so I can be smug about it.

When I smell all our delicious bakes and look at the snow outside the coffee shop, people walking past with bags filled with Christmas gifts, I feel like I'm living inside a Christmas postcard.

"What's going on?" Indy asks.

"What? Nothing," I say noncommittally.

"I'll take that cupcake after all, honey, and I hope your day gets better," the customer says as I give her the coffee and put the cupcake in a specialized box.

Indy sets the tray on the counter, and I help him transfer the cookies to a smaller tray in the display cabinet.

I try really hard, but I don't know if the cinnamon or the cloves remind me of my grandmother and her hugs and Christmas. I let out a very long sigh.

"Okay," Indy says. "Let's talk it out." He pulls me by my hand to one table and makes me sit. "What's up?"

"It's the coach. I keep giving him things, and nothing happens," I say, letting my frustration show. I tuck my hands in the front pocket of my Spilled Beans apron.

"I'm scared to ask. What *things* do you keep giving him?"

I shrug. "Cake. I don't know which is his favorite, so I've baked him a chocolate cake, pineapple, vanilla, birthday cake, fruitcake, cake with frosting, cake without frosting, cupcakes, muffins, special pastries from around the world—" Indy raises his hand to stop me.

"I get the idea."

"He returns the boxes I give him with those delicious cakes, and all there is inside is a sticky note that says thank you. There aren't even any heart-shaped confetti or paper flowers. *Nothing*."

Indy purses his lips, and I'm sure he wants to laugh. How can he want to laugh at the tragedy that is my life?

"Is that all?" he asks.

I stare at the table, and I'm sure my guilty look won't fool anyone, let alone Indy.

"I may have also bought him a few other gifts."

He gestures for me to expand on that.

"Okay, so maybe I've hung a few posters with inspirational quotes behind his desk at work. And he kept losing his pens, so I got him a pen holder."

"Was there anything printed on that pen holder?" Indy asks as if he's afraid of the answer.

I bite my thumbnail. "Um…*Stick it in me?*"

"Oh, Bubble." He holds his hands out, and I put my hand in his. He holds it tight like he's going to give me some bad news.

"Are you crushing on him?"

I snort and take my hand back. "No, of course not. Pfft. Me? Bubble doesn't crush. I crush strawberries for milkshakes, which, by the way, does not bring all the boys to the yard, but no…I'm not crushing…nope…"

Oh, who am I kidding?

Indy raises a brow.

"Okay, maybe a little bit." *Oh, who am I kidding? I have a crush on Coach the size of my bubble butt—thank you, squats—but I digress…* "It's just that my grandmother raised me with good manners, and she always said, *'Bubble, the way to a man's good graces is through his stomach.'"*

He sighs. "That only works if he's not straight, hun. You know that, right? Unless something changed? You told me you thought he was straight," Indy says.

"A guy can dream, right? Besides, he could come around." I raise my hands like I'm praying. "Never give up on something you can't go a day without thinking about."

"That's very insightful and true."

I stand and go behind the counter again. I'm sure we're due some customers any moment now. "I'm glad you agree. Winston Churchill said it, according to my inspirational quotes calendar."

"Wait," he says, following me. "So you're basically stalking him, so that *you're* all he's thinking about until he comes around?"

I try to ignore the pity in his voice.

"No. *He* is all I can think about. I can't give up until he specifically tells me to leave him alone. You know, like how vampires have to be invited in? I have to be invited out."

Indy laughs.

"Only a stupid man would send away someone who brings him cake daily."

I grin. "Precisely. My grandmother was right. Anyway, Lebanese week was great, and Dutch week is going well so far. Are we really going to try the stroopwafels?" I raise my hands in prayer.

Indy rolls his eyes and bites his lip. "We can't afford not to. It would be a sin to deprive this town of those beautiful thin wafers filled with that soft caramel melting over a cup of coffee."

"Stop, you're giving me a sugar boner," I joke.

The front doorbell rings, and my smile widens when I see two of my favorite customers.

"Mr. and Mrs. Crawford. How nice to see you."

"Good day, Bubble, my dear. Goodness, isn't it cold out there," Mrs. Crawford says.

Indy goes back to the kitchen, leaving me with them.

"You don't need to tell me. I was cold by the end of the summer. I lost the feeling of my lower limbs by fall, and I'm pretty sure I'm just a walking frozen ghost by now. Anyway, what can I get you?"

"We're going away until the new year but couldn't leave without having one or two of Indy's cinnamon rolls," Mr. Crawford says. "Keep 'em coming, Bubble."

"Dear, remember what the doctor said," his wife warns.

I smile at how they always warn each other about eating the treats they enjoy once a month at Spilled Beans. I never met my parents because they died when I was a baby, but I always thought they'd be a little like Mr. and Mrs. Crawford. Never taking each other too seriously and just enjoying life.

I prepare their coffees the way I know they like.

"Where are you going on this adventure, if I may ask because I'm totally nosy?" I ask.

"We're doing a tour of Europe. Revisiting all the places we saw on our honeymoon," Mr. Crawford says.

"But this time, we'll actually see them," Mrs. Crawford continues.

I chuckle and give them their drinks, returning to the counter for the cinnamon rolls.

"So you won't be spending Christmas with your family?" I ask.

Mrs. Crawford is the one to speak up. "Our son and his fiancé are taking the kids to Florida for Disney World, so we thought that instead of sitting at home like two old fogies, we'd have our own adventure."

I place the pastries on the table. "Oh shush, Mrs. Crawford," I say, running a hand over her sweater. "Look at your style. You're ageless. There's no old in your vocabulary."

"And how about you, dear? Are you doing anything special this Christmas?"

I beam. "As a matter of fact, yes. My best friend is coming all the way from the West Coast to visit. I haven't seen her since I moved to Connecticut."

"Sounds great. I bet you'll have loads of fun," Mrs. Crawford says.

I deflate a little. "I don't know. I'm afraid she'll find it a bit boring here. We'll obviously watch tons of Christmas movies and eat our body weight in cake, but I'm not sure what else to do."

I leave them to it to go check on Indy and see if he needs help in the kitchen. I find him jumping on the spot while holding his phone to his chest.

"Um…are you having an episode? Do I need to call someone? I should tell you I'm not good with blood, guts, or anything medical," I say.

Indy turns to me with the biggest smile. "Bubble, my dear, you've just gained yourself a two-week paid vacation."

I frown and look around to see if there are any cameras, and I'm being pranked.

"I, what?"

"You know Tyler is turning one this Christmas, right? Tate says it's time for us to take a family vacation. We're not going anywhere, but we're closing Spilled Beans, and he's handing his work to his partner so we can spend time together." His face becomes all dream-like. "Can you imagine sleeping in until six a.m.? Ahhh, bliss…so anyway, that's happening. So you're getting a paid vaycay."

He says it like it's final.

"Thank you. That's really generous of you, Indy."

And now I'm the one with the nervous energy. What will I do with myself for two weeks during the school break? Even Juju will only come for a few days.

I go back to the front of the coffee shop, and Mrs. Crawford stands and comes over to me, dangling a set of keys.

"My husband and I just had the best idea. How would you like to give your friend a true white-Christmas experience?" she says.

I'm feeling a little lightheaded and confused from Indy's vacation news and now Mrs. Crawford talking about a white Christmas. Did I eat something earlier that didn't agree with me?

"I don't understand."

"It's simple, dear. We have a cabin by the lake in Stillwater. It'll be sitting empty while we're in Europe and the kids are in Florida. It's yours for Christmas if you want it."

I feel tears prickling the backs of my eyes, and before I know it, I'm hugging Mrs. Crawford.

"Thank you so much. That's such a lovely gesture, and I promise I'll take the best care of your cabin."

She hugs me back, and I can barely contain my tears because she smells so comforting. This is the nicest thing anyone's done for me in a long time.

Apart from Indy giving me a two-week paid vacation that I now get to have in a lakeside cabin. Squee!

5

____

COACH

"Come on, guys, two more laps. I can't believe I'm barely breaking a sweat, and you're dropping like flies. I'm supposed to be the old man here."

"Yeah, Coach, but we've been playing for two hours," Jackson complains.

"You should be warm enough for this run then."

I'm running with the team. Something I enjoy occasionally doing after practice.

My career as a football player barely existed because I always wanted to be a coach, so after I had an injury that ended my playing days, I used it as a stepping stone after I graduated from college. It doesn't mean I don't enjoy playing.

I love being on the field and playing with the kids, especially when we don't have any games scheduled, so it's all just practice.

By the time we're finished, I'm keeping a straight face, but I'm definitely feeling the workout in my muscles. After all, I have a good thirty years on these kids.

I'm glad the coaches have their own locker room with a shower because that's exactly what I'll need.

"Off to the showers with you all, and have a Merry Christmas.

Don't overdo it. Trust me. You'll regret it on that first practice of the year," I say as we walk back into the building.

"Oh, come on, Coach. It's Christmas," one of the kids groans.

"It's also just a day."

"You say that because you never had my mom's meatloaf," he grumbles. "Damn, I'm already feeling January in my body."

I laugh.

The locker room becomes a noisy hub of teenagers talking over each other, messing about, and joking.

I've never let the teams know, but I've often just stood behind the door listening to the chatter, wondering what it would be like if I'd had my own kid.

Would they be like these kids? Or maybe they'd be more the kind to be found in the library with their nose in a book. Maybe even both.

I head off to the coaches' office. There's no point thinking about something that will never happen. I've made my peace with it, and that's that.

There are a couple of coaches and a gym teacher in the office. I nod to them as I come in.

"I see you have another box from Bubble," one of them says. "How come you're the only one that gets your own cake, and we have to share?"

"He must be special," the other one says.

"Do you put out?" the gym teacher says, and I throw a pen at him.

"Want to take it? At this rate, I'm going to end up six feet under before I'm fifty and, trust me, I'm not far off."

"Nah, Coach. I've seen you with the kids. You can still run circles around them," the gym teacher says as he high-fives me and heads off. "Merry Christmas, everyone."

"I'm grabbing a shower, so if you're gone before I'm back, I guess, well, Merry Christmas from me too," I say, picking up my gym bag.

"Wait," one of the coaches calls.

I stop and turn around.

The other coach hits his arm and shakes his head, making a weird face. "Never mind. It was about some stuff for the new year, but we'll deal in January."

"Ookay…" That's weird, but to each their own. I turn back and carry on to the locker room.

There's a semi-dark hallway we have to go through before we get to the locker room, and I've never understood if it just needs a new light bulb or if it's supposed to be like that. As soon as I open the door at the end, I'm met with billowing steam.

I can't see a foot in front of me. Thankfully, I know the bench by the lockers is close, so I feel my way and drop my gym bag on top of it.

Whoever is in the shower might be confusing it with a sauna because, within a minute, my T-shirt and shorts are sticking to me.

"Hey, buddy, are you going to take long?" I ask whoever is in here.

Jeez, it's even hard to breathe. I try looking for a window to let the steam out, but I can't find one.

There's no reply from the showers, so I sit on the bench waiting.

"Doo bee doo in a yellow submarine, yellow submarine…"

I can only vaguely hear, but it sounds like whoever is in there is singing. The misty steam subsides after a while, so hopefully, they're ending their shower soon.

After a few minutes, the water finally stops.

"Thank Christ," I mutter to myself. I don't want to be rude to whoever is in here, but did they need to turn the locker room into the scene of a bad horror movie for a shower?

I open the zipper of my gym bag to get my towel as the voice comes singing from the shower cubicle.

*"Would you still love me when I'm sixty-foo…*fuck!"

The guy clearly isn't expecting to see someone else in the room because he flails like he's trying to escape an attacker.

I can only move a step forward and hold him by his arms to stop him from slipping on the wet, tiled floor and breaking a leg, or worse.

"Fudging slippery squares of evil. I could have just died," he says breathlessly.

"Bubble. Are you okay?" I stare into his forest-green eyes, the scent of strawberries surrounding us, and that's when I realize Bubble is naked.

"So you *do* know my name."

His hair is sticking up in all directions and beads of water run down his skin.

Don't look. Don't look.

But I do because the steam must have gone to my head.

All I know is that Bubble is…well, thank god, not totally naked. The towel he probably had around his waist is now in his hands covering his…his…fuck…

Bubble is slim with a curved waist that is almost feminine, if it wasn't for the trail of light-brown hair leading from his belly button and disappearing under the towel.

He doesn't have any hair on his chest, just two very perky pink nipples.

My mouth goes dry. I know I need to say something, but somehow my brain has cut all communication with my mouth, and I can't utter a single word.

"Like what you see, Coach?" he asks in a teasing voice, and that's when I realize I've been staring longer than appropriate for a work colleague. Especially when said work colleague is basically naked. Or for a straight man to stare at a gay man.

I grab my bag and run out of the room, not stopping until I'm inside my car.

Even the cold outside does nothing to soothe the weird ache in my belly. And why is my dick so fucking hard?

I'm not attracted to men. I've always been with Mel, and I loved her and enjoyed having sex with her.

I grip my steering wheel hard. What the hell is happening to me?

Could it be the move to Connecticut? Maybe it's all this change. It's just a physiological reaction. Maybe I've been without sex for so long now that my body reacts to any naked adult.

I look in the rearview mirror and meet my own eyes. "Okay, change of plans. We go home, shower, and pack. Tomorrow, we do the grocery shopping and head over to the cabin. We need to get away from Windsor sooner than I thought. And the proof is that you're sitting in your car talking to yourself like you're someone else."

Fuck my life.

6

BUBBLE

THE DRIVE to Stillwater is pretty easy, even with the recent snow. Props to LA-born-and-raised Bubble for not crashing the car or killing an elderly person or animal along the way.

There's a woodland road to get to the cabin, as marked on the map, the navigation system, and the notes Mr. and Mrs. Crawford gave me.

I stop the car, but I'm sure I'm in the wrong place.

"Fudgesickles. I hope I'm not on the wrong side of the lake." I unfold the big map I brought and lay it over the steering wheel. At least it's nice and toasty inside the car.

With my finger, I trace the road I took from Windsor toward Stillwater and then out toward the lake.

I seem to be in the right place, but this cabin...well...it's much more than I expected.

When Mr. and Mrs. Crawford mentioned a cabin by the lake, I imagined something small and cozy, surrounded by trees. The kind of stuff fairytales are made of.

But this is more than just a little Hansel and Gretel-type cozy cabin in the woods.

"Well, only one way to find out if this is the real deal." I put my beanie on my head and scramble to put my coat on because I'm not stupid enough to go out there in just a sweater, no matter how close that front door is.

I turn off the car and brave the cold outside. This is the moment of truth.

"God, you're dramatic, Bubble." I pull the key from my pocket and put it in the keyhole. When it turns, and the door opens, I let out a little squeal.

I shake off most of the snow from my boots before going inside.

What I see when I open the door all the way is the magical wonderland of my dreams. I only remember to close the door behind me because it's still freaking freezing, but otherwise, I'm mesmerized by what I'm walking into.

"Grandma," I whisper. "Did you do this?"

I wait for a reply from heaven, but there are no noises.

The front door leads into a large open space with the biggest, comfiest-looking couch I've ever seen. It's facing a fireplace, which I'll need to figure out if I don't want to freeze to death.

But ignore all that. All houses have kitchens, couches, bedrooms, ceilings, whatever. This cabin though…is like my Christmas winter wonderland come true.

I take my phone out and video call Juju.

"Hey, Bubbs, what's up?" she asks, not even looking at the camera. "I'm packing right now. I'm so freaking excited. Do you think three pairs of heels is too much?"

"Juju, honey, look at me," I say.

She grabs the phone, and my view goes from the ceiling of her bedroom to her gorgeous face. She's wearing the off-shoulder slouchy top I gave her two years ago for her birthday. Oh, how I miss hot weather.

Anyway.

"Take those heels out of your suitcase. You don't need them unless you want to risk breaking your neck."

"But you said you're taking me to a place near the cabin. What if I find myself a sexy lumberjack?"

I laugh. "First of all, I doubt that lumberjacks are into heels. You wear those jeans, you know, the ones that make your ass pop out like it needs its own TV show? You'll get your attention. And second, it's just a diner. Please tell me you bought warm clothes."

She puffs. "Of course."

"Anyway, Juju, you are not going to believe this..." I flip the camera so she can see what I see.

"Fuck me sideways and make me into a Christmas garland. Is that a Christmas tree? It's fucking huge!" She says.

"I know. It has to be at least seven feet, and it's fully decorated. It even has presents underneath. They're probably fake, of course, but it looks so beautiful." I'm getting all emotional just talking about it. "I can't believe Mr. and Mrs. Crawford would go to all this trouble just for us."

"I always say you have good karma, sugarpie. This is the universe giving something back to you."

"And look at all the decorations on the walls and the ceiling." I move my phone around until Juju complains she's getting dizzy.

I take her on a tour of the rest of the house, the main room—where I'll be sleeping—and the second bedroom, which will be Juju's. It's clear Mr. and Mrs. C's grandchildren usually sleep in there because it's full of toys.

"Okay, I need to unload the car now and figure out how to get this place warm. I'll see you in a few days," I say, blowing her a kiss.

"Love you, babe."

I leave my phone on the kitchen counter and brace myself to go back out in the cold.

Thankfully, the temperatures kept all the food safe outside, so I bring all that in first, filling the fridge until it's stocked to the brim. I wonder for a moment if I have too much food, but then I just laugh. Never.

I go back to the car and take two smaller bags, but the suitcase is much heavier, so I leave it for later. I'm dying for a warm cup of coffee.

"Okay, Mr. and Mrs. C, how do you get this place warm?" I ask the absent couple.

I noticed the main bedroom has a fireplace but no wood, so I guess it's probably electric and works on a switch. But how about the one in the living room?

Oh lord, do I need to make fire?

Me. Bubble. A former cheerleader, who mostly wears pink, smells like strawberries, and sees the world through Bubble-tinted glasses… make fire?

"Oh, Grandma, this is not funny, you know?" A creaking noise startles me. "And don't freak me out either. Everyone knows there's only one degree of separation between fairytale woodland dwelling and horror movie cabin in the woods."

Okay, if they have a fireplace, they must have wood somewhere.

Step one, find wood.

I chuckle at my thoughts but put on my coat and boots and head outside.

Sure enough, there's a big pile of chopped wood under a tarpaulin on the side of the cabin. I carry a bunch inside.

"Step one achieved."

Step two is how to make the actual fire. I grab my phone, and there are a bunch of how-to videos. I watch a few until I understand how it works in principle.

There's a basket by the fireplace with some old newspapers and long matches, so I open the fireplace and start stacking all the elements. First, the scrunched-up papers and a few fire starters, and then the kindling, which are the smaller pieces of wood, followed by bigger ones.

"Okay, Bubble. This is it. You're about to maybe make fire."

I light a match and put it close to the newspapers until a few catch fire. When I see there are enough flames, I close the fireplace door.

"Shit, what was the next step?" I grab my phone quickly because I can see the flames already dying. "Why did Juju almost destroy my kitchen, making toast, and now I'm literally making fire, but the flames are going nowhere?" I say to myself, frustrated.

The man in the video talks about giving the fire some air. Huh? What?

"You want me to blow on it? Even *I* am not that good."

I look around the edges of the door until I see a little knob. I try to move it, and suddenly the flames inside the fireplace come up again.

"Oh my god! Oh my god!" I stand and dance on the spot. "I made fire. Did you see that, Grandma? I made fire!"

I take my Sailor Moon keychain from my pocket and hold it to my chest, staring at the flames for a while and taking in the warmth. So many emotions hit me. I'm happy to soon see Juju again. Sad my grandma is no longer with us. Lucky and grateful to Mr. and Mrs. C for letting me stay here for Christmas.

Before silly, sad tears try to escape my eyes, I prepare myself a coffee and eat a slice of my lemon-drizzle cake. A recipe I got from the wife of a well-known British TV chef. It works every time, and it's one of my favorites.

Once I'm done, I sit on the couch, staring at the flames again.

This Christmas vacation and the cabin are the perfect settings to help me refocus and regroup. I didn't think I needed to regroup, but after Coach ran out on me in the locker room, my confidence is a little bruised.

Indy is probably right. No amount of baked treats and flirting will get the big, sexy, almost-silver fox to be interested in me if he's not interested in men.

Why do I always go for the wrong ones?

As tiredness gets the best of me, I know I need to get my big suitcase from the car, but it's still early. I can take a little nap and do that later.

With my belly full of coffee and cake and surrounded by my beautiful Christmas winter wonderland and my self-made fire—hashtag smug—I close my eyes and relax.

I hear a car nearby. *Sounds like I'm getting some neighbors*, is my last thought before I drift off.

7

COACH

In the deep, harsh winter, I admit my fixer-upper cabin by the lake doesn't feel like the best place to spend Christmas. Especially for someone used to the warmer winters of San Diego.

But two days after the incident with Bubble, I'm still reeling from embarrassment, so I'll accept my punishment and take it on the chin.

As they say, what doesn't kill you makes you stronger. I'll either freeze to death or grow some more chest hairs. Or I could turn into a lumberjack because one thing's for sure, I'm gonna need a lot of wood to warm up this place.

Speaking of which, the first job is to get the fireplace going so I don't freeze to death, so once that's done, I finish bringing all my stuff inside.

The weather doesn't look too friendly. I'm glad I've brought enough food to last a while. I certainly don't want to drive to the nearest town to buy groceries.

There's a soft glow coming from the cabin next door. I guess the neighbors are spending Christmas here too. I bet their living conditions are a little more luxurious than mine.

"Don't moan, Riley. You wanted this."

I crack open a beer and take a swig. I made the rash decision to buy this cabin because there was no one to stop me. For the second time since I became an adult, whatever happened after I signed on the dotted line, I was doing something for myself. The first one being my divorce.

The couch in front of the fireplace is old but comfortable, and the comforter I bought covers the small tears.

There's a dining table with two chairs that I found in a yard sale. Once they're sanded and revarnished, they'll look like new. That's a summer job, but they'll do for now.

I finish the beer and take the bag with my clothes to the bedroom.

Again, it's a modest room with space for the bed, a chest of drawers, and a chair in the corner.

"Oh shit," I say when I look out the window. The old curtains looked like they belonged in a crime scene, so I threw them away. I have a new set at home, but I'm sure I didn't bring them with me. "I guess I'll be waking up with the sun."

After putting my clothes away, I head back to the living room.

"So, this is it. For the next two weeks," I say, doing a three-sixty turn and taking in all the details.

At least there's plenty to keep me busy. Maybe I should check out the storage shed outside and make sure it wasn't broken into while I was away. That's where I store my tools and everything I need to work on the cabin.

I grab my coat, boots, and gloves and head out. The one feature I love about my cabin that none of the other places around seem to have is a wrap-around porch. I guess at some point, the owners expanded the size of their properties and only kept the back decks facing the lake.

It may sound old-fashioned, but there's something really charming about being able to walk all the way around the cabin. You can set a chair or a bench anywhere you want.

You can follow the sun in the winter or the shade in the summer.

Maybe if I come over a few more times this spring, I can have the cabin fully finished by the summer. The thought gives me a new sense of purpose.

I'm glad to see the lock for the shed is still intact. I open it and grab my toolbox before closing it back up.

When I'm rounding back to the front door, I see the neighbor half-inside the trunk of his car, looking like he's struggling to get something out.

I set the toolbox by my front door and walk over to help. He doesn't look like a big person. Maybe it's the owner's kid.

"Hey, do you need help over there?" I ask.

The snow slows my steps but not by much, so I'm only a few feet from the guy when he pulls his head out of the trunk.

Pink cheeks and a bright-red nose from the cold, but those same forest-green eyes.

Who did I upset in a previous life?

"Coach!" Bubble says, with the biggest smile, as if he's just bumped into his best friend. "What are you doing here?"

"I live here…I mean…um, I own the cabin next door." Fuck. Why can't I string a whole sentence in the presence of this guy?

"Oh wow, that's…what a coincidence," he says, his smile widening. If that's even possible.

I'm pretty sure if Bubble was connected to a power source, he'd be lighting up the Christmas tree in the Windsor town square.

"I mean, I don't own that cabin. Have you seen the size of that? But I'm staying there. I know the most generous and stupendous couple, and they let me stay over Christmas."

The cabin is definitely an upgrade from mine. Up close, I can see it's been recently renovated. Even the wooden staircase leading to the front door seems new.

"You're here on your own?" I say tersely before catching myself, but he doesn't seem to notice my clipped tone.

It's none of my business what Bubble does or does not do, and with a cabin that size, I doubt someone as outgoing as he will be spending Christmas alone.

"Oh no, my best friend, Juju. She's coming from LA in a few days, and it's going to be great. She's never seen snow. Can you imagine? She's going to drop dead when she sees all these trees and the white."

I'm mesmerized by Bubble gesturing at the surrounding landscape, lost in his own bubble. If there was ever a time for his name to fit him perfectly, it would be now.

"It's quite magical, isn't it?"

"Yes. Very…anyway, I saw you struggling with something."

He pulls his beanie lower on his head. I wonder if he didn't grow up in a cold-weather state because he seems to struggle with it as much as I do.

"Oh yeah, I need to take my suitcase out of the trunk, but it's stuck. I had to push it all the way back because of all the food."

I should go back to my cabin and avoid Bubble at all costs, but since I came over to help, I can't exactly run away now.

"Okay, let me see." I go around him to the trunk to see where the case is stuck.

I try to wedge it out, but it's not budging.

"Christ, what do you have in here? A dead body?"

"Yeah, I like to carry them around. My therapist says I have attachment issues."

I snort-laugh and end up bumping my head on the inside of the trunk.

"Shit." I reach for my head to see if there's any sign of blood, but I think I'll only end up with a bump.

"Well, at least neither of us is naked this time," Bubble says.

I'm not sure if it's the bump on the head, the freezing cold, or Bubble's smiley eyes. Eyes that are basically all I can see under his coat, beanie, and scarf, but his quick comeback makes me laugh.

It surprises me, and it seems to catch Bubble too because he stares at me for a second too long before pointing at the suitcase.

"Come on, Coach, let's get Jeremy out of the trunk so we can have a hot cocoa by the fire," he says.

"Who's Jeremy?"

"He's the top boss in my dildo collection. What did you think? That I really did have a dead body in there?"

I stare at Bubble, dumbfounded because I don't even know what to say to that.

I sigh. "Let's get Jeremy home then."

Bubble claps as I rescue the suitcase.

He closes his trunk, and since the suitcase seems to weigh the same as three grown men, I also take it up the porch steps.

"Christ. How did you even get this from your place to the trunk?"

"Resilience and determination, Coach." He walks past me to open the door. "Also, a neighbor was walking past. I guess I'm lucky with neighbors, huh?"

Bubble's cabin is most definitely an upgrade from mine. He'd probably run a mile if he saw the old stained wooden floors and the lack of decent furniture.

"Can I treat you to a cup of hot cocoa for helping me?" he asks.

"I really should get going. I have a few jobs to do at my place. Thank you anyway."

He seems disappointed that I declined the invite, but just as I've seen him do several times around other people, he quickly turns it into a smile.

I leave his cabin and walk over to mine, picking up my abandoned toolbox before going inside.

The temperature inside is now considerably more comfortable.

I sit on the couch in front of the fireplace and think of Bubble. He acts like he's made of Teflon, but something tells me there's more to him than meets the eye.

Maybe I've been a little too quick to judge, but it's hard to think straight around the guy who has somehow found a way to rattle my cage like no one else.

I've managed football players, the press, and my ex-wife, and not once have I lost my composure. What is it about this guy that seems to shake my foundations like he's found the winning Jenga piece?

A crumbling tower of memories crashes inside my head, one over-riding them all.

Ben.

I can't remember the last time I thought of him.

He's who Bubble reminds me of. The boy who was so special, so alive, so beautiful, so generous, so kind that he was too good for this world.

My chest is suddenly too tight, but there's no point thinking about a past I can't change.

I just know I need to be careful around Bubble.

8

BUBBLE

I STIR the mint candy cane in my cup and take a sip of my cocoa, letting it warm me from the inside out. Hmm, I love mint-chocolate hot cocoa.

Shame Coach didn't want to stay to have one. Maybe I could have convinced him to have dinner with me or watch a Christmas movie.

He can say what he likes, but the way he keeps looking at me? It's giving me whiplash.

On the one hand, he runs. On the other, he stares at me like if I was a candy cane, he would lick me.

Of course, I had to go ruin it by being sassy.

"Not everyone can take your brand of crazy, Bubble. Sometimes you need to let them in gently," I say Juju's words aloud, like a mantra.

Speaking of which.

I put my phone on its love-heart stand and video call Juju.

This time when she answers, she's on her couch holding a glass of wine.

"What's up, babe? Afraid I've changed my mind about going?"

"I'm glad one of us has the stronger stuff," I say.

Her expression changes immediately, and she sits straighter. My bestest friend. Always ready to defend me. Always willing to kick someone's ass for me.

"Oh, Juju, what do I do? He's *here*. Like, just *there*. You know, before, I didn't know where he was when he wasn't there, but now he's just *there*," I say a little too dramatically, even for me.

"You're making as much sense as ice cream and fries," she says.

"What? That's gross."

"Hey, don't judge. It was the cheerleading finals, and I landed badly coming down from the pyramid. I hurt my ankle, and he-who-shall-not-be-named was a dick. I got home. There was drinking with my roomie. Thus, ice cream and fries ensued."

I shake my head. "Anyway. *He*. You know…"

She's staring at me. Her eyes narrow, and then it hits her.

"Oh! Your coach. Gotcha." She whispers. "He's there…*there*?"

I roll my eyes. "You don't need to whisper. He's not here in this cabin. He's in the cabin next door."

"How do you know? Did you see him through the window?"

"Ugh. Worse." I cover my face with my hands.

"Wait a minute."

She disappears off the screen and comes back a moment later with a bag of chips.

"You're unbelievable."

She stuffs a few chips into her mouth. "Nope. I'm just interested, and I want all the details so I can play matchmaker when I get there."

"You'll do no such thing, Jordana Silva," I say, full-naming her to convey the seriousness of the situation.

She laughs. "Go on, tell me what happened."

So I tell her about how Coach came to rescue me and the suitcase and how he turned down my offer of the most delicious, and in my opinion, un-refusable hot cocoa.

"Wait, you told a man you believe to be straight about the collection of dildos you're traveling with?"

I shrug. "Yes…? I'm such a mess."

"Oh, honey. You're not a mess. You just…love too easily. Actually, that's not right. You pick a person to love, and that's it. They're yours. It's what makes you, you, and I never want you to change."

I sag on the chair. "But I know I'm barking up the wrong tree with the coach. Hell, I'm probably barking up the wrong forest. It's just that sometimes there's something in his eyes that tells me he wants something. He just doesn't know what it is."

Juju finishes her wine. "You know my opinion on the fluidity of love. You never know. Maybe your coach might not even realize he's flowing toward you."

"Maybe…" I sigh.

"Gotta go, but keep me updated." She winks and then disconnects the call.

I walk up to the window that faces Coach's cabin. The curtains are closed, but I can see light through a little crack in the middle.

Is he going to spend Christmas on his own? I didn't have a chance to ask.

Outside, snow lightly falls. I look up at the sky.

"What do I do, Grandma? Why do I feel like this particular man is the one I can give my heart to? I know what you're gonna say. *He's older, and one day, you'll be left on your own again.* But what if this is my chance to be happy? To be loved? Doesn't that count? Isn't a few years of one hundred percent love more important than loads of years of fifty percent?"

I close the curtain and go to the main bedroom to take a shower. I've always liked really hot showers, even living somewhere warm like LA. Somehow, I feel more refreshed afterward, but in the cold weather, they really warm me.

As the steam builds around me, I can't stop thinking about the way Coach held on to my arms to save me from slipping on the tiles in the school.

His grip was strong, but it wasn't painful. I wish he'd run his hands over my body.

Goosebumps appear all over as I imagine how shy he'd be at first before he found his confidence, but then there would be no stopping him. He'd take charge, touching me everywhere, putting me at his mercy.

I reach for the soap to wash my body. My dick is so hard that I know a few strokes would make me come. This is so wrong. All these thoughts about a man I can't have.

But then there was his laughter when he bumped his head.

His joking about bringing Jeremy inside.

The bathroom is my sanctuary, and no one needs to know but me and my imagination.

I grab the soap and add a bit more to my hand, lathering it so I'm all nice and slippery.

Reaching behind me, I seek my hole, gasping as my finger teases the entrance.

What would it feel like to have his cock filling me up? Would he push harder when I demanded it, or would he always be gentle?

The coach in my mind seeks my little bundle of nerves with two fingers, knowing exactly how to take me to heaven and back.

I regret not bringing a toy into the shower, but my fingers are doing a good job. I wrap my hand around my cock, and after a few pulls, I'm coming so hard that I see stars in the backs of my eyes.

"Fuck me to the land of Oz and back. If this is what fantasy Coach does to me, real Coach will kill me."

I finish the shower and open the window to let the steam out while I dry myself.

Once everything is tidy, I close the window and settle into the big master bed.

I love that the fireplace is electric because I can have it on a comfortable setting all night.

I'm not sure what I'll do tomorrow. I'd planned on decorating the cabin for Christmas before Juju arrived, but since it's all done, maybe I should start baking.

The oven in the kitchen is top of the range, which is a luxury I'm only afforded at work, so I definitely want to make the best of it.

I open the book I bought at a book fair on the square in Chester Falls.

Maybe it's my recent orgasm or the day full of Coach, but I don't remember any of the words. All I know is that I spend the night dreaming of the big man that has me all twisted into knots.

The man has glued himself to my soul and won't let go.
Not that he knows it.
Which is a Bubbletastrophe.

655

9

COACH

I TOSS and turn all night. First, I'm cold, so I get some more blankets from the closet in the hallway. Then I'm too hot, so I push them down to the foot of the bed.

There's never been a time in my life when I've had trouble sleeping. Mel used to complain about it. She always liked to talk about her day and ask about mine while we were in bed.

She called it pre-sleep chit-chat. But I've always been an early riser, and because I am very active in my coaching practice, I usually fall asleep easily.

Since I can't get any shut-eye, I may as well start one of my many projects around here. One good thing about being married to Mel was that she never let me slack when it came to doing things around the house.

My status as an NFL team coach didn't matter as far as she was concerned. Whether there were games, press conferences, or trips away, I still needed to fix the sink or put a picture up when I was home.

So I have plenty of practice and skill when it comes to home projects. Not to mention all the years I spent helping my dad as a teenager. It seems the women in my life always have something that needs hanging.

I put on an old Marinos tracksuit I've worn more times than I can count and head over to the kitchen. The coffee machine, my one luxury here, brews a fresh pot in the time it takes me to push the couch aside to set up a work space in the middle of the living room.

This could wait until spring, but what else will I do here on my own?

Knowing me, I'll start regretting not taking my parents' offer to join them in St. Barts, and that's just a sad thought for a divorced forty-six-year-old man to have.

I pour the coffee into a cup and take a sip. "Ahh, baby, thank you for that. It's just what I need," I say to the coffee machine, who's currently the best relationship I have in my life.

"So, what shall we do today?" I look around. I could do the floor, but that requires moving more than just the couch, which is now in an even better position in front of the fireplace. I might leave it there for now.

I could change the faucets in the bathroom, but if it all goes wrong, I could end up having involuntary cold showers. Better do that in the spring.

"The kitchen cabinets. That's it." They're old but solid. They just need sanding and revarnishing, and they'll look brand new. I bet under that dark stain is a lighter wood.

I finish my coffee and go get my tools.

By midday, I have one door sanded and one half-done. It's taking longer, even with my handheld sander, because of some of the intricate details I'm finding on the edges of the doors, which were covered by years of grime.

Removing those with a small tool before sanding them isn't fun, but the result is worth it.

I'm finishing a sandwich I prepared for lunch when there's a knock on the door.

There's no need to guess who it is, just a need to prepare myself for the unpredictability that is my current new neighbor.

I open the door, and I'm immediately faced with a box that I guess has something edible inside. This is Bubble, after all.

"Are you hungry? I made you lunch," he says.

I stare at him in confusion.

"Good morning," I say.

He smiles, shyly holding the box to his chest. "Oh yeah. Good morning, Coach. What's your name, by the way? No one ever says it."

I raise a brow, but I'm not about to do an 'I'll show you mine if you show me yours' kind of thing. Especially not with Bubble. "It's Riley. Riley Dempsey."

He cranes his head sideways like he's inspecting me. "Hmm, yeah, I can see it. You're a Riley. You're also Coach though. Anyway. Food?"

"No, thank you. I've just had lunch."

He stares at me blankly. "But I didn't see any smoke coming out of your chimney."

I bite the inside of my cheek to keep from laughing. "Last I checked, adding some cold meat and lettuce to two slices of bread didn't require any special cooking skills."

"You had a sandwich?" His eyes bulge out like I've committed a cardinal sin.

"Yes. Now, can I help you with anything? I'm kinda in the middle of work here."

"No," he sighs, "I guess not."

He walks away, muttering something about nutrition and big chunky thighs. I have no fucking clue what he's talking about, but I'm not calling him back.

I take a deep breath to smell the forest air, but all I get is strawberries.

My dick stirs, so I slam the door shut and go back to work.

There's a TV in the cabin, but I need something louder. Something that'll penetrate my brain and push my thoughts aside.

I turn the radio to the loudest setting and continue my work.

As I see the kitchen cabinet doors lined up behind the couch, I know I made the right decision. It's getting darker outside, but now I can't stop.

My arms ache, and I need a hot shower. One more and all the upper cabinet doors will be sanded.

The wood beneath the dark stain is clear, as I suspected. I'm not a wood expert, but if I had to guess, I'd say it's pine or maybe a light oak.

I can't wait to put them up again. At least I don't have a huge amount of stuff inside the cabinets, so it won't take long to clean them inside and sand the frame.

My belly rumbles, so I prepare myself another sandwich and eat it in a few bites, downing it with a beer as I stand back. For the first time since I bought the cabin, I can see what it will look like when it's all finished.

The sense of pride takes me by surprise. I've had a long career of feeling proud of my achievements through my players' success. Whether it's a team win or a player getting a contract for a bigger team.

I've always felt proud of the barely out-of-high school kids who had never been away from their parents but still gave it their all. Going on to become amazing players and outstanding men, giving back to charity and their community.

But this thing in my chest is new, and I like it. Maybe next time my mom asks me if I've found my happiness, I can tell her I've located some of it.

With renewed energy, I continue to work on the doors until they're all sanded, and I have a neat row of light-wood doors ready to be stained with a clear varnish.

I put them to one side and brush the sanding dust into the trash before finishing it with the vacuum cleaner.

"Now, this is what I call a productive day. Maybe tomorrow I can take a break from work and walk around the lake. Get some fresh air and maybe stop talking to myself aloud."

I think I hear a thud, so I turn down the music and hear someone knocking.

"Bubble, how can I help?" I ask even before my door is fully open.

"Aww, you're using my name," he says.

"I don't have much choice since I don't know your real name."

He puts his finger to his chin like he's thinking about it. "Maybe soon. Anyway, how did you know it was me?"

I chuckle. "Could be a lucky guess, or it could be that I don't know anyone else around here."

He looks around and points at the cabin on the other side of mine. "Really? Why? Are they like…weird people or something?" he whispers.

"No," I whisper back. "I've never seen them before."

"Oh."

"Anyway, how can I help you?"

"You look like you need a shower," he says.

"Thanks?"

"Sorry, that was rude. I'm bringing you dinner since you refused your nutritious lunch."

I sigh. "Bubble, I don't need you to bring me food. I'm more than capable of making my own."

"Did you have a sandwich for dinner?" he asks, resting one hand on his hip while holding the box with the other.

"Yes, but—"

"I rest my case."

"Fine, I'll take it if it makes you happy."

He thrusts the box in my direction and leaves.

"Sorry, gotta run. Have a job to do."

I shake my head and go inside.

After a much-needed shower, I inspect the contents of Bubble's box, and I'm shocked to see a fully prepared meal of grilled chicken, steamed vegetables, and rice. Even though I had my sandwich earlier, I eat every single bite, and it's delicious.

The early day followed by all the work and a full belly makes me tired, so I clean up and retreat to the bedroom. Maybe I'll scroll through the sports news on my phone before I sleep.

I turn the lights out in the kitchen, and as I walk past the window that faces Bubble's cabin, I can't help but look in that direction.

His curtains are drawn back, and while his lights seem to be off, he must have some kind of smaller lamp, or maybe it's the glow from the fireplace.

He's lit from beneath, and he's dancing.

I'm frozen in place as I watch him move gracefully. He's wearing a tiny top that shows his abs and the shortest shorts I've ever seen. On a woman, I'd call them hot pants. But is that the same for men?

Suddenly, he grabs a hat out of nowhere and does some tricks with it before it ends up on his head, and then there's a chair. I don't know where it came from.

He stops, and I think he sees me, but he seems to be talking to someone.

He said he had a job. What kind of job?

I don't even want to think. He waves at something, and then the chair and the hat are gone.

A moment later, he's moving again, this time at a slower pace. He raises his arms above his head, twirling his hands.

It's so fucking sensual. One hand runs slowly down Bubble's arm toward the back of his neck before passing over his mouth. I see his lips follow the trail of his fingers.

He moves to the beat of whatever he's listening to, lost in his own world.

There's no doubt he's a man. For starters, there are no breasts. But he doesn't lack in lines or curves. His stomach is tight, just as you'd expect from an athlete, but when he turns around, there's an unmistakable curve leading to a round and very perfect ass.

I run my hand over my head. Why am I reacting to him? Is it because he's an artist? A dancer? Or is it *him*?

I've never looked at a man and thought about how sexy he is. Though in the past, whenever Mel commented on some of her favorite actors on TV, I couldn't deny they were attractive men.

Fuck, I'm too tired and horny. I haven't had sex with anything other than my right hand in over a year. My brain is fried, and Bubble's strawberry perfume probably has some kind of pheromone power mix.

In my semi-freaked-out state, I don't realize Bubble has stopped dancing and is staring at me through his window.

Naturally, my reaction is to drop to the floor, escape to the bedroom on my knees, and pretend this never happened.

BUBBLE

"Good morning, sky. Good morning, sunshine. Good morning, birds outside. Good morning, snow on the trees…hmm…" I stretch under the covers like a cat and burrow again into my fluffy warm world.

I look at the clock, but it's too early in LA to call Juju to tell her I caught Coach staring at me last night. Damn time zones.

"Okay, world, what shall we do today? Apart from being uh-mazing, of course?"

I get up from the bed and straighten the covers. There's an extra spring in my step, and nothing will burst Bubble's bubble today.

With Juju arriving tomorrow, I double-check that her room is ready for her. I've been turning on the electric fireplace in that room for two hours each day so it gets acclimated to the rest of the house. I know all too well how much colder the cold feels when you're not used to it.

I prepare a bowl of yogurt with my favorite granola and a cup of coffee before scrolling through the news on my phone.

There are some emails from the school and the kids sending pictures of the things they're getting up to over the Christmas break.

I head to the large double doors facing the lake and snap a few photos to send back as my replies.

Once I finish breakfast, I wrap up warm and go for a walk. There's fresh snow on the ground, but it should be okay as long as I don't go too far from the cabin.

I debate for a moment about asking Coach if he wants to come with me, but something tells me he's still hiding from me.

The path along the lake is well marked, and from the foot and paw prints, I can see it's already been well used this morning.

This place isn't too far from Windsor, so I might come over in the summer. I wonder if Mr. and Mrs. C would let me stay in the cabin again. This time I'd rent it out, of course.

More thoughts of the coach fill my head—as if they ever leave.

There's not a shadow of a doubt he watched me last night. I wasn't dancing like that for him on purpose.

If I had been, I would've put on a better show. But when I started the video call with a friend to show him some choreography moves for his audition, it was still daytime, and my curtains were drawn back. I didn't notice when it became dark outside.

The music I'd been playing changed from the upbeat tempo of my friend's audition song to something more mellow, and I felt like swaying to the sound of the melody.

Most days, I'm at the coffee shop, the school, or traveling between. I love both my jobs, but it can leave me with little time to do anything else. Enter my obsession with Coach Riley, and I have even less time.

Last night, I lost myself in the music. I stopped thinking about anything and just felt. It was beautiful, and then I opened my eyes and saw Coach watching me from his window.

He seemed lost while staring at me, so I wondered if he was even watching. When he vanished from the window, I knew I was right.

Now all I want to know is if he liked it. And I'm terrified that the next thing out of my mouth will be something that'll push him further away.

I stop and look up at the sky, filled with snow clouds. "Grandma, you need to give me a hand with this. If he's the one, I need something. Anything. Come on, it's Christmas, and you already owe me a bunch of presents from all the years you've been gone."

By the time I get back to the cabin, it's almost lunchtime, so I take a hot shower and then make myself a warm drink and something to eat.

I feel rejuvenated from my walk, so I think I'll make the cookie dough for the Christmas cookies this afternoon.

The cabin has a TV, but I don't feel like watching anything. I tune into a local radio station on the Crawford's stereo.

Christmas music fills the cabin, and I twirl around as I line up the ingredients I need to make the cookie dough.

There's no mixer in the cabin, but that's not a problem because I brought mine, just in case. I set it on the worktop, which is when I remember I'm not wearing my apron. And I'd rather not get flour all over my clothes.

I'm whistling along with the tune on the radio when my phone dings.

I grab it mindlessly and see a message from my friend.

Bubble, I owe you big time. I nailed the audition, and they've offered me a part. I'm going to be a backup dancer in an off-Broadway show.

I am going to kill that little bastard. My fingers fly over the keyboard as I type my reply.

Brandon, you sneaky little shit, why didn't you say THAT was what you were going for?

The speech bubbles start immediately.

Because you'd have been more nervous than I was. This way, I got pure unrestrained Bubble. And it worked. You really should come to New York.

I smile.

Nah. Too big for me. My bubble would burst too quickly, and there would be no more Bubble left.

I see the speech bubbles again, so while he's typing, I quickly run to my bedroom to get the apron from my suitcase.

As I return, I glance out the window and see smoke coming from one of the windows on Coach's cabin.

Oh shit. Shit. Shit.

I slide my feet into my boots, not bothering to tie them, and run over there as fast as possible. I knock on the door.

"Coach? Are you there?" There's no answer.

Ugh, can I knock the door off? I mean, I can do a bunch of cheer-leading stunts, so I can try.

I knock again. "Riley! Coach? Are you okay?"

I'm banging so hard on the door that when it opens, I fall forward and land with my hands on a chest. A naked, hairy chest.

Grandma, I never knew you had it in you, but thank you. Best. Christmas. Ever.

I take a step back, reluctantly letting go of that oh-so-de-ugh-licious chest, which is when I notice there's nothing but a towel around his waist.

Don't hyperventilate, Bubble. And for the love of all things sweet. Do. Not. Look.

I war with myself in front of the semi-nude man of my dreams while he's completely unaware that if he told me to roll over and bark, I'd do it.

And, of course, I fucking look. Who wouldn't?

He has the most perfect-looking bulge under that towel. I bite my lip.

"What's wrong? Why are you knocking on my door like the world's about to end?" Coach asks.

I open my mouth to talk, but it's as if the connection between the part of my brain that makes words and the part that instructs them to come out is broken.

"Can you not stare?" he asks.

"I'm sorry…um…I saw smoke…there was…"—I point to the area where the smoke disappears through the window— "smoke."

He scratches his head, which causes his pecks to flex, killing my two remaining brain cells.

"I put bread in the toaster before I jumped in the shower. It got stuck, so the toaster didn't turn off. Unfortunately, burned toast makes a lot of smoke, so I opened the window to let it out."

"Oh, so no imminent danger of your cabin burning down," I joke.

"Not today. Look, I feel a little underdressed here. Do you mind?" He gestures for the door.

"No, I don't mind at all. I guess we're even now, Coach. Although…" I take a step forward and whisper. "I had a lot less towel than you, so you still owe me." I wink.

"Get out," he says with a clipped tone, taking me so much by surprise that I step back and almost trip on my bootlaces.

I run back to my cabin.

When the door shuts behind me, I close my eyes, feeling every single bit of my pride dented, and then I close the curtains on the window facing Coach's cabin.

My phone is full of notifications, and I remember I was messaging Brandon before I saw the smoke. There's a bunch of worried texts, which I don't understand, so I scroll up to where I left off our conversation.

I know you won't want to see this, but I figured it'll be all over the news, so it may as well come from a friend. Click the link and call me after if you want to talk. Love you xx

I click on the link in the message below, which takes me to a sports news website. I almost fall to my knees when I read the headline.

Harley Bruce makes history as the first-ever NFL male cheerleader.

I skim through the article as the journalist gives a brief history of Harley's cheerleading career leading up to this key moment.

What they're missing are all the lies he told from the moment I met him until he ruined my dream.

11

COACH

THE MAN HAS BEEN FUCKING with my head since I met him. The fucking inspirational quotes. The fucking pen holder. All the fucking cakes.

And even when I came to the place I bought to be on my own, he's still fucking here.

I spent all morning chopping wood because it was the only activity I could do to expend the most energy. It wasn't until my back was killing me and my stomach demanded food that I stopped.

All fucking morning, I couldn't get the image of Bubble dancing from my head, and that was after a restless night where he seemed to be the main character in all my dreams.

And then, he turns up again to check on the non-fire I caused by leaving the toaster unattended for five minutes.

I get dressed and throw some shit between two slices of bread. I need to learn how to cook if I want to have more than sandwiches for lunch and frozen meals for dinner.

My phone rings and I answer without looking to see who's calling. "What?"

"Riley John Dempsey, is that how you answer a call from anyone, let alone your mother?"

Shit.

"I'm sorry, Mom. I wasn't thinking. Just having a bad day. That's all. How's your vacation?"

"It's wonderful. We're just calling because we saw the news about the weather up where you are and we're worried. It looks like there's a bad storm coming your way."

With all the thoughts of Bubble and working on the house, I haven't turned the TV on in days.

"I'll have a look at the news later. Don't worry. I have enough food and firewood to keep warm."

She relays the message to my father.

"As long as you're okay. We do worry about you, you know?"

I sigh. "Mom, I'm not a child. I can look after myself."

"I know, I know, but you've never really lived on your own. It's a big change."

"It's a change I needed, and I'll get used to it." Not to mention I'm forty-freaking-six years old.

Christ.

"Anyway, how are your projects going?" Mom asks.

"Well, I thank Dad for everything he's taught me about woodwork because my kitchen is starting to look as good as new." I can't hide my pride as I tell them about my progress with the kitchen and what I'm going to work on next.

"Just remember to also rest a little, honey. It's Christmas, after all."

Her mention of Christmas reminds me of the cabin next door with all the decorations. Or rather, the person staying in it.

"Mom, can I ask you a question?"

"Of course, dear."

"Do you remember my friend, Ben?"

She pauses. "Yes," she says, and I can hear the sadness in her voice.

"What do you remember about him?"

"He was one of those rare people with a special soul. Such a kind-hearted boy, always cheerful and wouldn't hurt a fly."

I remember Ben rescuing a baby bird that fell from a nest and spending the afternoon trying to climb a tree to put the bird back with its family.

"For a while, I thought…" Mom laughs.

"Thought what?"

"Oh, it's silly and doesn't matter anymore. I clearly got it wrong."

"What do you mean?"

She lets out one of her *this is a pointless conversation* sighs but answers my question.

"I just thought that you and he might have feelings for each other, you know? You two were inseparable. All you talked about was Ben this, Ben that. But then that god-awful accident happened and everything changed."

My breath catches. "Mom, say that again."

"Which part?"

"That last part. You thought I was gay?"

She sighs again. "I didn't know. You always kept everything so close to your chest unless you were talking about sports. When Ben came along, I wondered if maybe you were into boys. When Ben died, you closed off again and didn't speak about another person until Mel. I saw you were truly in love and she was the one for you, so that was that."

I'm not sure how to digest what my mom has said, so all I muster is, "Thank you, Mom."

"Well, I don't know what that was about. I hope you're feeling okay and not drudging up old memories and feeling sad. Especially this time of year."

I groan. "Mom."

"Yes, yes, you're forty-six. I'm just saying. I still worry about my only son. Anyway, we must go. Stay safe out there, honey."

"Bye, Mom. Love you."

The call with my mom leaves me paralyzed to my core. For the second time in a year, I feel like my whole life has been a lie. But this time, it's all my fault.

Did I repress my childhood memories? Was it because I was grieving for the friend I lost? Or was it because I felt more for him and didn't know it at the time?

Even though Ben has been hiding in the recesses of my memories all this time, now it's as if he was never gone. His floppy dark hair that wouldn't hold a style, no matter how much he tried. The happy brown eyes that always made me feel like life was an inside joke between the two of us.

Has Bubble reawakened something that's been lying dormant inside me? Did I repress my feelings for Ben to help me through the traumatic way he was taken from us?

"Fuck," I say aloud.

And what does this mean? Could I be gay? No. I loved Mel, and when we were together, I always desired her in every way. Am I bisexual? Pansexual?

I've never felt arousal in the presence of another man, and I've lived my life in locker rooms full of athletes that are desirable by anyone's standards.

But I get hard when Bubble is around. Just the smell of his strawberry shampoo, shower soap, or whatever it is, drives me insane. I got hard watching him dance yesterday. His sunny disposition never fails to make me smile, no matter how much I try to deny it.

And I fucking got hard earlier when I had nothing but a towel on. I was dangerously close to showing Bubble the effect his presence has on me.

I let out a long sigh.

It's not his fault that I'm so messed up.

All he's done is try to look after me, even when I didn't ask.

I owe him an apology.

It may be snowing outside, but I don't care. I grab my boots and coat and the keys to the shed where I keep my woodworking tools.

I can't cook a meal to make up for being a dickhead, but I can do something else.

Thirty minutes later—with both my nuts about to shatter into tiny frozen pieces—I've collected everything I need, and I head back to the cabin.

The snow is coming down heavier, so maybe my parents are right and we're on the path of a storm.

I wonder how Bubble is coping on his own in the cabin. He comes across as a social person, which is why I think he bakes for everyone. It's a good excuse to talk to people.

Does he feel bored on his own? Is he warm?

He said he's waiting for his friend to arrive. Is that tomorrow? Christmas is in just two days.

Now I feel guilty for being so wrapped up in my own world that I never checked on his. He came to me to offer food twice. He came when he thought my life was in danger, and I didn't even check if he knew how to keep a fire going.

No clue as to who wins the prize for asshole of the year.

I put all my work aside to focus on my apology gift for Bubble. It takes me the rest of the afternoon and into the evening, but I finish it.

12

BUBBLE

"Okay, world. It's a new day. Let's make sure we don't upset anyone. Let's not look at the news. And Juju is coming later, so yay!"

I push the bed covers down and get up.

"And, Grandma, I'm not talking to you today. Well, apart from this part where I'm telling you I'm not talking to you. And if you must know why, it's because after you gave me almost-naked Coach, he shouted at me. Not to mention the news about he-who-shall-not-be-named."

Along with my new positive outlook, I should also change the bedsheets. Tonight, I shall sleep in fresh linen and have nice dreams.

But first, clothes and then breakfast.

I pick the pink skinny jeans that make my ass look amazing and always make me feel like I can take on the world, and then I line up my Christmas sweaters.

"Which one shall I wear today?"

The red one with the pink hearts is perfect, but I'm not sure I'm feeling the love today. The green one is…too green. I open my suitcase again and find exactly what I want to wear. The sweater I knitted with my grandmother.

It's not the prettiest or perfect, but it's bubblegum pink, has

Christmas trees, and something tells me this one is the one I'll need today. I put it on over my cotton T-shirt with the pink rainbows and leave the room to face the day.

As soon as I get to the living room, I notice a heavier layer of snow on the back deck. It's a shame it's cold because I'd love to sit outside. But definitely not now. I shiver just at the thought, even though it's warm inside.

I've been waiting for Juju to arrive so we could turn on the Christmas tree lights together. It's so tempting to turn them on for a little bit, but I won't do it because the big reveal won't be as special.

Still, the tree is such a wonderful sight that I eat my pancakes while sitting cross-legged on the floor in front of it like I used to do when I was a kid.

Our tree wasn't like this one. It was much smaller, and all the ornaments were handmade and passed down through the generations. They're all in my car. Somehow it doesn't seem right to mix them with all these pretty store-bought ones.

But it's okay, I'll use mine again next year.

I clear my breakfast plate and quickly change my bedsheets, putting the dirty ones in the washer before I forget.

"That's one job ticked off the list. Well done, today-Bubble."

I remember Juju's favorite chocolate-chip cookies just in time. They need to cool in the fridge before baking, so I should prepare the dough now.

No need for recipes with this one. I watched my grandma make these cookies so often that even if she hadn't given me the recipe, I'd still know how to make them just from my heart. As easy as breathing.

I'm putting the batter to chill in the fridge when there's a knock on the door.

"Holy cake batter. Grandma, what have you done?"

There can be only one person on the other side of the door. My hands shake as I walk to answer it. I really don't like it when people are upset with me, and yesterday, Coach really was upset with me.

"Deep breaths, Bubble. Maybe he just needs to borrow a cup of sugar... or maybe he had a lobotomy and forgot how you've basically been throwing yourself at him for months in a not-very-subtle way. Yeah, he probably just needs sugar…"

Another knock.

"Bubble?"

I open the door slowly.

"H…hi? Do you need sugar?" I ask.

He stares at me and then laughs.

If he's laughing, maybe he's not too upset…right?

"No, I don't need sugar. But I do need to apologize to you. Can I come in?" he asks.

I stare at him. Wha…what?

"Bubble," he calls.

"Yes…"

"It's a bit cold out here."

"Sorry. Come in, I just…" I laugh. "For a moment, I thought you said you were coming to apologize. That's funny. Let me put some sugar in a small box for you."

I go back inside and leave the door open. He follows me, and I hear him shake the snow off his boots. When I turn around, he's right there in the kitchen with me. His boots are by the door.

"You didn't need to take your boots off. I could have brought you the sugar. I know those laces are a pain in the butt to do up. You would think a state that expects snow on a yearly basis would have invented some kind of slip-on boots or something."

"Bubble," he says, catching my arm and holding me in place. His nearness feels unsettling, especially because, this time, I'm not the one causing said nearness.

It also feels so good when his big hands hold my arms, just like that time in the locker room. Coach is strong but gentle, and my mind can't help thinking about other things.

Does everybody feel like this? Is this how people know they found their one? All the tingles from the tips of your toes to the ends of your hair. Your heartbeat going crazy. And you just want to get close to them.

And what happens when you find your one and they don't find you back? Do you just hurt forever? That…that would be so sad.

"Hey, Bubble. Where did you just go? You look like you're about to cry," Coach says.

"Oh, nothing. Just lost in thought. I don't know why you're here. I'm really sorry about yesterday…and all the days." I move my eyes away from his.

He sighs. "Come, let's sit." He leads me to the couch, adds another log to the fire, and sits next to me.

"We're sitting," I prompt, stating the obvious.

He smiles, but his expression changes as he looks into my eyes. "I've been an asshole to you and want to apologize. I shouldn't have spoken to you the way I did yesterday. You were worried about my safety at the expense of yours. For the love of god, you didn't even have a coat on."

"I'm sorry."

"No, please stop apologizing. You didn't do anything wrong."

"Okay," I say. "Can I ask you something?"

"Sure."

"Do I make you uncomfortable? Like…am I too much, too in your face"—I look away—"too gay?"

I don't know where the sudden courage to ask him these questions comes from, but it's out there now and can't be taken back. Maybe it's too much to hope he'll say what I want him to say. But if not, then I don't understand him.

Sure, most straight guys don't like getting attention from gay guys, but he hasn't exactly been pushing me away. He never told me to stop baking for him, never took down the inspirational posters. He didn't trash the pen holder.

"What's your real name?" he asks, and I don't know why this is important to him, but I give in.

"Curtis John Merroll."

"We have the same middle name," he says.

I smile. What an inconsequential piece of information, but somehow, I feel it opens the door between our worlds so we can finally meet.

"Why Bubble?"

"I was raised by my grandmother. She used to call me Bubble. Said

I was always in my own little world. Nothing and no one could ever burst my happiness. It was as if I floated under the power of my own special magic. It kinda stuck after that." I scrunch my nose. "And it's a thousand percent better than Curtis."

He laughs. "Thank you for telling me that, Curtis."

If he was anyone else, I'd punch him in the ribs until he called me Bubble, but hearing my real name for the first time in years coming from his lips is indescribable.

This man is going to grind my heart into dust, and worse, I'm going to let him.

"You didn't answer my question," I say.

He leans forward, resting his arms on his knees, staring at the fire in front of him.

"Yes, Bubble, you make me uncomfortable, but not—"

My phone rings, interrupting Coach. I want to throw it to the other side of the room because I need to know what he's going to say next, but when I see Juju's name come up, I freeze.

She's supposed to be mid-flight, and last I checked, you don't get Wi-Fi in Basic Economy.

"I need to get this," I say as I swipe the screen.

Coach nods.

"Juju, who did you flirt with to get an upgrade?" I ask.

"Huh?"

"You know," I say, stating the obvious, "your upgrade. Is he super sexy? Did you get his number to see him again?"

"Bubble, honey, my flight was canceled. Haven't you seen the news? Everything is closed because of the storm."

I'm glad I'm sitting because if I was standing, my knees would buckle.

"The…storm?"

She sighs. "You've been baking and singing Christmas songs and totally forgotten about the world, haven't you?"

"You're half right," I say.

"I'm so sorry, honey. I hate that you're all on your own out there. Maybe we can have our Christmas dinner and open our presents together via video call."

She's trying to sound positive, but I can hear the disappointment in her voice. She forgets I know her as well as she knows me, but I play along.

"Yeah, sure, let's do that," I say.

"Okay, speak to you later."

She ends the call, and I just stare at my phone for a moment.

"Is everything okay?"

I look up.

Crap, I forgot Coach was here. You're okay. You're strong. This is going to be okay.

"Yeah, sure. It's just my friend. Looks like her flight is canceled, so she can't come after all. Anyway, can I get you a coffee or something?"

I stand and walk to the kitchen before Coach answers. He follows me, but I ignore him. Maybe if I click my heels together, he'll disappear back to his cabin. Then I can feel sorry for myself for a little while until I can face him again to finish our conversation.

I mentally run through what I packed, and sadly, I don't think I have any red heels. I guess my fluffy pink slippers will have to do. And cake, of course.

"Bubble, are you okay?"

"Of course. Why wouldn't—"

Suddenly the front door to the cabin opens with a thud and the blondest child with the bluest eyes I've ever seen runs inside.

He stares at me and gasps.

"Are you our Christmas elf?"

13

———

COACH

THE KID's face is comical. He looks around the cabin, and with each thing his little blue eyes focus on, there's a new gasp of wonder.

A moment later, a little girl comes running in and almost bumps into the boy.

"Look, Megan, we have a Christmas elf," the kid says.

The girl gets closer to the boy and says in a hushed tone, "Are you sure he's not a stranger?"

"No, you silly. Look, he's small, wearing Christmas trees, *and* there's Christmas decorations everywhere."

"Oh yeah," the girl says, looking around the cabin and then turning to Bubble. "Do we need to go outside so you can finish your elf job? It's a little cold, but we can wait. Will we get in trouble with Santa?"

She holds the boy's hand and pulls him toward the door, but the boy doesn't budge.

Bubble looks up at the ceiling and mumbles something I can't make out before looking back at the kids.

"Sorry, kids…I'm not an elf. Also, not small," he says, going around the kitchen island with his hands on his hips, sounding quite indignant. "I'm perfectly formed, thank you very much."

I almost snort-laugh at his comment.

"Holy snakes, even his pants are pink," the girl says.

"They're awesome, right?" Bubble says, twirling on the spot. "Anyway, I'm Bubble. Who are you?"

"I'm George, but you can call me Gigi, and this is my sister, Megan."

I'm pretty sure I'm the only one in the room finding this situation a little…strange.

Bubble smiles and crouches to their level. "Are you twins?"

"No, silly. We're not really brother and sister yet. Our dads are getting married in the spring," the girl says like that explains everything.

"And where are your dads…?" Bubble starts.

"Don't worry. We can distract them," George says.

"Or maybe they can't see you because they're grownups, right?" Megan adds. "Only children can see you."

"Yeah. Don't worry, they're all kissy, kissy anyway, so you can finish deco—" George stops and looks at me. "Who's he? Is that your boss? He doesn't look like an elf."

Megan gasps. "Is that…Santa?" And then she hushes again. "Is he supervising you to make sure you do a good job? Are you going to get a promotion? My daddy got a promotion at work."

"Your dad works for Santa?" Bubble asks, and I groan.

"Curtis, has it occurred to you to question who these children are, where they came from, and how they got through the door?"

Bubble stares at me like he's about to state the obvious. "They're Gigi and Megan. They're probably staying in another cabin and got in because you didn't close the door all the way."

"And I'm also *probably* Santa Claus."

Both kids squeal. "Are you really?" George asks.

"Who's really what? In trouble for not helping out? You both are," a deep voice says before a tall guy comes into the cabin holding two large boxes.

A slimmer guy with long blond hair carrying a suitcase follows him. "I can't believe we made it, bab—"

Bubble is rooted in place as the two guys put their stuff down and slowly come to the realization they're not alone.

"Daddy," Megan says, pulling the hand of the bigger guy. He crouches to her level, and she whispers something in his ear. He frowns and then looks at the other guy holding onto George.

"We'll see, sweetheart. I'm not sure we have enough room for… um…elves to stay until Christmas…or Santa."

Bubble takes a small step backward like he's feeling intimidated or unsure, which I never thought I'd see in him. He always looks so confident and unrattled.

"Hi, I'm not sure what's happening, but who are you?" he asks.

"I'm pretty sure we're the ones who should be asking that, but for the sake of making this less awkward, I'm Fletcher Crawford, this is Harrison, and I own this cabin. You are?"

Bubble opens and closes his mouth, looking at both men and then at me before looking back at the Fletcher guy.

"You're Mr. and Mrs. Crawford's son and fiancé?"

Fletcher nods.

Bubble sags against the kitchen counter.

"I'm Bubble. I work at the coffee shop your parents often visit in Chester Falls. They kindly offered to let me stay here for Christmas. My friend was coming to stay with me, but her flight was canceled. They said you'd be in Florida."

Harrison shakes his head, and Fletcher looks apologetic.

"I'm so sorry. This is all my fault. When they told us about their traveling idea, we knew that if we said we were coming here for Christmas, they'd cancel their plans to stay with us. We knew how important this trip was to them." He looks at his partner. "So I made up a little white lie."

"We're going to Disneyworld in the spring, right, Daddy? After your honeymoon?" Megan asks.

"Yes, honey. We are."

"We're not allowed to lie," George says matter-of-factly. "It's a really bad thing, but Daddy explained it was okay just this one time because it was to help Grandma and Grandad."

Fletcher smiles at his kid, and I can't help smiling too.

"Well," Bubble says, a little too chirpy. "It's a good thing I've changed the bedsheets already, isn't it? Do you mind if I hang around to pack up my stuff? I'll be out of your way in no time." Then he crouches to the kids' level. "I'll even bake you some chocolate-chip cookies before I go." Then as if he remembers I'm in the room, he turns to me. "I'm sorry, Coach. It looks like I'm leaving earlier than I expected. Maybe we can catch up when school starts…or whenever?"

"Um…yeah, sure." I walk to the door and put my boots on, tucking in the laces instead of bothering to do them up since it's only a short walk to my cabin.

I take one last look at Bubble and leave.

The feeling of unease doesn't disappear when I get inside the warmth of my cabin and slip off my boots. I look around at all the tasks I have to do, but I don't feel like doing any of them.

I wanted to speak to Bubble and apologize. Maybe get to know him better. Who knows, maybe we could even be friends.

The gift I made for him is still on the kitchen table. I'd planned on giving it to him later.

I guess it'll be a post-Christmas present, I think as I put it away.

For the first time since arriving at the cabin, I turn the TV on but keep the volume low. Maybe that'll distract me from the fact that Bubble is leaving. I'm unsure why I don't like the idea that he won't be next door for Christmas.

It's not like we were going to spend the day together or anything.

Light snow has started falling again.

My stomach feels weird like I'm hungry but not. I stand again and walk to the fridge, opening and then closing it because I don't see anything I feel like eating.

"What the fuck is happening to me?"

Is this because of Ben? All the memories coming back? Is it because I didn't finish my conversation with Bubble?

Curtis.

I like his real name. It's such a grown-up name. He's right. It doesn't fit him the way Bubble does. I can't help feeling like sometimes Curtis wants to come out, but Bubble works hard to hide that part of himself.

My coffee maker starts spluttering into the pot, making me jump. I forgot I put it on a timer earlier so I'd have fresh coffee for lunch.

I look outside again, and the snow is coming down heavier. Bubble is dragging his huge suitcase down the cabin stairs with the big guy behind him.

What the fuck? How can he go anywhere in this snow?

He's going to get stuck somewhere, or worse, crash into a tree or ditch.

I slip my boots back on and run over to him.

"Where are you going?"

"Joseph, Mary, baby Jesus, and the three shepherds, Coach. Can you not jump a guy like that? I have a skin routine, and this has aged me at least a week."

I do a double-take at all the stuff he says and proceed to ignore it because he needs to see sense.

"You can't go anywhere in this weather."

"That's what we've been telling him," the tall guy says. "But he's adamant he's leaving. We've offered for him to stay in the spare room. The kids can share the couch."

I hold out my hand. "I'm sorry, we haven't been properly introduced. I'm Riley."

"Harrison. Pleasure to meet you."

I nod. "Harrison, are there any hotels or places where Bubble can stay so he doesn't have to drive all the way to Windsor?"

"No. That's what I was telling him. The next town is Stillwater, where we've just come from, and the roads were already getting too dangerous, even for those who know them well."

Bubble waves at me. "Hello? I'm here and can hear you. Thank you. I'm also an adult and can make my own decisions."

"What if the decisions you make are stupid ones?" I say, my voice rising. "Are we supposed to stand by and let you get on the road and kill yourself?"

"Pfft"—he waves me off—"I'm too pretty to die young. God wouldn't do that to me. Besides, what do you suggest? Would you like to share your bed with me?"

I stare at him. He takes a step forward, coming close enough that I can once again smell strawberries. "I'll be the little spoon if you want."

His eyes are filled with challenge. What he doesn't know is that he's challenging the most competitive person he'll ever meet. I wasn't the Marinos coach for nothing.

"Yes, that's exactly what I'm suggesting."

14

BUBBLE

Coach grabs the handle of my suitcase, picks it up like it weighs nothing, and starts walking to his cabin.

I look at Harrison, who shrugs. "Don't look at me. Last time I argued with a dude, I ended up falling in love with him. Let me get the rest of your stuff."

He goes back inside his cabin, and it takes me some time to process the situation.

Did Coach just say…what I think…he just said?

Surely not. "*Must be the cold, and the longer I stay out here, the more brain damage I'll sustain. Next thing I know, I'll be imagining Coach saying lunch is almost ready and we need to decorate a Christmas tree,*" I mutter to myself.

Harrison comes back out with the box containing my mixer and most of my groceries and walks past me toward the cabin next door.

I hurry after him, fresh snow crunching under my boots. Okay, maybe it would be a *really* bad idea to drive in these conditions, but I can't stay with Coach.

That would be horrible and wonderful all at the same time. I'm not sure I can handle it.

Hell, I'm not sure he can handle *me*.

I run up the steps of his porch and almost bump into Harrison as he comes out.

"Be back in a sec with the rest," he says.

"If I'd known you were so eager to get rid of me, I wouldn't have baked the cookies," I say in his direction.

He laughs. "But then you'd have to answer to the two little people in my cabin who still think you're Santa's elf. I'm not sure if I should thank you or hate you for that because it'll be impossible to tell them one day that Santa doesn't exist when they've seen a real-life elf."

I roll my eyes and go inside Coach's cabin.

"What's going on, Coach? First, you're running away from me, then you're coming to apologize, and now you're asking me to move in?" I put my hands on my hips, trying to look indignant, which I know is hard to pull off when you're dressed head to toe in pink with a Christmas tree print.

He ignores me and fills two cups with coffee before turning around and handing me one of the cups.

"I'm only trying to stop you from killing yourself out there by freezing to death. Case in point, you're shivering and you look like a strawberry popsicle."

"I wasn't supposed to stay outside that long. Just long enough to load the car and go."

Coach points to the couch, so I sit and drink my coffee. Harrison comes in a moment later with the rest of my groceries, my coat, and my smaller suitcase.

I feel my face warm at the thought of Jeremy in the middle of Coach's living room. He'll probably kick me out when he realizes, so I keep quiet about it. The coffee is not only delicious, but it's also doing a great job of reversing my frostbite.

"You have a lot of food here," Coach says, looking inside the boxes.

I sag into the couch.

"I was going to cook all of Juju's favorite meals."

He puts away everything that needs to be in the fridge and leaves the rest on the counter.

"I'm sorry the weather has ruined your Christmas plans," he says.

I shrug. "It shouldn't really surprise me. Bad things come in threes. That's what my grandma used to say. I have the first two down."

"Hey." Coach comes over and kneels in front of me. "What's happening? This isn't the Bubble I…well, barely know, but anyway, it's not you. You're positive. Full of energy. Nothing can push you down."

That draws a smile from me. "You're right, Coach. Let's turn the frown upside down, right?"

I stand and walk over to my suitcase. "Where's your spare room?"

Coach's face scrunches a little. "I don't have got one."

"You what now?"

"I only have one bedroom."

I look down at my suitcase. "Jeremy, this is about to become a little awkward." And then I turn to Coach. "When I said…outside…" I gesticulate to the vague area where my car is parked. "You know, me little spoon…"

Coach laughs. "Okay, first of all, I'm an awesome big spoon."

People of this kind planet. It's official. Bubble is deceased.

And then he continues, "But what I mean is that you can take my room. I'm happy sleeping on the couch. I've done it plenty of times before."

"Oh." And now I feel like a deflated merengue for thinking Coach might've actually been serious. I mean, I was also panicking a little at the thought, but mostly, I was hopeful.

Spending the night with those big arms wrapped around me? Where do I sign up? Who do I have to kill or inflict mild pain upon? I'll do it.

"Absolutely not. This is your cabin, and you're doing me a favor by taking me in. I should be the one sleeping on the couch," I say.

"I have a proposal."

"Go on…"

"Since you seem so insistent on feeding me, I'll exchange my bed for your hot meals."

Dammit. I can't fault his reasoning.

"Fine. But if I sleepwalk and end up on the couch anyway, it's your fault," I say.

"Do you sleepwalk a lot?"

No, but I have also never slept under the same roof as the man starring in all my dirty fantasies. I am not responsible for what my subconscious mind gets up to when I'm not awake.

I shrug and point to where I think the bedroom is. Coach nods, so I take my suitcase and make myself at home for the second time in a few days.

Coach changes the bedsheets while I arrange my clothes in color order, which is easy since eighty percent is pink. I leave Jeremy's suitcase closed. Coach doesn't need to see what's in there unless he asks very, *very* nicely.

By the time I come out of the bedroom, I'm feeling hungry and weirdly wired. I wonder if Coach will let me bake something.

I don't see him in the living room, and since the whole place is pretty small, I don't need to guess that he's not in the cabin.

A thudding sound comes from outside, so I look out the window and see Coach stacking wood logs against his shed.

"Holy lumberjacks. The man should come with a warning, and I need a cold shower." I look down at my dick. "You're lucky most of my jeans are too tight for you to give yourself away, you horny piece of Coach-addicted meat."

I step away from the window and fix myself a small sandwich since I'll be cooking Coach a nice dinner later.

Getting my bearings in the smaller cabin doesn't take as long as it did in the other. The place is strangely cozy, though it lacks any kind of personal touch.

There are no decorative pieces or picture frames on the walls. The couch looks old and worn, but the kitchen cabinets look like they've recently been renovated.

"Are you a work in progress?" I say, walking around, touching the bare walls. "I think Coach is a work in progress too."

While Coach is outside and I have free rein in the cabin, I rearrange the contents of the kitchen cabinets. Clearly, Coach doesn't like or know how to cook because most of the stuff here is canned. I take a peek in his freezer, and as I suspected, it's full of ready meals and frozen pizza.

If he thinks he's going to have anything but a good meal while I'm staying with him, he's got another think coming.

I play some music from my tablet and start taking out the ingredients I need for dinner. It's early enough that I can cook the pork slowly, and it'll be nice and tender by dinner. The only problem is that Coach only has one oven so I can't bake a cake.

"Okay, let's make a mousse instead. I think Coach is a chocolate man. What do you think, cabin?"

I sing along to the Christmas music as I create my chocolatey masterpiece. I have Indy to thank for the technique I use to make the mousse extra fluffy, and it never fails.

"You, my beautiful light and fluffy delight, are going to melt in Coach's mouth and make him beg for more."

I'm placing the ramekins with the mousse in the fridge when the video call app rings on my tablet. Juju's photo appears on the screen, so I rush to answer.

"Hey, honey," I say.

"Hey. You're…happy for someone who's been dumped by their best friend."

I put all the dirty dishes in the dishwasher and wipe the counter so it's all clean again.

"Don't make me sad again. I've had too much sad already," I pout and grab the tablet, taking her to the couch where I get cozy in front of Coach's fireplace.

"Hold on. You're in a different place. Where are all the Christmas decorations?"

I gasp. "Oh. My. God! That's what's missing. The Christmas decorations. Stay right there, honey."

"Where would I go?" She rolls her eyes, and I place the tablet on the couch.

One look out the window, and I see Coach is still stacking wood. There's a big pile of cut logs near him, so he might be a while.

I put my boots on and grab my car keys.

"What on earth is going on, Bubble?" Juju calls from the table.

"Shh," I say. "He can't hear us."

"Who's he?"

I ignore her and don't even bother putting on a coat before I step outside.

The biting cold takes my breath away, but this will be quick. I run over to the car and grab the only box that didn't make it into the other cabin. I take it back to Coach's place, but I'm missing one important element...

The thud from the other side of the cabin continues, which works perfectly to disguise my steps as I walk through the snow to the Crawford's cabin again.

After a couple of knocks, Fletcher opens the door.

"Um...sorry to bother you. Do you have an axe?"

He stares at me.

"Oh, I'm not murdering anyone. I just need a tree."

He tilts his head and narrows his eyes. "An axe murderer wouldn't admit to being an axe murderer."

"Have you ever heard of one asking around for an actual axe?"

"Fair point."

"Besides. How many axe murderers do you know that wear pink?"

He seems to think about it for a moment, which is a little scary. Does he actually know axe murderers? I shake my head to clear the ridiculous thoughts.

"Look, I just want to give Coach a Christmas tree. His cabin is like the saddest place on earth. It *needs* some Christmas cheer."

Fletcher goes inside, and a moment later, Harrison comes outside. I'm starting to shiver again, though not as badly as before. Maybe the adrenaline from wanting to make this a surprise for Coach is keeping me warm.

"Fletch says you want a tree?" Harrison asks.

"Yes. It doesn't need to be big."

I follow Harrison into the forest next to his cabin, and ten minutes later, I'm carrying the most perfectly imperfect small Christmas tree back to Coach's cabin. It's a bit wonky, some of the needles have fallen off, and quite honestly, it looks a little sad. It's absolutely perfect.

Harrison helps me place the tree by the fireplace using a spare stand he had in his cabin, then he leaves.

"Hello?"

"Fuck!" I screech.

"Curtis John Merroll. You never…or rarely curse. Which means you're doing something you're not supposed to do."

I pick up the tablet and catch Juju up with the events of the day while I quickly check on the pork. It's starting to smell divine inside the cabin.

"So let me get this straight," she says. "The guy who you have a crush on, but is straight and seems to keep running from you, has invited you to the cabin he owns where he has only one bedroom?"

"Uh-huh."

"Babe, that has bad romance written all over it. You be careful."

"Psht." I wave her off. "Nothing will ever happen. He's straight. But it seems that we can be friends, and friends would decorate each other's cabins if we thought they needed sprucing up, right? What kind of friend would I be if I didn't give my friend the best Christmas?"

She drinks the rest of her tea and quirks a brow. "How many times can you say friend in one sentence? The lady doth protest too much, methinks."

"And methinks it's time for you to go and…do something."

She laughs but blows me a kiss and hangs up the call. I put my tablet on the charger and pick up the box with the decorations.

I sit cross-legged on the floor in front of the tree with the box next to me. The last time I opened this box, Juju was with me. Last year, I couldn't bring myself to take them out.

"Grandma, you better have a plan because my gut feeling tells me this is the right thing to do."

15

COACH

I have no idea how long I stay outside stacking the wood under the tarpaulin on the side of the shed. Two things are certain, I'm definitely not cold anymore, and I have enough chopped wood to last me all winter if I lived here full time.

Sweat runs down my forehead as I grab the last few logs. I'll take those indoors to keep the fire going. Something tells me Bubble doesn't do well in cold weather, which I sympathize with.

I'm still not sure what came over me, basically demanding that Bubble stay in my cabin. I only have one fucking room.

But it's not like I could let him drive in this weather. I just hope I don't come to regret my decision.

The conversation with my parents. The memories of my childhood best friend that I'm starting to think could have been more if tragedy hadn't struck.

Everything runs on a loop in my head.

All because every cell in my body reacts when Bubble is around. Which is fucking annoying because most of the time, his endless positivity and happiness irritate the hell out of me.

I sit on the porch steps even though I can feel the cold snow seeping through my clothes. Christmas music plays inside the cabin, and the smell coming from the kitchen makes my mouth water.

I'll sleep on the floor for the chance to eat whatever Bubble is cooking in there.

So why am I so scared of going in?

I've survived making two of the hardest decisions of my life. Asking Mel for a divorce and leaving the Marinos. Going inside my own log cabin shouldn't be that scary.

After all, Bubble is all of five and a half feet of…

My traitorous brain brings up the memory of Bubble dancing like he was doing it for himself and no one else. The graceful way he moved, looking so free, like nothing can nail him down.

I let out a long breath, and even before I see it disappear in the cold air, I stand and walk inside, grabbing the basket with the logs.

"Dammit, I need to build a mud room or something," I mutter as the snow from my jacket and boots is too much to stay contained within the large matt I have inside the door.

I hang the coat and put the boots on a tray to catch the melting snow attached to the bottoms of the soles.

When I turn around, I wonder if I've stepped inside someone else's cabin.

There's a small Christmas tree by the fireplace with decorations and presents underneath. Twinkly lights are wrapped around the supporting beam in the middle of the room, tinsel hangs from the ceiling… How the hell did he get it that high up?

Is that mistletoe hanging above the couch?

My eyes zero in on Bubble, who's staring at me with a worried expression. He's holding one arm around his waist while the other is in front of his chest.

He's biting his nails nervously, but all I can see is that he's changed clothes. He's now wearing a tight pair of pink yoga pants that highlights every curve of his shapely legs to his slim waist. He's paired it with a wide-necked oversized sweater that falls off his shoulder.

His green eyes are open wide like a scared deer. One wrong move and he might bolt.

Except he's not the one that needs to bolt. I am.

I put my boots back on and pull the laces but don't bother tying them. I tuck them in and leave.

I run toward the forested area by the cabin and keep going until my lungs burn from the cold.

"Fuck." I shout, but it comes out like a cough. "What the hell is happening to me?"

My cabin is like a sensory overload of lights, smells, and everything that wasn't there before, but all my mind can think of is the exposed skin of Bubble's shoulder.

If I hadn't run out of the cabin, I'm afraid I'd have run toward him and done something really inappropriate.

"For fuck's sake, the kid is…a kid. He doesn't even know what he's doing when he throws himself at me."

My dick throbs in my pants. I lean against a tree and palm my erection.

Months of pent-up energy that I couldn't name before bursts to come out.

The heavy snowfall makes it unlikely someone else will be out in the woods. Before I think about it too much, I lower my zipper and take out my cock.

The relief of touching myself is counterbalanced by the cold. But my dick isn't bothered by it because whatever spell Bubble has put me under is enough to melt the ice caps.

The only way I can go back to the cabin is to take care of myself right here.

"It'll take the edge off so you can think clearly around him," I mutter as I stroke my length, trying to stop a moan. I don't know how far sound travels here, and the last thing I want is to be caught.

The tree is rough against my back. I lean my head against it and imagine how it would feel if Bubble was on his knees, wrapping his sweet lips around my cock and fulfilling all the promises he's eagerly teased me with.

The more I think about him, the more I question what the hell I've been doing my whole life.

His practically naked body in the shower, the exposed shoulder, his sweet face hidden by the wool hats, even his sheer determination to get his giant suitcase out of his car.

But even as those thoughts fill my head, I stroke myself furiously until I feel the build-up of my orgasm. I'm panting like a racehorse, my steamy breath floating away in the cold air.

I put my free hand to my mouth to muffle my sound. I can't help shouting his name when my orgasm hits me and I come all over the white snow in front of me, "*Curtis!*"

I put my hands on my knees to keep myself upright when my body wants to let go and relax. In my post-orgasmic trance, it's easy to forget the snow is cold, even if the air around me is finally seeping through my clothes.

When my breathing returns to a somewhat normal rate, I tuck myself in and zip my pants.

"Riley!"

Hearing the call, I move away from the tree and the evidence of what I've just done and walk toward the cabin. But Bubble isn't yelling from the cabin. He's running toward me.

"Riley."

He's holding my coat in his hands and looking at the ground. "I'm so sorry. I…shouldn't have done that without asking you first. I just thought the cabin needed to be cheered up, and I got carried away. I can take it all down. Please don't ask me to leave."

The last few words are an almost-silent plea.

I take the coat from him and put it on. It smells like firewood and a hint of strawberry. The last thing I want is for Bubble to think any of this is his fault, so I lean over a little to encourage him to meet my gaze.

"Hey, you didn't do anything wrong."

"Then why did you run?"

"Would you believe it if I said I forgot my hat outside?"

He rolls his eyes, and I chuckle.

"You're not wearing a hat."

I put my hand on my head. "Oh yeah. I couldn't find it."

He gives me a push, and I take a couple of steps back, laughing.

"I'm sorry. I didn't mean to worry you with my reaction. Honestly? The cabin looked a little sad. I'm happy you added some life to it."

He narrows his eyes. "Sooo, you ran away because you're happy I decorated the cabin…?"

"Let's go back inside. It smelled divine, and my belly is rumbling," I say, resuming my walk toward the cabin.

"No. Don't treat me like I'm dumb. I thought you were better than the rest. I'm leaving." He goes around me at a pace I almost struggle to keep up with.

"Bubble, wait. What do you mean? You're not dumb. You're anything but that."

"Then why are you avoiding my questions? Why are you behaving so weirdly? Do I gross you out or something? Did seeing me in your kitchen look too domestic and you're afraid to catch the gay from me? You know that's not how it works, right?"

He doesn't turn around, but he doesn't need to. I know exactly how fiery his eyes are. How flushed his cheeks are.

I grab his arm and pull him back. He crashes against me, which is when I forget about everything right or wrong. How old I am. How old *he* is. If I'm in the middle of a midlife crisis, or if I've just been asleep my whole life.

Everything dissipates in the cold air around us as I crash my lips against his.

16

BUBBLE

WHEN THE MAN of your absolute dreams slams their mouth into yours, there is only one course of action. Yours truly has broken it down into four easy steps for your convenience.

You're welcome.

Step one: make sure he really is attached to you. Lips to lips. You're a clam. Do not let go.

Step two: climb him like a tree.

Step three: thank your past self for all the squats that gave you those thunder thighs.

Step four: enjoy every second of that kiss before said man realizes what he's doing and has a freakout.

Please, god, let him not have a freakout.

With each pass of his tongue over my lips, I swear I lose a brain cell. Every time he sucks my lips between his, I see the pearly gates of heaven. When his tongue seeks entry into my mouth—spoiler alert, I let it in—I'm sure somewhere there's a headstone with my name on it.

Here lies Bubble. He lived a good life. Died young, but that kiss was so worth it.

Have I ever dreamed of kissing Coach? Duh.

Have I ever thought it would actually happen? Hell no.

Which is why even though he's kissing me, his tongue exploring mine, I still can't get out of my head.

Why am I the one freaking out?

Though not enough to stop the kiss. Stupid, I am not.

His big, strong hands on my ass hold me in place, and I wonder if he can tell what I'm wearing under my yoga pants. We move until I feel something rough against my back. A tree.

My lips must be three sizes bigger already from the way he's sucking them like I'm his favorite flavor of lollipop, but I can't stop kissing him. Or letting him kiss me. At this point, I'm not sure who's in charge here.

He moans, and I open my eyes. His are on me. Dark orbs, laser-focused but also filled with something. Questions? Desire? Who is this man?

Since I'm trapped between him and the tree, and I'm using my super thighs, he releases my butt. His hands cradle my face, and it's the first time he breaks the kiss.

My breathing is labored, and I'm terrified this is the moment something bad will happen.

"You're not dumb, Curtis. You're amazing, beautiful, free, graceful, creative, generous, and you make me feel things I've never felt before in my life. That's why I run. Because I don't know how to deal with all the feelings that constantly ping-pong around my body. Since the day you came into the school with your cheerful and upbeat mood and a box filled with cake, I haven't had a good night's sleep."

I roll my eyes. "Yeah right."

He shuts me up with another kiss, and I catalog all the stupid shit I can say for him to shut me up this way. Oh hell, I can have an encyclopedia before dinner.

I break the kiss. "Oh shit. Dinner."

"Huh?"

Coach stares at my swollen lips, dazed, as he runs his hand over his mouth.

"Dinner is ready," I say.

"Right. Yes, of course."

He puts me on the ground but takes a moment before he releases me.

"Are you okay?" I ask.

"Yes."

"We can talk about what happened later."

He nods.

I take his hand and pull him toward the cabin. Having just explored the back of my throat like he was looking for gold, he better not get funny about holding my hand.

"Do you want to grab a shower while I finish the vegetables?" I ask when we get in.

It's clear he's processing what happened. Hell, I'm processing what happened.

Although I'm sure we're processing it in very different ways.

When Coach goes into the bathroom, I lean against the kitchen counter and stare out the window. It didn't snow the whole time we were outside, but there are a few flakes falling again, and it's getting darker.

How did I miss that?

Apparently, the worst of the storm is due to hit any time now.

This is one of those times I would call Juju and tell her everything. She'd probably argue that I'm being stupid and putting my heart on the line or tell me to stay away from Coach.

I can't do that. I just can't. If there's a little part of him that wants me, I'm going to give myself. All of it.

I hear the shower going, so I start preparing the vegetables. The pork is cooked to perfection, if I say so myself, and the roasted potatoes are perfectly crispy.

"Grandma, I hope you're right on this one because if he doesn't ask me to marry him after this meal, then you've failed as my cooking teacher."

Coach comes out wearing a pair of sweatpants and an old Marinos T-shirt. His hair is still wet from the shower, sticking out in all directions like he got ready too quickly.

"Everything smells amazing. What is it?" he asks.

"Pulled pork belly with roasted potatoes and boiled vegetables."

His mouth literally gapes.

"You did all that today *and* you decorated the cabin?"

"Yup. Now sit and be prepared for the gastronomical orgasm of your life."

He coughs. "Did you just…? You know what? Never mind, let's eat."

He picks his seat while I bring the food over.

"How come there's a tablecloth? I don't have a tablecloth," he says.

"I didn't know how equipped Mr. and Mrs. Crawford's cabin was, so I overpacked. At least now I get to use all this stuff."

He takes a piece of pork, a few potatoes, and a considerable amount of vegetables.

I wait until he eats something.

Self-confidence has never been an issue for me. I can easily get wrapped up in my world and ignore what everyone else thinks about me if I believe I'm fabulous. Now, I'm second-guessing everything I do and think.

What if Coach doesn't like the way I seasoned the pork? What if the potatoes are too crispy? Or the vegetables not cooked enough?

"How did you learn to cook? And bake? Your cakes are amazing. I've had to start running with the kids to keep up with the amount of sugar you feed me."

I laugh. "Eating it is optional. But I'm glad you like my cakes. I've been trying to figure out which one is your favorite."

"I'll let you know one day."

"One day?"

He tastes the pork and moans. "It's in my best interests to keep my options open."

"I shouldn't be surprised since your job is literally to strategize for the winning outcome." I laugh.

He shrugs. "I'm not going to apologize for that. And this is delicious, by the way. You also still haven't answered my question."

"I learned to cook from my grandma. My parents died when I was young, so I was raised by my grandma in LA. She taught me everything I know."

"Sounds like a wonderful woman," Coach says.

"She was."

With the logs burning in the fire, the lights twinkling, and the Christmas tree in the background, I feel like I'm in my own personal Christmas dream.

"I'm really happy you like the food. Nothing gives me more pleasure than to see someone enjoying something I've cooked or baked."

"Oh my god, are you serious? This is the best thing I've had. My ex-wife was an okay cook, but when you spend half your life in hotels, you get to try all kinds of food."

I add a bit of everything to my plate, with a few extra potatoes because potatoes are life.

"I forgot you used to coach the Marinos. What was it like?"

He puts a piece of carrot in his mouth and chews while staring out the window. It's dark outside, so there's nothing to look at.

"It was great," he says. "My dream job. I loved every second of it."

"Why aren't you doing it anymore?"

He lets out a chocked laugh. "It'll take more than a make-out session to get to that topic."

I laugh. "Make-out session? Oh, Riley-Boo. You eat all your veggies like a good boy, and we'll have a make-out session so good you'll forget your name and social security number."

"So I guess we're talking about it then."

I put my elbows on the table and lean my head on my hands. "I guess we are."

17

COACH

I KNEW this moment would come. I replayed it in my head a million times while in the shower. Or at least how I'd imagined it would go.

But now, looking into Bubble's forest-green eyes, I don't know anything anymore.

We finish dinner, and I insist on doing the dishes since Bubble cooked everything.

He disappears into the bedroom, but he's back by the time I'm finished. I drink a glass of water and steady myself for the conversation I probably should have had with myself a long time ago. Except now I'm having it with someone else.

Someone twenty years my junior and who I can't stop thinking about doing things to. Even if I've never done those things before.

After I went to bed last night, I couldn't fall asleep. I still had so many questions. So I did what any respectable old man does. I went on a porn website, of course.

I started off with my usual but changed the category to gay porn.

The relief that came over me when I didn't get hard watching other men have sex almost made me laugh out loud. There I was, watching two men going to town on each other and feeling happy because I wasn't physically reacting to it.

But then one of them looked at the screen. He had green eyes, and soon enough, those green eyes were Bubble's. My dick hardened instantly as the green-eyed guy let his head fall back while his partner kissed his body until it reached his—

"Do you want dessert?"

"What?" I turn to face Bubble as he pulls me from my thoughts.

"I was asking if you wanted dessert." He looks at my crotch. "But if you're offering, then yes, please. I don't even need the cherry on top."

I look down at the outline of my erection in my sweatpants. At least I'm wearing underwear, or I'd be sporting a nice tent with these loose pants.

Bubble giggles but walks past me to the fridge. He grabs a couple of ramekins and then takes two spoons from the drawer.

"Come on, Coach. Let's use that nice couch of yours."

I draw a deep breath before following him, my eyes on the perfect curve of his ass. I've always been an ass man.

I guess that hasn't changed.

"What have you got there?" I ask.

"Not an erection, but if I catch you checking out my ass again, I can't promise it won't happen."

I groan. "Curtis."

I sit on the couch in my favorite spot. I'm not surprised when Curtis sits cross-legged so close to me that all I can smell is his strawberry scent and feel the warmth of his body.

Don't small people usually run cold?

He gives me one of the ramekins and a spoon.

"This is chocolate mousse," he says. "It's one of my favorite desserts, so I only have it on special occasions."

I scoop a portion of the mousse. It looks fluffy and light, like the kind I've had in restaurants.

When I taste it, though, there's a stark difference. It's so much better. The texture melts in your mouth, and the chocolate is rich without being too much. It's absolute perfection.

"Hmm, this is amazing, Curtis. I really don't know how you do everything so perfectly."

He stares at me. "What? Pfft. I don't. I just like making people happy."

"That may be so, but you're a talented baker and cook, and I've seen how you've built the cheerleading team at the school from the ground up."

I notice the skin on his neck reddening. He finishes his dessert and places the ramekin on the floor by the couch, and then looks at me.

The vulnerability in his eyes breaks my heart, especially because I'm probably the reason he's feeling like that to start with.

"I guess we should talk about what happened earlier," I say, placing my ramekin next to his.

"Can I ask one question before you say anything else?"

"Sure."

"Do you regret it?"

"No." I take his hand until he gets the message and straddles me. "I would do it again."

He smiles and puts his hands so lightly on my chest that it's like they're not even there.

"Do you want to touch me?" I ask.

He bites his lower lip. "Yes, but I don't want to make you uncomfortable."

I laugh. "This is about to be the most uncomfortable conversation of my life. I don't think anything you do can make it any worse."

He raises a brow. "Even a blowie?"

I drop my head back. "Fuck, Bubble. I need to think straight."

"I think that's the crux of it," he says. "Are you?"

I let out a breath and hold his hands, resting them against my chest. "I don't know, and that's the most honest answer I can give you. I married young and have only ever been with my ex-wife. I've always considered myself straight. I've never even looked at another woman."

"So...you tripped on a tree log because of the snow and lost consciousness. Sustained some mild brain damage, and when you came to, you decided you wanted to kiss me. Is that it?"

I laugh. "I'm not sure about the brain damage, but I think I've wanted to kiss you for a long time."

"That must have been difficult to get your head around."

He raises his hands to my face and circles my temples with his thumbs until he wraps his fingers around my hair.

"I've always known I like boys. I mean…I wanted to be like the girls. I envied them. But I always knew I wanted to kiss the boys. It wasn't easy growing up being me. I loved all the things no one else in my class loved, so I didn't have many friends. I guess that's when I turned to myself and decided I would be my own best friend."

He smiles, and I see no regret or sadness.

"I love every part of me. Yes, I'm a little crazy. Juju says I'm Bubblelicious. My boss and other friends may use different words to describe me—"

"Alive. That's what you look like to me, Curtis. You are life."

He lowers his gaze. "When you say things like that, you make me want to rip my clothes off and ride you like I'm the last cowboy in Texas. I've never even been to Texas."

I shake my head. "See? Who else would say that?"

"I'd hope no one. I don't deal well with competition." He frowns.

"Competition for what?"

"For you, you big, sexy, silly hunk of almost-silver sexy fox."

I bump his shoulder. "Hey, there's no silver in this fox."

He leans over so he's more on top of me and starts inspecting my hair.

My body, as usual, reacts to his nearness, and he's not immune either. I can tell he's pretending not to notice, but the slight shift in his voice when he tells me he found a gray hair tells me otherwise.

I run my hands up his back and inhale. He rests his head in the crook of my neck, and we just stay like that.

"You always smell like strawberries. It drives me insane," I whisper.

"It's my favorite scent. I use it in my shampoo and shower soap."

He feels so small on top of me. I know he's not fragile. He's an athlete who keeps a fitness regime. I felt the gripping power of his thighs earlier in the forest.

I slide my hands slowly toward the curve of his lower back. His loose sweater hides his shape, but in the position we're in, it's ridden up. When I feel warm skin under my fingers, I can't help wanting more.

"What do you want from me, Riley?" he asks.

Curtis places his hands on my chest and raises his head to meet my gaze.

"I don't know. I just know that you make me want things I've never wanted before, and I'm running out of excuses not to give in."

"Then give in, Riley."

I cup his ass, pulling him closer.

"I don't want to use you, Curtis. You deserve better than to be an experiment, and I can't promise I can give you more. Just because I'm discovering something new about myself doesn't mean I need to act on it."

He sits up, his eyes greener than ever. "Everyone deserves a chance to be themselves. If I can help you discover yourself, please let me do it. Trust me. It's not a hardship."

I laugh.

"I'm not joking, Riley. I'll ride you, blow you, aaanything you want, and I'll even feed you."

I shake my head at the ridiculousness of this conversation. My dick gets harder at his suggestions.

"Think about this as our own Christmas bubble. Whatever happens here stays here."

I look into his eyes to see how serious he is, and he's staring back with the same determination he's had when leaving gifts for me in the coaches' office or bringing me a new cake he's baked. Always confident I would never decline them.

"Our Christmas bubble?"

"Our Bubblelicious Christmas bubble," he says.

"So, how do you propose we start my journey of self-discovery?"

He bites his lip and points down at the very clear hardness in my sweatpants.

18

BUBBLE

I MIGHT BE VERY brave or very stupid, but I think I've just convinced a man, who up until today I thought was straight, to have free rein when it comes to using me.

Juju would definitely have my head cut off as well as my balls.

I know Riley's been hard from the moment he pulled me onto his lap. He may be confused about his attraction to men or me, but his body has no doubts about what it wants. That's a language I speak fluently.

"What do you"—he swallows—"mean?"

"I'm just going to help you take the edge off, okay?"

He nods.

I remove my sweater and help him take off his.

"Christ on a pedestal, Riley." I knew he kept in shape and often trained with his team, but this is a whole new level of sexy I wasn't prepared for.

"You're one to talk," he says. His hands run down my chest, tentatively touching my peaked nipples. "You're so graceful when you move. There's no doubt you're a dancer and an athlete. That day in the locker room...I had to run away because seeing you was too much. I think it was the first time I started wondering about my sexuality. Not consciously, but I was rock hard all the way home, and it didn't go away until I took care of myself."

I gasp. "Tell me what you did." I press my hips against his, and it has the desired effect. There's no need to remove any more clothes. I want him to feel comfortable, but there will be no mistakes here. He's getting the orgasm of a lifetime.

"I went inside my place," he says, leaning his head back on the couch.

"Any particular room?"

"The hallway. I was so hard that it was painful."

I pick up the pace of my thrusts, trying not to moan because what I'm doing to him feels good to me too.

"Did you take yourself in your hand right there and then?"

"Yes."

"Tell me how you like to stroke yourself."

"Curtis," he moans.

I lean forward so we're skin to skin. My nipples are painfully hard and so sensitive to every pass against the hairs of his chest.

"Fine. I like to grip it tightly, with long strokes. Sometimes I twist my wrist as I get toward the head."

I whisper in his hear. "I'll have that head in my mouth soon, Riley. It'll be so good it'll blow your mind."

"Fuck, Curtis."

"I know. Feels good, doesn't it?"

He doesn't answer. Instead, he puts his hands on my ass, turning the tables on us. Suddenly, I find myself lying on my back with Riley on top of me.

"Wrap your legs around me like earlier," he commands, and I obey.

What happens next is the best race to the finish line I've ever not entered.

"I'm sorry, I can't go slow. You feel too good," he says against my lips before taking them in a searing kiss that doesn't stop until we're both crying out through our orgasms.

I don't care that my cum seeps through my underwear and yoga pants. There's no way this won't be messy.

Coach moves only slightly, so most of his weight isn't on me, then peppers my neck with kisses until he reaches my mouth again. It's sweet and tender, and I don't want it to end.

"Riley?" I say when he releases my lips.

"Yeah?"

"I think it's safe to say we know each other well enough that you don't need to sleep on the couch anymore."

He gives a carefree laugh that settles in my chest as a good omen.

"Are you inviting me to your bed, Mr. Merroll?" he asks.

"Since it's your bed, I'm simply inviting you back, except now you get to be the big spoon to your own Christmas Bubble."

He snorts. "You are not going to start referring to yourself as my Christmas Bubble."

"Didn't I just bring you joy?" I pout.

He sucks my bottom lip into his mouth. My dick hardens again, especially as his thick leg is between my thighs, giving me the perfect position to rub against.

I moan. "Riley…"

"Hmm?"

"You keep kissing me like that and I'm not responsible for what might come next."

"Does it end in an orgasm?"

I nod, swallowing another moan. The man has discovered the sensitive spot on my neck. He might not know, but if he keeps licking and sucking my skin, I'll come again in about three seconds.

"Riley."

"Take what you want, Curtis."

Fuck, if I take what I want, I'll be riding his dick. I haven't seen it, but from what I felt when he was hard against me, Riley has top-of-the-range equipment down there.

It's not enough. I rub against him, but I can't get there. I love his weight on me. I love the way he's still sucking and kissing my skin. His hands explore me anywhere they can reach.

I know my pants are a mess, but I need to touch myself, and I'm too far gone to care. I need this orgasm now.

I reach for my pants, but Riley pushes my hand away.

"Let me do it. I've never touched another man's dick, but it can't be that different from mine, right?" The nervous but determined tone of his voice takes me back down a little.

"You don't have to, Riley. We can stop right now."

His eyes are on his hands traveling down my body. "I want to."

"It's going to be messy down there," I warn.

He laughs. "I'm a guy, remember? I know how messy it can get down there."

I want to argue because it's one thing to feel your own mess, but someone else's mess is different, especially when you've never been with a man. The last thing I want is for him to backtrack because of the ick factor.

"Hey, Bubble. Get out of your top head so I can rub your bottom head and give you an orgasm."

I stare at him. "Did you just Bubble me?"

"I did." He kisses me. "Now, let me make you feel good because we both need a shower, and it's getting late."

He pulls my pants down, and I cringe at the thought of my cool cum all over me. Riley truly doesn't seem to mind because the next thing I feel is his strong hand wrapped around my length. *Holy mother of Christmas hand jobs, the man has skills.*

We're practically glued head to toe, staring into each other's eyes as he seems to study my reactions.

I want to close my eyes and give in, but the competitor in me wants to challenge him.

He leans his forehead against mine and whispers, "You can resist all you want, Curtis, but you may as well let go before I make you."

My cock feels hard and flushed like I haven't come in a week.

"I like that you're soft everywhere," he says. "Not that I'd mind if you had hair, but all these places I'm touching with my hand, I want to taste them tomorrow. I want to see if you taste like strawberries all over, Curtis."

I'm practically rutting against him in rhythm with his strokes. Then he stops. I'm about to complain when his hand slides down until the pads of his big fingers touch my recently neglected hole, and I'm done.

I open my mouth to shout his name as I'm coming, but he slams his mouth onto mine and swallows my moans, kissing me as I ride the orgasm until I'm practically ready to pass out.

"You…Mister…Coach…" I say, breathing heavily, followed by a yawn. "…are the devil."

He chuckles and then gets up from the couch, taking me with him.

"Where are we going? Can't I just stay here in front of the fire, all cozy and warm?" I ask, struggling to keep my eyes open.

"Trust me. You'll thank me in the morning."

I'm pretty sure I fall asleep halfway through my shower…our shower. Holy ravioli, I'm taking a shower with Coach Riley Dempsey.

"Thanks, buddy, you did good today. We'll play some more tomorrow," I mutter.

"Are you talking to your dick?"

"Yes. Everyone needs a little praise, and tonight was a special night for him. He's been looking forward to this for a looong time."

Riley laughs, rinsing my shampoo, which was already in the shower because I cleaned up after cooking earlier.

When he's done, he tilts my head up. "Tonight was a special night for me too, Curtis. Thank you for listening and understanding. And thank you for making me feel so comfortable. I know we could have done other things that you're—"

"Don't finish that thought, Riley," I say, interrupting him. "Tonight was perfect. If you're discovering yourself, one of the most important things is to be accepting of yourself. Everything we did was beyond amazing. Now take me to bed because tomorrow is Christmas Eve, and we have a packed day."

"We do?"

"Yes. We have to bake cookies, build a snowman, turn on the lights on the Christmas tree, pick the perfect place to leave treats for the reindeer, and probably have some sexy time."

"Probably?" he asks, cupping my ass.

"Definitely. One hundred percent."

We dry out as much as we can be bothered to and then go to Riley's bed. I try not to overthink it because my mind and heart are pushing all these wonderful thoughts about a lifetime of bliss with my Coach. So before my brain starts planning my own wedding without my consent, I get under the sheets and cuddle up to him.

"Hmm, you're the perfect big spoon," I say, yawning again.

"You're perfect."

He wraps his arms around my waist, and as I drift off to sleep, I hope we haven't taken too many steps too fast. Because going from straight to sleeping naked with a man in less than twelve hours has to be a record.

Go, Bubble!

Thank you, Grandma. You really are the best.

19

COACH

I WAKE up lying on my back with Bubble wrapped around me as if he's afraid I'll run away while he's sleeping.

Mel was never a cuddler in bed. Always complained I was too hot and made her sweaty. She liked to talk before bed, and we never had an issue with our sex life. But when it came to sleeping, she turned away and fell asleep like I wasn't even there.

Bubble shivers a little, so I pull the covers up to his shoulders. He lets out a contented sigh.

Feeling someone in my arms in bed is nice. It's Christmas Eve, it's cold outside but warm under the covers, and I wonder how long we can stay like this before he wakes up. He seems to have quite an ambitious schedule for today, not including his plans for us.

Christ, what turn has the world taken that I have a man in my arms and everything feels just right? Why am I not freaking out over this? He called it our Christmas bubble. Is that why? Because while we're here, we're safe, and no one has to know?

I don't want to be that person. Too many of my players have been in that situation, and I've watched as fake girlfriends turned up for events while their long-term partners were at home.

While it wasn't my place to make them come out before they were ready, I have control over my life. From the conversation with my parents, I already know they'd accept me being with a man, and I have no doubts about my work.

It's really all down to me. Am I ready if the only person that makes me feel this way is young enough to be my son?

Bubble makes the cutest sound and stretches like a cat. When he opens his eyes and looks at me, his smile takes my breath away.

"Merry Christmas Eve, Riley."

"Merry Christmas Eve, Curtis."

He stretches up to kiss me, and I help him by placing my hands on my current favorite place on his body. His ass. I'm sure I'll find other favorite places, but I haven't had a chance to explore yet.

"My name doesn't sound so awful when you say it," he says.

"What people call you is an extension of who you are. Most people call me Coach because it's all I am."

He rests his chin on my chest. "No. It's all you let people see. Like Bubble. You're the only one who's seeing Curtis. I must be slipping."

"Maybe, but football has been my whole life. Nothing else has mattered as much, so I guess even I've started to see myself as only Coach."

He frowns, but then his expression changes again. "We should have breakfast. Come on, I'll make you pancakes." He jumps off the bed like he's on springs.

I sit up and watch as he debates on the perfect Christmas Eve outfit. When he's finally satisfied that his painted-on green jeans and white sweater with the Christmas decorations are it, he turns around.

"What are you doing still in bed?"

"Waiting for you to leave the room."

"Why?"

Because watching you saunter around naked has made me hard, and I'm slightly embarrassed about it?

He walks up to me and sits on the side of the bed. "What's wrong?"

"Nothing's wrong. I just need some privacy to get dressed."

"Oh…sorry. I'll get out then." He stands, but I hold his hand to stop him.

"Curtis, wait. I'm just embarrassed, okay?"

"Of what?"

I take his hand and place it on my lap.

He laughs and cops a feel.

"Do you think I don't have the same problem, Riley? Your dick has been poking my back all night, which resulted in me sleeping with a hard-on, which is fucking uncomfortable."

My mouth opens wide.

"The only reason I didn't jump your bones when we woke up is because we haven't had the safe-sex conversation, and I don't know if you're ready for that yet."

"I'm negative. I was tested when I ended my marriage and haven't been with anyone," I say.

It's his turn to look shocked. "I'm negative, and I'm on PrEP."

"I guess that answers one of the questions."

He swallows. "How about the other?"

I put my hand behind his neck and pull him in for a kiss. "Make me breakfast, and I'll tell you then."

He melts into the kiss, making me wonder if it's always like this with Bubble or if it's because this is all new to him. As he confessed, he's been wanting me for a while.

"You're a tease, but I'll make you breakfast. Ten minutes."

One last kiss and he leaves me and my considerably harder dick to get ready.

Are all young people this forward and at ease with their sexuality? Next to Curtis, I feel like a virgin, and not just because he's the first man I've ever been with.

It was a while before Mel and I took the step into penetrative sex because it felt like such a huge step for us at eighteen.

I scoff.

It was a huge step for me, at least.

I put that thought aside and get dressed to join Bubble in the open-plan living area. The cabin next door may have all the trimmings, but I do like how there are no frills to my cabin.

You come out of the bedroom and you're in the living space. It's small and cozy. At least it is now that Bubble is here. I'll have to think about bringing more decorative stuff when I come back in the spring.

I have some photos of my dad and me working in the garage together and of my family on vacation.

Curtis is already plating the pancakes. There are two cups of coffee on the table by the time I get to him, stealing a kiss before I sit.

He blushes, and I can't help feeling somewhat satisfied that I do that to him.

I shouldn't be surprised that his pancakes are fluffy, delicious, and leave me wondering about my need to increase my post-Christmas workouts. Especially if I keep eating at this rate.

"Okay, so what's next on your list of things that must be done today?" I ask.

He smiles with glee. "We need to build a snowman."

"A snowman. Outside. Where the temperature must have dropped considerably with the storm?" My pitch increases slightly with each word.

"Yup." He joins his hands together in excitement and then takes a box from under the table. "I have a scarf, a hat, and buttons, or maybe a tie. I haven't decided yet. Also, some extra accessories just in case."

"You are aware that we're both from the West Coast, the side that doesn't get snow, and we'll freeze our nuts out there."

"Aww, Coach, don't worry. I'll look after your nuts. Speaking of which." He gets up and comes to straddle me. "You owe me an answer."

My hands go instinctively to his waist. "I didn't exactly come prepared. I wasn't expecting to…you know…"

"End up having mind-blowing sex?"

I laugh. "You're setting a high expectation there."

Curtis tilts his head and sensually runs his hand up his neck, making my mouth dry and my balls tight.

"I know my skills," he says, letting his indicator finger skate over his lips before taking it in his mouth and sucking until it comes out with a pop.

"I was talking about mine," I swallow. I've never had doubts about my skills in bed, but Curtis is so different from anything I ever thought I'd experience.

He cups my face and looks into my eyes with the most earnest expression I've ever seen. "Riley, if you want this and I want this, it'll work. We'll fit together like cheese on pizza, like butter on bread, like icing on cake, like—"

"Are all your analogies food related? You're making me hungry, and I've just had breakfast."

He laughs. "How about we'll fit together because my ass has been waiting for that big dick of yours for months, so it'll fit. We'll not only fit, it'll be magical."

"Christ."

He cradles my face and looks into my eyes. "Do you want it? I'm not pushing you, am I, because Juju always says when I set my mind on something—"

Shutting him up with a kiss is my new favorite thing to do. The moment my lips touch his, there's an automatic switch in Curtis where his walls come down and he lets me in.

"I want it, Curtis." I close my eyes and say a silent little prayer. "Come on. Let's build that snowman. I need to cool down now."

He practically jumps off me and runs to the door. He puts on his boots, complaining about the laces, and then his coat, hat, and gloves.

"You forgot your box." I grab it and take it to him. I get ready, and we both leave the warmth of the cabin to face the freezing cold outdoors.

It's significantly colder than yesterday and the layer of snow is deeper. I'm not convinced we can do anything, but Bubble is like a kid in a candy store.

"Look, I found his arms!" He comes back from the edge of the forest with some twigs. He sets them by the box and puts his hands on his hips. "Okay. How do you build a snowman?"

I shrug. "I skipped that class to watch the cheerleaders practice."

He pushes me, and I lose my footing and end up sideways in the snow.

"You ass, you're going to pay for that." I bunch up some snow and throw it at him, but he's too fast and avoids being hit.

"Don't underestimate the cheerleaders." He sticks his tongue out at me.

"I wouldn't d—" A snowball hits me square in the face.

I stand and run to catch him, but the bastard is lean and fast.

"You've been overfeeding me on purpose," I shout. He's at least thirty yards away.

"It was all part of my master plan."

The door to the other cabin opens, and the two kids run out.

"Are you having a snowball fight? Can we join?" George asks.

His dad comes up behind him, shaking his head. "What did I say?"

George sighs and turns to Curtis. "Please?"

Curtis laughs. "I think I've already won the battle, troops. The old man over there won't take another one." I snort and watch as he leans to the kids' level. "But we could use your help with something else."

Both kids look like their days have been made. "We can help," they say in unison.

"Do you know how to build a snowman?" he asks.

"Yes!" Both kids scream excitedly, but Curtis's face of delight hits me unexpectedly in the one place of my heart I've been trying to keep buried.

"Hey, Riley, want a hot cocoa?" Harrison asks.

"Sure."

I walk up to Curtis. His smile is so genuine and carefree. At this moment in time, all he's thinking about is ticking off his list of things he's never done at Christmas. He has no idea of the turmoil he's just caused inside me.

"What's up?" he asks.

"Nothing. Go make the most Bubblelicious snowman this place has ever seen." I give him a quick peck on the lips and walk up the steps to Harrison's porch.

20

BUBBLE

I try not to look at Riley's ass as he walks away, but it's impossible. I may as well just give up right now. I'll never not watch his ass when he's walking away from me.

My head, my heart, and my belly are full of emotions, and I don't know what to do with them.

Waking up to Riley? Best thing ever. Hands down.

The only thing that would have topped that is if he'd topped me so we could start the day with a bone-melting orgasm. But somehow, not doing anything felt more intimate. Like there will be plenty more mornings of waking up together, so there's no need to rush.

The way he keeps looking at me is disconcerting. On one hand, it feels like he's stripping me naked every time his eyes so much as look in my direction. On the other, I feel his fear like it's a living, breathing thing.

I'm scared too. I'm scared I'll fall in love with him and be left to nurse my broken heart all alone, again. I love living in Windsor, my two jobs, and all the kids I work with. Moving again because of a broken heart would just restart the cycle.

Two little coughs pull me out of my head. I know Megan and Gigi aren't siblings, but in some ways, they're so alike. It's adorable.

"Yes?"

"You said we were going to build a snowman."

I chuckle. "I absolutely did. There's only one problem." I bend over a little to match their height. "I don't know how to build a snowman."

Megan frowns and elbows Gigi.

"What? Just because he can't build a snowman doesn't mean he's not a real elf. Elves are busy making toys. They don't have time to build snowmen," Gigi says matter-of-factly.

"I guess."

I bite my laugh. "So, are you going to help me?"

They both nod, and before I know it, I'm being pulled by each hand over to the space between the two cabins.

"Are you going to teach the other elves how to make a snowman?" Gigi asks.

"Absolutely." I may as well go with it. Who knows, I may have actually been an elf in my previous life, but I just don't remember. It would explain a lot about my current earthly presence.

"We have to start by making a snowball," Megan says.

We pack some snow together and shape it until we have a small ball.

"Now what?" I ask.

"Now we roll it around until more snow sticks to our ball and makes it bigger," George adds.

I'm surprised by how easy it is and how quickly we end up with a considerable-sized snowball. The kids pick the spot where they want the snowman to be and we leave the snowball there to start a new one.

The second and third balls are smaller, which is a good thing because I never considered they'd be so freakin heavy. I don't want the kids to get hurt, so I try my best to stack each of the balls on top of each other without their help.

"They're not perfect," Megan says, pouting.

I scratch my head over my hat. "You're right. It needs to be rounder. Do you think it helps if we add chunks of snow and then smooth it out?" I mean, it works with buttercream, so why not with snow?

"Uh-huh," they both say.

While the kids are distracted by smoothing out the snowman, I look in Riley's direction. He seems to be lost in conversation with Harrison. I don't know anything about the big guy, but considering his size, maybe he used to be a football player.

My stomach sinks a little at the thought of Riley finding more to talk about with a stranger than he could with me. I mean, what do I even know about football?

I know how to perform during a game, but it never interested me enough to figure out the football rules. At least not beyond hooking up with some of the many players in the closet.

But that's all in the past. I have no inclination to hook up with anyone.

Not true, Bubble.

I sigh. I'm totally inclined to hook up with Coach—Riley. My Riley.

He's not yours, Bubble.

I want to smack the voice in my head in the face. Riley is mine for now. At least until we go home after Christmas. And if that's all he can give me, then that's…sad, but I'll live.

Riley looks my way, and I wave. His smile is warm, and the way he looks at me is different now. Maybe it's too early to understand him, but I know something's changed.

We didn't wake up together in bed for nothing, right?

I look at the white sky that promises more snow and smile. My grandma is up there somewhere. She'll guide me in the right direction. I know it.

"Okay, my little helpers, are you ready to beautify our snowman?"

"Yes!"

I show the kids my box of delightful snowman clothing and decorations. They squee over all the options, taking everything out while they decide what goes best.

"Is Santa your boyfriend?" Megan asks.

"Who?"

She points to Riley on the porch with her dad, drinking cocoa.

"Oh. His name is Riley. He's…not really my boyfriend."

"But you're spending Christmas together. Mommy says Christmas and important holidays should be spent with our family. Boyfriends are family."

"Where's your mommy?" I ask, hoping I don't get some tragic reply like she's dead or something. I'd need to bake a dozen cakes to make up for upsetting the kids.

"Oh, she's going to meet Dr. Mike's parents. He's her boyfriend." She comes closer and whispers, "Did you know they are going to get married just like Daddy and Fletcher. Dr. Mike asked me if it was okay for him to ask Mommy to marry him, and I said yes. Mommy doesn't know yet." She clasps her gloved little hands in front of her in excitement.

I smile. "That's the coolest thing I've ever heard."

"We asked our dads for a baby brother or sister for Christmas," Gigi says.

"Oh really? And what did they say?"

Both kids shrug, and then Megan says, "Daddy looked really scared. Like his eyes opened reeeally wide, and Fletcher laughed." She chuckles. "Maybe my mommy and Dr. Mike can have babies soon."

"Would they still be my brother or sister?" Gigi asks.

"Duh," Megan replies.

I ruffle the beanies on their heads. "You two might be the most adorable people I've ever met. Fact."

They both smile wide, and then Gigi whispers something in Megan's ear. Megan's eyes go wide as she turns to me. "Does that mean we get what we want for Christmas?"

I shrug. "I don't have the right clearance with Santa to know that information. But I'll tell him you've been really good and so helpful teaching me how to build my very first snowman."

They seem happy with my answer and go back to picking the accessories for the snowman.

I stare at them. I've never thought much about having children before, but these two kids make me want to be a dad.

What would a couple of little Bubbles be like? I chuckle to myself. They'd be a handful, that's for sure.

I turn to Riley once more, and my heart skips a beat.

Be still. Be still.

21

COACH

I sip from the huge mug filled with steamy cocoa and marshmallows that Harrison gave me. "God, this is too good to be good for my health."

"Don't look at me. Fletch says at Christmas, all calories are free."

I laugh. "If only that were true."

"How are things going with you and Bubble? We really feel awful about the situation we put you both in."

I wave him off. "You had no way to know, just like Bubble couldn't have known. Things are working out okay."

He raises a brow. "Just okay? Was that a kiss I just saw before I went inside for the cocoa? Correct me if I'm wrong, but my impression when we arrived was that you weren't *that* close before." He takes a sip of his drink and sighs. "Christ, I'm spending too much time with Fletcher. I'm sorry. It's none of my business. You can ignore anything I say, and we can just supervise the kids to make sure they don't turn into icicles."

I chuckle. "It's okay. You read the situation right. We weren't that close. I'd go as far as saying we weren't even friends. When you arrived yesterday, I was here to apologize to Bubble for being an ass to him the day before."

Harrison laughs.

"What's funny?"

He clears snow off the porch rail and sets his mug down.

"I met Fletcher at a charity bachelor auction. He won me and was so forward about his intentions that I took an instant dislike to him, even though he was the sexiest thing I'd ever seen. A few months later, I moved to Stillwater with my ex and daughter." He takes another sip of his cocoa. "Guess who also lived in Stillwater? Guess whose kid was in my daughter's class? Let's just say we had a rocky start, but we found our way to each other in the end."

"What he means is that he was mine from the moment I bought him. He just took the longest time to figure out it was nonnegotiable. He's mine forever," Fletcher says, coming out of the cabin with his own drink and settling against Harrison's side.

They really look like they're in love. The kind of in love that you'd give up anything for.

The kind I'm not sure I ever had with Mel, no matter how much I loved her.

I look out at Curtis and the kids. They've rolled three giant balls of snow that Curtis stacked to make the snowman. Megan is sticking in the twigs to make the arms, and George is holding up a scarf and tie to Curtis, who looks like he's pondering the most important decision of his life.

The guys next to me talk about their plans to sneak the kids' Christmas presents under the tree that night. They also talk about some of the arrangements for their wedding.

It sounds so natural and domestic. I feel like I'm intruding in their personal space, so I keep quiet and observe the person turning my world upside down and making me consider a new start at forty-six.

Harrison's phone rings, but Fletcher takes it out of his hand before he has a chance to pick it up.

"Stella, honey, we need to talk," he says.

Harrison rolls his eyes.

"Is that Mommy?" Megan asks, running up the steps to meet us.

"It is, sweetheart," Fletcher says. "Do you want to talk to her?"

"Yes, please."

Megan takes the phone and runs back down the steps, apparently changing to a video call so her mom can see their snowman-making efforts.

"What's the point of being best friends with your ex-wife if you can't get past your fiancé to even say hello?" Harrison jokes, shaking his head at Fletcher.

"Stella and I have a lot of understandings."

Harrison rolls his eyes. "I bet."

"Wait. Your ex is a woman?" I ask before I realize how rude and inappropriate I sound. "I'm so sorry. That was out of line and not my business."

Harrison smiles. "Apology accepted. Yes, I'm bisexual, and so is Fletcher. We're used to people assuming we're gay because we're in a relationship. It's okay."

I nod. I always tell my team that if they have anything they need to talk about, they can talk to me. Family, personal, or school issues. It's sometimes easier to open up to a stranger than to someone you're too close to.

Curtis drapes a pink scarf carefully around the snowman.

Could I talk to these two guys? They've been with women. Maybe they understand this confusion, transition, or whatever this is going on inside me.

"You look like you're thinking too hard about something," Harrison says.

"Um…yeah. God, I don't know how to say this or why I'm even saying it. I'm straight. Or at least I've always considered myself straight. I was married for twenty-three years and never once looked at another person. And now?" I bring my hands to the bridge of my nose.

"You're attracted to someone who isn't a woman," Harrison says, glancing at Curtis.

I nod.

"Someone I never expected I'd be attracted to." I look at Curtis, too. "How can I get to my age and not know I'm attracted to men?"

"Are you attracted to men? Am I attractive to you? Or Fletcher?"

I think about it. Yes, they're good-looking, like most of the men

I've worked with throughout my career, but there's no other reaction. My body doesn't feel anything. I don't feel anything.

"No."

"I don't like labels, but since I realized I liked both guys and girls, I've found that the bisexual label is one I'm comfortable with. Maybe this is something for you to discover for yourself, but you might want to look into demisexuality or pansexuality."

I stare at the last of my cocoa. I've wondered about pansexuality but never demisexuality.

Since some of my players came out as part of the LGBTQ+ community, I made sure we supported not only the player but also their community. We did a lot of charity work and learned a lot about gender and sexuality. One of my regrets since leaving my job at the Marinos is that I miss doing that kind of community work.

"Hey, Coach, do you want to help us dress Mr. McChilly?" Curtis shouts.

"Are you really asking *me* for fashion tips?"

"Yeah, you're right." He winks. "Come on, my little elves. Let's see what else we have in the magical box of treats."

Once again, I watch in wonder as Curtis helps the kids pick the right accessories to dress up their snowman, and then he picks them up so they can reach the snowman's head. He's really good with them. I wonder if he wants to have children one day.

It's dawning on me that even though we tried so hard to have a baby for such a long time, Mel never took an interest in other people's children. How can you want to be a parent and not react to children around you? Then again, the foundation of our marriage was a lie, so nothing surprises me anymore.

"Thank you, Harrison," I say. "Sometimes you can walk your whole life blind to what's happening around you, can't you?"

"And sometimes all you have to do is open your eyes and everything you need is right in front of you," he says.

I let out a breath. "He's too young."

Harrison smirks. "Really? That's the excuse you're going with?"

"You can't deny there's a significant age gap between us. He's only twenty-six. I'll be a retired old man when he's still in his prime. He has so much life. I can't be the one to hold him back."

"That might not be your decision to make. Given how he keeps looking this way every few seconds, I'd say he might be more into whatever you have than you think."

That's what I'm afraid of. For so long, I didn't understand why Curtis got to me. Now it's starting to become clearer, but the air is still too misty, just like in the locker room at the school.

"Look, Daddy!" Megan shouts. "Is this the best snowman ever, or what?"

We all go over to inspect the hard work of the young team.

Curtis sidles up to me as soon as I'm close enough, and I wrap my arm around his shoulder. It feels so good that I pull him closer and kiss his temple.

In true Bubble fashion, the snowman isn't like other snowmen. The scarf around the neck is pink, of course, and it has Christmas decorations hanging from it. The buttons are black to match the hat, but there's a sparkly pink stripe around the hat to match the scarf.

The snowman even has a pair of snow boots.

"Is the snowman sparkly?" Fletcher asks.

"Yeah," Curtis answers. "I used edible glitter, so it'll all dissolve when the snowman melts."

"You did a great job," I say.

"Great? Megan, Gigi, did you hear that? Coach says we did a great job."

Both kids shake their heads, and I look at Curtis in confusion.

"What did we do?" he asks them.

"We built the most superlicious snowman ever," they say in synchrony.

I bow to them. "I see how that is a million times better than great. My apologies."

"Okay, you two," Harrison says. "Time for you to go back inside and warm up."

The kids run over to Curtis and hug him, and me by extension. "Thank you for making a snowman with us. Maybe tomorrow we can make Christmas snow angels," George says.

"I'd love that," Curtis says.

Some emotion lodges in my throat, and I know I need to take Curtis and go back inside the cabin. I need it to be just the two of us for a while.

Once the kids are out of earshot, I put my hand on his chin so I can look into his beautiful green eyes.

"Are you okay?" he asks, his eyes flicking between mine. I see worry etched in them.

"I need you, Curtis. All of you."

22

BUBBLE

THERE'S something raw in the way Riley looks at me. Like he wants to consume me and is both afraid and eager to get started.

"Okay, let's go inside." I take his hand, and he follows me.

We don't talk as we hang our coats and shake the snow off our boots before putting them on the tray.

The silence is killing me because I don't know what he's thinking. I want to know if he's really ready for this, if he's feeling what I'm feeling. It's okay if he's not, but I need to know.

"Are you hungry? I could make you something to eat," I say, walking over to the fridge.

"Curtis."

"Nothing too complicated. I'll give in and make you a sandwich. A proper one, not one of those things you call a sandwich."

"Curtis."

His voice is closer now. I shiver at his closeness. Why does taking this next step scare me so much?

Because you already care too much about him and you're afraid to get hurt.

Oh shut up, stupid brain.

"There's some leftovers from last night. Pulled pork and—"

I squeak as my sock-covered feet are lifted off the ground, and I'm taken to the bedroom over Riley's shoulder.

He drops me on the bed, making me bounce, and then follows, covering my body with his.

"Tell me you still want this, Curtis." His voice is raw, vulnerable.

"More than anything, Riley."

He closes his eyes like he's in pain. I reach over and massage his temples.

"Does it bother you that I'm much older than you?" he asks.

"What? No, not at all."

"I'll be fifty-six in ten years. Will you feel the same way then?"

I smile. "I've loved many things for a lot longer and haven't changed my mind. Riley, I might be Bubble, but remember, I'm also Curtis. Sometimes I don't want to be the one to cheer everyone up. Sometimes I want to cuddle in bed with a book. Sometimes I want someone to bake me a cake."

"I can't bake," he says.

"I know an excellent place in Chester Falls."

He smiles and leans his forehead against mine.

"I don't want to ruin this. You are too special, and I don't want to hurt you."

"You will only hurt me if you want me but refuse to follow your heart."

"I followed my heart once, and…" He closes his eyes like it's a painful memory. "Can I touch you?"

I whisper. "I'm yours."

He runs his hands through my hair. "I love how your hair smells and how soft it is." Then he kisses my forehead, my cheeks, my neck, but doesn't come anywhere near my mouth.

I raise my arms to encourage him to remove my shirt, which he does in the slowest way known to humankind. I'm burning from the inside out with how slow he's taking this.

When he kisses my sternum, I thread my fingers through his hair to encourage him to get closer to my nipples, but he grabs my hands and places them above my head.

"You're killing me, Riley."

"You said you're mine. I'm just savoring you."

"Can you savor me quicker?"

He chuckles but doesn't change what he's doing. His trail of kisses carries to my stomach, and I bite my lip to stop from moaning. Not that it helps much because his slow touches could make me come in my pants just from anticipation.

"FYI, if you pay attention to my nipples, I might like it," I say, trying to sound less bratty than it actually comes out.

He comes up and kisses me until I'm chasing his mouth when he lets go.

"FYI, making demands will only get you so far."

"But it'll get me *somewhere*."

When his lips meet mine, I feel his smile. I know he'll give me what I want.

When he *finally* pays attention to my nipples, I let out unrestrained moans because, fuck me, the man knows what he's doing. He licks and sucks them into peaks before biting them, blowing soft breaths, and then licking again.

"Fuck, fuck, Riley. I need more. Please."

He undoes the buttons on my jeans and pulls them down. Because they're so tight, my underwear follows.

My dick is flushed and leaking. He gives it a few slow strokes.

"I never thought I'd say another man's cock is beautiful. But looking at you, Curtis. Your body begging for release because of the way I'm touching you. It's the most beautiful thing I've seen in my life."

He raises himself on his knees and removes his pants and underwear too.

"Holy mother of well-endowed men. I'm going to start going to church."

He looks down at his engorged cock and gives it a long stroke.

"You saw it yesterday."

"*After* you came. I didn't think it was going to grow *that* big."

He smirks. "I didn't take you for a size queen."

I sit up to pull him back down on top of me, making sure his torpedo dick is in the right place. "I'm not, but I'm looking forward to spending the whole of January remembering this moment every time I so much as move an inch."

God, I love how giant and heavy he is. I hold on to his thick arms. They bulge as he holds himself, and I can't help running my hands over the straining muscles. He is totally fit for his age, and like the best of wines, he's going to get better and better.

"I'd like to try something," he says.

"Okay."

He doesn't take his eyes off mine as he scoots down my body, sucking on my skin here and there. I'm sure there will be bruising tomorrow.

Fuck, I hope there's bruising tomorrow and the day after because I'll need a reminder at some point in the future, when this is all over, that it really happened.

Maybe I should take photos. I make a mental note to do that.

Coach's mouth moves closer and closer to my flushed cock. My body hums with anticipation. Is he going to touch it again like he did yesterday?

As I hoped, he holds my cock and gives me a few strokes. Then he runs his tongue from the root to the tip and takes my mushroomed head in his mouth, and I cry out in pleasure.

"You taste like strawberries all over. Just like I thought," he says.

I want to make a joke and ask him to try my ass to verify if it's true, but my words become stuck in my throat when he takes more of my cock into his mouth.

He gags a little when my head hits the back of his throat, but that doesn't stop him.

This man. What is this man doing to me?

I open my legs wider to give him more space, but instead of getting more comfortable, he stops.

"What's wrong? Do you want to stop? It's okay if you do, but I'll kill you if you don't at least finish me with a hand job," I say, pouting.

He smiles, his lips glistening with his spit and some of my precum. He's never looked so sexy. He licks them as he looks down.

"I failed mind-reading class, Coach. What's happening down there?"

"Shh, give me a moment."

I lean my head back on the pillow. I did promise he had free rein of my body, so I guess, if I must, I could exercise *some* patience.

But I really want an orgasm.

I mean, I want two. I need the first to take the edge off before I'm relaxed enough to take Coach's power-rocket dick inside me.

My cock throbs at the thought of him filling me up. It's been such a long time since I had a good, satisfying fuck.

"What position will be more comfortable for you to take me?" he asks.

"On my belly with a few pillows under me or on all fours."

He seems to think about it for a moment and then flips me over. My face plops down on the pillow, so I use my elbows to get on all fours and watch what he's doing behind me.

I see him reach over to the nightstand and grab a bottle of strawberry-flavored lube. I raise a brow.

He has lube in his cabin that smells like strawberries? How long exactly has he been thinking about this?

"That was a coincidence," he says, "the store ran out of the nonflavored ones."

"Sure." I smirk, and he slaps my ass. It makes me hornier than it should, and it seems I make all the right noises because I get a slap on the other cheek to even it out.

My cock leaks onto the comforter underneath. "Nghh, fuck…"

He smooths the area with his hands, and I have no doubt my skin is all flushed. "In case you're wondering, I'm not into spanking."

"You could have fooled me," he says.

"Ass."

He runs his hand up and down my spine, humming. "You're wound up like a spring."

"That's because I need to come, and you're a fucking tease."

He laughs. "Okay, let me see if I can make it quick for you, Royal Highness Demander of Orgasms."

I bite my lip, wondering what he has in mind considering the position I'm in. Is he going to finger me until I come? That would certainly help get me ready to take his dream cock.

My mind is coming up with all the different scenarios when the least likely one happens. His wet, warm tongue covers my hole before he sucks and then proceeds to French-kiss my ass like I'm a can-can dancer.

"Cupcakes, fudge, sprinkles, and holy fucking stars," I shout. "Please don't stop."

My orgasm is teetering on the edge. As if he knows it, Riley strokes my cock at the same time that he penetrates my ass with this tongue, and that's it for me. I come on a string of curses like I'm starting a new religion.

"You…this…fucking hell…Riley." I fall onto the comforter, not caring that I'm basically lying in a puddle of my own cum.

He lies on his side, stroking my back. "Hey, I said I've never been with a man. I never said I didn't know what to do in bed."

"Smug bastard." I'm facedown on the pillow, so my insult comes out muffled and with zero malice. He can eat my ass any time he wants. I'll make a sign and everything.

Bubble's Ass Open for Business. Free buffet. Eat as much as you want.

I turn my face to him. "What do you propose we do now? Because you've noodled my legs."

He leans over for a kiss. "Let's test that young age recovery rate and do it the old-fashioned way."

"Like I said, Coach. I'm all yours."

23

COACH

I turn Bubble around, and sure enough, his stomach is coated in his release. It doesn't bother me. None of this bothers me.

Quite the opposite, I've never felt so horny for someone, so in tune with someone else's needs. Not that I have any experience beyond Mel, but I thought I'd feel more nervous or apprehensive.

I was in the beginning, but seeing Curtis react to my touch has removed every ounce of doubt about what I'm doing and how I feel about being with another man.

"Does it gross you out?" he asks, looking down at his stomach.

I run a finger over his release, feeling his taut muscles beneath, and then bring it over to my mouth to taste him.

He groans, and then he's on me. His tongue searches mine, tasting and teasing. I feel his cock harden again between us.

His kissing is so distracting that I don't even realize I'm on my back with him straddling me.

"Coach, you are a bag of dirty treats tied with a nice neat bow. No one would ever tell what's really inside. But now that I know, I want to keep looking to see what else you have."

I laugh. "It seems that you're ready for something else I have."

He looks down at where our cocks are sandwiched together. "I was born ready. Hand me the lube."

I grab it, and he steals it off me, uncapping it and squirting a good amount on his fingers before reaching behind himself.

"Turn around. I want to see," I ask.

His green eyes go impossible dark, and he does as I ask. We're in a reverse cowboy position, and I have a prime seat to watch the beauty that is his ass.

He adds one finger, and my cock jolts at the sight of it disappearing into his hole. It looks so small.

"I'll never fit in there."

He chuckles and then adds two fingers, letting out a moan. I grab his ass cheeks and spread them so I can see better.

"Enjoying the show, Coach?"

"It's exquisite."

"I promise it'll fit, and it'll feel so good."

A third finger goes in, and now Bubble is riding his fingers. His head is turned to face me, so I stroke my unattended cock to show him how much I can't wait to be inside him.

I grab the lube and generously coat my cock. He may have done a good job of preparing himself, but it's going to take some effort to take me.

"God, your ass is a work of art."

"All talk and no play makes Bubble an impatient boy." He pushes his ass back, and I take the hint.

I align my cock with his hole, holding it in place as he lowers himself on me.

My head feels like it's about to explode. I'm only an inch in and seriously doubting my staying power. He's so fucking tight.

"Jesus, Curtis, you're...fuck."

He doesn't say anything. His hands are on his legs, and I see his muscles flex as he slowly impales himself on me.

When he's fully seated, he lets out a breath.

"Are you okay?" I ask.

"Three cups of flour, three cups of sugar, four eggs—"

"What are you doing?"

He huffs. "What do you think? I'm trying not to fucking have an orgasm here because your torpedo dick is filling me up like a corndog at a football game. If I so much as think a sexy thought, I might just come."

I laugh because he almost sounds angry at the prospect.

He finishes what sounds like the recipe for a cake or something and then turns his head.

"Ready for the ride of your life, Coach?"

"I thought you were the one riding," I say.

He gives me a smile and licks his lips, which makes me want to pull him down for a kiss. Then he raises himself until it's just the tip of my cock inside him before coming back down again.

Sweat beads on my forehead as I try to keep it together.

"Fuuck, Bubble, you feel too good. So fucking tight." I grit my teeth.

He keeps a steady rhythm, but I see his thighs shaking. He's either tired from the position, or he's hanging by a thread as much as I am.

I sit up and hold his waist when he's fully seated.

"You're so amazing, Curtis." I suck the skin below his neck. He's so light and small I could move anywhere with me still inside him. I keep that thought for another time. For now, we both need to find relief.

I snake my hands around his back and gently pull him down so we're lying with his back to my front.

"Slide your feet forward and move now."

His skin reddens at my command.

"You like being told what to do?"

He bites his lip and nods.

"Then do it."

He raises his hips and comes down again.

"Riley," he shouts, and this is different from before. His body shakes as I meet his thrusts with mine.

"Baby, I'm so close," I say in his ear. "Will you come for me?"

I reach out to his cock, but he takes my hands and laces them with his. Our joint groans must be heard for miles, but we're both too far gone.

We keep the pace, me thrusting into him as he falls onto my cock like he's coming home. It doesn't take long before Curtis comes in the most beautiful full-body orgasm I've ever seen.

I hold him as he shakes through it, calling my name.

A couple more thrusts and my orgasm follows as I fill him over and over again. It's a pure raw, carnal release.

His head rests on my chest. His hair is wet with sweat, just like mine. We're sticky and will soon feel the cold, but neither of us seems ready to move.

"I think your cannon dick killed me, Coach."

I snort. "You'd certainly win gold at a rodeo, that's for sure."

He chuckles. "Damn right. Yeehaw."

My dick softens slowly and eventually slips out. Is it weird that I want to see my cum spill out of his hole?

What's happening to me? Why do I feel like I'm claiming this guy like a possessive animal?

I slowly raise to a sitting position, taking him with me and then lifting him so I can carry him to the bathroom.

His arms are folded close to his chest, and the way he looks at me makes my heart skip a few beats.

"You are adorable when you're tired, you know that," I say.

"Give me a twelve-minute halftime break, Coach, and I'll be ready for the second half."

I set him down on the bathroom tiles and turn the shower on. This cabin has an old system that takes a while to heat, so I turn back to my strawberry-flavored insatiable man.

Wait. Mine? Keep it cool, Riley. He's not yours. Christmas bubble, remember?

"Twelve minutes, you say?" I place my hands on either side of him, trapping him against the sink.

He narrows his eyes and bites his lips before licking them sensually. Then he looks down.

I follow his gaze, surprised to see he's already half-hard.

"Holy mother, what do you eat? I don't remember recovering that fast at your age."

He hooks his arms around my neck and lifts himself so he's

holding on to me like a koala. I smile and help him stay in place with my hands on his ass. It's definitely not a chore.

"First of all, Riley." He kisses my cheek. "You make me stupid horny. I can't help it." He kisses the other cheek. "Second of all, John, I've been waiting for you to notice me for about a billion years and five-hundred cakes." He kisses my lips, and this time he lingers until my own dick is at half-mast. I know I won't manage a full erection, but what this man does to me is beyond incredible.

"And third, Dempsey," he finishes with my surname. "I have no third. I just want you. Despite the storm and not seeing Juju, I feel like I've been given the best Christmas present ever."

"I'm sorry you can't see your friend this Christmas. I know you had a lot of plans. Will you tell me more about her?"

He looks at me for a moment and nods.

"Okay then. Let's get clean." I carry him inside the shower and then set him down.

We wash each other without any rush until both our stomachs rumble.

I change the bed while Bubble arranges something for us to eat. I made him promise he wouldn't do anything too complicated. He needs to relax a little too.

After we eat the sandwiches he makes—which taste like gourmet sandwiches because the man doesn't do anything by half-measure—we sit on the couch in front of the fireplace.

"So tell me about your best friend," I say.

He sits so his back is to the arm of the couch and his legs are on top of mine. He's now wearing a pair of lime-green yoga pants and a top that's so cropped I can see his abs. I put my arm over his shoulder, bringing him closer, and rest my other hand over his exposed skin.

"If you get me hard again, the only thing we'll be talking about is your submarine dick docking in my ass."

I laugh. "I'll behave."

He raises a brow and points at where I'm mindlessly running circles with my thumbs over his belly.

"Okay, okay. I'll stop."

He sighs. "Don't stop. Anyway, you want to know about Juju."

24

BUBBLE

RILEY IS DEFINITELY one-thousand times more comfortable than the couch. If only I could take him home with me at the end of this vacation. I'd sit on him all the time, and not always naked. I do have some self-control.

"I met Juju in college. We were both on the cheerleading team. I looked at her, and she looked at me, and it was as if the universe aligned itself. We became best friends that day."

Riley smiles. "That's such a strange concept because I can't see how I'd let someone in so quickly, but somehow, it's totally you, isn't it?"

I nod. "When you know, you know. We became inseparable. If I'd lived in student accommodation, we totally would have been roomies."

"Where did you live?"

"With my grandmother. She became ill when I finished high school, so I went to the local college so I could stay with her."

"Did you have other plans? If she wasn't sick, I mean," he asks.

"I did. I wanted to go to the University of Kentucky because it has the best cheerleading program, but then I switched. Grandma was so mad she didn't talk to me for days."

I smile, remembering how she even stopped cooking. As if it

would make a difference to the grandson she taught all of her recipes to, even her secret ones.

"I eventually won her back by baking her cookies. And she could never stay mad at me for too long. I'm too adorable."

Riley brings his hand up to my face and cradles it. "That you are. And persistent too."

I grin.

"Anyway, anytime I wasn't at school, I was home, so Juju came over a lot and also got to know my grandma. Juju doesn't get along with her family because they wanted her to work in the family diner like her sister, but she wanted to go to college and do something else. She spent so much time with me that my grandma kind of adopted her. I wouldn't have survived my grandma's death if it wasn't for Juju." I lean my head on Riley's chest. "She was everything. Made sure I ate, didn't miss class, and even went to all the cheerleading practices. We ended up winning our league championship that year."

"Wow, that's quite amazing. Congratulations."

I smile, but I don't feel it.

"With my grandma gone, I felt lost, so I put everything into cheerleading. My dream was to be the first male cheerleader to perform at an NFL game. Juju made me change colleges, and she came with me. We were the dream team."

"Why do I feel like this story doesn't have a happy ending?" he asks. His voice is gentle and soothing. I want to lean into it and let it lull me to sleep so I don't have to remember the bad times.

"I'm here with you, aren't I?" I ask, running my hand up his chest, smiling as his breath hitches under my touch. "That's as happy an ending as I could ever wish for."

"Curtis."

I'm not sure if he's saying my name as a warning to stop teasing him or bullshitting him.

"I had an injury eighteen months ago. The kind you don't recover from if you want to be a professional cheerleader."

"I'm so sorry, baby."

I shrug. "Nothing to be done. I decided on a fresh start in

Connecticut. I traveled a while before I settled on a place. I saw the advertisement to work as a barista at Spilled Beans in Chester Falls. When Indy, my boss, found out I could bake, he hired me on the spot. I love working there."

"But you live in Windsor, right?"

I elbow him lightly. "Want to stalk me, Coach?"

He chuckles.

"Yeah. I couldn't afford anything in Chester Falls, so I had to look farther out. It worked out well in Windsor because I overheard a few high school students mentioning cheerleading when I was out grabbing a coffee. I talked to them and then went over to the principal to ask if they were interested in starting a cheerleading program."

Riley stares at me with a look of pure awe.

"Just like that. You went to the principal, pitched a program, and that was it?"

"Did you forget the part where I mentioned I'm adorable? I'm also irresistible."

His brows furrow. "You and Principal—"

"What?" I stand from his lap and walk as far away from him as I can. "You think I'd sleep with someone to get a job?"

"No, of course not. Curtis."

"Really? Because that's what it sounded like to me. For your information, I was the best male cheerleader on my team. I was being fast-tracked for a special program at UK, until Harley..." I run to the bathroom and lock myself in. I can handle anyone making assumptions about me, but not Riley...not him.

Remembering what happened still makes me feel raw inside. Like I'm bleeding and someone keeps squeezing lemon juice on it.

"Don't worry, baby. I'll always be here for you," Harley says.

"I'll never cheer again." Tears stream down my face as I lie on the hospital bed. "I'll never dance. I'll never be...me."

"Hey, shh." He kisses my forehead. "Don't say those things. You don't know. Maybe the doctors can help. Let me go outside and see if I can speak to someone, okay? I think Juju is on the way."

"Thank you, Harley."

"Anything for you, baby."

Juju comes running inside the room. Her face pale and worried.

"Curtis. Please open the door."

I don't answer. I'm hurt by what he insinuated and angry that I've lowered my defenses to the point those words got to me. Words I've heard before and learned to ignore.

"Fight back with kindness, Bubble." My grandma used to say. *"Show them what you can do, and they can't argue with the evidence."*

If only it was that easy.

"Curtis, please."

His voice sounds broken, just like I feel.

Except I'm not broken. I'm strong. I fought, I recovered, and I have a new life.

I reach over to the door and unlock it.

Riley opens the door and comes inside. His eyes look wild, like he doesn't know what to do.

"I'm so sorry, Curtis. I was jealous. It's stupid. You said you were irresistible, which you are. Let's face it. I thought I was straight until you barreled into my life with your strawberry scent and your cakes. I'm sorry. I didn't want to think about you with anyone else."

He looks like he wants to touch me, so I take a step forward into his arms.

"You're forgiven, but you better not do it again. FYI, the principal is not only the straightest man ever, he's also so not my type."

He holds me tight. "What's your type?"

"You, you giant muscly with maybe just one gray hair duffus."

"I thought I was a fox," he says, stroking my hair.

"A foxy duffus."

He chuckles, and the rumble of his chest makes me feel better.

"Do you think maybe we could go to bed?" he asks.

"That would be nice."

We brush our teeth, peeking at each other and smiling. It's weirdly domestic.

Did we just have our first fight? Should we make out?

We're going to bed, so I'll suggest it.

"You're checking out my ass again," I say as I go to my side of the bed.

"You have a very checkable ass."

I remove my clothes until I'm fully naked, and he does the same. We stand on either side of the bed, staring at each other and smiling.

"I decided we should make out," I say.

"Oh really?"

"Yes, really."

"Why's that?"

"Because we just had a fight, so now we have to make out. It's the rules."

He brings his hand to his mouth.

"What?" I ask.

He shakes his head.

I put my hands on my hips, which isn't nearly as effective when you're naked and half-hard.

"Nuh-huh. I was married for twenty-three years. I know when to shut up and admit I'm wrong."

I get on my knees on the bed. "You better not be comparing me to your ex-wife, or we'll have serious issues."

He lies down and pulls me to lie on top of him. "It's clear in more ways than just the obvious ones how different you are from my ex-wife."

I pull the covers up and snuggle on his side.

"What was she like?"

"She's not dead," he says, laughing.

"You know what I mean."

He looks up at the ceiling. "She is beautiful, funny, strong-willed, and my parents love her."

"Can I ask what happened?"

Riley looks at me. "She lied about something unforgivable."

He doesn't say anything else. I'm curious, but I don't think it's the right time to ask. It may never be. It's in the past, after all, and if he asked me about Harley, I think I'd feel the same way.

I turn his head to face me and kiss him.

He tastes minty fresh and like my coach. This kiss is different. I don't know how I can tell, but I feel it.

When we part, I keep my eyes closed and bring up a memory of my grandmother when she was still healthy, cooking my favorite meal.

I still miss her so much, but with Coach by my side, it doesn't feel so bad.

I'm just scared of what will happen when Christmas is over and the bubble bursts.

25

———

COACH

When I wake up, I immediately know I'm alone because I'm cold, even with the covers over me. I rub my eyes and get up, putting on a pair of joggers, forgoing underwear.

There's a chill in the air, so I pick a warmer sweater. I look through the window and see a thicker layer of snow.

I don't need to guess where Bubble is because the cabin is small enough that there's only one possibility. That and I hear him curse like a sailor.

One quick trip to the bathroom, and I join the racket in the living room. It smells like Christmas has exploded in here. Cinnamon, spice, and all things nice.

"Freakin stale muffins and soggy breadsticks."

I hear him, but I don't see him until I get to the middle of the room and see his ass up in the air while he's halfway inside my fireplace.

He's wearing green tights, and whatever is over it has ridden up to give me a nice view of his shapely thighs and small but round bubble butt.

I clear my throat.

"Crumbs," he groans as he hits his head on the top of the fireplace. "Ouch."

I wince, hoping it didn't hurt because I didn't mean to scare him.

When he turns around to face me, I bite back a laugh. Bubble is wearing a long green sweater with a red Santa hat with a fluffy rim and tip. His face is covered in soot and ash, and he doesn't look happy.

"Did I catch you at a bad time, Santa?" I ask.

That gains me a smile, so I cross the space between us and start rubbing some of the soot from his cheek.

"Not at all. I was just checking if you were a good boy this year," he says, his hands snaking around my waist but landing on my butt.

"What do you think?"

He bites his lip and pretends to think for a moment. "I think you tried really hard to be good, but ultimately you gave in to temptation. I'm afraid you get a piece of coal in your sock."

I twist my nose. "Is there anything I can do to reverse this outcome?" I pull him closer so he feels my dick harden between us.

Curtis's breath catches. "You could let me see if I can fit up your chimney, but that would still make you a bad, bad boy for giving in to your temptations."

"Oh really?" I ask. "Because the last time I went up someone's chimney, they were praying like they found a new religion. That's a good thing, right?"

"I suppose you have a point." He releases his hold on me. "I should check on the cinnamon buns."

I reluctantly let him go. He goes toward the oven, stopping midway and turning back to me.

"Wait..." He shakes his head. "Hold on, cinnamon buns first."

I'm rooted in place until he's satisfied the cinnamon buns are ready to be out of the oven, which makes the whole cabin smell even nicer. He sets the tray on the stovetop to cool and then comes over to me.

"Did you say...what I think you...said? I mean...you said...your chimney..."

I laugh. "Yes, I said what you heard, and I meant it."

"But..."

I take his hand and lead him to the sink, getting a cloth wet so I can clean the soot from his face. He looks adorable, with his big green eyes, blinking like he can't believe me.

"Look, I don't know how to say this, but I'd like to try having you inside me. I understand if it's not your thing. If you prefer to bottom. I just thought that since we were experimenting, maybe I could do it with someone I trust."

His mouth is open. He closes and opens it again as if trying to find the right words.

"Um…I used to be more versatile when I was younger and mainly with guys my age. We all experimented both ways to figure out what we liked. I found that I prefer to bottom, but I don't mind topping." He takes a deep breath. "Holy Christmas morning."

"Shall I take that as a yes?" I ask to make sure this is really something he wants too.

"I'd be honored to be the first…um…person to go up your chimney."

"Good. Oh, there you are," I say, removing the last bit of soot from Curtis's face. I lower my lips to his, letting them linger and sucking his bottom one lightly. His breath hitches as he wraps his arms around my shoulders.

I lift him and set his ass on the counter. This way, he's taller than me, which gives him an advantage he doesn't often have. He takes over with a hunger that matches mine.

Fuck, why hasn't kissing been like this all my life?

When I break the kiss, we're both a little breathless. I'm hard and too hot for the clothes I'm wearing.

"Merry Christmas, Riley," he says. "Thank you for letting me spend this time with you."

"Merry Christmas, Curtis. I'm the one who should be thanking you. On my own, I would have spent all my time finding ways to keep busy, so I could stop thinking about you. Now I don't have to. This is the best Christmas I've had in a long time."

He holds me in a tight hug. "Me too." When he doesn't let go, I stay in place, running my hands up and down his back. It must be hard not seeing his friend again, especially now that his grandma isn't around anymore.

His eyes are a little red when he pulls away, but I don't see any tears. "Hey, today is a happy day, okay? Let's have breakfast. I'll fix the fireplace, and then we can do anything you want for the rest of the day."

"Can we watch Christmas movies?"

"Of course."

He beams. "Which one is your favorite?"

"*Die Hard.*"

He gasps. "*Die Hard* is *not* a Christmas movie." He jumps down from the counter and starts grabbing the stuff we need for breakfast.

"Of course it is," I argue. "It's set at Christmas. There's a Christmas party."

I check the fireplace, add a few logs, and start a fire.

"Is not. There are guns and people dying everywhere."

"People get hurt in *Home Alone*, and no one argues that it's a Christmas movie," I say.

He huffs.

I'll admit it's funny seeing him get all riled up over such a topic. But when he starts waving a knife at me before using it to spread the icing on the cinnamon buns, I get worried.

"Hey, baby," I say, coming up behind him. "Why don't you hold that anger in and let it out later in bed, huh?"

Bubble turns around after, thankfully, putting the knife down. "You like playing with fire, Mr. Dempsey."

I kiss him. "Only when it's you doing the burning." I take the plate with the cinnamon buns and put it on the table. He brings the coffee and two cups and announces that since it's Christmas morning, he's going to sit on my lap for breakfast.

We take our time feeding bites of still-warm cinnamon rolls to each other, drinking coffee, and talking about what Christmas used to be like when we were kids.

Bubble is so easy to talk to that I keep forgetting there's a twenty-year age gap between us. He may be bubbly, full of life, and seem care-free, but he's also responsible, caring, and very mature.

The way he put his grandmother first and his dream second says everything about the man he is.

He's talking about the decorations on the Christmas tree when my phone rings with a video call from my parents.

He starts to move from my lap, but I hold him in place. His cheeks redden. It's one of the few times I've seen him looking less confident.

"Hey, Mom. Hey, Dad," I say when I swipe to answer the call. I prop the phone against my empty coffee cup so I don't have to hold it.

"Hey, sweetie. Merry Christm—oh, you have company," Mom says.

"Merry Christmas, Mom. This is Curtis. He's the cheerleading coach at my high school. Remember the pie you had at Thanksgiving? You can thank him for that."

Curtis is as still as a mouse while my mom doesn't miss a beat.

"Nice to meet you, Curtis. Your pie was delightful. You'll have to share your recipe or let me know how I can get my hands on one next year."

I already have my arm around Bubble's waist, so I run my thumb in circles to reassure him that it's okay.

"Um, thank you, Mrs. Dempsey."

Mom waves him off. "Oh, pfft, call me Jan. So, what have you boys been up to? Has the storm passed already?"

It's my turn to blush. "Well, I…um…I've removed the doors from the kitchen cabinets, sanded them, and restained them. They look like new. Curtis decorated the cabin, so it looks like one of Santa's elves escaped the North Pole and is hiding here."

"For the last time, I'm not an elf. I'm small but perfectly formed," Bubble says, crossing his arms in front of his chest, looking outraged. Then he seems to catch himself, and his whole face goes an adorable shade of pink.

"It's been great having Curtis here. You know me, I'd have had sandwiches and frozen pizza for dinner every day," I say to my parents, trying to take some of the attention away from him.

"How exactly did he end up there? I thought you were going to be on your own," Dad says.

"Bubble…um, Curtis was in the cabin next door, but there was some confusion when the owners turned up. Because of the storm, it wasn't safe for him to drive home."

Mom leans her elbows on the table they're using to prop their tablet. "That's very generous of you, honey. How handy that you were there."

Curtis and I share a look. "Yes, very handy."

"Well, we'll let you enjoy the rest of your day. We just wanted to wish you a Merry Christmas. Be good, boys," Mom says, and Dad only has time to wave before the call ends.

"Oh my god, that was mortifying," Curtis says, hiding his face with his hands. "Your parents totally know we're fucking."

"How would they know?"

"I'm on your fucking lap, Riley. Do you have the habit of keeping your friends this close when you video call your parents?"

I hadn't thought of that. He feels so right on my lap that I don't want to let him go. I didn't think about how it would look to my parents. Although it is the first time since my divorce that they didn't bring up Mel. Maybe I should keep Curtis with me every time they call.

"Are you going to freak out?" he asks.

"No, why do you keep asking me that?"

He huffs and tries to get up. I keep him in place.

"Let me go, mountain man."

"Not until you tell me why you keep thinking I'm going to shout *no homo* anytime I so much as have a semi-serious expression."

26

BUBBLE

"No. It's Christmas Day, and the reason I sometimes say stupid things does not belong in this cabin," I say. "I am sorry though. This isn't about you. It's all me, okay?"

I really don't want to drag Harley and his shit in here. He doesn't deserve to occupy space here.

"I just met your parents." I repeat it because I can't believe that just happened. "They seem really nice."

"They are."

"Why didn't you spend Christmas with them?"

Coach picks a crumb of cinnamon bun and rolls it around the plate. "They were on a Christmas cruise in the Caribbean and stopped in St. Barts for Christmas."

"Do they travel a lot?"

He laughs. "Believe it or not, no, they don't. They've lived their whole life in Denver. Turned up out of the blue on Thanksgiving Day to tell me they were traveling over Christmas. I'm happy for them. They deserve to enjoy their retirement."

"How about you?"

He raises a brow. "I'm way, *way* off from retiring."

I pinch the muscles on his arms. "Hmm, I don't know, old man.

I'm not convinced. Maybe you should take me into the bedroom and show me how you're not quite ready for retired life."

The chair scrapes against the floor as he stands, taking me with him.

"I could get used to being carried everywhere, you know?" I say, wrapping my arms around his neck.

"I can't help it. You bring out my inner caveman."

"Take me to your cave then."

I don't think I've ever spent so much time in the bedroom over any Christmas vacation. There's something to be said about it, I think.

There are still plenty of cinnamon buns, and I can rustle up a quick dinner later. Go hungry, we will not. Even with all the sex.

Correction. All the best sex of my entire life.

Screw you, Harley. You were lousy in bed anyway.

Coach sets me on the bed but doesn't follow me.

"I'll be back in a moment," he says when I pout.

"Fine. I guess I'll undress myself. Don't blame me if I get the show running before you get back," I shout to the door he disappeared behind.

I remove my clothes, setting them carefully on the floor by the bed. I wanted to do my sexy elf dance for Coach, but it may have to wait for tomorrow. I missed a morning orgasm, and now that my belly is full of food, I want to satisfy my other needs.

He comes back, holding something wrapped in a piece of fabric.

"What's that?" I ask, sitting with my back toward the headboard of the bed.

He sits on the side of the bed next to me. "The day I realized I'd screwed everything up with you, I wanted to apologize, but I didn't know how. I couldn't face you without wanting to touch you, and I'd just been so rude to you."

I put my hand on his. "Hey, it's okay. We're past all that. Now when you shout at me, we're both naked, and I'm asking for it." I wiggle my brows, and he coughs, adjusting himself in his pants.

"Anyway. I made this to give you as a gift. I was going to take it to the cabin that morning when I went to apologize, but the glue hadn't set yet, so I hoped you'd still forgive me and I could give this to you later."

My chest expands, and I feel like I'm about to burst with emotion. All the emotions.

"Riley, you didn't have to do anything. Your apology was enough. Besides, you gave me a place to stay, and I'll say that living around your dick is a thousand times better than what I'd be doing at home alone."

He laughs. "What would you be doing?"

"Thinking about how I could convince you to let me impale myself on you permanently."

He shakes his head and places the fabric-wrapped gift on my lap. "It's nothing much but…I always enjoyed making things out of wood with my dad. It was the only gift I could make you here."

I unwrap the present to reveal a beautiful wooden book stand with hand-carved strawberries.

My throat feels tight, and I have to take a deep breath. "You…did all of this? On your own?"

"Yeah. It's not great. Carving isn't my best skill, but the wood had a few natural raised areas that made it perfect for it, so I couldn't resist. Since you always smell like strawberries, I figured you'd like it."

I run my fingers over the smooth wood. "I don't like it, Riley. I love it. This is the most thoughtful gift anyone has ever given me, other than my grandma's recipes. She had to give those to me because she had no other grandchildren to pass them on to, so she was kinda obliged."

"I'm sure she loved every minute of teaching you her recipes," he says. "I don't know if you have cookbooks or you use a tablet when you follow a recipe, but I thought this might be useful."

I put the gift to one side and wrap my arms around him. Slowly our mouths find their way to each other.

"I want to give you something else, Curtis." He looks into my eyes, and his are dark and needy. Afraid but full of trust.

"Are you sure?"

He pulls his sweater over his head and drags his sweatpants down. His cock stands thick against his stomach. "Absolutely."

I run my hands over his muscles. Is it strange to want to see what he'll look like with more silver hair? To want to see him grow older and even sexier than he is right now?

"Then let this be my gift to you, Riley. I'm going to make it so good."

"I know, baby. I know."

He puts my gift on the nightstand where the bottle of lube still sits, then jumps over me to the middle of the bed, taking me with him so I end up straddling his legs.

"I love it when you handle me like I'm super light."

"You *are* super light," he says.

I run my hands over all the deep ridges of his abs. He has such beautiful definition, and still, if this belly was flat or even round, I don't think I'd care.

His cock is hard and flushed. I want to make this so good for him. My hands shake a little as I give him a couple of strokes.

God, I love the way his breath catches when I touch him, like he's never been touched this way before. I want to be angry at a woman I don't even know because she had him for twenty-three years and couldn't make him feel this way.

Or maybe I'm assuming too much. He hasn't talked much about his marriage or why it broke down. Just like I haven't spoken about Harley. I guess we all have our past. Our secrets.

Coach wraps his hand over mine, tightening his grip. I lock eyes with him as we stroke him lazily. When he looks a little more relaxed, I point to the lube, and he hands it to me.

"I'm going to go slow, okay? At least my dick isn't as ginormous as yours."

He chokes a laugh. "Thanks."

"Open your legs."

He does, and I fit between them. He releases my hand and places both of his on either side of his body.

"You look like the best dessert, Riley. You're going to make me reconsider giving up my bottom crown, aren't you?"

"I'll tell you in a minute."

I uncap the lube, and once again, his whole body trembles. "Riley, we don't have to do this. Bottoming won't make you more or less gay or bi or whatever you are."

"I…just feel a little exposed like this. But I don't want to stop."

I look around, but he doesn't have a lot of pillows.

"I'll be back in a sec. Why don't you add a little lube to your hole and rub your finger around to get used to the feel of having something there?"

He nods. I run to the living room and grab the cushions from the couch and a blanket. It doesn't take me long, but I wait a few seconds to give him privacy to explore himself.

When I feel I've taken long enough, I go back into the bedroom. The sight of Riley naked in the middle of the bed, one hand stroking his cock, the other playing with the rim of his hole, almost makes me come on the spot.

He sees me by the door, but instead of stopping, he continues like he's enjoying it so much he can't stop himself.

"Scoot up against the board," I say, placing the pillows covered with the blanket behind him. I return to my place between his legs and add lube to my fingers.

I straddle one of his thick thighs, and he instantly opens his legs wider to give me room.

He pulls me for a kiss, so I take advantage and start exploring, just like I wanted.

I take it easy, testing my way around his rim, feeling as he contracts when I'm too close.

"I'm going to need you to relax, okay? Breathe out when I push in." We keep our gazes locked. I hope that not having my face down there makes him feel less open and vulnerable. He's in total control of the situation, but I'm not sure he understands how much power he really has.

He breathes out, and when I feel him relax, I push a finger in.

"You're doing good, baby," I say, distracting him with more kisses. Soon I'm able to slowly move my finger in and out. "That's it. You're doing great."

A small bead of sweat rolls down his forehead, and I lick it clean. God, what this man does to me that I'm now licking sweat.

He groans and plunges his tongue into my mouth. It's hard to keep my thoughts straight when he's doing that, but I manage to add another finger while he's distracted.

He moves on to kiss my neck and suck on my skin.

"You're so amazing, Curtis. I want to be all yours."

My heart thunders in my chest.

Focus on this, Bubble. Don't let the silly dreams get to you just yet.

Riley starts moving against my fingers, so I feel for his prostate. I know I've found it when he gasps like he's been hit in the chest.

"Holy fuck, what was that? Don't stop, please."

"That, my sexy coach, was your prostate." I add a third finger, but with the way he's moving, I know he's ready for me. "Just imagine when my cock rubs against that spot over and over again."

He groans and then holds my wrist. "I'm ready. Please, Curtis."

I have to take a slow breath before this next step. It's been years since I topped someone. It was with a friend who discovered then that he was definitely not a bottom. The experience isn't exactly something I want to remember.

Except it's all I can think about now. What if I can't do this right?

"What's the matter?" Riley asks.

"What? Nothing."

"You seemed lost for a moment there."

"Just a little nervous."

He takes the lube and squirts some directly onto my cock before spreading it around. Then he slides down on the bed, removing a couple of the pillows behind him, and aligns my cock with his hole.

"I'm all yours, baby."

"Okay," I whisper. "Breathe out and relax for me."

He does as I say, and maybe it's because my cock isn't that big—I mean, it's perfectly proportional to my body, thank you very much. But it's not a torpedo dick, that's for sure.

Maybe it's that, or maybe it's because we're really, truly meant for each other, but I slide in without any problems. I try to go slow, but Riley pulls me closer until I'm all the way inside him.

"God, I feel so full."

"It's amazing, isn't it?" I ask.

"It's…different."

I withdraw a little and then push back in. His mouth opens, letting out a breath with no sound, so I do it again and again until he's moaning and asking me to keep going.

His cock, which went flaccid when I first penetrated him, is hard again.

I take it as a sign he's enjoying this. I know I am. He's tight and hot, and even though my hole hasn't been invited to this party, I don't feel like I'm missing anything. The friction of my cock in his channel is enough to take me close to the edge.

"Fuck, Curtis. Faster. More."

I change the angle of my thrusts, and he cries out as I hit his prostate over and over.

27

COACH

My body is on fire and begging to roll around in the flames. I feel my orgasm cresting, like a group of firemen coming to relieve me from this pleasurable pain.

I want them to come, but I also want to send them away.

"Fuck…Curtis…don't…stop."

I'm holding on to him so tight that I'm not sure he has enough room to breathe. All I know is I've never felt like this before. I feel vulnerable but safe. Teetering on the edge but reluctant to jump.

"Riley, I'm getting close." His voice is muffled against my chest.

We're all groans and moans, curses and desperate touches. I don't know if I can come like this. Every time he hits my prostate, I feel like I'm going to burst, but then it goes away.

"I…can't."

He raises his head and meets my eyes. His hair is wet around his face, but he's never looked so beautiful. It hits me then. I could have this. More of this. More of his green eyes, his sunny personality, more of *him*.

"Riley," he whispers. He seems to want to say something else but catches himself. Instead, it's like he finds a renewed energy source and starts fucking me like his life depends on it.

My cock is so hard I'm afraid I'll do permanent damage to it if I don't come soon. Though it's my ass that I should be worried about because there's no doubt I'll be sore after this.

I try to reach for my cock, but we're practically glued together, and Bubble's focus on pounding my ass drives me insane.

How can someone so small have so much strength and staying power?

My orgasm builds again. This time there's nothing I can do to stop it.

"Curtis," I shout as I spill between us like I haven't come in a year. He follows me, digging his teeth into my peck, which I'm sure will leave a nice mark. Little fucker.

"Fuck a duck, Coach. I've earned all the candy I've hidden in my bag." He moves slightly to slide out of me, and I wince, feeling both the loss and the pain as he settles against my side.

"You have hidden candy?"

He doesn't move or look at me. Just shrugs. "I always have hidden candy. And glitter. You never know when the situation might call for it."

"Glitter?"

"Open your drawer and pass me the small pink bag inside."

I do as he says, and sure enough, there's a pink bag I've never seen before. I hand it to him. He opens it and takes out two pieces of candy. He puts one in his mouth and gives me the other. It tastes minty.

Then he takes something else out. He pulls a string, and before I can say anything, we have confetti raining down on us. It sticks to our skin because we're all sweaty.

"Thank fuck it's not glitter," I say.

"Congrats, Coach. You're no longer a butt virgin."

I slap his ass. "We need a shower. I can feel your cum seeping out of my ass."

He sighs. "It's wonderful, isn't it?"

He glances at me when I don't reply. "Fine, you can borrow the bottom crown occasionally, but you're a total top, aren't you?"

"I guess?" I say honestly. "That was more than amazing, and I want to do it again for sure, but the feeling of filling you and then leaving some of me behind? It makes me think things a man my age shouldn't."

Bubble stays silent against me, and I can't read him. Have I said too much? This is just temporary, isn't it? Our Christmas bubble. It'll be over when we go home. I have no right to want more. No matter how perfect it feels to be with him, age gap be damned.

"Come on, let's get you clean. I want to bake some cookies and take them to the kids next door. Then we'll do a Christmas movie marathon, but this time we'll do it for real. No distractions," he says.

I wince when I get up from the bed, feeling a lot sorer than I thought I would. "I can be on board with that…if you bake me some cookies too."

"Only if you help out."

I laugh all the way to the bathroom. Has he not seen already how I should not be allowed in the kitchen unless it's to fix something broken or to eat?

We end up taking our time in the shower, and I thank him for his gift by eating his ass until he comes again, this time against the bathroom tiles.

Note to self: Curtis thrashes around when he has really good orgasms. The bathroom tiles are a health hazard. Thankfully, I hold him in my arms as he loses control of his legs and slides down my body until we're both sitting.

Another note to self: well done for making the original shower cubicle much bigger.

Over the next few hours, I follow his orders as he tells me what to do in the kitchen with the precision of a military sergeant.

It's hot enough that my forty-six-year-old dick is ready to go again. A fact that doesn't go unnoticed, especially since I'm wearing a pair of sweatpants and nothing else.

Curtis? He's back to wearing his elf outfit and throwing heated looks in my direction.

While he decorates the cookies, he tells me what to do with dinner. Thankfully this only involves rubbing some spices and herbs onto a piece of meat and then putting it in the oven to cook on a slow heat.

By mid-afternoon, we're making our way across the snow to the cabin next door.

George cracks the door with Megan right behind him.

"Daddy!" Megan calls and opens the door for us to come inside.

Harrison peeks out from a hallway, holding a bunch of bedsheets in his arms. He waves for us to take a seat on the couch. "I'll be with you in a second, just need to get these in the wash."

"Daddy and Papa just had a shower," George says. "They said they had some messy Christmas presents from Santa."

"I think they spilled them on the bed too because they're doing the laundry again." Megan rolls her eyes.

I bite my lips so I don't laugh because I don't need two guesses as to what their parents were doing with whatever gifts Santa gave them.

"And what did Santa bring you?" Bubble asks.

"I got a new train set," George says.

"And I got five books," Megan says, adding, "Daddy said Santa knows we're going to Disneyworld in the spring, so he's giving more presents to children who need them because we're very lucky already. When I finish reading my books, I'm going to donate them to the Goodwill store."

"Yeah," George says, "and then she can play with my train set."

"Sorry, guys, we were...um..." Harrison looks a little flushed, coming out to the living room.

"Babe, I think they know," Fletcher adds.

"We don't want to interrupt your Christmas. It's just that Santa left these cookies at our place, but I think he really meant to leave them here," Curtis says, holding up a box filled with his cookies.

Megan and George look at each other with wide eyes and big smiles.

"That's very kind of Santa to do that. Are you sure it wasn't too much trouble?" Harrison asks.

"Absolutely not," Curtis says, and then he leans over like he's telling a secret. "I'm pretty sure I overheard one of the elves say that

Mrs. Claus baked these cookies herself. She made so many that she asked Santa to give them to the bestest boys and girls."

The kids look at their dads, who nod, and soon the box is taken from his hands.

"Don't eat too many, or you'll ruin your—" Harrison starts but doesn't finish. He likely knows it's hopeless on a day like today.

"Would you like to join us for coffee and some of those Mrs. Claus cookies?" Fletcher asks.

"Thank you, but we've got a Christmas movie marathon this afternoon, and I need to check on dinner. Thank you though," Bubble says.

"I don't suppose you know when the road out will be cleared," I ask.

"They're usually pretty good. As soon as they know the storm is over, they clear the roads. They know folks will need to get back home to their jobs since most of the cabins are vacation homes," Fletcher says.

"Thank you. That's useful to know."

We leave the family and walk back to my cabin. Curtis is strangely silent.

"You okay?" I ask.

"Yeah."

I laugh. "Really? You think you can fool me that easily?" I bend and pick up a chunk of snow and make it into a ball. "Maybe I can persuade you to tell me what's wrong."

"You should know by now there are much better ways to persuade me to do anything for you, Riley." He continues walking but goes toward the trees instead of the cabin.

I catch up to him and put my arm over his shoulder. He sags against me and lets out a deep sigh.

"Oh no. Not a sigh. This must be serious."

He elbows me. "I just…when you asked about the roads, it reminded me that at some point, we have to go home, that's all."

"You don't want to go home?"

He turns to face me. "Right now? No."

"Curtis." I'm not sure what to say.

"I'm sorry. I'm just being overdramatic. Juju says I do that a lot, but it's endearing…well, sometimes."

I take my gloves off so I can touch his face with my hands. "I like when you're dramatic. I like when you do a lot of things. And I don't want to go home either."

"You don't?"

I shake my head.

"I don't want the bubble to burst."

He narrows his eyes. "Bubble?"

"The Christmas bubble. I know you said what we do here stays here, but…"

Our breaths fog in the cold air. Curtis's cute nose is red, even though he's wearing a hat that covers almost his whole face.

"I thought you wanted to experiment," he says. His voice is small and unsure. "I didn't want to put any pressure on you. I know I was coming on too strong and you were straight."

I stop him with a kiss, loving how he responds immediately. Each pass of my tongue over his is met with a moan. When we part, his eyes are glassy and half-lidded.

"I think it's safe to say I'm not exactly straight. I spoke to Harrison when you were building the snowman. I think I may be demisexual, although I don't really care what label is attached to it. I just know that I like you, Curtis. I like you a lot."

He puffs out a breath and his cheeks redden. He's like the cutest elf I've ever seen.

"If my age doesn't bother you, then I don't want the bubble to burst, Curtis. I want to take you on an actual date when we get back home. See if we can make it out in the real world."

"Really? You don't think I'm too much, too over the top, too pink?"

I smile. "Baby, those were the things that made me want you. You never gave up. The gifts, the cakes. You burrowed under my skin with each day that passed. It's amazing I lasted this long."

"This really is the best Christmas ever." He holds me tight, so I kiss his head.

"I agree. We don't have to think about leaving just yet, so how about that movie marathon? We can cuddle naked under the blanket."

He releases me but pulls my hand and starts walking with purpose toward the cabin. "You have the best ideas."

28

BUBBLE

PACKING IS BITTERSWEET. I've had the best Christmas vacation ever and the best present. I mean, who gets a boyfriend for Christmas? At least, I think we're boyfriends. Riley wants to take me out on dates. If we're dating exclusively, then we're boyfriends.

Yes. I've decided.

Probably should tell him at some point.

The last couple of days have passed quicker than I wanted. Riley got me to agree that *Die Hard* is a Christmas movie by letting me ride his dick while we watched the movie. We both came during an explosion scene. I saw stars. Thus, it's a Christmas movie now.

I'm sure I should write a letter to the movie cast and director apologizing, but it was a damn good orgasm. We had hot cocoa with tiny marshmallows afterward. It was perfect.

I've never had so much good sex in my life, and what's even better is that I don't have to give it up. Because, as stated above, boyfriends.

Riley is outside making sure everything is in the right place and locked. He's a bit of a neat freak when it comes to his tools and all the stuff in his shed. It's kind of adorable.

It took me a while to pack because I really made myself at home in his cabin and had to rummage around for all my stuff.

He comes from the side of the cabin as I'm dragging my suitcase out.

"Hey, you should have called me. Let me help." He lifts the suitcase like it weighs nothing and takes it to my car. Since we ate most of the food I brought, I'm happy to travel home a lot lighter. The Christmas decorations are already in the trunk, so I'm almost done.

He closes the trunk and pulls me close. "Do you think Jeremy feels neglected? He spent all this time in the suitcase."

I laugh. "Nah. He doesn't have self-confidence issues. Besides, once I introduce you two properly, I'm sure you'll get along fine."

He raises a brow.

"What? Playing with toys isn't just for kids, you know," I say.

"Harrison sent a message to say the roads are clear from here to Stillwater. I'm sure they'll be fine the rest of the way to Windsor. Are you all packed up?"

"Yes, but I still don't want to go." I pout, but the only outcome is Riley pulling me in for a kiss, starting by sucking the pout straight out of me. Damn, he's so good at it.

I run my hands through his hair. "I'll miss you. Sorry if that sounds silly and desperate, but I don't care."

"I'll miss not having you around all the time too. Who'd have thought, huh?" He kisses my nose. "Get in your car and warm up. I'll just lock up and then follow you home, okay?"

"You don't have to, you know? I got here perfectly fine on my own," I say.

"I know, but I'll feel better knowing you're home safe. Besides, you have that big suitcase, and in case you missed them, I have a few muscles to spare."

I lick my lips. "Coach, your flirting game is on."

"Now that's something I've never heard before."

I poke his chest. "And never will again unless it's from me. Got it?"

He raises his hands. "Yes, sir."

"Ooh…park that thought for the end of our first date."

He gives me one last kiss and makes sure I'm in the car.

My phone rings with a call from Juju, but I don't want to answer now since we're about to get on the road. I'll call her back when I'm home. It's only a forty-minute drive.

I pick my playlist and turn the music on, singing along to my favorite songs as we leave our Christmas bubble and get ready to face the real world.

I'm just glad I still have until the new year off from Spilled Beans because I can spend some time with Riley before the start of the spring semester. No doubt we'll be busy once school starts again, but at least we'll both attend all the football games.

My mind drifts from thoughts about Riley to some ideas I had in the last few days for the cheerleading routine. Before I know it, I'm stopping in front of my building.

Riley parks behind my car and comes to help me with the suitcase.

"Bubble!" I hear a scream from a very familiar voice, and when I turn toward it, I almost faint.

"Juju! Oh my god, how are you here?"

"I tried calling, but you didn't answer. The airline offered to reschedule the flight, so I took the chance."

I hug her tight. She smells like airplane, flowers, and gummy bears, her favorite flying snack. "God, I missed you."

She looks behind me and her chin literally drops. "Wow."

"Oh, Juju, this is Riley." I turn to Riley. "Riley, this is my best friend, Juju."

"Nice to meet you, Juju," Riley says. "I've heard a lot about you."

"Everything he said is a lie," she says, pointing at me. "Unless it's true."

Riley laughs. "I guess I'll need to get to know you better to figure out which is which."

Juju meets my gaze, and I'm sure I'm melting on the spot, even in this cold weather. Yes, my boyfriend is being super-duper-sweet to my best friend. Is it legal to jump him in public and kiss his handsome face? Because I so want to do that right now.

She scratches her messy bun, her expression suddenly going serious. She spares a glance at Riley and then back at me. "Um, I'm not on my own. It wasn't my idea. It was more that I didn't have a choice.

Trust me, I wanted to cut off his balls during the flight, but I heard there's always an Air Marshall present, and I didn't want to get arrested."

"What are you talking about?"

My blood goes cold and my legs almost give out when I see the one person I swore I'd never want to see or hear from again in my life.

"Wha…what is he doing here?"

"Babe, are you okay?" Riley is there next to me, his strong arm keeping me steady.

Harley smiles like we're long-lost friends or lovers who haven't seen each other in a while and miss one another. "Boo-boo! Wow, you look fantastic."

He's dressed in clothes that are totally inappropriate for this weather. His leather shoes alone will get him killed if he doesn't die of frostbite first.

If only.

The closer he gets, the more my blood thaws until it reaches a boiling-rage temperature.

I don't want to make a scene, especially not in front of Riley. The last thing I want is for him to decide I'm far too much drama after all. Not to mention that my whole story with Harley is too humiliating.

Harley comes so close I can smell his cologne. The one that always made me nauseous. I should have known even then he wasn't right for me.

I freeze when he comes even closer, but Riley holds out his hand to him, effectively providing a safe barrier.

"Riley Dempsey. You are?"

Riley's voice is deeper and more assertive than I've heard it before.

Harley takes a step back and gives Riley an assessing look. He doesn't take Riley's hand, which is probably a smart move. "Harley Bruce. How's life been since you left the Marinos, Coach Dempsey?"

"Mr. Bruce. I read the sports news headlines too," Riley replies with a cryptic tone, and I swear I see some of Harley's color drain from his face.

What's that all about?

"Well, this was a nice little reunion, but you've seen Bubble, so you can get on your way, Harley. Ciao," Juju says, attempting to push him away.

"Not so fast. I'd like to catch up with Bubble," he says without taking his eyes off me.

"Bubble?" Riley's voice is gentle, and I love how he didn't call me by my name. Harley has no business knowing my name. I know Riley has my back if I want him to send Harley away. But now that he's here, I want to know what he has to say for himself before I kick his ass to Timbuktu.

I look up at Riley. "I'll text you later, okay?"

He stares into my eyes, and I wish I could tell him what I don't want to say aloud in front of Harley. "We're still on for tomorrow, yeah?"

"Of course." And with that, he returns to his car and leaves.

I watch as the car containing the person I want to be with disappears while the one I want to murder is still a few steps away.

"What the fuck are you doing here, Harley?"

"I came to see you, baby. You disappeared after I left the hospital. I was worried sick."

"You were so worried sick that you went and got my spot on the cheerleading team. Tell me, did you sleep with the coach to get in, or was it a straight knife in the back situation?"

I don't bother with my suitcase or any of the stuff in my car. I walk to my building, picking up Juju's suitcase by the door. Even though the last thing I want is to have Harley anywhere near my personal space, it's cold out. Juju is also wearing unseasonable clothing.

"I didn't stab you in the back, Bubble. You were injured. Someone else would have taken the spot. Wouldn't you have wanted that person to be me?"

I open my front door and walk inside my small apartment. It's cold because I haven't been in for a week, so I turn on the heat. My new personal goal is to get Harley out before the apartment gets warm.

Juju stays silent. I love her, but our conversation about this whole thing will happen later.

"You know what, Harley? You're right. I would have wanted you to have the spot. If you'd talked about it with me. If you'd asked me if I was okay with it. But I was in the hospital with my whole career destroyed in one single moment, and what did you do? As soon as you could stop playing the caring boyfriend, you left me."

He at least has the decency to look ashamed. "I did love you, you know?"

"You had a funny way of showing it. But you know what? I don't even care if it was real anymore. I just want you out of my life. I don't know why you're here, but you've seen me. The door is over there."

This is one of those rare times when I hate that my usually cozy apartment is too small. I can't make a dramatic exit unless I go hide in the bathroom or my bedroom, so I go to the kitchen and start brewing a pot of coffee.

"I know what I did was wrong, but I was hoping you'd put it behind us and—"

"And what? Want to get back together? Fuck no."

"I need your help," he says.

I laugh. "I have no money."

"It's not money I need."

I turn around and cross my arms. This should be good.

"I went out to celebrate my spot on the new team and someone spiked my drink. Nothing bad happened, but there was a random drug test the next day, and I failed. Now I have to audition again if I want to get back in."

I look at Juju. "Did you tell him I helped Brandon with his audition?"

"No. This dickwad just came over and refused to leave until I told him where you were. I already had my flight booked to surprise you, and he just followed me."

Harley stares at me. "You're the one who helped Brandon get his role?"

"No, asshole. Brandon helped Brandon get his role. When will you get through your head that only you can help yourself? No one else can do the work for you. I just gave him some choreography ideas, and he ran with them. Anyway, you're still here. Go away."

"So you're not going to help me?" He stares at me, and I see his vulnerability. But then I remember coming back from my surgery, and he wasn't there. Waiting for him to visit me at home, and he never did. Not a single flower, card, or wish that I would get better enough to follow my dream.

"No. Please leave. I'm not asking again."

"But I came all the way here," he says, like it's the grand gesture I've been waiting for all my life.

"I didn't ask you to come."

"I don't even have a suitcase or clothes."

"Believe it or not, there are shops in Connecticut too." I gesture to the door.

Harley looks at Juju, who's made herself comfortable on my couch under one of my many blankets. She's not even looking at us.

It's not until the door clicks shut that I finally take a breath.

I lean on the breakfast bar, and a moment later, Juju is there with her arms around me.

"I'm sorry. I tried to stop him, but he wouldn't listen. I tried to warn you, but you didn't pick up your phone all day."

"That's because I was busy having all the morning sex with my boyfriend before we came home."

She screeches and grasps her hands in front of her chest. "Fill me up with a cup of that coffee and *all* the details. Let's order in food. I can't believe you scored your Coach. He seemed pretty pissed when he left."

"I know. I'll call him later. Probably should cancel our date tomorrow. I don't want to leave you on your own."

She hits me in the head. "You will do no such thing. Did you see the way that man looks at you? You are not standing him up for me. I can take care of myself for one night. And you better stay over at his place if you're going to fuck like bunnies."

I hug her again. "Oh, how I missed you."

As I start pouring the coffee, the cup suddenly cracks. We both gasp and look at each other.

My grandmother used to say that was a sign something was about to happen.

"That's…just a delayed reaction from Harley turning up," Juju says.

A shiver runs down my spine. "Yeah…"

29

COACH

I REST my head against the back of my seat and close my eyes. I've barely slept over the last three days, but my body refuses to give me any kind of rest.

My suitcase is still by the front door of my place, abandoned.

"Are you okay, sweetie?" Mom asks.

"Yeah."

"You look tired."

"I'm good." I give her a smile and bring her hand up to my lips.

I'd barely arrived home after leaving Curtis with his friend and the other guy when I got a call from my mom. Dad slipped on a wet floor and broke his foot.

I'm glad it wasn't something more serious, but since they were about to leave St. Barts, they missed their flight back.

Her trembling voice over the phone is something I won't forget anytime soon. This was their first vacation abroad, so even though they had insurance to help with costs, I know this was a scary experience for my mom.

She may be brave most of the time, but she's a total mother hen to my dad and me. I can only imagine how helpless she felt seeing him in the hospital and not knowing what to do.

The only thing I could think to do on the spot was to fly out and bring them back home with me. I could arrange their flights back to Denver once we figured out what kind of support my dad would need at home.

Like me, he's not a small man, and with his mobility compromised, there's no way my mom can do everything for him.

"We'll be landing soon," I tell her, and she smiles. Dad is a few rows in front of us, reading a magazine. At least he's taking it all in his stride.

I stare at my phone. In the rush to pack clean clothes in a duffel bag, I forgot to grab the charger that was in my suitcase. Thank god for airport stores because I'd hate to think I couldn't have contacted Curtis to tell him I wouldn't make our date.

I pinch the bridge of my nose, willing my headache away.

God, I miss him so much.

It's been three days, and I can't stop thinking about him, worrying about if he's okay. I don't know what that thing between him and Harley Bruce was, but I didn't like how he looked at Curtis like he owned him or something.

I also didn't miss how Curtis tensed as soon as he saw Harley. The dickhead thought he'd be able to scare me off, but I know exactly who he is. I just don't know his connection to Curtis other than they're both cheerleaders. Maybe they used to be on the same team.

"Fuck," I say between gritted teeth, but it's loud enough that my mom puts her hand on my knee and pats it.

What if they were together? What if Harley wants to get back with Curtis?

"Honey, you look like you're about to jump out of your skin. Please tell me what's going on. Is it because you're having to deal with us at the last minute?"

"What? God no, Mom, of course not."

"Then what is it? We used to talk about everything, but you've closed yourself off from me." She sounds hurt, and she has reason to be.

I let out a sigh. The guy sitting on the other side of me is asleep. I turn in my seat slightly.

"Mom, if you found out that someone you love has a secret that could destroy your friendship but doesn't involve you, would you still want to know?"

She takes my hand in hers. "If the secret has the potential to destroy a friendship, then I'd say it already involves me. I'd want to know."

"Even if it's about Mel?"

"You are my only son. I'm so proud of the man you are. Nothing you could tell me would make me love you any less. Mel has become a daughter to us, but we know she's not perfect."

God, I want to hug her.

"Oh, Mom. I love you so much for being so open. You and Dad made me the way I am. You're always loving and accepting, which is why this is really difficult for me."

She squeezes my hand. "Let it out once, and we'll never speak of it again."

"I can't have children, Mom. I'm infertile."

Her eyes go red and fill with tears. "Oh, baby." She cradles my face, looking into my eyes until the information sets in.

"When did you find out?"

"Before I filed for divorce."

Her brows furrow because my mom has been there for twenty-three years of miscarriages and heartbreak. She was the shoulder Mel cried on like she would her own mother had she been alive.

"My whole life was a lie, Mom. When Mel got pregnant at eighteen, I was so scared about the prospect of being a father so young. We'd never…you know, had sex. Even though I was scared, I was devastated when she lost the baby. We both were."

"But if you can't have any children…?" Mom gasps. "She didn't know…" I see the pieces being put together in my mom's head. I don't need to tell her Mel cheated because it's obvious.

I nod. "We stayed together and got married and…then she lost another baby. I don't know why she did it, but since I'm infertile, you can guess how many times before and during our marriage she's been with other men and had unprotected sex. She put herself and me at risk. I couldn't forgive her."

"How did you find out?"

"A friend saw her leaving a hotel with a man while I was away with the team and told me. When I confronted her, she confessed to being lonely because I was always away. When I asked her about the first pregnancy, she couldn't even look at me. That's when I went to the doctor to get tested for STIs, and while I was there, I also asked about my fertility. It's ridiculous now to think we never considered one of us couldn't conceive. She probably just assumed those babies were mine."

Mom runs her hands through her hair. "My god, what have I done?"

"What are you talking about?"

She sighs. "I didn't want to be a burden to you, so I asked Mel if she could come to help us fly back home."

"What do you mean, Mom?"

"Oh, son. I'm so sorry. I shouldn't have done it. I'll call her when we land and cancel."

"Cancel what?"

"She's flying to Connecticut and staying in a hotel while we make the arrangements at home. Then she's flying back with us. I was just so scared of doing all of this with your dad on my own."

The announcement for the landing comes on.

"It's okay, Mom. It's probably a good idea. She's someone you know and trust to help you get home."

She scoffs. "Well, my trust in her has changed severely in the last few minutes, but if life has taught me anything, it's that sometimes we have to fight one fire at a time." She holds my hand in hers. "And what about that young man who was at the cabin with you? We may be old, but we're not blind. Dad and I talked about it. We think your age gap could be a concern in the future, but we saw how he looked at you when you weren't looking, even in that short call. If you two love each other, then we're happy for you and fully supportive."

I smile, bringing her hand up to my lips.

"Thank you, Mom." As soon as we're home, I'll call Curtis and set up another date. I don't want there to be any misunderstandings between us. I have to trust that what we had in the cabin was real, and

if I have to fight that shithead who turned up at his doorstep, then I'll
do it.

30

BUBBLE

I HEAR a noise at the front door and, soon after, steps approaching my room. I close my eyes.

"You can pretend all you want, but I know you're awake," Juju says. "I'm going to put a pizza in the oven unless you want me to destroy your kitchen with something a little more gourmet, like a salad?"

"Salad isn't gourmet. It's just stuff tossed in a bowl."

She jumps on the bed and tickles me. "So you *are* awake."

"Get off me, ridiculous woman."

"Make me."

I turn around and start tickling her back. We end up on the floor, tangled in my bed covers and laughing until we're crying.

"Thank you for being here," I say as we lie facing each other.

She grasps my hands close to her chest.

"Ew, I'm touching boob."

"Shut up," she says. "We're having a moment."

"We are?"

"Yes. The moment where I tell you that you need to stop moping around and pull yourself together. Okay, so you miss him. He'll be back soon, and you can get back to having all the hot sex."

"What if something bad happened?" My heart starts palpitating. "What if he's in the hospital and can't talk, and there's no one with him. Oh my god, Juju, we need to start calling all the hospitals."

I move to get up, but she grips me with the strength of a thousand vices.

"Stop being dramatic. Why would he be in the hospital? You said he went to get his parents from St. Barts."

"How do you know? He could have slipped on a wet floor and knocked himself out, and maybe he has a concussion and lost his memory. He'll never remember what we had this Christmas." My voice hitches and my lower lip wobbles.

Juju closes her eyes and takes a deep breath like she's giving up. "Okay, why don't you have a shower and get dressed in anything but yoga pants. We'll eat pizza and then go to his place. If he's not there, we'll ask his neighbors if they've seen him."

"Okay…I suppose that sounds like a reasonable plan."

We stand, and I take the opportunity of a messy bed to put the sheets in the wash. I quickly put fresh sheets on the bed and then jump in the shower.

When I come out, I smell the delicious scent of tomato, cheese, and garlic. If Juju also got us some buffalo wings, I might just have to smother her with kisses.

I'm getting dressed when my phone rings on the nightstand. I see Riley's name pop up and almost trip over myself to get the phone.

"Hello?"

"Curtis, baby."

The way he says my name like a prayer—god, it does things to me.

"Riley, god, I was so worried. Okay, I may have been a little dramatic about it too." He chuckles on the other side of the line. "But I'm really happy you're back, and I'm sorry your dad got hurt on vacation. Your mom must have been so scared."

"It wasn't easy for her. Dealing with all the insurance, the doctors. But we're all home now, and that's what matters. I need to help them arrange some support for my dad at home in Denver before they can fly out." He pauses. "Fuck, I miss you. I miss feeling your warm body against mine, your strawberry scent, your smile, your forest-green eyes."

I fall on the bed like an infatuated teenager. "I missed you too. And by the way, your phone voice is sexy as hell. Do you have five minutes to read the phone book while I get myself off?"

He laughs, and the sound reaches all the parts of my body that have been neglected in the last few days, especially my heart.

"I promise to make it up to you."

"You better."

"Listen, I gotta go. Call you later, okay?"

"Okay." I resist the urge to say *love you* at the end because it's ridiculous. We've been together a week, and we're not even officially boyfriends.

I jump off the bed with renewed energy.

"Wow, is there some kind of illegal substance in that new soap you bought?" Juju says when I come out of my room.

"Nope. Better. Let's eat because I'm starving, and then I need to bake a pie."

"Okaay."

Over lunch, I tell Juju about Riley's call, and she hits me on the head with her *I told you so* expression.

Riley's mom and dad liked the pie I made for Thanksgiving, so I check my cabinets, and I still have all the ingredients I need.

Juju turns the TV on, picking one of her reality TV shows to play in the background. I'm not letting her anywhere near my pie, so we chat about anything and everything.

When the pie is ready, I take it out of the oven and put it to one side to cool down. Then I go to the bedroom, pick my favorite outfit, and get ready.

"What do you think?" I ask Juju, doing a full twirl in front of her.

"I think that if I was your coach, I'd be eating that pie off your body."

I look at my pink cropped shirt with the oversized collar. "Should I tone it down?"

"No, babe. You be you. Go surprise your coach with your nice gesture."

"Okay. I've got this."

Despite my initial excitement, as I'm approaching Riley's place, nerves get the best of me. What if he doesn't want me to come over unannounced? What if he's not ready for me to properly meet his parents?

Shit. I didn't even think of that.

Well, it's too late now. Besides, I don't have to come in. I can just give him the pie and leave. Yeah, that's what I'll do.

I walk up to the door and ring the bell. A moment later, the door opens, but it's not Riley.

"Um…hi." I stare at the woman. It's not Riley's mom. I remember her from the call.

The woman stares at me in confusion. She's beautiful, with blonde hair and bright-blue eyes.

"Can I help you?" she asks.

"Um…I'm looking for Coach…I mean, Riley."

She smiles. "Oh, you must be one of his work colleagues. I'm Mel, his wife."

The way she says the words with such certainty and confidence almost knocks me sideways.

"Is Riley here?" I ask.

"He's gone out to do some shopping. We've all just flown in, so it's a bit of a mess." She straightens her long hair. "Is this work-related? Can I pass a message? Riley has always been a workaholic." She giggles.

"Um, no, it's not important. I heard his dad had an accident and thought he might want some pie to cheer him up."

She holds out her hands to take the pie from me. "Aw, that's very thoughtful of you. Thank you. We really appreciate your support. We'll write a note of thanks to the school."

I stand there speechless and confused.

"Was there anything else you wanted?"

"No. That was…no…" I walk back to my car.

I sit there for a while trying to process what just happened. He called me. He said he missed me.

But he never said his ex-wife was with him and never invited me to come over. It reminds me how little we really know about each other.

I'm on autopilot all the way home.

Juju runs to me as soon as I'm through the door.

"What happened?"

"I don't know."

"What do you mean?"

I sit on the couch with my coat and shoes still on. "His ex-wife was there. She referred to herself as his wife. He never said she was there when he called." I look at Juju. "Do you think he lied?"

"Why don't you call him?"

I shake my head.

"Fine, I'll call him." She grabs the phone from my hand before I can stop her and calls his number.

I hear the sound of the ringtone. It rings a few times until someone answers.

"Hello?"

Juju stares at me and mouths, "Is that her?"

I nod as tears start running down my face.

"Who is this? Your name comes up as Bubble, which must be a joke. Either way—"

Juju disconnects the call and wraps her arms around me.

"I fell in love with him, you know?"

"I know, sweetie. You have such a big heart."

"Why does no one want it?"

She rocks us in a soothing motion while running her hands up and down my back.

"I think it's time to open that bottle of wine you have in the fridge," she says.

"And then margaritas."

"Uh-huh."

"And rum punches?"

"Whatever you want, babe."

We collect all the alcohol I own plus what Juju's bought while she's been staying with me, and it all goes on the coffee table. I don't remember going to bed, but that's where I wake up the following morning.

And because it's New Year's Eve, we decide to remain drunk

because no one wants to be hungover on New Year's Eve before the party.

We eat and drink ourselves silly.

Within reason, of course. Juju, the saint she is, makes sure I keep drinking water and eating carbs.

New Year's Day passes in a flash, and then Juju is gone.

I'm left to patch my wounded heart on my own.

I haven't heard from Riley since our last call. Although, to be fair, I turned my phone off, so maybe there were calls. I don't know.

In a moment of weakness, when I know Juju is up in the sky flying back home, I turn it on.

There are some voicemails from Riley, but I can't bring myself to listen to them.

I'm too scared.

So I keep ignoring them and the new calls that come through.

The day before class starts, there's an email from the principal asking all teaching and administration staff to come in for a meeting.

I know I'll see Riley then and consider resigning from my job until Juju's voice in my head tells me to stop being dramatic.

There's only one thing to do.

I'm not Bubblelicious for nothing.

I'm going to fight fire with fire.

31

COACH

I END the call with my parents and get ready to go to school. I'm glad they've settled back at home fine and Dad is behaving.

It's time to get back to my life, including winning back the man I've fallen in love with.

When Mom told me about Curtis coming over with pie while I was shopping, I wanted to throttle Mel.

Thankfully, Mom did it for me by sending her back to her hotel before I got home. Mom had been helping Dad settle on the couch when the doorbell rang, so Mel answered the door.

I saw the pie on the kitchen counter as soon as I put the groceries down. For a moment, my heart soared, and I ran to the living room, thinking Bubble might be keeping my dad company.

Between arranging care and flights for my parents to return home after New Year's Day and making sure they were both comfortable in my much-smaller house, it didn't leave me with much time for anything else.

I called Curtis, but the phone seemed to be off. I left voicemails that were ignored.

In the end, Mom's parting words gave me the best idea.

"Your boy needs a grand gesture. Since you last saw him, you missed your date, but he still turned up with pie, and then he had to deal with facing your ex-wife. Show him you're deserving of his love."

So I made a few other calls and put a plan in place.

I look at the watch. It's time to leave, so I give myself another check in the mirror.

I'm wearing a white button-up shirt and the best pair of jeans I own. It's nothing special, but I know Curtis doesn't care about fancy stuff. He cares about being genuine and being yourself.

I grab my coat and leave.

When I get to the school, everyone is already there. The cheerleading team, the football team, and the school band. God, I love these kids.

"Hey, Justin. Everyone okay?" I ask Curtis's assistant coach.

"Coach, this is going to be epic." He goes to join the kids, holding a tablet in his hand.

Bubble should be arriving any moment now, so I take my place in front of the door leading to the locker rooms and our office.

My hands shake, so I put them in my pockets. This could go so fucking horribly wrong.

"He's here," I hear someone say.

I can't see anything because of the crowd of kids in front of me. I'm sure someone is recording this because the kids put so much work into practicing the routine at the last minute.

When I called Justin, he couldn't have been more excited to help.

He said there was some kind of unofficial bet going on among the cheerleading team because Curtis's crush wasn't that secret. They wondered when I'd finally break down and kill him or date him.

I don't know who's on the winning team, but I fell in love with the pint-sized, strawberry-scented, permanently cheerful man. I think I'm the one winning here. If he'll have me.

The band starts playing the song I heard him singing in the shower the day I first saw him almost naked, the Beatles' "When I'm Sixty-Four."

The lyrics have been slightly tweaked, which was Justin's idea, but the main part remains the same.

I hope he will still love me when I'm sixty-four.

Cheerleaders jump high in the air while the football team throws balls between each other. As Curtis walks through, they're supposed to create a walkway that leads directly to me at the end of the song.

I don't see much until he's closer, and then he's there. Only a few feet from me.

A few students stand between us. Cheerleaders doing their routine and blowing kisses at Bubble after they land on their feet. Footballs create an arch over his head.

It's amazing, but it doesn't compare to the shine in his eyes. The smile of pure joy seeing everything happen around him.

He covers his mouth with his hands when the cheerleaders do something particularly daring, and then he hugs them at the end. They push him toward me, which is when he finally sees me standing there.

He stops, and I can't read his face. The music is still playing. The cue for the kids to disperse and leave us alone is when the music ends.

When that happens, there will be nothing between us. No more lies or misunderstandings.

I mouth at him, "I love you," and his eyes fill with tears.

Please don't run from me. I need you.

He keeps walking forward until he crashes into my arms. I wrap mine around him and hold tight. He's not getting away from me anytime soon.

The music ends. He looks up at me.

"No. When you're sixty-four, I will love you more than I love you today because even after all the heartache and the things we need to talk about, you're still the only one I want."

I cradle his face and kiss him.

In seconds, we're surrounded by kids cheering, jumping, and clapping. It's insanity.

When we part, Curtis's cheeks are pink and his lips are red from me sucking on them.

"Go on, you've seen everything. You can go home," I shout so everyone can hear.

"Go, Bubble!" the cheerleaders shout.

"It's odd how they seem to have this weird vested interest in us being together," I say, placing my hand on his chin and turning his face back to me.

"How did you put all of this together?" he asks.

"Justin helped. He's a total enabler. My low-key surprise turned into a one hundred-people flash mob."

I take his hand and pull him inside the building, locking the door behind us.

Curtis raises a brow but doesn't ask questions.

His earthquake detection kits are still on the walls as we walk through the locker room, but it's the office I want him to see.

"Are you ready for it?" I ask.

"Is there another band and more music?"

"No."

"*Magic Mike*, but naked?" He wiggles his brows.

"What? No."

He shrugs. "That's okay. You can put on your own show for me."

I open the door and let him through.

"You moved my desk?" He runs his hand over his desk, where it joins with mine. They're side by side. His inspirational quotes have been moved so they cover the space behind both desks, and now I can see the paint on the wall.

"You belong next to me, Curtis. In every way possible." I pick him up and place him on his desk, pushing his coat off his shoulders so I can get closer to him. "I'm sorry about Mel. Anything she said or implied wasn't true. My mom was so angry when Mel said you'd dropped off a pie. She wanted to meet you."

"Mel didn't know who I was," he says.

"No. That is true. But the polite thing to do would have been to invite you in."

"Do you think she knew? That you maybe were with a guy."

I shrug. "No, and it doesn't matter. I came clean to my mom about what Mel did and the reason for our divorce. I will tell you the story later, but there's something more important that I think you should know."

"Okay."

God, his eyes hold so much trust.

"It's a few things, actually. The first and most important one is that I love you. I love you so much. I can't stand the thought of not seeing you every day, waking up to you, or hearing you mumble about ridiculous things. I love you to the point I want to know your best friend. I want her to visit you as often as she can. I want you to pursue your dreams and be happy. I just hope they also include me. I hope we can make our Christmas bubble last forever." He opens his mouth to talk, but I put a finger over his lips to stop him.

"I'm also infertile. I always wanted children but didn't know I couldn't have them until recently. When I got divorced, it became one of those things I accepted I'll never have. But I'll just put it out there, Curtis. If you want to be a dad, I'll be the best dad our children could ask for. If you don't, then that's also okay. Whatever we decide together will always be the right thing. I will never want anything more than you. Do you hear me?"

He looks up at the ceiling. "I always thought my grandma was up there looking out for me. Now I know it's true, and she really outdid herself this time."

Then he looks at me, his eyes red with unshed tears. "I ran away to Connecticut because someone I thought I loved made me feel like I was nothing more than a stepping stone to getting what he wanted. Now I know that every moment in my life was designed to take me to this exact spot where I can tell you that I love you back. I will give you as many children as you want because the only way I can see my future is with you, Riley Dempsey."

Our mouths meet in a soft, loving kiss that becomes hungry and desperate. Teeth clink together, nipping and biting. He tastes just how I remember. My favorite flavor of all time.

Strawberry Bubble.

"Take me home, Coach, and fuck me like you wanted that first time. Let's pretend we're in that shower."

"How did you know I wanted to fuck you then?" I nip at his neck, sucking his skin so it leaves a mark.

"It was in your eyes."

I grab his coat and help him put it on, zipping it up until he looks like the most delicious human burrito.

Before we leave, Curtis notices the new additions to our stationery. Pen holders. One that says *I'm his* with an arrow pointing to the other that says *He's mine.*

"Just so we're clear, this doesn't mean you get cake every day now," he says.

"What? Are you kidding me?"

He goes up on his toes to kiss me. "But you can eat my ass any time you want."

"I'll take that."

By the time we come out of the building, there's no one around.

Thank god the Principal is a Marinos fan, and I managed to get him a shirt signed by all the guys on the team.

I'd get shirts signed by all the teams in the NFL for the chance to get my Bubble back.

"God, I can't wait to be inside you again," I say, pulling him by the hand over to my car. We can get his tomorrow.

"Then we better be quick. Then again, my dick has been neglected for over a week. It won't take much for me to come as soon as I have your monster cock filling me."

"Christ, Bubble. You're going to make me come in my pants."

We get to my place in record time. Since my new favorite sport is carrying Curtis everywhere, I lift him up when we get out of the car and don't let him go until we're inside the bathroom in my bedroom.

Clothes are discarded, and I think my shirt is now missing a button or two. Curtis turns the shower on, and we wait until the water is warm before we go under the spray.

He puts his hands on the tiled wall and sticks his butt out for me. It's the most beautiful sight.

I drop to my knees and suck him until he's pushing back against my face.

"One of these days, you're going to sit on my face, and I'm going to eat you until you come, baby," I say.

He moans his reply as I replace my tongue with my lubed fingers.

"Fuck, I missed your fingers. Give me more, Riley."

"Patience, Curtis."

"Fuck that. I needed your dick inside me yesterday."

My dick thickens as I think of sinking into his tight hole. I stand and apply lube to my shaft before lining it up with his ass.

Using both hands, I open him so I can see as he takes me inch by inch.

"You look so good with my cock buried to the hilt inside you, Curtis."

"Ugh, why do you make my name sound like it's the sexiest name ever?"

"Because I love you, baby. Your name from my lips will always be a prayer."

He turns his face sideways to meet my gaze.

"Then take me to church, Riley."

I pull out and thrust back in one move. Curtis screams my name and more.

I need to see his face when he comes, so I pull out and turn him around.

"Wrap your legs around my waist."

His thighs pressing around me remind me of how strong he is. He may be small, but he's not weak. I grab my cock and put it back inside him.

With my hands on his ass, I don't even need the wall for support.

"Oh my god, Coach. This feels so good. God, you're hitting it right there every time. Fuck, don't stop."

I grit my teeth and use my hands to help him bounce on my dick until he's coming. Rope after rope of white cum coating our stomachs.

"I want to taste it," I say.

He runs his hand over his chest and then brings it to my mouth. The salty, bitter taste of his release and the fact I was already on the verge of coming take me over.

I fill him with more than a week's worth of cum. Just like him, I haven't touched myself. Even when all I could think about was Curtis, I needed my next time to be inside him.

Our breaths mingle in a lazy kiss. I pull us back under the water spray and put him down so we can wash each other.

I never thought I'd have a second chance at love at my age, but I know now I never stood a chance against Curtis. And I wouldn't have it any other way.

32

BUBBLE

A YEAR-ISH LATER

"It's enough, baby. Trust me."

I stare at the man I love above anything else, although right now, I wonder why.

I raise my hand, pointing at my fingers. "First, you can never have enough decorations. Second, yes, the cookies on the Christmas tree must be edible. Otherwise, what's the point. Third, we still need to hang the garland on the wood beam."

He takes his shirt off.

"What are you doing?" I grab his shirt and attempt to get him dressed. But his hands are already on the waist of his gray sweatpants. My traitorous dick reacts. "No. We are not having sex right now. Your parents will be here any moment, and we haven't finished decorating."

He's fully naked. His super-cannon dick pointing at me, taunting me.

I sigh and pinch the bridge of my nose. "Fine. But we'll need to be quick."

He lifts me over his shoulder and takes me to the bedroom.

Thank you, lord, for small mercies. I wouldn't want to have to clean cum from the couch cushions right before his parents arrive.

"Ass up," he commands, and I obey. I love it when he gets bossy.

I expect him to rim me, but instead, I feel cold lube on my ass. He opens me and something other than his fingers slides inside me.

"What the hell?"

"Relax, baby, it's only a plug."

"Why does it feel weird?"

He laughs. "You'll see. Now on your back."

Hmm, okay…

I don't know where this is going, but the more he touches me, the more I want to come, and the less I think about Christmas decorations or his parents coming with Juju from the airport.

We're staying at the cabin again this year, and after speaking to Mr. and Mrs. Crawford, they reassured me that no one was using their cabin this Christmas. We've rented it out for Riley's parents and Juju. It's going to be great.

Riley straddles me. He reaches behind his back and pulls a plug out of his own ass.

Sneaky bastard.

Then he aligns his hole with my cock and sits on me in one go.

"Fucking…fuck…" I scream. His weight makes the plug in my ass press against my prostate and the double stimulation is going to make this ridiculously quick.

"I'm going to move now, baby. It's going to be quick and dirty," he warns.

"Yes…please."

For a man who's just turned forty-seven, Riley has stupid stamina. I'm sure I'll die well before him. He rides my dick like a cowboy late for a rodeo.

His cock is flushed and leaking like a faucet. He's holding on to my legs behind him, so I know I'm hitting his prostate.

When his movements become jerkier, I know he's getting close.

"You ready, baby?" he asks.

"Fuck yeah." This is his show. I'm going to let him come before I allow myself to release, but the moment the first rope of cum hits my chest, the fucking plug in my ass vibrates and pushes me over.

I push my hips up with a strength I didn't know I had as my body gives in to the pleasure. I think I pass out for a moment because I don't remember the plug being turned off or removed from my ass.

Riley comes over with a warm cloth to clean his release from my chest. Some even hit my face. Then he lies beside me and pulls me into his arms.

"Was this you trying to kill me? Because you nearly succeeded," I say.

He chuckles. "No. That was me trying to relax you."

"Consider me relaxed." I lift one arm and let it fall back on the bed like it weighs a hundred pounds.

"You've been too stressed, baby."

"I know. I'm sorry. It's been crazy, hasn't it? I'm sorry I haven't been around as much."

He cradles my face. "I'm so incredibly proud of you, Curtis."

"I know. But I wish I had more time to spend with you."

This last year has been a total whirlwind. Brandon mentioned me to someone he worked with on Broadway, and they wanted me to move to New York to work with them.

Me. Curtis John Merroll. A choreographer on Broadway.

In.Sa.Ne.

I was excited at first, but right before I was supposed to meet them, I got a serious case of anxiety. Coach came with me to New York, and we had a great time.

He proposed to me in Central Park—*Yes, we're engaged!*—but I couldn't shake the feeling that something was off.

In the end, I decided it wasn't for me, but my meeting opened other possibilities, so I enrolled back in college to study choreography. I still coach the cheerleading team, but Justin does a lot of the work since I sometimes have class and miss training or games.

I suggested resigning, but the principal was having none of it, especially after the squad won their first national competition.

Coach is still with the team and loving it. Every so often, one of his old players comes to visit, which brings the reporters into town. It all becomes a circus for a few days until it all goes back to normal.

Juju is still in LA, but she's seriously considering moving to

Connecticut, especially after I graduate. We've been talking about opening a dance school together.

I haven't heard anything about he-who-shall-not-be-named since he left my apartment. That's not entirely true. Juju heard through the grapevine that the story he spun about his drink being spiked wasn't true. He was actually taking illegal drugs to help his performance on the mat.

As my grandma used to say, you make your own luck. I guess he thought he needed to steal it instead of working for it. I don't care anyway.

We grow and our dreams change. My dreams now include a lot of new changes in our lives.

I hear a car outside. "Oh shit. They're here." I jump off the bed and start picking up my clothes.

"Baby, calm down. They can't come in without a key, and they'll probably settle in next door first, anyway."

"But the decorations!"

Riley sighs, giving up the fight. "Come on, Bubblelicious. Tell me what I need to hang and where."

Riley's family and Juju send us a message to say they're unpacking and warming up the cabin and will join us for dinner. That gives us more time to put everything together.

I need it to be perfect.

We spent a lot of time at the cabin this summer, and Riley finished all his home-improvement projects. Then he indulged me with a shopping spree to buy new blankets, frames to hang our family photos, and decorations.

The cabin now feels like a home. Our little home away from home. A sanctuary we can escape to.

There's a knock on the door.

Riley opens the door, and the family spills in one by one.

Juju runs over to me straight away, hugging me tightly before stealing a piece of the meat I'm cutting for dinner.

Then it's Riley's parents, who are so adorably like Riley. I love them both.

"Did you make some more of that pie, son?"

"Sure did, Dad."

And that's another thing. They insist on me calling them Mom and Dad. The first time they said it, I cried like a baby and ran out of the room. After clarifying my reaction, they understood how special their request was to me. They've been Mom and Dad since.

"Dinner's ready," I announce.

Everyone takes their place while I bring all the food to the table.

Before we start filling our plates, Riley looks at me and smiles as he clears his throat.

"Mom, Dad, Juju," Riley says. "We have some news. If you look under your plates, there's a small envelope we want you to open."

They all lift their plates and look at what we left for them.

Riley puts his arm around my shoulders. We watch as the most important people in our lives find out that our family is about to become a little bigger, thanks to our amazing surrogate.

When we had a chance to talk about everything a year ago, Riley told me more about his attempts at having a family with his ex-wife. I know this is a big moment not just for him but for his parents too.

His mom comes around and gives me a tight hug. "My sweet child. Thank you for being everything our Riley needs."

"Mom, you know I'm not actually pregnant, right?"

They all laugh, and as everyone fills their plates with food, we talk about baby names, nursery decorations, and where the baby will go to school.

Mom and Dad announce they have no excuse not to move to Connecticut now. They visit us often enough, and the subject has come up in conversation. I guess all it took was one grandchild to make up their minds.

I think about my grandmother and smile to myself. I would love to have her with us, but I know she's around us. After all, she managed to push me toward my coach.

"I wish I'd met her," Riley says in my ear as if he can read my thoughts.

"Me too."

So here we are.

A year ago, I was single and pining for a man I thought was

straight. Little did I know that all I needed to do was invite him to my Christmas bubble, and he'd be mine forever.

Dear reader, I hope you've enjoyed Bubble and Coach's story. I had so much fun writing them, especially Bubble. He's one of the most delightfully funny characters I've written.

As a special treat for my readers I commissioned a piece of Bubble art. If you like coloring in scenes from your favorite books then sign up for my VIPs to receive a downloadable copy of Bubble and Coach's first kiss.

Click the link below to sign up to my newsletter and receive the scene in your inbox:

Sign up here (anawritesmm.com/sol-signup)
(if you signed up after How to Catch a Biker or Love Again you don't need to do it again, just check your inbox for you welcome email with the download link for all the bonus content!)

ROOM FOR 3
THE RESORT
ANA ASHLEY

1

JAKE

"Shit," I said between gritted teeth.

I ran my hands through my hair, making another mental note to have it cut soon.

This was the third time in a week I'd accidentally left cleaning supplies in one of the rooms. And not just any room. *The* room.

The double shift, just like the summer, had been too long, and I was feeling hot, bothered, and horny.

Most of the time, I saw the no-fraternization policy as a godsend. I wanted to finish my MBA and come back to the resort for a job that matched my skill set.

Hooking up with other staff was a bad idea, especially for me. I'd seen good people lose their jobs and their hearts because they hooked up with a colleague. Let's not even go there with guests. Not worth it.

That's why, with only a week to go before I was back to college on the other side of the country, I was sporting the biggest case of blue-balls-slash-guest-crush combo ever and counting down the days to the end of the season.

My phone buzzed in my pocket. I took it out discreetly and saw a message from my college roommate.

The supply closet was nearby, and the hallway was empty, so I pushed my cleaning cart inside and closed the door behind me before dialing his number.

He answered on the first ring. "Jake, I need to get laid. My mom is driving me nuts, and I swear if I'm told once again how so-and-so has a lovely single daughter, I might just rip off my own balls and feed them to the neighbor's dickhead cat."

"Tragic. And why do I want to hear this?" I said, trying to show disinterest but knowing already where the conversation was headed.

"Because, without my balls, what are you going to suck on before I shove my dick up your tight ass while you scream my name?"

"I guess you'd better hold on to your balls. It's only another week, Zak," I said.

"Hey, is everything okay?" he asked.

"Um, yeah? Why?"

"Don't know, you sound, I don't know…distant?"

"Nah, just tired. I'm ending a double shift."

"Damn, I don't know how you do it, Jake. Have you actually had a break since the end of term?"

"Yeah, of course, I have. I'm right on the beach, remember?"

I heard him sigh on the other side of the phone.

"Well then, use your beach and relax some because, in seven days, I'm going to unleash my pent-up sexual frustration on you."

"Can't wait," I said before ending the call.

I put the phone back in my pocket and started replenishing the cart for the next cleaner. No one expected me to do it, but I respected my colleagues enough to leave them with a cart ready to use at the start of their shift.

Fuck. The Lysol.

I looked inside all the cabinets but couldn't find a new can. Then I saw a note on the noticeboard asking staff to use Lysol sparingly because it was missing from the last delivery.

Just like the two mornings before, I had to return to the room.

Shit.

I made my way back down the hallway to the room. As I put the keycard in the door—after knocking and getting no response—I wondered if I would be as successful rescuing the products I left behind as I had been previously.

The room was still as tidy as I'd left it. Not surprising since I'd cleaned it only twenty minutes ago and the guests hadn't come back from breakfast.

With a single look, the sexy blue-eyed bear, who'd picked up the keys when the guests checked in, had all but invited me to join him and his equally gorgeous but brown-eyed younger husband for some under-the-sheets fun.

Although, if I ever dared to hook up with them, there would be no sheets, just some hard, sweaty fun.

Fuck, what was I thinking?

Great, and now I was hard. Just as I had been while cleaning their room earlier.

I hadn't been able to resist smelling the aftershave I'd seen in the bathroom, but it wasn't that scent that was driving me crazy. It was something else. Maybe it was the combination of both men, the aftershave, and the dirty thoughts that wouldn't leave my mind.

Hooking up with guests isn't allowed, I reminded myself.

If God knew the restraint it took to clean up after the two men without adding my own mess to it first, she'd definitely save me a spot in heaven.

Think of the consequences if this was to get out. Not worth it.

I froze when I heard the playful laughs as the room door opened all the way. I hadn't intended to get lost in my thoughts when I'd come in to rescue the Lysol.

Deep-blue eyes locked with mine before roaming south. I was held in place by his gaze, powerless to react as the magnetic power of those blues owned me like my body wasn't mine anymore.

The brown-eyed guy sidled up to his husband, who put his arm around him without looking away from me. He whispered something I couldn't hear and the blue-eyed bear smiled a slow, hungry smile.

I swallowed, gripping the can of Lysol harder in my hand.

The younger man, who looked to be around my age, crossed the short length of the room toward me. He was my height, which made it easier to look straight into his eyes, as hard as it was to look away from the bigger guy.

"What's your name?" he asked, his voice soft but confident as he gently placed a hand on my chest.

"Jake," I said.

"Nice to meet you, Jake."

I would have laughed at the polite greeting if his other hand hadn't pressed against the hardness in my work pants. He definitely wasn't shy about touching another man in front of his husband.

I swallowed and closed my eyes when he touched me, to stop myself from spontaneously combusting. Not that it mattered because if I was caught in the room with guests, I'd definitely get my ass fired, whether or not I was related to the owner of the resort chain.

The deep voice I'd met before spoke, "Jake, I'm Mal, and the man attached to your groin is my husband, Griff."

If I had any doubts that it was possible to orgasm from someone's voice alone, I was getting pretty close to proving that theory correct.

I opened my eyes and choked out a laugh. I already knew their names. I knew everything I could about them. I'd checked them in. I'd cleaned their room daily, trying not to build a picture of who they were based on the stuff they'd left out in the open in their room. It hadn't worked. The reality of the two men in front of me was so much better than my imagination.

"Fuck," I growled as Griff pulled the zipper down.

I held on to the chest of drawers behind me with one hand while holding the fucking can of Lysol with the other.

My body was like a coil, ready to spring at the lightest touch, and I couldn't resist pressing closer to Griff's hand.

He let out a soft giggle. "Baby," he said, looking behind at his husband. "Looks like we're going to use those after all."

He picked up a box of Trojan Magnum XL condoms and threw it on the bed.

I'd wondered about those every day I'd come in to clean the room. Why would they need condoms? And which one required the XL size?

Mal locked the door behind him and stalked toward me to claim my mouth.

How could a kiss be hard, soft, commanding, and reverent all at the same time?

I opened up for him, my body feeling like it would break in two, the bottom part begging for Griff's hand and the top part yielding to Mal's mouth.

"Tell us you want this," he said before he sucked on my bottom lip like it was candy.

"Yes," I said, sucking in a breath.

"Both of us."

"Yes."

I wrapped my arms around Mal. He picked me up like I was as light as a feather and dropped me on the bed, claiming my mouth with a desperation I hadn't felt from a lover in a long time.

The bed dipped on one side, and Mal turned us so Griff could come closer.

Behind me, Griff sucked on the skin of my neck while stretching his arm over me to touch Mal.

Strong hands groped my ass and pulled me closer. My erection pressed against Mal's. Yeah, he was definitely extra-large.

"Turn over," Griff said.

As hard as it was to give up Mal's lips, I was eager to taste Griff, so I did as I was told.

When my eyes met his, my heart skipped a beat, and once again, my body was torn in two.

I was burning red hot as Mal reached for the button of my pants and pulled them down to my knees, but I was also hypnotized by the pure innocence in Griff's eyes. It was like he'd been born to care about everything, care for his husband, care...for me.

"I...I need you to know I never do this," I said, my gut telling me I needed to say the words, especially for Griff. "I've never done it before."

Mal's hands stopped where they were resting on my stomach as he took his turn sucking on the skin behind my neck. I was now thankful I hadn't had time to have that haircut after all.

"You've never..." he trailed.

"Oh no. I have..." I blurted, looking behind me at him and

then turning to Griff. "I've had sex. I mean, I'm twenty-nine. I just...I've never done it with guests. Um...or with two guys at the same time."

Suddenly there was a bridge of communication passing over my head. My stomach sunk as I realized they were going to give me an out.

I thought back to my call with Zak. We'd been friends since we'd become roommates after I'd answered his ad on the college notice board. We'd been fucking just as long.

With Zak and me, there were no feelings, no mess. It was easy. We knew as soon as we graduated that we'd go our separate ways, and twenty years from now, when we met up, we'd be complaining about our spouses and reminiscing about the hot sex we had in college. That was our agreement, and it was still valid. I liked it because it was clean and easy.

"No," I said, louder than I expected. I didn't want clean. I didn't want easy. "I don't want to go. Please, I want to feel."

I looked into Griff's eyes as I pleaded. He caressed my face gently, and then his hand moved to the back of my neck to pull me in for a kiss.

Griff's mouth was everything I hoped for and more. Soft and sweet like cotton candy.

I gasped into his mouth when I felt cool lube and a thick finger pressing against my hole.

"Fuck, you look so good like this, Jake," Mal said in a thick, deep voice. I wanted to reach behind me to feel his erection, but Griff picked that moment to guide my hand toward his jeans.

His kiss became more insistent as I popped the buttons and took his cock into my hand. Okay...so they...were both extra-large.

"Take us both, Jake," Griff said, barely letting go of my mouth.

I cried out a curse when the velvety soft skin of Griff's cock rubbed against mine. I gripped us harder and pushed into him.

"Lift your leg over his, Jake."

This was what I wanted. No thinking required. Mal said, so I did. So simple, so good.

In this position, I was able to hold more of my cock and Griff's together and open up for Mal, which I realized was his intention when I felt a lubed finger push its way inside.

"Fuck," I shouted.

Mal's gentle hand on my back as he kept adding more fingers and stretching me was like being spanked and then caressed to take away the sting. Hard and soft at the same time.

Griff let go of my lips long enough for me to look behind and see Mal guide his thick cock inside me.

His eyes met mine when there was a little resistance. That blue ocean I was swimming in was destined to never be stormy. He too was born to look after others.

The position made it hard to kiss him. I tried to move, which was when I realized my pants were still halfway down my legs and my shirt was pulled up.

We were all still dressed. Which, in a perverted way, felt dirtier than if we'd all been naked.

Clothing implied the rushed need to get to that beautiful release. The one I hadn't had in weeks, from anything other than my own hand.

"You look so beautiful, Jake. That's it, take all of him. Mal is going to make you feel so good. We both are."

I nodded, powerless to do anything else but feel as both men took charge of my body.

Griff moved down the bed and took my cock in his mouth as Mal sped up his pace in and out of me.

He wrapped his arms around my waist and then moved so he was hitting my prostate with every thrust.

"I'm so close," I said. I shut my eyes tightly as if that would stop me from coming too soon.

"Baby, I want to come inside you."

For a moment, I thought Mal was speaking to me, but then I felt Griff nodding, and when I looked down, I saw him place his hand back on the bed.

His eyes were so dark and lustful, needy and warm. Griff was like walking through a door to shelter from the wind.

I thought I wanted red-hot, sexy, and dirty, but it was the way he looked at me that made the tingle I felt in my spine spread out to the rest of my body, which triggered my orgasm.

Mal held me as I spilled into Griff's mouth and then through the aftershocks when I was positive I'd died and gone to heaven.

He kept running his hands over my sensitive skin while pulling out of me gently.

As Mal removed the condom, I noticed he hadn't come. I was about to make a move, when Griff all but jumped onto Mal's lap and attacked him like he hadn't touched his husband in years.

Suddenly, I felt very much like that spare screw you always end up with after assembling flat-packed furniture.

The couple didn't notice as I pulled my pants up and walked toward the door.

"Jake," Griff called.

I looked at them, so beautiful in each other's arms, and something in my chest felt so tight that I had to bring my hand up to rub the spot in the middle of my ribs.

There was a look of uncertainty in Mal's eyes, and I thought I saw something that looked a lot like sadness in Griff's. Unfortunately, I didn't stay long enough to find out.

The cleaning cart was still in the supply closet, and I hadn't clocked out of my shift.

What I'd done was break all the rules, the resort's and my own, and after all that, I still forgot the can of Lysol in the room.

The taste of Griff's sweet tongue lingered in my mouth, and my ass stung deliciously, but there was no time to dwell on that because there was only one thing I could do.

It was time to go back to college.

Hopefully, by the time Zak arrived in a week, I'd be over whatever had just happened.

2

GRIFF

I looked around me at the mess. Despite the many moving boxes and packed items, our bedroom already looked empty. Devoid of any trace of everything that had happened within these four walls over the last two years.

The birthdays, the Christmas mornings, the breakfasts in bed, the late-night conversations, and lovemaking.

God, had it been two years already?

The only photo we had of our wedding day was still on top of the dresser. The date stamp on it confirmed that, two years ago tomorrow, I walked down the beach as the sun was setting, and in the presence of just two friends, married my best friend and love of my life.

My grandmother used to tell me, *you feel too much, my dear. There is no such thing as love at first sight. Love is like a seed, you need to water it to grow, but you also need the sun. You can't do it all on your own.*

Of course she was right. Every relationship or friendship I'd had was always about me giving. The time, the attention, the love.

I thought that was just the way it was going to be until I met Mal, but by then, it was too late to tell my grandmother that love at first sight did exist, alongside the kind of love she believed in.

I picked up our wedding photo. We were as in love now as we were then, maybe even more so. I hoped, wherever my grandmother was, she looked down at us and saw how happy and loved I was.

Strong arms wrapped around my waist.

"Hey, baby," Mal whispered before placing soft kisses behind my ear and all the way down my neck, pulling my shirt aside so he could carry on to my shoulder.

"This isn't how packing gets done," I teased even as I leaned back against his chest.

My brain tried to get control of the situation and tell me we had work to do, but when I was in Mal's arms, the only thing in control was my heart.

One of his hands snaked down past my stomach to cup my half-hard cock.

"Hmm, I like what *you're* packing. How about I give you a hand?"

I put the photo back down, turned around, and placed my hands on his chest. Mal's heart was steady, though maybe a tad fast because he was clearly in the mood for sex.

"How about we finish packing, order some food in, and then you can fuck me all the way to the east coast," I said.

He gave me a his smile I knew was only for me before claiming my mouth with a promising kiss.

God, I loved to kiss my husband.

From the moment I had my first stolen kiss with Ryan Schmidt in a supply cupboard at school when I was fourteen, I knew I'd found my new addiction.

I craved being so close to someone I could feel their heart beating against mine. I loved that feeling of losing yourself within a kiss because once you closed your eyes, all you could do was feel, and that was like a drug to me.

Everyone I'd kissed, from boyfriends to hookups, had their own taste. Some had been great and some not so much, but it wasn't until I kissed Mal that everything changed.

Kissing Mal wasn't just about how he always tasted like mint because he was addicted to the tiny candy pieces they gave out at reception. Kissing Mal was like levitating above the ground. Feeling so weightless that you became free from the shackles of being human.

"Fuck, Mal. You know I can't say no to anything when you kiss me like that," I said, trying to establish a regular breathing pattern, even as he nibbled on my bottom lip and peppered my chin and neck with kisses.

I felt his chuckle against my too-hot skin. "It's good to know that after two years of dating and two of marriage, I can still take you apart at the seams."

"Baby, I could be eighty-nine, and the effect would still be the same."

He stilled, so I pulled my head back to look at him.

"What's up?"

"When you're eighty-nine, I'll be long gone. Hell, I might even be gone by the time you're seventy-five."

Ugh, I hated when he brought up our age difference. Fifteen years wasn't even that big of an age gap. Yes, Mal had more gray hair than the mousy brown I'd seen in some of his younger photos, but he was a healthy and fit man who could give many guys my age a run for their money at the gym.

Besides, it was this Mal that I loved. I never even considered that I could have met him a decade earlier. And if I had, would we have had the same connection? The same love story? What was the point of wondering?

"What are you doing with me, Griff, when you could find someone much younger and with less annoying habits than me?" he said, equal parts teasing and needing reassurance.

"True. Do you have any idea how many lost socks I found at the back of the underwear drawer? I could open a shop," I said, pursing my lips. "Let's not even mention you're weird fetish with vegetarian pizza."

"Hey, veggie pizza is the one that rules them all."

"And those aren't your worst habits," I said, pointing at his chest. He put his arms back around me, locking his hands around my waist so I couldn't go anywhere.

"Oh really? What other habits make me such a terrible husband?"

I put my finger on my chin. "For starters, you treat all your staff nicely."

"How terrible of me."

"Yup, and don't think I haven't noticed you take a little longer chatting to the guests with children to make sure they really feel welcomed here."

"Truly despicable."

"I could go on, but—"

I couldn't finish my thought because Mal lifted me up and dropped me on our bed, covering my body with his bigger, sturdier one.

"But…"

I wanted to talk, but with his hands all over me, it was hard to concentrate.

"I…I, you…never mind, just make love to me. Fuck packing. We can pay someone."

He laughed, and I didn't need him to say anything else. We were back on track, and if I needed to stop packing to show my man how much he meant to me, then I'd do it today and every single day for the rest of our lives.

One of my favorite things to do was watch Mal sleep. Maybe it was because I didn't get to do it often, so when I had the chance, I didn't want to miss out.

He looked tired from working extra hours to ensure all his staff had the support they needed until his boss hired another resort manager.

When we met, he'd been upfront about his career goals and had told me he didn't see himself staying in Florida longer than two years.

I'd laughed at him and told him that if he was trying to find a way to put me off him, then he'd need to do better.

As an indie author, I could work from wherever I wanted, and despite never having left Florida, there was something about moving all the way across the country to the west coast that made me feel as though it opened a whole new world for me and my writing.

I was excited about the move and especially for Mal's new career opportunity.

Today was his official last day at this resort before we moved in a few days, but it was also our wedding anniversary. So I'd made a deal with his assistant manager, who promised we wouldn't be disturbed until after breakfast.

I wanted my husband for myself this morning. After I was done with him, they could spend the day saying goodbye to their boss.

Mal's eyelids moved as though he were dreaming. He reached out for me in his sleep and took a deep breath in when I scooted closer.

"I'm here, baby," I whispered. I ran my hands gently over his face and placed a soft kiss on his lips.

"Hmm, love you," he said into my mouth, deepening the kiss.

I could only moan my reply before I was flat on my back with his bigger body on top of mine.

"I thought you were asleep," I chuckled.

"I was, but you were in my dream, and I decided I wanted the real thing."

He rolled his hips, pressing his erection against mine. Enough to take my breath away, but not enough to give us any kind of relief.

"Here I am, baby. As real as I can be, and all yours." I wrapped my arms around his neck, licking my lips to entice him to kiss me again.

"Griff," he said, moving to lay by my side again. Mal's blue eyes had captivated me from the day I saw him across the grocery store aisle, but when they were as stormy as they were now, I worried for him.

"What's up? Are you okay?" I asked.

"Yeah…I just…I had a weird dream, that's all."

"Do you want to tell me about it?"

He scrunched his nose and shook his head.

"Come on, it's only a dream, but you may feel better sharing it."

He let his head rest on his bicep, and with his free arm, he pulled me so I was half-lying on top of him. Our erections were forgotten for the moment.

"Do you ever think about that day?"

I closed my eyes, thankful for Mal's chosen position because I didn't want him to read my face right now. Or, well, I didn't want him to misread me.

"Do you?" I asked.

"Yeah," he breathed out as if he'd let go of something that was weighing him down.

"What do you think about?"

"I'm mostly confused," he confessed. "I'm afraid that I liked it too much, worried about how Jake left and that we never had a chance to talk, and terrified that one day I may not be enough for you alone."

"Mal, you will always be enough for me."

I understood his worry. When we'd arrived at the Silver Sands Resort six months ago, Mal had been attracted to the guy that checked us in, Jake.

It wasn't unusual for either me or him to notice someone we thought was sexy and comment between ourselves. Once or twice we'd talked about having some fun with a third, but when I saw how Mal looked at Jake, I knew we'd found our guy.

I couldn't blame him. After all, I'd also felt a strange pull toward him. There was just something in his light-blue eyes that called to me.

At the time, Mal had been worried about his job interview with the resort owner, so I didn't mention anything until breakfast the morning after.

The morning we ended up having sex with Jake in our room.

"Your eyes that day," Mal said. "It was like you'd found something you didn't know you were looking for. I've never seen you like that, and it scares me. What if you find someone or something out there that makes you feel like that? I love you so fucking much, Griff. I couldn't bear to lose you."

My heartbeat increased with every word he said. How did I explain to someone who was feeling insecure about our relationship that he was right, but he was also wrong?

"Mal, I love you more than life itself. If it's just you and me for the rest of our lives as our little family of two, I will be happy. Hell, I will have lived my dream life," I said.

"But…"

I sighed.

"You're right. Being with Jake was special to me. Wasn't it to you?"

"Yeah…it was. I can't understand it. I already have you. We're enough, aren't *we* enough?"

"We are, baby. Those vows I said in front of the celebrant and our friends stood then, now, and forever. Maybe what we found was that we have more within our hearts to give. If we ever find someone that makes us feel like Jake did, we can talk about it and explore it. If not, then we are still living our happily ever after every single day, aren't we?"

Mal put his hand on my chin to pull me up for a kiss, and this time, I wasn't going to let his top head get in the way. His mouth had a way of removing all conscious thought from my brain, but I knew my husband well and had a trick or two up my sleeve.

"Come on," I said, putting some space between us so I could resume all brain activity again. "Let's jump in the shower. It's our anniversary, so I want to suck your cock for breakfast, fuck you against the wall, and then when we've both forgotten our names, we can have some real food."

"You make a compelling case. Who am I to argue?"

There were two quick knocks at the apartment door, followed by a single one. When I turned toward the door, Mal coughed.

"Are you going to answer it like that?"

I looked down at my naked body and hard cock—courtesy of my husband's sexiness—winked, and crossed our small living room toward the door, coming back to the bedroom seconds later with a bottle of champagne on ice and two glasses.

"Please tell me there was no one on the other side of the door," he said with a hint of possessiveness that made my cock twitch.

I shrugged teasingly as I placed the champagne bucket on the sink unit in the bathroom and started to tear the foil.

Mal put his hands on my hips from behind and bit the back of my neck at the hairline.

"Hmm, I love it when you go all caveman on me," I said.

"Oh yeah?"

"Yeah."

"Too bad because you made a promise, and I'm collecting."

Our eyes met in the mirror, and my heart skipped a beat.

Whatever challenges life threw at us, I knew we were strong enough to face them together. As he always did, Mal would excel in his new job because he cared about people and made sure they felt at home in his resort.

What we didn't expect was to arrive in LA days later to be told the resort Mal was going to manage wasn't Silver Palm, just south of Santa Monica, but their sister resort, Silver Sands on La Catarina Island.

The same resort we'd visited six months ago.

The same resort where Jake worked.

3

MAL

"So you want me to move people who are good at one job to somewhere else? Who's going to cover their job?"

"That's not what I'm saying, Pete."

"What are you saying, Hailey? Where am I supposed to get the manpower?"

I'd been listening to the same back and forth between Pete, my HR manager, and Hailey, one of the supervisors, for fifteen minutes.

It was a technique that had served me well throughout my career. Let them talk it out, and they'll come up with the solution. But this seemed an impossibility at Silver Sands.

I looked out of the shared office window toward the Pacific ocean. This was by far the best office I'd ever had in all the resorts I'd worked in. It was all open plan, which I loved even more because I never cared much for the whole boss-employee division. I didn't need an office of my own when there was plenty of space in the resort and a conference room to hold meetings in.

We stood right on top of the main restaurant, and the round shape of the building allowed me to look down at the guests, enjoying the pool and some of the activities, or out to the ocean and our beach.

As Pete and Hailey's discussion continued, my mind drifted off.

When Frank Marlow, my boss and the owner of Silver Resorts, called me a month ago—a day before we moved from Florida—I thought he was making sure everything was going to plan.

Finding out his plans had changed was…unexpected.

The resort was bigger. The pay package was better. The career opportunity was the best I could have hoped for.

The location?

How could I put it…? I was about to manage the same resort Jake worked at.

Griff had listened in to that conversation, and as Frank happily delivered the news, he was completely unaware that I was having a silent conversation with my husband over his excited voice.

For the first time in four years, neither of us could utter a word. I was terrified of meeting Jake again, and especially of being his boss, but what was really getting to me was that little flutter at the pit of my stomach that felt a lot like excitement.

Griff had bit his lower lip almost raw. His dark eyes saying what he didn't or couldn't.

I'd always been able to read his mood. Griff was a book with see-through pages and bold writing, and only I had access to the key to translate all the scribbles.

That time was no different. While his face showed worry, his eyes were full of the same excitement I felt.

When the day came, I didn't see Jake at the resort, nor on any of the following days. A search on the HR database didn't yield any results.

As the weeks went by, and I settled into my new job and our apartment, Jake became an almost mythical creature I thought I'd imagined.

Griff didn't talk about it, so I didn't talk about it.

The waves crashed onto the silver sand. It was still too cold to swim in the ocean, but it didn't stop our current guests from walking along the beach and dipping their toes in the chilly water.

"What do you think, boss?"

"Huh?" Shit, I should have been paying more attention.

Pete got up and walked to the window. "Look out there. The

maids have finished the main building, and they're heading toward the cabins. Would you get that kind of speed with new people?"

Hailey let out a frustrated groan.

Most of my team got along well enough, but for some reason, Pete and Hailey seemed to rub each other the wrong way.

"Okay, let's look at this from a different perspective," I said. "Maria started as a maid when she was sixteen. She's thirty-five now, and she's a supervisor."

"That's my point," Pete interrupted. "She's learned the job, and she did it well until she got a promotion."

I raised my hand. "You're right, Pete. But what if Maria wanted to work at reception. Do you know she speaks four languages fluently?"

"Does she?" he asked, looking doubtful.

"Yes," I said. "English, French, Portuguese, and Spanish. How many other Marias do we have out there in the resort, who are great at their job but have no prospects of growth in their section because we only have space for one Maria?"

Pete looked at Hailey, who straightened her shoulders and crossed her arms.

I continued, "My point is, this is a small island. Nowadays, kids have access to opportunities they never did before. The mainland is only a ferry away. Let's create the opportunities here on the island so we can retain them."

What I didn't say was what a lot of staff in the resort were thinking. My job should have been given to a local too.

It had been clear from day one. Some of the longtime service staff didn't like change. The old manager had been a born and bred Catarinian, while I'd come from Florida to steal the job of a hardworking local.

At least the community didn't seem to mind much that I was gay and married to a man. If anything, Griff had been well-received and had made friends even before he stepped a foot on the island.

Which reminded me that it was time for my daily wander around the resort before going home.

"I'm going to leave you to come up with a plan. See you in the morning," I said, closing my laptop and putting it in the bag before heading out of the office.

For me, one of the most important parts of my job was connecting with the staff, knowing them as people and not just the jobs they did. I knew as soon as we entered the peak holiday season, the most they'd have time for would be a wave from afar, so I was keen on making the most of the time I had.

I smiled as I walked down the steps and out of the building, remembering Griff's words about being nice to my staff.

A little movement in the corner of my eye caught my attention. I walked slowly as I approached the garden path, knowing any sudden movements tended to scare the cutest inhabitants of the island.

Long, floppy ears and cream fur popped from behind a small bush. Light-blue eyes stared at me, daring me to make a move.

"It's only me. Look, I've got treats," I said to the rabbit as I put my hand in the trouser pocket to retrieve the bag with a handful of pellets. I crouched and placed a few on the ground in front of me. "I know, it's not green, but I didn't want to risk stained pants if you missed our date."

The rabbit approached slowly, stopping to look behind him.

"Did you bring any friends today?"

He sniffed the air in my direction. We'd been doing this little dance almost daily, ever since I discovered the island was home to thousands of fluffy rabbits.

Tourists came to the island every year to see the rabbits who were so used to humans that some even let themselves be petted in exchange for food.

My little furry friend, however, seemed to distrust people. He never got too close, but that was okay.

"You must be special. Jake doesn't go near anyone, especially when his friends are nearby."

I turned to see my boss standing a few feet behind me. When I looked back at the rabbit, he was scurrying away, followed by two other rabbits I hadn't seen before.

"Jake?"

"My son named him a couple of years ago because of his light-blue eyes and cautious nature."

I got up and shook his hand.

"Hi, Frank, I didn't know you were on the island this week. Everything okay with Jessie?"

"Yeah, the old girl had a vet appointment, and she won't cooperate for anyone but the island doctor." He laughed. "Trust me to have all the money I need, and yet I live at the whim of a fourteen-year-old dog."

"You wouldn't have it any other way, would you?"

He shook his head with a fond smile.

"How are you settling in?"

For someone who owned multiple successful holiday resorts, Frank was one of the most down-to-earth people I'd ever met.

"All good. Silver Sands has the same issues all the other resorts have. I'm sure there's a resort management manual somewhere that lists it all. You can predict it down to the missing stationery." I laughed.

"Let me guess, the chefs want a pay rise, the managers can't agree on anything and blame each other for mistakes made, and the long-time staff thinks you're coming here to steal the jobs of good Catarinian people."

I chuckled as we started walking alongside the beach, still on the garden path.

"I've been in this business forty years, Mal. It's always the same. We can't please them all, or we'd have nothing to show for it. The youngsters want everything yesterday. No one wants to climb up the ranks. They want to go straight to the top."

"Nothing wrong with ambition, Frank."

"I agree, but the sign of a good leader is the will to put the work in, show you they're resilient, and appreciate a good day's work." He stopped and looked out toward the ocean, letting out a sigh. "And sometimes the lack of ambition is also problematic."

"Why do I get the feeling you're talking about someone in particular?"

He smiled. "You're a perceptive man, Mallory Prescott."

"Don't let my dashing good looks fool you, Frank. I've been around the block once or twice."

"Speaking of dashing good looks, how's that lovely husband of yours?"

In my whole fifteen-year career as a resort manager, none of my bosses had ever asked about my personal life.

Frank was different. Family was important to him. That much I could tell by how he handled his business.

"He's good. Thank you for asking. You'd think he's lived here all his life with how many people ask about him every day."

"It was the same with my Annie. Born and raised in LA, the moment she arrived on the island, she was home. Not a single day goes by that I don't miss her smile."

I put my hand on Frank's shoulder and squeezed tight. He'd lost his wife to cancer a few years ago, and her memory was still very much alive both in the resort and the small town around it.

"Tomorrow is your day off, right?" Frank asked.

"Yes, did you need me to come in? I was considering coming by first thing to talk to Hailey and Pete. They're locking heads over an issue, and I don't want it to escalate."

Frank let out a belly laugh.

"Oh, it will escalate, and poor Pete will no doubt sleep on the sofa for a couple of nights."

"What do you mean?"

"Didn't you know they're married?"

Huh…what?

"No. But they behave like…"

"An old married couple?" Frank added.

I smiled and shook my head. How had I not noticed?

I'd seen them come in together most days, but the unique rocky landscape of the island meant the resort was on the edge of one of the only two small towns in La Catarina. Many of the staff lived within walking distance of the resort, so I hadn't thought too much of it.

"In that case, I guess I'm spending the day with my husband. He's been on me to check out that new bakery that opened on Pebble street."

"Why don't you two come over for lunch? My son and nephew are back home from college, and I'd love to introduce you to them."

"Sounds good. I guess I'll see you tomorrow then."

An hour later, I was greeted by Griff, who jumped me as soon as I closed the front door of the apartment.

"Mm, baby," I moaned, setting my bag gently down on the floor so I wouldn't break the bottle of wine I'd bought on the way home.

I managed to keep focus only long enough to toe my shoes off. A sign that I was home and could finally relax.

"Are you still off tomorrow?" Griff asked, running his fingers through my hair without stopping our make-out session.

"Hmm."

"Is that a yes?"

"Hmm."

He pulled his head back to look at me.

"What?" I said, pressing him against the hallway wall and feasting on his neck.

"Mal…"

"Hmm…?"

He giggled when I sucked on the spot I knew drove him crazy. Even between layers of clothing, I could still feel his cock twitching.

I was pretty sure it wasn't dinner time. Who needed food anyway?

Fuck my rumbling stomach.

"Are. You. Off. Tomorrow?" he asked again.

I stood back so he could put his feet on the ground, but I didn't let him go.

"Yes. Frank asked us to have lunch with him. Apparently, his son and nephew are back from college."

"That's great. I like Frank. Should we go to the new bakery and buy dessert?"

I chuckled. "Why doesn't your suggestion surprise me?"

"I don't know what you mean." He shrugged, giving me his most *not guilty* look.

I picked up my bag and followed him to the kitchen, where the smell of dinner made my tummy rumble louder. Griff raised a brow.

I guess pre-dinner sex is out of the question.

"What did you make?"

"Three-bean chili and rice, and it's ready to eat, so you can go change while I get the food on the plates."

I pouted.

Griff dipped a little spoon in the chili sauce to taste it and then kissed me again. Delicious and with a hint of spice. Not too much, just how I liked it.

"Don't worry, baby. I plan on keeping you up later."

"I'm already up," I said, pressing closer to him.

"Go before I change my mind. I'm hungry and would rather eat this chili off a plate than off of you. But make no mistake, this chili is getting eaten."

I turned to go to the bedroom, shedding my clothes on the way and smiling as I heard Griff groan and curse.

Since Griff made good on his promise to keep me up, I decided it was only fair to indulge him with a breakfast out to the new bakery.

The last thing I needed was to become addicted to the delicious bread rolls they made and baked on-site using their own family recipe, but staring at my husband as he indulged his sweet tooth with one of the pastries after eating two rolls was an addiction in itself.

"You're not going to be hungry for lunch," I said as we walked out of the bakery with a box of mini-desserts in hand.

"Watch me."

We walked the length of the bay toward Frank's place without any rush. We stopped a few times to talk to people—thanks to my husband's magnetic social skills—collected some pebbles from the beach, and even stopped to take some photos.

It had been a while since we hadn't had one thing or another going on, so I allowed myself to enjoy walking with his hand in mine, listening as he told me about the research he was doing for his current book.

A couple of hours later, we stood in front of Frank's door, pressing the bell while joking about wishing for a light lunch because neither of us was hungry.

The door opened moments later, and I found myself staring at the light-blue eyes that had filled so many of my dreams in the past seven months.

Next to me, Griff gasped and squeezed my hand hard.

Mythical creature, my ass.

Jake was very much real, very much the same person we'd been with months ago, and very much *in* my boss's house.

4

JAKE

WHAT WAS the most appropriate reaction when you opened the door to your house and found the two men that had occupied most of your thoughts for months?

Gasp? Curse? Freeze?

Nope, clearly closing the door in their faces was the thing to do.

I mean, they weren't really there, were they? Maybe I needed a nap. I'd never hallucinated from jet lag before, but there was always a first.

"Did I hear the doorbell?" my uncle said, poking his head out of the kitchen.

"Um, yes…I'll get it," I said.

I opened the door slowly, my heartbeat increasing with each inch that revealed Mal and Griff, still there, looking every bit the sexy couple I'd hooked up with, and now also totally confused.

"Jake," Griff said with a shy, tentative smile before he looked at Mal.

Mal looked back at Griff.

Just like that day months ago, they were communicating only by looking at each other. It made me feel excluded, even though I had no right to feel that way.

"Um, how can I help?" I asked.

They both looked at me, but this time, Griff's smile was warm, calm, and inviting. Fuck if I didn't want to wrap myself up in it.

I definitely need to catch up with my sleep.

All my bad decisions happened when I was overtired, and I was done with making bad decisions. Case in point, the couple in front of me.

"Oh, boys, you're here. Come on in."

I jumped as my uncle seemed to have come out of nowhere and opened the door wider.

"I see you've met my nephew, Jacob. My son is around somewhere, but he promised to join us for lunch."

I stared open-mouthed as Mal and Griff followed my uncle inside.

What the actual fuck was going on?

"Jacob, this is Mallory and Griffin Prescott. Mallory is the new resort general manager," my uncle said.

"The new…general manager?" I asked. Surely I'd misunderstood.

"Yes. Now, let's go out back to the porch. It's a beautiful day, the sea is calm, and I have a bunch of steaks dying to meet the grill."

Mal and Griff followed my uncle as he laughed at his own joke.

I didn't miss Griff taking Mal's hand and giving it a little squeeze as they walked past me.

"I'm going to look for Gabe. I'll be right back," I said.

It wouldn't be hard to find my cousin since he was likely in his room sleeping, so I ran up the stairs and went to my room instead.

"Fuck!" I shouted between gritted teeth after I closed the door behind me.

I sat on my bed and grabbed my phone from the nightstand to dial the only person I could freak out with.

"Wow, you miss me already? Just say the word, and I'll be there with bells on, *and* it's not because I want to escape from my family—"

"Zak," I said, stopping him.

"What's up?"

"They're here."

"Who?" he asked.

"*Them!*"

"Oh…oh! Shit. Hold on, there, where? Your place? The resort?"

"Both. They're at my place for lunch, and my uncle says Mal is the new resort general manager."

"Fuck, Jake. That sucks."

I sighed.

"What do I do?" I asked.

"You tell them you've been horny for them for months and take them on a tour of the house, starting with your room."

"And now the serious answer, please," I said.

Zak laughed. "That *was* my serious answer. I've got blue balls because of those guys. The least you could do is nail them while they're there."

I groaned.

"You've been hooking up with a different guy every week for months. If anything, your balls could fall off from overuse."

"Yeah, but none of them were as good as you, so they don't count."

"Zak," I warned.

"Okay," he said. "Look, you're not going to say anything, right? And I doubt they will either because it could put Mal's job at risk. As I see it, you have all the power in this situation. Just remember, with great power comes great responsibility."

"I'm not feeling all that powerful." I sighed.

"But I bet you're sporting wood, amiright?"

"Bye, Zak," I said before I disconnected the call. Seconds later, I received a message with three eggplant emojis.

"Okay, let's regroup," I said to myself.

Zak was right. Both Mal and I could be in trouble if the truth came out. Maybe this lunch was a good opportunity to know more about them.

I knocked on my cousin's bedroom door before I opened it. As predicted, he was lying face-down on his bed.

"Fun night last night?" I asked, grabbing a ruler from his desk and swatting his butt with it.

"Fuck, that hurts." He groaned and turned around.

"You look a mess, Gabe. What time did you get in?"

"An hour ago?"

"Well, you're gonna have to sober up quickly because the general manager and his husband are downstairs for lunch, and you know your dad will want you there," I said, leaning against his desk and crossing my arms.

I loved my cousin, but sometimes his carefree attitude frustrated the hell out of me.

"His husband? I didn't know he was gay," Gabe said, getting up from his bed and looking for clothes. The room was so messy that I couldn't tell which clothes were clean and which were dirty, but he just grabbed a random pair of jeans and put them on before taking a clean shirt from his closet. "I must be getting rusty."

"What do you mean?"

"I was at his interview with Dad. He was Mr. Professional, said all the right things. Not for a split-second did I think he was gay."

I bit the inside of my cheek. Of course Gabe would have been at the interview. After all, he was in line to take over the business when my uncle finally decided to retire.

When we made it out to the back porch, my uncle was by the grill, talking to Mal.

"Look who's decided to join us," my uncle said. "Gabriel, why don't you get some drinks for our guests?"

"I'll get them," I said, glad to have an excuse to get away, but as soon as I turned back toward the kitchen, I came face to face with Griff.

"I'm um…getting drinks…" I said, squeezing past him into the kitchen.

"Wait, Jake."

I turned around, but not until I was safe and out of sight from my uncle and cousin.

"I won't say anything," I blurted out.

Griff stopped only inches away from me. His dark eyes bore into mine, once again giving me that strange feeling, so I looked away.

"That's not why I followed you here. I just want to know that you're okay. You know, after…" he said, trailing off.

I let out a strained laugh.

"I'm okay. Thanks for asking. As I said, I won't say anything to my uncle so—"

"Jesus, Jake, do you think I'm worried about Mal's job?"

"How about those drinks?" Gabe said, coming into the kitchen and opening the fridge. "Is there anything alcoholic in here?"

"There's beer, and I'm making a cranberry-and-white-wine spritzer," I said.

"Oh, fancy." He uncapped a beer and took a sip. "So, you must be Mal's husband. Nice to meet you."

Gabe extended his hand, and Griff took it. "Nice to meet you too, Gabriel. I'm Griff."

"Please call me Gabe. Only Dad insists on calling us by our full names," Gabe said.

Griff nodded and smiled.

"If you want to go back out, I'll be right out with the drinks," I said.

Griff looked my way and narrowed his eyes.

Yes, our conversation is over.

Because I couldn't stop looking at him without remembering that first kiss, I needed him to go out and join his husband, who was also my uncle's employee…and soon to be my boss.

I would do well to remember all those things.

When I went back out, everyone was sitting around the table, so I placed the tray with the spritzers and ice bucket on one end and started pouring the drinks.

"What are you working on at the moment, Griff?" my uncle asked. "I can't tell you how exciting it is to have a best-selling author living on the island."

Griff's an author?

"I'm finishing a novel I started a few months ago. Something a little different from what I normally do. After that, I'll have to see. The island is such a source of inspiration, and I've met so many great people here. I have a small-island series bubbling in the back of my mind already."

"Griff can literally go to the supermarket and find inspiration for a book," Mal said. "Don't be in his presence for long if you know what's good for you."

Both my uncle and Gabe laughed, but I was too preoccupied absorbing the information.

"Does that mean you're in all his books?" Gabe asked.

Mal looked at me as I stretched my arm out to give him his drink. He looked like he was going to speak, but then Griff laughed.

"No, Mal isn't in any of my books. Sometimes, the way someone makes you feel is too strong, too intense to put it in a book. If I ever wrote Mal into a book, it would be the last one I wrote because nothing else after that could do it justice."

My heart beat like it was going to run out of my chest and jump into the cold sea. The way Mal looked at Griff and then slowly met my gaze with the same intensity was overwhelming.

Mal moved his hand to take the glass at the same time I did, and the inevitable happened.

"Oh, my god…crap…I'm so sorry," I repeatedly said as if it would undo the fact that I'd just spilled a whole glass of cranberry-wine spritzer all over his lap.

I had a tea cloth next to the ice bucket, so I grabbed it and started patting his lap to absorb as much of the drink as possible before it soaked through.

"Ah…um…it's okay, don't worry," he said, shifting in his seat.

"No, I'll just clean it up a bit and—"

"Jake," he said, placing his hand over mine. "Honestly, it's okay."

I stared into his dark-blue eyes, and then I felt it. He was hard. His breath hitched up a little, and he looked at Griff.

I moved back like I'd been burned and nearly tripped on a flowerpot.

"Way to go, Jakey," Gabe said, laughing.

"I'll um…go get the red wine. Uncle Frank, do you think those steaks are almost done?" I said, not waiting for the reply before I ran inside.

I went straight to the bathroom and washed my hands. My dick was straining against my jeans. All it would take for me to get some relief would be a handful of strokes, but it felt wrong to do it.

Mal and Griff were a couple. They were married to each other. I was *not* part of them, and I had no business feeling so out of sorts around them.

"Focus, Jake," I said to the mirror. "Take a deep breath, go out there, and be the put-together person your uncle expects you to be."

I listened to my own words and ran some water over my face before I went back outside with the bottle of red wine my uncle had picked to go with the steak.

Mal went inside to clean up just as I came out. It took everything in me not to follow him in.

"You were right, son. Those steaks are done," my uncle said.

"Great, I'll grab the salad."

I went back into the kitchen, avoiding any kind of eye contact with Griff and hoping Mal took his time in the bathroom.

The rest of the lunch was a lot less awkward. I decided to focus on Gabe and keeping him busy, so he wouldn't drink too much, while my uncle kept the conversation going with Mal and Griff.

I also tried not to take in any of the information they shared, but I couldn't help being interested in Griff's writing or Mal's plans for the resort.

By the time they left, the shock of seeing them had worn off, even if I still felt strangely drawn to them. Mal had accepted my multiple apologies over spilling wine on him.

Luckily, he was wearing dark jeans, so once they dried out, any possible stains became invisible.

Gabe went straight back up to his room, so I made a cup of coffee for my uncle and took it to his office, approaching him with the practiced speech I'd been preparing for the last year.

"Hey, Uncle Frank, do you have a moment?" I said, placing the cup on his desk.

"Of course, son. What's up?"

I loved my uncle. He was the father I'd never had and my role model. He'd raised me ever since my mom had left me behind with him and my aunt before she decided to go and get herself killed.

"I love working at the resort. In all the summers I've worked here, I've gotten to know the staff and how things work. With my MBA finishing, I've been considering my options for the future."

My uncle nodded, taking a sip of the coffee.

"I'm incredibly proud of you, Jacob. You have a great work ethic, and I can't remember the last time I saw you go out with your friends to party and enjoy yourself."

I smiled. My uncle was the only person I knew that still called me Jacob, and Gabe, Gabriel. I once asked him why, and he simply shrugged and said those were our names.

"You know I've never been much of a party person," I said.

"Unlike your cousin. He's in line to inherit all of this and the business, and all he wants to do is party like it's going out of style."

"I think he's still grieving for Aunt Annie. I'll have a word with him and see how he's doing."

He nodded and picked up the photo he had on his desk of the four of us in New York the year before Aunt Annie died.

"We're all grieving, son. But we mustn't let the pain own us. Nothing good ever comes from that."

He put the frame back on the desk and looked at me. "So, tell me. What are your plans now that you've finished your MBA? Are you planning on heading out to the west coast again?"

"That's what I wanted to talk to you about. I've been offered a job with a company in Boston, but it doesn't start until September."

"That's great, Jacob. Congratulations. You should have said something earlier. We could have celebrated with champagne."

"It's okay, Uncle Frank. I don't want to make a big deal out of it. The truth is, I don't want to take that job."

"You don't? Why did you go for it?"

"Security. Uncle Frank, I want to work here, for you, at the resort. I know you just hired Mal, but I was hoping I could take on more responsibility and show you I have the skills to maybe one day run the resort for you."

My uncle leaned forward on his desk and rested his chin on his crossed hands.

"You have great potential, Jacob. Are you sure this is what you want?"

"Yes. The resort is my home, Uncle Frank. I love it more than anyone else you'll ever hire, but it's still a business, which is why I picked the right major and the MBA to give me the knowledge I can't get from cleaning rooms and working reception."

He smiled.

"That's how I started too. Your mother and me, cleaning rooms to the sound of her singing. The resort was still only a hotel, the only one on the island. Of course, she always wanted to leave. She never saw the potential." He sighed. We didn't talk about my mom often, and I tried to not think of her at all.

"Okay, let me speak to Mal and see if there's a management position for you."

"Thank you, Uncle Frank."

"What will happen in September?"

If I didn't fuck the job, or Mal and Griff, then I hoped I'd stay on. Which, of course, wasn't what I told my uncle.

"I guess we'll see, but for now, I want to focus on helping Silver Sands have the best summer season."

I left my uncle to his work and headed up to my room.

I didn't know how long I had until I started working at the resort again, but I had a feeling working with Mal was going to test my willpower, my work ethic, and my sanity.

5

GRIFF

"Oh fuck…nghh…yes, right there," Mal moaned.

I'd been pounding Mal's ass for the best part of the last hour, and every time I thought he was going to finally come…he didn't. It was fucking frustrating and perfect as hell.

"Are you going to give in, baby?" I whispered in his ear, even as I kept my relentless pace. I tried to keep my voice steady, but fuck if I wasn't so close to losing it.

The cock ring I'd put on had done a good job of keeping my orgasm at bay, but even that wouldn't last forever, and the way Mal's ass was squeezing my cock, I'd say we had a couple of minutes, tops.

"No, keep going…nghh…don't…stop," he growled.

The desperation in his voice went straight to my heart. Something wasn't right with my husband, but right now, the overwhelming need to come was taking over.

I pulled back, much to his pleading, and signaled for him to turn over to face me. Yep, in my dreams, I was strong enough to turn him over with little effort, but in reality, Mal was too heavy and bulky.

"Drama Queen *is not* a good look on you, baby," I said.

He looked like he was about to answer back or snarl, but I much preferred the roll of his eyes when I pushed my way back inside him.

"Oh fuck, Griff. You're gonna make me come."

"That's the goal. Now look at me. I want to see those beautiful blue eyes when you let yourself go."

Mal wrapped his arms around me so instead of holding myself up, I ended up plastered against him with his hard, thick cock between us.

I gave him open-mouthed kisses, keeping my eyes open as I worked my hips and rammed my cock into him over and over again.

"Griff," he pleaded, but there was no time to reach between us for his dick. Mal came so fiercely and so beautifully, I didn't think there was a better sight in the whole world.

My own orgasm threatened just below the surface. With heavy breaths and a slow move, he reached out to where our bodies were still connected and flicked the button of the cock ring open.

The sudden rush of blood to my already super-sensitive cock caused my body to convulse uncontrollably and push through my orgasm. There was nothing I could do but let my body ride the delicious wave of pleasure that coursed through me and forced me to keep rutting into Mal.

"Fuck…Jesus…holy…I think I'm dead," I breathed out.

Mal chuckled under me, but I didn't lift my head to face him. Instead, I let his steadying heartbeat guide mine.

"I was thinking we could go to the mainland this weekend," Mal said.

"Oh, yeah?"

I rested my head over my hands on his chest and winced as my dick slid out of his hole.

"Ugh, I hate this part." I got up to get a cloth to clean us both.

He laughed. "Is that the reason you don't top as often?"

Heat spread up to my face. "No. Um, well…maybe. I mean, who loves to clean their own cum out of someone else's ass?"

"I do. I love taking care of you after we make love."

Damn my sexy, sweet, loving man.

"Good for you. I'd rather show my love in other ways, like making your favorite pasta dish or being naked when I welcome you home from work," I said, finishing cleaning us both and settling right back into his arms.

He pulled me in for a kiss. "I love it when you do those things too."

"I knew you were with me because of the naked dinners."

"Among other things," he said, running his hand down my back and settling it on my ass before giving it a little squeeze.

I chuckled. "So tell me about these big weekend plans."

Mal tensed before he relaxed again. He may have thought I hadn't noticed, but I knew my husband better than he knew himself. I'd need to let him work up to telling me what was on his mind.

"We've been on the island six weeks, so I figured it would be nice to get the ferry to Long Beach, go for a long walk, eat nice food, find a hotel…make love all night…" he trailed off.

I didn't want to say that his idea sounded remarkably like what we did already, minus the hotel part. Clearly, he was in the mood to get away.

"I'm plotting a novel set in LA, so I wouldn't mind getting a feel for the city, even if it's just the beach," I said. "And the rest sounds acceptable enough. I mean, if I have to sit through a lovely meal and then have you ravage me all night long, I guess I can live with that."

I was on my back with Mal on top of me in two seconds.

"Finally," I sighed, loving the feel of his weight on me and wrapping my arms around his neck. He kissed me slowly, trapping my lower lip between his teeth, which totally woke up my dick again.

And then the alarm clock went off.

"Fuck." We both groaned.

"No round two for us," Mal said. "What are you up to today?"

"I'm going to El Pancito. I'm wrapping up the first draft of my new novel today with a celebratory cinnamon-and-raisin bagel."

We took a quick shower, and while Mal got ready for work, I checked my social media accounts. I was still adjusting to the three-hour time difference between Florida and LA, so I normally woke up to a bunch of notifications from the east coast readers.

Mal came into the kitchen ten minutes later. I openly gawked at the sight of him in his gray slacks and white button-down shirt with the sleeves rolled up to show his forearms.

"Damn, I'd totally tap your ass if I hadn't done that already this morning."

He laughed and came over, turning me around in the seat and placing himself between my legs. My sweatpants left nothing to the imagination.

"Save that for tonight. Make me that pasta dish you talked about yesterday, and I'll tap your ass in return."

My dick jerked its approval.

Mal filled his to-go cup with coffee and kissed me again.

"See you later. Love you."

"Love you too, Mal. Always."

After Mal left for work, I got dressed and made sure I had my laptop, charger, and favorite notebook all in my bag before I left the house.

Yesterday I'd spent all day writing in our small garden, so today, I definitely needed to be around people, and El Pancito was perfect.

"*Hola*, Griff. *¿Como estas?*" Elena, the owner of the small coffee shop, asked as soon as I walked in.

I laughed at her greeting in Spanish and went to the side of the counter to give her a kiss. Other than her name, there was nothing Spanish or Latino about Elena.

The daughter of a German engineer and an American teacher, the closest she was to any Spanish or Latino influence were the telenovelas she was obsessed with.

She'd told me when she opened her business that tourists thought they were in a bakery that had been passed from generation to generation ever since Elena's immigrant ancestors set foot on the island. She hadn't corrected them.

Elena had quickly become a good friend since I'd discovered she made the best bread in the world, and she discovered I was a romance author who also loved telenovelas.

I mean, all the love, hate, tension, and big hand gestures make for amazing romance, right? Let's not even mention how gorgeous people are in those shows.

"Pick your favorite spot because you're not leaving until you finish that book, you hear me?" she said, placing her hands on her hips.

"I'm going to need sustenance, honey," I replied and walked over to the table in the corner by the window.

"I've got you, babe."

I took my laptop out and opened my manuscript document.

Minutes later, I had a toasted cinnamon-and-raisin bagel and a big pot of coffee in front of me.

I poured the coffee into the cup and added one spoon of sugar.

My usual routine was to have the first cup of coffee while I watched people and let the story I was working on come back to me. Let the character's voices speak to me.

I smelled the delicious coffee, took a sip, and waited.

Nothing.

Even after reading through the last few chapters, I couldn't figure out how to write the final chapter.

"What's wrong, honey? You look lost," Elena said as she cleared the table next to mine.

I sighed. "I'm not sure. The words aren't coming. I mean, I know how to end the book, but nothing I write feels right."

Elena took a seat and rested her elbows on the table.

"Okay, let's talk this through. You have the whole book, correct?"

I nodded.

"So..." she trailed. "You just need the happy ever after."

"Thanks for telling me how books work," I said, trying to sound sarcastic and failing.

"Griff, you're living your own happy ever after. Honey, I've seen your husband. I bet you get a *happy ever after* every night," she said with the biggest wink ever to be winked.

I bumped her shoulder, and she laughed.

"Amiright, though?"

I thought back to this morning when I woke up to Mal sucking my dick like a vacuum cleaner before declaring he needed me inside him. That was definitely a very happy ever after.

"Damn, Griff. Say no more. *That* face tells me everything I need to know. I should charge you double for your breakfast on account of you having awesome sex and me having none."

I laughed.

"I think I'm going for a walk on the beach to clear my head. Can you wrap my bagel up for me?" I asked.

"Of course, sweetie."

According to the locals, the tourist season hadn't kicked in fully yet. There were people walking on the beach, but nothing like the numbers we could expect to see in a month.

It would be a shame to lose the peace and calm of the seaside, but I knew it would be good for all the local businesses, and especially Mal's resort.

At his last job, Mal had an apartment on-site, so I got to know everyone he worked with and felt like I was a part of their big family.

At La Catarina, we had our own house outside of the resort. I liked it because I could be myself and make friends without being worried that anything I said or did could affect Mal's work, but at the same time, I didn't get the scoop on what was happening.

I removed my shoes and walked to the shore, where the waves were flowing gently over the fine silver sand.

As the cold water of the Pacific hit my toes, realization hit *me*. I knew why I was blocked.

It had been a few days since we'd seen Jake again, and at Mal's boss's house, of all places.

Mal had refused to talk about it, but I'd seen how affected he'd been by Jake's presence. I'd felt it too, but unless he was willing to talk, I couldn't push it. I knew pushing Mal would only result in him clamming up.

I walked home via the market, where I bought the ingredients to make the pasta recipe I'd found online that had piqued Mal's interest.

By the time I turned the corner to our place, I felt a little more settled than I normally did after a walk.

I nearly jumped out of my skin and dropped the shopping bag when I was halfway up the path and saw Jake sitting on the grass by the rosebush.

"Sorry...I'm...um, I'm sorry, I didn't mean to startle you," Jake said, getting up. "There was no one here, and I used to look after the roses...um, before."

"Oh. Is it part of your job? I mean, no one came here before, so I've been looking after them ever since we moved in."

"Aunt Annie planted them years ago. She loved roses."

Jake didn't follow his statement with any kind of explanation for his presence in our front yard. He stood there staring at me. Was there longing in his gaze? Surely not.

Someone as gorgeous and young as Jake could have anyone he wanted. Even though he'd confessed that day that he'd never been with two guys before, he didn't seem like the kind of guy who struggled to find a boyfriend or hookups.

Not that I knew anything about him to make that kind of judgment. And why the fuck was I thinking about that day now?

Even without having the talk with Mal, I already knew that morning months ago was not to be repeated, especially not with Jake.

"I should go. I'm sorry. I shouldn't have come here," he said, taking a step before I caught his arm.

"Wait. Stay," I said.

"Why?"

I don't know. Fuck.

"Have a coffee with me."

He still looked unsure.

"Look, I had your dick in my mouth before. I promise my coffee can be just as good."

He laughed, and a little bit of the same look I saw that morning came back.

"Okay, sure."

Jake followed me inside and to the kitchen. He sat on one of the stools at the breakfast counter while I turned the coffeemaker on and started unpacking the groceries.

"Tell me about the roses," I said.

"Nothing much to tell. A few months after my aunt died, I needed to deliver some paperwork to the resort manager. He was a bit of a workaholic and was never home, so I was going to put the papers in the mailbox. That's when I saw the roses. They were growing all over the place, and the weeds were suffocating them. I started coming by to look after them. That's all."

I filled two cups of coffee and sat on a stool opposite Jake.

"Why me?" he asked. "Did you know who I was?"

"What? No, of course not." I took a sip of my coffee, followed by a deep breath. "We didn't plan anything if that's what you're asking. Since we came all the way to the west coast for the interview, we decided to take some time off. Mal had been a little stressed with some issues he'd had at work."

Jake nodded.

"Do you do that often?"

I shook my head. "No. We've never brought a third person into our bed before. I swear."

"Why then? Why me?"

"I'm polyamorous. Ever since I was young, my grandmother always told me I had too much love to give. I didn't understand any of it until I was in my late teens. I had a couple of boyfriends who got jealous whenever I said I was also attracted to other people, even though I never cheated on anyone."

"And Mal knows?"

I chuckled. "Of course. Our relationship relies on more than our love for each other. We promised to be truthful to each other and ourselves. Jake, you were the first person I'd been with since way before Mal came into my life and definitely the only one since. But I can tell you why we picked you."

I reached out to Jake and put my hand on top of his. "The way Mal looked at you the day we checked in. I've only seen it once, and it was directed at me. I can't speak for Mal, but I know how it feels to want more than one person at the same time. If my husband felt something when he saw you, I wasn't going to stop him from acting on it. *Especially* when I felt exactly the same way."

Jake took his hand back and ran it through his hair.

"This is too much. I never thought I'd see you again—"

The sound of keys in the door stopped Jake.

"Babe, are you in? Guess who forgot his papers, just like you—"

Mal stopped by the archway that divided the kitchen from the rest of the house.

He looked at Jake and then at me. I didn't need to be a mind reader to see the confusion in his eyes, the hurt in his body language, and the desire he was desperately trying to hide.

6

MAL

WHEN I REALIZED I'd left some papers at home, several options came to mind.

The first was that I could just work from home for the rest of the day. After that thought, more options came to mind.

Wait for Griff to come home and take him out to dinner.

Cook Griff a nice dinner…naked, of course.

Pick out a random sex scene from one of his books and reenact it later tonight. That option seemed to be compatible with all the other options, so I'd decided it was definitely happening.

What I had not expected when I got home was to see my husband and Jake sitting at the breakfast counter, with a coffee cup in hand, looking like they belonged there together.

Griff's loving smile as I turned the corner toward the kitchen had the same effect on me as on the very first day we'd met. It took my breath away.

Jake turned around slowly. His anxiety was clear in the way he gripped the coffee cup and his frame tensed.

"Hi," I said after what felt like a lifetime.

Griff came over to give me a small kiss. "Would you like a coffee?"

"Sure," I said. "Did you finish your manuscript?"

He groaned and pulled away. I grabbed his arm to pull him back to me.

"What's the matter?"

He gave me a look that said, *tell you later*, so I gave him a soft kiss on the lips and let him go.

"So, Jake, what brings you here?" I said, trying my best to be nonchalant.

He was still looking down at his now-empty coffee cup as Griff handed me mine. I took a sip and leaned against the counter. As if he knew I needed him there, Griff leaned right against my side.

"Jake was looking after the roses in the front garden when I got back. Did you know Annie planted them years ago?" Griff said.

Jake looked at Griff and then at me. The uncertainty in his eyes made him look so much younger than his twenty-nine years.

"Actually," Jake said, speaking for the first time. "I wasn't here just for the roses. I mean, I was, but not just…um, I came here before…"

"You did? When?" Griff asked.

"The day after the lunch at my uncle's place. I wanted to talk to you, but then…" he trailed off and looked down at his cup again.

"But then you didn't know how to do it," I said, finishing his thought for him.

"Yeah. I mean, this whole thing is weird, right?" He sighed. "I don't know, I just felt awkward, so I left and then came back a couple of times, but you weren't here. Today I got distracted by the roses, so I guess I was caught." He laughed.

"Jake, I hope you know you can come here and look after your aunt's roses anytime. We can see they're important to you. Besides, I don't know the first thing about flowers, so all I've done is make sure they're watered," Griff said.

Jake got up and took the empty cup to the sink, then he turned to face us but looked straight at me. "Look, I just wanted to reassure you that I have never and would never do anything with guests at the resort. I mean, again…I wouldn't do it again. And I'm not saying it because you obviously know I've done it now because—"

"Jake," I interrupted. "It's okay. I know what you mean. Why don't we start over like it never happened?"

Jake looked at Griff and then walked toward the door before turning back around. "Yeah...sure...never happened. I guess I'll see you at work tomorrow." And he was gone.

The noise of the front door closing was like a punch to the gut. And fuck me if I could understand why. I put my cup in the sink and leaned against it, looking out of the window toward the garden.

"What's wrong with you?" Griff said, his voice laced with unusual irritation.

"There's nothing wrong with me. Jake starts his new job at the resort tomorrow. He clearly doesn't want things to be awkward for us. I made it easy for everyone."

"Of course you did," Griff said, walking out of the kitchen.

I followed him to the spare room where he'd set up his office.

"What do you mean?" I asked. "Why do I feel like I've said something wrong?"

He sighed.

"Because you have, Mal."

"How was I supposed to have handled it? Should we have gone down memory lane? Remembered how amazing it felt to kiss him? Hold him? Fuck him? And how I nearly came just by watching you two together? Is that what you wanted? And how about the fact that we're going to be working together?"

I'd avoided this topic like the plague, but it seemed Jake's presence had opened that particular can and the worms were spilling out.

"Oh, Mal." Griff wrapped his arms around me. I kissed his hair and breathed in the familiar scent of his shampoo. "Do you remember when we talked about it before we moved here?"

I nodded, my words stuck in my throat.

"I need you to tell me what's on your mind and how you feel," he said.

"I thought I just did," I chuckled, and he shook his head. "I don't want to be around him," I finally confessed.

"Why?"

I pulled away a little so I could look into Griff's deep-brown eyes.

"You saw what happened at lunch with Frank. I'm attracted to Jake, and I'm terrified of it."

"Is it because you're going to be working with him?"

"Yes, but not just that. Griff, I'm…the thought that I want someone else makes me hate myself because I love you so much. I can't stand the thought that I could hurt you in any way."

Griff pulled me to the couch he had in his office and pushed me to sit down, then he straddled me and put his hands on either side of my face.

"Mal, I have no doubt that you love me. I trust you, and I know that you would never pursue anything with Jake or anyone else unless I agreed to it. The fact that you're struggling so much with your attraction to Jake tells me everything I need to know."

I nodded, and he carried on.

"Open your heart, baby. The same way you opened it for me. Just open it and see what happens. Would you be attracted to other people? Or just Jake? You need to know so you can decide what you want to do. Avoiding it will only make you hurt."

"I know that you're right. There's just so many elements to this. And whether or not I'm attracted to Jake, there's still the fact that we can't act on it."

"Tell you what, my sweet, gruff, gorgeous husband," he said, running his fingers through my hair and gripping it tightly.

"Who? Me?" I put my hands on his ass and pulled him closer so our dicks brushed against each other, which, even with clothes on, felt exquisite.

He gasped, his eyes going darker. "You were saying?"

"Um…yeah, I was saying…why don't we go away for the weekend as you suggested this morning? You don't need to do any hard thinking right now. Let's just enjoy each other."

"No *hard* thinking, you say?" I teased, catching his lips with mine as he melted into me. God, I loved kissing Griff. He always gave one hundred percent of himself to a kiss, as if it were a full-body experience.

I'd come to believe Griff had magical powers with the way he was able to settle my anxieties while also making me face my worst fears.

Yesterday was no different, and after a thorough make-out session, we cooked an early dinner together, and he'd been totally on board with reenacting a sex scene from one of his books.

He surprised me with one I hadn't read yet, so I just went along for the ride, which was how I found myself tied to the bed with Griff riding me until he came all over my chest. He made himself hard again and managed a second orgasm before I gave in and came inside my husband's tight heat.

It was also the thought of how we'd handled yesterday together that gave me the guts to ask Jake to see me in the conference room as soon as he came in.

"Knock, knock," Jake said, standing by the open door.

"Come in."

He closed the door behind him before he sat on the opposite side of the conference table.

"Jake, I want to apologize for yesterday and be honest with you. I hope you'll agree we're finding ourselves in a situation that is unprecedented for all of us."

He nodded.

"Yesterday, you said you've never broken the non-fraternization rule at work. Well, I can assure you neither have I. When we… when…" I took a deep breath. "Look, there was…is, something about you, and I can't understand it, but whatever it is, nothing else will happen now."

"Thank you for being honest with me, Mal. Working at the resort means more to me than anything else. The thought that I did something to jeopardize it was…" He shook his head, leaving the thought hanging.

Frank and I had met after the lunch at his place, and he'd told me about Jake's aspirations to work at the resort. He'd talked so glowingly about Jake that I'd started to wonder why he hadn't given his nephew my job.

"I'm glad we cleared that up. Frank talked wonders about you, but

I'd like to know more about you and your career aspirations from you, not secondhand," I said.

"How about we do it over a walk? There's someone I want you to meet."

I stood up and raised my hand for him to lead the way.

"Did Uncle Frank tell you I grew up here?" Jake said as we walked down the stairs outside the main restaurant to the gardens.

"No. You did?"

"Yeah, I grew up on the island, and I loved coming to the resort with my uncle. I knew all the staff, and they basically let me do anything I wanted."

The meek, uncertain Jake I'd seen yesterday in my kitchen was gone and replaced by a passionate young man that resembled me a lot. How it felt to visit my first resort and deciding this was what I wanted to do as a job.

"What kinds of things did you do?" I asked.

"When I was seven or eight, I used to follow the maids around. They'd give me little jobs like emptying the trash cans or making sure the minibars were stocked. The maids were also known gossips. Do you watch telenovelas?"

I shook my head. Griff also loved telenovelas.

He suddenly started laughing.

"One time, one of the maids told me to go help someone else. It was strange, but I did as I was told. As I was leaving, I noticed she snuck something wrapped in plastic into a separate bag on her cart. I thought she was stealing from my uncle, so I waited until she went into a room. I picked up the bag and ran to my uncle's office, so outraged that someone would steal from him."

"Did she steal something?"

"No, she'd found a purple dildo stuck in between the bedsheets. She had to take it to Lost Property and didn't want me to see it. Obviously, I didn't know what it was at the time. My uncle's face was priceless as I put the plastic-wrapped dildo on his desk, and it started vibrating all over the place. I was outraged when he refused to fire the maid and ran home to tell my aunt. Needless to say, I wasn't allowed to help the maids anymore. Believe it or not, it was safer for me in the kitchen. I learned a lot about cooking there."

How had I not noticed he had a little dimple on the side of his chin when he smiled? And why was I mentally cataloging both his face and what made him smile so I could work on making it happen again?

Fuck, Mal. Focus. You want to know about his career aspirations.

He stopped when we reached the grass and crouched down, gesturing for me to do the same. Then he put his hand up to his mouth and kissed the inside of his middle finger, which made a squeaking noise.

Seconds later, my furry old friend turned up and came right up to Jake.

"Hello, buddy. Do you want a treat? Of course you do," he said, talking gently to the bunny. He put his hand in his pocket and took out some rabbit treats, placing them on the grass in front of us.

"He's never come that close to me before," I said, amazed at how comfortable the usually skittish bunny was.

"He's about three years old. I found him after his mom abandoned him. I couldn't take him home because the bunnies here are wild, and apart from feeding them, we're not supposed to interfere with how they live. I had to keep coming back to feed him and hope he wasn't eaten by another animal."

The bunny finished his treat and then came up to Jake, who petted his gray fur.

"I've been giving him treats for weeks, and he's never come close to me," I said. "Your uncle called him Jake the other day. I mean, I get it with the blue eyes, but I have to say, that's where the resemblance ends."

Jake elbowed me, and I fell sideways, which scared bunny-Jake away.

"Gabe thinks he's funny, and my uncle went with it all too easily," he said, clearly not finding them naming the bunny after him funny at all.

"He normally has two friends with him, but they never come for the treats."

"The big one seems to have adopted Jake. It took me a while to gain his trust, so he'd let me feed him. The other one, who's about the same size as Jake now, he just likes cuddling up to the other two."

I stared into Jake's light-blue eyes. He looked relaxed, happy.

"Tell me how I can make your career dreams come true at the resort," I said.

As we walked along the beach, I got to know Jake, the hard-working young man who'd never taken a summer off to play around with his friends. Jake, the recent graduate who was willing to further his own education to complement his already extensive experience.

I itched to get to know Jake, the man. I thought about everything Griff had told me last night and decided to open my heart. Not to pursue anything with Jake, but to just let myself be me around him.

Griff sucked a patch of skin on my neck. I knew I'd get a mark, and I knew I'd need to be crafty about hiding it at work.

"Why are we still wearing clothes?" I groaned, raising my hips up to meet his and feeling his erection under his jeans.

"Because we can't take them off yet," he said, continuing kissing, licking, and sucking my skin.

"Baby…you're killing me." I was hard enough to pound nails and felt like I hadn't come in weeks.

The doorbell rang.

What the fuck?

Griff sat up and gave me a look that told me he was up to something. It was a look that got me hard every single time, but since it was impossible to get any harder than I already was, I tugged him back down to me and tried to pull his shirt off him.

"Nope, we need to get that." He got up and extended his hand for me to get up with him.

Hold on, how come we're in bed? We were making out on the couch.

Griff's mouth really did have magical powers if I was now losing track of time.

I grumbled but followed him to the door. And why did we both need to answer the door? Had we been getting solicitors? Griff hadn't mentioned anything before, and the island was so small, I doubted soliciting was even a thing here.

Before Griff answered the door, he looked at me. His bottom lip was trapped between his teeth. I released it with my thumb, and he smiled.

"I'm sorry," he said.

"Sorry about what?"

He opened the door so slowly, I worried about what was on the other side. And how did Griff know who or what it was?

"Jake," I said. "What are you doing here?"

He walked in, his eyes locked onto mine with a confidence I hadn't seen in him, and before I knew it, his lips were on mine.

My heart felt like it was beating out of my chest, initially because seeing Jake was unexpected, but as his tongue sought entry into my mouth, it was for a whole different reason.

Jake tasted like caramel. Sweet, rich, smooth.

I reached out for Griff. I needed him to ground me, bring me back to reality.

He held my hand, and as soon as Jake released me, their mouths met in a hungry kiss. Griff's hand tightened on mine while the other pulled Jake closer to him.

This was not happening. Not again.

I wanted to say something, to stop this, but it was as if all the words had deserted me.

If my cock had been hard earlier, now, watching Griff and Jake kiss, I was about ready to blow.

I don't know how long they stood there kissing in our strange three-way embrace, but when they stopped, there were no lingering looks. Or at least, I didn't have time to wonder about lingering looks because Griff pulled my face down for a kiss.

He tasted of chocolate.

When had he had chocolate?

Why did they, together, taste like my favorite ice cream: chocolate and caramel?

My heart raced. Hands touched me everywhere, apart from where I really ached to be touched.

Jake's mouth joined mine and Griff's in a three-way kiss I didn't think *was possible. The mix of tongues, flavors, soft lips, and their moans was heady.*

As it all started, so it ended. Griff was by my side and Jake by the front door.

"I'm sorry, I needed to know," he said.

"Know what?" I asked.

"If it was real. If it really happened all those months ago. If I still felt the same way."

And then he was gone.

I tried to chase after him, but all I saw outside on the lawn, lit up by our walkway light, were three bunnies.

Jake and the cuddly bunny scurried away, leaving only the bigger bunny staring at me a moment longer before he too left.

I woke up with a jolt. Griff was sound asleep next to me, and there was no Jake.

As stupid as it seemed, I got up and went to the front door. There was nothing there.

I leaned my head against the cold frame of the door, trying to get my breathing back.

What the fuck's happening to me?

7

———

JAKE

Working with Mal was great. He was professional but fair. He was a very hands-on manager, but let you get on with your work. He just liked to understand what you did.

I liked that approach, which was why I'd spent so many summers working in each of my uncle's resorts. I wanted to understand what made them different from each other, but also what made Silver Resorts *the* place to bring your family on vacation.

"Hey, Jake, do you have a second?" Hailey said, placing a glass of freshly squeezed juice in front of me.

I chuckled. "Take a seat. Is that for me?"

"Yes…consider it a bribe," she said, pulling a chair from a nearby desk.

The juice was delicious and fresh. Also, it was my favorite: mango and passionfruit.

"Hmm, it's nice, but not bribe-worthy. Now, if you'd added a poppy seed bagel from El Pancito…just sayin'."

"I'll make a note of that," she said, rolling her eyes.

"Good. Now, how can I help?"

"Mal mentioned you're working on our branding, what brings us together as a team and sets us apart from the other resorts, especially Silver Palms since it's our closest competitor," she said.

I wouldn't say they were a competitor as such since, at the end of the day, both resorts were Silver, but I understood what Hailey meant. She wanted our resort to succeed and not just be the poor relative to the glamor and luxury of LA's best resort.

"Yes, that's right."

When Mal had proposed that I work on a project rather than take on a role, it confused the hell out of me.

One thing I'd been adamant about when we'd talked about my work at the resort was that I didn't want to be here as a favor to my uncle. I wanted to be here because I had the experience and education to back it up.

I wasn't sure what to make of his decision, but he was my boss now, and since I reported directly to him, there was nothing I could do.

Regardless of Mal's plan, I was going to kick the hell out of this project and show him I deserved a place at the resort.

"Jake, we have a bunch of new hires this year. I love Pete, but I could kill him right now. Each contract states we hired them to do a specific job, except I need them to be flexible, and many of them don't want to."

"Because it's not in their contract or skill set," I added.

"Precisely, and that leaves us short in some areas and overstaffed in others. I understand that a fully flexible team isn't possible. It takes time to clean a room as fast as the maids do, and someone from another area might slow them down. But there must be a middle ground."

I thought about my experience in the other resorts, especially the one in LA. In my view, the issue hadn't been called out because they had a much bigger staffing budget and could afford to hire people that focused on a single job.

"It's interesting you should say that because I've seen the same problem in other resorts. I'm not sure how soon I could have a solution for you, but I can tell you it's part of what I'm looking at."

Hailey looked so relieved that I couldn't keep myself from joking.

"See? You didn't even need to bring me a bagel. But I'll just put it out there, you could have."

She laughed and got up to return the chair to its desk. There was no one else in the office, which was a rarity.

"Hailey?"

"Yes?"

"Can I ask you something personal?"

"Sure."

I'd known Hailey for years, even before she'd met Pete, so I knew if there was someone I could ask this question to, it was her.

"How do you do it? You and Pete working together and then going home."

She tilted her head before she winked and smiled.

"Oh no, if you're gonna tell me all the bickering you do at work is foreplay, then I don't want to know," I said, covering my ears and closing my eyes.

I heard a faint laugh before she pulled my hands away from my ears, and I opened my eyes.

"Well, sometimes, but it's more than that. We knew when he took the job that we would have our challenges. It's hard not to take work home sometimes, but we try to leave it all here. Home is our sanctuary. We pretend we work for different employers, so we're not tempted to discuss what happens at work. We try to have lunch together here so we can talk about work and not feel tempted to take it home."

"That sounds very…adult of you. Are you sure that's what really happens?" I asked, part teasing and part admiration.

"Believe it or not, it works most of the time. Why do you ask? Are you interested in anyone? I didn't think there was any—"

"Oh no," I said quickly. "I just wondered. You know, as part of my project. It's difficult recruiting on the island, and I'm thinking being in a relationship with someone else that works here might stop people from applying because of the no-fraternization rule."

The way she looked at me told me she didn't buy my excuse. Fortunately, Pete came into the office, taking Hailey's attention away from me.

If I were honest with myself, I didn't even know why I'd asked the question. It wasn't like I was considering dating anyone that worked with me. The no-fraternization rule applied to me as much as it applied to everyone else working at the resort, and I wasn't interested in breaking the rules. Well, not again.

My calendar app dinged with a new meeting notification, but it was the date on the corner of the screen that made my blood go cold.

How had I missed what day it was?

Well, that was easy to answer. I'd been so wrapped up in work, wanting to make a good impression on Mal, and just plain excited about working at the resort for more than a temporary assignment, that I'd completely shut off anything else in my life that wasn't related to work.

I picked up my cell phone to call my uncle but stopped before I tapped on his name. I called Gabe instead.

"Jake, bro, where are you?"

"Hi. I'm at work. Is Uncle Frank at the beach yet?"

"No, he said he'd wait for you."

I took a relieved breath.

"Okay, I'm leaving now. See you soon."

I scribbled an apology to Mal on a sticky note and put it on his desk. Not that he'd see it. If today was like any of the other days this week, he'd go straight home from wherever he'd been and wouldn't even stop by the office.

"Hey, Hailey, I'm heading off now. I just remembered I have to be somewhere this afternoon. I left a message on Mal's desk, but if you see him, can you tell him I'll explain tomorrow?"

"Sure thing. Is everything okay?"

"Yeah," I said, knowing my tight smile wouldn't convince her. "Just something I do with my uncle every year on this day."

Hailey nodded but said nothing else, so I grabbed my bag and left.

My uncle wasn't old by any means, but seeing him sitting at the kitchen table, suddenly his wrinkles seemed more pronounced, his eyes looked a little more tired, and his slim frame looked more like the age he was rather than the one we always believed him to be based on his youthful demeanor.

"Hey, Uncle Frank," I said, coming into the kitchen.

"Oh, hey, son. I was lost in time just now. Are you ready to go?"

"Yes, let me grab the speaker from my bedroom."

It was a warm late-spring day, so I quickly changed from my work slacks and dress shirt into jeans and an old college T-shirt before grabbing the bunch of daisies from the kitchen table and walking down to the beach with my uncle.

Thank goodness my uncle had remembered to get the flowers.

"It doesn't feel like it's already fifteen years since she's been gone," my uncle said, navigating the last few rocks before we arrived at the small sand beach at the bottom of the cliff.

"No, it doesn't, but some days it feels so much longer. I don't remember living with her in LA. I don't know if she took me out for ice cream on the beach, or if she dropped me at the school gate like the other moms."

My uncle put his hand on my shoulder and squeezed it. A lump formed in my throat, so I cleared it and turned the speaker on, connecting it to my phone and looking for the music app.

Her soulful voice filled the air around us and mixed with the sound of the waves, singing about love, destiny, and happiness. Tears ran down my face.

I read stories about people that kept voice messages from their loved ones after they died. Being able to listen to my mom's voice doing what she loved the most always hit me hard.

My mom had, in some ways, been very selfish. She'd had a dream and stopped at nothing to make it come true. She nearly made it too.

Had it not been for the drunk driver that had hit her car from behind on one of the rare days when she was on her way to the island to see me, she'd have seen her recently recorded album reach the charts.

"Some days, I want to hate her," I said. "She left me behind. Her music was more important than her own son."

My uncle let out a choked laugh. "I used to call her pig-headed, but I think we shared the same determination to succeed. The difference was that I wanted to give people an experience they couldn't forget through time away on vacation, and she wanted to do it using her beautiful voice."

"But you didn't abandon Aunt Annie or Gabe, and there was still space in your life to take me in." A sliver of anger threatened to rise, but I squashed it down. Anger toward my mom served no purpose.

"Do you think if she hadn't died, that one day she'd have come back for me and we'd be together? That we'd do all the things that she wasn't able to do with me when she was working hard to be noticed?"

The song was ending, so we grabbed the bunch of daisies, her favorite flowers, and threw them out into the water, one by one.

When all we could hear were the waves again, and all we could see were flowers floating away with the tide, my uncle turned to me.

"I know I don't say it enough, Jacob, but I love you as if you were my own son. I am grateful every day that your mom never brought your father into your life because we wouldn't have you otherwise." He put his arms around me and hugged me tightly. "You make me proud every day, and I know you are a good influence on Gabriel. We can spend a lifetime second-guessing what would have happened if things were different, but we can't change the past."

"I love you too, Uncle Frank, and not a day goes by that I don't feel thankful to you and Aunt Annie for raising me. Even if Gabe is a pain in the ass most of the time."

He laughed, and I realized that since I'd left for college, we hadn't had many times when it was just him and me.

"Now," he said, straightening up and putting on what Gabe and I liked to call his *dad-face*. "I believe Gabriel is at the top of the cliff waiting to take you out for a drink."

"Are you coming?"

"Nah, I'm gonna take Jessie for a walk and then settle in to watch a game on the TV."

It wasn't until we turned to leave that I saw a lone figure at the other end of the beach. There was rarely anyone here because of the rocky path down the cliff, and the sandy part was much smaller. Tourists, and even locals, preferred to go to the bigger beach on the other side.

I'd have ignored the person if I hadn't recognized him.

I told my uncle to go on up as I walked over to where Griff was sitting, looking out toward the horizon.

"Hey," I said, putting my hands in my pockets for something to do with them.

Between Griff and Mal, I was definitely a lot more comfortable with Griff. Attraction and everything else aside, he was such a warm, welcoming person. Not that Mal wasn't, but I didn't know what to make of the way he looked at me, of how intense it felt to be under his gaze.

"Hi, Jake. I hope I didn't interrupt anything. I didn't see you and Frank until I was halfway down the rocks. I'd have gone to say hi, but I saw you throw the flowers and figured you might not want to be disturbed."

I smiled and sat next to him on the rock.

"My mom died fifteen years ago, today. Uncle Frank and I always come here every year. Despite doing her best to leave the island, she loved the sea. This is our way to remember her."

Griff put his hand on mine and squeezed. "That's beautiful, Jake. I'm sure wherever she is, she's looking down on you and smiling."

I shook my head, unsure if my increased heart rate was because of Griff's words or his touch.

"Thank you. I like to think that too," I said, standing up. "Um, I better go. Gabe is waiting for me. I'll see you around."

Griff's warm smile made me want to hug him, burrow into him, and stay there until today wasn't today anymore.

"It was nice seeing you again, Jake."

I nodded and started making my way up the rocks to the top.

When I got to the parking lot, my cousin was leaning against a car with his sunglasses on, dressed like he was hoping to get undressed later. And not by his own hands.

"Come on, Sadface. I'm taking you to The Reef to put some food in you before we go to The Dive. We'll apologize to your liver tomorrow."

I laughed and followed him toward the best restaurant on the island. My cousin was never one to do anything by half measures.

It was a shame to have such delicious food when we knew we wouldn't remember it tomorrow, or it would end up at the bottom of the trashcan, but it didn't stop me from ordering the best steak on the menu and finishing my dinner with a chocolate mousse cake so delicious it should come with a warning for triggering orgasms.

The Dive was heaving, but somehow Gabe wove his way through the crowd to get to the bar and order our drinks while I scouted for a free table or just some space against a wall.

Considering how many people were in the small bar, we'd be lucky to find something to lean on.

A couple left just as I was going past, so I quickly grabbed their table. Next to us was another small table that had five guys sitting around it. There were so many empty glasses that you couldn't see the tabletop.

One of the guys caught me staring. He smiled and leaned forward.

"You can join us if you want."

I didn't miss the look of appreciation in his green eyes. He was cute. Maybe a little younger than me, but not by much.

"I'm here with my cousin," I said, pointing at the bar where Gabe was taking a tray from the bartender.

"If you change your mind…you're welcome to join us."

His smile as he turned back to his friends was a clear sign that he'd be up for sharing more than a drink.

I didn't have time to think about how I felt before Gabe came over and placed a tray overflowing with drinks on the table.

"Fuck, Gabe. Forget apologizing to my liver tomorrow. I should book myself in for a transplant instead."

He grinned and lined up the drinks in front of us.

"Okay, so we're starting with some shots to warm up. We've got a white gummy bear, a kamikaze, a lemon drop, and a lemon ball."

I shook my head but followed his lead as he downed the shots one by one.

By the time we switched to beer, I was feeling all warm and fuzzy, happy, and also a little horny. Something my neighbor from the other table didn't seem to miss.

"I'll be right back," I said and got up to go to the restroom.

The floor seemed a little unstable. It had been a while since I'd been to The Dive, so maybe they'd had renovations.

Thank fuck for men's big bladders because the restroom was more or less empty. I stared at the funny pattern on the tiles while I considered the benefits of peeing standing up versus sitting down.

I decided on standing up because who knew when these restrooms were last cleaned.

I bet they never lose their Lysol cans in this place.

An image of Griff's brown eyes, the feel of his soft lips, and Mal's commanding voice whispering in my ear filled my brain.

"Fuck, how can I pee with a fucking boner?"

"Want a hand?"

I looked up to see the guy from the other table. Somehow the fact he wasn't Griff or Mal made my dick deflate enough I could finish and tuck myself away.

That pissed me off. Who the fuck did they think they were to come inside my head and mess up with me? I wanted to have a boner for the guy standing in front of me looking like he was ready to be dragged into one of the stalls for a quick fuck. I *did not* want a boner for the married couple I couldn't have.

I took the guy by the hand and pulled him into the nearest stall. I didn't even bother locking the door before I slammed my mouth on his.

He let out a moan that spurred me on. I unzipped his jeans and took his cock out. It felt good…hard, long, and it already had some precum beading from the head.

I wondered if he just wanted me to suck him or if he'd be up for getting fucked.

"What's your name?" he asked.

"Jake, you?"

"Sam."

"Nice to meet you, Sam," I said, tugging his lips between my teeth before I sucked them.

Fuck, they were soft like Griff's.

Shit. Fuck.

He put his hands on my shoulders, which I took as a sign he wanted me to get on my knees and suck him.

I started moving, but he stopped me.

"What's up?" I asked.

"Jake, are you sure you want this?"

I frowned. *Huh?*

"What do you mean?"

"I mean that you're coming at me like a starved man, but you're not even hard. I'm all for some fun, but I'm not a jerk. I'm not going to take advantage of you, and I'm also not the guy for you to take your issues out on."

I took a step back and leaned against the wall.

"I'm sorry. I'm…sorry, Sam."

He placed his hand on the handle of the door that was closed but unlocked.

"You're cute, Jake. I'm sure you'll work it all out." And then he left.

When I got out of the restroom, I saw Gabe on the dance floor eating some guy's face while grinding against him to the beat of the music.

I needed to get some air, so I headed toward the door. Once I was out, I didn't stop until I found myself on the beach.

It was dark already. The sky was clear and full of stars, and there was a slight chill in the air I hadn't noticed after leaving the bar.

I pulled my phone out and sent Gabe a text.

Jake: I'm going home. Sorry to leave you, but you seemed happily occupied.

Gabe: Nah, he was too handsy. I'm off toward home too. Are you okay?

Jake: I'm good. Just needed some air.

Gabe: See you at home then.

I pocketed the phone and looked one more time to the sky.

"I still miss you, Mom."

Despite the foggy mist of my grief and alcohol-induced self-pity, I managed to get home and crash in my own bed.

What I didn't manage to do was set my alarm for the next day, so when Gabe knocked on my door, sounding like he'd just run a triathlon and was ready to start a marathon, I was ready to grab the closest thing to me, which was my phone, and throw it at him.

It wasn't until I noticed the time that I jumped out of bed like it was on fire.

My head was killing me, and I felt queasy, but it was nothing a shower couldn't fix.

"Hey, Gabe," I shouted from the bathroom. "Can you make me a coffee to go? I'll owe you."

"I'll go one better, big bro. I'll take you to work too."

I wasn't sure if he felt bad because we got drunk last night, or if he was still pitying me over the reason we always got drunk together on the same day each year, but I didn't care. Coffee and a ride to work were like my birthday and Christmas thrown together at this point.

Please let Mal not be in the office. Please let Mal not be in the office.

I gave a sigh of relief when Mal was indeed not in the office, but my already delicate stomach sank when I saw a note on my computer to meet him in the conference room.

"What time do you call this?" he said.

"I'm sorry, Mal. I didn't mean to be late, but—"

"I didn't call you to hear excuses. You said you wanted to learn the ropes and one day run this place. Well, you just missed the opportunity to sit in on a conference call with me and the general managers of Silver Palms and Silver Springs."

My head felt like it was going to explode, but it was the disappointment in Mal's voice that really got to me.

"I don't know what to say, Mal. I'm so sorry. It won't happen again."

"I hope not."

He stood up and left the room.

If it were possible to feel any worse than I already did, I would, but in my uncle's words, *we can't change the past.*

I filled my coffee cup to the brim and took an Advil before turning my computer on.

8

GRIFF

As I TYPED the last words on my manuscript, I felt that familiar rush that always came whenever I finished a book. It was only the first draft, and I'd do a revision before sending it to my editor, but reaching the end was an accomplishment in itself, and it didn't matter how many books I'd published, ten or a hundred, that feeling would never go away.

I saved the document and made a few copies, making sure to also email a copy to myself, and then closed everything down.

It was close to lunchtime, so I made myself a sandwich and considered what to do for the rest of the day. I didn't have a routine for when I finished a book, but I knew once the euphoria passed, I'd feel low for a few hours until my brain reset itself.

Today, I didn't want to feel down. I wanted to look forward to the next stage in the production of this book. I wanted to look forward to starting the series I'd been thinking about and researching ever since we moved to the west coast.

I picked up my phone to call a friend I hadn't seen in a while, but when I saw the photo I had on my locked screen of Mal and me on the beach, I had to do something else first.

Griff: Finished another one.

Mal: Wow, baby. Well done! I'm so proud of you. Celebrate tonight?

Griff: Definitely. How does naked sound to you?

Mal: Naked…you want to expand on that?

Griff: Naked…anything naked. Just naked.

Mal: Lol. Well, when you put it that way, I'm very UP for that.

Griff: I bet. See you later, baby. Love you.

Mal: Can't wait. Love you too.

I scrolled through some photos we took a few days ago on the beach.

La Catarina was such a beautiful place. I still pinched myself every time I looked outside and saw the ocean in the distance, or whenever I remembered that I could walk everywhere and it took as long to get to my favorite bakery as it did to get to my newly found favorite spot.

My phone rang, and I saw my friend's name displayed on the screen.

"Maya, my beautiful, warm ray of sunshine. I was just about to call you," I said.

"Liar."

I laughed. "No, I truly was. How are you doing?"

She sighed on the other side of the line, and I could just imagine her running her hand through her long, straight black hair.

"Finished a book this morning. I've got the downsies now," she said.

"Girl, you're living my life. That was the reason I was calling you too."

She laughed. "You were calling me because you're down? Gee, thanks."

"Pot. Kettle," I said.

"Oh, Griff, we should do this over a bucket of coffee and one of those decadent cakes from Il Fornaio."

I hummed my thoughts on that particular experience as I refilled my coffee cup and walked to the couch. Decadent didn't even begin to explain how good those cakes were.

"When are you coming to visit?" I asked. "There's a bakery here that you'd love. Now that I think of it, it's not only the bakery you'd love."

"Hmm? I'm intrigued," she said. "Tell you what, you come to the Romance Lovers Con, and I'll go back with you."

"When is that? Gosh, I've been so absorbed by the move and this book that everything else has slipped my mind."

Not to mention the whole thing with Jake.

"Mid-August. I'll email you the information. Now tell me about this baker you're saving for me."

I tucked my feet under my legs and got comfortable. My chats with Maya could go on for a while, and since we'd both just finished projects, we could take the time to catch up.

"Her name is Elena, and you'd love her. You can come here, fall in love, have pretty babies, and live happily ever after."

"Jesus, Griff, you're worse than my mother."

I gasped.

We stayed on the phone until Maya had to go. It was still early enough, and the phone call left me energized and restless, but in a good way.

I got dressed and decided a walk on the beach was the next thing on my list. I wasn't planning on doing any work, but I never left home without my notepad, so I put it in my bag with my phone and left.

On my way to the beach, I walked past El Pancito. Elena was busy, so I bought a pretzel to go.

The cliff beach was quiet as usual, which was such a striking difference from the main beach on the other side that was full of colorful beach umbrellas and sun loungers.

To get down to the beach, you had to use the rickety wooden stairs that didn't go all the way down to the sand but stopped on a flat rock. Once you were on that rock, you could easily navigate the rest of the way down using the other rocks. But if you were carrying all the usual beach paraphernalia, it would be challenging, if not downright dangerous.

When my feet landed on the packed sand of the small beach, I looked out into the ocean and took a deep breath, inhaling the salty air and listening to the seagulls in the distance. This place was so beautiful, and I wanted to write about it.

I went to the end of the beach to my favorite rock and got my notepad out. From the rock, I could see how the island's shape curved in the distance. I couldn't see the main beach, but I could tell there were similar beaches to this one along the coast.

Frank had said that one reason the island wasn't overdeveloped was that it was mainly rocky and lacked the miles of uninterrupted beach you got on the coast of LA. Silver Sands Resort was in lots of ways perfectly positioned on one of the lower points of the island and with access to the largest beach.

I took my phone out, snapped a photo, and sent it to Mal. Maybe on his next day off, we could bring a packed lunch and spend the day here.

Little sparks of arousal traveled up my spine as I imagined Mal in his swimming shorts, sunbathing on this rock. He didn't relax as often or as much as I thought he should, despite all my best efforts.

We had a good life, and we were happy, but there was no denying we could still work a little more on the old work-life balance.

My dick hardened as I thought about running my hand over the warm skin of Mal's chest, feeling the salt-and-pepper hairs, the toned muscles leading to the most perfect cock I'd ever seen. I still felt the same rush of energy when I thought about Mal today as I did when I first met him over four years ago.

I loved kissing him, making love to him, talking to him. He was my whole world.

Did I tell him that often enough?

I thought I did, but was it enough? Lately, Mal had been a little lost. I knew working with Jake wasn't easy on him.

On the plus side, he'd recognized the attraction and talked about it with me. On the downside, he was avoiding contact with Jake so he wasn't tempted. I figured as much two nights ago when he told me how he'd been a little short with Jake.

I sighed and lay back on the rock. The warm sun on my face was nice, healthy, and rejuvenating.

Maybe somewhere there was an alternative world where Mal, Jake, and I could be together.

I opened my eyes and sat up immediately, looking for my notepad.

A story of three men who loved each other in alternate universes, in different combinations, until they find a way to be together. Romantic Fantasy? Paranormal?

I'd just had the plot bunny of my life, and now I needed to figure out the genre because I wasn't sure this would fit in my normal contemporary romance.

Maybe I should ask my readers on social media. I made a note on my pad to spend an hour or so later working on that.

Laughter caught my attention. I thought I was alone on the beach, but it seemed that since my introspections, a couple and their photographer had joined me.

The woman was heavily pregnant and wearing a long floaty dress while the man had on shorts and a T-shirt. I couldn't take my eyes away from them. The way they looked at each other and touched each other was as if the photographer wasn't there.

My phone rang, and I saw Mal's name come up on the screen together with the photo we took on our non-honeymoon honeymoon.

I smiled and picked it up. "Hey, baby. Miss me already?"

"I always miss you," he said, and I could almost feel the warmth of his smile coming through the call.

"Is everything okay?"

"Yeah…um, Jake and I have to go to the mainland for a meeting."

"Okay. Will you be back in time for dinner?"

"Um…I'm…um…"

What was going on? Mal was never afraid of telling me anything work-related.

"Mal?"

"We will need to stay there overnight. There's a dinner event."

I cleared my throat.

"Okay, I'll see you when you're back then. Have a good trip."

Mal went quiet on the other side, but I didn't know what to say. Normally it was my job to reassure him, let him know I had his back, but my words were stuck in my throat and didn't want to come out. I looked out to the couple who had taken a break from their photo shoot and were sitting on the sand chatting to the photographer.

"I love you so much, Griff. See you when I'm back, okay?"

"Love you too, baby," I said before we ended the call.

This was a good thing. Mal and Jake taking a trip together. Wasn't it?

I knew nothing would happen between them. Mal was too stubborn to give in to what he wanted if he felt it was the wrong thing to want.

There was a small part of me that wished they would get closer, however selfish that was. And an even bigger part of me that wished I was there with them.

But I wasn't invited, which in itself was unusual. Unless…Mal didn't invite me because my presence there would bring back the memories of that day and the temptation to repeat.

I got up and walked to the water's edge, cursing myself for not bringing swim trunks, even though I'd known I was going to the beach.

The water was inviting, so I removed my shoes and socks, rolled my jeans up to my knees, and went in.

As soon as the water touched my toes, I instinctively jumped back because I wasn't expecting it to be so cold. That earned me some laughs from my neighbors on the warm sand.

"You try it out," I said. "It's deceivingly cold."

"I love the cold water. As soon as this little guy or girl comes out, I'll be counting the days until I can surf again," the woman said. "I'm Stacey, by the way. This is Carlos, my husband, and Sam, my brother and the photographer."

I waved. "Hi, I'm Griff. Do you have long to go?"

Carlos's face panicked a little. "The baby is overdue, actually, but since it's our first, the doctors said even when we go into labor, it could take hours until the baby is out. We've been told to make the best of it."

I laughed. "You looked like you were having fun earlier. Sorry to be a creepy voyeur, but you looked great. I bet those photos will come out perfect."

"Thank you. Do you want to join us? We're waiting for the sun to go down a little to finish the photo shoot," Stacey said.

"Sure."

Listening to Stacey and Carlos talk about their preparations for the arrival of their baby was the best thing to put my own thoughts to the back of my mind. I never intended on staying on the beach until the sun was setting, but now that I knew I'd go home to an empty house, I was glad I'd stayed.

Sam was packing up his camera when we heard a loud rumble. It sounded a lot like thunder, but then the ground moved. It didn't last long, but it was definitely unsettling to feel the ground shaking beneath.

"Fuck, was that an earthquake?" Sam said.

"I think it was," Carlos said, and then he picked up his phone. "I just got an alert. There could be more on the way. We need to get out of here."

Sam quickly grabbed all the belongings on the sand and stuffed them into his backpack. I looked at where my bag with my notepad and phone were. It was probably a risk going there to get them, but I couldn't leave them behind.

"Guys," Stacey said with a surprisingly calm voice. "My water broke."

"Are you in pain?" I asked. Fuck, I had no clue what happened when someone went into labor.

She shook her head but looked at Carlos with an apologetic look.

"You had contractions today?" he asked.

Carlos looked like he was about to have a baby, and Stacey would probably end up having the baby if we didn't hurry.

"Come on," I said. "Let me help get you to the top."

The sun was low in the sky, but there was still plenty of light. Enough to help Stacey to a safe place and then run back down for my stuff.

We got to the big rock where the wooden stairs started fairly easily. Sam ran up to get their car as close to the stairs as possible so Stacey didn't have to walk far.

"Fuuuck, motherfucking shit-balls..." Stacey shouted as she

squeezed my hand with more strength than any human being should have.

She held her belly and breathed hard. Carlos helped lean her against another rock until the contractions stopped.

"Baby, you can do this. You're a badass surfer, and now you're gonna be a badass mom," Carlos said, holding Stacey's face with his hands.

She nodded, showing some of her fierceness, despite the small tear that ran down her cheek.

"Come on, beautiful, let's get you up there," I said, holding out my hand.

Stacey took it, and with Carlos' help, she walked up the wooden steps.

"What's taking you so long?" Sam shouted from the top. "I got places to be, you know. It's not every day your niece is born."

Stacey chuckled and mumbled under her breath about it being a boy.

I was about to make a joke about her naming the baby after me when the ground shook again.

Carlos pulled Stacey to him, but I was still on the rock. The rock moved, taking me with it. Everything was too quick. I slipped off onto another rock, grazing my arm on the way down.

Like the first two tremors, this one was over quickly, but it was far more devastating because now I was midway through the cliff on a rock I wasn't sure was stable and too far away to reach the stairs.

"Griff," Stacey called.

"Go, please go, you need to get to the hospital," I shouted back.

"Are you hurt?" Carlos asked.

"No, I'm good. You go up. You need to get Stacey to the hospital. You can call someone to help me on the way."

I saw how torn Carlos was between his instinct to protect his wife and unborn child and leaving someone behind.

"Carlos, go. If there's another tremor, the stairs might not make it," I said.

The intention was to scare him into action, but as I said it, I realized it could really happen.

Please go quickly. Please.

I didn't take my eyes off them until I saw they were at the top with Sam.

"I've called for help," Sam shouted down.

"Griffin is a wonderful name," I shouted back and then laughed when I heard Stacey say, "No chance."

When they were out of sight, I turned around to assess the situation.

Fuck.

The last tremor had displaced all the rocks that made the path down to the beach. With the sun disappearing on the horizon, it would be stupid to make my way down to the beach. I'd probably be better off staying where I was and waiting until someone could throw me a rope or something to get me up to the stairs.

At least I hadn't been alone at the beach. Sam had asked for help, so it was only a matter of time until someone came.

A chill ran through me. What had the impact of the earthquakes been in town? Was everyone okay? Was anything damaged?

Mal. Jake. Did they make it out before the earthquakes?

Unlike my grandmother, who was a woman of faith, I rarely prayed, but this was an occasion that called for it because I couldn't think of anything else I could do while I was stuck here.

I needed Mal and Jake to be safe. I needed to go home to them.

Them.

I heard it before I felt it. Another loud rumble, and then the rain of dust and small rocks started falling. I leaned against one of the big boulders to avoid getting hit. And then the worst happened.

Even in the dim dusk light, I saw the wooden stairs collapsing onto the rocks below, causing a wave of more dust and more rocks to come in my direction.

I jumped over the rocks to get away, hoping I wouldn't make it worse and land on an unstable rock.

And because today really wasn't my day, I slipped and fell between two big boulders.

The good news? Nothing was broken. I was still alive.

The bad news? I was completely stuck.

9

MAL

"Hey, baby," I said to the phone's voicemail. "I missed you today when I went home to pack my overnight bag. I hope you're out celebrating your book. I'm so fucking proud of you, Griff." I looked out of the window to the setting sun and in the direction of the island. You couldn't see it from here, obviously, but it didn't matter. Just knowing that Griff was out there, probably having some fun with Elena, was enough.

I could just imagine the welcome home party tomorrow. We weren't apart often, so when we had to be, we always did something to remind us of how good it was when we were together.

Most times, it meant we'd spend the day or night in bed, getting reacquainted. Okay, not most times. All the time. I laughed, and then the phone beeped before ending the message.

I redialed his number, and it went to voicemail again. "Hey, me again. I got distracted thinking of you. I hope to be back by lunchtime tomorrow. You know the drill. Oh, and as usual, I can't do my fucking tie properly. I might have to go to dinner without it...I said it in my other message, but I'll say it again. I miss you, baby, and I love you. See you tomorrow."

I turned to the mirror again after ending the call. The tie knot wasn't right, and I'd clearly overestimated the length of the shorter end.

There was a knock on the door, so I had a quick look around to make sure the room wasn't a mess before I answered. Griff teased me for it, but there was something about respecting the work of the maids that made me want to keep my room as tidy as possible whenever I was in a hotel or resort.

"Hey, are you ready?" Jake said as I opened the door.

He looked great. Dark-blue suit, white shirt, hair perfectly styled, and a pink tie that not only brought out the blue color of his eyes, it was also perfectly tied.

How could I attend a dinner with the other resort managers *not* wearing a tie?

"Yeah, almost." I gestured for him to come inside and went back to the mirror to fight with the fucking knot.

"You were great today, Mal. I mean, I've never been to one of those meetings before, but it was like you've been working in the company for years, not just a couple of months."

I lined up the two ends of the tie again before throwing the top over the bottom. Or was that the other way round?

"Don't let that fool you," I said. "It's years of watching people and understanding when is the best time to speak up. Your uncle hired good people to manage his resorts, which makes things a lot easier."

I put the slim end of the tie through the knot and pulled it down until it was tight. Okay, so it looked a lot more like a tie knot should, but it also looked like a five-year-old had done it.

Jake came over and put his hands on mine to stop me from choking myself out of frustration.

"Can I help?" he asked.

I nodded, my mouth going dry and my words failing to take shape.

Jake smelled good, like shower soap and only a hint of cologne. I let the tie go and watched in the mirror as he came from behind me to tie a perfect knot.

"I used to watch Uncle Frank when I was a kid. Back then, I

thought people looked really smart when they wore a suit and tie, and I wanted to be smart, so I asked him to teach me."

My eyes were on the practiced moves of his hands. "And now?"

He chuckled. "Now, when I see a guy in a suit, his intelligence isn't necessarily the first thing I notice."

Our eyes met in the mirror and held there for a few seconds before he looked away.

"There. You're all set," he said.

I looked at my reflection and smiled at how perfectly straight my tie was.

"Thank you," I said. "Griff always does my tie. I really am hopeless at it."

He smiled. "Now you have a go-to tie man at home and at work."

"Come on, let's make sure we're not too late for this dinner. Are you ready to answer more questions from them about your project?" I asked.

He winked. "I was born ready."

Silver Palm Resort was twice the size of Silver Sands. We'd had a full tour of the resort when we arrived. Of course, Jake was already familiar with the location, but their state-of-the-art conference facility was brand new.

We were both amazed by the capacity of the resort to host events on a scale I hadn't seen before at a resort whose primary focus was the tourist trade.

"I'm glad you're with me because I think I'd be lost already," I said as we turned what felt like the tenth corner into another large hallway.

Jake laughed, "It's normally not that difficult to go from your room to the dining areas, but we're not dining in a customer area. Besides, this is the shortcut."

"*This* is the shortcut?"

Jake looked at me and winked.

I smiled and shook my head. We'd been working together a few weeks now, and attraction aside, Jake was a perfect work partner. He listened, had good ideas, and wasn't afraid to volunteer them, even when he wasn't sure if they could work.

We'd even found ourselves working through meal breaks because we were so engrossed.

There was definitely something special about Jake. I just hoped I could help channel his drive to build a career in his uncle's company without interference from my personal feelings about him.

And those feelings, that attraction that lived under the surface every second we were together, needed to stay under the surface.

The room that was set up for our dinner was a private meeting room conveniently located near the resort's main kitchen. The smell coming from it made my mouth water.

"I'm so sorry to have to host you here rather than the main restaurant, but we have a wedding there tonight, and I'm not sure they'd be happy with us crashing the party," Mason, the resort manager, said. "Please, take a seat. We may not be part of the wedding party, but the chef has reassured me he has some of his specialty dishes for us nevertheless."

We took our seats, and a server came over to offer us fresh rolls.

"Mal, Jake, you got here a minute too late to be part of the decision-making so you'll have to go with it," Trey, the manager of Silver Springs, said.

"What did we miss?" I asked.

"Lose the tie," Mason said. "We may talk business at the table, but we can damn well be comfortable while we do it."

It was only then I realized Jake and I were the only ones wearing a tie, while everyone else had lost their jackets and looked relaxed in their unbuttoned shirts.

"To think Mal spent the last three hours doing his tie," Jake joked.

I hit him with my elbow, and everyone laughed, including me.

"My absentee vote agrees with the majority," I said, removing my tie twice as fast as it took Jake to tie it. I looked at him from the corner of my eye and saw his dimpled smile.

"Then I think we're ready to get started on food and business." Morgan nodded to the server to indicate we were ready and then turned to Jake. "Jake, we all know you well. You've worked with all of us in the past, and I'm impressed to hear about both you finishing your MBA and the ideas you're bringing to the table."

"Thank you," Jake said.

We'd discussed this particular moment before. Jake was afraid everyone would see him as his uncle's nephew and not someone with credentials. I was ready for my show of support for his ideas, but it seemed we didn't need to.

"Tell us more about your project. I'm particularly interested in how we can tighten the Silver brand to offer a consistent customer experience," Morgan continued.

Jake looked at me, and I gave him a reassuring smile.

Throughout dinner, I sat back and watched Jake take in all the questions from my colleagues, seeming to consider them carefully before answering or making notes to take away.

By the end of the dinner, Jake had won everyone over, and I was wondering if I needed to keep him closer or risk losing him to a sister resort.

"I just need to use the restroom before we head back," he said, leaning in and whispering in my ear.

"Okay, I'll wait here."

"Mal," Trey said, sitting in Jake's vacant chair. "The boy is good."

"That he is. And don't think I won't be keeping my eye on you, Trey. You're not poaching him," I said.

He put his hand on my shoulder and said, "Something tells me nothing would take him away from you."

What?

"What do you mean?"

"He looks at you like you're the source of all knowledge. That kind of loyalty can't be bought." He patted my shoulder and left.

I stood up and grabbed my jacket and tie from the chair while I waited for Jake. Trey's parting words ran through my head. Should I take them at face value? Did Trey read anything in our behavior that was a sign that something more was going on?

Not that anything was going on, because it wasn't.

And fuck, they all knew I was happily married. The last thing I wanted was rumors to get out among the upper management team of the company.

"Okay, I'm ready," Jake said.

As soon as we were out of the room and out of earshot, Jake squeezed my arm and all but squealed. "Oh my god, did that just happen?"

"You mean, you knocking them off their seats? Yes, I believe it did."

"They really want this, right? Cross-training, staff exchange, growth programs."

"You have planted the seed, Jake, and I don't think it'll be long until it takes root."

I was so absorbed by Jake's ramblings about the dinner as we navigated all the hallways that I didn't even notice we were right in front of my room door.

We stopped, and I saw the same realization in Jake's eyes.

He stared at me, going quiet as if suddenly all the words had left him, which made me laugh because I hadn't been able to get a word in edgeways as he was talking about the dinner so passionately. It was as if I hadn't been there, and he didn't want me to miss out on what had happened.

"Do you want to come in for a coffee?" I asked, swiping the key card and turning the handle.

He opened his mouth and closed it again before looking to both sides of the hallway.

"Um…I…we shouldn't," he said.

"Jake, I really do mean coffee."

He took a deep breath and nodded. "Okay."

I put my jacket and tie on the bed and went to the coffee machine. There was a box with coffee pods, so I took two out and turned the machine on to warm up.

Jake sat on one of the two armchairs that faced the glass door to the balcony.

"What made you want to work in this industry?"

The question was one that I'd been asked so many times before that I didn't need to think before the words came out. From my first work placement to every interview for all the jobs I'd applied for, it was always the first question to come up. It was as if my answer to that particular question dictated how suited I was to the job.

My mouth opened, but those familiar words refused to come out. I placed both coffees on the small table between the two chairs and sat down.

Jake looked at me with those big blue eyes, lighter than mine, full of youth, life, energy, and passion. In some ways, he was so similar to Griff. Was that why I felt so drawn to him?

"My mom was a maid at a resort on the coast of Maine. That's where I grew up."

"You're a long way from Maine," he said, taking a sip of his coffee.

I added sugar to mine and stirred it. "Sometimes I'm not sure if I'm in a different state, country, or lifetime from those days."

"Why's that? Do you not go back there?"

"No, I don't have any family there. My dad died when I was a baby, and we moved to Maine for my mom's job. She had no help, but she was the nicest person you could ever meet. I remember she always had friends from work over for coffee or dinner. I used to think she was very sociable, but I think it was her way of connecting to people and having a support network. Let's put it this way, she never struggled to get a free babysitter for me."

"Why don't you think she was sociable?"

"Because when it was just the two of us, she was always quiet. The TV was turned off, we didn't play music. To this day, I'm not sure if she was an introvert and the quiet times were when she recharged or if she struggled with depression. I never had a chance to find out."

Jake reached out with his hand to take mine.

"I'm sorry, Mal." He squeezed my hand and then let go. I missed his touch as soon as it was gone.

I never talked about my past or my mom. Why was I opening up to Jake?

"Why do I get the feeling you know exactly how I feel?" I asked.

Jake smiled, but it didn't reach his eyes, and the dimple on the side of his chin didn't show up. I met his gaze and waited for his answer.

The lights flickered and then went out.

"What the—" was all I managed to say as I felt the ground shaking.

Jake grabbed my hand again, and in the semi-darkness of the room, I saw he was pulling me toward the door.

"Won't it be worse outside?" I asked.

"It's ok. We're only standing in the doorway because it's the safest place."

I wasn't sure how long the tremor lasted. I was still holding on to Jake's hand when the backup lights came on.

"Sorry," I said, letting go.

He took my hand again. "It's okay. We'll be okay."

How did he know? We'd just been in a freakin' earthquake.

Other guests who'd been in their rooms had done the same thing. I did a quick count to see how easy it would be to take them all to safety if we needed to get out of the building.

"I need to go to my room to get my phone," Jake said.

"No, it's not safe. What if there's more?"

How was he as calm as a cucumber, while I was on the verge of a panic attack?

"It's only a few doors down. I'll be back before the next shake."

"There will be more?"

He chuckled. "Usually, yes. Welcome to California."

He ran to his room and was back a minute later.

"Why do you need your phone?" I asked.

"I have the earthquake warning app."

"The what?"

"I'll explain another time. Hold on, there's another one coming."

As predicted by Jake's phone, there was another tremor, this time stronger. It was hard to stand up because other than the frame of the door, there was nothing to hold on to.

I sat on the floor and pulled Jake to me, not letting go until the tremor ended.

I was terrified, but for some reason, having him pressing against me was comforting. Knowing we were both warm meant we were both alive.

"Griff!" I screamed and scrambled over to the bed where I'd left my jacket with my phone in its pocket. How could I have forgotten him?

My hands shook as I took the phone out and dialed his number.

Please pick up, baby. Please pick up.

The phone rang until it went to voicemail again.

"Hey, um…baby. I just need to talk to you. Can you call me when you get this message? Love you."

I sat on the floor with my back to the bed frame.

Jake was right there next to me. One hand over my shaking one and the other scrolling through his phone for news.

"Fuck," he said.

"What?" I asked.

He turned to me and took both my hands.

"Mal, listen to me carefully, okay? I need you to not panic. I know you've probably never been in an earthquake before, but they happen all the time here. That's why I have the app on my phone. This was probably just a level three. You feel it, but there's likely no major damage."

"Do you think the island has been affected?"

Even in the dim emergency lights, his face gave me the answer his words hadn't yet voiced.

"I need to go home, Jake. I need to make sure Griff is okay. He hasn't answered his phone since this afternoon. Oh my god, Jake, what if something happened to him?"

Jake put his hands on either side of my face. I stared into his eyes, which in the dim lights were darker than the usual light blue.

"Hey, it's going to be okay. Trust me?" he said, so close I could smell the coffee on his breath.

I nodded.

"He's everything, Jake. I will have nothing if I lose him."

"You won't," he whispered.

"You can't know that for sure."

"You're right. But we can get back on the island as soon as possible and verify for ourselves."

Frank and Gabe.

"Can you get through to Frank and Gabe?" I asked.

"No, the mobile signal is probably out. It doesn't take much on the island for that to happen."

I'd experienced that before, a few weeks ago when a storm cut off all power and it took a few days until both the internet and cell signal were working fully.

"How do we get back on the island?"

"Did you know the resort is a designated shelter for the island?" he asked.

"Yes. In cases of emergency, we can offer shelter and food to the entire population of the island."

"Who needs to be at the resort when that happens?"

"Me." Thank fuck for Jake being here because my panic over Griff's safety was affecting my ability to keep calm under pressure. "I have the number for the fire department on my phone. They can airlift us there."

Jake smiled and nodded.

"You're a fucking genius," I said, and before my brain caught up with me, I pulled Jake in and pressed my lips against his.

JAKE

It happened quicker than the blink of an eye.

One moment Mal's lips were on mine, and the next, they were gone. It could barely be called a kiss. I mean, our lips touched, but it wasn't a soft, slow kiss. It was hard and so fast my brain didn't catch on until it was over.

But I felt it, oh man, I felt it…but it wasn't really a kiss, was it?

It was Mal releasing the tension he was holding from worrying about Griff. The relief of finding a solution to getting back to the island.

The proof of that was in how he was already up and packing his few belongings in his overnight bag, the fear of future tremors seemingly gone.

"Aren't you going to grab your bag?" he asked, looking over his shoulder at me, still sitting on the floor.

I stood up, feeling off-balance, and walked to my room.

Get a grip, Jake.

His reaction wasn't out of character for someone going through a difficult experience, but from the little I knew of Mal, it was out of character for him. The calm, composed Mal, who always seemed in control, always knew what was going on, always armed with a solution.

Still, I understood how he felt. All my life, I'd been worried about someone in one way or another. I'd worried about my mom. If she was happy. If she would ever find what she wanted so she could come home for me.

I'd worried about Aunt Annie when she got sick until we eventually lost her, and after she died, I started worrying about Uncle Frank and Gabe. Uncle Frank, who'd lost the love of his life, and Gabe, who sometimes seemed to be just lost.

Even Zak. Thousands of miles away. I worried that one day his incessant search for happiness in someone else's body would get him into trouble.

My life was one big pot full of worry. There was very little I could control, so I mostly dabbed between constant crippling worry and pretending nothing bad could ever happen to anyone.

And now I was adding Griff and Mal to my already long list.

Two safety marshals came over to escort everyone to the safest place within the resort a few minutes later. I cringed when I saw Mal and I were the only ones carrying our belongings. So much for all the training that told us to stay put until someone came for us.

I checked my phone for further information on the earthquake. We were still in a state of alert, but the last tremor was quite small. It could be hours until another one hit, or we could be lucky and that would be the last one.

"I'll call the fire department. Can you see if you can find Mason or one of the other guys? They're probably helping," Mal said. I left my bag by his feet and scanned the large hall for a familiar face.

All around, there were people in various states of dress. Some looked like they'd been getting ready for bed when the earthquake hit, and then there were the wedding guests who, in comparison, were overdressed.

Some people had minor injuries, but I couldn't see anyone needing medical help beyond first aid. I was glad Mason had the other resort managers here to help. A few additional pairs of first-aid-trained hands were always good, especially when they were probably looking at staying in the safe location of the resort's main restaurant until safety could be assessed in the morning.

"Jake!"

I looked around for who called my name and saw Mason waving a few feet away. He was kneeling next to a woman and a little girl.

The little girl wasn't crying, but her cheeks had streaks of dried tears and her chest was still heaving as her mother ran her hand over her hair.

"Look," Mason said. "This is Dr. Jake. Shall we ask him for his opinion?"

The little girl nodded.

Mason gave me a look that said to go with it, so I smiled and kneeled down too.

"Hello, what's your name?" I asked.

"Melody."

"Hello, Melody. That's a beautiful name. I'm Dr. Jake. Do you want to tell me what happened?"

She shook her head and put her thumb in her mouth.

Mason put his finger gently on the girl's chin to tilt her head. "Do you see that big nasty bump, Dr. Jake? When the ground started shaking, Melody was so brave trying to get to her mommy to help her that she bumped her head on the bedside table."

"Oh, I see, that is definitely a sign of the utmost bravery. I think you'll be okay, Melody. But just to be sure, why don't we put a band-aid on your bump?"

She smiled and nodded. Mason took out a kid's band-aid from his kit and put it on Melody's forehead.

"There you go," Mason said. "Are you going to stay here with your mommy to make sure she doesn't get hurt?"

The little girl nodded. Her mom looked relieved to have a calmer child on her hands and mouthed a thank you over Melody's head.

"Thanks for that, Jake."

"It's Dr. Jake to you," I joked. "Mason, we need to get to the island. There's no phone signal, and we don't know the impact of the earthquake on the resort or the community. Mal is trying to get through to the fire department."

"You remember where my office is?" Mason asked.

"Yeah."

"My car keys are on the top drawer of my desk. I'm not going to leave here anytime soon, so take my car to the fire department and leave it there. My brother-in-law is a firefighter there, so he can make sure I get the car back."

I looked at Mason. "Are you sure?"

"Absolutely. It's a little chaotic here, but we've certainly had worse earthquakes. There's nothing here we can't handle, but both you and Mal should be on the island."

"Mason, your guys here are good. I've never seen such organized emergency procedures. I'm gonna have to pick your brains when this has calmed down," Trey said, coming out of nowhere.

Suddenly an idea came to mind. I just hoped I wasn't out of line.

"Hey, Trey, the procedure here is actually modeled after ours at Silver Sands because we have a similar layout, just smaller. If you've got nothing better to do, we could probably use an extra hand out there."

"Sweet. You haven't heard this, Mason, but I'm heading up to my room to grab my stuff," Trey said. Mason closed his eyes and shook his head.

I laughed. "Great, meet us out front."

When I looked over at Mal, I saw he was on his phone, so instead of getting back to him, I went to Mason's office to get the key to his car.

Mal looked lost by the time I got back to him. His eyes scanned the room as if he were looking at everything for the first time, and I could see panic settling over him.

"Hey," I said, placing my hand on his elbow to get his attention.

"Did you find Mason? I spoke to the fire department chief, and he said they'd be able to fly us out at the break of dawn."

"Okay, that gives us a few hours of waiting. We have Mason's car, so we can wait here, or we can head over there. There's a diner next to the fire department that's always open."

Mal nodded.

I ran my hand over my hair and scratched my day-old scruff.

"What's up?" Mal asked.

Jeez, was he a mind reader?

Or maybe he could just read my mind because it seemed that, around Mal, I was totally see-through.

"Trey was keen on knowing more about our emergency procedures, so I invited him to come over to the island to help us out. I'm sorry. I know I should have asked first, but I just figured that before you get to the resort, you'll want to make sure Griff is okay. And I want to check in on Uncle Frank and Gabe too. Trey could go to the resort and meet Hailey and—"

Mal stopped my ramble by placing his hand on the back of my neck. It was warm and settled me like nothing else could.

His dark-blue eyes met mine, and he smiled.

"Thank you, Jake. I know I should be in control and know what to do, but honestly, I feel like a hole has opened under my feet and is dragging me down. You're so young, and here you are, thinking on your feet, preemptively knowing what we might find when we get to the island, and taking the initiative."

I didn't know what to say, so I did the only thing I could. I took a step forward and hugged him.

This wasn't like the kiss. Mal didn't let go of me straight away. If anything, I could swear his arms tightened around me.

Mal still smelled of the shower he'd had earlier. No aftershave. Just soap and Mal.

My dick would have gotten hard, but it didn't because my heart was taking over.

Not that it would take much for that to happen with Mal pressing against me like this, but all of my blood was pumping around my heart, making it beat extra hard.

Could Mal feel it? If he could, he said nothing. He just held me, with one arm around my back and the other hand still on my neck, keeping me close.

I forced myself to step back, but I couldn't look him in the eye for fear of what he might see.

"Let's head out front. Trey is meeting us there."

Mal took his bag from the floor and said, "Let's go."

As I'd hoped, there were no additional tremors. By all means, this had been quite a non-event as far as earthquakes in California go.

It still didn't mean there was any less urgency to get to the island, and the longer we waited, the more anxious Mal became.

Not that you could tell. We'd sat in the diner across the fire station waiting for the sun to rise, and throughout all that time, Mal had been a chatterbox.

By the time we got the go-ahead to leave, Trey had been briefed on the layout of the resort, who was in charge, and where everything was.

Trey made notes as they discussed a plan based on the eventuality that we just needed to reassure people that everything was okay and get them back to normal, or in the case of any casualties or damages.

The calm, collected Mal was focused on doing the right thing for everyone. But I could see beyond the plans.

He hadn't stopped playing with his wedding ring. There were times when he suddenly stopped talking, and I knew he was thinking about Griff, but then he'd come back to us with yet another piece of information Trey needed.

As the helicopter lifted off, I held Mal's hand in mine and squeezed. I'd ended up sitting between Mal and Trey, so I knew no one could see us.

Mal looked at me, his gaze so full of vulnerability that I wanted to put my arms around him and just hold him.

I knew he couldn't hear me over the noise of the helicopter, so I just mouthed, "He's okay."

He mouthed back, "Thank you," and then squeezed my hand back but didn't let go.

As soon as the island was in sight, I looked out of the window. The closer we got, the clearer it was that the earthquake hadn't destroyed any buildings, but I noticed a couple of beaches had been lost to landslides and rockfalls.

I just hoped that the timing of the earthquake meant there had been no rock climbers in the area.

The chief of the fire department met us as soon as we landed. We followed him from the roof and into the building.

"Morning, folks. Can I get you a coffee? I understand you've been up all night waiting to get here."

"We're good, Chief," Mal said. "Can you give us an update?"

He nodded, taking us into a small kitchen and going straight to the coffee machine.

"The good news is that there are no casualties, and I haven't yet heard of any damage to buildings. The LA Fire Department is kindly lending us the chopper you've just flown in for the day, and the guys are now getting ready to do a flyover of the island to check on the remote areas."

"Is there any bad news, Chief?" Mal asked.

The chief took a sip of his coffee before answering.

"Our hospital is already quite small, so whenever something like this happens, we tend to run out of beds pretty quickly. People are still coming in with small injuries, so we set up a triage room at the resort. My guys have done a check of the resort, and everything's fine. Hailey and Pete have been there all night, and they have a couple of my guys helping and taking anyone that needs medical attention to the hospital."

"How about power?" I asked.

"We never lost it, which is good, but cell signal is still down, which is making it tricky to get ahold of people to check that they're okay."

The way the chief said it and then looked at Mal made me feel like I was going to be sick.

"Do you boys want to head toward the resort? I just need to have a quick word with Mal."

No, I didn't want to walk away and leave Mal on his own to hear whatever news the chief had for him, but I couldn't exactly justify my request to stay either, so I walked out of the station with Trey following me.

"I'm very impressed," Trey said. "Shocked, actually. If this was back home, I'd have the chief of police and the fire chief fighting over who was in charge.

"This is a small island. The chief of police is the fire chief's son-in-law. They know to play along, or they'll both be in trouble with the mayor. And that's one woman you don't want to cross."

Trey laughed.

"Hey, do you mind if we wait out here for Mal? He's been worried about Griff, and I don't want him to come out on his own if he's getting bad news," I said.

"Sure, I was thinking the same. So why's the Mayor so scary?"

"Would you ever cross your wife or your mother-in-law?"

"Hell no," Trey said with a mock shiver.

St. Harbor was the largest of the two main populated areas on the island. But even then, we could walk the length of the town in thirty minutes.

The fire department was at one end of town and a short walk to the gated driveway leading to the resort.

As soon as I saw Mal leave the station, I knew something bad had happened. I walked over to him, but he stopped me before I could ask questions.

"Let's go."

I looked at Trey, who also seemed to notice Mal didn't look right.

"Mal, what did the chief say?" I asked.

"Not now. We need to get to the resort and find Hailey and Pete."

His behavior only fed my already high tendency to worry. My mind ran over all the possible scenarios as I did my best to keep up with Mal's pace toward the resort.

Did he have news about Griff? Or was it Uncle Frank and Gabe?

Oh god.

What if he had bad news about my family, and he was waiting for the right moment to tell me?

We found Hailey outside the resort's main restaurant, helping the staff manage the line of people waiting to go in. She looked tired but still had a smile on her face. A smile that became wider when she saw us.

"What time do you call this," she said, looking at her watch. "You know you missed out on all the fun, right? But don't worry. Pete's compiling a list of customer complaints, and he promised the juiciest ones will land on your desks."

Considering how tightly wound Mal had been since he left the station, I was surprised to see a smile on his face.

"Hailey, I can't begin to thank you for the work you've done here. Do you have someone to relieve you so you can go home?" Mal asked.

"Who do you take me for, boss? We run a tight ship out here. Brian went home as soon as it was safe last night, so he'll be here shortly, and Alana was off this weekend, but she's coming in too. Most of the staff are okay, and we've redeployed them to wherever is most needed. We've had a few grumbles, but let's just say my resting-bitch-face is getting quite a workout at the moment."

I raised a brow, which Hailey didn't miss, so I got a punch in the stomach for it.

"We have some help for you," Mal said. "Trey is my counterpart at Silver Springs in Colorado. He apparently leads a very boring life and swapped his vacation time for helping us out."

Hailey stretched out her hand to greet Trey. "Nice to meet you, Trey. I love your resort. Pete and I honeymooned there. Follow me, and I'll show you the ropes. Mal, go home. We're all good here. To be honest, we'll need some help to handle the customer queries and complaints, but that's not our priority for now."

Mal raised his hands and smiled. "I guess I've been told. I'll catch you later then."

As soon as Hailey and Trey were out of sight, Mal all but ran toward the driveway and then turned a corner where we had the pump room for the water supply.

I called out to him, but he didn't look like he heard me or even noticed I was following him. I sped up my pace when he went behind the building and found him leaning against the wall, his chest heaving and his hands covering his face.

"Hey," I whispered.

Part of me was afraid he'd shut me down like he did outside of the fire station, but I couldn't handle seeing him struggle and not try to help.

When he raised his head, his face was wet with tears.

"Please tell me what's going on? Is it what the chief told you?" I asked.

Mal nodded. "Griff is in the hospital. He was rescued from the cliff beach last night."

I had to lock my knees because I felt as though the weight of my body was suddenly too much and my legs would give in any moment.

"No, please tell me he's okay."

Mal straightened up and took a deep breath, running his hands through his short hair and scruff.

"He's okay. Sorry, I didn't mean to…I just needed a moment to gather myself. I'm going to the hospital now."

"I'll come with you." There was no choice to be made there. I didn't know why, but my gut told me my family was okay. The same gut feeling that told me I needed to be with both Griff and Mal right now.

Mal looked at me, and I could see he was torn.

I put my hand on the back of his neck and made him look at me. "I wasn't asking, Mal. I'm coming with you."

He stared at me, still looking confused, but I didn't miss how his shoulders lost a little of the tension they were holding.

The hospital was busy, as expected. We went straight to the reception desk, which fortunately didn't have a line of people in front of it.

"Hi, I'm here for Griffin Prescott. I'm his husband, Mallory Prescott."

The girl behind the desk looked at her computer.

"Oh yes, he's in one of the rooms on the second floor." Then she looked at me. "I'm afraid we only allow spouses or next of kin."

Mal looked at me.

"That's okay. I'll wait here," I said.

"No, he can come in," Mal said.

The receptionist let out an annoyed sigh, but Mal interrupted her before she could say anything.

"He's our boyfriend and next of kin. Griff will be really upset if he can't see Jake."

The girl opened her mouth and closed it again, opting instead to point toward the hallway that led to the elevator. "Room fifteen."

My brain struggled to catch up with what Mal had said and then totally gave up the fight when he took my hand and pulled me away from the reception desk.

When we were alone in the elevator, he took my other hand and brought them both up to his chest.

"Don't ask me to explain what I just did, Jake. I can't. All I know is that I need you right now." He took a deep breath, closing his eyes before opening them again. There was so much vulnerability and fear in his gaze.

I smiled and shook my head. "I can't understand it either, Mal. But I'm here. I'm here for you both."

He kissed my cheek. As soon as the doors to the elevator opened, we were out like lightning looking for room fifteen. Considering the size of the hospital, it didn't take long.

Griff looked so small, lying on the bed with his eyes closed. He wasn't connected to any machines, which I took as a good thing.

Mal took the side of the bed Griff's head was turned to, and I took the other side.

He ran his hand over Griff's hair and kissed his forehead.

"I'm home, baby," he said gently. I felt like an intruder, and the coldness that seeped through my bones after we'd had sex months ago came back to me. Except this time, it was worse. Because now I knew them.

The room was silent, and all I could hear were the noises of machines, people talking, and activity outside.

Mal reached out his hand. I looked at it, unsure of what he wanted but held my hand out. He took it and then placed both our hands over Griff's.

In the silence of the room, both my heart and Mal's gesture were louder than a firework display.

But fireworks were nothing compared to looking at Griff's beautiful face as he woke up, saw both Mal and me, and smiled as if everything was finally right.

11

GRIFF

My head felt like it had an army of tiny people trapped inside, trying to escape by chiseling away at my skull.

There was a warm weight on my hands. It was grounding, reassuring, and it meant I was no longer at the beach, trapped between the rocks.

That memory made my head hurt more, so I pushed it away and forced my eyes to open so I could see for myself that I really wasn't at the beach anymore.

Easier said than done when the men wouldn't stop the chiseling. Come on. Lunch break, anyone?

Another memory came to me. Someone throwing a rope and telling me to tie it around my waist. Being pulled up. Slipping and hitting my head.

I must be at the hospital.

Everything was fuzzy at first, and my eyes didn't seem able to focus. I could tell there were two things next to me, but I couldn't tell what they were.

I blinked a few times and willed my eyes into focus. It happened slowly, and as the faces became clear, the headache subsided a little. Or maybe I imagined it.

Was this real? Were Mal and Jake really here? Together?

I smiled at them, and they smiled back.

"Man, whatever drugs they gave me, can I have a daily dose? Like, forever?"

Their hands were on mine, so that explained the warm weight. I brought them up to my face and inhaled before gripping tighter and resting them on my chest.

They weren't going to get away from me. Ever.

Mal leaned over and caressed my face with his free hand before giving me a kiss. Oh, how I'd missed him. So much.

I needed Jake too, so I reached out for him. He looked at Mal, who nodded, and when I pulled him in for a kiss, he came.

My two favorite pairs of lips.

"Hmm, that's better. I can die now."

I closed my eyes again. They felt heavy, and I was glad I'd managed to keep them open long enough.

Mal chuckled. "You're not dying, baby. As for the drugs, I'm not sure yet, but sleep if that's what you need. I'll be here when you wake up."

"Promise?" I slurred.

"With my whole heart. Always."

I was going to collect on that promise later, but there was somewhere else I needed to be first. I just hoped there was a dream Mal and a dream Jake to keep me company because I didn't want to have to wait to wake up again to see them both.

The next time I came back to consciousness, my head didn't hurt as bad. Maybe the tiny men had finished for the day. I could only hope.

This time the weight on top of me was Mal's head. He was asleep.

I ran my hand over his forehead and the crease between his brows relaxed until he opened his eyes and smiled when he met mine.

"Hey, sleepyhead," he said. "How do you feel?"

"Much better."

"Good," he said before standing up and then lying on the bed next to me and pulling me into his arms.

"I was so scared," he said. "I don't think I've ever been so scared in my life...when I couldn't get ahold of you..."

"Hey, it's okay, I'm here, and you're here," I said.

Mal kissed my head and ran his free hand down my cheek until it rested over my heart.

"Do you know when we can go home?" I asked.

"The doctor came in earlier while you were asleep. You have a concussion, which you apparently sustained not when you were falling down a bunch of rocks, but when they rescued you." He chuckled, and I felt him shake his head.

"What can I say? A damsel isn't truly in distress until she knocks herself out."

"No more knocking yourself out. It's a rule from now on, okay?" he demanded.

"I think I can do that."

Mal was so warm and strong. I just wanted to go home so I could cuddle him in our own bed.

"Anyway, we're just waiting for the doctor to do the rounds. He said if you're awake when he comes back, he'll discharge you."

I nodded.

"Mal...was Jake here earlier? Or did I dream that?"

"You didn't dream it, but you were a little out of it. Yes, he was here. He's gone to check in on Frank and Gabe and will be back."

I groaned when another memory came to me.

"Um...Mal, did I kiss Jake?"

"Yes, you did."

I looked up at him, but he didn't look upset like I'd expected. Quite the opposite.

"I have my own confession to make," he said. I felt his heart rate increase under my hand but waited to hear what he wanted to say. "Last night, when we were in the middle of the earthquake, I panicked. All of my training, common sense, everything...just left me. I froze. Jake kept calm and reassured me everything was going to be okay. When he found a way for us to get on the island, I was so relieved, and I didn't think, I just...I kissed him. I'm so sorry, Griff."

"Wait, hold on. You saw me kiss Jake right here in front of you, and it's like the most natural thing in the world, but you think I'm going to be upset because you kissed him too? I'm only upset that I wasn't there."

Mal took a deep breath and pulled me even closer.

There was a knock on the door before it opened, and Sam walked in but stopped when he saw I wasn't alone.

"I'm sorry. I didn't know you had company. I can come back another time," he said.

"No, come in, Sam. Sam, this is my husband, Mal. Mal, it's a long story, but Sam is the one that called for help for me yesterday."

"In that case, I owe you more than you'll ever know. If you ever want a weekend stay at the resort, just let me know. I'll even throw in full catering and a spa treatment," Mal said.

"You work at the resort?" Sam asked. "That's amazing. I'll take you up on that, not to stay overnight, although that would be great, but to photograph the bunnies. I've heard the ones that live closer to the resort are very friendly."

"Sam is a photographer," I said. "That's what he was doing at the beach. Taking photos of his sister, Stacey, and her husband. Oh my gosh, how are Stacey and the baby?"

Sam broke into the biggest smile.

"That's why I came. Stacey is fine, although Carlos fainted and knocked his head on a table, so he had to have stitches, which Stacey and I will ever let him live down."

He pulled out his phone and then gave it to me.

"Let me introduce you to Griffin Samuel Cortano. Isn't he gorgeous?"

I looked at the photo of the tiny baby all wrapped up. He looked a lot like Stacey.

"She really named him after us?" I said, my words stuck in my throat.

"She did. She was going with Samuel first, but when I saw him, I thought Griffin was more fitting. Besides, we'd have to compete for all the personalized gifts every Christmas," he said, laughing.

Sam told Mal how we got Stacey off the beach before the stairs collapsed while I stared adoringly at baby Griffin.

I looked at Mal, wondering how long he'd want to wait until we got a baby of our own.

As if he could read my mind, he smiled and said, "I want one too."

"Well, that's my cue to go. From the way you're looking at each other, I wouldn't be surprised if you started trying now, and one baby named after me is enough," Sam said, and we all laughed.

Sam took his phone back and was about to leave when Jake came in.

When Jake saw Sam, he froze, and his eyes darted between the three of us in panic.

Sam grinned and said, "Oh! So, *they* were the reason you couldn't… Good choice, man…good choice." And then he walked past Jake, squeezing his shoulder. "Nice to bump into you again."

I looked at Mal, who was just as confused.

Jake was still wide-eyed even after Sam left, and stood by the door, so Mal got out of the bed and went to Jake.

"Hey, are you okay? Frank and Gabe?" he asked.

"Yes…um, yes, my uncle and Gabe were both at home when the earthquake hit. They're safe. Jessie is still a little shaken, but she'll be fine too." Jake looked at Mal and then at me. "Nothing happened between Sam and me. I mean, it almost did, but I couldn't go through with it."

"Hey, come here," I said, extending my hand to him. He came and stood by the bed.

I grabbed his hand and squeezed it. Jake was a free single man, and I didn't want him to feel bad for being with other people, but at the same time, I was beyond happy that nothing had happened between him and Sam.

We were on the verge of something, but a hospital room was not the place to have this conversation, and under the current circumstances, I felt too vulnerable to push anything. Knowing my luck, all of this was a dream caused by my concussion, and in a minute, I'd wake up alone in the hospital room.

Mal and Jake talked about their meetings and evening the day before and how they got back on the island. It felt so natural to have them together, talking, laughing. I wondered if they could see what I saw. Feel what I felt.

The doctor came in shortly after to discharge me. I couldn't be left alone over the next forty-eight hours, and I had to have plenty of rest and no stress. Doctor's orders.

Jake took us home in his car, and I was surprised to see him come inside.

He and Mal shared a look, and as much as it warmed me to see they had a connection, I was wondering what it was about.

"Okay, guys, what's going on?" I asked with my hand on my hips, which was probably not as menacing as if I was standing up instead of sitting on the couch.

"When the doctor said you couldn't be alone, Jake offered to take turns staying with you if Frank and Gabe were okay. And since they are…" He shrugged.

I wasn't sure I was happy with this development or annoyed that I apparently needed a babysitter.

"Wait, are you leaving?" I asked Mal.

I sat next to him. "I need to get to the resort and see what's going on. We had one of the other managers fly in with us, but he probably needs a rest. It'll only be a few hours, okay?"

"Okay."

He kissed me quite thoroughly and then left.

"Great, and now I have a hard-on," I said aloud before I caught myself.

"You're not the only one." Jake groaned. "You guys are too sexy together. It's unfair to the rest of humanity."

I laughed. "Since you're stuck with me, how about we watch a movie? After all that sleep…and that kiss, I'm wide awake."

"Sure, how about I order some food?" he asked.

"You can order food on the island?"

"You can when you have a younger cousin that owes you a million favors."

I laughed. Half an hour later, Gabe showed up with a bunch of Chinese food containers, declaring he was staying to watch a movie with us because Frank wanted to watch *Dancing with the Stars*.

The excuse was valid. I wasn't keen on the show myself, but it was the way Gabe sat next to Jake and looked so proud of himself for remembering Jake's favorite dishes that made me wonder if there was more to it.

The day I'd met Gabe, he was full of charm and exuded confidence and swag, but there was clearly another side to him.

I don't know at what point I fell asleep during the movie, but I woke up to Mal caressing my face and whispering.

"Hey, gorgeous," he said. "How do you feel?"

"Okay, headache is definitely not as bad now, and I don't feel as dizzy."

He smiled at me in the most adoring way and then cocked his head.

"You know, if you wanted to host an orgy, all you needed to do was ask."

I didn't get what he was talking about until he pointed at Jake and Gabe, both asleep on the other sofa, leaning against each other.

"That is wrong in so many ways, I said, slapping him gently. "Are you here to stay? Can we go to bed?"

He kissed me and nodded and then went over to the guys and woke them up gently.

"We have a spare room with a big bed. Why don't you crash here?" he said.

Gabe yawned and stretched out like a cat.

"Thanks, I think I'll just head home," he said before turning to Jake. "Your car's outside, so I take it you don't need a lift."

"I'm good, thanks," Jake said.

"All right. See you guys. Hope you're better soon, Griff," Gabe said and then left.

Jake rubbed his face from sleep and turned to Mal. "How're things at work? I should probably head out there to help."

"Everything's okay. We've had to move a few guests because some worrying cracks appeared in the walls on the west side. I'll need to find a structural engineer to check it out before we allow people on that side. Fortunately, the resort wasn't at full capacity, and some guests cut their holiday short."

"How are Hailey and Pete?"

"They're both taking turns with Alana and Brian. Why don't you grab a good night's sleep? If you want to head out there first thing tomorrow, maybe you can help Hailey with her admin. I spoke to Frank earlier and briefed him on what happened."

I found myself drifting off as they talked. Why were their voices so soothing? And could I have this all the time but without clothes?

"Right, mister. Off to bed with you," Mal said.

I opened my eyes and met Mal's. He must have been crouching right by the arm of the couch, where I was leaning.

The way he looked at me was everything. Even in the dimmed lights, I still saw my heart reflected back at me, with all the love it contained.

Mal stood and helped me to my feet. I leaned on him and put my arm around his waist, feeling his warm strength.

He then did the last thing I ever expected him to do, but also the one I'd hoped the most. He stretched out his hand to Jake.

Jake took Mal's hand slowly as if he were afraid it was going to be taken back and let out a small sigh when Mal pulled him closer to us.

"Let's just sleep, okay?" Mal said, placing a gentle kiss on Jake's lips.

Jake nodded and then looked at me as if asking for permission. I gave it with my lips and then pulled Mal in for the same.

We walked to the room and undressed in silence. I got a T-shirt for Jake to sleep in since we were about the same size.

I swallowed at the sight of the two men I was about to spend the night with, even if it was just sleeping.

Mal guided me to the middle of the bed and took his place on one side. Jake took the other side and pulled the blanket over us.

I turned to Jake and pulled Mal's arm over me. Then I took Jake's hand, laced his fingers with mine, and tucked our joined hands in the space between my neck and my shoulder.

This was the most complete I'd felt in my life, which was unfair to Mal because I knew I didn't need anyone else but him. Or at least I didn't think I did. But what can you do when your heart is selfish and wants more?

When Mal reached out for Jake, I thought I was going to cry, but the tears didn't come. All I felt was peace and completeness.

Well, that, and a stupid erection.

I thought people with concussions weren't supposed to be under any kind of stress?

12

MAL

I DIDN'T NEED to open my eyes to know I was exactly where I needed to be. At home, in my bed, with Griff sleeping soundly against me.

His hair smelled of coconut and holidays on the beach. I inhaled the scent, allowing myself a moment to indulge until movement on the bed took my attention from Griff.

Jake.

Our eyes met over Griff's head. It didn't take any special powers to see what was going through Jake's mind at that moment.

Panic. Confusion. Lust. Hope. Longing.

He looked at Griff sleeping against me and then ran his hand over Griff's hair and the bandage on his arm. Griff moved a little and let out a small, contented sigh but didn't wake up.

Jake's hand froze over Griff when he moved. So without thinking, I took it and brought it to my lips. His eyes closed as I placed a kiss on his palm.

I didn't know what to say to him. Why did we have to use words to communicate when actions always spoke louder? And then I remembered one of the many things my wiser-beyond-his-age husband said to me once. *Sometimes we need to hear what's in someone's heart because we're too scared to trust our eyes.*

Jake had followed us to our bed last night because I'd asked him to. Not with my words but with my actions.

I'd be lying to myself if I denied the effect that small, barely-there kiss at the LA resort had on me. I'd be lying if I denied that watching as Griff pulled Jake in for a kiss at the hospital didn't settle something in the pit of my stomach.

Maybe it was time to listen to my heart, my body, and my soul, not to mention my husband.

"Jake," I whispered.

He took his hand back and sat up in bed slowly, looking down at the T-shirt Griff had given him last night. It was red with the words, *No one loves like a romance author*, printed on the front. It was such an old T-shirt that some letters were faded from being washed, but they were as true today as when I saw Griff wearing it for the first time.

Griff loved like no one else I'd met before. Maybe it was also time to give him what he needed too.

"I…um…I'll head to the resort now," Jake said in a low voice.

"Will you be back later?" I asked.

"Yes. I'm happy to keep Griff company while you go to work."

"Jake," I said, stretching my arm to reach his over Griff. "I would like to see you later too."

I didn't want Griff to wake until he was ready. After what he'd been through, he needed as much rest as possible, especially with the concussion.

Jake looked at me, searching for the meaning behind my words, so I said it again.

"I want you here, Jake. Not just for Griff."

"Okay."

I smiled and squeezed his arm to make sure he really heard me.

He nodded and got up from the bed, picking up his clothes from the chair and leaving the room.

My focus went back to Griff, who'd somehow slept through my exchange with Jake. He looked so peaceful, with his full lips slightly parted, letting out tiny puffs of breath, his long dark lashes, and perfect nose.

I always thought it wasn't possible for me to love Griff more than I already did, but somehow, every morning I woke up to him, I felt more. Like our love was growing with us.

Beyond the bedroom door, I heard Jake using the bathroom to get ready for work, and I could be mistaken, but I thought I heard the coffee machine too.

I must have fallen asleep again because the next time I opened my eyes was to gaze into Griff's deep-brown ones.

He smiled and pulled me in for a kiss before I had a chance to check how he was feeling. Sneaky bastard.

I chuckled and tickled his sides before he got any ideas about turning the kiss into something else. As much as I was dying to get my hands on him, I needed to know first how he really was. And by that, I meant his top head, not the one lower down that was currently poking my thigh.

"You're no fun," he said, pouting after I put a safe distance between us.

I raised my brow. "That's not what you said two days ago when I rim—"

He put his hand on my mouth and said, "Don't say it unless you're going to do it."

I winked and licked his palm, and then laughed as he groaned and lay on his back.

"How do you feel?" I asked.

Griff turned his face to me and smiled. "Surprisingly good. My head hurts a little."

"Any dizziness?"

"No."

I ran my hand over his chest, letting it come to rest on his waist.

"Jake is coming back later," I said.

"Did he sneak out?"

"No, he was okay. We didn't talk because I didn't want to wake you, but I asked him to come back later."

Griff took my hand and raised it to his mouth, doing the exact same thing I did to Jake earlier.

"I think I'm ready to try," I said. "I'm terrified it'll end badly, that we'll both end up hurting, but…"

"It'll hurt more if we don't try."

"Yeah."

"Shower?"

"Only if you promise to behave," I warned.

Griff snorted, but he behaved. Well, mostly.

"So, what do you want to do today?" I asked, pouring coffee into Griff's cup. The coffee that Jake had started for us earlier, even though he hadn't stayed long enough to have any.

"Can we just cozy up on the couch watching telenovelas?"

"Of course." I'd watch anything if it meant Griff had a chance to relax and get better, even telenovelas.

"What are you smiling for?" he asked. "You hate telenovelas."

"No reason. I remembered that Jake also watches them."

He smiled, tilted his head, and narrowed his eyes. I ignored him and instead put some toast and scrambled eggs on our plates and took them to the table, sitting next to him.

"Thank you, baby," he said.

"You're welcome. Now eat up so you can have some painkillers if you need them, and then we're watching *The Beautiful and the Beast.* Or is it the Bitch?"

Griff let out a belly laugh that went straight to my heart.

"You mean *The Beautiful and the Rich?*"

"Yeah, I guess. I liked mine better though," I teased and then kissed his head.

When we finished breakfast, I cleared our plates. I thought Griff might get settled on the couch, but he stayed at the table watching me as I worked.

I may have put on a little show for him by pulling my sweatpants lower on my hips and pushing my ass out as I put everything away in the cupboards.

He had his arms crossed and a pout on his face by the time I turned around to face him.

"Who are you, and what have you done to my husband?" he said, narrowing his eyes.

I ignored his comment but strolled over to him and pulled him to me before I picked him up. He wrapped his legs around my waist and took my mouth greedily.

"Hmm, now we're talking," he moaned against my lips.

I walked us to the couch and placed him in the middle while I grabbed the remote and sat next to him.

"You're such a tease," he said but burrowed against me until we were both half-lying on the couch.

I turned the TV on and looked for the right channel, but when I found it, Griff took the remote and muted the sound.

"What's up? You want to watch something else? Like…the diving competition or the swimming trials on the sports channel?" I asked.

"You mean, men in Speedos," he chuckled. "Nice try, but no. Melissa finds out today that her mother is really her twin sister, and we can't miss that."

I stared at him. "How does that even work?"

"The same way everyone has great hair in telenovelas. Magic."

He was silent for a moment, and I could tell he was working up to something he either wasn't sure how to voice or was worried about my reaction.

"Mal?"

"Yeah?"

He moved a little, so he was face to face with me.

"What made you change your mind?"

"About Jake?"

He nodded.

"I don't know. I guess I'm tired of fighting it, and I think I finally understand you."

"What do you mean?"

It was hard to explain because it hadn't been just a single flashbulb moment. It was a combination of lots of little things.

"When I look at Jake, I want to pull him into my arms. I want to tell him how amazing he is, how much I respect his hard work and his ideas. I want to kiss him, and god, that day in LA is imprinted in my mind. Every time I see him, I want to do it all over again, but I don't want to do it just once. I want to keep on doing it."

"And how about Griff?"

Jake's voice from the living room door made me jolt. My words got stuck in my throat as I realized he'd heard everything I said.

I opened and closed my mouth, but suddenly I was afraid that I'd say all the wrong things and lose Jake even before we got him.

He raised his hand to show us a bag he was carrying and went to the kitchen. Less than a minute later, he came back to the living room and sat on the coffee table facing Griff and me.

"I'm sorry I came in like that. I took your spare key earlier because I wasn't sure if you'd be asleep when I came back, or…" he trailed.

"It's okay, Jake," Griff said. "You did the right thing."

Griff reached for Jake, who held out his hand.

Jake looked at me. "All those things you said."

"They're all true, Jake," I said.

"But how about Griff? He's your husband. You love him."

I looked at Griff and smiled. "Yes, that's right. I love Griff more than I ever thought I could love another person, and it seems he kinda loves me back the same way."

I laughed when Griff elbowed me.

"But you see, Jake," I continued. "I thought what I felt for you was wrong. Even though Griff told me from the start of our relationship that he's polyamorous, I didn't get it. How could he be poly if he was with me and no one else? I was afraid I wasn't enough for him. And then we met you, and my fear stopped being about Griff."

"You were afraid to like me?" he asked.

"I was afraid to lose Griff, and I was confused about my feelings for you." I shook my head. "I don't even know how to explain it, but after the earthquake, maybe even before, I started realizing that my growing feelings for you didn't diminish my feelings for Griff."

I reached out for him, and he came forward a little on the table so he could hold both my hand and Griff's.

His eyes flickered between Griff and me as he bit his lip. I felt myself harden at the thought of using my mouth to release his lip and then suck on it while Griff paid attention to the smooth skin of his neck.

Griff shifted a little, which I knew was on purpose because he could tell how hard I was, but we weren't ready to take things further.

Not until Griff was well enough, anyway. No matter how much he pushed.

"I'm scared," Jake confessed. "I've never been in a relationship before. I don't want to come between you, and I don't want to be left hurting and alone when this ends…whatever this is…or will be."

"The most important thing in a poly relationship is communication. It's also the hardest," Griff said. "Jake, do you feel something for me? Attraction? Maybe something else you can't yet put your finger on?"

Jake nodded.

"And how about Mal? Do you feel the same?"

"Yes."

"I do too," Griff said and then looked at me. I nodded.

It was true. One of the reasons I'd struggled with my attraction to Jake was that it brought back all the feelings I had toward Griff when we first met.

"Maybe we don't have to figure everything out just yet," I said.

"Can I…can I kiss you?" Jake asked.

It didn't matter who he was speaking to because the answer was hell yes.

"Come here," I said, pulling him toward us, where he ended up half straddling Griff and me.

When his lips touched mine, it was as if I'd lived my entire life in a beautiful, cozy home that had just been extended to add a new sunroom.

Jake's lips were soft, but he wasn't afraid to go for what he wanted, and it seemed he wanted a taste of me. His tongue sought mine, gently licking and massaging as his lips closed over mine.

I heard a moan and opened my eyes to see Griff kissing Jake's neck until Jake broke our kiss and put his hand on the back of Griff's neck to take his turn with him.

Watching them kiss wasn't second to kissing each individually. Not at all. Watching them was better, and I knew the only thing that could ever beat it would be if we could all kiss at the same time.

I also knew we needed to stop before we got too carried away, but my body was in charge now, and it told my brain to fuck off.

I leaned forward and kissed their necks in turn as they kissed each other. My lips were in charge as they moved closer and closer to theirs until we were all kissing.

I thought it would be awkward, but as soon as we found our rhythm, it was the most beautiful and erotic thing I'd done with clothes on in my entire life.

Griff pulled us closer with the desperation of someone who needed more. Jake followed, and I wanted to. Fuck, how I wanted to.

I pulled away, panting, and tried to regain my brainpower. Griff and Jake were both struggling to get hold of themselves too.

For a moment, we sat in silence, our faces only inches apart, breathing hard. I couldn't speak for them, but I was so hard that if either of them so much as sneezed in my direction, I'd come in my pants.

"That… that was amazing," Jake said.

Griff let out a contented sigh and leaned against me.

"How am I going to watch a telenovela with a hard-on?" he asked.

"Oh, which one are you watching?" Jake asked with interest.

"The Beauty and the Bitch," I answered, rolling my eyes.

Jake gasped, and Griff laughed.

And there it was. The moment. Sometimes you had to pick your battles, and this time my victory came with my retreat.

"Well, I guess I should head on to the resort and check in on things. You guys get cozy and watch Melinda and her twin sister-slash-mom."

"Melissa," they both said at the same time.

I laughed and got up from the couch, not missing how both of their eyes were trained hungrily on my cock tenting my pants.

"No," I said, pointing at them. "No messing around until we know Griff is fully recovered."

"Are we allowed to make out?" Griff asked as I reached the living room door.

I groaned, wondering if sticking my head in the freezer would help me cool down sufficiently to be able to function at work, knowing what I'd be leaving behind.

I took a quick cold shower and got dressed for work. Before I left, I stepped into the living room to say goodbye to my men.

The thought that they were both mine, made me smile, and when they both looked away from the TV to smile back at me, I knew I'd need to go, or I'd never leave the house.

"I'll be back as soon as I can," I said, kissing each in turn. "Jake, you're staying tonight?"

"After that kiss? Hell yeah, I'm staying," he said.

"You never answered my question," Griff said.

I kneeled to his level on the couch and ran my hand over his cheek.

"Make sure you rest. But yeah, the thought of you two here making out is going to keep me hard all day."

Griff gave me a victorious smile and turned to kiss Jake. Then they settled back on the sofa with Griff leaning against Jake in the same way he'd leaned on me earlier.

Maybe not so unsurprisingly, the only jealousy I felt was that I couldn't spend the day with them.

I gave them each one last kiss and left.

Tomorrow morning. That was as long as we'd need to wait to make sure Griff was fully recovered from his concussion.

We could wait that long, couldn't we?

13

———

JAKE

"Dad, call the police. We have a stranger in the house," Gabe shouted from my bedroom door. Uncle Frank had gone for a walk with Jessie, so I knew there was no one else in the house.

It had been a week since the earthquake and Griff's injury. Six days since Mal, Griff, and I acknowledged our attraction for each other and decided to explore it.

Not that anything had happened, which was both frustrating and a relief.

Despite Griff's rapid recovery, things at the resort had become too busy, and as soon as he could be home on his own, both Mal and I increased the number of hours we spent at work. Especially since Trey had returned to Colorado a few days before.

Okay, so there had been a few intense make-out sessions every night, but even without talking about it, we'd all silently agreed we didn't want our first time together to be rushed.

I'd also slept at their place every night, which was likely the reason for my cousin's little theatrics.

I closed the chest drawer, turned around, and leaned on it.

"Oh, it's my big bro!" he exclaimed with ridiculous exaggeration. "I'd almost forgotten what you looked like."

"And somehow, you didn't forget where my room is or where I keep my shirts." I pointed at the gray shirt he had on. One I'd picked up from a store next to the college campus last year.

He shrugged and walked inside the room, throwing himself on my bed and sitting cross-legged.

"So, are you going to tell me what's going on with you? Or do I have to guess? And you know that I have a very colorful imagination…" He let his words hang.

"Nothing's going on. It's been very busy at the resort."

"I know. Dad's been glued to his computer, trying to figure out a way to keep the resort open while we repair the west-side building."

Gabe played with the hem of his jeans, where they were a little worn and fraying, his face changing from playful to serious.

"What's the matter?" I asked, sitting on the edge of the bed next to him.

He looked at me, but there was none of his usual demeanor. As much as it frustrated me to see Gabe sail through life as if he had no worries or responsibilities, sometimes I wondered if it was just for show.

Gabe had never had any problems opening up to me, but even I couldn't deny that between finishing my masters, working at the resort, and keeping my mind occupied with Griff and Mal, I may have neglected our relationship a little.

"I think I want to move back home," he said.

"It's a hell of a commute to Berkeley," I said, joking, but stopped when I saw Gabe's pained look. "Hey, you know you can talk to me, right?"

He took a deep breath and leaned back on the headboard of my bed.

"I spoke to my advisor, and he said I can do most of my classes remotely. I don't want to quit," he blurted. "I just don't want to go back there."

"Did something happen? You loved it out there. All the parties, the guys…the girls. What changed?"

"No, nothing dramatic happened," he said, rolling his eyes. "I guess I just prefer to be home near Dad, and he keeps talking about me working with him when I graduate and…I'd like to do that."

I nodded. I knew my uncle could be a little relentless with his eagerness to get Gabe to take over the business one day.

Most of the time, I wasn't sure Gabe actually wanted to do it, but then I'd catch him reading up on stuff or listening to Uncle Frank talk about the business with such rapture that I knew the same passion for Silver Resorts ran in his blood.

"Have you told your dad?"

"No." He went back to inspecting his jeans.

I put my hand on his to stop him from fraying the hem further. "He'll be okay with it, you know?"

"Yeah, I just don't want to let him down."

"You won't, Gabe. I promise."

"Okay, enough with the depressing. Don't think I've forgotten about your escapades. Who have you been fucking every night that we haven't seen you for a week?"

I wasn't expecting him to change the subject so swiftly. My skin heated, and I didn't know where to look or what to do that wouldn't give me away.

Not that he was completely wrong, of course. I had slept with someone, just not slept *slept* with them…yet.

In the last week, Griff, Mal, and I stole many moments to kiss, touch, and be close, but at no point did we discuss how to handle it if our relationship, or arrangement, or whatever it was, went public.

"I'm not fucking anyone." The crude words felt wrong coming from me, but also because I wanted nothing more than to be fucking someone. Two someones.

"Fine, don't tell me." He shrugged and got up from the bed.

"Gabe," I called as he got near the door.

"It's…um…it's new. I'm not sure what it is yet, but I'll tell you when I can, okay?"

He nodded and blew me a kiss before disappearing toward his own room.

Sneaky bastard.

I packed some more clothes in a bag and left the house before I bumped into my uncle on his way back from the walk with Jessie. I could handle Marlow Junior, but Marlow Senior had special powers, and I wasn't sure how convinced he'd be that my absence was because of my increased workload.

A wave of anxiety rolled through my stomach as I pulled up to Mal and Griff's house.

Was this all a mistake?

Every time I took a step toward their house, I knew we could be on the verge of something that would cause more damage and harm than good.

Equally, every time I looked into their eyes, I couldn't walk away. Mal with his big presence, sometimes broody but always reliable, and Griff with his calm, welcoming demeanor.

Why these two men?

I'd already decided to forget the strangeness of wanting two men at the same time. Poly relationships were more common than most people thought. Who was I to fight against something I felt so strongly about?

But why Griff and Mal?

They were an established couple, already married and with their own lives put together. I was fresh out of college, trying to prove myself in my first real job. What could I offer them they didn't already have?

A knock on the window got my attention. I hadn't even noticed I was still in the car.

I opened the door and got out, meeting an anxious-looking Griff.

"Is everything okay?" he asked, running a hand up my arm and letting it rest on my neck.

It felt warm, settling. His welcoming brown eyes roamed over me, looking for the source of my worry.

"Yeah, everything's okay." I smiled at him and saw his immediate relief. That settled my nerves a little more too.

He grabbed my hand and pulled me toward the front door. "Come on, I need your help with something."

We went straight to the bedroom, so I placed my bag on the floor next to the chest of drawers.

The bag hadn't even landed safely when I was pulled once again. Though not toward the kitchen or living room as I'd expected. No, Griff led me to the bathroom.

"Did something break here?" I asked. "I know I worked housekeeping at the resort, but I'm totally hopeless at maintenance stuff."

Griff laughed and then tilted his head, looking me up and down in a way that raised my body temperature by one hundred degrees, not to mention other parts of my body.

"I think you're wrong. The kind of maintenance I need you to carry out is not only essential, but I'm also pretty sure you're great at it," he said.

He pushed me against the sink and pulled my shirt over my head, then he pulled his off and leaned against me.

His lips ghosted over the skin of my neck. "Is this okay?"

"Fuck yeah," I breathed out, pulling him even closer by his hips. I was impossibly hard, and so was he, judging from the jean-covered hardness pressed against mine.

I needed to kiss him, feel his soft lips on mine, taste him, but he had other plans. He worshiped every inch of my skin until he reached my nipples, where he sucked them into hard peaks.

"If you keep doing that, you're gonna make me come," I rasped.

"Are you serious?" he asked, looking at me with the kind of smile that said he was dying to test that theory. I nodded.

Griff licked a path up my sternum, onto my neck, and over my Adam's apple until his lips claimed mine.

I put my hand behind his head to keep him in place while I sucked his lips with mine until he opened his delicious mouth for me. I swirled my tongue around his until we were both struggling for breath.

"One day, we'll see if that's true, but not today," he said between kisses.

"What are we doing today?"

"Getting naked," he said, opening the front of my jeans and drawing my cock out. "And staying naked." He gave it a teasing tug before releasing it and helping me out of my jeans, shoes, and socks.

"I can be on board with that," I chuckled.

The rest of his clothes came off, and in no time, we were back to kissing and touching each other. I felt so hot. Even the cold sink behind me didn't bother me in the least.

Griff let go of me to turn the shower on, so I made the best of him being temporarily turned away and sunk to my knees.

"Fuck." Griff cried when I all but buried my face in his ass. He smelled freshly cleaned, so I went straight for the kill. I squeezed and then held his butt cheeks open so I could see my prize.

He relaxed his hole for me, which was an invitation to go for it. As if I needed it.

I saw him grip the door to the shower before licking a path from his taint all the way up his crease, taking my time rimming his hole.

The more Griff pushed back against my tongue, the more I denied him what he wanted. He groaned in frustration. "Jake."

I looked at the tiled floor beneath me and saw a trail of precum from my cock to the tile, and he wasn't doing any better because, in his eagerness to get more of my tongue, he'd neglected his own cock.

"Could you come like this?" I asked.

"Try me," he rasped.

I stood up and turned him around, slamming my mouth on his as I walked him back inside the shower.

Our cocks were hard and desperate for relief.

"When's Mal getting home?" I asked into his mouth.

"Anytime now." He smiled into my lips.

So that was his plan, to work us both up and get us ready for Mal.

Mission accomplished.

The warm water cascaded over us as we continued to make out under the spray.

I grabbed the soap and squirted a good amount onto my hand, then lathered it and ran it over my chest and then Griff's, feeling his muscles contract under my touch.

It was a heady feeling to see him as desperate for my touch as I was for his, and somehow, it still wasn't enough. We needed Mal here.

"You keep doing that to my cock, and this show will be over soon."

He laughed. "Maybe, in hindsight, we shouldn't go without sex for so long again."

"I agree."

The bathroom was so steamed up I had to run a hand over the glass. Not that I needed it to know who'd just arrived.

Mal stood by the bathroom door, fully naked, stroking his cock.

"Fuck," I rasped.

"He's gorgeous, isn't he?" Griff said into my ear even as he peppered me with kisses.

"Yes…" my voice was no louder than a whisper. I tried to keep my eyes open and focused on Mal, but when I felt the pad of Griff's finger run down my crease and press into my hole, I couldn't help closing them and resting my head on his shoulder.

"Look at him, baby. He's so ready for you."

I didn't know if Griff was talking to Mal or me, but it didn't matter. Whether I was topping or bottoming, I knew I was in for one hell of a ride.

I groaned when Griff removed his finger, but when I looked up, I saw he had his hand stretched out as an invitation to Mal.

Mal took one step forward, but then he stopped, and I knew he was contemplating the merits of watching Griff and me together. I couldn't blame him in the slightest because I would soon stand back for the chance to watch them too.

How many times had I woken up in the middle of the night, my cock hard enough to pound nails, all because of the one image I'd had stuck in my head.

That split-second before I fled the resort room all those months ago when Griff had leaped into Mal's arms just after he'd given me the best orgasm of my life.

I'd often wondered if they'd carried on after I left, but while I had decided it wasn't worth revisiting that and asking, it didn't stop my mind from imagining them together, drawing out their own pleasure from each other.

Fortunately, Mal took a few more steps forward until he was within reach. Griff and I pulled him into the shower and between us.

Mal was facing me, so I couldn't resist pulling him in for a kiss. I needed it as much as I needed breath. Fuck me if I could understand why, but it didn't matter. All I wanted was to taste Mal.

His kisses were so different from Griff's. While Griff's kissing was a full-body experience that you could feel from the top of your head down to the tips of your toes, Mal made me forget I had a body. The way he wrapped his hand behind my neck to keep me in place as he plunged his tongue into my mouth was like a pirate protecting his treasure chest. Focused, determined, and greedy.

Mal took it all, and in the process, he gave it all back too. Okay, so maybe not so much like a pirate.

I felt weightless by the time he was finished with me and turned to kiss Griff the same way.

While they kissed, I took my time to explore Mal's body. He was softer than Griff and a lot hairier. I never thought I'd be turned on by an older man, but the dark hair on his back with a peppering of gray and white and the softness of his body over the hard muscle I felt underneath made me want to lick every inch of his body.

From Griff's earlier demands, I could tell he was happy bottoming, but I wasn't sure about Mal.

"Yes," he said.

"What?" I asked.

"I'll bottom for you." He kissed me again, and my brain went into overdrive at the thought of being caught appreciating his gorgeous ass, and the realization that not only was Mal happy to bottom, but that he wanted me to top him was almost more than I could handle.

Fortunately, my brain was too mushy, so I was unable to process all the information and have time to let any kind of nerves settle over me.

The only thing I could do was feel.

I didn't know when we changed positions, but suddenly I was no longer the bread in our Mal sandwich. I was the filling.

Mal was behind me, his thick cock running up and down my crease while Griff went on his knees.

My next thought before my cock was engulfed in the wet heat of Griff's mouth was how come we hadn't run out of hot water. After that, I didn't fucking care because the sight of Griff's mouth wrapped around my cock while Mal's dick was pushing gently against my hole was enough to make my orgasm build faster than I expected.

There was no time to warn Griff as I released into his mouth. My legs were jelly, and I was only held up because Mal had wrapped his arm around my waist.

"Fuck, I'm so sorry...I...fuck." It seemed that my capacity for cognitive speech may have left me through my dick.

Griff stood up and kissed me, giving me a taste of myself, and then it was Mal's turn.

"Hmm, you taste amazing," Mal moaned into my mouth. I reached over my shoulder to keep him right where he was, with his mouth on mine.

I didn't need to look to see that Mal's free arm went around me to wrap around Griff because I felt him closer.

His lips latched onto my neck again and sucked. I knew I'd get a mark there, but I did absolutely nothing to dissuade him. Instead, I threaded my hand through his wet hair to keep him in place.

Somehow my spent cock still had enough life in it to twitch under the touch of both my men.

I opened my eyes and stilled at my thought.

"What's the matter, baby?" Mal asked.

They weren't my men, were they? Did I want them to be? Hell yeah, but what happened now? Last time, I'd run the moment they latched on to each other.

A small wave of panic rolled through me.

But they weren't doing that now. I'd had my orgasm, and throughout it and after, they were still showering me with affection.

I could still feel Griff and Mal's erections against my skin, but they hadn't pushed for more. They needed their own relief, but they'd put it aside for me.

One of them turned the water off, and then I was pulled out of the shower and wrapped into a fluffy towel.

"Hey," Griff said, placing his hands on my face and caressing my cheeks. "Are you okay?"

I nodded. My words were stuck in my throat, but I was too afraid to voice them, anyway.

Behind us, Mall was running a towel over Griff to dry him off. Even as Griff focused on me, his eyes never leaving mine, I saw Mal's caring nature, making sure Griff's wet hair dried.

He gave Griff another towel, and he did the same to me.

How ridiculous that I'd just had an amazing orgasm at the hands of these two amazing people, and now I was freaking out. Even more ridiculous was that they were caring for me while waiting for me to calm down.

"I don't know how to say this, but suddenly I was scared," I whispered. Afraid that if I said it any louder, my words would carry some kind of destructive power.

"What were you scared of, sweetheart?" Griff asked.

"My first thought after I came was that I was lucky to have you as my men. But then the image of you two together before I left last time…" I lowered my head, and Griff moved so it was resting on his shoulder. Mal came around the side to put his arms around me too.

"We are," Mal said. "We are yours, Jake." He ran his hand through my hair gently.

I felt Griff nod against me, and then he whispered in my ear, "Will you be ours too?"

14

————

GRIFF

My eyes met Mal's over Jake's head.

I always knew navigating a three-way relationship would be complex. There would be times when we wouldn't be on the same page. Maybe we'd all have self-doubts at the same time. Or maybe, just as one of us found our place, another would suddenly struggle. It could really make your head hurt to think of the rollercoaster of emotions.

But I knew it was worthwhile because the moment we'd just had in the shower was real. We were real. Maybe we just needed to help each other get there.

I saw Mal's eyes dim a little the longer we waited for Jake's answer to my question.

When Jake raised his head from my shoulder, his eyes were full of uncertainty.

He looked at Mal and me as if he were steeling himself before he said, "I don't want to be an extra. I don't want to be left behind."

Mal was quicker than me to react because my own brain was busy trying to understand the depth of his words and his worry that we would push him aside at some point, or that he wouldn't be on equal footing.

I stood aside as Mal placed a small kiss on Jake's lips and lifted him until Jake had his legs wrapped around Mal's waist before he walked to the bedroom.

Mal placed Jake on the bed and removed all the towels, including the one he had wrapped around his waist. Mine had fallen off at some point between the bathroom and the bed, and I didn't care to pick it up.

There were more important things to focus on.

Like watching the way Mal kissed Jake's stomach, and how Jake reacted with a shy laugh before Mal settled his weight over him.

I watched Jake's cock come back to life under Mal's touch, but I knew that wasn't his end goal. He was just doing what he'd done to me countless times. Grounding me with the power of his love and his body.

My own nerves settled a little, knowing that, at this moment, Mal wasn't the one who needed care. Somehow he'd come to accept what we all had together.

I lay on my side next to Jake, cradling his head. He was warm and smooth. It felt good to run my hand down his sides and then up and over Mal as if they were one complete entity.

"Do you feel how hard I am, Jake?" Mal asked. He wasn't grinding or moving over Jake. He was simply there.

"Yes," Jake answered, and then he looked at me. I smiled at him.

"It's for you too," Mal said as he nuzzled Jake's neck, placing soft kisses on his skin. "I want to be with you as much as I want to be with Griff. You are no second best, no extra, no leftover."

Jake nodded.

"It's okay to have doubts," he carried on. "God knows I've been struggling with this for a long time now, but someone very smart once told me to follow my heart because he'd always be there with me. So that's what I'm doing. Neither of us can make any promises, but I hope we can all trust that at least what we all feel is real, and it won't go away."

"I tried," Jake said. "I tried to make it go away, but every night I dreamed about you. I dreamed I was part of you, and every morning I woke up to the same reality that I wasn't—"

Mal cut off Jake's words with a claiming kiss while I whispered in his ear, "You are part of us now. Trust us. Let us be part of you too."

As I hoped, the combination of my reassuring words and Mal's grounding weight was enough to settle Jake. But only for a moment because he soon began to move his hips and grind against Mal.

His increasingly desperate moans reawakened my dick, and as much as I'd happily take myself in hand while I watched, I wanted to be a part of them.

I moved down the bed and settled behind Mal. As if he knew what I had in mind, he opened his legs. Jake, who'd already given Mal enough space between his legs, tightened them around his waist.

The image in front of me was the stuff of my teenage dreams.

I was looking at the yin and yang of Jake's smooth hole, glistening with Mal's precum and Mal's round, soft, and much hairier butt. They were smooth and rough, soft and hard, and if I didn't get a move on, I was going to come on the spot just by looking at them.

"You guys should see what you look like from here," I said.

I ran my hands up the back of Mal's thighs, feeling his hairs under my fingers until I reached his cheeks and opened them up to reveal his hole.

He didn't stop grinding against Jake, but he did look over his shoulder.

"What do we look like?"

"Hot. Sexy. Slippery. And so fucking fuckable I wish I had two dicks to take you at the same time."

Jake groaned under Mal. "Guess what my next internet search is going to be."

I chuckled.

"Maybe we should get a few mirrors so we can watch everything from all angles," Mal said.

My cock was fully hard and ready for anything, and Mal's words didn't make it any easier to keep myself under control.

While I reached over to the bedside table to grab the bottle of lube and a couple of condoms, Mal flipped them over so Jake was on top.

"What—" he gasped.

"I told you, baby. I want to feel you inside me."

Jake looked at me, his gaze full of need. I pulled him up and slammed my mouth on his. And since I was on my knees, all I had to do was sit back on my heels and let Jake straddle me.

"Fuck yeah," Mal said. "Watching you two is the most fucking arousing thing I've ever seen."

"Am I missing out on something here?" Jake chuckled.

"Not for long, sweetheart," I said into his ear. "Can I fuck you while you fuck Mal?"

Jake sat up and fell back on the bed, staring at the ceiling. "Please, God, make this be true. I'm not dreaming, am I? Pleeeease?"

I laughed and lay down next to him. "Is that a yes?" I asked, running my hand down his chest. He sucked in a breath when I tugged one nipple and nearly jumped off the bed when Mal latched on to the other with his tongue.

"Nhnn fuuck," Jake moaned.

"Baby, you might need to go easy on him if you ever want him inside you," I warned Mal.

He raised his brows. "Really?"

I nodded.

Jake suddenly sat up and pushed Mal on the bed. "One day, you can both go to town on my nipples…and other sensitive areas, but not now." He kissed Mal. All his earlier fears were seemingly gone, or at least sidelined.

Their temporary distraction with each other was perfect because Mal's cock stood thick and heavy over his stomach, and my mouth was salivating for a taste.

I grabbed the lube and squirted a small amount on my fingers. My dick jumped at the sound of Mal's moan when I sought his hole. Jake's hungry eyes were trained on Mal's cock, but he was mine now.

"I'm going to open him up for you, Jake. Just watch him. See how he loves it," I said.

I took Mal's cock and gave it a few strokes before wrapping my lips around the head and sucking it like the best candy. I knew I couldn't go too far because Mal, like me, was already wound too tight.

When I was ready to add a third finger, I released his cock and took Jake's in my mouth. He probably hadn't even realized he'd been grinding against Mal all that time.

They both hissed. One from pleasure, and the other from short-lived pain because when I hit Mal's soft bundle of nerves, a trail of precum pooled in his stomach, and I released Jake's cock to lick it.

Despite having come earlier, Jake sounded as desperate as Mal and I, so I unwrapped the condom and rolled it down his cock before adding a little more lube.

Mal held his hands out to Jake, who took them without question, letting me guide his length into Mal's hole.

I wasn't a spectator for long because as soon as he was as far as he could be inside Mal, Jake released one hand and wrapped it around the back of my neck to pull me in for a kiss.

The move forced me to half fall on Mal's chest so I was between them, which Mal didn't seem to mind, from the way he held on to me.

Every sound and every move was amplified. Mal's jerky moans, Jake's heavy breathing, the way their bodies moved with each other.

I had my eyes closed, but I didn't need to open them to know how beautiful they were together. I could feel it.

"I need you inside me, Griff. Please."

I opened them to stare straight at Jake's desperate gaze. He needed this, and I knew there was nothing that would ever stop me from giving him anything.

They paused long enough to allow me to suit up and prep Jake. Thank fuck I wasn't as thick as Mal because I couldn't wait to be inside Jake.

"Are you ready, sweetheart?" I asked, running my hand down his back.

"Yes," he pleaded.

I had to take more than one deep breath and think of all the unsexy things I could think of—my grandmother's roast chicken or laundry—because watching as my cock disappeared into Jake's tight hole was almost too much.

He moved forward so he was lying on Mal, and as soon as I was all the way in, I saw Jake rest his head on Mal's chest.

Every thrust into Jake felt like I was inside Mal too. It was everything I'd ever hoped being with two men at the same time would be and more.

We stared into each other's eyes. I was desperate to say the words I'd said so many times during our lovemaking, but I couldn't say them aloud now because I knew they didn't apply just to Mal.

The consequences of crossing yet another barrier in such a short time could be devastating, so I put my focus and energy into giving my two men the pleasure they deserved.

"Fuck, Griff, you feel so good," Jake moaned. "I'm so close."

I helped Jake to a straight position against my chest and turned his face for a kiss that was meant to claim, but it felt that it was more of me losing myself to him.

With each pass of his tongue over mine, I tasted his moans, so I increased my pace. We were all so close that, with one move, I sealed our fate.

I wrapped my hand around Mal's cock, not that he needed that much to trigger his orgasm.

"Fuuuck!" he cried as he spilled into my hand. I never stopped moving in and out of Jake.

"Let go, sweetheart," I said into Jake's mouth. "We'll be here to catch you."

He groaned, and screamed, "Mal!"

I couldn't tell if Mal did anything or just held Jake because as soon as Jake's orgasm started, I couldn't stop mine. My body took over as I rutted into him until I had nothing left.

Jake was breathing heavily under me. How soon would I need to move? Because every muscle in my body had gone on holiday and left me in a jellified form.

Someone ran a hand through my hair. It was probably Mal.

Shit, we're crushing him.

I placed a kiss on Jake's back as I slowly pulled away from him and removed my condom. I only needed to find enough energy to grab a towel to clean Mal and dispose of the condoms.

When I returned to the bedroom, Jake was snuggled up against one side of Mal, and they were kissing lazily. When I joined them, I kissed him over Mal and then kissed Mal before I settled next to them.

My eyes were suddenly too heavy.

"I know we're supposed to have dinner, but I think I'm dead, and dead people don't eat."

That was all I remember saying before I heard a few chuckles and let sleep take me.

There wasn't a single cloud in the sky, the temperatures had risen to the kind of heat that makes you want to jump in the ocean, and I could swear the flowers on the small square next to El Pancito were smiling at me.

Gosh, what an afternoon followed by a long night of lovemaking could do to a man's mood. It wouldn't surprise me at this rate if those rabbits we saw all over the island suddenly jumped out from behind the bushes and started singing and talking to me.

I laughed to myself and crossed the road to my favorite bakery. I hadn't seen Elena since the day of the earthquake, so I readied myself to be attacked by one of her tight hugs.

We'd messaged during the week, but with Mal and Jake doing all sorts of weird hours at the resort, I'd opted for working from home all week and got started on the first round of edits for my new novel.

Jessie was on her lead tied to the bike rack outside El Pancito. She stood up and wagged her tail as soon as she saw me.

I stopped in panic. How could I face Frank, knowing the things I'd done and how I felt about his nephew? The nephew he'd raised as his own son?

The topic of telling people about us hadn't come up yet. Hell, we were still figuring it out ourselves.

I was about to turn to go back the other way when Frank waved at me from inside the bakery. I smiled and waved back.

Cross the road and talk to him like nothing happened.

I went straight to Jessie, who was impatiently waiting for me.

"Hey, girl, whatcha doing here?" I cooed, scratching behind her furry ears.

She let out a bark as Frank came out of the bakery holding a drink and a pastry bag.

"Griffin. How are you doing, son?"

"I'm good, Frank. How are you?"

"Well, this old girl keeps me on my toes, that's for sure," he said.

I stood up and leaned closer to him, and whispered, "She's also a good excuse to grab one of Elena's pastries, right?"

He winked. "Would you like to join us for our walk? I'd love to ask you about something."

"Um…yeah, sure." I coughed to cover up my nerves and said, "I'd love to."

"Great. Go get your snack. We'll wait here for you," he said, and Jessie followed with her own bark of agreement.

As I expected, Elena near enough jumped from behind the counter. I had to apologize to the rest of her customers for her exaggerated reaction.

No, I wasn't anyone famous. And no, I wasn't dying.

Once that was settled, she returned to serving the customers while I waited my turn.

"So…tell me what put that lovin' smile on your face. That has to be more than just a good dickin' from Mal," she said when I got to the front of the line. Fortunately, there was no one behind me.

"Good morning, my dear Elena. Could I have a coffee and a chocolate-pecan-caramel cookie to go, please?"

"You can ignore me all you want, but you're gonna spill the beans at some point."

She put the coffee and cookie on the counter and then her hands on her hips.

"Don't give me attitude woman, I nearly died last week," I said, sticking my tongue out at her.

"And for your efforts to stay alive, you're getting that coffee and cookie. Now go off and be happy somewhere else if you're not gonna share it."

I laughed and blew her a kiss before I grabbed my things and left.

Frank had finished his pastry, so he held on to Jessie's lead with one hand and his drink with the other.

"So, what did you want to ask me?"

"I've been reading your books, and there's one where three guys—"

My coughing fit interrupted Frank. He tapped his hand on my back to help me clear my throat.

"Sorry…I was too eager to eat my cookie," I said. It was an excuse even I didn't buy.

"So nothing to do with a straight old man asking you about three-way gay sex?"

My mouth was literally agape, and I was in shock.

I shook my head and took a sip of my coffee, trying to compose myself.

"I'm afraid to ask again, Frank, but what's your question?"

"You have a wonderful way with words. My Annie would have loved your books too. So much love and romance. I read all your books—"

"You did?"

"Of course," he said as if I were crazy for even thinking he wouldn't. "I've read nearly all of them, and in order. Anyway, I got to this, what do you call it? Oh yeah, poly romance, and I don't get it. Don't they get jealous?"

I looked around us. The sky was still blue, the flowers still looked beautifully blooming, but I was pretty sure I'd stepped into some kind of separate dimension.

"Many people see it that way because western society educated us to see just the love between two people and nothing more. Many cultures allow for more than one spouse, and even in the animal kingdom, a lot of species have multiple partners. Of course my romance is fiction, but those relationships happen in real life too."

Frank scratched his chin and looked pensive.

"Does it bother you?" I asked.

"No, at all, son. When I met my Annie, I felt like the luckiest man on earth, and I'm grateful for every day we spent together. Love is more precious than the rarest gem. To have one person loving you with everything they have is the most wonderful thing. To have more than one…well, that's just being a lucky bastard. No one should throw that away."

He laughed, and I couldn't help joining him.

"When's that next book coming out? I'm nearly finished with your backlist. You can't leave me hanging."

"Tell you what, Frank. As soon as this next one is ready, you can have an advance copy."

"Perfect," he said. "Now tell me, how are your husband and my nephew?"

Fuck.

15

MAL

"THERE'S NO OTHER OPTION. We have to do it," Hailey said, leaning against the windowsill in the conference room.

"If we do it, we may as well kiss goodbye to this year's profits," Pete said, raising his hands.

Brian sat forward on the large conference desk. "I think the safety of our guests is more important."

"I'm not disputing that, but we don't want to lay off people," Pete argued.

"What do you think, Mal?" Jake asked.

I looked around the room. This was decision time. We'd looked for all the alternatives to keep the resort open while we repaired the west building, but a survey had uncovered a few other structural issues that needed to be dealt with.

"Frank will be here soon, so we need to reach a consensus. What's our biggest worry? Profits and layoffs, right?"

Everyone agreed.

"The fastest way to get the resort up and running is to do all the repairs while we're closed because then we don't need to worry about disruption to our guests. We all agree with that?"

"Yes," Pete said. "But if we close, will we reopen? I just can't see how it would work."

"For once, I agree with Pete," Hailey said and then raised her finger. "Don't get used to it though."

Pete smiled, and Hailey continued. "I can't see months of working around disruptions, closed-off areas, and the health and safety implications alone are giving me the hives. But at the same time, what do we do with our current staff? The impact on their income, their families, and the island can't be ignored."

"I agree wholeheartedly," I said.

Brian snorted.

"Is there something you'd like to add, Brian?" I asked.

Out of the management team, Brian was the only one who'd been openly reluctant to accept me. I'd found out through Hailey that Brian had wanted the promotion but was unsuccessful. That hadn't surprised me because, at his level, Brian still had a lot to learn before he was ready to manage the whole resort. It wasn't about capability. It was simply about exposure to any real kind of experience stepping up from his role.

We'd made a plan to increase his responsibility so he'd be ready to step up when the opportunity came, but so far, I had seen little initiative from him.

"No, nothing," he said under his breath.

"Good, because if you have any doubt about my loyalty and dedication to the resort or the people of this island, then we can take that conversation elsewhere. This isn't the time or place for it."

Brian gave me a defiant stare before sitting back in his chair.

"Okay, where were we?" I asked the room.

Jake raised his hand. "I have an idea, which may or may not work. I guess it'll depend on the budget, but if it does work, then we could come back stronger than before."

"Let me worry about the budget. Give us your idea," I said.

Jake went over to the whiteboard and drew a grid with the various colored pens. I couldn't help admiring the way his slacks hugged his ass and thighs. Even from behind, Jake was a striking man, and if we weren't in a room full of people and at work, I'd be fucking him against that whiteboard right now.

Get your head in the right place, Mal. Both of them.

The last thing I wanted was to sport wood in front of my boss and uncle of one of the men I was currently in a relationship with.

Erection sufficiently deflated.

Jake finished his chart, and it was so well designed I already had a clue what he was about to propose.

"I told Alana about my proposal to upskill our staff using other resorts for training. She commented the other day at lunch how it would take forever for all the staff to have their turn at working in a different resort because usually, we'd only afford a few to be away from work at one time, and that's assuming we don't have anyone on a long-term absence."

"Are you saying we should relocate everyone to the other resorts? How do you suggest they'll afford the accommodation near the other resorts? Not to mention being away from home," Brian said.

I wanted to hit him with something hard, but he did have a point, so I let Jake take the challenge. The difference between Jake and Brian was one hundred percent work ethic, experience, and attitude. If I left the resort tomorrow, I knew Jake could do the job, and he'd learn as he went. Brian would run it into the ground.

Not that I was thinking of leaving. If anything, my long-term career plans were taking a different route to what I'd expected.

"I took your concerns on board, Brian. You are right. Not everyone can travel and be away from home. What I propose is a resourcing matrix where we record everyone's work aspirations, travel requirements, family responsibilities, et cetera. In a nutshell, this is how it could work. Mike in catering wants to move up a level. He's single and lives with his family, and he's happy to travel. We can relocate him to Silver Springs, where he can rent a small apartment while he works there. His salary will increase accordingly because there is a higher pay band in Colorado, and if with the additional money he can't pay his living expenses, then we will supplement it."

"And if they can't travel?" Brian asked.

"A different example. Mrs. Solano looks after her grandchildren when her daughter is at work, so she can't travel. We can offer her a mix of paid holiday, unpaid leave, and some shifts at the Silver Sands. Silver Sands is the closest, so I'd imagine we'll have a majority of staff requesting to work there. We can work with Morgan to provide a free shuttle from the ferry to the resort. Once again, the salary at Silver Sands would be higher so no one would be out of pocket with the additional expense of the ferry."

I walked up to the board and looked at the matrix where Jake had written some information off the top of his head but given us a picture of the options we could offer.

"I really like this, Jake. We can work on the details, but this is a really cost-effective solution to upskill our staff using someone else's payroll. We could refresh all our skills in one go. Staff will feel valued. We could even lose some along the way to the other resorts if they secure a promotion, but that's a hit I'd love to take. Well done, Jake."

Everyone around the room had a smile on their face. Apart from Brian, of course.

"Good afternoon, everyone. My apologies for the delay. I was having a wonderful conversation with Griff and lost track of time," Frank said as he came in the room and took a seat at one end of the table.

From the corner of my eye, I noticed Jake tense up.

"Welcome, Frank. I hope Elena didn't kick you both out of El Pancito for emptying her pastry shelf," I joked.

"Don't know what you're talking about," he said, waving his hand dismissively. Which also meant guilty as charged.

I laughed. "Actually, Frank, you came at the right time. Jake was just describing the potential of his resourcing matrix, and I'd love to book a meeting for us to go through the numbers."

"Fantastic," Frank said and then gestured for Jake to carry on.

There were no two ways about it. Jake's passion and great ideas were sexy as hell. While he gave Frank an abridged version of his earlier speech, I sat back to admire him. Pride swelled in my chest. He'd done all this on his own. Yes, it needed refining, and I was sure not everyone would be happy with it, but it was a solid idea.

Frank was beaming when Jake finished, and everyone around the room was on board, even Brian. Well, semi on board.

"Do you have time to crunch some numbers with me, Frank? Or do you want to sleep on it?" I asked Frank after everyone left the room.

"I'm happy to do it now."

I glanced at the rest of the office and saw Jake go toward the restroom.

"Frank, will you excuse me for a moment? I just remembered I need to catch Jake about something. Would you like me to grab you a coffee or tea on the way back?"

"No thanks, Mal. But if there's one of those fruit tarts from Chef Silva, then I wouldn't mind taking one home. Jessie has been craving them."

I laughed out loud, knowing Frank's dog would get nowhere near that tart. "You got it. Gotta keep the girl happy."

The great thing about my team was that no one liked to spend much time cooped up in the office, so after the meeting, everyone disappeared. It helped that it was a gorgeous early summer day.

As I'd hoped, there was no one else in the restroom, so I waited for Jake to come out of the cubicle.

"Oh, hey," he said before looking under the other cubicles, but I shook my head to let him know there was no one else around.

Then he walked over until he had me pressed against the wall. His hands gripped my waist as he nuzzled my neck.

"I've been dying to touch you all day, Mal. When you looked at me earlier, I nearly came in my pants." His voice was low and sexy, and his lips ghosting my skin without actually touching me was torture.

"How do you think I felt, watching you command that room with your sexy brain?"

"Sexy brain?" He chuckled.

"Oh yeah, your brain turns me on so much. Your ideas, your creativity…"

"Nothing to do with my tailored slacks then?"

"Hmm…"

This time he sucked a spot on my neck as his hands roamed to cup my cock, which by now was fully hard. How I was going to leave this restroom with any kind of decorum, I didn't know.

"Jake, we're playing with fire."

He let out a sound between a laugh and a sigh and settled his hands on my chest. I pulled him in for a kiss but didn't let it get too heated.

"God, I can't wait to get home," he said before he caught himself. "Um, sorry, I shouldn't assume…"

I kissed him again until he was like putty in my hands.

"Assume, Jake. Always assume. You can come and go as you please. Keep the spare key you've been using." I ran a finger down his cheek and traced his lips. He parted them and sucked my finger in. "When I got home yesterday, and you and Griff were in the shower, it was one of the most arousing things I've ever seen. One day I want him to edge you so you can't come until I get home, and then I'll watch you spill your hot cum all over me before I've even removed my clothes."

He let out a breathy moan I caught with my mouth.

When we parted, Jake took a step back and adjusted his erection in his pants. I sighed and did the same.

"Later," I whispered.

"Later." He nodded.

I went over to the sink to run some water over my face and wash my hands.

"So you think my idea is really that good?" Jake asked.

"Good? Baby, it could save the resort."

At that moment, the door to the restroom opened, and Brian came in. Thankfully, there was a respectful distance between Jake and me.

"What's this? Staff meeting in the men's room? People will talk, you know," he said with a snigger.

"What exactly is your problem, Brian?" Jake asked.

"No problem at all," he said, looking Jake up and down and then walking to the cubicle at the far end.

I shook my head to warn Jake to not react.

"I'll get started on that report you asked for," Jake said to me before he left the restroom.

Frank was outside the conference room talking to Hayley by the time I got back with his fruit tart.

"I'm sorry for the delay, Frank. Chef was just finishing these off, so you have a fresh one to take home."

"Perfect. Let's talk numbers then."

I spent the rest of the afternoon with Frank, feeling more hopeful with each minute that passed and each detail we ironed out.

We had a busy few months ahead of us, but if we made this work, we could reopen just in time to catch the late summer holidaymakers.

My only problem during the meeting was that I had to keep myself in check every time I thought about going home after work to spend some time with Griff and Jake.

"Mal, can I ask you a question?"

"Sure."

"I know the earthquake was a tough event for you, especially with Griff getting caught in it. I just wanted to check in and make sure you were okay."

There weren't many times I thought about the father I'd never met, but there was something about Frank that always caught me off guard whenever he went personal.

I tried to shake the feeling off.

"The earthquake was definitely a new experience," I said. "But we're okay. Griff is okay. In fact, he won't stop talking about having a baby boy named after him."

"Oh yes, he told me about that earlier. What a wonderful thing."

I got up to tidy up the markers and clean the whiteboard while Frank gathered his things.

"Um…Mal, this may seem like a strange question, but how's Jake doing?"

My hand froze mid-wiping the board, and I turned around.

"What do you mean?"

"Well, he was so excited to work here, and I know you guys get along. But he's not been home much, and sometimes I worry about him. Do you think maybe he's seeing a new boy?"

Frank referring to Jake as young enough to date boys didn't feel right, and the thought that Jake could be out there meeting other men felt even worse, despite me knowing it wasn't true.

"Jake's a grownup, Frank. Maybe he's just having fun. He's a very responsible person and has done a wonderful job. I'm not worried about my position here, so I can tell you this, he's talented and hard-working, and I couldn't have picked anyone better to work with."

"It's not his work ethic that I'm worried about. It's his heart." Frank went over to the window facing the gardens and the beach beyond. "I loved my sister dearly, but Jake deserved better than her. He's always been such a good boy. I'm proud to have raised him as my son, but…I'd hate to see him with his heart broken again."

I wasn't sure what Frank meant, but if it was something personal and important, I hoped that one day Jake felt comfortable enough with Griff and me that he would open up and share it.

How could I reassure Frank that Jake was okay without giving us away?

"Frank, um…Jake has been staying with us. I mean, I don't know everything he does, but we've been working closely, and he's become a friend to Griff and me. When we've worked late, he's stayed at our house."

He looked at me. His brows were a little furrowed, but he nodded and then smiled.

"Okay, if he's with you, then he's okay. Thank you."

I nodded.

My head was still all over the place when Jake met me in the staff parking lot later.

"Hey, everything okay?" he asked. I saw his hand move to touch me, but he stopped himself in time. We were in plain sight, and it wouldn't be smart to show any kind of affection.

"Yeah, we'll talk about it when we get home."

"Okay."

As soon as we were outside the resort, I grabbed Jake's hand and laced our fingers together before resting our hands on my leg. Jake sighed, and when I looked at him, he was more relaxed.

"I missed Griff today. Wouldn't it be nice if he worked at the resort too?" Jake said.

I laughed out loud.

"No. I'd never get any work done, and I'd be sporting wood all day. It's bad enough as it is. Do you know what it does to me when you walk past smelling of our shower soap and Griff's aftershave? It's like a multisensory explosion goes off inside of me."

He chuckled.

"And if you're not careful, I'll have to fire you," I threatened.

"Oh yeah? And what kinds of things would I have to do to get fired?" he asked, leaning over the console to get closer to me. "Should I do this?" He ran his other hand from my shoulder all the way down to rest on my crotch.

"Jake," I warned.

"Well, tell me then. How naughty would I have to be?"

He was so lucky that we were pulling into the driveway, and it wasn't overlooked, so as soon as I put the car in park, I pulled him to me and slammed my mouth onto his.

Our tongues swirled around each other with the desperation of someone on the edge of life.

"Wow," Jake said. "It's a good thing we didn't do this earlier because I'd have fainted."

I gave him another, smaller kiss and said, "Come on, let's see if we can get dirty before dinner."

He was by the front door with his keys ready before I even locked the car.

The first thing I noticed as we went inside was the stereo playing Vivaldi's Four Seasons. That wasn't a good sign. Griff only played this kind of music when he was stress cleaning.

We followed the smell and found Griff facing the cooker, wearing nothing but his sweatpants and a backward cap. It was fucking hot, but I was more curious to find out why our kitchen looked like a restaurant kitchen and a bakery had an affair.

"Griff?" I called softly so I wouldn't startle him.

He turned around, smiled, and came straight at us. His kiss was frantic, and even Jake noticed because he came closer to us, putting his hand on the small of Griff's back.

"Baby, what's wrong?" I asked.

"Nothing. Everything is right because you're both here, and I'm so ready to get naked." He looked down at himself and laughed. "Well, more naked."

I cradled his face with my hands. "Griffin, what's wrong?"

He huffed and walked away from us to turn the rings off on the stove and check the oven.

"Frank knows about us," he said.

"What?" Jake shrieked.

"No, he doesn't," I said. "What makes you think that?"

He wrung the tea towel tight in his hands. "I met him today at El Pancito. We went for a walk, and he started talking about romance and poly relationships. He said he read my books and asked stuff, and then he wanted to know how you two were. I didn't know what to say, so I excused myself and came home. Well, I went to the market first and bought all the ingredients to make this."

He was breathless by the time he finished.

Jake had gone white.

"Okay, let's all calm down. Frank spoke to me earlier. Jake, he's worried about you because you haven't been home. I told him we've been working late and sometimes you crash here," I said.

"But then why all the questions?" Griff asked.

"Could it be that he was just curious? I mean, baby, your books are amazing. It's nice he felt comfortable enough to ask you those questions directly."

"As weird as that is, please don't add any details because I don't need to know. But it's nice that he asked," Jake said.

Griff finally smiled.

"Okay, so this is how it's going to be. We're going to all have a shower because I'm dying to get naked, and this one has been edging me all day." I pointed to Jake, who rolled his eyes. "Fine, he was just breathing. Same difference. Then we're going to pick a starter, entree, and dessert from this wonderful spread and have dinner. And after that, we're going around the neighborhood to offload some of this before it spoils. Got it?"

Griff bit his lip. "God, I love it when you go all bossy." He sidled up to me and pressed his lips against mine, then he kissed Jake.

"I'm so on board with that plan, it's not even real," Jake said.

"Great. Off you go then," I ordered.

I followed behind them, watching as they removed each other's clothes with each step they took toward the bathroom.

At this rate, we wouldn't make it that far.

16

JAKE

How do you know it's been too long since you've been home?

No one notices when you've arrived. Not even the dog.

I couldn't blame them. The last few weeks had been so busy at work that I'd gotten into a routine of going home with Mal so we could continue working after hours.

Most days, we'd do a couple of hours of work after dinner until we all collapsed together on the couch in a tangle of limbs watching a TV show before going to bed.

Some days we didn't even pretend to be interested in whatever was on TV and just went straight to the bedroom.

Sex with Griff and Mal was unlike anything I'd ever experienced before. We had amazing chemistry and somehow were able to read each other perfectly.

Despite my initial fears, I hadn't for one second felt like an extra or an addition to their relationship.

Maybe it was because Mal and I had our own dynamic from working together. We had our inner jokes, and I loved to tease him and work him up throughout the day. The payback was always so worth it.

I also had a great relationship with Griff. Maybe it was because we were the same age, but we just had an amazing connection, and I couldn't imagine not being around him. He was like the sun that shone brightly on everyone around him.

It had only been a few weeks, but walking through the door to the house I'd called home for most of my life now felt strange.

I put that thought aside. I knew I was already in way too deep with Griff and Mal. Entertaining the thought that our relationship could be permanent was as scary as the possibility that it wouldn't last.

My footsteps on the tiled floor must have given me away because before I could turn around the corner to the den where I'd heard voices coming from, I was attacked by Jessie.

I kneeled because, for all her excitement, she was an old girl, and as much as she'd be happy to jump at me, I knew it was easier if we were on the same level.

"Girl, we need to talk about your stinky breath," I said as she ran her slobbery tongue over my chin.

She barked.

"I don't care if you disagree with me. No dog's gonna want to kiss you with that breath."

"I don't know. She's pretty adorable."

My head snapped up to the sound of my best friend's voice.

"Zak. What the hell, man?" I gave Jessie a parting kiss on her head and stood up to pull him into a hug. "What are you…when did you get…how long are you staying?"

"Calm down, Oprah. Nice to see you too."

We walked to the den, where my uncle and Gabe sat watching a game.

"What did I tell you about letting strangers in?" I asked my family.

"Dude, he knew about the birthmark on your butt cheek. He can't be that much of a stranger," Gabe said, and my uncle snorted.

Jesus fuck.

"Speaking of strangers. When were you going to tell us you moved out, son?" my uncle asked.

Zak looked at me with a face I knew all too well. It was as if the questions were bubbling up under the surface, ready to come out.

"I haven't moved out," I protested.

"Could have fooled me," my uncle said.

Wait, was he upset?

Gabe got up and left toward the kitchen, and Zak followed him. I took that as their way to give me some time, so I went around the U-shaped sofa and sat next to my uncle.

"Hey, Uncle Frank, is everything okay? Does it bother you that I've been staying with Mal and Griff?"

He turned the game off and looked at me.

"A little…no, really, it doesn't bother me. I just miss you, that's all."

"You've seen me every day for the past three weeks."

"I've seen my nephew, the hardworking young man who's putting everything he has into the resort. But I haven't seen my son. He's the one I miss."

I finally understood. Because I hadn't been home, he'd missed all the things we used to do together that were just ours, like tending to my aunt's flowers in the garden, cooking together, talking about my mom.

"I'm sorry, Uncle Frank. I guess I got too focused on work and forgot about everything else. I can stay here more often. Mal and I won't have that much work all the time. The resourcing matrix is nearly complete."

He placed his hand on top of mine.

"Don't mind me, son. I'm only an old man with far too much time on my hands. You and Gabriel are young. You both need to be out there having fun."

"Uncle Frank, you're not old, and I promise I'm out there having fun. But I am also enjoying my job at the resort. It's making me think about what I always thought I wanted from my career."

"How so?"

I wasn't sure I was ready to have this conversation just yet, especially since I hadn't been doing my job long enough to talk about the future.

"We'll talk about it another time, but I want to ask you something."

Jessie, who'd followed Gabe and Zak to the kitchen, no doubt hoping for treats, came back and jumped on the sofa on the other side of my uncle. Laying her head on his lap.

He instinctively scratched her fur.

"Have you ever thought about dating?"

He let out a belly laugh.

"There's only one woman in my life now."

"As much as she may warm up your bed nicely, I'm talking about the two-legged kind of female, Uncle Frank. I know no one will ever replace Aunt Annie, but I think she'd like you to be happy."

"She made me promise I'd open up my heart to someone else after she was gone." His voice was so wistful, it almost broke my heart. "But you two boys were young, and I had a company to run. Maybe now it's a little late. Who'd want an old man set in his ways?"

"Just think about it," I said. "You might not want to tell Gabe, though, or he'll have a line of women at the door by the end of the week."

My uncle looked absolutely terrified.

"I should be a better guest and see my friend. I still can't believe he's here. Will it be okay if he stays with us?"

"Of course, son. He sounds like a good man. Are you two...?"

"Oh, no. We're just friends. There's nothing between us."

"*The Lady Doth Protest Too Much.*"

I laughed. "Zak and I are close, and I love him dearly, but what we were is in the past."

"Is that because there's someone in your present?"

"Time out," I said, getting up. "I'll see you at breakfast. If you want me to stay, there better be some of your special scrambled eggs on the menu."

"Got it," he said, waving his hand and turning the game back on.

When I got to the kitchen, Gabe and Zak were sitting on opposite sides of the island, each with a beer in hand.

I grabbed a beer from the fridge to join them, but Gabe got up. "I'll leave you alone to catch up. I have to study for my finals."

"When are you leaving for Berkeley?" I asked Gabe.

Even though I hadn't been home, we'd spoken on the phone and messaged each other. He was nervous about his finals.

"Next week."

"You'll do great. You know that, right?"

"Yeah…"

He didn't sound too sure of himself.

I walked over to him and wrapped my arms around him. He hugged back tight.

"Are you staying here this week?" he asked.

I hadn't planned on it, but Zak was here, so that had taken the decision out of my hands.

"Yeah, I am, little bro."

He nodded and left.

"So…" Zak started, but I held my hand up.

"Do we need to go somewhere else for this conversation?"

He raised his eyebrows.

"Oh…you want to rehash the old times?" he asked, drinking the rest of his beer and placing the bottle next to the sink.

"Hell no. Do I look like I need to rehash the old times?"

I was joking, but he looked me up and down and whistled.

"No, you most definitely don't. Are you working out? You look a lot—"

"Let's go to my room."

I left my half-drunk bottle next to Zak's and indicated for him to follow me.

On the way past the staircase, I saw Zak's suitcase and grabbed it, leaving it in the spare room next to mine before leading us to my room.

Zak sat on my bed, and I could swear I saw something pass through his eyes before he smiled wide. "So this is where all your wet dreams happen…nice."

He jumped a little on the mattress, impressed with the lack of noise. That had been one of the worst things about our old place. Both our beds creaked so much, the neighbors used to bang on the wall when we had sex until we started using far more creative and fun places in the apartment.

"What's that smile on your face?" he asked.

"Nothing. Just remembered the fun we had at the old apartment."

He laughed. "Should I be offended that with such amazing memories, there's no hint of even a semi under your slacks?"

"We did have a lot of fun, but strangely, it's easy for me to separate that time from now. We always knew our time together served a purpose, and it would end after graduation. I'm not going to say I love you like a brother because…ew…but I do love you. I just don't want to get naked with you."

"Speaking of getting naked. Damn, man, you never said how hot your cousin is. I mean, there's hot, and then there's *him*."

"You're not hooking up with Gabe."

Zak straightened up.

"Why not?"

"Because…because you're both as wild as each other, you're both hurting, and I'm afraid that if you use sex as a distraction, you'll both end up destroying each other."

He stared at me. Shock and hurt were written all over his face.

"Zak…I'm—"

"That's okay, I get it." He got up from the bed. "Are you sure it's okay for me to stay here? It's only for a few days. I have a thing in LA, and after that, I'll be out of your way."

"Of course you can stay. As long as you like."

I broke the distance between us with only a few steps. "Zak, wait. I'm sorry. Look, you know I've always been honest with you."

He nodded.

"This isn't some kind of big brother thing with Gabe. I can't stop you from hooking up. You're both adults. I just don't want either of you to hurt at the end."

His big brown eyes were sad as he shrugged. "He's probably not even gay, and if he is, he might not be interested. You said he goes to Berkeley, right? There's probably a load of hot, smart people for him out there."

What the hell?

"Who are you, and what did you do with my confident, overbearing best friend?"

"Still me," he mumbled. "Just brought down a few notches. About time, right?"

I shook my head. What had happened since I last saw him?

Guilt filled my conscience. I'd been so focused on work and enjoying this thing with Mal and Griff, I'd neglected my best friend.

He'd always been so self-sufficient. A go-getter. Nothing could bring him down.

Had that been a mask? And how had I missed it?

"Hey, Zak…"

"Yeah?"

He was almost by the spare bedroom door.

"You know what happens next week?"

He narrowed his eyes in deep thought before a smile worthy of the old Zak graced his face.

"We're having the party of all motherfucking parties?" He squealed.

"Whoa." I shook my head.

"Nope. This is just what we need. Leave it to me."

He went inside the room, closing the door behind him and leaving me full of apprehension.

I hadn't given any thought to my birthday. I guessed I should celebrate it since I was turning thirty, but Uncle Frank hadn't mentioned it, Gabe would probably be gone by then, and the thought of spending the night wrapped around my men was more appealing than a party.

My phone rang in my bedroom, so I ran back in to get it, pressing the green button as soon as I saw Griff's name on the screen.

"Hey."

"Hey, baby, are you staying at your house tonight?" Griff asked.

"Yeah, I'm sorry, my best friend is here."

There was a short silence.

"Is that the guy you…" Griff didn't finish, and I didn't like that his voice had changed.

"Yes. Griff, I meant what I said three weeks ago. I'm yours and Mal's. You have nothing to worry about, okay?"

"We trust you, Jake. We're just going to miss you like crazy, that's all."

Sigh. So was I. My bed looked so empty and big. Too big just for me.

I'd gotten used to waking up in the middle of both men or cuddling with one of them while reaching out for the other.

I closed the bedroom door and sat on the edge of the bed.

"It's going to feel weird sleeping on my own. Is that strange? I mean, we've only been together a few weeks," I said.

"It's okay to feel how you feel, baby. Maybe it's good for you to spend some days back at Frank's. Hang out with your friend."

"I'll still see Mal at work, but how about you?"

Did I sound too whiny? When did I become so desperate for someone's company?

"How about I meet you at the resort tomorrow for lunch? Just the two of us. I'll bring food from El Pancito."

"Damn, you know the way straight to my heart."

"I hope so, baby. I hope so."

"And that's why I need to exercise more. Griff is far too good at finding his way into people's hearts...and waistbands." Mal groaned

I laughed, knowing he wouldn't have it any other way.

"By the way...um...there's something I may have forgotten to mention," I said.

"What's that?"

"Um, next week...it's my birthday."

Griff gasped. "Why didn't you tell us? Are you turning thirty? Oh, baby, we need to celebrate big time, and when I say big time, I mean—"

"Griff?"

"Yeah, sorry, I got excited. What's up?"

"Zak, my friend, wants to throw me a party. I'm kinda scared about it, but...I think it'll also be fun."

"That's great. Let me know if he needs any help with the preparations."

He cleared his voice. "Will there be an...after party? You know...a more intimate affair for a couple of select guests? Maybe at an undisclosed location?"

The husky tone of his voice made my cock stand at attention. Mal was normally the one who could command my body with his deep voice, but fuck, Griff's voice was like a caress. A teasing feather running smoothly over my body.

"Fuck, Griff," I rasped, my voice thick with need.

"Are you hard?"

"What do you think?"

I heard a rustling sound and then a moan.

"What are you guys doing?" I asked.

"Griff is straddling me, and he has both our cocks in his hand. Will you take yourself out too, baby?"

My hand was already halfway to undoing the zipper before Mal finished speaking.

I wrapped my hand around my cock, imagining it was Griff's hand, stroking and twisting, running his blunt nail over my slit.

"Fuck, yeah," I said. "Is he doing that thing you like?"

Mal's groan told me I was right on the money. He loved it when we pulled his balls at while stroking the head of his cock.

I balanced the phone on my shoulder, which freed my hand. I ran my fingers over my belly, closing my eyes and imagining I was looking into Mal's eyes.

I pulled on my nipple, forgetting that my door was unlocked and it wouldn't take much for Zak to catch on to what I was doing.

For moments, the only noises were the ones coming from the phone. Moans, breaths that caught as the pleasure built up. I was so close to the edge.

"Are you going to come for us, Jake? Just imagine Griff stroking you as you let yourself go and spill into my mouth."

His words were enough to send me over. My phone fell from my shoulder onto the bed as my orgasm tore through me, leaving me spent, sated, relaxed, and floating on air.

When I recovered some of my energy, I grabbed the phone and held it to my ear.

There was nothing but heavy breathing on the other side.

"That was hot as fuck," I said. "I'll spend a few more nights away from you just so we can do this again."

They both laughed.

"Next time we get to edge you with toys," Mal said.

I closed my eyes at the thought. My door would definitely need to be locked next time.

"I'm going to grab a shower and sleep. See you tomorrow?" I said.

"Looking forward to it," Mal said, and Griff followed with a, "Can't wait."

I showered quickly, suddenly feeling as though I'd sleep like a stone.

When I grabbed my phone to set my alarm, there was a message from Zak.

Zak: Fucker. I still know your sounds, and your uncle's walls are paper-thin. Next time invite me in or do it somewhere else.

I laughed.

Jake: Your parents didn't teach you eavesdropping is not polite?
    Zak: You mean the king and queen of zero boundaries?
    Jake: We need to talk, don't we?
    Zak: Yeah…tomorrow. I'm beat. Night, dude.
    Jake: Night.

Zak hadn't said much about the reason for his visit, and something told me there was more to it than just whatever he had to do in LA.

Whatever was going on with my best friend, I'd be there for him.

I also needed to remember that while my uncle and Gabe didn't know about my relationship with Mal and Griff, Zak knew.

He wouldn't knowingly out us, but he knew I was close with my family and probably assumed this wasn't a secret.

I put a clean pair of underwear on and got under the sheets.

Weaving a web of lies didn't sit well with me, especially when it came to my family, but I also wasn't sure I was prepared to be open.

Sometime later, there were still no solutions, but sleep eventually took over.

I could worry another day.

17

GRIFF

WALKING through the resort was a strange experience. We'd lived on-site in the last one, so everyone knew me. Now, I'd been stopped by staff several times and had to explain my presence.

It was reassuring that everyone was mindful of security, but more than a few staff members had raised a brow when I'd explained I was Mal's husband, but I was here to see Jake.

There was nothing wrong with meeting a friend for lunch, so I ignored them and went looking for the man who'd made himself a nice cozy place inside my heart, right alongside Mal.

Jake was talking to a girl at the reception desk and didn't see me as I walked in, so I stopped to take him in before I gave my presence away.

He wore the navy slacks I always thought brought out his amazing ass, paired with a white button-down, with the sleeves rolled up his forearms.

More than once, I saw the girl's eyes scan over Jake's arms and chest.

I know, honey. He's gorgeous.

But it wasn't just his looks that made me feel hot all over or made my heart rate increase a little when I saw him.

Jake had a quiet but confident presence. His body language as he spoke to his colleague was open, calm, and also totally unaware that she was hitting on him.

Nice try, honey. He's taken.

"Ogling my staff is not permitted on the premises."

Mal's voice from behind me made me jump a little but also gave me a shiver up my spine.

"Oh really? I guess I'll have to remove your staff from the premises," I said, turning around to face my husband.

His hair was a little disheveled, as if he'd been running his hands through it a lot.

"Is everything okay?" I asked.

"Yeah, just some teething problems with the construction work company."

The dark circles under his eyes told me otherwise, but I knew him well. If he wanted to talk about anything, he'd do it when he was ready.

"There's a gorgeous guy coming this way. About your height, light-brown hair, or dark blond, depending on the lighting, bright blue eyes, and I bet he's packing a nice one too. Play your cards right, and you might get lucky," he said before he walked away.

"Tease," I said back, smiling as his shoulders moved with his laughter.

"What's he teasing you about?" Jake asked, coming up to me.

"Apparently, you're a sure thing if I play my cards right."

He tilted his head and smiled. His eyes, light blue like the ocean on a summer's day, shone brightly.

"Come on, follow me," he said.

We walked in silence through the reception area of the building toward a landscaped garden. I wanted to hold his hand so bad. I held the strap of my backpack with one hand and put the other hand in my pocket.

"Where are we going?" I asked.

"My favorite place…well, second favorite place."

"What's your favorite place?"

"Your house."

"You mean our house."

I looked at Jake to see his reaction to my words. He blushed and met my eyes briefly.

"I like that…I like that a lot," he said.

"I'm serious, Jake. Any place that is mine and Mal's is also yours."

He didn't say anything, so I matched his pace out of the garden onto a graveled path. We had the beach on our right and a grassy area to the left.

The main building of the resort was behind us, and all I saw were smaller buildings, which I guessed served as storage areas or for laundry.

I remembered Mal mentioning once that the laundry house was always away from the main resort because of the constant noise of the washers and dryers.

We walked past only one other member of staff going toward the main building. Otherwise, the area was deserted.

The graveled path gave way to a wooden deck.

"Uncle Frank made this deck for the staff to hang out during break times, but most people stay in the dining area because it's closer to the resort," Jake said. "That's why there are no chairs or tables here at the moment."

"They have more time to enjoy their break, but they don't get to enjoy the view."

"Yeah. The part-timers have shorter breaks because they work fewer hours and the full-timers spend too much time on their feet to do the walk."

We sat at the edge of the deck with our feet on the grass, and Jake took his shoes off immediately. It looked like something he did without even thinking. I did the same.

The grass was soft, the ocean was calm, and there wasn't even a small breeze in the air. It was a perfect day. And I had the perfect company for an alfresco lunch.

"Elena baked these rolls especially for us. They're filled with prosciutto, pesto, and parmesan," I said, opening my backpack and taking out the box I'd borrowed from Elena so the rolls wouldn't get squashed in the bag.

"Wow, sounds delicious. I love her bread," Jake said.

I took out two sodas and closed the bag again so sand wouldn't get inside.

"So, why is this your second favorite place?" I asked.

"Because it's peaceful. I like watching the small waves kissing the shore, the seagulls having conversations about whose lunch they're going to steal. But mostly, it's because here I feel like I'm at home, right between the sea and the resort."

I stared at him in awe. The way he'd put it made so much sense. I'd always felt Jake had a very special connection to the island, but I never thought it ran so deep.

A dark thought filled my mind. I wanted to banish it, but it refused to leave me.

One day when Mal's time at the resort came to a natural end, we'd move somewhere else. That was the way. Our life. What we'd chosen.

But what about Jake? Would he come with us if we had to move? Could we make him follow us? Could we live with ourselves if we had to make him choose between his home and his roots? His heart?

"Hey, what's on your mind? You look like you went somewhere unpleasant."

There was no point in thinking about what could happen in the distant future.

"No, just a passing thing. Nothing major. How's your roll?"

"Absolute perfection, and just what I needed after the morning I've had."

"Is it very busy?"

"Busy is an understatement, but I don't want to talk about work. I want to listen to my boyfriend while I check him out and imagine he's saying every word naked."

I laughed and leaned a little toward him. "I won't argue against that. Is this place safe?"

He looked behind us even though I hadn't seen anyone.

"Sadly, no. Anyone can walk past anytime."

I couldn't touch him physically, but there was another way.

"Close your eyes," I said.

"What?"

"Just do it. Lean back on your hands and close your eyes. I'm not going to touch you, so anyone walking by will just think we're talking."

"Okay."

I liked that even his short agreement was laced with so much need.

"Tonight, when you're in your bedroom, I want you to think of this moment. Think of the warmth of the sun on your face and imagine that it's my hand caressing you. The pads of my fingers tracing your lips. You lick them, hoping to feel me, but I've moved on. My fingers are now running a line down your chest. My nails scratching your beautifully smooth skin."

Jake had closed his eyes, and his mouth was slightly parted. His breathing came in short bursts, and the erection in his slacks was unmistakable.

"You like it when I run my nail over your nipples, don't you?"

"Yes…" he rasped.

"I do it and then smooth the pain away with my thumb. My hand travels down, opening your shirt one button at a time until I reach your slacks. What do you want me to do, Jake?"

"Take me out, please take me out."

I loved the desperation in his voice. He moved his hips to grind against an invisible hand.

"You want it so much, Jake. I want you so much. Listen to the sound of the ocean. Each wave breaking against the shore is like my hand stroking you. Slowly but firmly, and every so often, the water recedes only to break out again with more force. It builds with you. My hand moves faster, and you can feel it building inside you—"

"Griff…I'm so close. Fuck, I could come right now."

"Look at me, baby."

The intensity of his gaze took my breath away. If we weren't in danger of being seen by anyone, I'd have impaled myself on his cock, prep be damned.

"Griff, fuck. What are you doing to me?"

I dared to caress his cheek just for a moment before I took it back.

"Take a breath. Remember this later. The wait will be worth it."

He groaned. "God, we have to talk about something…anything else, or it'll be an embarrassing walk back."

I laughed. "Anything you like."

I opened the backpack and brought out a box with a chopped mango I got in the market first thing this morning.

"How did you become a writer? Was it something you always wanted to do?"

"I guess talking about my grandmother *is* a boner killer," I chuckled.

Jake bit his lips as if to stop himself from laughing and gestured for me to continue.

"Okay…let me see if I can give you the short version. I always loved reading, and as a kid, I used to make up stories a lot. My grandmother made me write them down because she was afraid that if I kept saying them aloud, I'd get in trouble."

"Why's that?"

"Let's say that making up a story about the next-door neighbor and the mailman going on an adventure in a hidden room inside her house would cause all kinds of trouble with her husband."

Jake snorted.

"So anyway, by the time she was sick with cancer, I was already living with her. My mom had died a few years before, so it was just us. I started by reading her the books she liked, but she got bored with them and told me to write her a real romance. One where she could imagine someone like me having a happy ever after. So I did. I wrote three full novels before she died."

"Did you publish them?"

"Not initially. I was too upset to publish them at first, but the practice of writing made it easier to write my first published romance. After I met Mal, I finally published the three books. They're my *Because I Love You* series."

Jake turned to me. "That's the first series you wrote with poly characters."

"Yeah."

"And you wrote that for your grandmother?"

I smiled. "I added the sexy parts after if that's what you're wondering. But yeah, even though she didn't believe that a happy relationship between three or more people was possible, she didn't want me to stop believing in it myself."

"She sounds like an amazing woman."

"She was."

Jake gazed back at the ocean and was quiet for a moment.

"I'm scared."

I took his hand, not caring in the least if anyone walked and saw us. If there was one thing I couldn't stand, it was watching one of my men hurt.

"What scares you?"

"That this thing between us won't last because I'm already in way too deep. That it could last, but that the world isn't ready for us. That we might have to hide, or worse, that we won't be able to hide."

"Hey, hey, take a deep breath, baby."

I heard a rustling noise, so I let go of his hand, thinking someone was walking nearby, but when I looked around, I saw it wasn't a person.

"Look, baby. We have a curious visitor."

I hadn't come across many of the island bunnies because they lived mostly on the side of the resort and into the grassy area beyond, so it always amazed me when I saw them come so close.

"Oh, that's Jake."

"Huh?"

"I didn't name him," Jake grumbled.

The bunny stared at me. "I can see the resemblance. It's the big blue eyes."

He sniffed the air in my direction. "Oh, you think I have snacks? You might be lucky, buddy."

I grabbed the small box of pellets from my bag and put a few in front of the bunny.

"You have pellets?" Jake asked.

"Yeah, Mal told me we might see bunnies today. I was hoping we would."

Bunny-Jake sniffed the pellets and ate one, but then he kept looking around as if he were waiting.

"This is a minor miracle," Jake said. "Look over there to the taller grass patch."

Two sets of bunny ears popped up from between the green grass.

"Are they your friends, Jake?" I asked the bunny. "Here. Take some pellets for them."

As if he understood what I meant, he put a few pellets in his mouth and hopped away from us. The two bunnies came out from behind the grass to meet him halfway.

Jake gasped.

"What?"

"They've never done that."

"What do you mean?"

"I've known them for a couple of years, and I've never seen the three of them properly together. They're so beautiful, aren't they?"

They were. One of the bunnies was a little bigger than Jake, and the third one was the same size. It was as if the big one looked over the other two, but clearly, Jake was the social one.

"Look at them, Jake. They're like you, me, and Mal. See how happy they look together?"

Jake's eyes were wide as they met mine.

"The bunnies..." he said. "They stick together. They've been looking after each other all this time."

I nodded. There was nothing else I could add. Jake got it.

It wouldn't be easy to live on a small island like this as a throuple, especially with both Jake and Mal working in the largest business on the island.

Sticking together and protecting each other might not be enough, but the starting point was acknowledging that there was an us. That we were real and valid. Then we'd deal with the next step.

"I think I'm in love with you, Griff."

I gasped. Surely he didn't...I didn't... "What?"

His honest blue eyes reflected all that love back to me. No way I misunderstood.

"I love you, Griff. Mal too. I think I probably have for a long time, but I was afraid. Afraid my feelings were confused, afraid I could never be part of what you two have—"

"I love you too, Jake. And I can guarantee Mal feels the same way. Although you should probably tell him yourself."

He smiled. "I will."

"God, I want to kiss you so much right now," I said.

Jake's eyes darkened, and he looked behind us for a hot second before he put his hand on the back of my neck and slammed his mouth onto mine.

It was dirty and quick, but the kiss left me wanting more—as if I'd ever not want more of Jake—and tasted a lot like revenge for earlier.

"You fucker," I said, palming my erection and willing it to go down. "You better wipe that grin off your face before I jump you, and then no hell or heaven will get me off you before we both get off."

He laughed and stood up.

"Where are you going?"

"Work. Believe it or not, sleeping with the boss doesn't make my breaks magically longer, and I'm already late."

I put our leftovers in a bag and closed the backpack before standing up.

"You're late?"

"A little, but it's okay."

We started our walk back, side by side, just like before, but now it was different. Jake was different, and I was different. He loved me, and he loved Mal.

I looked at the line where the ocean met the sky and smiled. If my grandmother was watching, she'd be so happy to be wrong. That I knew for sure.

Mal was talking to someone outside the building as we approached. He looked tense.

Jake must have also noticed because he picked up his pace.

"What happened?" Jake asked.

"The contractors pulled out," Mal said.

"What? Why? They've done work for us before, and there's never been an issue."

"Well, it seems that there is an issue now, but they won't tell me what it is. It doesn't matter anyway because knowing what their problem is doesn't fix ours. Now we have to find a new contractor, which will delay the start of the work by weeks. The knock-on effect could be disastrous for us."

I looked at both my men, feeling helpless. At least I could show my affection openly to one of them.

Mal didn't stop me when I put my hand on his cheek to get him to look at me.

"Listen to me, baby. You can do this. Both of you. You go out there and find a contractor, and if you don't, I'm sure there's an entire island full of people out there with some of the skills you need to make this happen. This resort isn't just a job. It's their home. People will come through to support you. You just need someone to do the heavy lifting."

He smiled at me. "Fuck, I love you so much, Griff."

From the corner of my eye, I saw Jake stare at Mal with a shy smile. I couldn't wait for the day we could all be together again in a less public space. Hopefully, it wouldn't be long.

"I better leave you to work. My procrastination knows no bounds, so another five minutes here, and I'll be volunteering for laundry services just so I don't have to work on my edits."

"I heard that. Run while you can."

I turned around to face a petite woman with long blond hair tied in a ponytail.

"Hailey, this is my husband, Griff. Baby, this is Hailey, one of my managers. And she's right, you better run, or she'll take your offer, and I won't stop her."

Hailey gave me a hug and whispered, "I wouldn't put you in the laundry room, but I do have a bunch of filing up in the office. There's an amazing view from up there."

I placed a small kiss on Mal's lips, regretting I couldn't do the same to Jake, and turned to leave.

"That is my cue to escape. Between filing and editing, I'll take editing. At least there are naked men in my paperwork."

Hailey laughed as Mal and Jake groaned.

"Jake, call me later. I want to hear about your birthday party."

I saw the murderous look he gave me just before Hailey squealed something about mocktails and nineties' music.

18

MAL

I ADMIRED Griff's perky ass for a second before turning back to an overworked and overexcited Hailey.

"How are you feeling? Do you need to take the afternoon off?" I asked.

She rolled her eyes at me and looked around to make sure we weren't overheard.

"You know this child has another six months inside me before they come out. Stop acting like if I sneeze, you'll end up with a litter of babies in your lobby."

Jake snorted.

We'd only found out this morning that Hailey was pregnant, and it seemed I'd turned out to be a papa bear when it came to her.

I put one arm around her. "I'm so happy for you, Hailey. You're gonna be a great mom. Anything you need, just let me know, okay?"

She pulled away and made a face. "You might want to change your cologne." And then she made a run toward the restroom.

"What's wrong with my cologne?"

Jake came a little closer and sniffed the air around us. His eyes darkened. "I have absolutely no issues with how you smell. Maybe you should stick to me and leave Hailey alone."

"I can be on board with that idea. Come on, let's see if we can fix this contractor mess."

The resort was so much calmer than usual. Most of our customers were happy to move their booking to another date, or another resort. As a whole, the business hadn't lost out, but I was worried that if we didn't find a contractor that was ready to move in, we could be in trouble.

Both Alana and Pete were huddling over a computer in the office, and Brian was at his desk.

"Hey, the storage containers have arrived. I'm assembling a team to start stripping the rooms," he said as we walked past.

"That's great, thanks. At least some things are moving on schedule," I said.

Jake turned to Brian. "Have you filled in your matrix yet?"

"I thought the matrix was complete," I said.

Brian turned on his chair and crossed one leg over the other. "I've been thinking about it, and I changed my mind, so I cleared my information from the matrix."

"Okay," I said. "So long as your final option is there before the deadline, that's not a problem. We want everyone to have the chance to reflect and make the best decision for themselves, considering the unexpected and unprecedented situation we're finding ourselves in."

He nodded and turned back to his work. Jake followed me to the conference room in silence. He didn't need to talk for me to know deep down he was seething, and he had all reason to be.

Like the professional he was, Jake waited until I'd closed the door before letting out a groan.

"I'm sorry...sorry, I don't...he just frustrates me."

"Hey, that's okay. You don't need to put on a front with me. I know how it feels. I've dealt with many Brians before."

"If I knew what his problem was, I could talk to him, but other than him being a regular jackass, I'm drawing a blank."

I chuckled. "Come on, forget about him. Tell me about your lunch date."

Jake smiled, and a little bit of color appeared on his cheeks.

"That good, huh?"

"Yeah, it was nice. Griff is…fun."

"That he is."

He didn't seem to want to share more, so I opened the database where we had information on all the contractors that had been approved to work for the resort already.

It was an extensive list. The majority of them were on the mainland, which explained the preference for the contractors we went for because they were based on the island.

They'd been recommended by Frank, who apparently had a personal relationship with the owner.

I'd still done my own checks before hiring them, cross-referencing when they'd last worked for us with the quality of the work and how it stood the test of time.

There had been no reason for concerns, so it was a real disappointment that they pulled out.

"Jake, who owns Melville?"

"The contracting company? John Melville, why?"

"Frank told me they go back a long way, and since my checks came through without concerns, I don't understand why they'd pull out, especially without giving a reason when they have a personal relationship with us. This is an expensive contract, so I can't imagine it would hurt their bottom line."

"I know. John and Uncle Frank were partners a long time ago. When John's first wife was sick, he sold his share of the resort to Uncle Frank, who apparently paid him above the market rate to help them out. After she recovered, Uncle Frank asked if he wanted back in the business, but he decided to start up a contracting company with his three brothers. Running a smaller company between four people gave him extra time with his wife. He's a nice man, very much like Uncle Frank."

"I can't help feeling like there's more to this, and we're missing something. Maybe I should speak to Frank about it."

"Sure, but in the meantime, we should probably start making some calls," Jake said.

I smiled, admiring his focus, especially after coming back from a lunch with Griff. I knew all too well the power of the Griff effect. I just hoped whatever they'd gotten up to, they hadn't been seen.

Strangely enough, I didn't feel an ounce of jealousy. Sure, I wanted to have been there with them, but it was good for us to spend time with each other individually, and since Jake didn't live with us, that was even more important.

Maybe I should take him out on a date too.

"And then I sucked him like a hoover until he came so hard the bunnies got scared and ran away…"

"Huh?" What was he talking about?

He laughed. "I've been talking to you, but you were all spaced out."

"Please tell me you didn't actually do what you just said."

"What if we did?" He moved his eyebrows up and down in a suggestive manner.

Fuck, the need to touch Jake was overwhelming. I loved it when he teased me, but knowing he wasn't coming home with me left me feeling frustrated. When the three of us were together, we were explosive, but I also loved the times we spent together cuddling on the sofa or talking over dinner.

"I'm contemplating if there's enough budget to build some fucking walls in this office," I said.

Jake winked as if he knew exactly what I'd do to him if we had the chance and a safe space.

Hours and dozens of phone calls later, and we still hadn't found a contractor able to step in to do the job. A couple said they could rearrange things with their current clients for a price.

I wasn't willing to be the reason someone else's work got delayed, and I definitely couldn't stretch the budget.

"What if we ask Uncle Frank to talk to John?" Jake asked. His hair was all messy, and his eyes looked tired.

I looked toward the office, and there was no one out there, so I rolled my chair over to him.

"Come here." I took his hand, and he didn't argue when I pulled him to my lap but did look around to make sure there was no one around.

"How may I be of assistance, boss?" he asked. He sounded light-hearted but tense, and I couldn't put my finger on the reason.

Was it the situation with the contractor? Or was it something else?

He hadn't said much about his lunch with Griff, but they were both smiling and looking relaxed on their way back.

"You can kiss me," I said, straightening his hair.

"Oh, really? And I won't get in trouble with the boss?"

"You certainly won't get in trouble with this boss."

As soon as our lips touched, Jake melted into me. His little sighs mixed with my own breath as we kissed over and over again.

My dick hardened, and I knew Jake could feel it because he pulled away from the kiss and leaned his forehead against mine with a groan.

"Could we maybe go out on a date sometime?" he asked.

"Of course. I was thinking about it earlier. I'd love to spend time with you outside of work."

His smile lit up the office. Had he been working himself up to asking me out?

I wanted to laugh at the thought because, in so many ways, Jake was quite forward and open, and after his initial concerns about being an extra part in my relationship with Griff, he'd fit in perfectly with us.

"Come on, let's shut down and go home."

He stood up and then froze, looking toward the office.

"What's up?"

"Nothing. I thought I saw something out there, but maybe I imagined it."

I hated the hiding and especially hated all the time I'd recently spent with Frank while hiding my relationship with Jake.

But I wasn't sure I was ready to tell the world I was with two men.

Was it selfish to want to keep this to ourselves for a little longer? It probably was. It's not like Griff or I had any family left to care or have an opinion. But Jake did, and they were important to him.

"I'm sorry, baby, that was my fault. I shouldn't have done that. It was inappropriate to do it here in the office," I said.

Jake smiled. "No, you should totally have done it. I needed it. But yes, we need to be careful. The moment we become careless is when we'll be found out."

I nodded. He was saying all the right things, but fuck if I didn't hate that this was the situation.

We walked together to the staff parking lot, where our cars were next to each other. I opened the door to my car and leaned over the roof.

"We miss you. You know that, right?"

"I know. I miss you too. Zak has shit timing. I might have to kill him."

I smiled and waved goodbye.

It was too quiet when I got home, so I put my bag down in the hallway and went searching for Griff.

I found him asleep, hunched over his laptop in the office. He'd likely been working all afternoon.

"Hey, sleepyhead," I said, running my hand down his back gently.

He woke up, taking a deep breath and then opening his eyes, smiling when he saw me.

"What time is it?"

"Just after seven, baby. Want to join me in the shower? I'll cook you dinner after."

He smiled and gave me a quick kiss. "That would be great. I started a new book today."

"Really? That's amazing, but I thought you were still editing the last one, and you always say you can't handle two things at the same time."

He snorted. "Books, baby. I can't handle two books at the same time. There are plenty of things I can handle in pairs."

I picked him up, so his ass was on the edge of the sink, and he wrapped his legs around me.

I pulled his shirt off and kissed his collarbone, inhaling the scent of his soft skin. Coconut, holidays, and Griff. He was delicious.

"Can we…just have a shower?" he asked.

"Of course. Is everything okay?"

"Yeah, I just want to wait. Maybe Jake will call later."

I helped him out of the rest of his clothes. Last night we'd ended up making each other come while Jake was on the phone. It was as perfect as it could have been without him here.

Thinking about what we could do later made me impossibly hard.

"I like your thinking. Maybe I'll let you ride me while you tell him exactly how it feels to have me buried all the way inside your gorgeous ass."

He took my hand and guided it to his cock. We wouldn't do anything, but I couldn't help closing my hand around it and giving it a few tugs before I let him go.

We made the shower quick to avoid getting carried away, and then I made us a pasta dish for dinner while Griff did his usual backing up of all his work before he turned his laptop off for the day.

We were on the couch watching one of Griff's soap operas when we heard a key in the door.

Griff jumped up off the couch and ran out of the living room. I turned the TV off and followed him.

By the time I got to the door, Griff had his legs wrapped around Jake, who had him leaning against the wall. The photo frames around them were in danger of falling down as they consumed each other as if they hadn't seen one another for months.

I approached and pressed against Jake's back, sucking on the skin on the back of his neck.

A hand tugged on my hair, pulling me closer, and I had to assume it was Griff's because Jake's were firmly on Griff's ass, holding him up.

"Bedroom," Griff rasped.

Jake put Griff down and turned around to kiss me.

"I had to come. Sorry."

"Hey, what are you apologizing for?" I cradled his face with my hands, feeling the rough scruff of his unshaven beard.

"I don't know. It's embarrassing to be this needy, right?"

Griff met my eyes and took Jake's hand, leading us to the bedroom. When they were both on the bed naked, I took off my clothes and covered Jake's body with mine.

"Don't ever feel bad or embarrassed about needing anything, and definitely not about needing us. In case you can't feel it, I'm pretty needy right now, and look at Griff. What do you see in his eyes?"

"He wants it too," Jake said.

"No, baby. He *needs* it."

Jake gazed into Griff's eyes, and I could swear there was some kind of exchange between them, but I couldn't tell what it was.

"I came here because…I wanted…" He looked between Griff and me. "I was hoping you…ugh…can I have you both at the same time?"

Griff let out a breath at Jake's words. "Are you sure?" he asked.

Jake nodded.

"Baby…"

"Please, Mal, please."

The desperate tone of his voice had me concerned. "But—"

"I just want to feel you both. Zak is going to stay at least until after my birthday. If all I can have with you both are a few stolen moments, then I want to make them count. I want you to make sure I can feel you both for days, so I don't forget how amazing we are together."

I pressed my lips against Jake's in a bruising kiss that would probably leave us both with a rash, but I didn't care.

Griff leaned over to grab supplies, leaving me to explore Jake. We needed him relaxed enough to take us both.

I remembered how sensitive Jake's nipples were and went in for the kill, flattening my tongue against them.

"Fuck, fuck…arghh…"

Griff took Jake's mouth, drinking in every single moan that I drew out of him.

I kissed and sucked on his skin, making my way down to his cock. He was leaking a trail of precum that I was eager to taste.

"Mmhmm, you're delicious, Jake," I said, releasing his cock.

Griff was conveniently close, so without warning, I sucked his crown, almost gagging when he involuntarily raised his hips to meet my mouth.

"Fuck, Mal. Warn a guy."

"Where would the fun in that be, baby?"

They both laughed.

When I was satisfied that they were both ready for more, I crawled up to meet their mouths. I had each of my legs between them, which left my cock rubbing against the outside of their thighs.

The friction caused by all of us grinding against each other was wonderfully painful.

"How do you want us, Jake?" I asked.

"Can I ride you and have Griff from behind?"

Griff nodded and got up straight away. I grabbed a few pillows and placed them on the head of the bed, so I had something to lean against.

Jake straddled me. His eyes were an ocean of emotions. A swirling dark blue, so full of desire.

"We're going to make this so good for you, Jake."

"I know."

He leaned to kiss me, and I saw Griff's hungry eyes as he stared at Jake's ass.

Maybe he decided that he was already wound too tight to rim Jake because he took the bottle of lube, and the next thing I knew, Jake was moaning into my mouth.

Jake's cock rubbed against mine as he pushed back to take more of Griff's fingers.

"Griff, please…" Jake groaned. "More."

I wasn't sure this was going to work because between Jake writhing against me, his moans, and what my imagination could conjure about what was about to happen, I was as close to blowing as a teenager looking at their first porn magazine.

As if he could read my mind, Griff asked Jake to lift a little so he could roll a condom down my length.

I stared into Jake's eyes as he lowered himself down on my dick. His arms were around my neck, so Griff held my dick in place until I was all the way inside Jake.

He let out a little breath and closed his eyes. Griff was right behind him, so Jake leaned back, resting his head on Griff's shoulder.

Looking at how beautiful they were was the only thing taking my mind away from how warm and tight Jake felt. How would it be when Griff joined me?

When Jake opened his eyes, it was as if I was staring at a different version of him. The version of Jake I'd been attracted to when I first saw him. The version of him that I got to feel *that* morning at the resort.

With one hand on my chest and the other holding Griff's arm in place around his chest, Jake started moving.

For the longest time, there was nothing but Jake riding me. Soft moans, skin sliding against skin. His cock was so hard I was surprised he hadn't come already.

Griff had his eyes closed. From the look on his face and the movement of his shoulder, he was using his hand to get himself ready for Jake.

I reached out to him. "Griff, come here, baby."

19

JAKE

My body was a swirl of conflicting emotions. I wanted to chase the orgasm, and I wanted to feel both of them inside me, but I was also nervous about it, and not just because I was afraid it would be too painful and that I'd need to stop.

There was this visceral need to claim them. Yes, I was the one being fucked, but this was my way of telling my body and my mind that there would never be anyone else but these two men.

There was no need to tell my heart because that ship had sailed a long time ago. My heart knew who it wanted, whether my brain liked it or not. And since my body was on board with my heart, all it was left was for my brain to get with the program.

Griff placed a kiss on my neck and stood up on the bed, moving around and placing his cock level with Mal's head.

"Fuck, that's so sexy." I groaned, watching Griff's cock disappear into Mal's hungry mouth.

I ran my hands up Griff's legs, massaging each butt cheek, sought out his crease, and found his hole. My intention wasn't to go in but just to tease him.

Mal was close, I could tell. And I knew as soon as Griff was also inside me, I wouldn't last, so I needed Griff to be right there with us.

When I added a little pressure with my finger, Griff cursed and pushed further into Mal's mouth.

"Jake," he begged.

"I need you now, Griff," I said.

Mal released Griff's cock, and he went back around, kneeling behind me. I heard the foil tearing, and my nerves shot up.

Mal must have sensed it because he placed his hands on my face and pulled me down for a kiss.

I let myself get lost in it until I felt pressure against my hole.

"It's okay, baby. He's starting with some lubed fingers to make sure you're okay."

I nodded, unable to say a word.

My ass was on fire, but every time I moved even a little, Mal's cock put pressure against my prostate, and my body lit up, needing more.

"Griff...I'm ready." I looked behind me, our eyes meeting and sharing the declarations we'd said earlier.

He kissed me and then pushed me gently so I was chest to chest with Mal.

The pain was undeniable as Griff's cock fought its way in. I relaxed and focused on Mal's eyes. That deep, rich, dark blue that often said more than his words conveyed.

Did he know how much his eyes gave him away?

"Mal...I...fuck...god...so good. So, so good." I gasped for air as Griff bottomed out inside me.

"So perfect, Jake," Griff said. "You look so perfect. You feel so perfect. I'm going to let you adjust before I move, okay?"

"No, do it, Griff. Please."

My cock had gone soft but was hardening back up under Mal's touch. I felt so deliciously full, and it was as if every inch of my being was touched by these two men.

I felt Griff's breaths on my back, and his hands gripped my sides so hard I knew I'd have bruises tomorrow.

He was already moving in and out of me, but Mal had remained still. His face was full of focus, but then something snapped, and he pulled out a little before pushing back in.

I stopped being able to tell which one was moving as I became a giant ball of need, ready to burst, to be taken to a new existential plane where I could float.

Groans, mingled breaths, sweat, skin slapping against skin. Even without the visual, I knew we were beautiful. We were perfect together.

My orgasm hit me before I could even tell it was coming. Rope after rope of cum spilled onto Mal's chest.

My eyesight went dark for a moment, and then there was nothing but stars and happiness. I heard both of them come in turn, but I couldn't feel anything else other than lightness.

I winced when Griff pulled out slowly, and I felt empty when Mal's cock slid out, but I couldn't move.

Griff took care of the condoms. That much I could tell from the rustling of the bedsheets behind me.

I was still straddling Mal. My head resting on my arms over his chest.

His heart was beating so fast, and his breathing was still erratic.

His hands on my damp hair were like heaven, and then Griff joined us, adding his hand to Mal's on my head, soothing me and making me feel all the feelings I'd never thought were possible.

All of my life, I'd been an extra. Sure, I'd been picked up, looked after, and loved, but never before had I felt so much like I belonged.

Belonging was more than love. Belonging meant you had a place, you were important, worthy. And now I belonged. I belonged in the arms of these two wonderful men that had been ready to open their bubble up to include me.

I didn't realize I was crying until Mal wrapped his arms around me, and I opened my eyes to meet Griff's as he wiped the tears off my face.

"I love...I love you so much," I said. My voice was strained, but I needed them to know. "Mal, I love you. I...I'm sorry if this is too much, too heavy, too...I don't know...just too..."

"Shh..." he said, rubbing his arms up and down my back.

Griff looked like he was on the verge of crying too. Something in his eyes told me he knew exactly how I felt, how important this moment was. I held his hand and kissed it.

Then I looked up at Mal. His face was full of wonder and confusion.

I'd had the words back from Griff already, but Mal hadn't said anything yet.

Then again, we were just coming down from the orgasm of a lifetime, and I sprung a love declaration on him, tears and all.

We stayed in silence for a long time. It was comfortable…until it wasn't.

At some point, Mal stopped his caress on my back, and when I looked at him, his head was turned away, and he looked like he was a thousand miles away.

I stood up. "I…um, I should go back home."

"Jake…" Griff said, reaching out to me.

"I'll just clean up in the bathroom, and then I'll go."

It took me a minute to locate all the clothes we'd discarded on the floor earlier, and then I closed myself in the bathroom.

I peed and then cleaned as much of the dried cum as I could before I put my clothes back on.

My butt hurt, my leg muscles were sore from holding the position while riding Mal, and my dick was dead to the world.

I looked in the mirror. I was the same person as before…wasn't I?

Who was I before I met Mal and Griff? It felt like such a long time ago.

Maybe I really should make the best of having Zak around. Talk shit about the old times. Talk about the present and what I've been missing, and also about the future.

There was a small knock on the door.

"It's open."

"Hey, are you okay?" Griff asked.

"Yeah, a little sore."

"That's not what I meant." He came closer, looking straight into my eyes and searching for the answers even I didn't have yet.

I sighed. "It's okay. I know he's struggled with us, with adding me to your relationship."

"Jake, you're not an extra. This is a brand-new relationship for us all. We have to remember that. He cares about you. You know that, right?"

"Yeah, I do."

And it was true. I knew how Mal felt. Even if he hadn't said it in words, he'd definitely said it with his actions. The way he respected me at work, respected my limited experience and my ideas, and the way he looked at me as if he still couldn't understand why he couldn't take his eyes off me or stop wanting to touch me.

That wonder I'd seen in his eyes after I told him I loved him. That was love.

I kissed Griff and left the bathroom. Mal wasn't in bed anymore, but I found him sitting on the couch in the living room.

When he saw me, he stood up and came to me, claiming my mouth with a kiss that was everything I needed at that moment.

"Hey, I'm not upset, okay?" I said when he finally released me.

He stared at me much in the same way Griff had in the bathroom.

"I promise." I smiled. "And let's face it. It's not like you're gonna want to live without this fine ass, anyway."

His shoulders relaxed, and he wrapped his arms around me, kissing my neck.

"You're an amazing man, Jake," he said.

"Well, duh."

He kissed me again, and then I was the one to stop it because as much as I'd love to stay here kissing Mal and Griff, I did need to go home.

"Hey, do you think I could take tomorrow morning off? I'd like to hang out with Zak, and if I don't rein him in, he's going to plan a birthday party to rival the Kardashian weddings."

"What's a Kardashian?"

Griff snorted from behind us and came over to kiss me goodbye too.

"A fire-breather."

"No."

"A casino."

"No."

"A carnival."

"No."

"Karaoke."

"No."

"This is going to be the most boring party ever," Zak said, turning over on his beach towel to face me.

"You're forgetting that I don't want a party."

"Bah, everyone wants a party. What are you going to tell your grandchildren when they ask you what wild things you did in your youth?"

I looked at him with a raised brow.

"Oh yeah, I forget you're fucking two guys. Can't get wilder than that. Although you might not want to tell your grandchildren that."

I laughed. "Can we stop talking about my grandchildren and focus on this thing you want to plan? Why can't I just have a bunch of friends over, grill some steak, have drinks, music, and hang out?"

"That's the daytime program. I'm talking about the *nighttime* program. Unless you were planning on…oh my god, you were totally planning on sneaking out of your own party to go do the horizontal dance with the boss and the hot writer."

"How do you know Griff's hot?"

Zak rolled his eyes. "Social media, you dumbass. Shame he doesn't have any photos of his husband on his page, but I bet he's hot too, amiright?"

I grabbed a shell from the sand and threw it at him.

"Now, stop deflecting. I know exactly what you're doing," I said.

"What do you mean?"

"Come on, Zak, this is me. Whatever is going on, you can talk to me."

He rolled onto his back and shielded his eyes from the sun with his hands.

"The thing I have in LA tomorrow. It's a job interview."

"That's amazing, Zak. It'll be great to have you closer."

"Yeah, well…my parents may not feel the same way," he said. There was a strange edge to his voice.

"Why's that? I mean, I know you said they're a little overbearing, but—"

"I came out to them."

The way he said it told me things hadn't exactly gone well for him.

"What happened?"

"It was like I was talking to a wall. I told them I'm gay, and the next words out of their mouth were that the daughter of this woman in my mom's Shodo club is back home from college. Now that we're both home, maybe they should invite her to come over for dinner."

I reached out and squeezed his arm.

"I always knew they wouldn't accept me, but in a perverted way, I think it would have been better if they'd shouted at me or even kicked me out. I couldn't have felt more invisible to my parents if I actually were invisible."

"I'm so sorry, Zak. What are you going to do?"

He looked at me. "Get the job in LA, move out here, and live my life on my own terms."

"I hope you get the job, and I know I'm partial to this place, but if you can commute to the island, then this is the best place to live, cheaper than in the city, and well, your best friend is already here. What else could you possibly want?"

"Sex? You're not putting out these days, and I'm not cutting myself off from my parents to live like a monk."

I laughed. "Sounds like Gabe and I need to show you around."

He shrugged.

"Let's get in the water one last time. You need to go to work soon, don't you?" he asked.

I looked at the time on my phone screen.

"Yeah, let's do it. You go ahead, let me just send a couple of messages."

"Man, you're so whipped."

I took a picture of the beach and sent it to Mal and Griff with a caption saying I knew a couple of secret beaches on the island and then added a wink emoji.

"Every time I see you, you're with a different hot guy. I have questions."

I looked up at the man standing between me and the sun.

"One of them is my cousin, so he doesn't count, and neither does my college roommate," I said, standing up. "Hi, Sam. Nice to see you again."

"How about the other two?" he asked, a knowing smile spreading through his lips.

"It's complicated."

He laughed. "It didn't look too complicated that day at the hospital."

I shrugged.

"So, which one's this one?" He nodded to the beach where Zac was playing as if it were his first time at the beach.

"Roommate."

"Free agent?"

"Hmm, I'm having a birthday party next weekend. Why don't you come along?"

He looked out to the water and then back at me.

"Why do I get the feeling you want to use me to get your friend off your back?"

I shrugged. "I mean, would you feel *really* bad being used?"

"Hell no. Give me the address, and I'll be there with bells on."

"Give me your phone."

I tapped my address and my phone number into Sam's phone.

We'd only had a couple of awkward encounters, and I tried not to think of the drunken kiss we'd had when I'd been avoiding my feelings for Griff and Mal, but Sam seemed like a nice guy.

Maybe it was just what Zak needed.

And if they kept each other busy, maybe I *could* sneak out of the party earlier with my men and get to the real celebration. After all, it wasn't every day you turned thirty.

But I was still twenty-nine. So, to prove I could still be as immature as Zak, I ran to the water and threw myself onto him, making us dive under the water.

Maybe it would be okay to be a little late for work just this once.

20

GRIFF

"How do I look?"

Mal perused me from head to toe, scratching his short beard and squinting.

"Come on, don't be a dick. I want to look good. Am I okay?" I asked.

He didn't have time to answer before the door to Frank's house was opened by Frank himself.

"Gentlemen, come on in," he said with great flourish, gesturing for us to go inside. "Hello, Mal. And what a pleasure to see you again, Griff. How's business?"

"Everything's great, Frank. Thanks for asking. In fact…" I opened my backpack that held Jake's birthday present and took out a large envelope.

"Oh my goodness, is that what I think it is?"

He smiled as if it were his own birthday.

"It is indeed. An early copy of *Tough Love*."

"You make an old man very happy, Griff. Who knew I'd get into gay romance in my old age, hey?"

"You're definitely not old, Frank. And I think you could score a nice girl if you wanted to," I said, winking at him.

"Oh no, not you too. Jacob's onto me to join one of those dating apps."

His face made it clear what he thought of Jake's suggestion. I actually could imagine Frank with a nice woman who'd be there for him but also challenge him. He definitely still had a lot of life in him. Goodness, he was barely sixty.

"Frank, I hate to bring up business today, but do you think we could catch up for a moment?" Mal asked.

"Of course, follow me to the office."

"I'll go find the birthday boy if that's okay?" I asked.

Mal leaned over to kiss my cheek and whispered, "You look stunning. Go get him, baby."

While Mal and Frank disappeared down a hallway to Frank's office, I went toward the kitchen to see if I could find Jake or Gabe.

I'd only been in the house once, but the kitchen was fairly easy to find, especially since there was music coming from that direction.

As soon as I turned into the kitchen and saw a small crowd of people, my nerves shot up. I didn't exactly have social anxiety, but walking into a party on my own was my version of my worst nightmare.

I thought Jake was only having a few friends over, not this many people. I stood by the door, scanning all the faces and hoping to find someone familiar, without success.

Stepping back out and leaning against the wall, I tried to get my heart rate down a little. Maybe Jake was in the garden.

After all, how hard could it be to find the birthday boy at his own party?

"Griff? Is that you?"

I looked up to see Sam standing in front of me with a drink in hand.

"Sam! Hi. Nice to see you. I didn't know you knew Jake."

"I don't, not really. We had a…well, never mind. We met at the beach a few days ago, and he invited me. My mission is to find Jake's friend and keep him busy, but I haven't seen him anywhere. Hell, I don't even know what he looks like. How about you? What are you doing out here on your own?"

I shrugged. "I'm not great with big crowds. I was hoping to find Jake to give him his present while Mal is with Frank."

He leaned over to look through the doorway.

"He's definitely not in the kitchen. How about we go out there together? We might actually find our men in the same place."

He froze and then looked at me. "I'm sorry. I didn't mean to imply that Jake is your...or his friend is my...anything...it was just...oh fuck, I hope I didn't offend you."

I laughed. "You didn't offend me at all. By the way, how's baby Griffin and his sleep-deprived parents?"

"You're right. Very sleep-deprived, but Griffin is the cutest baby ever. I'm actually sad. I have a job on the mainland and will be away for a few months. He's growing so fast, and I don't want to miss out on anything."

"That's why God invented video calls," I said. "Congrats on the job. Anything exciting?"

Sam walked into the kitchen, and I followed him.

"Some. I'm photographing rich people's houses for a magazine, but since I'll be in San Francisco, a friend hooked me up to photograph his friends in drag. He's doing a super-cool project on toxic masculinity, stereotypes, and gay culture."

"Wow, that sounds really interesting. I hope we'll get to see those photos somewhere," I said.

"Let's see if I do a good enough job first. Oh, I see Jake's friend over there."

I looked at the spot Sam pointed out and saw Gabe with a guy. They were sitting on a round couch that had a fire pit in the middle. That must be Zak.

Jake had said they'd been best friends and fuck buddies throughout college, but looking at Zak now, I couldn't help feeling a little insecure. He was all sharp jaw, smooth skin, wide-set eyes, and perfect teeth.

He wasn't just beautiful. They had a shared history, a long-term relationship, and that meant more than something fleeting.

What we had wasn't fleeting, was it?

I tried to shake the thoughts off. Jake had told me he loved me,

Mal had as well, and he'd been clear from the start that there was nothing between him and his friend.

"He's stunning, right?" Sam said. "I don't know how Jake expects me to grab his attention when he's clearly interested in the equally gorgeous guy next to him."

"Who? Gabe?"

We walked past a station with drinks, so I grabbed a glass of chilled white wine.

"You know who he is? I was hoping to see Jake first. I've seen the blond guy with Jake before at a bar."

"That's his cousin, Gabe. He's a sweetheart," I said. "That means the other guy must be Jake's friend, Zak."

"Ahh, that's his name. Very sexy."

I laughed.

"What?" Sam asked.

"Look at us like two teenagers trying to figure out the hot kids. Come on, let's go say hi."

The sun was getting lower in the sky, and with the lights turning on, the backyard looked cozy and a lot more like what I'd expected from this party.

I was glad that more people seemed to gather inside than outside. I'd heard someone mention a game on TV when we passed through the kitchen, so that could be the reason.

Gabe and Zak seemed lost in their conversation, but when we approached, they moved away from each other.

"Hi, Griff, how are you?" Gabe asked, standing up to give me a hug.

"Good, and you? How is your exam prep?"

"God, don't ask. This is my one night off. I'm going to make the best of it."

As if he'd just noticed I wasn't alone, he looked at Sam, pausing for a moment.

"Hi, have I seen you before?"

Sam smiled wide. "Kind of, but not really. You were at The Dive with Jake one time?"

"Oh yeah, you were the guy that…" Gabe stopped himself, which was strange, but then he stretched his hand out to Sam. "I'm Gabe. Nice to meet you. This is Zak, Jake's friend from college."

Zak smiled and stood up to shake Sam's hand. "Now, I definitely know I've not met you before because I'd have remembered."

Sam smiled back. "Likewise."

Gabe looked at both Sam and Zak with confusion. And maybe a little disappointment.

My little romantic poly heart burst with giddiness because it was clear that the three guys found each other attractive.

I made the first move to sit on the couch, and they followed.

"Do you live here?" Zak asked Sam.

"Yeah. I take it you're visiting."

"I am, but if all the natives are as cute as you, I might rethink my life choices," Zak said.

Sam laughed. "Are you always this forward?"

"Yes."

They stared at each other for a moment.

Gabe stood up again. "Excuse me, I'll be right back."

I put my wine down on a side table and chased after him.

"Hey, are you okay?"

"Sure. Just not in the mood to play third wheel."

"I think you're reading that situation wrong," I said.

"Did you hear them? They basically just hit on each other within half a second of meeting. I've been hanging out with Zak for almost a week and haven't so much as had one flirtatious comment. They're clearly way out of my league."

I wondered if he noticed he'd said they rather than he.

"Just because they're more forward with each other doesn't mean they're not into you. It just means there's a different dynamic between you and them."

He looked at Zak and Sam, who were talking to each other, but I'd noticed each of them stealing glances at Gabe.

"How do you know this stuff?"

"I'm a romance author. It's my job."

He laughed.

"Why don't you go back there and just hang out. By the way, have you seen Jake?"

"I'd put my money on him being with Uncle Frank in the office working. This party wasn't exactly his choice. Zak can be very…"

"Persuasive?"

"I was going to say stubborn but persuasive works. He cares a lot for Jake, so that's all that matters."

I nodded.

"Who cares a lot for Jake?"

I turned around and saw Mal and Jake approaching.

"No one. No one cares about you, so stop having a big head just because it's your—" That was all Gabe could say before Jake had him in a chokehold.

"Can you do that with your clothes off?" Zak shouted, and Jake gave him the bird without releasing his cousin.

"In my day, birthday parties weren't this much fun," Mal said.

I wrapped my arm around his waist and leaned into him. "Back in the day, you didn't even have butter or flour to make a cake, babe. Those were dark days."

He poked me in the ribs.

"Hey! Come on, let's sit down so we can give Jake his present."

Jake released Gabe immediately. "I get presents?"

He looked so happy and carefree. All I wanted was to bridge the gap between us and kiss him.

I held on to Mal to stop myself from reaching out, and he squeezed me tight. We hadn't been with Jake since the night he had us both, but we were hoping he'd be able to sneak out and spend the night with us.

No doubt Zak would cover for him at home.

The thought left me with a bad taste in my mouth. Jake shouldn't have to do this, and neither should we. I understood the reasons for us to be discreet, but it didn't mean I had to like it, especially when I missed Jake so much.

Would there be a day when we could all live under the same roof? I really hoped so.

Gabe added some more wood to the fire pit and declared we all needed s'mores, so he disappeared to the kitchen.

"Are you ready for your present, birthday boy?" I asked Jake.

"I was born ready."

I grabbed my backpack and took out the gift box.

"You know you didn't have to give me anything, right?"

I shrugged. "Yeah, we know. But what's the point of going to a birthday party if you don't get to indulge in some retail therapy?"

Mal snorted, and I elbowed him.

"What?" Jake asked, looking at us.

"Nothing, just open the present." I couldn't exactly tell him about the additional stuff I'd also bought at the same time.

Jake unwrapped the box slowly, removing each bit of sticky tape individually.

"Oh god, you're one of those people," I said.

Zak leaned forward with an all-knowing expression. "You should see the box of old wrapping paper he had in our apartment. After a while, I started wrapping his presents with the paper he'd used to unwrap them."

Jake gave him a murderous look. "You're a heathen. You placed the sticky tape in different places so the paper couldn't be reused."

"Guilty as charged."

Jake removed the lid of the box and gasped. He took out the notebook, running his fingers over the smooth leather and the hand-painted image I'd glued to the front cover.

"The bunnies." He looked at us with the biggest smile. "How?"

"I told Elena what I was planning, and she has a friend that makes those beautiful drawings. Mal said that at work, you're a planner, and you write everything down on your notepad," I said.

"I am. This is the perfect gift. Thank you so much."

We shared a silent moment full of promise, and I knew Mal's hand on mine as he looked at Jake was his way of saying he wanted to be touching him too.

The drawing on the notebook had so much meaning. The three bunnies symbolized the island and everything it had to offer. Jake's home. It also symbolized the three of us looking out for each other, protecting each other, and also always up for it.

What a major life bonus when the people you connected with were also amazing in bed, I thought.

"Happy birthday to you…happy birthday to you…"

Gabe and Frank walked toward us with a big birthday cake filled with candles, singing at the top of their lungs.

The people that had been inside the house were suddenly all around us, and as if he could feel my tension, Mal came even closer and put his arm around me.

Even though he was reluctant to have a party, it was nice to see Jake looking so happy.

When everyone stopped singing, he blew out all the candles and then went around hugging everyone.

"I see where your priorities are," he said to the people grabbing a slice of cake and disappearing back inside.

"Damn right," one guy said.

"Put on your high school football uniform, and we'll watch you instead," a girl said.

There were a few hurrah's from other girls before they all went inside.

"Before he was popular with the boys, my boy here was popular with the girls," Frank said proudly. "Just like his uncle."

"Ew, Dad." Gabe groaned.

"Do you really know all those people?" I asked.

Jake had always come across as a homebody who preferred spending time with his uncle and cousin than out partying. The fact that he'd had Zak as his constant hookup during college supported that theory. There was no need to go out with lots of people when you had all you needed at home.

"Most of them. I haven't seen the majority for years, and some are Gabe's friends. When you grow up on a small island, you end up knowing most people. I'm sure some weren't even invited. They just heard about the party and decided to come along."

That was such an alien concept to me. I'd been one of those kids that kept to himself. I'd traveled the world with my grandmother every day when we read books together, but I had less than a handful of friends at school.

"This cake is wonderful," Mal said. "Here, babe. Try a bit." He fed me the cake, winking when I wrapped my lips around the fork.

You're playing with fire, Mal.

And he absolutely knew it because he'd done it when Jake was looking.

"Oh, is that the doorbell?" Frank asked.

"Don't worry, Dad. I'll get it," Gabe said, running inside.

Moments later, he came back out. A man that looked around the same age as Frank walking alongside him.

"Well, if it isn't John Melville. Did you hear there was cake, John?"

The man laughed and shook Frank's hand.

Mal tensed up, and when I looked at him, he was staring at Jake.

Jake met Mal's eyes, and I saw an imperceptible nod pass between them.

What was going on?

21

——

MAL

"You know I'll never say no to cake, Frank," John said.

"You asked for seconds of our wedding cake…before everyone else even had their first slice." Frank cut a piece of the cake and put it on a plate for John.

"I remember that. And your Annie left the guests waiting so she could ask the caterers for a box to put an extra piece of cake for me. She was a good woman."

The last thing I imagined John Melville to be was a friendly guy with a thick beard and a smile that reached his eyes.

Jake stared at John with a frown. Was he as confused by this exchange as I was?

"So, are you going to make the introductions? I remember little Jacob here and Gabriel. You both used to run to the door every time I came over and check my pockets for candy."

Frank laughed. "They haven't changed much. They can sniff out one of Elena's cakes a mile off." Then he turned to me. "This is Mallory Prescott. He runs the resort, and this is his husband, Griffin."

John held his hand up to shake mine, his eyes boring into me, but he didn't say anything. Just a simple smile and a nod.

He ignored Griff before turning to Frank. "As you know, there is an issue with the contract to work at the resort. If you have a moment, I'd like to talk to you about it."

"John, in case you didn't notice, we're hosting people. This is not a day for business," Frank said.

He glanced at me, and I gave him a small nod. When I'd spoken to Frank earlier, he'd been shocked to hear that John's company had backed out of the contract.

He'd even suggested that maybe this had been a decision made by one of John's brothers, not himself.

Had John come over to clarify things and get the contract back on? I didn't want to ruin Jake's party by having a business meeting, but I finally had the owner of Melville Construction and didn't want to miss the opportunity to fix things.

"I promise this won't take long, and we don't even need to bother the birthday boy," John said.

"Uncle Frank, if I may," Jake interrupted. "Mal and I have been working on this for days. I think we should hear what John has to say."

"Yes, I hear you've been working extra hard. You always were a people pleaser, Jacob."

What the fuck did John mean?

"I'm not sure," Frank said.

Gabe turned to Frank. "Dad, I'll keep an eye on the party. Why don't you do what you need to? I'm sure Zak will help," he said, pointing to where Zak and Sam had retreated to talk to other people in the party.

"I'll be back in a bit. Will you be okay?" I asked Griff. He hated big gatherings, especially when he didn't know most people, which was the case on this occasion.

When I'd joined the party earlier and noticed how many people were there, I immediately panicked until I saw he was with Gabe and seemed to be okay.

"Your husband should join us, Mallory. This might concern him too. After all, Silver Resorts is a family business, isn't that right, Frank?"

Everyone stared at John.

"But I don't work for the resort," Griff said.

"If you'll indulge an old man," John replied.

Frank led the way, and we followed him inside. Jake held back a little to get into step with me.

"I don't like this," he whispered. "Something doesn't feel right."

I nodded. "I guess we're about to find out."

Jake closed the office door behind him.

Frank's office was also his private library, so he had two sets of couches and a chair around a large coffee table.

I sat on one couch with a confused Griff next to me. Jake sat on the opposite couch with John while Frank took the chair.

"So," Frank started. "I learned today that your company pulled out of the contract to work on the structural damage of one of our buildings. I understand Mal and Jacob have been trying to get through to your company to work things out, but they've not been successful, and now you visit out of the blue, John. We have a friendship that goes back over forty years. I hope this was a misunderstanding."

John sat back, crossing one leg over the other.

"Frank, you know how much I value our friendship. You were there for me in my darkest times. Without your help, I wouldn't have been able to stand up, let alone walk on my own two feet."

"You say that, and here we are, discussing why your company withdrew the contract," Frank said.

"Indeed. As I said earlier, your business is all about family. It's sad that your sister is no longer with us. She'd have been so proud of you."

Jake stilled. "Can we leave my mother out of this, please? I appreciate your friendship with my uncle, but please get to the point."

John looked taken aback by Jake's abruptness, but Frank's lips twitched with a small smile. Griff had his hand on mine and squeezed lightly.

Yeah, our man can stand up for himself.

"As I was saying," John continued. "We were practically family by the time we took over the resort, and even after I left to look after my late wife, I always felt welcome. I am no longer confident that's the case."

What the fuck was he talking about? The resort was welcoming of everyone. Until a few days ago, I didn't know his name, let alone his friendship with Frank.

I had to bite my tongue so I wouldn't speak out of turn.

"Frank, you take pride in welcoming families into your resort, but I no longer believe the resort is the most appropriate environment for the traditional American family."

What the fuck?

Was he saying what I thought he was saying? Had he withdrawn the contract because the resort was managed by a married gay man?

I straightened up in my seat. I could take a lot of things, but I'd outgrown homophobic pricks a long time ago. And for once, I knew my boss would have my back.

Frank scratched his chin, clearly eager to see where this was going. From the tapping of his finger on the arm of his chair, I could tell he wasn't impressed with John's slow and drawn-out speech.

"My business is also my family, and as such, there are things I don't stand for. My reputation is everything, and I cannot afford to lose business if I'm associated with people with alternative lifestyles—"

"John, you're walking a fine line," Frank threatened.

"Look, it's no one's business but their own what people do in the privacy of their own home. I don't care who or what people do in their bedrooms, but this island has always been a safe and wholesome place for families. I'll say this because I care about you enough to be upfront. You need to look into how your business is being run."

That was it. I was about to lose it. I took a deep, steady breath before I spoke up. "John, with all due respect, you are making comments that have no place in this day and age, and I'm certain they have no place in this house either. Not only are you being homophobic, but you are also saying that gay men are in some way a danger to the people of this island?"

"I'll agree with Mal," Frank said. "I thought we were having a business meeting. I thought you came here to talk through the contact and maybe ask for more money. I didn't expect my family to be insulted, and I'm certain that it is you I don't want to do business with, not the other way round."

John raised his hand. "I came as a friend, Frank. I have a vested interest in seeing the island and the businesses within prosper."

He put his hand in his jacket and took out a photo, placing it on the coffee table.

The photo had been taken days ago when Griff and Jake had their lunch date. They were looking at each other and smiling.

"I don't understand, John. I know Jake is friends with Mal and Griff, so I'm failing to see an issue here."

"Maybe this might clarify things a little better." John placed another photo on the table, and in that one, Jake and Griff were kissing.

It was clear that it wasn't just a kiss. Griff's hand was cradling Jake's face lovingly.

"What is this?" Frank asked.

"That…is the kind of example your management team sets for the rest of your business."

"Jacob, what is this? Are you having an affair with Griff?"

Jake had gone as white as a sheet. I had to resist my instinct to get up and go to him, especially when Griff had stiffened up next to me.

"Maybe this one will give you the full picture. Pardon the pun," John said.

The next photo he laid out on the table was of Jake and me. We were in the conference room. Jake sat on my lap, and he was looking at me and smiling. That was just before he'd said he thought he saw something out in the office.

Someone had been there and taken a photo of us. Undoubtedly the same person who took the other photo.

Frank's brows were furrowed as he stared at Jake as if he were seeing him for the first time.

I wanted to say something to clarify that neither Griff nor I were cheating on each other with Jake. But how was telling Frank we were all in a relationship any better?

"Who took these photos?" Frank asked.

John straightened up. "Well, I…um…I always knew Jacob was a smart boy, and he loves the resorts as much as you do. It's a shame that he's fallen prey to a predator, a climber that took advantage of him not after joining your team, but all the way back when Mallory was at the resort for his job interview."

"Jacob, is this true?"

"Yes, Uncle Frank. I met Mal and Griff when I was working before my last college term. I didn't know who they were or what they were doing at the resort. I thought they were regular guests."

"Since when do you make it a habit of engaging in…whatever you did, with guests?"

Jake looked down at the floor. His hands were in his lap.

"For goodness' sake," I said. "Jake is an adult. Yes, we met months ago. Neither of us knew who each other was. We didn't speak or meet again until I started my job. I don't understand how any of this is relevant to the contract between Melville Construction and Silver Resorts."

"How do you explain those photos, Mal?" Frank asked.

"Frank, I would prefer to discuss those in private, not in front of someone who I not only don't know, but who also has no business in my or my husband's personal life."

"Fair enough," Frank said. "John, you still haven't answered my question. Who took the photos?"

"My stepson."

"Brian?"

Wait. Brian is John's stepson?

Jake looked at John in shock and then at me.

"It's all making sense now," I said. "I'm going to take a guess you didn't know Brian was John's stepson, did you, Jake?"

"No, of course not. He's much older than me, and I finished school on the mainland. Besides, I don't know everyone on the island."

"Frank, Brian has been a major contradictory force in the team. I've been managing him, but I wasn't able to pinpoint the reason for his behavior other than him having a sour feeling toward me for getting the job he wanted."

John stood up. "Brian has been overlooked for promotion more times than I care to count. He's given years of dedication to your company, and he's gotten peanuts back. Then you hire someone like him," he said, pointing at me. "Who then goes and betrays your trust by getting involved with your nephew."

His voice got louder as he continued. "And as if that's not enough, his husband is also in on it and seduces your nephew too. Hell, at this stage, I wouldn't be surprised if they were all in some kind of disgusting threesome. When I came into this information, I wanted to advise you as a friend. If anyone should run the resort, it's Jacob, but now I doubt even he's going to do a good enough job if he lets what's in his pants get in the way of his work."

"John, out of respect for our friendship, I'd like you to go now," Frank said.

"I will go, but I'll just leave you with this…if you want to keep the reputation of the resort, you will promote Brian, who's happily married to a woman, with one child and another on the way. He'll do a good job because he's focused, and he wants it. Do that, and the contract is back on."

"And if I don't?"

"Good luck finding a contractor to do the job. This is a small island, and the world outside of it isn't that big."

And with those parting words, John left the room.

Frank stood up and went over to the drinks tray by the window. He poured scotch into a glass and drank it straight up.

"Pardon my French, but what the fuck is going on?"

22

JAKE

I LOOKED into my uncle's eyes and saw nothing but disappointment.

I'd done everything right in my life until I hadn't.

Bile rose in my stomach, and I had to run.

"I'm sorry."

I didn't stop until I got to the nearest bathroom and emptied the contents of my stomach down the toilet until there was nothing but dry heaving.

"Hey, are you okay?" Gabe asked. "You didn't drink that much. Are you getting sick?"

I shook my head.

Standing up was a challenge, but I made it with his help so I could rinse my mouth.

He opened the cabinet over the sink and passed me the small bottle of mouthwash. I took it and mixed some of it with water from the glass.

"Jake, you're shaking."

I looked at him.

"And you're crying."

Was I? Maybe that's why Gabe was a little blurry.

"What happened? I was walking the last guest to the door when I saw John leave and you run out of the office.

"Everyone left?"

"The game finished, but Sam is still here. He, Zak, and I were going to watch a movie, but I can send him home."

"No, no, you should do that. You've been studying too hard. You need a night off."

He smiled. "You really are the best big brother-slash-cousin anyone could ever ask for, aren't you? Tell me what's wrong. Did you fight with Griff and Mal?"

"What?"

"Oh, come on, don't pretend it's not happening. I know you're together."

"What? Ho…how?"

"It's not hard to guess. You never came home that night after Griff left the hospital. I thought you just crashed there because you were too tired to drive, but then you kept staying there every night. At first, I thought you were seeing someone, but you never talked about anything else but them."

"Christ, was I that obvious?"

"Only to me. I don't think threesomes are on Dad's radar."

I sighed. "They are now."

"What do you mean?"

"John outed us. The whole meeting was a shit storm."

I sat on the edge of the bathtub and rested my elbows on my knees. "Uncle Frank looked so disappointed."

Gabe kneeled in front of me. "I don't know what went on in there, but I know Dad. He loves you so much. Sometimes I think he loves you more than he loves me."

"Don't be silly. Of course he doesn't. You're his son."

What made him think his dad loved me more than he loved him?

"Come on, you're so perfect all the time. You've always known what you wanted. I…I just feel like I'll never meet his expectations, and I'm terrified I'll fail if I try."

"Oh, Gabe." I pulled him into my arms. He wrapped his around my waist.

"So…two guys, huh?" he asked.

I shrugged. "I didn't expect it, but yeah, I guess the heart wants what it wants, but I may have to let them go."

"Why? Dad will accept it, you know?"

"I know…I think I know. But there's more to it. This isn't just about us."

Gabe sat back on his heels and messed up my hair. "Don't be afraid to fight for what you want. You never have, so don't start now."

I smiled at him. When did my little brother become so wise?

"Okay. I have to go back in there. Did you know there are two insanely hot men in the living room?" He wiggled his eyebrows.

I laughed. "And I guess I have to go face the music."

Gabe squeezed my shoulder and gave me an encouraging smile before leaving me by the office door.

I turned the handle and walked in, but what I found wasn't exactly what I was expecting.

Mal and Griff were still on the couch. Griff sat forward with his head resting in his hands, and Mal seemed to be comforting him.

"Where's my uncle?"

"Jake." Griff ran to me and held me tight. "I'm sorry. I'm so sorry. This is all my fault. I shouldn't have met you for lunch, and I shouldn't have come on to you so strong."

"Griff," Mal said.

"No, it's true. You don't know. I was basically fucking him with my eyes. No wonder that Brian guy noticed us."

Mal sighed. He didn't disagree with Griff.

"I shouldn't have touched you in the office either. Even if Brian already had photos of you two kissing, seeing us in the conference room just gave him more ammunition."

I understood what they were saying, but the words didn't sit well with me.

"Do you regret it? Both of you?" I pulled away from Griff and took a step back to look at them. "Of course you do."

"No," Mal said. "We don't. I don't regret a single thing we did together, Jake. But we have to be realistic here. How are people going to accept us? *We've* barely had time to figure things out ourselves, and now Frank's business and his reputation are at risk because of us."

What was he saying? I looked at Griff. His eyes were full of pain and unshed tears.

"Please leave. I need to…I can't do this right now."

Griff reached out to me. "Jake."

"Please…if you care about me at all, just give me some space. I need to talk to my uncle."

I left them and walked toward the stairs, but I stopped before I reached the first step.

What was I going to do? What was I going to say?

I turned around and went outside. Machine gun noises came from whatever movie Gabe, Zak, and Sam were watching, and I was glad they masked my footsteps on the tiled floor of the kitchen.

The air outside was cool, but I welcomed the chill. It meant we were in for another hot day tomorrow, but for now, I craved the cold.

I breathed in and smelled the grass and the remains of the fire. If it wasn't for the glasses and bottles scattered around the garden, you'd never know there had been a party only an hour ago.

The sky was clear and full of stars. I lay on one of the couches and stared up at the dark vastness. We were far away enough from the mainland that we didn't get as much light pollution.

My head was all over the place, trying to make sense of what had happened.

I'd known John since I was a kid, and even though I hadn't seen him for years, I knew he was close to my uncle.

How could he do this?

I'd seen the betrayal in my uncle's eyes. It was right there with the disappointment.

Betrayed by his friend of over forty years at the hands of his nephew.

How could I take this all back? How could I make it better for him?

I don't know how long I stared at the sky, looking for answers in the stars, but at some point, I must have fallen asleep because when I opened my eyes, the sky was no longer dark. There was a blanket over me, and my face was warm from the rising sun.

"Good morning." Gabe held a cup of coffee in his hand, so I sat up and accepted it.

"This is great, thanks. I can't believe I fell asleep out here."

"Zak came out to check on you, but you were out cold. You were lucky. Any other time of year, we'd have dragged your sorry ass inside."

"Thanks...I think." I took another sip of the coffee. "Is Uncle Frank awake?"

"Yeah. He went out with Jessie, so he should be back any time now."

As if on cue, Jessie came out from the kitchen and ran toward us.

"Hey, baby girl. Good walk?" She licked my face in answer and then jumped on the couch, settling next to me.

Uncle Frank came out, holding a cup of coffee.

Gabe gave me a reassuring smile and went back inside.

I couldn't face my uncle. Not before I apologized.

He sat next to me.

"Uncle Frank...I...I'm so sorry." A lump formed in my throat, and I gripped the cup tighter. "I didn't mean to lie or deceive you. I understand if you don't believe me or trust me anymore."

"Are you with Griff, Mal, or both?" he asked.

"Both. I'm with both...was...with both. I don't know anymore."

"Why?"

I met his eyes. The same hazel color as my mother's and Gabe's. I'd always been the odd one out with clear blue eyes.

"All I've ever wanted was to work at the resort and make you proud, make you not regret taking me in. And I've thrown it all away. This...this thing with Mal and Griff. It could ruin your reputation. As it is right now, it means we'll need to stay closed for longer or only keep part of the resort open."

"The earthquake isn't your fault, Jacob."

"No, but everything else is. If I didn't work at the resort, I wouldn't have met them again. There would be no photos of us together, and John wouldn't have pulled the contract."

That was it. It all became clear at that moment. As painful as it was, it was the right thing to do.

"Uncle Frank, I'd like to resign."

"What?"

"I resign."

"Why?"

"Because without me, you don't have to fire Mal. He's a great manager, and I think he's just what the resort needs."

"Is that it?"

"I don't want to disappoint you, Uncle Frank. You are like a father to me. If you want, I'll give them up. We'll go back to how it was, except I'll look for another job."

It was all so clear in my mind. So why did it hurt so much to say it?

Because I was lying again. I didn't want to give them up. I wanted them as much as I'd ever wanted to make my uncle proud.

"Jacob, look at me. First of all, I don't know what makes you think I'm firing Mal. Second, you could never disappoint me. Sometimes I wish you didn't try so hard to be the perfect son. My love isn't conditional. I'm not going to send you away. I *am* your father. Maybe not totally by blood, but one hundred percent in my heart."

"I'm so sorry, Uncle Frank." I cried in his arms.

"Me too, son. I'm sorry that what your mother did has stayed with you all this time."

"I know she didn't want to abandon me. Deep down, I know she loved me. She just didn't know what to do with a child when her dreams were so big."

He squeezed my shoulders. "It is possible to dream big and still love and care for your family, Jacob. This is all on your mother. I loved my sister dearly, but she failed us all. Wherever she is, this is something for her to carry. Our only job is to be happy in this life because it can be very short. Tell me, Jacob. How do you feel about Mal and Griff?"

Warmth spread through my chest.

"I love them. I never thought I'd love two men at the same time, but I do. I feel at home, safe, and loved every time I'm with them."

"Do they love you back?"

I sighed. "Griff said he loves me, but Mal hasn't said it yet."

"He's a man of few words. His actions speak louder."

"Then he definitely loves me." I laughed.

My uncle finished his coffee and sat back on the couch.

"This is all new to me. I've read Griff's books, so let's say my mind has been truly opened when it comes to relationships between men. I wanted to be there for you and Gabriel as you grew up, but you're both so different from me and from each other. But one thing is universal, we all need someone to love, and there are no rules that say there's a limit on how many people you can love."

"I want to love them, Uncle Frank. So much. What you had with Aunt Annie? I want it with them, but I'm not sure this island is ready for it. And from John's actions yesterday, I'm afraid of what might happen if this comes out."

"Once upon a time, people looked down on your mother because she was pregnant out of wedlock. But they always still came when she sang at The Dive. When you give people something they love, they tend to forget the details. It may take some people longer to accept it, but they'll come around eventually."

I couldn't believe everything I was hearing from my uncle. Did he really accept my relationship with Griff and Mal? Was he really ready to stand up for us?

"Thank you, Uncle Frank. You have no idea how much this means to me. I feel like I've been in this fog of lies, and it's clearing up finally. But there's still the issue with the resort and the lack of contractors willing to do the work."

"I don't know how we solve it, son. But I know what the first two steps are."

"What are they?"

"Brian will no longer be welcome at the resort. If he had any concerns, he had plenty of opportunities to do the right thing and speak to me. Spying and taking photos of his colleagues and then helping John with his ridiculous blackmail is not the culture I want to breed in my business."

I nodded. He was right. Firing someone who had a family to feed was always difficult, but Brian hadn't thought of his family when he decided to spy for his stepdad. He thought he'd find an easy way up the career ladder.

There was a big difference between being driven and stabbing someone in the back, and Brian was firmly in the second camp.

"I also accept your resignation," he said.

What?

He laughed. "Don't look at me like that. It's not appropriate for you to work for Mal if you're in a relationship."

"Of course. I understand. I mean, I have plenty of experience and my MBA. I'm sure I'll find something on the mainland."

"That's not necessary. I want you to work for me as a consultant. The work you did for Mal with the skills matrix, the cross-training, and efficiency? I want you to do it for the whole business. John was right. Silver Resorts is all about family, and it's time we invest our time and money in our family. Of course this would require you to be away at times when you need to visit other resorts, but never for long, I imagine."

I stared at my uncle. My mouth opened, but no sounds came out.

"Of course you don't have to accept it—"

"I do. I really do. I've been thinking about it for a while, but I was going to wait until Mal didn't need me at the resort anymore. I always thought I wanted to run this resort, but now I know what I wanted was to be part of it, part of your business. That job would give me a lot more satisfaction, and I hope it gives me enough scope to support Gabe when he takes over the business from you one day."

Uncle Frank stood up from the couch. "That's settled, then. Come on, Jessie, let's see what we have left in the fridge to feed the troops. Do you know that your friend Sam stayed over last night?"

"Um, no, I crashed out here."

My uncle looked up at the sky and sighed. "Ah, to be young and able to sleep anywhere. I remember those days."

I laughed. "Trust me, my back isn't particularly happy right now."

"I think you should go see your men. I'm sure they'll have a cure for that." He chuckled.

I groaned. "Ugh, you need to stop reading Griff's books."

Our eyes met, and I finally saw what I'd been searching for all my life.

"Uncle Frank…may I call you Dad?"

He covered his mouth with his hand and nodded.

"Oh, son, you always could have called me Dad."

I walked over to him.

"I think I was afraid that if I did, then you too would go away. I don't think I could handle not having you around."

His eyes were full of unshed tears as he took my hands in his.

"Maybe you needed to find your own home before you could learn or accept that you always had one here. This will always be your home, Jacob. Whatever happens. I don't need to promise you that because, as a parent, that is just the way it is. Unconditional shelter."

I nodded, letting a few tears finally fall down my cheek, and hugged my father fiercely.

"Now go see your guys and make sure you're all back here for dinner."

"I love you, Dad."

"Love you too, son."

23

GRIFF

I CONNECTED my phone to the speakers and scrolled down my playlists until I found the right one.

The kitchen cabinets needed a good clean, so I filled a container with water, added some soap, and started emptying the contents onto the countertop.

Then the music stopped.

"What the—"

"No," Mal said. "This is not one of those moments."

"I can't just sit here, Mal. I need to move, to do something, and if I'm doing something, I need my music."

He took the set of plates I was holding and placed them on the countertop before settling his hands on my shoulders.

I sighed.

"Baby, if you're stressed, use me. I'm here. Talk to me."

"What do you mean, use you?" I asked.

He stared at me, raising a brow.

"No! How can you even think about sex at a time like this?"

"I wasn't thinking of sex, Griff. I was talking about us supporting each other and figuring out what to do together, but clearly, that doesn't work for you anymore."

I didn't like his accusatory tone. "What do you mean?"

"Never mind."

He turned the music back on and left me in the kitchen.

I turned it back off and followed him.

He was in the living room, sitting on the couch, leaning forward with his head in his hands.

I sat on the coffee table in front of him and waited, my heart breaking every time Mal took a breath that turned into a sob.

"I'm sorry," I said when after ten minutes, he still hadn't looked up. "I just don't know what to do. I want to call him, go over there and bang on the door until he sees us."

Mal shook his head.

"What if he doesn't? What if he doesn't want to see us? What if Frank's company is more important? Could we blame him? That's his family business, his dream. Could we blame him for wanting to protect his family?"

I shook my head. We couldn't. No matter how much it hurt, we'd support his decision.

"The question is, am I still enough for you? After having him too. If he doesn't come back to us. Am I enough? Are we enough?"

"What? Of course you are. Mal, I love you more than life itself. Feeling upset because Jake isn't here doesn't mean that if he doesn't come, I'll be sad forever. I'm sorry if I made you feel that way. I was just doing what I do when I'm stressed."

I stood up and pushed him back into the sofa until I was straddling him.

"I love you so much, Mal."

"I love you too. And I miss him so much. It's taking every ounce of willpower I have in me to not do what you said. Go out there, knock the door off, and claim him like I should have done days ago."

I used my thumbs to clean the wetness from his cheeks.

"I should have told him then. When he said he loved me, I should have said it back," he confessed.

"Why didn't you?"

"I was overwhelmed. I was forty when we met, Griff. I always believed that I'd meet someone in my twenties or early thirties, and that would be it. But when none of my relationships worked, I thought there was something wrong with me. I had accepted that I would be on my own and sticking to casual encounters. Then you came into my life and stole my heart."

I smiled, recalling the exact moment we'd accidentally bumped into each other on the beach walk.

"Baby, I thought you stole my whole heart. And then Jake came along, and I realized you'd left some behind for him. I went from having no one to having the best husband I could ever wish for to having another man I love as much as I love you."

"You should tell him that. He needs to know."

He nodded and smiled.

"He asked for time. We can give him today, then we'll swoop in and kidnap him."

"I like that idea. I like it a lot…"

That could be a great plot starter. Regular Joe is kidnapped by a criminal for hire. When the criminal figures out the guy isn't who was supposed to be kidnapped, he needs to run from the people that hired him for the job. *Love on the Run*. That would be the title.

"Baby?"

"Hm, what?"

"Are you writing a book in your head?" Mal asked.

"Yeah, why?"

"Because I think you should be kissing me instead."

I laughed. "I can do that."

Our kiss was interrupted by the doorbell.

"Are we expecting someone?" he asked.

"It's Sunday, so, no. Unless…" I ran to the door with Mal on my heels.

When I opened the door, I didn't know if I should laugh or cry.

Jake stood at the doorstep, wearing a resort uniform and holding a can of Lysol and a box of extra-large Trojan condoms.

"You called for room service?"

I stood there with a grin on my face, staring at one of the two most beautiful men on the planet. He'd come. He was ours.

He took my hand when I stretched mine out and pulled him inside, pushing him against the wall.

The Lysol and box of condoms fell on the wooden floor of the hallway as Jake held on tight, but when I stepped back to look at him, he was gazing into Mal's eyes.

Something was passing between them. A secret communication. A silent declaration.

I ran my hands over Jake's chest and felt my way down until I cupped his erection. He bit his lip, pushing into my hand.

"What's your name?" Mal said behind me. His deep, warm, aroused voice wrapping around us.

"Jake."

"Jake, I'm Mal, and the guy attached to your dick is my husband, Griff."

Jake looked at me and smiled. I couldn't wait any longer to taste him.

It felt like forever since I'd touched him, and my body was craving him, craving being touched and taken to heights I could only reach when I was with my two men.

He kissed me back with all he had, and then he reached behind me to pull Mal into a kiss. I sucked on the warm skin of his neck until he groaned.

"You can mark me all you want, but you're going to have to explain that to my dad later," he said.

Mal and I looked at each other.

"What?"

"Do we need to talk first?" Mal asked.

"Fuck no," Jake said. "Bedroom first. Talk later."

Mal pulled me away from Jake and grabbed both our hands, dragging us to the bedroom until we all fell in a mess of limbs on top of the comforter.

One by one, all clothes were removed until we were blissfully naked. *Finally.*

Jake ended up facing Mal with me against his back.

I touched, kissed, licked, and felt every inch of skin I could get my hands and mouth on. Their moans as they kissed only made my cock harder.

"Jake," Mal said, breaking their kiss breathlessly. "I know you said no talk, but I can't let this be unsaid any longer. I do love you. So much. I've been attracted to you from the moment you checked us in at the resort, but the day you held me through the earthquake and told me everything would be okay. The day you showed me that I didn't need to be the strong one all the time. That was the day I fell in love with you."

"I know," Jake whispered. "I know."

My heart soared hearing Mal open his heart to Jake.

This was the moment everything I'd hoped for—but didn't imagine I'd have—slotted nicely into place. Like that final move in a Rubik's Cube, we became perfectly aligned.

And sometimes, we'd shift a little. We'd argue because we weren't perfect, and we would disagree because we were individuals. But in the end, we'd always fit because we were always meant to be complete. It had just taken a long time to figure out how many sides there were to us and how we fit together.

Suddenly I remembered we hadn't given Jake all of his birthday presents.

"Mal," I said. "I'm going to grab the…you know…"

"The what?" Jake asked, turning over to face me. "Oh my god, why are there mirrors everywhere?"

"It's part of your birthday present," I said. "The part we couldn't give you yesterday."

I grabbed the box from the dresser while Mal got up to get his phone from the living room.

When I went back to bed, I sat against the headboard and settled Jake against me.

His weight on me when he leaned back against my chest was perfection. I kissed his shoulder and then his mouth when he turned his head to me.

"Got it," Mal said. He unlocked the phone and gave it to Jake. "What's this?"

"Our test results. We're both negative. We did it a few days ago, hoping at some point we could forego condoms," Mal said.

"We can," Jake said. "I was tested as soon as we had sex. I wanted to bring it up, but I wasn't sure if it was too early. I can show you the results."

"Are they negative?" I asked.

"Yes."

"Then your word is all we need. Now open this one."

He laughed at my eagerness, but he'd soon find out why I was dying for him to open the box.

He shook the box first and then looked carefully for all the sticky tape.

"Oh, for the love of God. I'll buy you five hundred boxes. Just open the damn thing before I expire with need." I groaned.

Mal laughed, and I growled back.

"Does he always get like this when he's horny?" Jake asked.

"Just wait until he's spent an afternoon writing a sex scene. He'll jump you and have you naked before you even know it."

Jake turned to me. "I like that." And then he kissed me.

Ten million years later, he removed the lid of the box and discarded the paper inside.

"Oh, my…is this…"

"It sure is."

After our first time together, I'd researched how either of us could fuck the other two at the same time. The answer had been glaringly obvious and sexy as fuck. A strap-on dildo that we could use to fuck one of us while buried deep in the other. It even had a special feature included, but that was my secret for now.

Jake's cock, already hard from rutting against Mal, twitched. He was so ready for this.

"What's it gonna be, baby? Your birthday, your choice," I whispered in his ear, taking the strap-on and discarding the box.

His gaze flickered between me, Mal, and the strap-on. He bit his lip, a cute pinkish hue gracing his cheeks.

"You want to fuck us like we fucked you?" Mal asked.

Jake shook his head. "No. I want to make you feel like I felt when

I had you both. Full, loved, complete. So it's much more than fucking."

I kissed his neck, making sure to not leave marks that would be visible.

"Baby, if you ever want to become a writer, just say the word."

He sat up and turned around, claiming my mouth. Mal joined us in a three-way kiss that was tender, hot, and promising at the same time.

"I'll say one word," Jake gasped. "Now."

"You got it, baby," Mal said.

I couldn't tell which way was the head or the feet of the bed when my men pressed me down and kissed every inch of my skin.

When I didn't think I could take any more teasing, they went to town on my cock.

My head nearly blew off when I raised it and saw they had their mouths around my cock. Their lips touched, and they looked into each other's eyes as they sucked up and down my length.

"Jesus, fucking…you're gonna kill…I can't even…"

Mal pulled away first. "As much as I'd love to see you let go this way, I think Jake is dying to be inside you, baby."

"And inside you…now the question is…who's going to get me, and who's going to get the dildo…" He moved his brows up and down.

"I really don't care as long as I get cock," I said, pulling him so he covered my body.

He gave me a bruising kiss as our cocks rubbed against each other.

Jake jumped off the bed to grab the lube, and while Mal explored my skin, biting and sucking on my nipples, I watched Jake put on the strap-on.

When he was done, he looked at me with enough heat to power an entire village.

"Check the box again," I said.

He did and widened his eyes when he saw it. I shook my head, and he nodded his understanding.

"I hope you're both ready for this because I'm nuclear horny. I missed you, and the sight of me fucking both of you might just cause spontaneous combustion. Just sayin.'"

Despite his words, Jake made sure to prep us thoroughly.

"Look at us, Mal."

We'd taken some time two days ago to position the mirrors carefully so wherever we were on the bed, we'd be able to see our reflection.

"So hot. So fucking hot," he said.

My legs were wrapped around his waist, and he'd raised his so our holes were completely exposed.

Our breaths mingled as we tried to keep it together. With Jake doing a thorough job of prepping us and our cocks trapped together between us, it was going to be a challenge.

In the mirror, I saw Jake apply lube to his cock and the dildo and then edge forward.

Mal let out a breath and then moaned when the head of the dildo breached through the ring of muscles.

"Ugh, fuck."

Because of the angle, I could see that Mal would have more of the dildo inside him before Jake could get inside me.

"God, Mal, you look so gorgeous. That cock filling you up. I just want to bite your butt cheeks," Jake said.

I chuckled, thinking about Mal's very biteable butt cheeks. I loved how round and soft they were. There were plenty of angles between Jake and me. We needed Mal's softness to balance us.

My laugh was stuck in my throat when I felt Jake seeking entrance into my body.

Slowly, he edged his way in until his balls were flush with mine.

Our eyes met in one of the mirrors: mine, Jake's, and Mal's. What a beautiful image.

"I'm going to move now," he said. It felt like a warning, but nothing could have prepared me for it.

I was used to feeling. Whether I was fucking or being fucked, all I could do was feel, but now there was a visual, and oh my goodness in heaven, what a visual.

Mal grunted every time Jake pulled out and pushed back in, and our bellies were wet with precum.

Jake's thrusts became sharper but shorter. He wasn't pulling out as much because he needed to keep his hands free.

I reached over Mal's shoulder, and he took my hand, lacing our fingers together.

The other hand held the remote for the dildo.

I couldn't take my eyes off him as he looked at the mirror and focused on Mal.

"Ugh fuck…fuck, Jesus fuck, what's that…ugh!" Mal's reaction to the vibration was to cant his hips.

He couldn't move much because of our position, but by now, every single tiny movement was blown out of proportion.

My eyes rolled back, and I squeezed Jake's hand tight. Any moment now, I'd either pass out or come. Hopefully, I'd come before I passed out because I was wound so tight that I needed release like my next breath.

I'D PLAYED with dildos and butt plugs enough to know and appreciate the difference between that and being filled by a real, warm, pulsing cock.

I also appreciated Griff's creativity in bed. Many times he'd asked to try positions, toys, or food during sex for research.

His books had all the feels, but they were also hot as fuck.

If it was possible to have a Ph.D. in sex, I was pretty sure we were halfway to graduating. But every so often, Griff still surprised me, and this was one of those times.

Not that I'd never had a vibrating sex toy inside me.

He'd once added a vibrating bullet when he was already inside me, and I was about to come.

To say I lasted less than a second the moment the vibrations hit my prostate was an understatement. That had been the day I'd learned about full-body orgasms.

Having a vibrating dildo controlled by Jake, who was fucking both me and Griff with short thrusts, was another kind of sensation altogether.

Griff shook under me. "God, I can feel you vibrating. How...is that possible?" he asked.

"Don't know, baby. But our man sure does have some tricks up his cock."

"Don't make me laugh," Jake said.

"Or what?"

I felt his answer in my ass, my prostate, in my fucking soul.

Fighting the orgasm was pointless because I wasn't the one in control. My body had given itself to Jake, and with Griff's cock rubbing against mine, I was on a sensory overload.

I came with the power of a thousand orgasms, with stars in my eyes and wonder for the sheer amount of pleasure the human body was capable of.

Jake stopped the vibrations as soon as I came. Everything was over-sensitive, and I didn't have the power of speech to ask him to stop.

Griff let out a contented sigh, and I could tell from how relaxed he was and the amount of cum between us that he'd also come.

I opened my eyes to look in the mirror. Jake had a pained look. He'd been doing his very best to give us our pleasure, and now it was his turn.

He pulled out of Griff and the dildo out of me simultaneously. His self-restraint and care for us made me fall in love all over again.

As soon as he'd stepped out of the strap-on, he brought his hand to his hard, flushed cock, and with only a few expert strokes, he came all over Griff and me, marking us.

"Wow. I may be dead," he said, collapsing on top of us. "I don't have a gym membership, but if I did, I'd be canceling it right now because this right here…best workout ever."

"Amen," Griff said.

"How about we move this to the locker room? I believe the policy in this establishment is that you're allowed to check out other customers," I said.

"How about groping?" Jake said.

"Yup."

"Blowjobs in the shower room?" Griff asked.

"All kinds of ogling, groping, sucking, and anything else leading to a happy ending are permitted," I said.

"We need to move, or we'll be stuck like this forever." Jake groaned.

"You won't hear me complain," I said, slapping his butt.

We took a lazy shower, taking turns washing each other. Between kissing and touching, we didn't do much talking, but I knew it was coming.

I left my gorgeous guys making out in the shower and stepped out to dry myself.

After I put on a pair of shorts, I got the coffee machine going and put clean sheets and a fresh comforter on the bed.

The noises coming from the bathroom got my attention, and I got there just in time to see Jake come inside Griff's mouth while he stroked himself until he came.

"Thank you for the show."

They cleared the foggy glass of the shower and kissed until my own cock attempted to come back to life.

I turned on the sink faucet, which made their water run cold. They swore at me but turned the shower off and came out.

"You'll thank me when you don't turn into prunes."

We finally settled on the couch with much-needed coffee.

Griff settled against Jake's chest, and I was on the opposite end with both their feet in my lap.

"Where do you want to start?" I asked Jake.

"I hope what happened just now is a dead giveaway as to how things are going to be."

Griff closed his eyes with a contented sigh. If he were a cat, he'd be purring as Jake brushed his still-wet hair away from his face.

"If this is how it's going to be, I need to look into a better life insurance policy, baby."

"Aww, look, Griff. Grandpa over there can't keep up with us."

"Don't worry. He'll manage. I've been pushing his limits for four years, and he always comes through."

"But there's two of you now. My poor heart won't make it." I pouted but then smiled. I'd keep up with them for as long as I could, and one day when my poor dick gave up, I'd happily watch them go at it.

"What's that smug smile for?" Griff asked.

"I just realized I have free porn for life with you two."

"Damn right you do," Jake said.

I loved this quiet after the storm. The teasing, the talking. I had a feeling it wouldn't be easy, but nothing in life was. What mattered was that we'd have each other, even if some things would have to change.

"I hate to bring this up, but if Frank isn't about to fire my ass for being with you, then we still have a problem with you working for me."

"No problem. He fired me instead," Jake said.

"He what?"

"Hold your guns, big guy. He hired me back. I'm going to work directly for him, not the resort. It's a really exciting job, and I can't wait to get started."

"Really? That's…that's amazing. Does that mean he…"

"Won't chop your balls off?" Griff finished for me.

"Yeah." I choked.

"That I can't promise," Jake said. "But I guess you'll find out over dinner later."

"Don't look so smug," I said, tickling Griff's foot.

"Hey, he already loves me. I gave him an early copy of my book, remember? And I taught him all he needs to know about threesomes."

Both Jake and I groaned. I did not need to know what Frank knew or imagined went on between us in the bedroom.

"The most important thing is that he accepts us. Nothing is ever guaranteed in life, but while I love you and you love me, we have everything we need right here. Dad understands that," Jake said.

"Dad?"

Jake smiled. "He's been there for me all my life, but it's like I couldn't see it because I was too afraid he'd stop wanting me. I figured it's time to let him be what he's always been: a father."

I scooted over to steal a kiss from Jake. "I'm so happy for you and Frank." And then, since Griff was within range, I kissed him too.

The three of us ended up making out for a while, which was their sneaky way of making me so horny I'd agree to anything for a blowjob.

Even watch an episode of *The Beauty and the Bitch*, or whatever the thing was called.

Jake had a key to his place, of course, but it didn't feel right for him to use it to let us in, especially after what had happened yesterday.

We rang the bell and heard Jessie barking on the other side for a moment until Gabe answered the door with a giant smile.

"Hey, guys. Come on in. I'll just warn you, Dad is in a foul mood since he realized Jake is moving out."

"Huh, who says I'm moving out?" Jake asked.

Gabe raised his brows and pointed at the three of us.

"Babe, you're moving out," I said matter-of-factly.

"Oh, really?" he said, crossing his arms.

What? He didn't want to move in with us?

"You aren't?" I asked.

"Gabe, tell Dad we'll be down in a minute," Jake said and dragged Griff and me up the stairs to his bedroom.

He closed the door behind us and then turned around, placing his hands on his hips.

"Anything you want to ask me?"

I looked at Griff, who had a partly amused, partly confused expression going on.

"What do you mean?"

"What do you mean, what do I mean? Have you actually asked me to move in with you? Or am I supposed to assume?"

He sounded mad and hurt. I thought it was a good thing.

"Don't you want to live with us?"

"Of course I do."

"I'm confused."

Griff sidled up to me and wrapped his arms around my waist. "Baby, we need to learn to communicate better. We've been together a while, but this is all new to Jake. What you might assume my answer or reaction would be might be different for Jake."

I held my hand out to Jake, and he came easily. It felt right holding them both, one under each arm.

"I'm sorry for assuming, baby. Do you want to move in with us?"

Jake avoided my gaze.

"Um…yeah, but…does it have to be now? Uncl…my dad just got me back a few months ago. Gabe's going back to Berkeley for his exams, and if I leave…"

Griff looked at me. I knew he'd be upset without Jake, as would I, but he wasn't going anywhere. We could wait.

"We understand, sweetheart. You do what you need to do. Spend some more time with your dad, and when you're ready, we'll be waiting."

He kissed me and then Griff. "Thank you. I will still spend as much time with you as I can, and I'll stay over some nights."

Griff caressed Jake's cheek. "We're in this together for the long haul. We'll miss you, but it'll just make the times we're together all the more special."

Jake nodded.

"Okay, we probably should go down there before Frank kills me."

"Why do you think Dad will only kill you?" Jake asked as we walked down the stairs.

"Have you looked at Griff's adorable face? No one can stay mad at that," I said. "Besides, I'm older, and you're his kid."

They both laughed.

"Come on, pay up," Griff said.

"Damn you, Mal."

"What's going on?"

Jake sighed. "We made a bet in the shower as to how long it would take you to bring up our age difference. I had faith in you. Six hours? You couldn't even make it a whole day."

I shook my head. "I'm in so much trouble with you two."

"I sincerely hope so, Mal. Being kept on our toes is good for your heart," Frank said, coming out of nowhere.

God, if even Frank was on their side, I *really* was in trouble.

Not that I'd have it any other way.

As we sat around the table with Frank, Gabe, Zak, and Griff and I on either side of Jake, all I could do was hope that we'd have many more moments like this.

We enjoyed Frank's home-cooked butter chicken and vegetables with the bottle of wine we'd brought with us.

Frank's good disposition had returned when Jake reassured him he wasn't moving out just yet. After dinner, we sat around the fire pit outside, enjoying the dessert Griff had prepared.

"Okay, family, we have a problem we need to resolve," Frank said.

"Can I be the one to fire Brian?" Gabe said, raising his wine glass.

We all laughed.

"Any other time, son, I'd see it as a good experience, but I want to make sure the message is loud and clear and reconvened to my former friend."

"Oh, but, Dad, I've been practicing." And then he stood up and pointed at no one. "You're fired, you weak, sleazy, backstabbing shit-head. Leave."

He sat back down. "What do you think?"

I couldn't help laughing at his proud face. He was clearly joking, but Brian totally deserved that kind of delivery when he lost his job.

"We have a bigger problem than Brian, Frank. We still don't have a contractor. We'll be one manager down. Two if we include Jake, who got himself fired—ugh." I coughed when Jake hit me in the ribs.

"All we can do is keep looking, Mal. There will be someone out there ready to do the work. I'm not going to compromise on safety, and I'd rather have the resort closed than have the building collapse and hurt someone."

We all agreed, but the financial hit could be too much.

"Can we afford it though? You'll have the same overhead costs with one resort down. As it is, we're already missing the summer peak trade."

"If you're asking if we can afford it financially, I'll need to check with my accountant," Frank said. "The question is, can we afford to do nothing?"

The surrounding mood became heavier. I couldn't believe we'd overcome so many hurdles, and it came down to this.

I always thought the challenge would be to organize resources.

What to do with people who needed a steady paycheck, how to retain staff during such a long period.

Those had been my worries. Getting the actual job done was never a concern.

"I may have an idea."

Everyone looked at Griff. He seemed a bit unsure after speaking up, but I put my hand on his knee to support him.

"I hope I'm not speaking out of turn, and I apologize for putting anyone on the spot, but I've been thinking about this a lot," he said.

"Go on, son, sometimes we need a fresh perspective to help us find the solution," Frank said.

Griff nodded. "I've seen how hard Jake has been working to relocate people to other resorts and make sure everyone has what they need. It's because the resort is important to this island. And if the resort looks after the people of the island, why can't the island take care of the resort?"

"How?" Jake asked.

"You need a structural engineer with a license who can also manage the project, right?"

"That's right," I said.

Griff looked at Zak, who'd been staring at the fire but suddenly looked up. "I can do it. I have the right licenses to work in California. I just don't have the workmen."

"That's where the island comes in. If we spread the word, I'm sure there's a bunch of builders, electricians, and anyone else you need, right here, on the island. Think of it as a GoFundMe, but with skilled people."

There was a moment of silence until Frank laughed.

There were a few puzzled looks until he spoke. "I like it. Of course we'll have to make sure everything is compliant, but if Zak wants to take on the job, then we can find the people. And this right here, gentleman, is the reason why people like John and Brian will never have what we have. Because they're so busy tripping each other up that they miss the opportunities to achieve something great."

I wondered if Frank was referring to John's missed opportunity when he was invited to rejoin the business and decided against it. But that was all in the past and irrelevant.

Now, I was just proud of my smart husband, who'd saved more than the day with the best idea.

I hugged him tightly, stopping myself from showing affection in front of everyone, but Jake had no such concerns when he pulled Griff in for a kiss.

"And that is my cue to retire with my girl. Come on, Jess, let's watch the news in the bedroom."

We said goodbye to Frank and spent the rest of the evening in animated conversation, making plans as if we were the fantastic five. Six, if you counted Frank.

I didn't miss the way Zak and Gabe kept looking at each other when the other wasn't watching.

Gabe became frustrated when he realized he'd miss all the action because he was going back to college, but everyone promised to keep him updated.

Griff was visibly disappointed when Jake said he was staying at home because Zak was leaving in a couple of days, but when he took us up to his bedroom and kissed us until we were both breathless, we knew that our reunion would be well worth the wait.

25

JAKE

Four months later

"Mmhmm, such a nice ass," I said.

"Soft, round, bitable…it's perfection," Griff agreed.

"Do you think we killed him?"

"It's possible."

"Do you think he'll be up for a repeat later?"

"Absolutely."

We stood in the bedroom door watching Mal. He was face-down on the bed, star-fished and completely dead to the world.

It had been a long day already, and it was only lunchtime, but we'd been up working since before dawn.

Mal and I had gone to the resort to finalize some work, and Griff had taken the opportunity to get up and work on his book.

An unexpected burst pipe put an end to our plans for the day, but Zak had insisted he'd oversee the workmen and sent us home.

A long lovemaking session and a shower later, we were all feeling a lot more relaxed, but I hadn't been able to sleep because it was the middle of the day, and Griff had wanted to deadhead Aunt Annie's rose bushes.

I looked behind us at the clock in the hallway.

"Should we wake him up?" I asked.

"Wait, let's ogle him a little longer," Griff said. "God, I could lick that salt-and-pepper fuzz on his legs all day long."

"Right? He's going to want a haircut soon, but I like his hair longer."

"Word."

"Do you think he'll notice if we take turns eating his ass?" I asked.

"It's lunchtime, right?" Griff shrugged.

When Mal's foot twitched, Griff and I locked eyes and smiled. That was his giveaway. Mal couldn't stay still in bed for long. Even when he was tired and wanted to rest, his feet seemed to have a will of their own.

He could pretend all he wanted, but we knew he'd likely heard most if not all of our conversation.

I winked at Griff to follow my lead. "Yeah, but look at him. He's fast asleep. Maybe I should eat your ass instead."

"You won't hear me complain."

"Turn around and drop those shorts," I commanded.

Griff rustled his shorts but didn't move. I was trying so hard not to laugh.

"Look at your hole, so eager to feel my tongue."

"Hmm, like that, Jake."

Mal turned his head to face us, smiling when he was caught.

"Fucking teasers." He groaned.

We laughed and ran to the bed, jumping on top of him.

"What do you think is the punishment for peeping Toms?" Griff asked.

"Hmm, don't know…maybe tie him to the bed and have our way with him?" I suggested.

Mal grabbed my waist and turned me over so I ended up under him, and then he threw his leg over Griff's thighs.

"I'm the peeping Tom? You two were the ones staring at my ass for the last ten minutes."

Griff and I looked at each other and grinned. "No regrets," we said at the same time.

We all laughed, exchanging lazy kisses.

How perfect was my life? Being with two men who loved me as much as I loved them. The three of us couldn't be more different. Griff was this force of nature that was made for love. His job as a romance author couldn't be more suited for someone like him.

He lived and breathed love, and every day I woke up in his arms and saw his happy smile, I knew that he was truly happy.

Mal was our rock. The solid presence that always calmed us down. Maybe it was because he was a little older, had lived more, but he always seemed to have a way of bringing us back together and reminding us we were strong and good.

As for me, I didn't feel like an abandoned child anymore. It hadn't been until my conversation with my dad that I'd realized how much hurt I'd been carrying all my life. Everything I'd done was to make sure I was worthy of being kept. I didn't even see that my constant strive for perfection was also hurting my brother.

We'd talked about that too. My relationship with Gabe had become stronger, and I was starting to see him grow into the person he was meant to be.

The oven timer went off.

"I love you both, but right now, I may love my roast chicken a little more," I said.

They both gasped and exchanged a look that meant I was in trouble.

Ten minutes later, they'd worked me up so much I could have sworn I'd never need food again in my life. Their hands explored, and their mouths mapped every inch of my skin.

Have you ever had four hands touching you all over? Ten out of ten, absolutely recommend.

I came in someone's mouth. I couldn't tell whose because my eyes were closed, and when they kissed me, I could taste myself in both their mouths.

Have I said yet how much I loved my life?

Griff held my hand as we walked inside the resort's main dining hall.

He didn't enjoy big crowds, so I was ready to go full-on protective mode and take him outside if he wasn't enjoying himself. But as he took in all the new changes in the large room, all I could see was his big smile and relaxed features.

This was it, the culmination of four months of hard work.

There was plenty of food and drink available, live music from a local band, and everyone seemed to be enjoying themselves.

Tonight was family night. Everyone attending either worked here at the resort or was a contractor or worker that helped us with the renovations.

I saw Hailey and Pete at one of the tables and went to greet them.

"You look radiant, Momma," I said, bending down to give her a hug.

"Ugh, I'm the size of a house, and apparently, I'm still due to grow more. How much space does this kid need, anyway?"

She grumbled, but I knew it was all for show because she was dying to meet her baby. We still didn't know if it was a boy or girl. They'd decided to wait until the baby was born to find out.

"Hey, have you seen your boss?" I asked.

"You mean…your *boyfriend*? I still can't believe you scored not one but two of the cutest gay men on the island," she said.

I shrugged. "It's my charm."

"Among other things," Griff said under his breath.

I was still amazed by how people on the island didn't care that Mal, Griff, and I were together.

It could have something to do with Griff baking endlessly to feed all the workers at the resort with all kinds of muffins and brownies. Or maybe it was because, like a true family, we supported each other. People that lived on the island were our key workers. The resort and the island were codependent. It was a line we'd used many times when recruiting people to work with us.

John had placed a complaint with the mayor's office, accusing us of poaching his workers, malpractice, and even carrying work without a license.

All those accusations were disproved very easily, so eventually, he'd given up.

It was upsetting to see how that had affected my dad. After losing his sister, then his wife, now he'd lost one of his oldest friends.

But as he'd stated, he'd gained two son-in-laws and another additional son in Zak, who'd moved into the house at Dad's request.

It had made sense because we all spent so much time together working and socializing that he'd have wasted money renting out his own place.

I suspected there were other intentions there too.

Zak and Gabe had become close, even though Gabe had left for Berkeley shortly after my birthday party and had only returned a few days ago.

"Hey, mind if I steal my men away?"

I turned around when I heard Mal's voice. As if by design, both Griff and I took our place on either side of Mal, who was conveniently tall enough to hold us both under his arms.

"Aww, you guys are too adorable," Hailey said, gushing. "I like the new look, boss. It's a lot less…grumpy."

We all laughed.

"I don't have time for that, Hailey. I'm too tired to be grumpy."

"You won't sleep that much tonight either," Griff said under his breath, but this time, a little too loud, so everyone heard him over the music.

He blushed an adorable shade of pink, and if we weren't in public, I'd have kissed him until he was full-on red.

"Come on," Mal said. "I have something to show you."

We followed him out of the dining hall.

"Where are we going?" Griff asked.

"It's a surprise."

We left the main buildings behind us and followed the path through the garden toward the private cabins. The family cabins were the ones closest to the resort and the children's playground, then there was a tropical garden, and on the other side, the honeymoon cabins.

Each had its own front yard with a bathtub, and it led directly to the beach. There were also taller hedges and strategically placed trees to give the couples more privacy to enjoy their special time.

As we walked past the tropical garden, I could see where we were headed.

"I wanted to take you both somewhere, but the resort reopens in a week, and I can't be away. So this is the next best thing," Mal said, opening the door to the last cabin on the row.

He turned on the lights to show the brand-new decor. We'd made the best of being closed to do other smaller redecoration jobs and replace units that were looking a little tired.

All in all, Silver Sands was looking stunning and ready to welcome all the guests onto the island. Considering we were already fully booked until the spring, I wasn't sure the low season was going to feel that low.

Griff walked further inside the cabin, taking in all the features. The living room with a large couch and a fireplace, the small kitchen with some essentials so the honeymooners wouldn't need to leave their cabin if they so wished.

We followed him into the room.

"Wow. Can we get a bed that size at home?" he asked.

"We probably should," I said. "We're gonna need it."

Mal looked at me. "Are you saying…?"

I nodded. "I'm moving in. That is if you still want me, but considering Griff can't let go of my cock the moment I walk in, and you sleep half on top of me when I stay over…I think it's a sure thing."

He picked me up in a fireman's lift and dropped me on the bed. Griff followed us.

"Are you serious, baby?" Mal asked.

"I've got my stuff packed. I was going to tell you tonight so we could move my stuff tomorrow. I've been dying to move in, but with Gabe away, it didn't feel right leaving Dad on his own with Zak."

"He'd have Frank joining a sex cult in no time," Griff said.

I shivered. "First, I don't want to hear the words Frank and sex together in the same sentence. Ever. Second, what kind of conversations have you been having with Zak?"

"You don't want to know, but he has some kind of imagination."

Oh, I knew, but I didn't want to say it in front of our overprotective and slightly prone to jealousy boyfriend.

Mal liked Zak a lot when he forgot that Zak and I knew each other very well beyond our friendship. When he remembered? Well, let's just say that grumpy Mal made an appearance and would only go away with a magical blowjob.

"We have some food in the fridge, and I packed clothes and some…stuff from home. After the party, we can come here and have our own celebration. Let's say that checkout time in the morning is very flexible."

We exchanged some heated kisses, and I wondered if we really needed to get back to the party, but Mal's phone ringing answered that question.

Mal went ahead while Griff and I had a better snoop around the cabin. I'd mostly been dealing with staffing and development as well as building my new role with my dad, so I hadn't gotten as involved with the renovations.

After we locked the cabin, we made our way back but decided to take the beach walk.

With the sun long gone, the sand was cold, but it was still bearable. The moon was full and high up in the sky, making the sand and the waves look the silver color the resort was named after.

"The resort looks beautiful in this lighting, almost surreal and magical," Griff said.

He was right. The twinkling lights of the dining hall in the distance gave it an extra dimension.

Suddenly Griff stopped, grabbing my arm.

"What?"

"Look, isn't that Gabe and Zak? Is there someone else with them?"

I turned to where Griff pointed, and sure enough, my brother was locked in an embrace with Zak, and was that…Sam?

It was hard to see clearly in the dark, and they were quite a ways away from us, but it looked like they were engaged in conversation, and then Gabe pulled Sam into a kiss.

Griff gasped.

I covered his mouth with my hand. "We can't tell anyone, okay? We don't know what's going on. They're just friends."

He rolled his eyes, so I removed my hand and gave him a quick kiss.

"Are you sure you don't know what's going on? Because I never kissed my friends like that."

When I looked again, they had parted but were walking together toward the tropical gardens.

"I didn't know Sam was back. Wasn't he in San Francisco on a job?" I asked.

"Clearly, he's not in San Francisco anymore, babe."

"Come on, let's go back to the party before someone sends out a search party for us and finds them instead."

The rest of the evening was great. We danced, laughed, and ate cake.

I loved hearing from staff how much they enjoyed their time at the other resorts. Some people had taken time off and were eager to return to work.

It was sometime later that I noticed Gabe and Zak coming back into the hall. Sam wasn't with them.

"Great party, hey, boys?" Dad said, holding a champagne glass.

"The best, Dad. It's great to see everyone here. Well, almost everyone."

We'd lost a handful of staff to other resorts. Something I was immensely proud of, and my meetings with the resort managers had been productive and gave me much hope that we could create the culture my dad had worked for his whole life.

"I'm going to miss you at home, son."

"I'll miss you too, but you know we'll come over all the time, right?" I said.

"Frank, you keep making that chicken dish we all love, and we might all just move in with you," Griff said.

Mal joined us again after doing another round around the room and talking to everyone.

I took a sip of my drink.

A year ago, almost to the date, I broke one of my rules because two men got under my skin with their sheer presence.

A year later, all my dreams were coming true. I was loved. I belonged. I had a career, goals, and prospects. Most of all, I had a family.

All because I'd forgotten the bottle of Lysol in their room.

All because I'd worked at the resort.

I hope you enjoyed The Resort. The story of Mal, Jake and Griff started off as a newsletter serial I sent my newsletter subscribers every two weeks over a year.

This was my first MMM story, so I was naturally nervous, but since the story came to an end I've received so many emails from my VIPs saying how much they loved following Jake, Mal and Griff's journey to their happy ever after.

And you know what's best?

It doesn't end here!!

I've got a short story in the same world and you can have it for free. Not only that…the next newsletter serial will start shortly.

Want to know what happens to Gabe, Zak and Sam?

Be sure to subscribe to my newsletter so you don't miss out on The Island (serial) and The Vacation (Free short).

Click the link below to sign up to my newsletter and receive the scene in your inbox:

Sign up here (anawritesmm.com/sol-signup)
(if you signed up after How to Catch a Biker, Love Again or Christmas Bubble, you don't need to do it again, just check your inbox for you welcome email with the download link for all the bonus scenes! And since you're subscribed, you'll automatically receive The Island serial when it starts.)

Be sure to follow me on Bookbub (bookbub.com/authors/ana-ashley) to be notified of new releases, and look for me on Facebook (facebook.com/anawritesmm/) for sneak peaks of upcoming stories.

For giveaways, sneak peaks, ARC opportunities and general caffeinated fun times, please join my facebook group! Café RoMMance - Ana's Reader Group (facebook.com/groups/CafeRoMMance/)

Hi there,

Are you an Ana Ashley fan looking for:

✔ backstage access

✔ Special perks

✔ Free books

✔ Giveaways

✔ exclusive fiction created for you

You can get all these things and more by joining my member's club, Ana's Attic. Click the link below to sign up with a 25% discount and a 7-day free trial.

Sign up for Ana's Attic on my website! (anawritesmm.com/attic)

Discount code: MAYDEC

BOOKS BY ANA ASHLEY

Single Dads of Stillwater

A spin off series from Chester Falls that can be read on its own. Each book features one or more single dads in this community of friends, family and found family. In this contemporary MM romance series you'll find heat, emotion and a guaranteed happy ever after.

Newcomer

Antagonist

Breakthrough

Heartstring

Datebook (Coming late 2023)

Finding You Series

A standalone series set across the Atlantic between New York and Portugal. Find your way home with this contemporary MM romance series with friends to lovers, star-crossed lovers and age gap with plenty of heat, feels and always a happy ever after.

Home Again

Together Again

Love Again

And for a special short story, Complete Again, plus bonus scenes, grab the Finding You boxset now.

Room for 3 series

This is a high heat MMM contemporary romance series set in an island resort.

The Resort

The Vacation (Free short story)

Chester Falls Series

From a Prince to a Happy Ever After for all, enjoy this small town MM romance series that's as sweet as they come, with plenty of heat, humor and everything in between.

How to Catch a Bookworm (Prequel short)

How to Catch a Prince

How to Catch a Rival

How to Catch a Bodyguard

How to Catch a Bachelor

How to Catch the Boss (a Christmas novella)

How to Catch a Biker

How to Catch a Vet

How to Catch a Happy Ever After

You can now have all the books in the series and the prequel all in two boxsets.

Chester Falls Collection Volume I

Chester Falls Collection Volume II

Standalone books

Christmas Bubble: a low angst, standalone, Christmas novel featuring a petite but larger-than-life cheerleader, an older demisexual football coach and a winter cabin by the lake with only one bed. With cameos from Chester Falls and Stillwater.

Midnight Ash: a sweet Cinderella fairytale retelling with a sexy kinky twist on the side, and a cast who don't quite behave as you'd expect.

Stronghold: a sweet and sexy romance in Sarina Bowen's World of True North, Vino & Veritas series. This is a standalone story between two childhood friends who reunite after as decade apart, with some creative use of maple syrup.

FREE READS

My Fake Billionaire - Amazon

My Fake Billionaire - All stores

The Vacation (Free short story)

AUDIOBOOKS BY ANA ASHLEY

A lot of my books are now available on audiobook through Amazon/Audible and iTunes.

Dads of Stillwater narrated by John Solo

Newcomer

Antagonist

Breakthrough

Heartstring

Chester Falls narrated by Nick Hudson

How to Catch a Bookworm (a short prequel)

How to Catch a Prince

How to Catch a Rival

How to Catch a Bodyguard

How to Catch Bachelor

How to Catch the Boss (a Christmas novella)

How to Catch a Biker

How to Catch a Vet

How to Catch a Happy Ever After

Stronghold narrated by John Solo

ABOUT THE AUTHOR

Ana Ashley was born in Portugal but has lived in the United Kingdom for so long, even her friends sometimes doubt if she really is Portuguese.

After getting hooked on reading gay romance, Ana decided to follow her lifelong dream of becoming an author.

These days you can find her in front of her laptop bringing her stories to life, or in the kitchen perfecting her recipe for the famous Portuguese custard tarts.

Ana Ashley writes sweet and steamy gay romance set in America, often in small towns where everyone knows everyone.

You can follow Ana on the usual social media hangouts.

For access to exclusive teasers, content, and general book and food related goodness you can now join Ana in her Facebook Group, Café RoMMance - Ana's Reader Group

Email - ana@anaashley.com

9 781915 031051